John Irving was born in Exeter, New Hampshire, in 1942, and he once admitted that he was a 'grim' child. Although he excelled in English at school and knew by the time he graduated that he wanted to write novels, it was not until he met a young Southern novelist named John Yount, at the University of New Hampshire, that he received encouragement. 'It was so simple,' he remembers. 'Yount was the first person to point out that anything I did except writing was going to be vaguely unsatisfying.'

In 1963, Irving enrolled at the Institute of European Studies in Vienna, and he later worked as a university lecturer. His first novel, *Setting Free the Bears*, about a plot to release all the animals from the Vienna Zoo, was written between 1965 and 1967 and was followed by *The Water-Method Man* (1972), an hilarious tale of a man with a complaint more serious than Portnoy's, and *The 158-Pound Marriage* (1974), which exposes the complications of spouse-swapping. Irving achieved international recognition with *The World According to Garp*, which he hoped would 'cause a few smiles among the tough-minded and break a few softer hearts.'

John Irving has a life-long passion for wrestling, and he plays a wrestling referee in the film of *The World According to Garp*. He now writes full-time, has two children and lives in the United States.

John Irving

The Hotel New Hampshire

CORGI BOOKS
A DIVISION OF TRANSWORLD PUBLISHERS LTD

THE HOTEL NEW HAMPSHIRE

A CORGI BOOK 0 552 12040 5

Originally published in Great Britain by
Jonathan Cape Ltd.

PRINTING HISTORY
Jonathan Cape edition published 1981
Corgi edition published 1982
Corgi edition reprinted 1982 (twice)

Corgi Books are published by
Transworld Publishers Ltd,
Century House, 61–63 Uxbridge Road,
Ealing, London W5 5SA

Printed and bound in Great Britain by
Cox & Wyman Ltd, Reading

For my wife Shyla,
whose love provided
the light and the space
for five novels

The novelist is indebted to the following works and wishes to express his gratitude to the authors: *Fin-de-Siècle Vienna*, by Carl E. Schorske; *A Nervous Splendor*, by Frederic Morton; *Vienna Inside-Out*, by J. Sydney Jones; *Vienna*, by David Pryce-Jones and the Editors of Time-Life Books; *Lucia di Lammermoor*, by Gaetano Donizetti, the Dover Opera Guide and Libretto Series, (introduced and translated by Ellen H. Bleiler); and *The Interpretation of Dreams*, by Sigmund Freud.

With special thanks to Donald Justice. And with special thanks – and special affection – to Lesley Claire and the Sonoma County Rape Crisis Center of Santa Rosa, California.

On July 18, 1980 the Stanhope Hotel on Eighty-first and Fifth Avenue changed management and ownership and became the American Stanhope – a fine hotel currently not beset by the problems of the Stanhope described in this fiction.

CONTENTS

1

The Bear Called State
O'Maine

The summer my father bought the bear, none of us was born
—we weren't even conceived: not Frank, the oldest; not Franny,
the loudest; not me, the next; and not the youngest of us, Lilly
and Egg. My father and mother were hometown kids who knew
each other all their lives, but their 'union,' as Frank always
called it, hadn't taken place when Father bought the bear.

'Their "union," Frank?' Franny used to tease him; although
Frank was the oldest, he seemed younger than Franny, to me,
and Franny always treated him as if he were a baby. 'What you
mean, Frank,' Franny said, 'is that they hadn't started screwing.'

'They hadn't consummated their relationship,' said Lilly, one
time; although she was younger than any of us, except Egg,
Lilly behaved as if she were everyone's older sister—a habit
Franny found irritating.

' "Consummated"?' Franny said. I don't remember how old
Franny was at the time, but Egg was not old enough to hear talk
like this: 'Mother and Father simply didn't discover sex until
after the old man got that bear,' Franny said. 'That bear gave
them the idea—he was such a gross, horny animal, humping
trees and playing with himself and trying to rape dogs.'

'He *mauled* an occasional dog,' Frank said, with disgust. 'He
didn't *rape* dogs.'

'He tried to,' Franny said. 'You know the story.'

'*Father's* story,' Lilly would then say, with a disgust slightly
different from Frank's disgust; it was *Franny* Frank was disgusted with, but Lilly was disgusted with Father.

And so it's up to me—the middle child, and the least
opinionated—to set the record straight, or nearly straight. We
were a family whose favorite story was the story of my mother
and father's romance: how Father bought the bear, how Mother

and Father fell in love and had, in rapid succession, Frank, Franny, and me ('Bang, Bang, Bang!' as Franny would say); and, after a brief rest, how they then had Lilly and Egg ('Pop and Fizzle,' Franny says). The story we were told as children, and retold to each other when we were growing up, tends to focus on those years we couldn't have known about and can see now only through our parents' many versions of the tale. I tend to see my parents in those years more clearly than I see them in the years I actually can remember, because those times I was present, of course, are colored by the fact that they were up-and-down times—about which I have up-and-down opinions. Toward the famous summer of the bear, and the magic of my mother and father's courtship, I can allow myself a more consistent point of view.

When Father would stumble in telling us the story—when he would contradict an earlier version, or leave out our favorite parts of the tale—we would shriek at him like violent birds.

'Either you're lying now or you lied the last time,' Franny (always the harshest of us) would tell him, but Father would shake his head, innocently.

'Don't you understand?' he would ask us. 'You imagine the story better than I remember it.'

'Go get Mother,' Franny would order me, shoving me off the couch. Or else Frank would lift Lilly off his lap and whisper to her, 'Go get Mother.' And our mother would be summoned as witness to the story we suspected Father of fabricating.

'Or else you're leaving out the juicy parts on purpose,' Franny would accuse him, 'just because you think Lilly and Egg are too young to hear about all the screwing around.'

'There was no screwing around,' Mother would say. 'There was not the promiscuity and freedom there is today. If a girl went off and spent the night or weekend with someone, even her peers thought her a tramp or worse; we really didn't pay much attention to a girl after that. "Her kind sticks together," we used to say. And "Water seeks its own level." ' And Franny, whether she was eight or ten or fifteen or twenty-five, would always roll her eyes and elbow me, or tickle me, and whenever I tickled her back she'd holler, 'Pervert! Feeling up his own sister!' And whether he was nine or eleven or twenty-one or forty-one, Frank always hated sexual conversations and demonstrations of Franny's kind; he would say quickly to Father, 'Never mind that. What about the motorcycle?'

'No, go on about the sex,' Lilly would tell Mother, very

12

humorlessly, and Franny would stick her tongue in my ear or make a farting noise against my neck.

'Well,' Mother said, 'we did not talk freely of sex in mixed company. There was necking and petting, light or heavy; it was usually carried on in cars. There were always secluded areas to park. Lots more dirt roads, of course, fewer people and fewer cars—and cars weren't compact, then.'

'So you could stretch out,' Franny said.

Mother would frown at Franny and persevere with her version of the times. She was a truthful but boring storyteller—no match for my father—and whenever we called on Mother to verify a version of a story, we regretted it.

'Better to let the old man go on and on,' Franny would say. 'Mother's so serious.' Frank would frown. 'Oh, go play with yourself, Frank, you'll feel better,' Franny would tell him.

But Frank would only frown harder. Then he'd say, 'If you'd begin by asking Father about the motorcycle, or something concrete, you'd get a better answer than when you bring up such general things: the clothes, the customs, the sexual habits.'

'Frank, tell us what sex is,' Franny would say, but Father would rescue us all by saying, in his dreamy voice, 'I can tell you: it couldn't have happened today. You may think you have more freedom, but you also have more laws. That bear could not have happened today. He would not have been *allowed*.' And in that moment we would be silenced, all our bickering suddenly over. When Father talked, even Frank and Franny could be sitting together close enough to touch each other and they wouldn't fight; I could even be sitting close enough to Franny to feel her hair against my face or her leg against mine, and if Father was talking I wouldn't think about Franny at all. Lilly would sit deathly still (as only Lilly could) on Frank's lap. Egg was usually too young to listen, much less understand, but he was a quiet baby. Even Franny could hold him on her lap and he'd be still; whenever I held him on my lap, he fell asleep.

'He was a black bear,' Father said; 'he weighed four hundred pounds and was a trifle surly.'

'*Ursus americanus,*' Frank would murmur. 'And he was unpredictable.'

'Yes,' Father said, 'but good-natured enough, most of the time.'

'He was too old to be a bear anymore,' Franny said, religiously.

That was the line Father usually began with—the line he

13

began with the first time I remember being told the story. 'He was too old to be a bear anymore.' I was in my mother's lap for this version, and I remember how I felt fixed forever to this time and place: Mother's lap, Franny in Father's lap beside me, Frank erect and by himself—sitting cross-legged on the shabby oriental with our first family dog, Sorrow (who would one day be put to sleep for his terrible farting). 'He was too old to be a bear anymore,' Father began. I looked at Sorrow, a witless and loving Labrador, and he grew on the floor to the size of a bear and then aged, sagging beside Frank in smelly dishevelment, until he was merely a dog again (but Sorrow would never be 'merely a dog').

That first time I don't remember Lilly or Egg—they must have been such babies that they were not present, in a conscious way. 'He was too old to be a bear anymore,' Father said. 'He was on his last legs.'

'But they were the only legs he had!' we would chant, our ritual response—learned by heart—Frank, Franny, and I all together. And when they got the story down pat, eventually Lilly and even Egg would join in.

'The bear did not enjoy his role as an entertainer anymore,' Father said. 'He was just going through the motions. And the only person or animal or thing he loved was that motorcycle. That's why I had to buy the motorcycle when I bought the bear. That's why it was relatively easy for the bear to leave his trainer and come with me; the motorcycle meant more to that bear than any trainer.'

And later, Frank would prod Lilly, who was trained to ask, 'What was the bear's name?'

And Frank and Franny and Father and I would shout, in unison, 'State o' Maine!' That dumb bear was named State o' Maine, and my father bought him in the summer of 1939 —together with a 1937 Indian motorcycle with a homemade sidecar—for 200 dollars and the best clothes in his summer footlocker.

My father and mother were nineteen that summer; they were both born in 1920 and raised in Dairy, New Hampshire, and had more or less avoided each other through the years they were growing up. It is one of those logical coincidences upon which many good stories are founded that they—to their mutual surprise—ended up having summer jobs at the Arbuthnot-by-the-Sea, a resort hotel that was, for them, far away from home,

14

because Maine was far from New Hampshire (in those days, and to their thinking).

My mother was a chambermaid, although she dressed in her own clothes for serving dinner, and she helped serve cocktails under the tents to the lawn parties (which were attended by the golfers, the tennis and croquet players, and the sailors home from racing on the sea). My father helped in the kitchen, carried luggage, hand-groomed the putting greens, and saw to it that the white lines on the tennis courts were fresh and straight and that the unsteady people who should not have been on board a boat in the first place were helped on and off at dockside with a minimum of injury or getting wet.

They were summer jobs both my mother's and father's parents approved of, although it was a humiliation to Mother and Father that they should discover each other there. It was their first summer away from Dairy, New Hampshire, and they no doubt imagined the posh resort as a place where they could present themselves—total strangers—as also somewhat glamorous. My father had just graduated from the Dairy School, the private boys' academy; he'd been admitted to Harvard for the fall. He knew it would be the fall of 1941 before he'd finally get to go, because he'd set himself the task of making money for his tuition; but at the Arbuthnot-by-the-Sea in the summer of '39 my father would have been happy to let the guests and other help think he was headed for Harvard straight away. My mother being there, with her hometown knowledge of his circumstances, forced Father to tell the truth. He could go to Harvard when he made the money for what it would cost; it was some accomplishment that he could go at all, of course, and most of the people of Dairy, New Hampshire, had been surprised to learn he'd even been admitted to Harvard.

The son of the football coach at the Dairy School, my father, Winslow Berry, was not quite in the category of a faculty child. He was a jock's only son, and his father, whom everyone called Coach Bob, was not a Harvard man—he was thought incapable, in fact, of producing Harvard material.

Robert Berry had come East from Iowa when his wife died in childbirth. Bob Berry was a little old to be single and a first-time father—he was thirty-two. He came searching for an education for his baby boy, for which he offered himself, in trade, for the process. He sold his physical education abilities to the best prep school that would promise to take his son when his son was old

15

enough to go. The Dairy School was not a bastion of secondary school education.

It might have once wished for a status equal to Exeter's or Andover's, but it had settled, in the early 1900s, for a future of compromise. Near to Boston, it admitted a few hundred boys who had been turned down by Exeter and Andover, and a hundred more who shouldn't have been admitted anywhere, and it gave them a curriculum that was standard and wise—and more rigorous than most of the faculty who were employed to teach there; most of them had been turned down elsewhere, too. But, even second-rate among New England prep schools, it was far better than the area public schools and especially better than the only high school in the town of Dairy.

The Dairy School was just the kind of school to make deals, like the one it made with Coach Bob Berry, for a piddling salary and the promise that Coach Bob's son, Win, could be educated there (for free) when he was old enough. Neither Coach Bob nor the Dairy School was prepared for how bright a student my father, Win Berry, would turn out to be. Harvard accepted him among the first class of applicants, but he was ranked below scholarship level. If he'd come to them from a better school than Dairy, he probably could have won some kind of Latin or Greek scholarship; he thought he was good at languages and at first wanted to major in Russian.

My mother, who (being a girl) could never go to the Dairy School, attended the private female seminary also in town. This was another second-rate education that was nonetheless an improvement over the public high school, and the only choice of the town's parents who wished their daughters to be educated without the presence of boys. Unlike the Dairy School, which had dormitories—and 95 percent boarding students—the Thompson Female Seminary was only a private day school. My mother's parents, who for some reason were even older than Coach Bob, wished that their daughter would associate only with the Dairy School boys and not with the boys from the town—my mother's father being a retired Dairy School teacher (everyone called him Latin Emeritus) and my mother's mother being a doctor's daughter from Brookline, Massachusetts, who had married a Harvard man; she hoped her daughter might aspire to the same fate. Although my mother's mother never complained that *her* Harvard man had whisked her away to the sticks, and out of Boston society, she did hope that—through meeting one

16

of the proper Dairy School boys—my mother could be whisked back to Boston.

My mother, Mary Bates, knew that my father, Win Berry, was not the proper sort of Dairy boy her mother had in mind. Harvard or no Harvard, he was Coach Bob's son—and a delayed admission was not the same thing as being there, or being able to afford to go.

Mother's own plans, in the summer of '39, were hardly appealing to her. Her father, old Latin Emeritus, had suffered a stroke; drooling and addled, and muttering in Latin, he would totter about the Dairy house with his wife ineffectually worrying about him unless young Mary was there to look after them both. Mary Bates, at nineteen, had parents older than most people's grandparents, and she had the sense of duty, if not the inclination, to pass up the possibility of her own college education to stay at home and care for them. She thought she would learn how to type and work in the town. This summer job, at the Arbuthnot, was really meant to be an exotic summer vacation for her before she settled into whatever drudgery the fall would bring. With every year, she looked ahead, the Dairy School boys would get younger and younger—until none of them would be interested in whisking her back to Boston.

Mary Bates had grown up with Winslow Berry, yet they had never given each other more than a nod or a grimace of recognition. "We seemed to be looking beyond each other, I don't know why," Father told us children—until, perhaps, they first saw each other out of the familiar place where they'd both grown up: the motley town of Dairy and the barely less motley campus of the Dairy School.

When the Thompson Female Seminary graduated my mother in June of 1939, my mother was hurt to realize that the Dairy School had already had its graduation and was closed; the fancier, out-of-town boys had gone home, and her two or three 'beaus' (as she called them)—who she might have hoped would ask her to her own graduation dance—were gone. She knew no local high school boys, and when her mother suggested Win Berry to her, my mother ran out of the dining room. 'Or I suppose I could ask Coach Bob!' she shouted to her mother. Her father, Latin Emeritus, raised his head from the dinner table where he'd been napping.

'Coach Bob?' he said. 'Is that moron here to borrow the sled again?'

Coach Bob, who was also called Iowa Bob, was no moron,

17

but to Latin Emeritus, whose stroke seemed to have fuddled his sense of time, the hired jock from the Midwest was not in the same league with the academic faculty. And years ago, when Mary Bates and Win Berry had been children, Coach Bob had come to borrow an old sleigh, once notorious for standing three years, unmoved, in the Bates front yard.

'Does the fool have a horse for it?' Latin Emeritus had asked his wife.

'No, he's going to pull it himself!' my mother's mother said. And the Bates family watched out the window while Coach Bob put little Win in the driver's seat, gripped the whiffletree in his hands behind his back, and heaved the sleigh into motion; the great sled skidded down the snowy yard and into the slippery street that was still lined with elms, in those days—'As fast as a horse could have pulled it!' my mother always said.

Iowa Bob had been the shortest interior lineman ever to play first-string football in the Big Ten. He once admitted to being so carried away he *bit* a running back after he tackled him. At Dairy, in addition to his duties with football, he coached the shot put and instructed those interested in weight lifting. But to the Bates family, Iowa Bob was too uncomplicated to be taken seriously: a funny, squat strongman with hair so short he looked bald, always jogging through the streets of town—'with a ghastly-colored sweatband around his dome,' Latin Emeritus used to say.

Since Coach Bob would live a long time, he was the only grandparent any of us children would remember.

'What's that sound?' Frank would ask, in alarm, in the middle of the night when Bob had come to live with us.

What Frank heard, and what we often heard after Coach Bob moved in, was the creaking of push-ups and the grunting of sit-ups on the old man's floor (our ceiling) above us.

'It's Iowa Bob,' Lilly whispered once. 'He's trying to stay in shape forever.'

Anyway, it wasn't Win Berry who took Mary Bates to her graduation dance. The Bates family minister, who was considerably older than my mother, but unattached, was kind enough to ask her. 'That was a long night,' Mother told us. 'I felt depressed. I was an outsider in my own hometown. But in a very short while that same minister would marry your father and me!'

They could not even have imagined it when they were 'introduced,' together with the other summer help, on the unreal green of the pampered lawn at the Arbuthnot-by-the-Sea. Even the staff introductions were formal, there. A girl was called out, by name, from a line of other girls and women; she would meet a boy called out from a line of boys and men, as if they were going to be dance partners.

'This is Mary Bates, just graduated from the Thompson Female Seminary! She'll be helping in the hotel, and with hostessing. She likes sailing, *don't* you, Mary?'

Waiters and waitresses, the grounds crew and caddies, the boat help and the kitchen staff, odd-jobbers, hostesses, chambermaids, laundry people, a plumber, and the members of the band. Ballroom dancing was very popular; the resorts farther south —like the Weirs at Laconia, and Hampton Beach—drew some of the big-name bands in the summers. But the Arbuthnot-by-the-Sea had its own band, which imitated in a cold, Maine way the big-band sound.

'And this is Winslow Berry, who likes to be called Win! *Don't* you, Win? He's going to *Harvard* in the fall!'

But my father looked straight at my mother, who smiled and turned her face away—as embarrassed for him as she was for herself. She'd never noticed what a handsome boy he was, really; he had a body as hard as Coach Bob's, but the Dairy School had exposed him to the manners, the dress, and the way with his hair that Bostonians (not Iowans) were favoring. He looked as if he already went to Harvard, whatever that must have meant to my mother then. 'Oh, I don't know what it meant,' she told us children. 'Kind of cultured, I guess. He looked like a boy who knew how to drink without getting sick. He had the darkest, brightest eyes, and whenever you looked at him you were sure he'd just been looking at you—but you could never catch him.'

My father maintained that latter ability all his life; we felt around him, always, the sense that he'd been observing us closely and affectionately—even if, when we looked at him, he seemed to be looking elsewhere, dreaming or making plans, thinking of something hard or faraway. Even when he was quite blind, to our schemes and lives, he seemed to be 'observing' us. It was a strange combination of aloofness and warmth—and the first time my mother felt it was on that tongue of bright green lawn that was framed by the gray Maine sea.

STAFF INTRODUCTIONS: 4:00 P.M.

That was when she learned he was there.

When the introductions were over, and the staff was instructed to make ready for the first cocktail hour, the first dinner, and the first evening's entertainment, my mother caught my father's eye and he came up to her.

'It will be two years before I can afford Harvard,' he said, immediately, to her.

'So I thought,' my mother said. 'But I think it's wonderful you got in,' she added quickly.

'Why *wouldn't* I have gotten in?' he asked.

Mary Bates shrugged, a gesture learned from never understanding her father (since his stroke had slurred his speech). She wore white gloves and a white hat with a veil; she was dressed for 'serving' at the first lawn party, and my father admired how nicely her hair hugged her head—it was longer in back, swept away from her face, and clamped somehow to the hat and veil in a manner both so simple and mysterious that my father fell to wondering about her.

'What are you doing in the fall?' he asked her.

Again she shrugged, but maybe my father saw in her eyes, through her white veil, that my mother was hoping to be rescued from the scenario she imagined was her future.

'We were nice to each other, that first time, I remember that,' Mother told us. 'We were both alone in a new place and we knew things about each other nobody else knew.' In those days, I imagine, that was intimate enough.

'There wasn't *any* intimacy, in those days,' Franny said once. 'Even *lovers* wouldn't fart in front of each other.'

And Franny was forceful—I frequently believed her. Even Franny's language was ahead of her time—as if she always knew where she was going; and I would never quite catch up to her.

That first evening at the Arbuthnot there was the staff band playing its imitation of the big-band sound, but there were very few guests, and even fewer dancers; the season was just beginning, and it begins slowly in Maine—it's so cold there, even in the summer. The dance hall had a deck of hard-shined wood that seemed to extend beyond the open porches that overlooked the ocean. When it rained, they had to drop awnings over the porches because the ballroom was so open, on all sides, that the rain washed in and wet the polished dance floor.

That first evening, as a special treat to the staff—and because

20

there were so few guests, and most of them had gone to bed, to get warm—the band played late. My father and mother, and the other help, were invited to dance for an hour or more. My mother always remembered that the ballroom chandelier was broken—it blinked dimly; uneven spots of color dappled the dance floor, which looked so soft and glossy in the ailing light that the floor appeared to have the texture of a candle.

'I'm glad someone I know is here,' my mother whispered to my father, who had rather formally asked her to dance and danced with her very stiffly.

'But you don't know me,' Father said.

'I said that,' Father told us, 'so that your mother would shrug again.' And when she shrugged, thinking him impossibly difficult to talk to—and perhaps superior—my father was convinced that his attraction to her was not a fluke.

'But I *want* you to know me,' he told her, 'and I want to know you.'

('Yuck,' Franny always said, at this point in the story.)

The sound of an engine was drowning out the band, and many of the dancers left the floor to see what the commotion was. My mother was grateful for the interruption: she couldn't think of what to say to Father. They walked, not holding hands, to the porch that faced the docks; they saw, under the dock lights swaying on the overhead wires, a lobster boat putting out to sea. The boat had just deposited on the dock a dark motorcycle, which was now roaring—revving itself, perhaps to free its tubes and pipes of the damp salt air. Its rider seemed intent on getting the noise right before he put the machine in gear. The motorcycle had a sidecar attached, and in it sat a dark figure, hulking and still, like a man made awkward by too many clothes.

'It's Freud,' someone on the staff said. And other, older members of the staff cried out, 'Yes! It's Freud! It's Freud and State o' Maine!'

My mother and father both thought that 'State o' Maine' was the name of the motorcycle. But then the band stopped playing, seeing its audience was gone, and some of the band members, too, joined the dancers on the porch.

'Freud!' people yelled.

My father always told us he was amused to imagine that *the* Freud would any moment motor over beneath the porch and, in the high-strung lights lining the perfect gravel driveway, introduce himself to the staff. So here comes Sigmund Freud, Father thought: he was falling in love, so anything was possible.

21

But this was not *that* Freud, of course; it was the year when *that* Freud died. *This* Freud was a Viennese Jew with a limp and an unpronounceable name, who in the summers since he had been working at the Arbuthnot (since 1933, when he'd left his native Austria) had earned the name Freud for his abilities to soothe the distress of the staff and guests alike; he was an entertainer, and since he came from Vienna and was a Jew, 'Freud' seemed only natural to some of the odd, foreign wits at the Arbuthnot-by-the-Sea. The name seemed especially appropriate when, in 1937, Freud arrived for the summer on a new Indian motorcycle with a sidecar he'd made all by himself.

'Who gets to ride behind and who gets to ride in the sidecar, Freud?' the working girls at the hotel teased him—because he was so frightfully scarred and ugly with pockmarks ('holes from the boils!' he called them) that no woman would ever love him.

'Nobody rides with me but State o' Maine,' Freud said, and he unsnapped the canvas canopy from the sidecar. In the sidecar sat a bear, black as exhaust, thicker with muscles than Iowa Bob, warier than any stray dog. Freud had retrieved this bear from a logging camp in the north of the state and had convinced the management of the Arbuthnot that he could train the beast to entertain the guests. Freud, when he emigrated from Austria, had arrived in Boothbay Harbor, by boat, from New York, with two job descriptions in capital letters on his work papers: EXPERIENCE AS ANIMAL TRAINER AND KEEPER; GOOD MECHANICAL APTITUDE. There being no animals available, he fixed the vehicles at the Arbuthnot and properly put them to rest for the non-tourist months, when he traveled to the logging camps and the paper mills as a mechanic.

All that time, he later told my father, he'd been looking for a bear. Bears, Freud said, were where the money was.

When my father saw the man dismount from the motorcycle under the ballroom porch, he wondered at the cheers from the veteran members of the staff; when Freud helped the figure from the sidecar, my mother's first thought was that the passenger was an old, old woman—the motorcyclist's mother, perhaps (a stout woman wrapped in a dark blanket).

'State o' Maine!' yelled someone in the band, and blew his horn.

My mother and father saw the bear begin to dance. He danced away from Freud on his hind legs; he dropped to all fours and did a short lap or two around the motorcycle. Freud stood on the motorcycle and clapped. The bear called State o' Maine began to

22

clap, too. When my mother felt my father take her hand into his —they were not clapping—she did not resist him; she gave back equal pressure, both of them never taking their eyes from the bulky bear performing below them, and my mother thought: I am nineteen and my life is just beginning.

'You felt that, *really?*' Franny always asked.

'Everything is relative,' Mother would say. 'But that's what I felt, yes. I felt my life *start.*'

'Holy cow,' said Frank.

'Was it me or the bear you liked?' Father asked.

'Don't be silly,' Mother said. 'It was the whole thing. It was the start of my life.'

And that line had the same fix-me-to-the-spot quality of Father's line about the bear ('He was too old to be a bear anymore'). I felt rooted to the story when my mother said that this was the *start* of her life; it was as if I could *see* Mother's life, like the motorcycle, after long revving, finally chunk into gear and lurch forward.

And what must my father have imagined, reaching for her hand just because a bear was brought by a lobster boat into his life?

'I knew it would be *my* bear,' Father told us. 'I don't know how.' And perhaps it was this knowledge—that he saw something that would be his—that made him reach for my mother, too.

You can see why we children asked so many questions. It is a vague story, the kind parents prefer to tell.

That first night they saw Freud and his bear, my father and mother did not even kiss. When the band broke up, and the help retired to the male and female dormitories—the slightly less elegant buildings separate from the main hotel—my father and mother went down to the docks and watched the water. If they talked, they never told us children what they said. There must have been a few classy sailboats there, and even the private piers in Maine were sure to have a lobster boat or two moored off them. There was probably a dinghy, and my father suggested borrowing it for a short row; my mother probably refused. Fort Popham was a ruin, then, and not the tourist attraction it is today; but if there were any lights on the Fort Popham shore, they would have been visible from the Arbuthnot-by-the-Sea. Also, the broad mouth of the Kennebec River, at Bay Point, had a bell buoy and a light, and there might have been a lighthouse

23

on Stage Island as long ago as 1939—my father never remembered.

But generally, in those days, it would have been a dark coast, so that when the white sloop sailed toward them—out of Boston, or New York: out of the southwest and civilization, anyway —my mother and father must have seen it very clearly and watched it undistracted for the time it took to come alongside the dock. My father caught the mooring line; he always told us he was at the point of panic about what to do with the rope—tie it up to something or tug it—when the man in the white dinner jacket, black slacks, and black dress shoes stepped easily off the deck and climbed the ladder up to the dock and took the rope from my father's hands. Effortlessly, the man guided the sloop past the end of the dock before he threw the rope back on board. 'You're free!' he called to the boat, then. My mother and father claimed they saw no sailors on board, but the sloop slipped away, back to the sea—its yellow lights leaving like sinking glass—and the man in the dinner jacket turned to my father and said, 'Thanks for the hand. Are you new here?'

'Yes, we both are,' Father said.

The man's perfect clothes were unaffected by his voyage. For so early in the summer he was very tanned, and he offered my mother and father cigarettes from a handsome flat black box. They didn't smoke. 'I'd hoped to catch the last dance,' the man said, 'but the band has retired?'

'Yes,' my mother said. At nineteen, my mother and father had never seen anyone quite like this man. 'He had obscene confidence,' my mother told us.

'He had money,' Father said.

'Have Freud and the bear arrived?' the man asked.

'Yes,' Father said. 'And the motorcycle.'

The man in the white dinner jacket smoked hungrily, but neatly, while he looked at the dark hotel; very few rooms were lit, but the outdoor lights strung to illuminate the paths, the hedgerows, and the docks shone on the man's tanned face and made his eyes narrow and were reflected on the black, moving sea. 'Freud's a Jew, you know,' the man said. 'It's a good thing he got out of Europe when he did, you know. Europe's going to be no place for Jews. My broker told me.'

This solemn news must have impressed my father, eager to enter Harvard—and the world—and not yet aware that a war would interrupt his plans for a while. The man in the white dinner jacket caused my father to take my mother's hand into

24

his, for the second time that evening, and again she gave back equal pressure as they politely waited for the man to finish his cigarette, or say good night, or go on.

But all he said was, 'And the *world's* going to be no place for *bears!*' His teeth were as white as his dinner jacket when he laughed, and with the wind my father and mother didn't hear the hiss of his cigarette entering the ocean—or the sloop coming alongside again. Suddenly the man stepped to the ladder, and only when he slipped quickly down the rungs did Mary Bates and Win Berry realize that the white sloop was gliding under the ladder and the man was perfectly in time to drop to its deck. No rope passed hands. The sloop, not under sail but chugging slowly under other power, turned southwest (toward Boston, or New York, again)—unafraid of night travel—and what the man in the white dinner jacket last called to them was lost in the sputter of the engine, the slap of the hull on the sea, and the wind that blew the gulls by (like party hats, with feathers, bobbing in the water after drunks had thrown them there). All his life my father wished he'd heard what the man had to say.

It was Freud who told my father that he'd seen the *owner* of the Arbuthnot-by-the-Sea.

'*Ja,* that was him, all right,' Freud said. 'That's how he comes, just a couple of times a summer. Once he danced with a girl who worked here—the last dance; we never saw her again. A week later, some other guy came for her things.'

'What's his name?' Father asked.

'Maybe *he's* Arbuthnot, you know?' Freud said. 'Someone said he's Dutch, but I never heard his name. He knows all about *Europe,* though—I can tell you that!'

My father was dying to ask about the Jews; he felt my mother nudge him in his ribs. They were sitting on one of the putting greens, after hours—when the green turned blue in the moonlight and the red golfing flag flapped in the cup. The bear called State o' Maine had his muzzle off and was trying to scratch himself against the thin stem of the flag.

'Come here, stupid!' Freud said to the bear, but the bear paid no attention to him.

'Is your family still in Vienna?' my mother asked Freud.

'My sister is my only family,' he said. 'And I don't hear nothing from her since a year ago March.'

'A year ago March,' my father said, 'the Nazis took Austria.'

'*Ja,* you're telling *me?*' Freud said.

State o' Maine, frustrated by the lack of resistance the flagpole gave him—for scratching—slapped the flagpole out of the cup and sent it spinning across the putting green.

'Jesus God,' said Freud. 'He's going to start digging holes in the golf course if we don't go somewhere.' My father put the silly flag, marked '18,' back into the cup. My mother had been given the night off from 'serving' and was still in her chambermaid's uniform; she ran ahead of the bear, calling him.

The bear rarely ran. He shambled—and never very far from the motorcycle. He rubbed up against the motorcycle so much that the red fender paint was shined as silvery as the chrome, and the conical point of the sidecar was dented in from his pushing against it. He had often burned himself on the pipes, going to rub against the machine too soon after it had been driven, so that there were ominous patches of charred bear hair stuck to the pipes—as if the motorcycle itself had been (at one time) a furry animal. Correspondingly, State o' Maine had ragged patches in his black coat where his fur was missing, or singed flat and brown—the dull color of dried seaweed.

What exactly the bear was trained to do was a mystery to everyone—even something of a mystery to Freud.

Their 'act' together, performed before the lawn parties in the late afternoon, was more of an effort for the motorcycle and Freud than it was an effort for the bear. Around and around Freud would drive, the bear in the sidecar, canopy snapped off —the bear like a pilot in an open cockpit without controls. State o' Maine usually wore his muzzle in public: it was a red leather thing that reminded my father of the face masks occasionally worn in the game of lacrosse. The muzzle made the bear look smaller; it further scrunched up his already wrinkled face and elongated his nose so that, more than ever, he resembled an overweight dog.

Around and around they would drive, and just before the bored guests returned to their conversation and abandoned this oddity, Freud would stop the motorcycle, dismount, with the engine running, and walk to the sidecar, where he would harass the bear in German. This was funny to the crowd, largely because someone speaking German was funny, but Freud would persist until the bear, slowly, would climb out of the sidecar and mount the motorcycle, sitting in the driver's seat, his heavy paws on the handlebars, his short hind legs not able to reach the footposts or the rear-brake controls. Freud would climb into the sidecar and order the bear to drive off.

Nothing would happen. Freud would sit in the sidecar, protesting their lack of motion; the bear would grimly hold the handlebars, jounce in the saddle, paddle his legs back and forth, as if he were treading water.

'State o' Maine!' someone would shout. The bear would nod, with a kind of embarrassed dignity, and stay where he was.

Freud, now raging in a German everyone loved to hear, climbed out of the sidecar and approached the bear at the controls. He attempted to show the animal how to operate the motorcycle.

'Clutch!' Freud would say: he'd hold the bear's big paw over the clutch handle. 'Throttle!' he would shout: he'd rev the motorcycle with the bear's other paw. Freud's 1937 Indian had a gearshift mounted alongside the gas tank, so that for a frightening moment the driver needed to take one hand from the handlebars to engage or change gears. 'Shift!' Freud cried, and slammed the cycle into gear.

Whereupon the bear on the motorcycle would proceed across the lawn, the throttle held at a steady low growl, neither accelerating nor slowing down but moving resolutely toward the smug and beautifully attired guests—the men, even fresh from their sporting events, wore hats; even the male swimmers at the Arbuthnot-by-the-Sea wore bathing suits with tops, although the thirties saw trunks, on men, prevailing more and more. Not in Maine. The shoulders of the jackets, men's and women's, were padded; the men wore white flannels, wide and baggy; the sportswomen wore saddle shoes with bobby socks; the 'dressed' women wore natural waistlines, their sleeves frequently puffed. All of them made quite a colorful stir as the bear bore down on them, pursued by Freud.

'*Nein! Nein!* You dumb bear!'

And State o' Maine, his expression under the muzzle a mystery to the guests, drove forward, turning only slightly, hulking over the handlebars.

'You stupid animal!' Freud cried.

The bear drove away—always through a party tent without striking a support pole or snagging the white linen tablecloths that covered the tables of food and the bar. He was pursued by waiters over the rich expanse of lawn. The tennis players cheered from the courts, but as the bear drew nearer to them, they abandoned their game.

The bear either knew or didn't know what he was doing, but he never hit a hedge, and he never went too fast; he never drove down to the docks and attempted to board a yacht or a lobster boat. And Freud always caught up with him, when it seemed that the guests had seen enough. Freud mounted the cycle behind the bear; hugging himself to the broad back, he guided the beast and the '37 Indian back to the lawn party.

'So, a few *kinks* to work out!' he'd call to the crowd. 'A few flies in the ointment, but *nichts* to worry! In no time he will get it right!'

That was the act. It never changed. That was all Freud had taught State o' Maine; he claimed it was all that the bear could learn.

'He's not so smart a bear,' Freud told Father. 'I got him when he was too old. I thought he'd be fine. He was tamed as a cub. But the logging camps taught him nothing. Those people have no manners, anyway. They're just animals, too. They kept the bear as a pet, they fed him enough so he wouldn't get nasty, but they just let him hang around and be lazy. Like them. I think this bear's got a drinking problem because of them loggers. He don't drink now—I don't let him—but he acts like he wants to, you know?'

Father *didn't* know. He thought Freud was wonderful and the 1937 Indian was the most beautiful machine he had ever met. On days off, my father would take my mother driving on the coast roads, the two of them hugged together and cool in the salt air, but they were never alone: the motorcycle could not be driven away from the Arbuthnot without State o' Maine in the sidecar. The bear went berserk if the motorcycle tried to drive away without him; it was the only event that could make the old bear run. A bear can run surprisingly fast.

'Go ahead, you try to get away,' Freud told Father. 'But better push it down the driveway, all the way out to the road, before you start the engine. And the first time you try it, don't take poor Mary with you. Wear lots of heavy clothes, because if he catches you, he'll paw you all over. He won't be mad—just excited. Go on, try it. But if you look back, after a few miles, and he's still coming, you better stop and bring him back. He'll have a heart attack, or he'll get lost—he's so stupid.

'He don't know how to hunt, or anything. He's helpless if you don't feed him. He's a pet, he's not a real animal no more. And he's only about twice as smart as a German shepherd. And that's not smart enough for the world, you know.'

'The world?' Lilly would always ask, her eyes popping.

But the world for my father, in the summer of '39, was new

28

and affectionate with my mother's shy touches, the roar of the '37 Indian and the strong smell of State o' Maine, the cold Maine nights and the wisdom of Freud.

His limp, of course, was from a motorcycle accident; the leg had been set improperly. 'Discrimination,' Freud claimed.

Freud was small, strong, alert as an animal, a peculiar color (like a green olive cooked slowly until it almost browned). He had glossy black hair, a strange patch of which grew on his cheek, just under one eye: it was a silky-soft spot of hair, bigger than most moles, at least the size of an average coin, more distinctive than any birthmark, and as naturally a part of Freud's face as a limpet attached to a Maine rock.

'It's because my brain is so enormous,' Freud told Mother and Father. 'My brain don't leave room on my head for hair, so the hair gets jealous and grows a little where it shouldn't.'

'Maybe it was bear hair,' Frank said once, seriously, and Franny screamed and hugged me around the neck so hard that I bit my tongue.

'Frank is so weird!' she cried. 'Show us *your* bear hair, Frank.' Poor Frank was approaching puberty at the time; he was ahead of his time, and he was very embarrassed about it. But not even Franny could distract us from the mesmerizing spell of Freud and his bear; we children were as caught up with them as my father and mother must have been that summer of 1939.

Some nights, Father told us, he would walk my mother to her dorm and kiss her good night. If Freud was asleep, Father would unchain State o' Maine from the motorcycle and slip his muzzle off so the bear could eat. Then my father would take him fishing. There was a tarp staked low over the motorcycle, like an open tent, which protected State o' Maine from the rain, and Father would leave his fishing gear wrapped in the flap of that tarp for these occasions.

The two of them would go to the Bay Point dock; it was beyond the row of hotel piers, and choppy with lobster boats and fishermen's dinghies. Father and State o' Maine would sit on the end of the dock while Father cast what he called spooners, for pollack. He would feed the pollack live to State o' Maine. There was only one evening when there was an altercation between them. Father usually caught three or four pollack; that was enough—for both Father and State o' Maine—and then they'd go home. But one evening the pollack weren't running, and after an hour without a nibble Father got up off the dock to take the bear back to his muzzle and chain.

'Come on,' he said. 'No fish in the ocean tonight.'

State o' Maine wouldn't leave.

'Come on!' Father said. But State o' Maine wouldn't let *Father* leave the dock, either.

'Earl!' the bear growled. Father sat down and kept fishing. 'Earl!' State o' Maine complained. Father cast and cast, he changed spooners, he tried everything. If he could have dug for clam worms down on the mud flats, he could have bottom-fished for flounder, but State o' Maine became unfriendly whenever Father attempted to leave the dock. Father contemplated jumping in and swimming ashore; he could sneak back to the dorm for Freud, then, and they could come recapture State o' Maine with food from the hotel. But after a while Father got into the spirit of the evening and said, 'All right, all right, so you want fish? We'll catch a fish, goddamn it!'

A little before dawn a lobsterman came down to the dock to put out to sea. He was going to pull his traps and he had some new traps with him to drop, and—unfortunately—he had bait with him, too. State o' Maine smelled the bait.

'Better give it to him,' Father said.

'Earl!' said State o' Maine, and the lobsterman gave the bear all his baitfish.

'We'll repay you,' Father said. 'First thing.'

'I know what I'd like to do, "first thing," ' the lobsterman said. 'I'd like to put that *bear* in my traps and use *him* for bait. I'd like to see him *et up* by lobsters!'

'Earl!' said State o' Maine.

'Better not tease him,' Father told the lobsterman, who agreed.

'*Ja*, he's not so smart, that bear,' Freud told Father. 'I should have warned you. He can be funny about food. They fed him too much at the logging camps; he ate all the time—lots of junk. And sometimes, now, he just decides he's not eating enough —or he wants a drink, or something. You got to remember: don't ever sit down to eat yourself if you haven't fed him first. He don't like that.'

So State o' Maine was always well fed before he performed at the lawn parties—for the white linen tablecloths were everywhere burdened with hors d'oeuvres, fancy raw fish, and grilled meats, and if State o' Maine had been hungry, there might have been trouble. But Freud stuffed State o' Maine before the act, and the bloated bear drove the motorcycle calmly. He was placid, even bored, at the handlebars, as if the greatest physical need soon to seize him would be an awesome belch, or the need to move his great bear's bowels.

'It's a dumb act and I'm losing money,' Freud said. 'This place is too fancy. There's only snobs who come here. I should go someplace with a little cruder crowd, someplace where there's bingo games—not just dancing. I should be places that are more *democratic*—places where they bet on dog fights, you know?'

My father *didn't* know, but he must have marveled at such places—rougher than the Weirs at Laconia, or even Hampton Beach. Places where there were more drunks, and more careless money for an act with a performing bear. The Arbuthnot was simply too refined a crowd for a man like Freud and a bear like State o' Maine. It was too refined, even, to appreciate that motorcycle: the 1937 Indian.

But my father realized that Freud felt no ambition drawing him away. Freud had an easy summer at the Arbuthnot; the bear simply hadn't turned out to be the gold mine Freud had hoped for. What Freud wanted was a different bear.

'With a bear this dumb,' he told my mother and father, 'there's no point in trying to better my take. And you got other problems when you hustle them cheap resorts.'

My mother took my father's hand and gave it firm, warning pressure—perhaps because she saw him imagining those 'other problems,' those 'cheap resorts.' But my father was thinking of his tuition at Harvard; he *liked* the 1937 Indian and the bear called State o' Maine. He hadn't seen Freud put the slightest effort into training the bear, and Win Berry was a boy who believed in himself; Coach Bob's son was a young man who imagined he could do anything he could imagine.

He had earlier planned that, after the summer at the Arbuthnot, he would go to Cambridge, take a room, and find a job—perhaps in Boston. He would get to know the area around Harvard and get employed in the vicinity, so that as soon as there was money for tuition, he could enroll. This way, he imagined, he might even be able to keep a part-time job *and* go to Harvard. My mother, of course, had liked this plan because Boston to Dairy, and back again, was an easy trip on the Boston & Maine —the trains ran regularly then. She was already imagining the visits from my father—long weekends—and perhaps the occasional, though proper, visits she might make to Cambridge or Boston to see him.

31

'What do you know about bears, anyway?' she asked. 'Or motorcycles?'

She didn't like, either, his idea that—*if* Freud was unwilling to part with his Indian or his bear—Father would travel the logging camps with Freud. Win Berry was a strong boy, but not vulgar. And Mother imagined the camps to be vulgar places, from which Father would not emerge the same—or would not emerge at all.

She needn't have worried. That summer and how it would end were obviously planned more hugely and inevitably than any trivial arrangements my father and mother could imagine ahead of them. The summer of '39 was as inevitable as the war in Europe, as it would soon be called, and all of them—Freud, Mary Bates, and Winslow Berry—were as lightly tossed along by the summer as the gulls knocked about in the rough currents at the mouth of the Kennebec.

One night in late August, when Mother had served at the evening meal and had only just had time to change into her saddle shoes and the long skirt she played croquet in, Father was called from his room to assist with an injured man. Father ran past the lawn for croquet where Mother was waiting for him. She held a mallet over her shoulder. The Christmas-like light bulbs strung in the trees lit the lawn for croquet in such a ghostly way that—to my father—my mother 'looked like an angel holding a club.'

'I'll be right with you,' Father said to her. 'Someone's been hurt.'

She came with him, and some other running men, and they ran down to the hotel piers. Alongside the dock was a throbbing big ship aglow with lights. A band with too much brass was playing on board, and the strong fuel smell and motor exhaust in the salt air mixed with the smell of crushed fruit. It appeared that some enormous bowl of alcoholic fruit punch was being served to the ship's guests, and they were spilling it over themselves or washing the deck down with it. At the end of the dock a man lay on his side, bleeding from a wound in his cheek: he had stumbled coming up the ladder and had torn his face on a mooring cleat.

He was a large man, his face florid in the blue wash of the light from the moon, and he sat up as soon as anybody touched him. '*Scheiss!*' he said.

My father and mother recognized the German word for 'shit'

32

from Freud's many performances. With the assistance of several strong young men the German was brought to his feet. He had bled, magnificently, over his white dinner jacket, which seemed large enough to clothe two men; his blue-black cummerbund resembled a curtain, and his matching bow tie stuck up straight at his throat, like a twisted propeller. He was rather jowly and he smelled strongly of the fruit punch served on board ship. He bellowed to someone. From on board came a chorus of German, and a tall, tanned woman in an evening dress with yellow lace, or ruching, came up the dock's ladder like a panther wearing silk. The bleeding man seized her and leaned on her so heavily that the woman, despite her own obvious strength and agility, was pushed into my father, who helped her maintain her balance. She was much younger than the man, my mother noted, and also German—speaking in an easy, clucking manner to him, while he continued to bleat and gesture, nastily, to those members of the German chorus left on board. Up the dock, and up the gravel driveway, the big couple wove.

At the entrance to the Arbuthnot, the woman turned to my father and said, with a controlled accent: 'He *vill* need stitches, *ja?* Of course you *haf* a doctor.'

The desk manager whispered to Father, 'Get Freud.'

'Stitches?' Freud said. 'The doctor lives all the way in Bath, and he's a drunk. But I know how to stitch anybody.'

The desk manager ran out to the dorm and shouted for Freud.

'Get on your Indian and bring old Doc Todd here! We'll sober him up when he arrives,' the manager said. 'But for God's sake, get going!'

'It will take an hour, *if* I can find him,' Freud said. 'You know I can handle stitching. Just get me the proper clothes.'

'This is different,' the desk manager said. 'I think it's different, Freud—I mean, the guy. He's a *German*, Freud. And it's his *face* that's cut.'

Freud stripped his work clothes off his pitted, olive body; he began to comb his damp hair. 'The clothes,' he said. 'Just bring them. It's too complicated to get old Doc Todd.'

'The wound is on his *face*, Freud,' Father said.

'So what's a face?' said Freud. 'Just skin, *ja?* Like on the hands or foots. I've sewn up lots of foots before. Ax and saw cuts—them stupid loggers.'

Outside, the other Germans from the ship were bringing trunks and heavy luggage the shortest distance from the pier to the entranceway—across the eighteenth green. 'Look at those

33

swine,' Freud said. 'Putting dents where the little white ball will get caught.'

The headwaiter came into Freud's room. It was the best room in the men's dorm—no one knew how Freud ended up with it. The headwaiter began to undress.

'Everything but your jacket, dummy,' Freud said to him. 'Doctors don't wear waiters' jackets.'

Father had a black tuxedo jacket that more or less agreed with the waiter's black pants, and he brought it to Freud.

'I've told them, a million times,' the headwaiter said—although he looked strange saying this with any authority, while he was naked. 'There should be a doctor who actually lives at the hotel.'

When Freud was all dressed, he said, 'There *is*.' The desk manager ran back to the main hotel ahead of him. Father watched the headwaiter looking helplessly at Freud's abandoned clothes; they were not very clean and they smelled strongly of State o' Maine; the waiter, clearly, did not want to put them on. Father ran to catch up with Freud.

The Germans, now in the driveway outside the entrance, were grinding a large trunk across the gravel; someone would have to rake the stones in the morning. 'Is der not enough help at dis hotel to help us?' one of the Germans yelled.

On the spotless counter, in the serving room between the main dining hall and the kitchen, the big German with the gashed cheek lay like a corpse, his pale head resting on his folded-up dinner jacket, which would never be white again; his propeller of a dark tie sagged limply at his throat, his cummerbund heaved.

'It'z a *goot* doctor?' he asked the desk manager. The young giantess in the gown with the yellow ruching held the German's hand.

'An excellent doctor,' the desk manager said.

'Especially at stitching,' my father said. My mother held his hand.

'It'z not too civilized a hotel, I tink,' the German said.

'It'z in der *vilderness*,' the tawny, athletic woman said, but she dismissed herself with a laugh. 'But it'z *nicht* so bad a cut, I tink,' she told Father and Mother, and the desk manager. 'We don't need too goot a doctor to fix it up, I tink.'

'Just so it'z no *Jew*,' the German said. He coughed. Freud was in the small room, though none of them had seen him; he was having trouble threading a needle.

34

'It'z no Jew, I'm sure.' The tawny princess laughed. 'They *haf* no Jews in Maine!' When she saw Freud, she didn't look so sure.

'*Guten Abend, meine Dame und Herr,*' Freud said. '*Was ist los?*'

My father said that Freud, in the black tuxedo, was a figure so runted and distorted by his boil scars that he immediately looked as if he had stolen his clothes; the clothes appeared to have been stolen from at *least* two different people. Even his most visible instrument was black—a black spool of thread, which Freud grasped in the gray-rubber kitchen gloves the dishwashers wore. The best needle to be found in the laundry room of the Arbuthnot looked too large in Freud's small hand, as if he'd grabbed the needle used to sew the sails for the racing boats. Perhaps he *had*.

'Herr *Doktor?*' the German asked, his face whitening. His wound appeared to stop bleeding, instantly.

'Herr Doktor Professor Freud,' Freud said, moving in close and leering at the wound.

'Freud?' the woman said.

'*Ja,*' Freud said.

When he poured the first shot glass of whiskey into the German's cut, the whiskey washed into the German's eyes.

'Ooops!' said Freud.

'I'm blind! I'm blind!' the German sang.

'*Nein,* you're *nicht* blind,' Freud said. 'But you should have shut your eyes.' He splashed another glass in the wound; then he went to work.

In the morning the manager asked Freud *not* to perform with State o' Maine until after the Germans left—they were leaving as soon as ample provisions could be loaded aboard their large vessel. Freud refused to remain attired as a doctor; he insisted on tinkering with the '37 Indian in his mechanic's costume, so it was in such attire that the German found him, seaward of the tennis courts, not exactly hidden from the main hotel grounds and the lawns of play, but discreetly off to himself. The huge, bandaged face of the German was badly swollen and he approached Freud warily, as if the little motorcycle mechanic might be the alarming twin brother of the 'Herr Doktor Professor' of the night before.

'*Nein,* it'z *him,*' said the tanned woman, trailing on the German's arm.

35

'What's the Jew doctor fixing this morning?' the German asked Freud.

'My hobby,' Freud said, not looking up. My father, who was handing Freud his motorcycle tools—like an assistant to a surgeon—took a firmer grip on the three-quarters-inch wrench.

The German couple did not see the bear. State o' Maine was scratching himself against the fence of the tennis courts—making deep, thrusting scratches with his back against the metal mesh, groaning to himself and rocking to a rhythm akin to masturbation. My mother, to make him more comfortable, had removed his muzzle.

'I never heard of such a motorcycle as *dis*,' the German told Freud, critically. 'It'z *junk*, I tink, *ja?* What's an Indian? I never heard of it.'

'You should try riding it yourself,' Freud said. 'Want to?'

The German woman seemed unsure of the idea—and quite sure that *she* didn't want to—but the idea clearly appealed to the German. He stood close to the motorcycle and touched its gas tank and ran his fingers over its clutch cable and fondled the knob to the gearshift. He seized the throttle at the handlebars and gave it a sharp twist. He felt the soft rubber tube—like an exposed vital organ among so much metal—where the gas ran from the tank into the carburetor. He opened the valve to the carburetor, without asking Freud's permission; he tickled the valve and wet his fingers with gasoline, then wiped his fingers on the seat.

'You don't mind, *Herr Doktor?*' the German asked Freud.

'No, go on,' Freud said. 'Take it for a spin.'

And that was the summer of '39: my father saw how it would end, but he could not move to interfere. 'I couldn't have stopped it,' Father always said. 'It was *coming*, like the war.'

Mother, at the tennis court fence, saw the German mount the motorcycle; she thought she'd better put State o' Maine's muzzle back on. But the bear was impatient with her; he shook his head and scratched himself harder.

'Just a standard kick starter, *ja?*' the German asked.

'Just kick it over and she'll start right up,' Freud said. Something about the way he and Father stepped away from the motorcycle made the young German woman join them; she stepped back, too.

'Here goes!' the German said, and kicked the starter down.

With the first catch of the engine, before the first rev, the bear called State o' Maine stood erect against the tennis court fence,

36

the coarse fur on his dense chest stiffening; he stared across center court at the 1937 Indian that was trying to go somewhere without him. When the German chunked the machine into gear and began, rather timidly, to advance across the grass to a nearby gravel path, State o' Maine dropped to all fours and charged. He was in full stride when he crossed center court and broke up the doubles game—racquets falling, balls rolling loose. The player who was playing net chose to *hug* the net instead; he shut his eyes as the bear tore by him.

'Earl!' cried State o' Maine, but the German on the throaty '37 Indian couldn't hear anything.

The German woman heard, however, and turned—with Father and Freud—to see the bear. '*Gott!* Vut vilderness!' she cried, and fainted sideways against my father, who wrestled her gently to the lawn.

When the German saw that a bear was after him, he had not yet got his bearings; he was unsure which way the main road was. If he'd found the main road, of course, he could have outdistanced the bear, but confined to the narrow paths and walkways of the hotel grounds, and the soft fields for sports, he lacked the necessary speed.

'Earl!' growled the bear. The German swerved across the croquet lawn and headed for the picnic tents where they were setting up for lunch. The bear was on the motorcycle in less than twenty-five yards, clumsily trying to mount behind the German —as if State o' Maine had finally learned Freud's driving lesson, and was about to insist that the act be performed properly.

The German would not allow Freud to stitch him up *this* time, and even Freud confessed that it was too big a job for him. 'What a mess,' Freud wondered aloud to my father. 'Such a lot of stitches—not for me. I couldn't stand to hear him bawl all the time it would take.'

So the German was transported, by the Coast Guard, to the hospital at Bath. State o' Maine was concealed in the laundry room so that the bear's mythical status as 'a wild animal' could be confirmed.

'Out of the *voods*, it came,' said the revived German woman. 'It must haf been *incensed* by der noise from der motorcycle.'

'A she-bear with young cubs,' Freud explained. '*Sehr* treacherous at this time of year.'

But the management of the Arbuthnot-by-the-Sea would not allow the matter to be dismissed so easily; Freud knew that.

'I'm leaving before I have to talk with *him* again,' Freud told Father and Mother. They knew that Freud meant the owner of the Arbuthnot, the man in the white dinner jacket who occasionally showed up for the last dance. 'I can just hear him, the big shot: "Now, Freud, you knew the risk—we discussed it. When *I* agreed to have the animal here, *we* agreed he would be *your* responsibility." And if he tells me I'm a lucky Jew—to be in his fucking America in the first place—I will let State o' Maine *eat* him!' Freud said. 'Him and his fancy cigarettes, I don't need. This isn't my kind of hotel, anyway.'

The bear, nervous at being confined in the laundry room and worried to see Freud packing his clothes as fast as they came out of the wash—still wet—began to growl to himself. 'Earl!' he whispered.

'Oh, shut up!' Freud yelled. 'You're not my kind of bear, either.'

'It was my fault,' my mother said. 'I shouldn't have taken his muzzle off.'

'Those were just love bites,' Freud said. 'It was the brute's claws that really carved that fucker up!'

'If he hadn't tried to pull State o' Maine's fur,' Father said, 'I don't think it would have gotten so bad.'

'Of course it wouldn't have!' Freud said. 'Who likes to have hair pulled?'

'Earl!' complained State o' Maine.

'That should be your name: "Earl!" ' Freud told the bear. 'You're so stupid, that's all you ever say.'

'But what will you do?' Father asked Freud. 'Where can you go?'

'Back to Europe,' Freud said. 'They got smart bears there.'

'They have Nazis there,' Father said.

'Give me a smart bear and fuck the Nazis,' Freud said.

'I'll take care of State o' Maine,' Father said.

'You can do better than that,' Freud said. 'You can *buy* him. Two hundred dollars, and what you got for clothes. *These* are all wet!' he shouted, throwing his clothes.

'Earl!' said the bear, distressed.

'Watch your language, Earl,' Freud told him.

'Two hundred dollars?' Mother asked.

'That's all they've paid me, so far,' Father said.

'I know what they pay you,' Freud said. 'That's why it's only two hundred dollars. Of course, it's for the motorcycle, too. You've seen why you need to keep the Indian, *ja?* State o'

Maine don't get in cars; they make him throw up. And some woodsman chained him in a pickup once—I saw that. The dumb bear tore the tailgate off and beat in the rear window and mauled the guy in the cab. So don't *you* be dumb. Buy the Indian.'

'Two hundred dollars,' Father repeated.

'Now for your clothes,' Freud said. He left his own wet things on the laundry room floor. The bear tried to follow them to my father's room, but Freud told my mother to take State o' Maine outside and chain him to the motorcycle.

'He knows you're leaving and he's nervous, poor thing,' Mother said.

'He just misses the motorcycle,' Freud said, but he let the bear come upstairs—although the Arbuthnot had asked him not to allow this.

'What do I care now what they allow?' Freud said, trying on my father's clothes. My mother watched up and down the hall; bears *and* women were not allowed in the men's dorm.

'My clothes are all too *big* for you,' my father told Freud when Freud had dressed himself.

'I'm still growing,' said Freud, who must have been at least forty then. 'If I'd had the right clothes, I'd be bigger now.' He wore three of my father's suit pants, one pair right over the other; he wore two suit jackets, the pockets stuffed with underwear and socks, and he carried a third jacket over his shoulder. 'Why trouble with suitcases?' he asked.

'But how will you *get* to Europe?' Mother whispered into the room.

'By crossing the Atlantic Ocean,' Freud said. 'Come in here,' he said to Mother; he took my mother's and father's hands and joined them together. 'You're only teen-agers,' he told them, 'so listen to me: you are in love. We start from this assumption, *ja?*' And although my mother and father had never admitted any such thing to each other, they both nodded while Freud held their hands. 'Okay,' Freud said. 'Now, three things from this follow. You promise me you will agree to these three things?'

'I promise,' said my father.

'So do I,' Mother said.

'Okay,' said Freud. 'Here's number one: you get married, right away, before some clods and whores change your minds. Got it? You get married, even though it will cost you.'

'Yes,' my parents agreed.

'Here's number two,' Freud said, looking only at my father.

39

'You *go* to Harvard—you promise me—even though it will cost you.'

'But I'll already be married,' my father said.

'I said it will cost you, didn't I?' Freud said. 'You promise me: you'll go to Harvard. You take *every* opportunity given you in this world, even if you have too many opportunities. One day the opportunities stop, you know?'

'I want you to go to Harvard, anyway,' Mother told Father.

'Even though it will cost me,' Father said, but he agreed to go.

'We're up to number three,' Freud said. 'You ready?' And he turned to my mother; he dropped my father's hand, he even shoved it away from him so that he was holding Mother's hand all alone. 'Forgive him,' Freud told her, 'even though it will cost you.'

'Forgive me for what?' Father said.

'Just forgive him,' Freud said, looking only at my mother. She shrugged.

'And *you!*' Freud said to the bear, who was sniffing around under Father's bed. Freud startled State o' Maine, who'd found a tennis ball under the bed and put it in his mouth.

'Urp!' the bear said. Out came the tennis ball.

'You,' Freud said to the bear. 'May you one day be grateful that you were rescued from the disgusting world of *nature!*'

That was all. It was a wedding and a benediction, my mother always said. It was a good old-fashioned Jewish service, my father always said; Jews were a mystery to him—of the order of China, India, and Africa, and all the exotic places he'd never been.

Father chained the bear to the motorcycle. When he and Mother kissed Freud good-bye, the bear tried to butt his head between them.

'Watch out!' Freud cried, and they scattered apart. 'He thought we were eating something,' Freud told Mother and Father. 'Watch out how you kiss around him; he don't understand kissing. He thinks it's *eating.*'

'Earl!' the bear said.

'And please, for me,' Freud said, 'call him Earl—that's all he ever says, and State o' Maine is such a dumb name.'

'Earl?' my mother said.

'*Earl!*' the bear said.

'Okay,' Father said. '*Earl* it is.'

'Good-bye, Earl,' Freud said. '*Auf Wiedersehen!*'

They watched Freud for a long time, waiting on the Bay Point dock for a boat going to Boothbay, and when a lobsterman finally took him—although my parents knew that in Boothbay Freud would be boarding a larger ship—they thought how it *looked* as if the lobster boat were taking Freud to Europe, all the way across the dark ocean. They watched the boat chug and bob until it seemed smaller than a tern or even a sandpiper on the sea; by then it was out of hearing.

'Did you do it for the first time that night?' Franny always asked.

'Franny!' Mother said.

'Well, you said you *felt* married,' Franny said.

'Never mind when we did it,' Father said.

'But you *did,* right?' Franny said.

'Never mind that,' Frank said.

'It doesn't matter *when,*' Lilly said, in her weird way.

And that was true—it didn't really matter *when.* When they left the summer of 1939 and the Arbuthnot-by-the-Sea, my mother and father were in love—and in *their* minds, married. After all, they had promised Freud. They had his 1937 Indian and his bear, now named Earl, and when they arrived home in Dairy, New Hampshire, they drove first to the Bates family house.

'Mary's home!' my mother's mother called.

'What's that *machine* she's on?' said old Latin Emeritus. 'Who's that with her?'

'It's a motorcycle and that's Win Berry!' my mother's mother said.

'No, no!' said Latin Emeritus. 'Who's the *other* one?' The old man stared at the bundled figure in the sidecar.

'It must be Coach Bob,' said my mother's mother.

'That moron!' Latin Emeritus said. 'What in hell is he wearing in this weather? Don't they know how to dress in Iowa?'

'I'm going to marry Win Berry!' my mother rushed up and told her parents. 'That's his motorcycle. He's going to Harvard. And this . . . is Earl.'

Coach Bob was more understanding. He liked Earl.

'I'd love to know what he could bench-press,' the former Big Ten lineman said. 'But can't we cut his nails?'

It was silly to have another wedding; my father thought that Freud's service would suffice. But my mother's family insisted

41

that they be married by the Congregational minister who had taken Mother to her graduation dance, and so they were.

It was a small, informal wedding, where Coach Bob played the best man and Latin Emeritus gave his daughter away, with only an occasional mumbling of an odd Latin phrase; my mother's mother wept, full of the knowledge that Win Berry was *not* the Harvard man destined to whisk Mary Bates back to Boston—at least, not right away. Earl sat out the whole service in the sidecar of the '37 Indian, where he was pacified with crackers and herring.

My mother and father had a brief honeymoon by themselves. *'Then* you surely must have done it!' Franny always cried. But they probably didn't; they didn't stay anywhere overnight. They took an early train to Boston and wandered around Cambridge, imagining themselves living there, one day, and Father attending Harvard; they took the milk train back to New Hampshire, arriving at dawn the next day. Their first nuptial bed would have been the single bed in my mother's girlhood room in the house of Latin Emeritus—which was where my mother would still reside, while Father sought his fortune for Harvard.

Coach Bob was sorry to see Earl leave. Bob was sure the bear could be taught to play defensive end, but my father told Iowa Bob that the bear was going to be his family's meal ticket and his tuition. So one evening (after the Nazis took Poland), with the earliest nip of fall in the air, my mother kissed my father good-bye on the athletic fields of the Dairy School, which rolled right up to Iowa Bob's back door.

'Look after your parents,' my father told Mother, 'and I'll be back to look after you.'

'Yuck!' Franny always groaned; for some reason, this part bothered her. She never believed it. Lilly, too, shivered and turned up her nose.

'Shut up and listen to the story,' Frank always said.

At least I'm not opinionated to the degree of my brothers and sisters. I could simply see how Mother and Father must have kissed: *carefully*—Coach Bob amusing the bear with some game, so that Earl would not think my mother and father were eating something that they weren't sharing with him. Kissing would always be hazardous around Earl.

My mother told us that she knew my father would be faithful to her because the bear would maul him if he kissed anybody.

'And *were* you faithful?' Franny asked Father, in her terrible way.

'Why, of course,' Father said.

'I'll bet,' Franny said. Lilly always looked worried—Frank looked away.

That was the fall of 1939. Although she didn't know it, my mother was already pregnant—with Frank. My father would motorcycle down the East Coast, his exploration of resort hotels —the big-band sounds, the bingo crowds, and the casinos —taking him farther and farther south as the seasons changed. He was in Texas in the spring of 1940 when Frank was born; Father and Earl were at that time touring with an outfit called the Lone Star Brass Band. Bears were popular in Texas—although some drunk in Fort Worth had tried to steal the 1937 Indian, unaware that Earl slept chained to it. Texas law charged Father for the man's hospitalization, and it cost Father some more of his earnings to drive all the way East to welcome his first child into the world.

My mother was still in the hospital when Father returned to Dairy. They called Frank 'Frank' because my father said that was what they would always be to each other and to the family: 'frank.'

'Yuck!' Franny used to say. But Frank was quite proud of the origins of his name.

Father stayed with my mother in Dairy only long enough to get her pregnant again. Then he and Earl hit Virginia Beach and the Carolinas. They were banned from Falmouth, Cape Cod, on the Fourth of July, and back home with Mother in Dairy—to recover—soon after their disaster. The 1937 Indian had thrown a bearing in the Falmouth Independence Day Parade, and Earl had run amok when a fireman from Buzzards Bay tried to help Father with the ailing motorcycle. The fireman was unfortunately accompanied by two Dalmatian dogs, a breed not known for intelligence; doing nothing to disprove their reputation, the Dalmatians attacked Earl in the sidecar. Earl beheaded one of them quite cleanly, then chased the other one into the marching unit of the Osterville Men's Softball Team, where the foolish dog attempted to conceal himself. The parade was thus scattered, the grieving fireman from Buzzards Bay refused my father any more help with the Indian, and the sheriff of Falmouth escorted Father and Earl to the city limits. Since Earl refused to ride in cars, this had been a most tedious escort, Earl sitting in the sidecar of the motorcycle, which had to be towed. They were five days finding parts to rebuild the engine.

Worse, Earl had developed a taste for dogs. Coach Bob tried

to train him out of this maiming habit by teaching him other sports: retrieving balls, perfecting the forward roll—even sit-ups —but Earl was already old, and not blessed with the belief in vigorous exercise that possessed Iowa Bob. Slaughtering dogs didn't even require much running, Earl discovered; if he was sly —and Earl *was* sly—the dogs would come right up to him. 'And then it's all over,' Coach Bob observed. 'What a hell of a linebacker he could have been!'

So Father kept Earl chained, most of the time, and tried to make him wear his muzzle. Mother said that Earl was depressed —she found the old bear increasingly sad—but my father said that Earl wasn't depressed in the slightest. 'He's just thinking about dogs,' Father said. 'And he's perfectly happy to be attached to the motorcycle.'

That summer of '40 Father lived at the Bates house in Dairy and worked the Hampton Beach crowd at night. He managed to teach Earl a new routine. It was called 'Applying for a Job,' and it saved wear and tear on the old Indian.

Earl and Father performed in the outdoor bandstand at Hampton Beach. When the lights came on, Earl would be seated in a chair, wearing a man's suit; the suit radically altered, had once belonged to Coach Bob. After the laughter died down, my father entered the bandstand with a piece of paper in one hand.

'Your name?' Father would ask.

'Earl!' Earl said.

'Yes, Earl, I see,' Father said. 'And you want a job, Earl?'

'Earl!' said Earl.

'Yes, I *know* it's Earl, but you want a *job,* right?' Father said. 'Except it says here that you can't type, you can't even read—it says—and you have a drinking problem.'

'Earl,' Earl agreed.

The crowd occasionally threw fruit, but Father had fed Earl well; this was not the same kind of crowd that Father remembered from the Arbuthnot.

'Well, if all you can say is your own name,' Father said, 'I would venture to say that either you've been drinking this very night or you're too stupid to even know how to take off your own clothes.'

Earl said nothing.

'Well?' Father asked. 'Let's see if you can do it. Take off your own clothes. Go on!' And here Father would pull the chair

44

out from under Earl, who would do one of the forward rolls Coach Bob had taught him.

'So you can do a somersault,' Father said. 'Big deal. The clothes, Earl. Let's see the clothes come off.'

For some reason it is silly for a crowd of humans to watch a bear undress: my mother hated this routine—she said it was unfair to Earl to expose him to such a rowdy, uncouth bunch. When Earl undressed, Father usually had to help him with his tie —without help, Earl would get frustrated and *rip* it off his neck.

'You sure are hard on ties, Earl,' Father would say then. The audience at Hampton Beach loved it.

When Earl was undressed, Father would say, 'Well, come on —don't stop now. Off with the bear suit.'

'Earl?' Earl would say.

'Off with the bear suit,' Father would say, and he'd pull Earl's fur—just a little.

'Earl!' Earl would roar, and the audience would scream in alarm.

'My God, you're a *real* bear!' Father would cry.

'Earl!' Earl would bellow, and chase Father around and around the chair—half the audience fleeing into the night, some of them stumbling through the soft beach sand and down to the water; some of them threw more fruit, and paper cups with warm beer.

A more gentle act, for Earl, was performed once a week in the Hampton Beach casino. Mother had refined Earl's dancing style, and she would kick off the big band's opening number by taking a turn with Earl around the empty floor, the couples crowded close and wondering at them—the short, bent, broad bear in Iowa Bob's suit, surprisingly graceful on his hind paws, shuffling after my mother, who led.

Those evenings Coach Bob would baby-sit with Frank. Mother and Father and Earl would drive home along the coast road, stopping to watch the surf at Rye, where the homes of the rich were; the surf at Rye was called 'the breakers.' The New Hampshire coast was both more civilized and more seedy than Maine, but the phosphorescence off the breakers at Rye must have reminded my parents of evenings at the Arbuthnot. They said they always paused there, before driving home to Dairy.

One night Earl did not want to leave the breakers at Rye.

'He thinks I'm taking him fishing,' Father said. 'Look, Earl, I've got no gear—no bait, no spooners, no *pole*—dummy,' Father said to the bear, holding out his empty hands. Earl looked

45

bewildered; they realized the bear was nearly blind. They talked Earl out of fishing and took him home.

'How did he get so old?' my mother asked my father.

'He's started peeing in the sidecar,' Father said.

My mother was quite pregnant, this time with Franny, when Father left for the winter season in the fall of 1940. He had decided on Florida, and Mother first heard from him in Clearwater, and then from Tarpon Springs. Earl had acquired an odd skin disease—an ear infection, some fungus peculiar to bears —and business was slow.

That was shortly before Franny was born, late in the winter of 1941. Father was not home for this birth, and Franny never forgave him for it.

'I suspect he knew I would be a girl,' Franny was fond of saying.

It was the summer of '41 before Father was back in Dairy again; he promptly impregnated my mother with me.

He promised he would not have to leave her again; he had enough money from a successful circus stint in Miami to start Harvard in the fall. They could have a relaxed summer, playing Hampton Beach only when they felt like it. He would commute on the train to Boston for his classes, unless a cheap place in Cambridge turned up.

Earl was getting older by the minute. A pale blue salve, the texture of the film on a jellyfish, had to be put in his eyes every day; Earl rubbed it off on the furniture. My mother noticed alarming absences of hair from much of his body, which seemed shrunken and looser. 'He's lost his muscle tone,' Coach Bob worried. 'He ought to be lifting weights, or running.'

'Just try to get away from him on the Indian,' my father told his father. 'He'll run.' But when Coach Bob tried it, he got away with it. Earl didn't run; he didn't care.

'With Earl,' Father said, 'familiarity *does* breed a little contempt.' He had worked with Earl long and hard enough to understand Freud's exasperation with the bear.

My mother and father rarely talked of Freud; with 'the war in Europe,' it was too easy to imagine what could have happened to him.

The liquor stores in Harvard Square sold Wilson's 'That's All' rye whiskey, very cheap, but my father was not a drinker. The Oxford Grill in Cambridge used to dispense draft beer in a glass container the shape of a brandy snifter and holding a gallon. If you could drink this within some brief amount of time, you got a free one. But Father drank one regular beer there, when his week's classes were over, and he'd hurry to the North Station to catch the train to Dairy.

He accelerated his courses as much as possible, to graduate sooner; he was able to do this not because he was smarter than the other Harvard boys (he *was* older, but not smarter, than most of them) but because he spent little time with friends. He had a pregnant wife and two babies; he hardly had time for friends. His only recreation, he said, was listening to professional baseball games on the radio. Just a few months after the World Series, Father listened to the news of the attack on Pearl Harbor.

I was born in March of 1942, and named John—after John Harvard. (Franny had been called Franny because it somehow went with Frank.) My mother was not only busy taking care of us; she was busy taking care of old Latin Emeritus, and helping Coach Bob with the aged Earl; she didn't have time for friends, either.

By the end of the summer of 1942, the war had really obtruded on everyone; it was no longer just 'the war in Europe.' And although it used very little gas, the 1937 Indian was retired to the status of living quarters for Earl; it was no longer used for transportation. Patriotic mania spread across the nation's campuses. Students were allowed to receive sugar stamps, which most students gave to their families. Within a three-month period, every acquaintace Father had at Harvard either was drafted or had volunteered into some program. When Latin Emeritus died—and, in her sleep, my mother's mother quickly followed him—my mother came into a modest inheritance. My father accelerated his induction voluntarily and went off in the spring of 1943 for basic training; he was twenty-three.

He left behind Frank, Franny, and me with Mother in the Bates family house; he left behind his father, Iowa Bob, to whom he trusted the tedious care of Earl.

My father wrote home that basic training was a lesson in ruining the hotels of Atlantic City. They washed down the wood floors daily, and marched off down the boardwalk for rifle training on a sand dune. The bars on the boardwalk did a booming business with the trainees, except my father. No one inquired about age; the trainees, most of them younger than my father, wore all their marksman's medals and drank on. The bars

47

were full of office girls from Washington, and everyone smoked unfiltered cigarettes—except my father.

Father said everyone romanticized about 'a last fling' before going overseas, although far fewer realized it than boasted of it; Father, at least, had his—with my mother, in a hotel in New Jersey. This time, fortunately, he did not make her pregnant, so Mother would not be adding to Frank, Franny, and me for a while.

From Atlantic City my father went to a former prep school north of New York, for cryptographic training. He was then sent to Chanute Field—Kearns, Utah—and then to Savannah, Georgia, where he'd earlier performed, with Earl, in the old DeSoto Hotel. Then it was Hampton Roads, Port of Embarkation, and my father went to 'the war in Europe,' having a vague idea that he might find Freud there. Father felt confident that by leaving three offspring with my mother he was ensuring his safe return.

He had Air Force assignment at a bomber base in Italy, and the greatest danger was shooting someone when drunk, being shot by someone who was drunk, or falling into the latrine when drunk—which actually happened to a colonel my father knew; the colonel was crapped on several times before he was rescued. The only other danger involved acquiring a venereal disease from an Italian whore. And since my father did not drink or screw, he had a safe passage through World War II.

He left Italy via Navy transport and Trinidad to Brazil —'which is like Italy in Portuguese,' he wrote my mother. He flew back to the States with a shell-shocked pilot who buzzed a C-47 up the broadest street of Miami. From the air, my father recognized a parking lot where Earl had vomited after a performance.

My mother's contribution to the war effort—although she did secretarial work for her alma mater, the Thompson Female Seminary—consisted of hospital training; she was in the second class the Dairy Hospital gave to prepare nurses' aides. She worked one eight-hour shift per week and was on call for substitutions, which were frequent (there being a great shortage of nurses). Her favorite stations were the maternity ward and the delivery room; she knew what it was like to have a baby in that hospital with no husband around. That was how my mother spent the war.

Just after the war, Father took Coach Bob to see a professional football game, which was played in Fenway Park, Boston. On their way to the North Station to take the train back home to

Dairy, they met one of Father's Harvard classmates, who sold them a 1940 Chevy coupe for 600 dollars—a bit more than it cost new, but it was in fair shape and gasoline was ridiculously cheap, maybe twenty cents a gallon; Coach Bob and my father split the cost of insurance, so at last our family had a car. While Father finished his degree at Harvard, my mother had a means to take Frank, Franny, and me to the beaches on the New Hampshire shore, and Iowa Bob drove us once to the White Mountains, where Frank was badly stung by yellow jackets when Franny pushed him into a nest.

Harvard life had changed; the rooms were overcrowded; the Crimson had a new crew. The Slavic studies students claimed responsibility for the American discovery of vodka; no one mixed it with anything—you drank it Russian style, cold and straight in little stemmed glasses—but my father stuck with beer and changed his major to English literature. That way he tried, once again, to accelerate his graduation.

There were not many of the big bands around. Ballroom dancing was declining as a sport and pastime. And Earl was too decrepit to perform anymore; my father's first Christmas out of the Air Force, he worked in the toy department of Jordan Marsh and made my mother pregnant, again. This time, it would be Lilly. As concrete as the reasons were for calling Frank Frank and Franny Franny and me John, there was no specific reason for calling Lilly Lilly—a fact that would bother Lilly, perhaps more than we knew; maybe for all her life.

Father graduated with the Harvard class of 1946. The Dairy School had just hired a new headmaster, who interviewed my father at the Harvard Faculty Club and offered him a job—to teach English and coach two sports—for a starting salary of twenty-one hundred dollars. Coach Bob had probably put the new headmaster up to it. My father was twenty-six: he accepted the position at the Dairy School, although it hardly struck him as his life's calling. It would simply mean he could finally live with my mother and us children, in the Bates family house in Dairy, near to his father and near to Earl—his ancient bear. At this phase in his life, my father's dreams were clearly more important to him than his education, perhaps even more important to him than we children, certainly more important to him than World War II. ('At *every* phase of his life,' Franny would say.)

Lilly was born in 1946, when Frank was six, Franny was five, and I was four. We suddenly had a father—as if for the first time, really; he had been at war, at school, and on the road with Earl all our lives, so far. He was a stranger to us.

The first thing he did with us, in the fall of 1946, was to take us to Maine, where we'd never been before, to visit the Arbuthnot-by-the-Sea. Of course, it was a romantic pilgrimage for my father and mother—an expedition for old times' sake. Lilly was too young to travel and Earl was too old, but Father insisted that Earl come with us.

'The Arbuthnot is his place, too, for God's sake,' Father told Mother. 'It wouldn't be the same—to be at the Arbuthnot without old State o' Maine!'

So Lilly was left with Coach Bob, and Mother drove the 1940 Chevy coupe, with Frank, Franny, and me, a big basket of picnic food, and a mountain of blankets. Father got the 1937 Indian running; he drove it, with Earl in the sidecar. That was how we traveled, unbelievably slowly, up the torturous coast highway, many years before there was a Maine Turnpike. It took hours to get to Brunswick; it took another hour past Bath. And then we saw the rough, moving, bruise-colored water that was the mouth of the Kennebec meeting the sea, Fort Popham, and the fishing shacks at Bay Point—and the chain drawn across the driveway to the Arbuthnot. The sign said:

CLOSED FOR THE SEASON!

The Arbuthnot had been closed for many seasons. Father must have realized this soon after he took down the chain and our caravan drove up to the old hotel. Bleached colorless as bones, the buildings stood abandoned and boarded-up; every window that was showing had been smashed or shot out. The faded flag for the eighteenth green had been stabbed into a crack between the floorboards of the overhanging porch, where the ballroom was; the flag drooped from the Arbuthnot-by-the-Sea as if to indicate that this had been a castle taken by siege.

'Jesus God,' Father said. We children huddled around my mother and complained. It was cold; it was foggy; the place scared us. We'd been told we were going to a resort hotel, and if this was what a *hotel* was, we knew we wouldn't like it. Great clots of grass had pushed their way through the ruptured clay of the tennis courts, and the lawn for croquet was knee-high, to my father, with a saw-edged kind of marsh grass that grows wildly by salt water. Frank cut himself on an old wicket and began to snivel. Franny insisted on Father's carrying her. I hung to my mother's hips. Earl, whose arthritis affected him disagreeably, refused to move away from the motorcycle and threw up in his muzzle. When Father took his muzzle off, Earl found something in the dirt and tried to eat it; it was an old tennis ball, which Father took from him and tossed far away, toward the sea. Gamely, Earl started to retrieve the ball; then the old bear seemed to forget what he was doing and just sat there squinting at the docks. Probably he could barely see them.

The hotel piers were sagging. The boathouse had been washed out to sea in a hurricane during the war. The fishermen had tried to use the old docks to bolster up their fishing weirs, which were strung together down at the lobstermen's dock at Bay Point, where a man or a boy appeared to be standing guard with a rifle. He was stationed there to shoot seals, Father had to explain —because the far-off figure with the gun startled my mother. Seals were the number one reason why weir fishing would never be too successful in Maine: the seals broke into the weirs, gorged themselves on the trapped fish, and then broke out. They ate a lot of fish this way, and destroyed the nets in the process, and the fishermen shot them whenever they could.

'It's what Freud would have called "one of the gross rules of nature," ' Father said. He insisted on showing us the dormitories where he and Mother had stayed.

It must have been depressing to both of them—it was simply uncomfortable and foreign to us children—but I think my mother was more upset at Father's reaction to the fall of the Arbuthnot than she was upset by what had happened to the once great resort.

'The war changed a lot of things,' Mother said, showing us her famous shrug.

'Jesus God,' Father kept saying. 'Think of what it *could* have been!' he cried. 'How could they have blown it? They weren't *democratic* enough,' he told us baffled kids. 'There ought to be a way to have standards, to have good taste, and still not be so exclusive that you go under. There ought to be a livable compromise between the Arbuthnot and some hole like Hampton Beach. Jesus God!' he kept calling out. 'Jesus God.'

We followed him around the beaten buildings, the mangled and grown-amok lawns. We found the old bus that the band members had traveled in, and the truck the grounds crew had used—it was full of rusty golf clubs. They were the vehicles Freud had fixed and kept running; they wouldn't run anymore.

'Jesus God,' Father said.

We heard Earl calling to us from far away. 'Earl!' he called.

We heard two shots from the rifle, from far away—down on the Bay Point dock. I think we all knew that it was not the sound of a seal being shot. It was Earl.

'Oh no, Win,' my mother said. She picked me up and started running; Frank ran in agitated circles around her. Father ran with Franny in his arms.

'State o' Maine!' he cried.

'I shot a bear!' the boy on the dock was calling. 'I shot a whole bear!' He was a boy in dungaree coveralls and a soft flannel shirt; both knees were gone out of the coveralls and his carrot-colored hair was stiff and shiny from saltwater spray; he had a curious rash on his pale face; he had very poor teeth; he was only thirteen or fourteen years old. 'I shot a bear!' he screamed. He was very excited, and the fishermen out on the sea must have wondered what he was yelling about. They couldn't hear him, over their trolling motors and the wind off the water, but they slowly gathered their boats around the dock and came bobbing in to land, to see what the matter was.

Earl lay on the dock with his big head on a coil of tarred rope, his hind paws crumpled under him, and one heavy forepaw only inches from a bucket of baitfish. The bear's eyes had been so bad for so long, he must have mistaken the boy with the rifle for Father with a fishing pole. He might even, dimly, have remembered eating lots of pollack off that dock. And when he wandered down there, and got close to the boy, the old bear's *nose* was still good enough to smell the bait. The boy, watching out to sea—for seals—had no doubt been frightened by the way the bear had greeted him. He was a good shot, although at that range even a poor shot would have hit Earl; the boy shot the bear twice in the heart.

'Gosh, I didn't know he *belonged* to anybody,' the boy with the rifle told my mother, 'I didn't know he was a *pet*.'

'Of course you didn't,' my mother soothed him.

'I'm sorry, mister,' the boy told Father, but Father didn't hear him. He sat beside Earl on the dock and raised the dead bear's head into his lap; he hugged Earl's old face to his stomach and cried and cried. He was crying for more than Earl, of course. He was crying for the Arbuthnot, and Freud, and for the summer of

52

'39; but we were very worried, we children—because, at that time, we had known Earl longer, and better, than we really knew our father. It was very confusing to us—why this man, home from Harvard, and home from the war, should be dissolved in tears, hugging our old bear. We were, all of us, really too young to have *known* Earl, but the bear's presence—the stiff feel of his fur, the heat of his fruity and mud-like breath, the dead-geranium and urine smell of him—was more memorable to us, for example, than the ghosts of Latin Emeritus and my mother's mother.

I truly remember this day on the dock below the ruined Arbuthnot. I was four, and I sincerely believe that this is my first memory of life itself—as opposed to what I was *told* happened, as opposed to the pictures other people have painted for me. The man with the strong body and the gentleman's face was my father, who had come to live with us; he sat sobbing with Earl in his arms—on a rotting dock, over dangerous water. Little boats chugged nearer and nearer. My mother hugged us to her, as tightly as Father held fast to Earl.

'I think the dumb kid shot someone's dog,' a man in one of the boats said.

Up the dock's ladder came an old fisherman in a dirty-yellow oil-skin slicker, his face a mottled tan beneath a dirty-white and spotty beard. His wet boots sloshed and he smelled more strongly of fish than the bucket of bait by Earl's curled paw. He was plenty old enough to have been active in the vicinity in the days when the Arbuthnot-by-the-Sea had been the grand hotel it was. The fisherman, too, had seen better days.

When this old man saw the dead bear, he took off his broad sou'wester hat and held it in one hand, which was big and hard as a gaff. 'Holy cow,' he said, reverently, wrapping an arm around the shoulders of the shaken boy with the rifle. 'Holy cow. You kilt State o' Maine.'

2

The First
Hotel New Hampshire

The first Hotel New Hampshire came about this way: when the Dairy School realized it had to admit women to its student body, in order to survive, the Thompson Female Seminary was put out of business; there was suddenly a large, unusuable piece of real estate on the Dairy market—a market that was forever depressed. No one knew what to do with the huge building that had once been an all-girls' school.

'They should burn it,' Mother suggested, 'and turn the whole area into a park.'

It was something of a park, anyway—a high plot of ground, maybe two acres, in the dilapidated heart of the town of Dairy. Old clapboard houses, once for large families and now rented piecemeal to widows and widowers—and to the retired Dairy School faculty—surrounded by dying elms, which surrounded the four-story brick monster of a school building, which was named after Ethel Thompson. Miss Thompson had been an Episcopal minister who had successfully masqueraded as a man until her death (the Reverend *Edward* Thompson, she'd been called, rector of the Dairy Episcopal parish and notorious for hiding runaway slaves in the rectory). The discovery that she was a woman (following an accident in which she was crushed while changing a wheel of her carriage) came as no surprise to a few of the Dairy menfolk who had taken their problems to her at the height of her popularity as rector. She had somehow acquired a lot of money, not a penny of which was left to the church; it was all left to found a female seminary—'until,' Ethel Thompson wrote, 'that abomination of a boys' academy is forced to take in girls.'

My father would have agreed that the Dairy School was an abomination. Although we children loved playing on its athletic fields, Father never ceased reminding us that Dairy was not a 'real' school. Just as the town of Dairy had once been dairy land, so had the athletic fields of the school been a pasture for cows; and when the school had been founded, in the early 1800s, the old barns were allowed to stand beside the newer school buildings, and the old cows were allowed, like the students, to wander freely about the school. Modern landscaping had improved the fields for sports, but the barns, and the first of the original buildings, still occupied the scruffy center of the campus; some token cows still occupied the barns. It had been the school's 'game plan,' as Coach Bob called it, to have the students care for the dairy farm while going to school—a plan that led to a lax education and poorly cared-for cows, a plan that was abandoned before the First World War. There were still those on the Dairy School faculty—and many of them were the newer, younger faculty—who believed that this combination of a school and a farm should be returned to.

My father resisted the plan to return the Dairy School to what he called 'a barnyard-experiment in education.'

'When my kids are old enough to go to this wretched school,' he would rage to my mother, and to Coach Bob, 'they will no doubt be given academic credit for planting a garden.'

'And varsity letters for shoveling shit!' said Iowa Bob.

The school, in other words, was in search of a philosophy. It was now firmly second-rate among conventional prep schools; although it modeled its curriculum on the acquiring of academic skills, the school's faculty grew less and less able to teach such skills and, conveniently, less convinced of the need for such skills—after all, the student body was decreasingly receptive. Admissions were down, hence admission standards fell even lower; the school became one of those places you could get into almost immediately upon being thrown out of another school. A few of the faculty, like my father, who believed in teaching people how to read and write—and even punctuate—despaired that such skills were largely wasted on students like these. 'Pearls before swine,' Father ranted. 'We might as well teach them how to rake hay and milk cows.'

'They can't play football, either,' Coach Bob mourned. 'They won't *block* for each other.'

'They won't even run,' Father said.

'They won't *hit* anybody,' said Iowa Bob.

'Oh yes they will,' said Frank, who was always picked on. 'They broke into the greenhouse and vandalized all the

55

plants,' said Mother, who read of this incident in the school paper, which was, Father said, illiterate.

'One of them showed me his thing,' Franny said, to cause trouble.

'Where?' Father said.

'Behind the hockey rink,' Franny said.

'What were you doing behind the hockey rink, anyway?' Frank said, disgusted as usual.

'The hockey rink is warped,' Coach Bob said. 'There's been no maintenance since that man, whatever his name was, retired.'

'He didn't retire, he *died,*' Father said. Father was often exasperated with his father, now that Iowa Bob was getting older.

In 1950 Frank was ten, Franny was nine, I was eight, and Lilly was four; Egg had just been born, and in his ignorance was spared *our* dread that we would one day be expected to attend the much accused Dairy School. Father was sure that by the time Franny was old enough, they would be admitting girls.

'Not out of anything resembling a progressive instinct,' he claimed, 'but purely to avoid bankruptcy.'

He was right, of course. By 1952 the Dairy School's academic standards were in question; its admissions were steadily falling, and its admission standards were even further in question. And when the admissions continued to go down, the tuition went up, which turned away even more students, which meant some faculty had to be let go—and others, the ones with principles *and* other means, resigned.

The 1953 football team went 1–9 for the season; Coach Bob thought that the school couldn't wait for him to retire so that they could drop football altogether—it was too costly, and the alumni, who had once supported it (and the entire athletic program), were too ashamed to come back and see the games anymore.

'It's the damn uniforms,' Iowa Bob said, and Father rolled his eyes and tried to look tolerant of Bob's approaching senility. Father had learned of senility from Earl. But Coach Bob, to be fair, had a point about the uniforms.

The colors of the Dairy School, perhaps modeled on a now-vanished breed of cow, were meant to be a deep chocolate brown and a luminous silver. But with the years, and the increasingly synthetic quality of the fabrics, this rich cocoa and silver had become dingy and sad.

'The color of mud and clouds,' my father said.

56

The students at the Dairy School, who played with us kids —when they were not showing Franny their 'things'—informed us of the other names for these colors, which were in vogue at the school. There was an older kid named De Meo—Ralph De Meo, one of Iowa Bob's few stars, and the star sprinter on Father's winter and spring track teams—who told Frank, Franny, and me what the Dairy School colors really were. 'Gray like the pallor of a dead man's face,' De Meo said. I was ten and scared of him; Franny was eleven, but behaved older with him; Frank was twelve and afraid of everybody.

'Gray like the pallor of a dead man's face,' De Meo repeated slowly, for me. 'And brown—cow-brown, like manure,' he said. 'That's shit to you, Frank.'

'I *know*,' said Frank.

'Show it to me again,' Franny said to De Meo; she meant his thing.

Thus shit and death were the colors of the dying Dairy School. The board of trustees, laboring under this curse—and others, going back to the barnyard history of the school and the less-than-quaint New Hampshire town the school was plopped down in—decided to admit women to the student body.

That, at least, would raise admissions.

'That will be the end of football,' said old Coach Bob.

'The *girls* will play better football than most of your boys,' Father said.

'That's what I mean,' said Iowa Bob.

'Ralph De Meo plays pretty good,' Franny said.

'Plays with *what* pretty good,' I said, and Franny kicked me under the table. Frank sat sullen and larger than any of us, dangerously close to Franny and across from me.

'De Meo is at least fast,' Father said.

'De Meo is at least a *hitter*,' Coach Bob said.

'He *sure is*,' Frank said; Frank had been hit by Ralph De Meo several times.

It was Franny who protected me from Ralph. One day when we were watching them paint the yard-line stripes on the football field—just Franny and I; we were hiding from Frank (we were often hiding from Frank)—De Meo came up to us and pushed me into the blocking sled. He was wearing his scrimmage uniform: shit and death Number 19 (his age). He took his helmet off and spit his mouthpiece out across the cinder track, letting his teeth gleam at Franny. 'Beat it,' he said to me, still looking at Franny. 'I got to talk to your sister in the worst way.'

57

'You don't have to push him,' Franny said.

'She's only twelve,' I said.

'Beat it,' De Meo said.

'You don't have to push him,' Franny told De Meo. 'He's only eleven.'

'I got to tell you how sorry I am,' De Meo said to her. 'I won't still be here by the time you're a student. I'll be graduated already.'

'What do you mean?' Franny said.

'They're going to take in girls,' De Meo said.

'I know,' Franny said. 'So what?'

'So, it's a pity, that's all,' he told her, 'that I won't *be* here by the time you're finally *old* enough.'

Franny shrugged; it was Mother's shrug—independent and pretty. I picked De Meo's mouthpiece up from the cinder track; it was slimy and gritty and I tossed it at him.

'Why don't you put that back in your mouth?' I asked him. I could run fast, but I didn't think I could run faster than Ralph De Meo.

'Beat it,' he said; he zipped the mouthpiece at my head, but I ducked. It sailed away somewhere.

'How come you're not scrimmaging,' Franny asked him. Behind the gray wooden bleachers that passed for the Dairy School 'stadium' was the practice field where we could hear the shoulder pads and helmets tapping.

'I got a groin injury,' De Meo told Franny. 'Want to see it?'

'I hope it falls off,' I said.

'I can catch you, Johnny,' he said, still looking at Franny. Nobody called me 'Johnny.'

'Not with a groin injury you can't,' I said.

I was wrong; he caught me at the forty-yard line and pushed my face in the fresh lime painted on the field. He was kneeling on my back when I heard him exhale sharply and he slumped off me and lay on his side on the cinder track.

'Jesus,' he said, in a soft little voice. Franny had grabbed the tin cup in his jock strap and twisted its edges into his private parts, which is what we called them in those days.

We both could outrun him, then.

'How'd you know about it?' I asked her. 'The thing in his jock strap? I mean, the cup.'

'He showed me, another time,' she said grimly.

We lay still in the pine needles in the deep woods behind the

58

practice field; we could hear Coach Bob's whistle and the contact, but we were hidden from all of them.

Franny never minded when Ralph De Meo beat up Frank, and I asked her why she minded when Ralph beat up me.

'You're not Frank,' she whispered fiercely; she wet her skirt in the damp grass at the edge of the woods and wiped the lime off my face with it, rolling up the hem of her skirt so that her belly was bare. A pine needle stuck to her stomach and I picked it off for her.

'Thank you,' she said, intent on getting every last bit of the lime off me; she pulled her skirt up higher, spit in it, and kept wiping. My face stung.

'Why do we like each other more than we like Frank?' I asked her.

'We just do,' she said, 'and we always will. Frank is weird,' she said.

'But he's our brother,' I said.

'So? You're my brother, too,' she said. 'That's not why I like you.'

'Why *do* you?' I asked.

'I just do,' she said. We wrestled for a while in the woods, until she got something in her eye; I helped her get it out. She was sweaty and smelled like clean dirt. She had very high breasts, which seemed separated by too wide an expanse of chest, but Franny was strong. She could usually beat me up, unless I got completely on top of her; then she could still tickle me hard enough to make me pee if I didn't get off her. When she was on top of me, there was no moving her.

'One day I'll be able to beat you up,' I told her.

'So what?' she said. 'By then you won't want to.'

A fat football player, named Poindexter, came into the woods to move his bowels. We saw him coming and hid in the ferns we'd known about for years. For years the football players crapped in these woods, just off the practice field—especially, it seemed, the fat ones. It was a long run back to the gymnasium, and Coach Bob harangued them for not emptying their bowels before they came to practice. For some reason the fat ones could *never* get them entirely empty, we imagined.

'It's Poindexter,' I whispered.

'Of course it is,' Franny said.

Poindexter was very awkward; he always had trouble getting his thigh pads down. Once he had to take off his cleats and remove the entire bottom half of his uniform, except his socks.

59

This time he just struggled with the pads and pants that bound his knees precariously close together. He kept his balance by squatting slightly forward with his hands on his helmet (on the ground in front of him). This time he crapped messily on the insides of his football shoes and had to wipe the shoes as well as his ass. For a moment, Franny and I feared he would use the ferns for this purpose, but Poindexter was always hurried and panting, and he did as good a job as he could with the handful of maple leaves he'd gathered on the path and brought into the woods with him. We heard Coach Bob's whistle blowing, and Poindexter heard it, too.

When he ran back toward the practice field, Franny and I started clapping. When Poindexter stopped and listened, we stopped clapping; the poor fat boy stood in the woods, wondering what applause he had imagined—*this* time—and then rushed back to the game he played so badly and, usually, with such humiliation.

Then Franny and I snuck down to the path that the football players always took back to the gym. It was a narrow path, pockmarked from their cleats. We were slightly worried where De Meo might be, but I went up to the edge of the practice field and 'spotted' for Franny while she dropped her pants and squatted on the path; then she spotted for me. We both covered our rather disappointing messes with a light sprinkling of leaves. Then we retreated to the usual ferns to wait for the football players to finish practice, but Lilly was already in the ferns.

'Go home,' Franny told her; Lilly was seven. Most of the time she was too young for Franny and me, but we were nice to her around the house; she had no friends, and she seemed entranced by Frank, who enjoyed babying her.

'I don't have to go home,' Lilly said.

'Better go,' Franny said.

'Why's your face so red?' Lilly asked me.

'De Meo put poison on it,' Franny said, 'and he's looking around for more people to rub it on.'

'If I go home, he'll see me,' Lilly said seriously.

'Not if you go right away,' I said.

'We'll watch out for you,' Franny said. She stood up out of the ferns. 'It's all clear,' she whispered. Lilly ran home.

'Am I really all red in the face?' I asked Franny.

Franny pulled my face up close to hers and licked me once on my cheek, once on my forehead, once on my nose, once on my lips. 'I can't *taste* it anymore,' she said. 'I got it all off you.'

60

We lay together in the ferns; it wasn't boring, but it took a while for the practice to be over and for the first football players to come down the path. The third one stepped in it—a running back from Boston who was doing a postgraduate year at Dairy, basically to get a little older before he played football in college. He slid a short ways in it, but caught his balance; then he regarded the horror in his cleats.

'Poindexter!' he screamed. Poindexter, a slow runner, was well to the rear of the line of players heading for the showers. 'Poindexter!' screamed the running back from Boston. 'You *turd*, Poindexter!'

'What'd I do?' Poindexter asked, out of breath, forever fat —'fat in his genes,' Franny would say, later, when she knew what genes were.

'Did you have to do it on the path, you asshole?' the running back asked Poindexter.

'It wasn't me!' Poindexter protested.

'Clean my cleats, you shit-for-brains,' the running back said. At a school like Dairy, the linemen, although bigger, were the weaker, fatter, younger boys, often sacrificed for the few *good* athletes—Coach Bob let the good ones carry the ball.

Several rougher members of Iowa Bob's backfield surrounded Poindexter on the path.

'They don't have girls here yet, Poindexter,' said the running back from Boston, 'so there's nobody but you to clean the shit off my shoes.'

Poindexter did as he was told; he was, at least, familiar with the job.

Franny and I went home, past the token cows in the falling-down school barns, past Coach Bob's back door, where the rusty fenders of the 1937 Indian were inverted on the porch—to scrape your shoes on. The motorcycle fenders were the only outdoor remains of Earl.

'When it's time for us to go to the Dairy School,' I said to Franny, 'I hope we're living somewhere else.'

'*I'm* not going to clean the shit off anybody's shoes,' Franny said. 'No way.'

Coach Bob, who ate supper with us, bemoaned his terrible football team. 'It's my last year, I swear,' the old man said, but he was always saying this. 'Poindexter actually took a dump on the path today—during practice.'

'I saw Franny and John with their clothes off,' Lilly said.

'You did not,' Franny said.

'On the path,' Lilly said.

'Doing what?' Mother said.

'Doing what Grandpa Bob said,' Lilly told everyone.

Frank snorted his disgust; Father banished Franny and me to our rooms. Upstairs Franny whispered to me, 'You *see?* It's just you and me. Not Lilly. Not Frank.'

'Not Egg,' I added.

'Egg isn't anybody yet, dummy,' Franny said. 'Egg isn't a human being yet.' Egg was only three.

'Now there's two of them following us,' Franny said. 'Frank and Lilly.'

'Don't forget De Meo,' I said.

'I can forget him easy,' Franny said. 'I'm going to have lots of De Meos when I grow up.'

This thought alarmed me and I was silent.

'Don't worry,' Franny whispered, but I said nothing and she crept down the hall and into my room; she got into my bed and we left my door open so we would hear them all talking at the dinner table.

'It's not fit for my children, this school,' Father said. 'I know that.'

'Well,' Mother said, 'all your talk about it has certainly convinced *them* of that. They'll be afraid to go, when the time comes.'

'When the time comes,' Father said, 'we'll send them away to a *good* school.'

'I don't care about a good school,' Frank said, and Franny and I could sympathize with him; although we hated the notion of going to Dairy, we were more disturbed at the thought of going 'away.'

' "Away" *where?*' Frank asked.

'Who's going away?' Lilly asked.

'Hush,' Mother said. 'No one is going away to school. We couldn't afford it. If there's a benefit to being on the faculty at the Dairy School, it's at least that there's someplace free to send our children to.'

'Someplace that's not any good,' Father said.

'Better than average,' Mother said.

'Listen,' Father said. 'We're going to make money.'

This was news to us; Franny and I kept very still.

Frank must have been nervous at the prospect. 'May I be excused?' he asked.

'Of course, dear,' Mother said. '*How* are we going to make money?' Mother asked Father.

'For God's sake, tell *me*,' Coach Bob said. '*I'm* the one who wants to retire.'

'Listen,' Father said. We listened. 'This school may be worthless, but it's going to grow; it's going to take on *girls*, remember? And even if it *doesn't* grow, it's not going to fold. It's been here too long to fold; its instincts are only to survive, and it will. It won't *ever* be a good school; it will go through so many phases that at times we won't recognize the place, but it's going to keep going—you can count on that.'

'So what?' said Iowa Bob.

'So there's going to be a school here,' Father said. 'A private school is going to go on being here, in this crummy town,' he said, 'and the Thompson Female Seminary *isn't* going to go on being here, because now the girls in town will go to Dairy.'

'Everybody knows that,' said Mother.

'May I be excused?' Lilly asked.

'Yes, yes,' Father said. 'Listen,' he said to Mother and Bob, 'don't you see?' Franny and I didn't see anything—only Frank, sneaking by in the upstairs hall. 'What's going to become of that old building, the Thompson Female Seminary?' Father asked. And that's when Mother suggested burning it. Coach Bob suggested it become the county jail.

'It's big enough,' he said. Someone else had suggested this at Town Meeting.

'Nobody wants a jail here,' Father said. 'Not in the middle of town.'

'It already looks like a jail,' Mother said.

'Just needs more bars,' said Iowa Bob.

'Listen,' Father said, impatiently. Franny and I froze together; Frank was lurking outside my door—Lilly was whistling, somewhere close by. 'Listen, listen,' Father said. 'What this town needs is a *hotel*.'

There was silence from the dining room table. A 'hotel,' Franny and I knew, lying in my bed, was what did away with old Earl. A hotel was a vast ruined space, smelling of fish, guarded by a gun.

'Why a hotel?' Mother finally said. 'You're always saying it's a crummy town—who'd want to come here?'

'Maybe not *want* to,' Father said, 'but *have* to. Those parents of those kids at the Dairy School,' he said. 'They visit their kids, don't they? And you know what? The parents are going to get richer and richer, because the tuition is going to keep going up and up, and there won't be any more scholarship students—there will *only* be rich kids coming here. And if you visit your kid at this school now, you can't stay in town. You have to go to the beach, where all the motels are, or you have to drive even farther, up toward the mountains—but there's nothing, absolutely nothing to stay in *right here*.'

That was his plan. Somehow, although the Dairy School could barely afford enough janitors, Father thought it would provide the clientele for one hotel in the town of Dairy—that the town was so motley, and no one else had dreamed of putting up a place to stay in it, didn't worry my Father. In New Hampshire the summer tourists went to the beaches—they were half an hour away. The mountains were an hour away, where the skiers went, and where there were summer lakes. But Dairy was valley land, inland but not upland: Dairy was close enough to the sea to feel the sea's dampness but far enough away from the sea to benefit not in the slightest from the sea's freshness. The brisk air from the ocean and from the mountains did not penetrate the dull haze that hung over the valley of the Squamscott River, and Dairy was a Squamscott Valley town—a penetrating damp cold in winter, a steamy humidity all summer. Not a picture-pretty New England village but a mill town on a polluted river—the mill now as abandoned and as ugly as the Thompson Female Seminary. It was a town with its sole hopes hung on the Dairy School, a place no one wanted to go.

'If there was a hotel here, however,' Father said, 'people would stay in it.'

'But the Thompson Female Seminary would make a dreadful hotel,' Mother said. 'It could *only* be what it is: an old school.'

'Do you realize how cheaply one could buy it?' Father said.

'Do *you* realize how much it would cost to fix it up?' Mother said.

'What a depressing idea!' said Coach Bob.

Franny started to pin my arms down; it was her usual method of attack—she'd get my arms all tied up, then tickle me by grinding her chin into my ribs or my armpit, or else she'd bite me on the neck (just hard enough to make me lie still). Our legs were thrashing under the covers, throwing the blankets off —whoever could scissor the other's legs had the initial advantage—when Lilly came into my room in her weird way, on all fours with a sheet over her.

'Creep,' Franny said to her.

64

'I'm sorry you got in trouble,' Lilly said under the sheet. Lilly always apologized for ratting on us by completely covering her body and crawling into our rooms on all fours. 'I brought you something,' Lilly said.

'Food?' Franny asked. I pulled Lilly's sheet off and Franny took a paper bag that Lilly had carried to us, clutched in her teeth. There were two bananas and two of the warm rolls from supper in it. 'Nothing to drink?' Franny asked. Lilly shook her head.

'Come on, get in,' I said to her, and Lilly crawled into bed with Franny and me.

'We're going to move to a hotel,' Lilly said.

'Not quite,' said Franny.

But they seemed to be talking about something else downstairs at the dining table. Coach Bob was angry with my Father, again—for the same old thing, it seemed: for never being satisfied, as Bob put it, for living in the future. For always making plans for the *next* year instead of just *living*, moment by moment.

'But he can't help it,' my mother was saying; she always defended my father from Coach Bob.

'You've got a wonderful wife, and a wonderful family,' Iowa Bob was telling my father. 'You've got this big old house—an inheritance! You didn't even have to pay for it! You've got a job. So what if the pay's not great—what do you need money for? You're a lucky man.'

'I don't want to be a teacher,' Father said quietly, which meant he was angry again. 'I don't want to be a coach. I don't want my kids to go to a school this bad. It's a hick town, and a floundering school full of rich kids with problems; their parents send them here in a desperate effort to arrest their already considerable sophistication—*run-amok* sophistication on the part of the kids, run-amok *hick*ness on the part of the school and the town. It's the worst of both worlds.'

'But if you just spent more time with the kids *now*,' Mother said, quietly, 'and worried a little less about where they're all going to be in a few *years*.'

'The *future* again!' said Iowa Bob. 'He *lives* in the future! First it was all the traveling—all so he could go to Harvard. So he went to Harvard, then, as fast as he could—so he could be *through* with it. For what? For this job, which he's done nothing but complain about. Why doesn't he *enjoy* it?'

'Enjoy *this*?' Father said. '*You* don't enjoy it, do you?'

65

We could imagine our grandfather, Coach Bob, fuming; fuming was how he ended most arguments with my father, who was quicker than Iowa Bob; when Bob felt outwitted, but still right, he fumed. Franny and Lilly and I could imagine his knotty, bald head smoldering. It was true that he had no higher regard for the Dairy School than my father had, but Iowa Bob had at least committed himself to something, he felt, and he wished to see my father *involved* with what he was doing instead of involved—as Bob would say—with the *future*. After all, Coach Bob had once bitten a running back; he had not seen my father ever so engaged.

He was probably distressed that my father never became passionate about any sport, although Father was athletic and liked exercise. And Iowa Bob loved my mother very much; he had known her all the years my father was away at the war, away at Harvard, and away with Earl. Coach Bob probably thought that my father neglected his family; in the last years, I know, Bob thought Father had neglected Earl.

'Excuse me,' we heard Frank say; Franny locked her hands around my waist at the base of my spine; I tried to force her chin up, off my shoulder, but Lilly was sitting on my head.

'What is it, dear?' Mother said.

'What's up, Frank?' Father said, and we could tell by the sharp creak of a chair that Father had grabbed for Frank; he was always trying to loosen Frank up a little by wrestling with him, or trying to get him to play, but Frank wouldn't go for it. Franny and I loved it when Father would roughhouse with us, but Frank didn't like it at all.

'Excuse me,' Frank repeated.

'You're excused, you're excused,' Father said.

'Franny is out of her room, she's in bed with John,' Frank said. 'And Lilly's with them. She brought them something to eat.'

I felt Franny slide away from me; she was out of my bed and out of my room, her flannel nightie ballooning like a sail in the draft from the upstairs hall by the stairwell; Lilly grabbed her sheet and crawled into my closet. The old Bates family house was huge; there were so many places to hide, but my mother knew them all. I thought Franny was dashing back to her room, but I heard her going *downstairs,* instead, and then I heard her screaming.

'You weirdo fink, Frank!' she screamed. 'You fart! You turd in a birdbath!'

'Franny!' Mother said.

I ran to the stairwell and hugged the banister; the stairs were carpeted, deep and soft, the same carpet that covered the house. I could see Franny go straight for the headlock on Frank in the dining room. She took him down fast—Frank was slow-moving and not very physical; he was badly coordinated, although bigger than Franny, and much bigger than me. I rarely fought with him, even in fun; Frank did little in the way of fighting for fun, and even in fun he could hurt you. He was too large, and despite his distaste for the physical life, he was strong. He had a way, too, of finding your ear with his elbow, or your nose with his knee; he was the kind of fighter whose fingers and thumbs always found an eye, whose head bobbed up and split your lip against your own teeth. There are people who are so physically uncomfortable with themselves that they seem to jar against any *other* body. Frank was like that, and I left him alone; it was not just because he was two years older.

Franny occasionally couldn't stand not testing him, but they almost always hurt each other. I watched her locked in a death grip with Frank under the dining room table.

'Stop them, Win!' my mother said, but Father hit his head on the table trying to drag them out where he could separate them; Coach Bob went under the table from the other side.

'Shit! Father said.

I felt something warm against my hip at the banister; it was Lilly, peering out from under her sheet.

'You rat's asshole, Frank!' Franny was screaming.

Then Frank got Franny's hair and yanked her head against the dining table leg; although I did not have breasts of my own, I could feel it in my chest when Frank dug his knuckles into Franny's breast. She had to let go of her headlock and he rapped her head against the table leg twice more, snarling her hair around his fist, before Coach Bob got three of their four legs in his huge hands and hauled them out from under the table. Franny lashed out with her free foot and caught Bob with a good blow to the nose, but the old Iowa lineman hung on. Franny was crying now, but she managed to strain against her hair hard enough to bite Frank on the cheek. Frank grabbed one of her breasts in his hand; he must have squeezed her hard because Franny's mouth opened against Frank's cheek and a losing sob broke from her. It was so terrible and defeated a sound that it sent Lilly running back to my room with her sheet. Father knocked Frank's hand from Franny's breast and Coach Bob got a headlock on Franny,

67

so that she couldn't bite Frank again. But Franny had a hand free and she went for Frank's private parts; whether you were in a cup, in or out of a jock, or wearing nothing at all, Franny could get to your private parts when the chips were down. Frank was suddenly all arms and legs jerking, and a moan so blue escaped him that I shivered. Father slapped Franny in the face, but she wouldn't let go; he had to claw her fingers open. Coach Bob dragged Frank free of her, but Franny took a last kick with her long leg and Father was forced to slap her, hard, across the mouth. That ended it.

Father sat on the dining room carpet, holding Franny's head against his chest and rocking her in his arms while she cried. 'Franny, Franny,' he said to her softly. 'Why does everyone have to hurt you to stop you?'

'Easy, son, just breathe easy,' Coach Bob told Frank, who lay on his side with his knees up to his chest, his face as gray as one of the Dairy School colors; old Iowa Bob knew how to console somebody who'd been felled by a blow to the balls. 'Feel kind of sick, don't you?' Coach Bob inquired, gently. 'Just breathe easy, lie still. It goes away.'

Mother cleared the table, picked up the fallen chairs; her determined disapproval of her family's inner violence registered on her face as enforced silence, bitter and hurt and full of dread.

'Try a deeper breath, now,' Coach Bob advised Frank; Frank tried and coughed. 'Okay, okay,' said Iowa Gob. 'Stick with the little breaths awhile longer.' Frank moaned.

Father examined Franny's lower lip while her tears streamed down her face and she made those gagging kinds of sobs, half strangled in her chest. 'I think you need some stitches, darling,' he said, but Franny shook her head furiously. Father held her head tightly between his hands and kissed her just above the eyes, twice. 'I'm sorry, Franny,' he said, 'but what can I *do* with you, what can I *do?*'

'I don't need stitches,' Franny mourned. 'No stitches. No way.'

But on her lower lip a jagged flap protruded and Father had to cup his hand under Franny's chin to catch her blood. Mother brought a washcloth full of ice.

I went back to my room and coaxed Lilly out of the closet; she wanted to stay with me and I let her. She fell right asleep, but I lay in bed thinking that every time someone said 'Hotel,' there would be blood and sudden sorrow. Father and Mother drove Franny to the Dairy School infirmary, where someone would

68

stitch her lip together; no one would blame Father—least of all Franny. Franny would blame Frank, of course, which—in those days—was my tendency, too. Father would not blame himself —or at least not for long—and Mother would blame herself, inexplicably, for some while longer.

Whenever we fought, Father usually cried at us, 'Do you know how this upsets your mother and me? Imagine that *we* fought all the time, and you had to live with it? But *do* your mother and I fight? *Do* we? Would you like it if we did?'

We would not, of course; and they didn't—most of the time. There was only the *old* argument, the living-in-the-future-and-not-enjoying-today argument, which Coach Bob expressed more vehemently than Mother, though we knew it was her opinion of my father, too (that, and that Father couldn't help it).

It didn't seem like a big thing, to us kids. I rolled Lilly on her side so that I could stretch out flat on my back with both my ears off the pillow, so that I could hear Iowa Bob coaching Frank upstairs. 'Easy, boy, just lean on me,' Bob was saying. 'The secret's in the breathing.' Frank blubbered something and Coach Bob said, 'But you can't grab a girl's tit, boy, and not expect to take a shot in the balls, now, can you?'

But Frank blubbered on: how Franny was terrible to him, how she never let him alone, how she was always turning the other kids against him, how he tried to avoid her but she was always there. 'She's in the middle of everything bad that happens to me!' he cried. 'You don't *know!*' he croaked. 'You don't know how she teases me.'

I thought *I* knew, and Frank was right; he was also rather unlikable, and that was the problem. Franny was *awful* to him, but Franny was not awful; and Frank was not really awful to any of us, except he (himself) was, somehow, awful. It bewildered me, lying there. Lilly began to snore. I heard Egg shuffle down the hall and wondered how Coach Bob would handle it if Egg woke up hollering for Mother. Bob had his hands full with Frank in the bathroom.

'Go on,' Bob said. 'Just let me see you do it.' Frank sobbed. 'There!' cried Iowa Bob, as if he'd just discovered a fumble in the end zone. 'See? No blood, boy—just piss. You're okay.'

'You don't know,' Frank kept saying. 'You don't know.'

I went to see what Egg wanted; being three, he wanted something unobtainable, I thought, but I was surprised that he was cheerful when I came into his room. He was obviously surprised to see me, and when I returned all the soft animals to his bed—he had thrown them all over his room—he proceeded to introduce me to each of them: the frayed squirrel he had vomited on, many times; the worn elephant with one ear; the orange hippopotamus. He was upset whenever I tried to leave him, so I took him into my room and put him in my bed with Lilly. Then I carried Lilly back to her room, although that was a long way for me to carry her and she woke up and became irritable before I got her in her own bed.

'I never get to stay in your room,' she said; then she was asleep again, instantly.

I went back to my room and got in bed with Egg, who was wide-awake and talking nonsense. He was happy, though, and I heard Coach Bob talking downstairs—at first, I thought, to Frank, but then I realized Bob was talking to our old dog, Sorrow. Frank must have gone off to sleep, or at least gone off to sulk.

'You smell worse than Earl,' Iowa Bob was telling the dog. And, in truth, Sorrow was dreadful to smell; not only his farting but his halitosis could kill you if you weren't careful, and the old black Labrador retriever seemed viler to me, too, than my faint memory of the foul odors of Earl. 'What are we going to do with you?' Bob mumbled to the dog, who enjoyed lying under the dining room table and farting all through mealtimes.

Iowa Bob opened windows downstairs. 'Come on, boy,' he called to Sorrow. 'Jesus,' Bob said, under his breath. I heard the front door open; presumably Coach Bob had put Sorrow out.

I lay awake with Egg crawling all over me, waiting for Franny to get back; if I was awake, I knew she'd come and show me her stitches. When Egg finally fell asleep, I carried him back to his room and his animals.

Sorrow was still outside when Father and Mother drove Franny home; if his barking hadn't woken me up, I'd have missed them. 'Well, that looks pretty good,' Coach Bob was saying, obviously approving of Franny's lip job. 'That won't leave any scar at all, after a while.'

'Five of them,' Franny said, thickly, as though they had given her an additional tongue.

'Five!' Iowa Bob cried. 'Terrific!'

'That dog's been farting in here again,' Father said; he sounded grouchy and tired, as if they'd been talking, talking, *talking* nonstop since they'd left for the infirmary.

'Oh, he's so sweet,' Franny said, and I heard Sorrow's hard tail wagging against a chair or the sideboard—*whack, whack,*

70

whack. Only Franny could lie next to Sorrow for hours and be unaffected by the dog's various stenches. Of course, Franny seemed to notice smell, in general, less than the rest of us. She had never objected to changing Egg's diapers—or even Lilly's, when we were all much younger. And when Sorrow, in *his* senility, would have an accident overnight, Franny never found the dog shit displeasing; she had a cheerful curiosity about strong things. She could go the longest, of any of us, without a bath.

I heard all the grown-ups kiss Franny good night and I thought: Families must be like this—gore one minute, forgiveness the next. Just as I knew she would, Franny came into my room to show me her lip. The stitches were a crisp, shiny black, like pubic hair; Franny *had* pubic hair, I did not. Frank did, but he hated it.

'You know what your stitches look like?' I asked her.

'Yeah, I know,' she said.

'Did he hurt you?' I asked her, and she crouched close by my bed and let me touch her breast.

'It was the other one, dummy,' she said, and moved away from me.

'You really got Frank,' I said.

'Yeah, I know,' she said. 'Good night.' Then she peeked back in my door. 'We *are* going to move to a hotel,' she said. Then I heard her going into Frank's room.

'Want to see my stitches?' she whispered.

'Sure,' Frank said.

'You know what they look like?' Franny asked him.

'They look gross,' Frank said.

'Yeah, but you know what they look like, don't you?' Franny asked.

'Yes, I know,' he said, 'and they're gross.'

'Sorry about your balls, Frank,' Franny told him.

'Sure,' he said. 'They're okay. Sorry about . . .' Frank started to say, but he had never said 'breast,' much less 'tit,' in his life. Franny waited; so did I. 'Sorry about the whole thing,' Frank said.

'Yeah, sure,' Franny said. 'Me too.'

Then I heard her testing Lilly, but Lilly was too soundly asleep to be disturbed. 'Want to see my stitches?' Franny whispered. Then after a while I heard her say to Lilly, 'Sweet dreams, kiddo.'

There was, of course, no point in showing stitches to Egg. He

71

would assume that they were remnants of something Franny had eaten.

'Want a ride home?' my father asked his father, but old Iowa Bob said he could always use the exercise.

'You may think this is a crummy town,' Bob said, 'but at least it's safe to walk at night.'

Then I listened some more; I knew when my parents were alone.

'I love you,' my father said.

And my mother said, 'I know you do. And I love you.' I knew, then, that she was tired, too.

'Let's take a walk,' Father said.

'I don't like to leave the children,' Mother said, but that was no argument, I knew; Franny and I were perfectly capable of looking after Lilly and Egg, and Frank looked after himself.

'It won't take fifteen minutes,' Father said. 'Let's just walk up there and look at it.'

'It,' of course, was the Thompson Female Seminary—that beast of a building Father wanted to turn into a hotel.

'I went to school there,' Mother said. 'I know that building better than you do; I don't want to look at it.'

'You used to like walking with me at night,' Father said, and I could tell by my mother's laughter, which was only slightly mocking, that she was shrugging her shoulders for him again.

It was quiet downstairs; I couldn't tell if they were kissing or putting on their jackets—because it was a fall night, damp and cool—and then I heard Mother say, 'I don't think you have any idea how much money you're going to have to sink into that building to make it even *resemble* a hotel anybody would ever want to stay in.'

'Not necessarily *want*,' Father said. 'Remember? It will be the only hotel in town.'

'But where's the money going to come from?' Mother said.

'Come on, Sorrow,' Father said, and I knew that they were on their way out the door. 'Come on, Sorrow. Come stink up the whole town,' Father said. Mother laughed again.

'Answer me,' she said, but *she* was being flirtatious now; Father had already convinced her, somewhere, sometime before —perhaps when Franny was taking the stitches in her lip (stoically, I knew: without a tear). 'Where's the money going to come from?' Mother asked him.

'*You* know,' he said, and closed the door. I heard Sorrow barking at the night, at everything in it, at nothing at all.

72

And I knew that if a white sloop had pulled up to the front porch and the trellises of the old Bates family house, my mother and father would not have been surprised. If the man in the white dinner jacket, who owned the once exotic Arbuthnot-by-the-Sea, had been there to greet them, they wouldn't have blinked an eye. If he'd been there, smoking, tanned and impeccable, and if he'd said to them, 'Welcome aboard!'—they would have set out to sea on the white sloop there and then.

And when they walked up Pine Street to Elliot Park and turned past the last row of the houses lived in by the widows and widowers, the wretched Thompson Female Seminary must have shone in the night to them like a château, or a villa, throwing a gala for the rich and famous—although there couldn't have been a light on, and the only soul around would have been the old policeman in his squad car, cruising every hour or so to break up the teen-agers who went there to neck. There was just one streetlight in Elliot Park; Franny and I would never cross the park after dark in our bare feet for fear of stepping on beer bottle glass—or used condoms.

But how Father must have painted a different picture! How he must have taken Mother past the stumps of long-dead elms—the glass crunching underfoot must have imitated the sound of pebbles on an expensive beach, to them—and how he must have said, 'Can't you just imagine it? A family-run hotel! We'd have it to ourselves most of the time. With the killing we'd make on the big school weekends, we wouldn't even have to advertise —at least, not much. Just keep the restaurant and bar open during the week, to attract the businessmen—the lunch and cocktail crowd.'

'Businessmen?' my mother might have wondered aloud. '*What* lunch and cocktail crowd?'

But even when Sorrow flushed the teen-agers from the bushes, even when the squad car stopped Father and Mother and asked them to identify themselves, my father must have been convincing. 'Oh, it's you, Win Berry,' the policeman must have said. Old Howard Tuck drove the night car; he was a moron and smelled of cigars extinguished in puddles of beer. Sorrow must have growled at him: here was an odor to conflict with the dog's own highly developed smell. 'Poor Bob's having a rough season,' old Howard Tuck probably said, because everyone knew my father was Iowa Bob's son; Father had been a backup quarterback for one of Coach Bob's *old* Dairy teams—the teams that used to win.

'Another rough season,' my father must have joked.

'Wutcha *doin'* here?' old Howard Tuck must have asked them.

And my father, without a doubt, must have said, 'Well, Howard, between you and me, we're going to buy this place.'

'You *are?*'

'You betcha,' Father would have said. 'We're going to turn this place into a hotel.'

'A hotel?'

'That's right,' Father would have said. 'And a restaurant, with a bar, for the lunch and cocktail crowd.'

'The lunch and cocktail crowd,' Howard Tuck would have repeated.

'You've got the picture,' Father would have said. 'The finest hotel in New Hampshire!'

'Holy cow,' the cop could only have replied.

Anyway, it was the night-duty town patrolman, Howard Tuck, who asked my father, 'Wutcha gonna call it?'

Rembmber: it was night, and the night inspired my father. He had first seen Freud and his bear at night; he had fished with State o' Maine at night; nighttime was the only time the man in the white dinner jacket made an appearance; it was after dark when the German and his brass band arrived at the Arbuthnot to spill a little blood; it must have been dark when my father and mother first slept together; and Freud's Europe was in total darkness now. There in Elliot Park, with the patrol car's spotlight on him, my father looked at the four-story brick school that indeed resembled a county jail—the rust-iron fire escapes crawled all over it, like scaffolding on a building trying to become something else. No doubt he took my mother's hand. In the darkness, where the imagination is never impeded, my father felt the name of his future hotel, and our future, coming to him.

'Wutcha gonna call it?' asked the old cop.

'The Hotel New Hampshire,' my father said.

'Holy cow,' said Howard Tuck.

'Holy cow' might have been a better name for it, but the matter was decided: the Hotel New Hampshire it would be.

I was still awake when Mother and Father came home—they were gone much longer than fifteen minutes, so I knew that they'd encountered at least the white sloop, if not Freud *and* the man in the white dinner jacket, along the way.

'My God, Sorrow,' I heard Father say. 'Couldn't you have done that *outside?*'

The vision of them coming home was clear to me: Sorrow snorting through the hedges alongside the clapboard buildings of the town, rousing the light-sleeping elderly from their beds. Confused with time, these old people might have looked out and seen my father with my mother, hand in hand; unaware of the years gone by, they would have gone back to bed, muttering, 'It's Iowa Bob's boy, with the Bates girl and that old *bear*, again.'

'Just one thing I don't understand,' my mother was saying. 'Will we have to sell *this* house, and move out of it, before we're ready to move in *there?*'

Because that was the only way he could afford to convert a school into a hotel, of course. The town would be glad to let him have the Thompson Female Seminary, dirt-cheap. Who wanted to have the eyesore left empty, where children could get hurt, smashing the windows and climbing the fire escapes? But it was my mother's family house—the lush Bates family house—that would have to pay for the restoration. Perhaps this was what Freud meant: what Mother must forgive Father for.

'We may have to *sell* it before we move there,' Father said, 'but we may not have to move *out*. Those are just *details.*'

Those details (and others) would take us years, and would cause Franny to say, long after the stitches were out of her lip and the scar was so thin that you thought you could brush it away with your finger—or that one good kiss would erase the mark from her mouth—'If Father could have bought another bear, he wouldn't have needed to buy a hotel.' But the first of my father's illusions was that bears could survive the life lived by human beings, and the second was that human beings could survive a life led in hotels.

3

Iowa Bob's Winning Season

In 1954 Frank joined the freshman class at the Dairy School—an uneventful transition for him, it seemed, except that he spent even more time in his room, by himself. There was a vague homosexual incident, but a number of boys, all from the same dormitory, had been involved—all older than Frank—and the assumption was that Frank had been the victim of a rather common prep school joke. After all, he lived at home; it's not surprising that he was naïve about dormitory life.

In 1955 Franny went to the Dairy School; that was the first year women went there, and the transition was not so smooth. Transitions would never be too smooth when Franny was involved, but in this case there were many unforeseen problems, ranging from discrimination in the classrooms to not enough showers in the wing of the gym they had partitioned for the women to use. Also, the sudden presence of women teachers on the faculty caused several tottering marriages to fall, and the fantasy life of the *boys* at Dairy was no doubt increased a thousand-fold.

In 1956 it was my turn. That was the year they bought an entire backfield and three linemen for Coach Bob; the school knew he was retiring, and he hadn't had a winning season since just after the war. They thought they'd do him a favor by stocking his football team with one-year postgraduate athletes from the toughest Boston high schools. For once Coach Bob not only had a backfield; he had some beef up front, for blocking, and although the old man disliked the idea of a 'bought' team —of what (even in those days) we called 'ringers'—he appreciated the gesture. The Dairy School, however, had more in mind than making Iowa Bob's last year a winning season. They were shooting every angle they could, to attract more alumni money and a new and younger football coach for the next year.

76

One more losing season, Bob knew, and the Dairy School would drop football forever. Coach Bob would rather have gone out a winner with a team he built, over several years, but who wouldn't rather go out a winner almost any way possible.

'Besides,' said Coach Bob, 'even good talent needs a coach. These guys wouldn't be so hot without me. Everybody needs a game plan; everybody needs to be told what they're doing wrong.'

In those years, Iowa Bob had lots to say to my father on the subject of game plan and doing wrong. Coach Bob said that the restoration of the Thompson Female Seminary was 'a task akin to raping a rhinoceros.' It took a little longer than my father had expected.

He had no trouble selling Mother's family house—it was a beauty, and we made a killing on it—but the new owners were impatient to take possession and we paid them a stiff rent to live there for a full year after all the papers were signed.

I remember watching the old school desks being removed from what was going to be the Hotel New Hampshire—hundreds of desks that had been screwed down to the floor. Hundreds of holes in the floor to fill, or else carpet the whole thing. That was one of the details Father had to deal with.

And the fourth-floor bathroom equipment was a surprise to him. My mother should have remembered: years before her time at the Thompson Female Seminary, the toilets and sinks for the top floor had been misordered. Instead of outfitting bathrooms for high school-sized students, the toilet and sink people delivered and installed *miniatures*—they were meant for a kindergarten in the north of the state. Since the mistake cost less than the original order, the Thompson Female Seminary had let it pass. And so generations of high school girls had stooped and cracked their knees while trying to pee and wash—the tiny child-sized toilets breaking the girls' backs if they sat down too fast, the little sinks hitting them at knee level, the mirrors staring straight at their breasts.

'Jesus God,' Father said. 'It's an outhouse for elves.' He had hoped simply to disperse the old bathroom equipment throughout the hotel; he had enough sense to know that the guests wouldn't want to share communal bathrooms, but he thought he could save a lot of money by using the toilets and sinks that were already there. After all, there wasn't much equipment that a high school and a hotel had in common.

77

'We can use the mirrors, anyway,' Mother said. 'We'll just mount them higher on the walls.'

'And we can use the sinks and toilets, too,' Father insisted.

'*Who* can use them?' Mother asked.

'Dwarfs?' said Coach Bob.

'Lilly and Egg, anyway,' Franny said. 'At least for a few more years.'

Then there were the screwed-down desk chairs that had matched the desks. Father wouldn't throw them out, either.

'They're perfectly good chairs,' Father said. 'They're very comfortable.'

'It's sort of quaint how they have names carved in them,' Frank said.

'*Quaint*, Frank?' Franny said.

'But they have to be screwed down to the floor,' Mother said. 'People won't be able to move them around.'

'Why should people have to move hotel furniture around?' Father asked. 'I mean, we set the rooms the way they should be, right? I don't want people moving the chairs, anyway,' he said. 'This way, they can't.'

'Even in the restaurant?' Mother asked.

'People like to shove back their chairs after a big meal,' said Iowa Bob.

'Well, they can't—that's all,' Father said. 'We'll let them push the tables away from them instead.'

'Why not screw down the tables, too?' Frank suggested.

'That's a quaint idea,' Franny said. She would say, later, that Frank's insecurity was so vast that he would have preferred all of life screwed down to the floor.

Of course, the partitioning of rooms, with their own baths, took the longest. And the plumbing was as complex as a freight yard of tracks in a city railraod station; when someone flushed on the fourth floor, you could hear it coursing through the entire hotel—trying to find a way down. And some of the rooms still had blackboards.

'So long as they're clean,' Father said, 'what's the harm?'

'Sure,' said Iowa Bob. 'One guest can leave messages for the next guest.'

'Things like "Don't ever stay here!" ' Franny said.

'It will be all right,' Frank said. 'I just want my own room.'

'In a hotel, Frank,' Franny said, 'everybody gets a room.'

Even Coach Bob would get a room; after his retirement, the Dairy School wouldn't let him go on living in campus housing,

Coach Bob was cautiously warming to the idea; he was ready to move in when we were ready. He was interested in the future of the playground equipment: the cracked-clay volleyball court, the field-hockey field, and the basketball backboards and hoops —the nets were long since rotted away.

'There's nothing that looks more abandoned,' Bob said, 'than a basketball hoop without a net. I think that's so sad.'

And one day we watched the men with the pneumatic drills chipping THOMPSON FEMALE SEMINARY off the death-gray face of stone, sunk in the bricks, above the great front door. They stopped work for the day—I'm sure on purpose—leaving only the letters MALE SEMIN over the door. It was Friday, so the letters stayed that way over the weekend, to my mother's and father's irritation—and to Coach Bob's amusement.

'Why don't you call it the Hotel Male *Semen?*' Iowa Bob asked my father. 'Then you'll only have to change one letter.' Bob was in a good mood, because his team was winning and he knew he was about to get out of the wretched Dairy School.

If my father was in a bad mood, he rarely let it show. (He was full of energy—'Energy begets energy,' he would repeat and repeat to us, over our homework and at sports practices for the teams he coached.) He had not resigned from the Dairy School; he probably didn't dare, or Mother wouldn't let him. He was going ahead with the Hotel New Hampshire, but he was teaching three classes of English and coaching track winter and spring, so he was going ahead at half-speed.

Frank seemed to disappear at the Dairy School; he was like one of the token cows. You didn't notice him after a while. He did his work—he seemed to find it hard—and he attended the required athletics, although he favored no particular sport and wasn't good enough for (or didn't try to make) any of the teams. He was big and strong and as awkward as ever.

And (at sixteen) he grew a thin moustache on his upper lip, which made him look much older. There was something floppy and puppylike about him—a certain heavy cloddishness in his feet—that suggested he would one day be a very large and imposing dog; but Frank would wait forever for the poise that must attend imposing size in order for the animal to *be* imposing. He had no friends, but no one worried; Frank had never been much for having friends.

Franny, of course, had lots of boyfriends. Most of them were older than Franny, and one of them I liked: he was a tall, red-haired senior at the school—a strong, silent type who

79

stroked the first boat of the varsity crew. His name was Struthers, he had grown up in Maine, and except for the blisters on his hands, which were painted a rust-brown with benzoin—to toughen them—and the fact that he smelled, at times, like wet socks, he was acceptable to everyone in our family. Even Frank. Sorrow growled at Struthers, but that was a smell thing: Struthers threatened Sorrow's dominance of our house. I didn't know if Struthers was Franny's favorite boyfriend, but he was very fond of her, and nice to the rest of us.

Some of the others—one of them was the leader of that pack of Boston ringers who'd been hired to play for Coach Bob —were not so nice. In fact, the quarterback of that imported backfield was a boy who made Ralph De Meo look like a saint. His name was Sterling Dove, although he was called Chip, or Chipper, and he was a cruel, angular boy from one of the posher Boston suburban schools.

'He's a natural leader, that Chip Dove,' Coach Bob said.

He's a natural commander of someone's secret police, I thought. Chipper Dove was blondly handsome, in a spotless, slightly pretty sort of way; we were a dark-haired family, except for Lilly, who was not so blond as she was washed-out—all over; even her hair was pale.

I would have enjoyed seeing Chip Dove play quarterback *without* a good line to protect him—and when he had to throw a lot of passes to catch up several touchdowns—but the admissions office had done a good job for Coach Bob; Dairy's football team never fell behind. When they got the ball, they kept it, and Dove rarely had to pass. Although it was the first winning season that any of us children could remember, it was dull—watching them grind down the field, eating up the clock and scoring from three or four yards out. They were not flashy, they were simply strong and precise and well coached; their defense was not so strong—the other teams scored back on them, but not too often: the other teams rarely got to have the ball.

'Ball control,' crowed Iowa Bob. 'First time I've had a ball-control team since the war.'

My only comfort in Franny's relationship with Chipper Dove was that Dove was such a team boy he was rarely in Franny's company without the rest of the Dairy backfield—and often a lineman or two. They menaced the campus that year like a horde, and Franny sometimes was seen in their camp; Dove was attracted to her—every boy, except Frank, seemed attracted to Franny. Girls were cautious in her company; she simply outshone them, and perhaps she was not a very good friend to them. Franny was always meeting more and newer people; she was probably too curious about strangers to be loyal in the way girls want their girl friends to be loyal.

I don't know; I was kept in the dark about that. At times Franny would fix me up with a date, but the girls were usually older and it didn't work out. 'Everyone thinks you're cute,' Franny said, 'but you have to *talk* to people a little bit, you know —you can't just *start out* necking.'

'I *don't* start out necking,' I'd tell her. 'I never *get* to the necking.'

'Well,' she said, 'that's because you just sit there waiting for something to happen. Everyone knows what you're thinking.'

'*You* don't,' I said. 'Not always.'

'About *me*, you mean?' she asked, but I didn't say anything. 'Listen, kid,' Franny said. 'I know you think about me too much —if that's what you mean.'

It was at Dairy that she started calling me 'kid,' although there was just a year's difference between us. To my shame, the name stuck.

'Hey, kid,' Chip Dove said to me in the showers at the gym. 'Your sister's got the nicest ass at this school. Is she banging anybody?'

'Struthers,' I said, although I hoped it wasn't true. Struthers was at least better than Dove.

'Struthers!' Dove said. 'The fucking *oarsman?* The clod who *rows?*'

'He's very strong,' I said; that much was true—oarsmen are strong, and Struthers was the strongest of them.

'Yeah, but he's a clod,' Dove said.

'Just pulls his oar all day!' said Lenny Metz, a running back who was always—even in the showers—just to the right of Chip Dove's hip, as if he expected, even there, to be handed the ball. He was as dumb as cement, and as hard.

'Well, kid,' said Chipper Dove. 'You tell Franny I think she's got the nicest ass at this school.'

'And tits!' cried Lenny Metz.

'Well, they're okay,' Dove said. 'But it's the ass that's really special.'

'She has a nice smile, too,' Metz said.

Chip Dove rolled his eyes at me, conspiratorially—as if to show me he knew how dumb Metz was, and he was much, much

81

smarter. 'Don't forget to use a little soap, huh, Lenny?' Dove said, and passed him the slippery bar, which Metz, instinctively —a non-fumbler—slapped against his belly in his bearish grip.

I turned off my shower because some bigger person had moved under the stream of water with me. He shoved me out of his way altogether and turned the water back on.

'Move on, man,' he said, softly. It was one of the linemen who kept other football players from hurting Chipper Dove. His name was Samuel Jones, Jr., and he was called Junior Jones. Junior Jones was as black as any night in which my father's imagination was inspired; he would go on to play college football at Penn State, and pro ball in Cleveland, until someone messed up his knee.

I was fourteen, in 1956, and Junior Jones was the largest organization of human flesh I had ever seen. I moved out of his way, but Chipper Dove said, 'Hey, Junior, don't you know this kid?'

'No, I haven't met him,' said Junior Jones.

'Well, this is Franny Berry's brother,' Chip Dove said.

'How do you do?' said Junior Jones.

'Hello,' I said.

'Old Coach Bob is this kid's grandfather, Junior,' Dove said.

'That's nice,' said Junior Jones. He filled his mouth with a froth of lather from the tiny bar of soap in his hand, then tipped his head back and rinsed his mouth out in the downstream of the shower. Perhaps, I thought, this was what he did instead of brushing his teeth.

'We were talking,' Dove said, 'about what it was we *liked* about Franny.'

'Her smile,' Metz said.

'You said her tits, too,' Chipper Dove said. 'And *I* said she had the nicest ass at this school. We didn't get to ask the kid, here, what *he* likes about his sister, but I thought we'd ask you first, Junior.'

Junior Jones had lathered his bar of soap away to nothing; his huge head was awash with white froth; when he rinsed himself under the shower, the suds lapped around his ankles. I looked down at my feet and felt the close presence of the remaining twosome from Iowa Bob's backfield. A burnt-face boy named Chester Pulaski, who spent too much time under the sun lamp —even so, his neck blazed with boils; his forehead was studded with them. He was primarily a blocking back—not by choice; he simply didn't run quite as well as Lenny Metz. Chester Pulaski was a natural blocking back because he tended to run *at* his opponents more than he tended away from them. With him, and flitting near to me, like a horsefly that won't leave you alone, was a boy as black as Junior Jones; any comparison, however, was over with their color. He sometimes lined up as a wide receiver, and when he ran out of the backfield it was only to catch Chipper Dove's short and safe little passes. His name was Harold Swallow, and he was no bigger than I was, but Harold Swallow could fly. He had moves like the bird he was named for; if anyone ever tackled him, he might have broken in half, but when he wasn't catching passes and flying out of bounds, he was just hiding in the backfield, usually behind Chester Pulaski or Junior Jones.

They were all there, standing around me, and I thought that if a bomb were to be dropped on one spot in the shower room, Coach Bob's winning season would be over. Athletically, at least, I was the only one who wouldn't have been missed. I was simply not in the same category with Iowa Bob's imported backfield, or with the giant lineman Junior Jones; there were other linemen, of course, but Junior Jones was the main reason Chipper Dove never even fell down. He was the main reason there was always a hole for Chester Pulaski to lead Lenny Metz through; Jones made a hole big enough for them to run through side by side.

'Come on, Junior, *think,*' Chip Dove said, dangerously —because the tone of mockery in his voice implied his doubt that Junior Jones *could* think. 'What is it *you* like about Franny Berry?' Dove asked.

'She's got nice little *feet,*' said Harold Swallow. Everyone stared at him, but he just pranced around under the falling water, not looking at anybody.

'She's got beautiful skin,' said Chester Pulaski, helplessly drawing even more attention to his boils.

'Junior!' Chip Dove said, and Junior Jones shut off his shower. He stood and dripped for a while. He made me feel as if I were Egg, years ago, still learning to walk.

'She's just another white girl, to me,' Junior Jones said, and his look paused a second on each of us before moving on. 'But she seems like a good girl,' he added, to me. Then he turned my shower back on and shoved me under it—it was too cold—and he walked out of the shower room, leaving a draft.

I was impressed that even Chipper Dove would go only so far with him, but I was more impressed that Franny was in trouble

—and still more impressed that I was helpless to do anything about it.

'That scum Chipper Dove talks about your ass, your tits, even your *feet!*' I told her. 'You watch out for him.'

'My *feet?*' Franny said. 'What's he say about my feet?'

'All right,' I said. 'That was Harold Swallow.' Everyone knew Harold Swallow was crazy; in those days, when someone was as crazy as Harold Swallow, we said he was as crazy as a waltzing mouse.

'What did Chip Dove say about me?' Franny asked. 'I just care about him.'

'Your *ass* is all he cares about,' I told her. 'And he talks about it to everyone.'

'I don't care,' she said. 'I'm not that interested.'

'Well, *he's* interested,' I said. 'Just stick with Struthers.'

'Oh, kid, let me tell you,' she sighed. 'Struthers *is* sweet, but he is boring, boring, *boring.*'

I hung my head. We were in the upstairs hall of what was now only a rented house, although it still felt like the Bates family house to us. Franny rarely came into my room anymore. We did our homework in our own rooms and met outside the bathroom to talk. Frank didn't even seem to use the bathroom. Every day, now, in the hall outside our rooms, Mother would stack up more cartons and trunks; we were getting ready to move to the Hotel New Hampshire.

'And I don't see why you have to be a cheerleader, Franny,' I said. 'I mean, you, of all people—a *cheerleader.*'

'Because I like it,' she said.

In fact, it was after a cheerleading practice that I met Franny, not far from our place in the ferns we didn't see so much of —now that we were students at the school—when we encountered Iowa Bob's backfield. They had accosted someone on the path through the woods that was the shortcut back to the gym; they were working someone over in the large mud puddle that was drilled with football cleats—holes like machine-gun fire in the mud. When Franny and I saw who they were—the boys in the backfield—and that they were beating up on someone, we started to run the other way. That backfield was always beating up on someone. But we hadn't run more than twenty-five yards before Franny caught my arm and stopped me. 'I think it was Frank,' she said. 'They've got Frank.'

So of course we had to go back. For just a second, before we could actually see what was going on, I felt very brave; I felt

84

Franny take my hand and I gave her a strong squeeze. Her cheerleading skirt was so short that the back of my hand brushed her thigh. Then she pulled her hand out of mine and screamed. I was in my track shorts and I felt my legs turn cold.

Frank was wearing his band uniform. They had stripped the shit-brown pants (with the death-gray stripe down the leg) clean off him. Frank's underwear was yanked down to his ankles. The jacket of his band uniform had been tugged up to the middle of his chest; one silver epaulette floated free in the mud puddle, alongside Frank's face, and his silver cap with the brown braid —almost indistinguishable from the mud itself—was squashed under Harold Swallow's knee. Harold held on to one of Frank's arms, fully extended; Lenny Metz stretched Frank's other arm. Frank lay belly down with his balls in the heart of the mud puddle, his astonishing bare ass rising up out of the water and submerging again, as Chipper Dove pushed it down with his foot, then let it up, then pushed it down. Chester Pulaski, the blocking back, sat on the backs of Frank's knees with Frank's ankles locked under his arms.

'Come on, hump it!' said Chipper Dove to Frank. He pushed down on Frank's ass and drove him deep into the mud puddle again. The football cleats left little white indentations on Frank's ass.

'Come on, you mud-fucker,' said Lenny Metz. 'You heard the man—hump it!'

'Stop it!' Franny screamed at them. 'What are you doing?'

Frank seemed the most alarmed to see her, although even Chipper Dove couldn't conceal his surprise.

'Well, look who's here,' Dove said, but I could tell he was thinking about what to say next.

'We're just giving him what he likes,' Lenny Metz told Franny and me. 'Frank likes to screw mud puddles, don't you, Frank?'

'Let him go,' Franny said.

'We're not hurting him,' Chester Pulaski said; he was forever embarrassed about his complexion and he chose to look at me, not at Franny; he probably couldn't stand to see Franny's fine skin.

'Your brother likes *boys*,' Chipper Dove told us. 'Don't you, Frank?' he asked.

'So what?' said Frank. He was angry, not whipped; he'd probably stuck his fingers in their eyes—he'd probably hurt one or two of them, here or there. Frank always put up a fight.

85

'Putting it up boys' asses,' said Lenny Metz, 'is *disgusting.*'

'It's like stickin' it in *mud,*' Harold Swallow explained, but he looked as if he'd really rather be *running,* somewhere, than holding Frank's arm. Harold Swallow always looked uneasy —as if he were crossing a busy street, at night, for the first time.

'Hey, no harm done,' said Chipper Dove. He took his foot off Frank's ass and took a step toward Franny and me. I remembered what Coach Bob was always saying about knee injuries; I was wondering if I could take a swipe at Chip Dove's knee before he beat the shit out of me.

I didn't know what Franny was thinking, but she said to Dove, 'I want to talk with you. Alone. I want to be alone with you, right now,' Franny told him.

Harold Swallow shrieked with a laughter as nasal and high-pitched as the song of any waltzing mouse.

'Well, that's possible,' Dove said to Franny. 'Sure, we can talk. Alone. Anytime.'

'Right now,' Franny said. 'I want to do it right now—or never,' she said.

'Well, right now, sure,' said Dove. He rolled his eyes to his backfield men. Chester Pulaski and Lenny Metz looked mortified with envy, but Harold Swallow was frowning at a grass stain on his football uniform. It was the only mark on him: a small grass stain, where Harold Swallow must have flown too close to the ground. Or perhaps he was frowning because Frank's outstretched body blocked his view of Franny's feet.

'Let Frank go,' Franny told Dove. 'And make the others go —to the gym,' she said.

'Sure we'll let him go,' Dove said. 'We were just going to, anyway, *right?*' he said—the quarterback: giving signals to his backfield. They let Frank go. Frank stumbled getting up and tried to cover his private parts, which were thick and sodden with mud. He dressed himself, furiously, without a word. At that moment I was more afraid of him than I was afraid of any of the others—they were doing what they'd been told to do, anyway: they were trotting down the path to the gym. Lenny Metz turned to leer and wave. Franny gave him the finger. Frank pushed wetly between Franny and me and started tramping home.

'Forget something?' Chip Dove said to him.

Frank's cymbals were in the bushes. He stopped—seemingly more embarrassed for forgetting his band instrument than he appeared to be humiliated for all the rest of it. Franny and I hated

86

Frank's cymbals. I think it was wearing a uniform—*any* uniform—that had attracted Frank to the band. He was not a social creature, but when Coach Bob's winning season prompted the resurrection of a marching band—no band had marched at Dairy since shortly after World War II—Frank could not resist the uniforms. Since he could play nothing, musically, they gave him the cymbals. Other people probably felt foolish with them, but not Frank. He liked marching around, doing nothing, waiting for his big moment to CLASH!

It was not like having a musical member of the family, always practicing and driving the rest of us nuts with the screeching, tooting, or plinking of an instrument. Frank didn't 'practice' the cymbals. Occasionally, at odd hours, we would hear one shattering clang from them—from Frank's locked room—and we had to imagine, Franny and I, that Frank had been marching in place in his uniform, sweating in front of his mirror until he couldn't stand the sound of his own breathing and had been inspired to put a dramatic end to it.

The terrible noise made Sorrow bark and, probably, fart. Mother would drop things. Franny would run to Frank's door and pound on it. I would imagine the sound differently: it was remindful of the suddenness of a gun, to me, and I always thought, for an instant, that we had just been startled by the sound of Frank's suicide.

On the path where the backfield had ambushed him, Frank dragged his muddy cymbals from the bushes, clanking them under his arm.

'Where can we go?' Chip Dove asked Franny. 'To be *alone*.'

'I know a place,' she said. 'Nearby,' she added. 'It's a place I've known forever.' And I knew, of course, that she meant the ferns—*our* ferns. To my knowledge, Franny hadn't even taken Struthers there. I thought she could only be mentioning them this clearly so that Frank and I would know where to find her, and rescue her, but Frank was already heading home, stomping down the path without a word to Franny, or one look at her, and Chip Dove smiled at me with his ice-blue eyes and said, 'Beat it, kid.'

Franny took him by the hand and pulled him off the path, but I caught up to Frank in no time. 'Jesus, Frank,' I said, 'where are you going? We've got to help her.'

'Help Franny?' he said.

'She helped you,' I said to him. 'She saved your ass.'

'So what?' he said, and then he started to cry. 'How do you

87

know she *wants* our help?' he said, sniveling. 'Maybe she *wants* to be alone with him.'

That was too terrible a thought for me—it was almost as bad as imagining Chipper Dove doing things to Franny that she didn't want done to her—and I grabbed Frank by his one remaining epaulette and dragged him after me.

'Stop crying,' I said, because I didn't want Dove to hear us coming.

'I want to talk with you, just *talk!*' we heard Franny screaming. 'You rat's asshole!' she yelled. 'You could have been so nice, but you had to go and be such a super *shit* of a human being. I *hate* you!' she cried. 'Cut it *out!*' she screamed.

'I think you *like* me,' we heard Chipper Dove say.

'I might have,' Franny said, 'but not now. Not *ever,*' we heard her say, but she stopped sounding angry; suddenly she was crying.

When Frank and I reached the ferns, Dove had his football pants down at the knees. He was having the same trouble with the thigh pads that Franny and I had observed, years ago, while spying on the crapping posture of the fat football player named Poindexter. Franny had *her* clothes *on,* but she seemed curiously passive, to me—sitting in the ferns (where he'd pushed her, she told me later) with her hands over her face. Frank clashed his damn cymbals together—so startlingly loud that I thought an airplane was flying into another airplane above us. Then he swung the right-hand cymbal smack into Chip Dove's face. It was the hardest hit the quarterback had taken all season; we could tell he wasn't used to it. Clearly, too, he was impeded by the position of his pants. I dropped straight on him as soon as he was down. Frank continued to clash his cymbals together—as if this were a ritual dance that our family always practiced prior to slaughtering an enemy.

Dove threw me off him, the way old Sorrow could still knock Egg down—with a good toss of his big head—but the clamor Frank was making seemed to paralyze the quarterback. It seemed to awaken Franny from her moment of passivity, too. She made her usual unbeatable move for the private parts of Chipper Dove, and he made the sickly motions of quitting this life, forever, that surely Frank must have recognized—and, of course, *I* remembered from the days of Ralph De Meo. She really grabbed him good, and when he was still on his hip in the pine needles, with his football pants still around his knees, Franny pulled his jock and cup halfway down his thighs before releasing it with a snap. For just a second, Frank, Franny and I got to see Dove's small, frightened private parts. 'Big deal!' Franny screamed at Dove. 'You're such a big deal!'

Then Franny and I had to restrain Frank from going on and on with his banging cymbals; it seemed that the sound might kill the trees and drive small animals from the forest. Chipper Dove lay on his side with one hand cupping his balls and the other hand holding one ear shut against the noise; his other ear was pressed to the ground.

I saw Dove's helmet in the ferns and took it with me when we left him there to recover himself. Back at the mud puddle, on the path, Frank and Franny filled the quarterback's helmet with mud. We left it brimming full for him.

'Shit and death,' Franny said, darkly.

Frank couldn't stop tapping his cymbals together, he was so excited.

'Jesus, Frank,' Franny said. 'Please cut it out.'

'I'm sorry,' he told us. And when we were nearer home, he said, 'Thank you.'

'Thank you, too,' Franny said. 'Both of you,' she said, squeezing my arm.

'I really *am* queer, you know,' Frank mumbled.

'I guess I knew,' Franny said.

'It's okay, Frank,' I said, because what else could a brother say?

'I was thinking of a way to tell you,' Frank said.

And Franny said, '*This* was a quaint way.'

Even Frank laughed; I think it was the first time I'd heard Frank laugh since the time Father discovered the size of the fourth-floor toilets in the Hotel New Hampshire—our fourth-floor 'outhouse for elves.'

We sometimes wondered if living in the Hotel New Hampshire would always be like this.

What seemed more important to know was who would come to stay in our hotel after we moved in and opened it for business. As that time approached, Father became more emphatic about his theories for the perfect hotel. He had seen an interview, on television, with the head of a hotel-management school—in Switzerland. The man said that the secret to success was how quickly a new hotel could establish a pattern of advance bookings.

'Advance Bookings!' Father wrote on a shirt cardboard and

stuck it to the refrigerator of Mother's soon-to-be-abandoned family house.

'Good morning, Advance Bookings!' we would greet each other at breakfast, to tease Father, but he was rather serious about it.

'You laugh,' he told us one morning. 'Well, I already have two.'

'Two what?' Egg asked.

'Two advance bookings,' Father said, mysteriously.

We were planning to open the weekend of the Exeter game. We knew that was the first 'advance booking.' Every year the Dairy School concluded its miserable football season by losing to one of the big schools, like Exeter or Andover, by a big score. It was always worse when we had to travel to those schools and play them on their own well-kept turf. Exeter, for example, had a real stadium; both Exeter and Andover had smart uniforms; they were both all-boys' schools then—and the students wore coats and ties to classes. Some of them even wore coats and ties to the football games, but even if they were informally attired, they looked better than we did. It made us feel terrible to see students like that—altogether clean and cocky. And every year our team stumbled out on the field, looking like shit and death —and when the game was over, that was how we all felt.

Exeter and Andover traded us off; each one liked to use us for their next-to-last game—a kind of warm-up exercise—because their last game of the season was with each other.

But for Iowa Bob's winning season we were playing at home, and this year it would be Exeter. Win or lose, it would be a winning season, but most people—even my father and Coach Bob—thought that this year's Dairy team had a chance of going all the way: undefeated, and with a last-game victory over Exeter, a team the Dairy School had never beaten. With a winning season, even the alumni were coming back, and the Exeter game was made a parents' weekend. Coach Bob wished he had new uniforms to go with his imported backfield, and Junior Jones, but it pleased the old man to imagine that his tattered shit-and-death squad just might knock Exeter's crisp white uniforms with crimson letters, and crimson helmets, all over the field.

Exeter wasn't having too hot a year, anyway; they were poking along about 5–3—against better competition than we usually saw, to be sure, but it was not one of their *great* teams.

Iowa Bob saw that he had a chance, and my father took the entire football season as a good omen for the Hotel New Hampshire.

The weekend of the Exeter game was booked in advance —every room reserved, for two nights; and reservations for the restaurant on Saturday were already closed.

My mother was worried about the chef, as Father insisted on calling her; *she* was a Canadian from Prince Edward Island, where she'd cooked for a large shipping family for fifteen years. 'There's a difference between cooking for a family and cooking for a hotel,' Mother warned Father.

'But it was a *large* family—she said so,' Father said. 'And besides, we're a small hotel.'

'We're a *full* hotel for the Exeter weekend,' Mother said. 'And a full restaurant.'

The cook's name was Mrs. Urick; she was to be assisted by her husband, Max—a former merchant seaman and galley cook who was missing the thumb and index finger of his left hand. An accident in the galley of a vessel called the *Miss Intrepid*, he told us children, with a salty wink. He had been distracted imagining what Mrs. Urick would do to him if she knew about his time ashore with an intrepid lady in Halifax.

'All at once I looked down,' Max told us—Lilly never taking her eyes from his maimed hand. 'And there was my thumb and my finger amongst the bloody carrots, and the cleaver was hacking away with a will of its own.' Max flinched his claw of a hand, as if recoiling from the blade, and Lilly blinked. Lilly was ten, although she didn't seem to have grown much since she'd been eight. Egg, who was six, seemed less frail than Lilly—and sturdily unimpressed with Max Urick's stories.

Mrs. Urick didn't tell stories. For hours she scrutinized crossword puzzles without filling in the squares; she hung Max's laundry in the kitchen, which had been the girls' locker room of the Thompson Female Seminary—thus it was familiar with drying socks and underwear. Mrs. Urick and my father had decided that the most fetching menu for the Hotel New Hampshire would be family-style meals. By this Mrs. Urick meant a choice of two big roasts, or a New England boiled dinner; a choice of two pies—and on Mondays a variety of meat pies, made from leftover roasts. For luncheons there would be soups and cold cuts; for breakfasts, griddle cakes, and so forth.

'Nothing fancy, but just plain good,' said Mrs. Urick, rather humorlessly; she reminded Franny and me of the kind of boarding-school dietician we were familiar with from the Dairy

School—a firm believer that food was no fun but, somehow, morally essential. We shared Mother's anxieties about the cooking—since it would be our standard fare, too—but Father was sure Mrs. Urick would manage.

She was given a basement room of her own, 'to be close to my kitchen,' she said; she expected her stockpots to simmer overnight. Max Urick had a room of his own, too—on the fourth floor. There was no elevator, and my father was happy to use up a fourth-floor room. The fourth-floor rooms had the child-sized toilets and sinks, but since Max had done his bathroom business for so many years in the cramped latrine of the *Miss Intrepid,* he was not insulted by the dwarf facilities.

'Good for my heart,' Max told us. 'Good for pumping the blood—all that stair-climbing,' he said, and whacked his stringy gray chest with his damaged hand. But we thought that Max would go to great lengths to keep as far from Mrs. Urick as possible; he would even climb stairs—he would pee and wash in anything. He claimed to be 'handy,' and when he wasn't helping Mrs. Urick in the kitchen he was supposed to be fixing things. 'Everything from toilets to locks!' he claimed; he could click his tongue like a key turning in a lock, and he could make a terrible whooshing sound—like the tiny fourth-floor toilets in the Hotel New Hampshire sending their matter on an awesome, long voyage.

'What's the *second* advance booking?' I asked Father.

We knew there'd be a Dairy School graduation weekend, in the spring; and maybe a big hockey-game weekend in the winter. But the small, if steady, visits from parents of students at the Dairy School would hardly require any booking in advance.

'Graduation, right?' Franny asked. But Father shook his head.

'A giant wedding!' Lilly cried, and we stared at her.

'Whose wedding?' Frank asked.

'I don't know,' Lilly said. 'But a *giant* one—a really big one. The biggest wedding in New England.'

We never knew where Lilly thought up the things she thought up; Mother looked worriedly at her, then she spoke to Father.

'Don't be secretive,' she said. 'We all want to know: what's the second advance booking?'

'It's not until summer,' he said. 'There's a lot of time to get ready for it. We have to concentrate on the Exeter weekend. First things first.'

'It's probably a convention for the blind,' Franny said to

92

Frank and me, when we were walking to our classes in the morning.

'Or a leprosy clinic,' I said.

'It will be all right,' Frank said, worriedly.

We didn't take the path through the woods behind the practice field anymore. We walked straight across the soccer fields, sometimes throwing our apple cores into the goals, or else we walked down the main path that bisected the campus dormitories. We were concerned that we continue to avoid Iowa Bob's backfield; none of us wanted to be caught alone with Chipper Dove. We hadn't told Father of the incident—Frank had asked Franny and me not to tell him.

'Mother already knows,' Frank told us. 'I mean, she knows I'm queer.'

This surprised Franny and me only for a moment; when we thought of it, it made perfect sense, really. If you had a secret, Mother would keep it; if you wanted a democratic debate, and a family discussion lasting for hours, maybe weeks—perhaps months—then you brought up whatever it was with Father. He was not very patient with secrets, although he was being silent enough about his second advance booking.

'It's going to be a meeting of all the great writers and artists of Europe,' Lilly guessed, and Franny and I kicked each other under the table and rolled our eyes; our eyes said: Lilly is weird, and Frank is queer, and Egg is only six. Our eyes said: We're all alone in this family—just the two of us.

'It's going to be the *circus*,' said Egg.

'How'd you know?' Father snapped at him.

'Oh no, Win,' Mother said. 'It *is* a circus?'

'Just a little one,' Father said.

'Not the descendants of P. T. Barnum?' said Iowa Bob.

'Of course not,' Father said.

'The King Brothers!' Frank said; he had a King Brothers tiger-act poster in his room.

'No, I mean *really* small,' Father said. 'A sort of *private* circus.'

'One of those second-rate ones, you mean,' Coach Bob said.

'Not the kind with freaky animals!' Franny said.

'Certainly not,' said Father.

'What do you mean, "freaky animals"?' Lilly asked.

'Horses with not enough legs,' said Frank. 'A cow with an extra head—growing out of her back.'

'Where'd you see that?' I asked.

'Will there be tigers and lions?' Egg asked.

'Just so they're on the *fourth* floor,' said Iowa Bob.

'No, put them with Mrs. Urick!' Franny said.

'Win,' my mother said. '*What* circus?'

'Well, they can use the *field*, you see,' Father said. 'They can pitch their tents on the old playground, they can eat in the restaurant, and some of them might actually stay in the hotel, too —although most of those people have their own trailers, I think.'

'What will the animals be?' Lilly asked.

'Well,' said Father, 'I don't think they have too many animals. It's *small*, you see. Probably just a few animals. I think they have some special *acts*, you know—but I'm not sure what animals.'

'What *acts?*' said Iowa Bob.

'It's probably one of those *awful* circuses,' Franny said. 'The kind with goats and chickens and those everyday junky animals everyone's seen—some dumb reindeers, a talking crow. But nothing big, you know, and nothing exotic.'

'It's the exotic ones I'd just as soon *not* have around here,' Mother said.

'*What* acts?' said Iowa Bob.

'Well,' Father said. 'I'm not sure. Trapeze, maybe?'

'You don't know what animals,' Mother said. 'And you don't know what acts, either. What *do* you know?'

'They're *small*,' Father said. 'They just wanted to reserve some rooms, and maybe half the restaurant. They take Mondays off.'

'Mondays off?' said Iowa Bob. 'How long did you book them for?'

'Well,' Father said.

'Win!' my mother said. 'How many weeks will they be here?'

'They'll be here the whole summer,' Father said.

'Wow!' cried Egg. 'The circus!'

'*A* circus,' said Franny. 'A weirdo circus.'

'Dumb acts, dumb animals,' I said.

'Weird acts, weird animals,' Frank said.

'Well, you'll fit right in, Frank,' Franny told him.

'Stop it,' Mother said.

'There's no reason to get anxious,' Father said. 'It's just a small, private circus.'

'What's its name?' Mother asked.

'Well,' said Father.

'You don't know its name?' asked Coach Bob.

'Of course I know its name!' Father said. 'It's called Fritz's Act.'

'Fritz's *act?*' Frank said.

'What's the act?' I asked.

'Well,' Father said. 'That's just a *name*. I'm sure there's more than one act.'

'It sounds very modern,' Frank said.

'*Modern,* Frank?' Franny said.

'It sounds kinky,' I said.

'What's kinky?' said Lilly.

'A kind of animal?' Egg asked.

'Never mind,' said Mother.

'I think we should concentrate on the Exeter weekend,' Father said.

'Yes, and getting yourselves, and me, all moved in,' said Iowa Bob. 'There's lots of time to discuss the summer.'

'The whole summer is booked in advance?' Mother asked.

'You see?' Father said. 'Now, *that's* good business! Already we've taken care of the summer, *and* the Exeter weekend. First things first. Now all we have to do is move in.'

That happened a week before the Exeter game; it was the weekend when Iowa Bob's ringers rang up nine touchdowns—to match their ninth straight victory, against no defeats. Franny didn't get to see it; she had decided not to be a cheerleader anymore. That Saturday Franny and I helped Mother move the last things that the moving vans hadn't already taken to the Hotel New Hampshire; Lilly and Egg went with Father and Coach Bob to the game; Frank, of course, was in the band.

There were thirty rooms over four floors, and our family occupied seven rooms in the southeast corner, covering two floors. One room in the basement was dominated by Mrs. Urick, that meant that, together with the fourth-floor resting place of Max, there were twenty-two rooms for guests. But the head-waitress and head maid, Ronda Ray, had a dayroom on the second floor—to gather herself together, she'd said to Father. And two southeast-corner rooms on the third floor—just above us—were reserved for Iowa Bob. That left only nineteen rooms for guests, and only thirteen of those came with their own baths; six of the rooms came with the midget facilities.

'It's more than enough,' Father said. 'This is a small town. And not popular.'

It was more than enough for the circus called Fritz's Act,

95

perhaps, but we were anxious how we were going to handle the full house we expected for the Exeter weekend.

That Saturday we moved in, Franny discovered the intercom system and switched on the 'Receiving' buttons in all the rooms. They were all empty, of course, but we tried to imagine listening to the first guests moving into them. The squawk-box system, as Father called it, had been left over from the Thompson Female Seminary, of course—the principal could announce fire drills to the various classrooms, and teachers who were out of their homerooms could hear if the kids were fooling around. Father thought that keeping the intercom system would make it unnecessary to have phones in the rooms.

'They can call for help on the intercom,' Father said. 'Or we can wake them for breakfast. And if they want to use the phone, they can use the phone at the main desk.' But of course the squawk-box system also meant that it was possible to listen to the guests in their rooms.

'Not *ethically* possible,' Father said, but Franny and I couldn't wait.

That Saturday we moved in, we were without even the main-desk phone—or a phone in our family's apartment—and we were without linen, because the linen service that was going to handle the hotel laundry had also been contracted to do ours. They weren't starting service until Monday. Ronda Ray wasn't starting until Monday, either, but *she* was there—in the Hotel New Hampshire—looking over her dayroom when we arrived.

'I just need it, you know?' she asked Mother. 'I mean, I can't change sheets in the morning, *after* I wait on the breakfast eaters —and *before* I serve lunch to the lunch eaters—without having no place to lay down. And between lunch and supper, if I don't lay down, I get feeling nasty—all over. And if you lived where I lived, you wouldn't wanna go home.'

Ronda Ray lived at Hampton Beach, where she waitressed and changed sheets for the summer crowd. She'd been looking for a year-round arrangement for her hotel career—and, my mother guessed, a way to get out of Hampton Beach, forever. She was about my mother's age, and in fact claimed to remember seeing Earl perform in Earl's casino years ago. She had not seen his ballroom dancing performance, though; it was the bandstand she remembered, and the act called 'Applying for a Job.'

'But I never *believed* it was a real bear,' she told Franny and me, as we watched her unpack a small suitcase in her dayroom.

96

'I mean,' Ronda Ray said, 'I thought *nobody* would get a kick out of undressing no *real* bear.'

We wondered why she was unpacking *night*clothes from the suitcase, if this *day*room was not where she intended to spend the night; she was a woman Franny was curious about—and I thought she was even exotic. She had dyed hair; I can't say what color it was because it wasn't a real color. It wasn't red, it wasn't blond; it was the color of plastic, or metal, and I wondered how it felt. Ronda Ray had a body that I imagined was formerly as strong as Franny's but had grown a little thick—still powerful, but straining. It is hard to say what she smelled like, although —after we left Ronda—Franny tried.

'She put perfume on her wrist two days ago,' Franny said. 'You following me?'

'Yes,' I said.

'But her watchband wasn't there then—her brother was wearing her watch, or her father,' Franny said. 'Some man, anyway, and he really *sweated* a lot.'

'Yes,' I said.

'Then Ronda put the watchband on, over the perfume, and she wore it for a day while she was stripping beds,' Franny said.

'What beds?' I said.

Franny thought a minute. 'Beds very strange people had slept in,' she said.

'The circus called Fritz's Act slept in them!' I said.

'Right!' said Franny.

'The whole summer!' we said, in unison.

'Right,' Franny said. 'And what *we* smell when we smell Ronda is what Ronda's watchband smells like—after all that.'

That was coming close to it, but I thought it was a slightly better smell than that—just slightly. I thought of Ronda Ray's stockings, which she hung in the closet of her dayroom; I thought that if I sniffed just behind the knee of the pair of stockings she was wearing I would catch the true essence of her.

'You know why she wears them?" Franny asked me.

'No,' I said.

'Some man spilled hot coffee on her legs,' Franny said. 'He did it on purpose. He tried to boil her.'

'How do you know?' I asked.

'I've seen the scars,' Franny said. 'And she told me.'

At the squawk-box controls, we switched off all the rooms and listened to Ronda Ray's room. She was humming. Then we heard her smoke. We imagined how she'd sound with a man.

'Noisy,' Franny said. We listened to Ronda's breathing, intermixed with the crackles of the intercom system—an ancient system that ran on the power from an automobile battery, like a clever electric fence.

When Lilly and Egg and Father came home from the game, Franny and I put Egg in the dumbwaiter and hauled him up and down the four-story shaft until Frank ratted on us and Father told us that the dumbwaiter would be used only for removing linen and dishes and other *things*—not humans—from the rooms.

It wasn't safe, Father said. If we let go of the rope, the dumbwaiter fell at the speed imposed by its own response to gravity. That was fast—if not for a *thing*, at least for a human.

'But Egg is so light,' Franny argued. 'I mean, we're not going to try it with *Frank*.'

'You're not going to try it at *all!*' Father said.

Then Lilly got lost and we stopped unpacking for almost an hour, trying to find her. She was sitting in the kitchen with Mrs. Urick, who had seized Lilly's attention by telling her stories of the various ways she'd been punished when she'd been a girl. Her hair had been cut out in hunks, to humiliate her, when she forgot to wash before supper; she'd been told to go stand barefoot in the snow whenever she swore; when she'd 'snitched' food, she'd been forced to eat a tablespoon of salt.

'If you and Mother go away,' Lilly said to Father, 'you won't leave us with Mrs. Urick, will you?'

Frank had the best room and Franny complained; she had to share a room with Lilly. A doorway without a door connected my room to Egg's. Max Urick dismantled his intercom; when we listened to his room, all we heard was static—as if the old sailor were still far out to sea. Mrs. Urick's room bubbled like the stockpots on the back of her stove—the sound of life held steadily at a simmer.

We were so restless for more guests, and for the Hotel New Hampshire to actually be open, that we couldn't keep still.

Father paced us through two fire drills, to tire us out, but it only roused us to wanting more action. When it was dark, we realized the electricity hadn't been turned on—so we hid from each other, and searched for each other, through the empty rooms with candles.

I hid in Ronda Ray's dayroom on the second floor. I blew my candle out and, with my sense of smell, located the drawers where she'd put her nightclothes away. I heard Frank scream from the third floor—he'd put his hand on a plant in the dark

—and what could only be Franny laughing in the echo chamber that the stairwell was.

'Have your fun now!' Father roared from our apartment. 'When there are *guests* here, you can't have the run of the place.'

Lilly found me in Ronday Ray's room and helped me put Ronda's clothes back in the chest of drawers. Father caught us leaving Ronda's room and took Lilly back to our apartment and put her to bed; he was irritable because he'd just tried to call the electric company to complain that the power was off and had discovered that our phones weren't connected, either. Mother had volunteered to take a walk with Egg and make the call from the railroad station.

I went looking for Franny, but she had made it back to the lobby, undetected; she switched all the intercoms to 'Broadcasting' and broadcast an announcement throughout the hotel.

'Now hear this!' Franny boomed. 'Now hear this! Everyone out of bed for a sex check!'

'What's a sex check?' I wondered, running down the stairwell to the lobby.

Frank fortunately missed the message; he was hiding in the fourth-floor utility closet, where there was no squawk box installed: when he heard Franny's announcement, the message was garbled. He probably thought that Father was pacing us through another fire drill; in his haste to leave the utility closet, Frank stepped in a pail and fell on all fours, his head hitting the floor and one hand touching, this time, a dead mouse.

We heard him scream again, and Max Urick opened his door at the end of the fourth-floor hall and bellowed as if he were out to sea and going down.

'Shut up your God-awful screeching, or I'll hang you by your little fingers off the fire escape!'

That put Frank in a bad mood; he declared that our games were 'childish' and he went to his room. Franny and I watched out over Elliot Park from the big corner window in 3F; that would be Coach Bob's bedroom, but Bob was out at an Athletic Department banquet, celebrating all but the last game—yet to be played.

Elliot Park was typically deserted, and the unused playground facilities stuck up like dead trees against the dull glow from the one streetlight. The last of the construction equipment was still there, the diesel machines and the workmen's shack, but the Hotel New Hampshire was finished, now, except for landscaping, and the only machine that had been in use, for days, was the backhoe that crouched near the front flagstone path like a starving dinosaur. There were still a few stumps from the dead elms to dig out of the ground, and a few holes to fill around the periphery of the new parking lot. A soft, glossy light came from the windows of our apartment, where Father was putting Lilly to bed, by candlelight, and Frank was, no doubt, looking at himself in his band uniform in the mirror of his room.

Franny and I saw the squad car come into Elliot Park—like a shark cruising forsaken waters for an unlikely meal. We speculated that the old patrolman, Howard Tuck, would 'arrest' Mother and Egg as they were walking back from the railroad station. We speculated that the candlelight in the Hotel New Hampshire would convince Patrolman Tuck that there were ghosts of old Thompson Female Seminary students haunting the hotel. But Howard parked the patrol car behind the most obvious pile of construction rubble and shut off his engine and his lights.

We saw the head of his cigar, like the shimmering red eye of an animal, in the dark car.

We saw Mother and Egg crossing the playground undetected. They came out of the darkness, and out of the scant light, as if their time on earth were that brief and that dimly illuminated; it gave me a twinge, to see them like that, and I felt Franny shudder beside me.

'Let's go turn all the lights on,' Franny suggested. 'In all the rooms.'

'But the electricity is out,' I said.

'It is now, dummy,' she said, 'but if we turn on all the lights, the whole hotel will light up when they turn the power on.'

That sounded like a fine idea, so I helped her do it—even the hall lights outside Max Urick's room—and the outdoor floodlights, which would one day illuminate a patio extending from the restaurant but now would shine only on the backhoe, and a yellow steel hard hat that dangled by its chin strap from a small tree the backhoe had left alone. The workman whose hat it was seemed gone forever.

The abandoned hat reminded me of Struthers, strong and dull; I knew Franny hadn't seen him in a while. I knew she had no favorite boyfriends, and she seemed sullen on the subject. Franny was a virgin, she'd told me, not because she wanted to be but because there wasn't a boy at the Dairy School who was (as she put it) 'worth it.'

'I don't mean I think *I'm* so great,' she told me, 'but I don't

100

want some clod ruining it for me, and I don't want someone who'd laugh at me, either. It's very important, John,' she told me, 'especially the first time.'

'Why?' I asked.

'It just is,' Franny said. 'It's *the first time*, that's why. It stays with you forever.'

I doubted it; I hoped not. I thought of Ronda Ray: what had the first time meant to her? I thought of her nightclothes, smelling—ambiguously—like her wrist under her watchband, like the back of her knee.

Howard Tuck and the patrol car hadn't moved by the time Franny and I accomplished turning on all the lights. We snuck outdoors; when the power went on, we wanted to see the whole hotel ablaze. We climbed into the driver's seat of the backhoe and waited.

Howard Tuck sat so still in the squad car, he looked as if he were waiting for his retirement. In fact, Iowa Bob was fond of saying that Howard Tuck always looked 'at death's door.'

When Howard Tuck cranked the ignition of the squad car, the hotel lit up *as if he'd done it*. When the patrol car's headlights blinked on, every light in the hotel came to life, and Howard Tuck seemed to lurch the car forward and stall—as if the sight of the bright hotel had dazed him and his foot had slipped off the gas or off the clutch. Actually, the sight of the Hotel New Hampshire blazing with light the instant he started his car had been too much for old Howard Tuck. His life in Elliot Park had been less illuminated—only occasional sexual discoveries, inexpert teen-agers caught in his spotlight, and the odd vandal interested in doing trivial damage to the Thompson Female Seminary. Once the Dairy School students had stolen one of the school's token cows and tied it to the goal at one end of the field-hockey field.

What Howard Tuck saw when he started his car had been a four-story shock of light—the way the Hotel New Hampshire might look the precise second it was bombed. Max Urick's radio came on with a blast of music that caused Max to shriek in alarm; a stove timer chimed in Mrs. Urick's underground kitchen; Lilly cried out in her sleep; Frank came to life in the dark mirror; Egg, anxious at the hum of electricity he felt throb through the hotel, shut his eyes; Franny and I, in the backhoe, held our hands over our ears—as if the sight of this much sudden light could only be accompanied by an explosion. And the old patrolman, Howard Tuck, felt his foot slip off the clutch at the moment his heart stopped and he departed a world where hotels could spring to life so easily.

Franny and I were the first to get to the squad car. We saw the policeman's body slumped against the steering wheel and heard the horn blaring. Father and Mother and Frank ran out of the Hotel New Hampshire, as if the police car were sounding the signal for another fire drill.

'Jesus, Howard, you're *dead!*' Father said to the old man, shaking him.

'We didn't mean to, we didn't mean to,' Franny said.

Father thumped old Howard Tuck on the chest and stretched him out on the police car's front seat; then he struck him on the chest again.

'Call somebody!' Father said, but there was no working phone in our unlikely house. Father looked at the puzzling maze of wires and switches and ear- and mouthpieces in the squad car. 'Hello? Hello!' he said into something, pushing something else. 'How the fuck does this thing work?' he cried.

'Who's this?' said a voice out of the tubes of the car.

'Get an ambulance to Elliot Park!' my father said.

'Halloween alert?' said the voice. 'Halloween trouble? Hello. Hello.'

'Jesus God, it's *Halloween!*' Father said. 'Goddamn silly machine!' he cried, slamming the dashboard of the squad car with one hand; he gave a fairly hard thump to the quiet chest of Howard Tuck with his other hand.

'We can get an ambulance!' Franny said. 'The *school* ambulance!'

And I ran with her through Elliot Park, which was now glowing in the stunning light that poured from the Hotel New Hampshire. 'Holy cow,' said Iowa Bob, when we ran into him at the Pine Street entrance to the park; he was looking at the bright hotel as if the place had opened for business without him. In the unnatural light, Coach Bob looked years older to me, but I suppose he really looked only as old as he was—a grandfather and a retiring coach with one more game to play.

'Howard Tuck had a heart attack!' I told him, and Franny and I ran on toward the Dairy School—which was always up to heart-attack tricks of its own, especially on Halloween.

4

Franny Loses a Fight

On Halloween, the Police Department of the town of Dairy sent old Howard Tuck to Elliot Park, as usual, but the State Police sent two cars to cruise the campus of the Dairy School, and the campus security force was doubled; although short on tradition, the Dairy School had a considerable Halloween reputation.

It had been Halloween when one of the token cows had been tied to the goal at the Thompson Female Seminary. It had been another Halloween when another cow had been led to the Dairy School field house and indoor swimming pool, where the beast suffered a violent reaction to the chlorine in the water and drowned.

It had been Halloween when four little kids from the town had made the mistake of going trick-or-treating in one of the Dairy dorms. The children were kidnapped for the night; they had their heads shaved by a student costumed as an executioner, and one child was unable to speak for a week.

'I *hate* Halloween,' Franny said, as we noted there were few trick-or-treaters on the streets; the little kids of Dairy were frightened of Halloween. An occasional cringing child, with a paper bag or a mask on its head, cowered as Franny and I ran by; and a group of small children—one dressed as a witch, one as a ghost, and two as robots from a recent film about a Martian invasion—fled into the safety of a lit doorway as we charged up the sidewalk toward them.

Cars with anxious parents were parked here and there along the street—spotting for would-be attackers as their children cautiously approached a door to ring a bell. The usual anxieties about the razor blades in apples, the arsenic in the chocolate cookies, were no doubt passing through the parked parents' minds. One such anxious father put his headlights on Franny and me and leaped from his car to give chase. 'Hey, you!' he yelled.

'Howard Tuck had a heart attack!' I called to him, and that

seemed to stop him—cold. Franny and I ran through the open gate, like the gate to a cemetery, that admitted us to the playing fields of the Dairy School; past the pointed iron bars, I tried to imagine the gate for the Exeter weekend—when they would be selling pennants and blankets and cowbells to bash together at the game. It was a rather cheerless gate, now, and as we ran in, a small horde of children rushed by us, running *out*—the other way. They were running for their lives, it seemed, and a few of their terrified faces were as shocking as the Halloween masks some of the other kids had managed to keep on. Their plastic black-and-white and pumpkin-colored costumes were in shreds and tatters, and they wailed like a children's hospital ward —great gagging snivels of fear.

'Jesus God,' Franny said, and they fled away from her—as if *she* were in costume and *I* wore the worst mask of all.

I grabbed a small boy and asked him, 'What's happening?' But he writhed and screamed in my hands, he tried to bite my wrist—he was wet and trembling and he smelled strange, and his skeleton costume came away in pieces in my hands, like soggy toilet paper or a decomposing sponge. 'Giant spiders!' he cried, witlessly. I let him go.

'What's happening?' Franny called to the children, but they were gone as suddenly as they'd appeared. The playing fields stretched in front of us, dark and empty; at the end of them, like tall ships across a harbor shrouded by fog, the dorms and buildings of the Dairy School seemed sparsely lit—as if everyone had gone to bed early, and only a few good students were burning, as they say, the midnight oil. But Franny and I knew that there were very few 'good' students at Dairy, and on a Halloween Saturday night we doubted that even the good ones were studying—and we doubted that any of the dark windows meant that anyone was sleeping. Perhaps they were drinking in the blackness of their rooms; perhaps they were violating each other, and some captured children, in their dark dorms. Perhaps there was a new religion, the rage of the campus, and the religion required total night for its rituals—and Halloween was its day of reckoning.

Something was wrong. The white wooden goal at the near end of the soccer field seemed *too* white, to me, although it was the darkest night I had been in. Something was too stark and apparent about the goal.

'I wish Sorrow was with us,' Franny said.

Sorrow *will* be with us, I thought knowing what Franny

104

didn't know: that Father had taken Sorrow to the vet's this very day, to have the old dog put to sleep. There had been a sober discussion—in Franny's absence—of the need for this. Lilly and Egg weren't with us, either. Father had told Mother, Frank and me—and Iowa Bob. 'Franny won't understand,' Father had said. 'And Lilly and Egg are too young. There's no point in asking their opinion. They won't be rational.'

Frank did not care for Sorrow, but even Frank seemed saddened by the death sentence.

'I know he smells bad,' Frank said, 'but that's not exactly a fatal disease.'

'In a hotel it is,' Father said. 'That dog has terminal flatulence.'

'And he *is* old,' Mother said.

'When *you* get old,' I told Mother and Father, 'we won't put you to sleep.'

'And what about *me?*' Iowa Bob said. 'I suppose I'm the next one to go. Got to watch my farting, or it's off to the nursing home!'

'You're no help at all,' Father told Coach Bob. 'It's only Franny who really loves the dog. She's the one who's *really* going to be upset, and we'll just have to make it as easy for her as we can.'

Father no doubt thought that anticipation was nine-tenths of suffering: he was not really being cowardly by *not* seeking Franny's opinion; he knew what her opinion would be, of course, and he knew that Sorrow had to go.

And so I wondered how long we would be moved into the Hotel New Hampshire before Franny would notice the old farter's absence, before she would start sniffing around for Sorrow—Father would have to put all his cards on the table.

'Well, Franny,' I could imagine Father beginning. 'You know that Sorrow wasn't getting any younger—or any better at controlling himself.'

Passing the dead-white soccer goal, under the black sky, I shuddered to think how Franny would take it. 'Murderers!' she would call us all. And we would all look guilty. 'Franny, Franny,' Father would say, but Franny would make an awful fuss. I pitied the strangers in the Hotel New Hampshire who would waken to the variety of sounds Franny was capable of.

Then I realized what was wrong about the soccer goal: the net was gone. End of the season? I thought. But no, if there was one week more of football, surely there was a week more of soccer, too. And I recalled in past years how the nets would stay on the goals until the first snow, as if it took the first storm to remind the maintenance crew what they had forgotten. The nets in the goals held the drifted snow—like spider webs so dense that they trap dust.

'The net's gone—off the goal,' I said to Franny.

'Big deal,' she said, and we veered into the woods. Even in the dark, Franny and I could find the shortcut, the path the football players always used—and everyone else, because of them, stayed off it.

A Halloween prank? I thought. Stealing a net to a soccer goal . . . and then, of course, Franny and I ran right into it. Suddenly the net was over us, and under us, and there were two other people trapped like us: a Dairy School freshman named Firestone, his face as round as a tire and as soft as a kind of cheese, and a small trick-or-treater from town. The trick-or-treater was wearing a gorilla suit, though he was closer, in size, to a spider monkey. His gorilla mask was backwards on his head, so that when you saw the back of his head you saw a monkey, and when you saw his screaming face you saw him for the frightened little boy he was.

It was a jungle trap, and the monkey thrashed in it wildly. Firestone tried to lie down, but the net kept jiggling him out of position—he collided with me and said, 'Sorry'; then he collided with Franny and said, 'God, awfully sorry.' Every time I tried to get back on my feet, the net would jerk my feet out from under me, or the net over my head would jerk my head back and I'd fall. Franny crouched on all fours, keeping her balance. Inside the net with us was a large brown paper bag, spewing forth the Halloween hoardings of the child in the gorilla suit—candy corn and sticky balls of coagulated popcorn, breaking apart under us, and lollipops with their crinkly cellophane wrappers. The child in the gorilla suit was screaming in that breathless, hysterical way, as if he were about to choke, and Franny got her arms around him and tried to calm him down. 'It's all right, it's just a dirty trick,' she said to him. 'They'll let us go.'

'Giant spiders!' cried the child, slapping himself all over and twitching in Franny's grasp.

'No, no,' Franny said. 'No spiders. They're just *people*.'

But I thought I knew *what* people they were; I would have preferred the spiders.

'Got *four* of them!' said someone—a voice with a locker-room familiarity to it. 'Got fucking four of them at once!'

'Got a little one and three big ones,' said another familiar voice, a ballcarrier's voice or a blocking back's voice—it was hard to tell.

Flashlights, like the blinking eyes of rather mechanical spiders in the night, looked us over.

'Well, look who's here,' said the voice in command, said the quarterback called Chipper Dove.

'Got pretty little feet,' said Harold Swallow.

'Got beautiful skin,' said Chester Pulaski.

'She has a nice smile, too,' said Lenny Metz.

'And the best ass in the whole school,' said Chipper Dove. Franny rested on her knees.

'Howard Tuck had a heart attack!' I told them all. 'We've got to get an ambulance!'

'Let the fucking monkey go,' said Chip Dove. The net shifted. The thin black arm of Harold Swallow snatched the kid in the gorilla suit out of the spider's web and released him into the night. 'Trick or treat!' said Harold, and the little gorilla was gone.

'Is that you, Firestone?' Dove asked, and the flashlight shone on the bland boy named Firestone, who looked as if he were trying to fall asleep at the bottom of the net, his knees drawn fetus-tight up to his chest, his eyes closed, his hand over his mouth.

'You fag, Firestone,' said Lenny Metz. 'What are you doing?'

'He's suckin' his thumb,' said Harold Swallow.

'Let him go,' the quarterback said, and Chester Pulaski's painful complexion blossomed, momentarily, in the flashlight; he dragged the dormant Firestone from the net. After a slight pounding sound, of flesh on flesh, we heard the awakened Firestone trot away.

'Now look who's left,' said Chipper Dove.

'A man had a heart attack,' Franny said. 'We really *are* going to the infirmary for the ambulance.'

'You're not going there now,' said Dove. 'Hey, kid,' he said to me, holding a flashlight on my face. 'You know what I want you to do, kid?'

'No,' I said. And someone kicked me through the net.

'What I want you to do, kid,' Chipper Dove said, 'is stay right here, in our giant spider web, until one of the spiders tells you you can go. You understand?'

'No,' I said, and someone kicked me again, a little harder.

'Be smart,' Franny said to me.

'That's right,' said Lenny Metz. 'Be smart.'

'And you know what I want *you* to do, Franny?' said Chipper Dove, but Franny didn't respond. 'I want you to show me that place, again,' he said. 'That place where we can be alone. Remember?'

I tried to crawl closer to Franny, but someone was tightening the net around me.

'She stays with me!' I yelled. 'Franny stays with me.'

I was down on my hip, then, with the net growing tighter and someone was kneeling on my back.

'Leave him alone,' Franny said. 'I'll show you the place.'

'Just stay here and don't move, Franny,' I said, but she let Lenny Metz pull her out from under the net. 'Remember what you said, Franny!' I cried to her. 'Remember—about the first time?'

'It probably isn't true,' she said, dully. 'It probably isn't anything.'

Then she must have made a break for it, because I heard a scuffle in the dark, and Lenny Metz cried out, '*Nuff!* Son of a bitch, you bitch!' And there was that familiar sound of pounding —flesh on flesh again—and I heard Franny say, 'All right! All right! You bastard.'

'Lenny and Chester are going to *help* show me the place, Franny,' Chipper Dove said. 'Okay?'

'You turd in a birdbath,' Franny said. 'You rat's asshole,' she said, but I heard flesh on flesh again, and Franny said, 'Okay! Okay.'

It was Harold Swallow who was kneeling on my back. If the net hadn't been all tangled around me, I might have been a match for him, but I couldn't move.

'We'll be back for you, Harold!' Chipper Dove called.

'Hang in there, Harold!' said Chester Pulaski.

'You'll get your turn, Harold!' said Lenny Metz, and they all laughed.

'I don't want no turn,' said Harold Swallow. 'I don't want no trouble,' he said. But they were gone, Franny occasionally cursing—but farther and farther away from me.

'You're going to *get* in trouble, Harold,' I said. 'You *know* what they're going to do to her.'

'I don't want to know,' he said. 'I don't get in no trouble. I come to this shit-ass school to get *outa* trouble.'

'Well, you're in trouble now, Harold,' I said. 'They're going to *rape* her, Harold.'

108

'That happens,' said Harold Swallow. 'But not to me.' I struggled briefly under the net, but it was easy for him to keep me pinned down. 'I don't like to fight, either,' he said.

'They think you're a crazy nigger,' I told him. 'That's what they think you are. That's why they're with her and you're here, Harold. But it's the same trouble,' I told him. 'You're in the same trouble they're in.'

'They never get in no trouble,' Harold said. 'Nobody ever tells.'

'Franny will tell,' I said, but I felt the candy corn pressed against my face, and into the damp ground. It was another Halloween to remember, for sure, and I felt as weak and small as I'd ever felt—on every Dairy Halloween I could recall, scared to death by bigger, always *bigger* kids, stuffing my head in my trick-or-treat bag and rattling it until all I heard was cellophane, and then the bag bursting around my ears.

'What did they look like?' Father would always ask us.

But every year they looked like ghosts, gorillas, skeletons, and worse, of course; it was a night for disguises, and nobody ever was caught. Not for tying Frank to the fire escape of the biggest dorm, where he wet his pants; no one ever caught anyone for that. Not for the three pounds of cold, wet pasta someone threw on Franny and me, crying, 'Live eels! Run for your lives!' And we lay writhing on the dark sidewalk, the spaghetti sticking to us, beating each other and screaming.

'They're going to *rape* my sister, Harold!' I said. 'You got to help her.'

'I can't help nobody,' Harold said.

'*Somebody* can help,' I said. 'We could run and get somebody. I know you can *run*, Harold.'

'Yeah,' he said. 'But who's going to help you with *those* guys?'

Not Howard Tuck, I knew, and by the sound of sirens, which I heard now—from the campus and the town—I guessed that Father had figured out the police car enough to use its radio for help. So there would be no authorities available to help Franny, anyway. I started to cry, and Harold Swallow shifted his weight on my shoulder.

It was quiet for a second, between the deep breaths the sirens take, and we heard Franny. Flesh on flesh, I thought—but it was different now. Franny made a sound that moved Harold Swallow to remember who *might* help her.

'Junior Jones could handle those guys,' Harold said. 'Junior Jones don't take no shit from *nobody*.'

'Yes!' I said. 'And he's your friend, isn't he? He likes you better than them, doesn't he?'

'He don't like *nobody*,' said Harold Swallow, admiringly; but suddenly his weight was off me, and he was pawing at the net, unwinding it from around me. 'Get up off your ass,' he said. 'Junior *does* like somebody.'

'Who's he like?' I asked.

'He likes everybody's sister,' said Harold Swallow, but this thought did not reassure me.

'What do you mean?' I asked him.

'Get up on your feet!' said Harold Swallow. 'Junior Jones likes everybody's sister—he told me so, man. He said, "Everybody's sister is a good girl"—that's just what he said.'

'But what's he *mean?*' I said, trying to keep up with him, now, because he was the *fastest* organization of human flesh at the Dairy School. As Coach Bob said, Harold Swallow could fly.

We ran toward the light at the end of the footpath; we ran past where I knew I'd last heard from Franny—where the ferns were, where Iowa Bob's backfield was taking turns. I stopped there; I wanted to run into the woods there, and find her, but Harold Swallow pulled me along.

'You can't do nothing to those guys, man,' he said. 'We got to get Junior.'

Why Junior Jones would help us, I didn't know. I only thought that I would die before I found out—trying to keep up with Harold Swallow—and I thought that if Jones indeed liked 'everybody's sister,' as he apparently claimed, that didn't necessarily mean good news for Franny.

'*How* does he like everybody's sister?' I panted to Harold Swallow.

'He likes them like he likes his *own* sister,' Harold Swallow said. 'Man!' he said to me. 'Why are you so *slow?* Junior Jones has got a sister *himself*, man,' Harold said. 'And some dudes raped her. Shit,' he said. 'I thought everybody knew that!'

'There's a lot you miss, not living in the dorms,' Frank was always saying.

'Did they catch them?' I asked Harold Swallow. 'Did they catch the guys who raped Junior's sister?'

'Shit,' said Harold Swallow. '*Junior* caught them! I thought everybody knew that.'

'What'd he do to them?' I asked Harold Swallow, but Harold had beaten me to Junior Jones's dorm. He was flying up the stairwell and I was easily a full flight of stairs behind him.

'Don't ask!' Harold Swallow yelled down to me. 'Shit,' he said. 'Nobody knows what he did to them, man. And nobody asks.'

Where the hell does Junior Jones *live?* I wondered, passing the third floor and climbing higher, my lungs breaking, Harold Swallow nowhere in sight. But Harold was waiting for me at the landing of the fifth and topmost floor.

Junior Jones lives in the *sky,* I thought, but Harold explained to me that most of the black athletes at the Dairy School were quartered on the top floor of this one dorm. 'Where we're out of sight, you know?' Harold asked me. 'Like fucking birdies in the nests in the tippy-tops of the trees, man,' said Harold Swallow. 'That's where the black people get put at this shit-ass school.'

The fifth floor of the dorm was dark and hot. 'Heat rises, don't you know?' said Harold Swallow. 'Welcome to the fuckin' jungle.'

Every light in every room was out, but *music* was playing and escaping from under the doors; the fifth floor of that dorm was like a tiny street of nightclubs and bars in a city observing blackout conditions; and from the rooms I heard the unmistakable shuffling of feet—dancing and dancing in the dark.

Harold Swallow pounded on a door.

'What you want?' said the terrifying voice of Junior Jones. 'You want to die?'

'Junior, Junior!' said Harold Swallow, pounding harder.

'You *do* want to die, don't you?' said Junior Jones, and we heard a series of locks, as if from a jail cell, unlocking the door from inside.

'If some mother wants to die,' said Junior Jones, '*I'll* help him.' More locks unlocked; Harold Swallow and I stepped back from the door. 'Which one of you wants to die first?' said Junior Jones. Heat and a saxophone throbbed from his room; he was backlit by a candle burning on his desk, which was draped—like the coffin of a President—with the American flag.

'We need your help, Junior,' said Harold Swallow.

'You sure do,' said Junior Jones.

'They've got my sister,' I said to him. 'They've got Franny,' I said. 'And they're raping her.'

Junior Jones seized me by my armpits and hoisted me up to

111

him, face to face; he leaned me, gently, against the wall. My feet felt a foot or two off the floor; I didn't struggle.

'Did you say *rape*, man?' he asked.

'Yeah, rape, rape!' said Harold Swallow, darting around us like a bee. 'They're raping his sister, man. They really are.'

'Your *sister?*' Junior asked me, letting me slide to the floor against the wall.

'My sister Franny,' I said, and for a moment I feared he would say, again, 'She's just another white girl, to me.' But he didn't say anything; he was *crying*—his big face as shiny and wet as the shield of a warrior left out in the rain.

'Please?' I said to him. 'We have to hurry.' But Junior Jones started shaking his head, his tears spraying Harold Swallow and me.

'We're not gonna be in *time*,' Junior said. 'No way are we going to be in *time*.'

'There's *three* of them,' said Harold Swallow. 'Three times takes time.' And I felt sick—I felt like Halloween, again and again, with a bellyful of junk and trash.

'And I know *which* three of them, don't I?' said Junior Jones. I noticed he was getting dressed: I *hadn't* noticed he'd been naked. He pulled on a baggy gray pair of sweat pants, he pulled on his high-topped white basketball shoes over his huge bare feet. He put on a baseball cap, with the visor turned backwards; that was all he was going to wear, apparently, because he stood in the fifth-floor hall of the dorm and shouted suddenly. 'Black Arm of the Law!' he said. Doors opened. 'Lion hunt!' Jones yelled. The black athletes, quarantined on the top floor, peered out at him. 'Get your shit together,' said Junior Jones.

'Lion hunt!' cried Harold Swallow, flying up and down the hall. 'Get your shit together! Black Arm of the Law!'

It was then that it occurred to me that I didn't know any black students at the Dairy School who *weren't* athletes—of course: our shit-ass school wouldn't take them if they couldn't be of some *use*.

'What's a lion hunt?' I asked Junior Jones.

'Your sister's a good girl,' Jones said. 'I know she is. Everybody's own sister is a good girl,' he said, and I agreed with him, of course, and Harold Swallow bumped my arm and said, 'You see, man? Everybody's sister is a good girl.'

And we flew down the stairwell with remarkable silence, considering how many of us there were. Harold Swallow led us, waiting impatiently on every landing. Junior Jones was surprisingly quick for his size. On the second-floor landing we encountered two white students coming home from somewhere; they saw the black athletes descending the stairs and fled down the hall on their floor. 'Lion hunt!' they cried. 'Fucking Black Arm of the Law!'

Not a door opened; two lights went out. And then we were outside in the Halloween night, heading for the woods and the place just off the footpath that I would recognize and remember all my life. There's not a day when I couldn't locate those ferns, where Franny and I were first and always alone.

'Franny,' I cried out, but there was no answer. I led Jones and Harold Swallow into the woods; behind us, the black athletes fanned out along the footpath and entered the woods all up and down the path—shaking the trees, kicking the dead leaves, some of them humming a little tune, *all* of them (I suddenly noticed) wearing those baseball caps turned backwards, all of them bare-chested; two of them wore catchers' masks. The sound they made coming through the woods was like the whirring of a large rotary blade cutting through a field. Flashlights blinked, and like a swarm of large fireflies we came upon the ferns where Lenny Metz, his pants still off, held my sister's head pinched between his knees. Metz was kneeling on Franny's arms, stretched over her head, while Chester Pulaski—who, no doubt, had been third in line—was finishing his turn.

Chipper Dove was gone; he had been first, of course. And like the careful quarterback he was, he hadn't held the ball too long.

'Of course I knew what he was going to do,' Franny told me, much later. 'I was prepared for him—the first time—somehow. But I never thought he'd let the others even *see* me with him. I even *told him* that they didn't have to force me, that I'd let *him*. But when he *left* me with them—I wasn't prepared for that at all. I never even imagined that.'

It seemed to my sister that she'd been made to pay disproportionately for her mischief with the lights in the Hotel New Hampshire and her inadvertent contribution to Howard Tuck's departure from our world. '*Boy*, are you ever made to pay for a little fun,' Franny said.

And it seemed to me that Lenny Metz and Chester Pulaski hardly paid enough for the 'fun' they'd had. Metz released my sister's arms when he first caught sight of Junior Jones; he pulled his pants up and made a break for it—but he was a running back used to good blocking in front of him and a relatively open field. In the dark woods he could barely see the dark bodies of the humming black athletes, and although he ran with power and with some speed, he struck a tree as big around as his thigh, and was dragged back to the holy ground in the ferns, where Junior Jones ordered all his clothes stripped off him and had him tied to a lacrosse stick; he was then carried, naked, to the Dean of Men. I learned, later, that the lion hunters always delivered up their prey with a certain flair.

Once they'd caught an exhibitionist who'd been bothering the girls' dorm. They hung him by his ankles to the shower head in the most populated of the girls' bathrooms—wrapped naked in a transparent shower curtain. Then they called the Dean. 'This is the Black Arm of the Law,' said Junior Jones. 'this is the sheriff of the fucking fifth floor.'

'Yes, Junior, what is it?' the Dean asked.

'There's a male nudist in the females' dorm, first-floor bathroom, on your right,' Jones said. 'The lion hunters captured him in the act of exhibiting himself.'

Thus Lenny Metz was lugged to the Dean of Men. Chester Pulaski got there ahead of him. 'Lion hunt!' Harold Swallow had screamed in the woods, and when Lenny let go of Franny's arms, Chester Pulaski slipped out of my sister's arms and made a break for it, too. He was completely undressed, however, and on his tender bare feet he trotted slowly between the trees, not striking them. Every twenty yeards or so, he was scared to death by the Black Arm of the Law, the black athletes who crept through the woods, swishing the trees, snapping sticks, and humming their tune. It had been Chester Pulaski's first gang bang, and the jungle ritual had completely colored the night for him—he thought the woods were suddenly full of *natives!* (cannibals! he imagined)—and he stumbled whimpering and bent over, appropriate to my imagination of Earl Man, not quite upright, mostly on all fours. He was naked and scratched by branches, and mostly on all fours, when he arrived at the dormitory apartment of the Dean of Men.

The Dean of Men had not been happy at the Dairy School since the school had admitted women. Before then he'd been Dean of Students—a prim, fit man with a pipe and a fondness for racquet sports; he had a pert, fit wife of the youthful, cheerleader variety, her age betrayed only by an alarming pouchiness about her eyes; they had no children. 'The boys,' the Dean of Students liked to say, 'are all my children.'

When the 'girls' arrived, he never felt the same about them and quickly appointed, to assist himself, his wife in the role of

114

Dean of Women. His new title, Dean of Men, pleased him, but he despaired at all the new sorts of trouble his boys got into now that there were girls at Dairy.

'Oh no,' he probably said, when he heard Chester Pulaski clawing at his door. 'I hate Halloween.'

'I'll get it,' his wife said, and the Dean of Women went to open the door. 'I know, I know,' she said, cheerfully, 'trick or treat!'

And there was a naked and cringing Chester Pulaski, the blocking back—blazing with boils, smelling of sex.

The scream of the Dean of Women was said to have awakened the bottom two floors of the dorm the two deans lived in—and even Mrs. Butler, the night nurse, who was sleeping at her desk in the infirmary next door. 'I hate Halloween,' she probably said to herself. She went to the infirmary door and saw Junior Jones and Harold Swallow and me; Junior was carrying Franny.

I had helped Franny get dressed in the ferns and Junior Jones had tried to untangle her hair while she cried and cried, and finally he'd said to her, 'You want to walk or ride?' It was a question Father used to ask us children when we were years younger, which meant did we want to walk or did we want to take the car. Junior, of course, meant he would carry her, and that's what Franny wanted—so he did.

He carried her past the spot in the ferns where Lenny Metz was being lashed to a lacrosse stick and prepared for a different kind of travel. Franny cried and cried, and Junior said, 'Hey, you're a *good* girl, I have very good judgment about that.' But Franny kept crying. 'Hey, listen,' said Junior Jones. 'You know what? When someone touches you and you don't *want* to be touched, that's not really *being* touched—you got to believe me. It's not *you* they touch when they touch you that way; they don't really *get* you, you understand. You've still got *you* inside you. Nobody's touched you—not really. You're a really good girl, you believe me? You've still got *you* inside you, you believe that?'

'I don't know,' Franny whispered, and went on crying. One of her arms lolled down Junior's side and I took her hand; she squeezed; I squeezed back. Harold Swallow, darting through the trees, guiding us like a hush up the path, found the infirmary and opened the door.

'What's all this?' said the night nurse, Mrs. Butler.

'I'm Franny Berry,' said my sister, 'and I've been beaten up.'

115

'Beaten up' would remain Franny's euphemism for it, although everyone knew she had been raped. 'Beaten up' was all Franny would admit to, although no one missed the point; this way it would never be a *legal* point, however.

'She means she was raped,' Junior Jones told Mrs. Butler. But Franny kept shaking her head. I think that her way of interpreting Junior's kindness to her, and his version of how the *her* in her had not been touched, was to convert her sexual abuse into the terms of a mere fight she had lost. She whispered to him—he still held her against his chest and in his arms—and then he put her down on her feet and said to Mrs. Butler, 'Okay, she was beaten up.' Mrs. Butler knew what was meant.

'She was beaten up *and* raped,' said Harold Swallow, who couldn't stand still, but Junior Jones cooled him down with a look and said to him, 'Why don't you fly away, Harold? Why don't you fly off and find *Mr. Dove?*' That put the gleam back in Harold's eye, and he flew away.

I called Father, before I remembered there was no working phone in the Hotel New Hampshire. Then I called Campus Security and asked them to give Father the message: Franny and I were at the Dairy School Infirmary; Franny had been 'beaten up.'

'It's just another Halloween, kid,' Franny said, holding my hand.

'The worst one, Franny,' I said to her.

'The worst one so far,' she said.

Mrs. Butler took Franny off, to fix her—among other things—a bath, and Junior Jones explained to me that if Franny cleaned herself there would be no evidence that she was raped, and I went after Mrs. Butler to explain it to her, but Mrs. Butler had already explained this to Franny, who wanted to let it go. 'I've been beaten up,' she said, although she would listen to Mrs. Butler's advice about checking, later, to see if she was pregnant (she wasn't)—or infected with a venereal disease (someone had passed on a little something, which was eventually cured).

When Father arrived at the infirmary, Junior Jones had gone to lend his assistance to the delivery of Lenny Metz to the Dean, Harold Swallow was combing the campus, like a hawk, looking for a dove—and I was sitting in an all-white hospital room with Franny, fresh from her bath, her hair in a towel, an ice pack on her left cheekbone, her right ring finger bandaged (she'd torn out a nail); she wore a white hospital smock and was sitting up in

116

bed. 'I want to go home,' she told Father. 'Tell Mother I just need some clean clothes.'

'What did they do to you, darling?' Father asked her, and sat beside her on the bed.

'They beat me up,' Franny said.

'Where were *you*?' Father asked me.

'He got help,' Franny said.

'Did you see what happened?' Father asked me.

'He didn't see anything,' Franny said.

I saw the Third Act, I wanted to tell Father, but although we *all* knew what 'beaten up' meant, I would remain faithful to Franny's term for it.

'I just want to go home,' Franny said, although the Hotel New Hampshire seemed, to me, to be a large and unfamiliar place to curl up in. Father went to get her clothes.

It was a pity he missed seeing Lenny Metz trussed up on the lacrosse stick and carried through the campus to the Dean like a poorly prepared piece of meat on a spit. And a pity Father didn't witness the precociousness of Harold Swallow searching for Dove, gliding up to every dorm room like a shadow. Until Harold ascertained that Chipper Dove could only be in the girls' dorm. After that, he thought, it would be just a matter of time until he found whose room Dove was hiding in.

The Dean of Men, covering Chester Pulaski with his wife's camel's-hair coat—it was the nearest thing handy—cried out, 'Chester, Chester, my boy! *Why?* Only a *week* before the Exeter game!'

'The woods are full of niggers,' Chester Pulaski said, mournfully. 'They're taking over. Run for your life.'

The Dean of Women had locked herself in the bathroom, and when the second set of clawing sounds, and banging, reached her ears, she cried to her husband, '*You* can answer the goddamned door *this* time!'

'It's the *niggers,* don't let them in!' Chester Pulaski cried, clutching the Dean of Women's coat around him. The Dean of Men bravely opened the door; for some time he'd had an arrangement with Junior Jones's secret police, which was Dairy's highly underground and very good arm of the law.

'For God's sake, Junior,' the Dean said. 'This is going too far.'

'Who *is* it?' cried the Dean of Women from the bathroom, as Lenny Metz was brought into the Deans' living room and stretched out on the hearth before the fireplace; his broken collarbone was killing him, and when he saw the fire he must have thought it was meant for him.

'I confess!' he cried.

'You bet you do,' said Junior Jones.

'I did it!' cried Lenny Metz.

'You sure did,' said Junior Jones.

'I did it, too!' cried Chester Pulaski.

'And who did it *first?*' asked Junior Jones.

'Chipper Dove!' sang the boys in the backfield. 'Dove did it first!'

'There you have it,' said Junior Jones to the Dean of Men. 'You got the picture?'

'What did they do—and to *whom?*' the Dean asked.

'They gang-banged Franny Berry,' said Junior Jones, just as the Dean of Women emerged from the bathroom; she saw the black athletes swaying in the doorway, like a choral society from an African country, and she screamed again; she shut herself back up in the bathroom.

'Now we'll bring you Dove,' said Junior Jones.

'Gently, Junior!' cried the Dean. 'For God's sake, *gently!*'

I stayed with Franny; Mother and Father came to the infirmary with her clothes. Coach Bob was left to baby-sit with Lilly and Egg—like the *old* days, I thought. But where was Frank?

Frank was out on a 'mission,' Father said mysteriously. When Father had heard that Franny was 'beaten up,' he'd never doubted the worst. And he knew that Sorrow would be the first thing she'd ask for when she was home in her own bed. 'I want to go home,' she would say; and then she'd say, 'I want Sorrow to sleep with me.'

'Maybe it's not too late,' Father had said; he'd left Sorrow at the vet's before the football game. If it had been a busy day for the vet, perhaps the old farter was still alive in some cage. Frank had undertaken the mission to go and see.

But it was like the rescue mission of Junior Jones; Frank arrived too late. He woke up the vet with his pounding on the door. 'I hate Halloween,' the vet probably said, but his wife told him it was one of the Berry boys asking about Sorrow. 'Oh-oh,' the vet said. 'I'm sorry, son,' the vet told Frank, 'but your dog passed away this afternoon.'

'I want to see him,' Frank said.

'Oh-oh,' the vet said. 'The dog is dead, son.'

'Have you buried him?' Frank asked.

'It's so sweet,' the vet's wife told her husband. 'Let the boy bury his own dog, if that's what he wants.'

'Oh-oh,' the vet said, but he led Frank to the hindmost room of the kennel, where Frank was treated to the sight of three dead dogs in a pile, with a pile of three dead cats beside them. 'We don't bury things on the weekends,' the vet explained. 'Which one is Sorrow?'

Frank spotted the old evil-smeller instantly; Sorrow had begun to stiffen up, but Frank was still able to force the dead black Labrador into a large trash bag. The vet and his wife couldn't have known that Frank had no intention of *burying* Sorrow.

'Too late,' Frank whispered to Father, when Mother and Father and Franny and I arrived home—at the Hotel New Hampshire.

'Jesus God, I can walk by myself, you know,' Franny said, because all of us were trying to walk next to her. 'Here, Sorrow!' she called. 'Come on, boy!'

Mother started to cry and Franny took her arm. 'I'm *okay*, Mom,' she said. 'Really I am. Nobody touched the *me* inside me, I guess.' Father started to cry and Franny took his arm, too. I had been crying all night, it seemed, and I was all cried out.

Frank pulled me aside.

'What the fuck is it, Frank?' I said.

'Come see,' he said.

Sorrow, still in the trash bag, was under the bed in Frank's room.

'Jesus God, Frank!' I said.

'I'm going to *fix* him for Franny,' he said. 'In time for Christmas!'

'*Christmas*, Frank?' I said. '*Fix* him?'

'I'm going to have Sorrow *stuffed!*' Frank said. Frank's favorite course at the Dairy School was biology, a weird course taught by an amateur taxidermist named Foit. Frank, with Foit's help, had already stuffed a squirrel and an odd orange bird.

'Holy cow, Frank,' I said, 'I don't know if Franny will like that.'

'It's the next-best thing to being alive,' Frank said.

I didn't know. By the sudden outburst we heard, from Franny, we knew that Father had broken the news to her. A slight distraction to Franny's grief was caused by Iowa Bob. He insisted on going out and finding Chipper Dove himself, and it took some persuading to talk him out of it. Franny wanted another bath, and I lay in bed listening to the tub filling. Then I

119

got up and went to the bathroom door and asked her if there was anything I could get her.

'Thank you,' she whispered. 'Just go out and get me yesterday and most of today,' she said. 'I want them back.'

'Is that all?' I said. 'Just yesterday and today?'

'That's all,' she said. 'Thank you.'

'I would if I could, Franny,' I told her.

'I know,' she said. I heard her sinking slowly in the tub. 'I'm okay,' she whispered. 'Nobody got the fucking *me* in me.'

'I love you,' I whispered.

She didn't answer me, and I went back to bed.

I heard Coach Bob, in his rooms above us—doing push-ups, and then some sit-ups, and then a little work with the one-arm curls (the barbells' rhythmic clanks and the old man's enraged breaths)—and I wished he had been allowed to find Chipper Dove, who would have been no match for the old Iowa lineman.

Unfortunately, Dove *was* a match for Junior Jones and the Black Arm of the Law. Dove had gone straight to the girls' dorm, and to the room of a doting cheerleader named Melinda Mitchell. She was called Mindy and she was gaga over Dove. He told her he'd been 'fooling around' with Franny Berry, but that when she started fooling around with Lenny Metz and Chester Pulaski, too, it had put him off. 'A cock tease,' he called my sister, and Mindy Mitchell agreed. She had been jealous of Franny for years.

'But now Franny's got the black bunch after me,' Dove told Mindy. 'She's pals with them. Especially Junior Jones,' Dove said, '—that goody-goody spade who's a fink for the Dean.' So Mindy Mitchell tucked Dove into her bed with her, and when Harold Swallow came whispering at her door ('Dove, Dove —have you seen Dove? Black Arm of the Law wants to know'), she said she didn't let *any* boy into her room and she wouldn't let Harold in, either.

So they didn't find him. He was expelled from the Dairy School in the morning—along with Chester Pulaski and Lenny Metz. The parents of the gang-bangers, when they heard the story, were grateful enough that nothing criminal was being charged that they accepted the expulsion from school rather graciously. Some of the faculty, and most of the trustees, were upset that the incident couldn't have been suppressed until after the Exeter game, but it was pointed out that Iowa Bob's backfield was a less embarrassing loss than losing Iowa Bob himself—for the old man surely would have refused to coach in a game with those three still on his team.

It was an incident that was hushed up in the best private school tradition; it was remarkable, really, how a school as unsophisticated as the Dairy School could at times imitate exactly the decorum of silence in dealing with distasteful matters that the more sophisticated schools had learned like a science.

For 'beating up' Franny Berry—in what was implied to be merely an extension of the general roughhouse quality of a Dairy School Halloween—Chester Pulaski, Lenny Metz, and Chipper Dove were expelled. Dove, it appeared to me, got off scot-free. But Franny and I had not seen the last of him, and perhaps Franny already knew that. We had not seen the last of Junior Jones, either; he became Franny's friend, if not exactly her bodyguard, for the duration of his stay at Dairy. They went everywhere together, and it was clear to me that Junior Jones was responsible for helping Franny feel that she was, indeed, a good girl—as he was always telling her. We had not seen the last of Jones when we left Dairy, although—once again—his style of rescuing Franny would distinguish itself by his late arrival. Junior Jones, as you know, would play college football at Penn State, and professional football for the Browns—until someone would mess up his knee. He would then go to law school and become active in an organization in New York City—which would be called, at his suggestion, the Black Arm of the Law. As Lilly would say—and one day she would make this clear to us—Everything is a fairy tale.

Chester Pulaski would suffer *his* racist nightmares most of his life, which would be over in a car. The police would say that he must have had his hands all over someone while he was supposed to be paying attention to the steering wheel. The woman was killed, too, and Lenny Metz said he knew her. When his collarbone healed, Metz went right back to carrying the ball; he played college football somewhere in Virginia and introduced Chester Pulaski to the woman he killed over one Christmas vacation. Metz would never be drafted by the pros —for a pronounced lack of quickness—but he was drafted by the U.S. Army, who didn't care how slow he was, and he died for his country, as they say, in Vietnam. Actually, he was not shot by the enemy; he did not step on a mine. It was another kind of combat that Lenny Metz succumbed to: he was poisoned by a prostitute, whom he had cheated.

Harold Swallow was both too crazy and too fast for me to

keep up with. God knows what became of him. Good luck to you, Harold, wherever you are!

Perhaps because it was Halloween, and Halloween's atmosphere pervades my memory of Iowa Bob's winning season, they have all become like ghosts and wizards and devils and creatures of magic, to me. Remember, too: it was the first night we slept in the Hotel New Hampshire—not that we slept for most of it. Any night in a new place is a little uneasy—there are the different sounds of the beds to get used to. And Lilly, who always woke up with the same dry cough, as if she were a very old person—and we'd be constantly surprised to see how small she was—woke up coughing differently, almost as if she were as exasperated with her own poor health as Mother was. Egg never woke up unless someone woke him, and then he behaved as if he'd been awake for hours. But the morning after Halloween, Egg woke up by himself—almost peacefully. And I had heard Frank masturbate in his room for years, but it was different hearing him do it in the Hotel New Hampshire—perhaps because I knew that Sorrow was in a trash bag under his bed.

The morning after Halloween, I watched the early light fall in Elliot Park. There'd been a frost, and through the frozen rinds of someone's mangled pumpkin I saw Frank trudging to the bio lab with Sorrow in the trash bag over his shoulder. Father saw him out the same window.

'Where the hell is Frank going with the garbage?' Father asked.

'He probably couldn't find the trash barrels,' I said, so that Frank could make good his escape. 'I mean, we don't have a phone that works, and we *were* out of electricity. There probably aren't any trash barrels, either.'

' 'There are so,' Father said. 'The barrels are out at the delivery entrance.' He stared after Frank and shook his head. 'The damn fool must be going all the way to the dump,' Father said. 'Jesus, that boy is queer.'

I shivered, because I knew that Father didn't know that Frank really *was* queer.

When Egg was finally out of the bathroom, Father went to use the facilities and found that Franny had beaten him to the door. She was drawing *another* bath for herself, and Mother told Father, 'Don't you say a word to her. She can take all the baths she wants.' And they went away, arguing—which they rarely did. 'I told you we'd need another bathroom,' Mother said.

I listened to Franny, drawing her bath. 'I love you,' I whispered at the locked door. But—over the sound of the healing water—it is unlikely that Franny ever heard me.

5

Merry Christmas, 1956

I remember the rest of 1956, from Halloween to Christmas, as
the length of time it took Franny to stop taking three baths a day
—and to return to her natural fondness for her own good, ripe
smell. Franny always smelled nice to me—although at times she
gave off a very strong smell—but from Halloween to Christmas,
1956, Franny did not smell nice to herself. And so she took so
many baths that she did not smell at all.

In the Hotel New Hampshire, our family took over another
bathroom and sharpened our skills at Father's first family
business. Mother took charge of the cranky pride of Mrs. Urick,
and the plain-but-good production of Mrs. Urick's kitchen; Mrs.
Urick took charge of Max, in spite of his being well hidden from
her, on the fourth floor. Father handled Ronda Ray—'not
literally,' as Franny would say.

Ronda had a curious energy. She would strip and make up all
the beds in a single morning; she could serve four tables in the
restaurant without botching an order or making anyone wait; she
could spell Father at the bar (we were open every evening, except
Monday, until eleven) and have all the tables set before
breakfast (at seven). But when she retired, to her 'dayroom,' she
seemed either in hibernation or in a deep stupor, and even at the
peak of her energy—when she was getting everything done, on
time—she *looked* sleepy.

'Why do we say it's a *dayroom?*' Iowa Bob asked. 'I mean, if
Ronda goes back to Hampton Beach, when does she do it? I
mean, it's all right that she lives here, but why don't we *say* she
lives here—why doesn't *she* say so?'

'She's doing a good job,' Father said.

'But she's *living* in her dayroom,' Mother said.

'What's a dayroom?' Egg asked. It seemed everyone wanted
to know that.

Franny and I listened to Ronda Ray's room on the intercom

for hours, but it would be weeks before *we* learned what a dayroom was. At midmornings we would switch on Ronda's room and Franny would say, after listening to the breathing for a while, 'Asleep.' Or sometimes: 'Smoking a cigarette.'

Late at night, Franny and I would listen and I would say, 'Perhaps she's reading.'

'Are you kidding?' Franny would say.

Bored, we would listen to the other rooms, one at a time, or all together. Checking out Max Urick's static, over which we could—occasionally—hear Max's radio. Checking the stockpots in Mrs. Urick's basement kitchen. We knew that 3F was Iowa Bob, and we would tune in the sound of his barbells every once in a while—often interrupting him with our own comments, like: 'Come on, Grandpa, a little quicker! Let's really snap those babies up—you're slowing down.'

'You damn kids!' Bob would grunt; or at other times he would slap two iron weights together, right next to the speaker-receiver box, so that Franny and I would junp and hold our ringing ears. 'Ha!' Coach Bob would cry. 'Got you little buggers *that* time, didn't I?'

'Lunatic in 3F,' Franny would broadcast on the intercom. 'Lock your doors. Lunatic in 3F.'

'Ha!' Iowa Bob would grunt—over the bench presses, over the push-ups, the sit-ups, the one-arm curls. 'This hotel is *for* lunatics!'

It was Iowa Bob who encouraged me to lift weights. What happened to Franny had somehow inspired me to make myself stronger. By Thanksgiving I was running six miles a day, although the cross-country course at Dairy was only two and a quarter miles. Bob put me on a heavy dose of bananas and milk and oranges. 'And pasta, rice, fish, lots of greens, hot cereal, and ice cream,' the old coach told me. I lifted twice a day; and in addition to my six miles, I ran wind sprints every morning in Elliot Park.

At first, I just put on weight.

'Lay off the bananas,' Father said.

'And the ice cream,' said Mother.

'No, no,' said Iowa Bob. 'Muscles take a little time.'

'Muscles?' Father said. 'He's fat.'

'You look like a cherub, dear,' Mother told me.

'You look like a teddy bear,' Franny told me.

'Just keep eating,' said Iowa Bob. 'With all the lifting and running, you're going to see a change in no time.'

'Before he *explodes?*' Franny said.

I was going on fifteen, as they say; between Halloween and Christmas I gained twenty pounds; I weighed 170, but I was still only five feet six inches tall.

'Man,' Junior Jones told me, 'if we painted you black and white, and put circles around your eyes, you'd look like a *panda.*'

'One day soon,' said Iowa Bob, 'you're going to drop twenty pounds and you'll be hard all over.'

Franny gave an exaggerated shiver and kicked me under the table. 'Hard all over!' she cried.

'It's gross,' Frank said. 'All of it. The weight lifting, the bananas, the panting up and down the stairs.' In the mornings when it rained, I refused to run wind sprints in Elliot Park; I sprinted up and down the stairs of the Hotel New Hampshire, instead.

Max Urick said he was going to throw grenades down the stairwell. And on a very rainy morning, Ronda Ray stopped me on the second-floor landing; she was wearing one of her nightgowns and looking especially sleepy. 'Let me tell you, it's like listening to lovers go at it in the room next to mine,' she said. Her dayroom was nearest the stairwell. She liked to call me John-O. 'I don't mind the sound of the feet, John-O,' she told me. 'It's the breathing that gets me,' she said. 'I don't know if you're dying or trying to come, but it curls my hair, let me tell you.'

'Don't listen to any of them,' said Iowa Bob. 'You're the first member of this family who's taken a proper interest in his body. You've got to *get* obsessed and *stay* obsessed,' Bob told me. 'And we have to beef you up before we can strip you down.'

Thus it was, and so it is: I owe my body to Iowa Bob—an obsession that has never left me—and bananas.

It would be a while before those extra twenty pounds came off, but they would come off, and they have stayed off ever since. I weigh 150 pounds, all the time.

And I would be seventeen before I finally grew another two inches, and stopped for life. That's me: five feet eight inches tall and 150 pounds. And hard all over.

In a little while I will be forty, but even now, when I work out, I remember the Christmas season of 1956. Now they have such fancy weight machines; there's no more sliding the weights on the bar, and forgetting to tighten the screws and having the weights slide together and mash your fingers, or fall off the end

126

of the bar on your toes. But no matter how modern the gymnasium, or the equipment, it only takes a little light lifting to bring back Iowa Bob's room—good old 3F, and the worn oriental rug where his weights were, the rug Sorrow used to sleep on: after weight lifting on that rug, Bob and I would be covered with the dead dog's hair. And after I've been pushing the weight for a while, and that long-lasting, luxurious ache starts creeping over me, I can bring to mind every scruffy person and every stain on the canvas that dotted the horsehair mats in the weight room of the Dairy School gym, where we would always be waiting for Junior Jones to finish *his* turn. Jones took all the weights in the room and put them on one barbell, and we would stand there with our empty bars, waiting and waiting. In his days with the Cleveland Browns, Junior Jones weighed 285 and could bench-press 550. He was not *that* strong when he was at the Dairy School, but he was already strong enough to suggest to me a proper goal for the bench press.

'What you weigh?' he'd ask me. 'Do you even know?' And when I'd tell him what I weighed, he'd shake his head and say, 'Okay, double it.' And when I'd doubled it—and had put 300 pounds or so on the barbell—he'd say, 'Okay, down on the mat, on your back.' There were no benches for doing bench presses at the Dairy School, so I'd lie down on the mat on my back and Junior Jones would pick up the 300-pound barbell and place it gently across my throat—there was just enough room so that the bar depressed my Adam's apply only slightly. I gripped the bar in both hands and I felt my elbows sink down into the mat. 'Now lift it over your head,' said Junior Jones, and he'd walk out of the weight room, to get a drink of water, or go take his shower, and I'd lie there under the barbell—trapped. Nothing happened when I tried to lift 300 pounds. Other, bigger people would come into the weight room and see me lying there, under the 300 pounds, and they'd respectfully ask me, 'Uh, you gonna be through with that, after a while?'

'Yeah, just resting,' I'd say, puffing up like a toad. And they'd go away and come back later.

Junior Jones would always come back later, too.

'How's it going?' he'd ask. He'd take off twenty pounds, then fifty, then one hundred.

'Try that,' he'd keep saying; he kept going away, and coming back, until I could extricate myself from under the barbell.

And all 150 pounds of me has never bench-pressed 300 pounds, of course, although twice in my life I have done 215, and I believe that doubling my own weight is not impossible. I can get in a marvelous trance under all that weight.

Sometimes, when I'm really pumping, I can see the Black Arm of the Law moving through the trees, humming their tune, and sometimes I can recall the smell of the fifth floor of the dorm where Junior Jones lived—that hot, jungle nightclub in the sky—and when I run, about the third mile, or the fourth, or sometimes not until the sixth, my own lungs remember, vividly, the feeling of keeping up with Harold Swallow. And the sight of a slash of Franny's hair, fallen across her open mouth—no sound coming from her—as Lenny Metz knelt on her arms and pinched her head between his heavy, running-back's thighs. And Chester Pulaski on top of her: an automaton. I sometimes can duplicate his rhythm, exactly, when I am counting out the push-ups ('seventy-five, seventy-six, seventy-seven'). Or the sit-ups ('one hundred and twenty-one, one hundred and twenty-two, one hundred and twenty-three').

Iowa Bob simply introduced me to the equipment; Junior Jones added his advice, and his own marvelous example; Father had already taught me how to run—and Harold Swallow, how to run harder. The technique and routine—and even Coach Bob's diet—were easy. The hard part, for most people, is the discipline. As Coach Bob said, you've got to get obsessed and stay obsessed. But for me, this was also easy. Because I did it all for Franny. I'm not complaining, but it was all for Franny—and she knew it.

'Listen, kid,' she told me—from Halloween to Christmas, 1956—'you're going to throw up if you don't stop eating bananas. And if you don't stop eating oranges, you're going to have a vitamin overdose. What the hell are you pushing so hard for? You'll never be as fast as Harold Swallow. You'll never be as big as Junior Jones.

'Kid, I can read you like a book,' Franny told me. 'No way is it going to happen *again*, you know. And if it does—and you actually *are* strong enough to save me—what makes you think you'll even *be* there? If it happens again, I'll be someplace far away from you—and I'll hope you never know about it, anyway. I promise.'

But Franny took the purpose of my workouts too literally. I wanted strength, stamina, and speed—or I desired their illusions. I never wanted to feel, again, the helplessness of another Halloween.

There was still the evidence of a mangled pumpkin or two —one at the curb of Pine Street and Elliot Park, and another that had been thrown from the bleachers and burst upon the cinder track around the football field—when Dairy hosted Exeter for the last game of Iowa Bob's winning season. Halloween was still in the air, although Chipper Dove, Lenny Metz, and Chester Pulaski were gone.

The second-string backfield appeared under the influence of a spell: they did everything in slow motion. They ran to the holes that Junior Jones had opened, after the holes had closed; they lobbed passes into the sky, and the passes took forever to come down. Waiting for one such pass, Harold Swallow was knocked unconscious and Iowa Bob wouldn't let him play the rest of the long day.

'Somebody rang your bell, Harold,' Coach Bob told the speedster.

'I ain't got no bell,' Harold Swallow complained. 'Who rang?' he asked. 'What somebody?'

At the half, Exeter led 24–0. Junior Jones, playing both offense and defense, had been involved in a dozen tackles; he caused three fumbles and recovered two; but the second-string Dairy backfield had coughed up the ball three times, and two looping passes had been intercepted. In the second half, Coach Bob started Junior Jones at a runningback position, and Jones made three consecutive first downs before the Exeter defense adjusted. The adjustment was simply recognizing that as long as Junior Jones was *in* the backfield, he would carry the ball. So Iowa Bob put Junior back in the line, where he had more fun, and Dairy's only score, which came late in the fourth quarter, was properly credited to Jones. He broke into the Exeter backfield and took the ball away from an Exeter running back and ran into the Exeter end zone with it—and with two or three Exeter players clinging to him. The extra point was wide to the left and the final score was Exeter 45, Dairy 6.

Franny missed Junior's touchdown: she had come to the game only because of him, and she had gone back to being a cheerleader for the Exeter game only to yell her lungs out for Junior Jones. But Franny got involved in an altercation with another cheerleader, and Mother had to take her home. The other cheerleader was Chipper Dove's hiding place, Mindy Mitchell.

'Cock tease,' Mindy Mitchell called my sister.

'Dumb cunt,' Franny said, and whacked Mindy with her

129

cheerleader's megaphone. It was made of cardboard, and it looked like a large shit-brown ice cream cone with a death-gray *D* for Dairy painted on it. '*D* is for Death,' Franny always said.

'Smack in the boobs,' another cheerleader told me. 'Franny hit Mindy Mitchell with the megaphone smack in the boobs.'

Of course I told Junior Jones, after the game, why Franny wasn't there to walk with him back to the gym.

'What a good girl she is!' Junior said. 'You tell her, won't you?'

And of course I did. Franny had taken *another* bath and was all dressed up to help Ronda Ray wait on tables; she was in a pretty good mood. Despite the rather landslide conclusion of Iowa Bob's winning season, nearly everyone seemed in a good mood. It was opening night at the Hotel New Hampshire!

Mrs. Urick had outdone herself at plainness-but-goodness; even Max was wearing a white shirt and tie, and Father was absolutely beaming behind the bar—the bottles winking in the mirror, under his fast-moving elbows and over his shoulders, were like a sunrise Father had always believed was coming.

There were eleven couples and seven singles for overnight guests, and a divorced man from Texas had come all the way to see his son play against Exeter; the kid had gone out of the game in the first quarter with a sprained ankle, but even the Texan was in a good mood. Compared to him, the couples and the singles seemed a little shy—not knowing each other, just having children at the Dairy School in common—but after the kids went back to their dorms, the Texan got everyone talking to each other in the restaurant and bar. 'Isn't it *great* having kids?' he asked. 'God, it's something how they all grow up, isn't it?' Everyone agreed. The Texan said, 'Why don't you all pull your chairs over here to my table and have a drink on me!' And Mother stood anxiously in the kitchen doorway, with Mrs. Urick and Max, and Father stood poised but confident behind the bar; Frank ran out of the room; Franny held my hand and we held our breath; Iowa Bob looked as if he were suppressing an enormous sneeze. And one by one the couples and the singles got up from where they were sitting and attempted to pull their chairs over to the Texan's table.

'Mine's stuck!' said a woman from New Jersey, who'd had a little too much to drink; she had a sharp, squeaky giggle of the mindless quality of hamsters running miles and miles on those little wheels in their cages.

A man from Connecticut turned bright red in the face, trying

130

to lift his chair, until his wife said, 'It's nailed down. There are nails that go right into the floor.'

A man from Massachusetts knelt on the floor by his chair. 'Screws,' he said. 'Those are *screws*—four or five of them, for each chair!'

The Texan knelt down on the floor and stared at his chair.

'*Everything's* screwed down here!' Iowa Bob shouted, suddenly. He had not spoken to anyone since after the game, when he told the scout from Penn State that Junior Jones could play anywhere. His face was unfamiliarly red and shining, as if he'd had one more drink than he usually allowed himself—or the sense of his own retirement had finally come to him. 'We're all on a big ship!' said Iowa Bob. 'We're on a big cruise, across the world!'

'Ya-*hoo!*' the Texan shouted. 'I'll drink to that!'

The woman from New Jersey clutched the back of her screwed-down chair. Some of the others sat down.

'We're in danger of being swept away, at any time!' Coach Bob said, and Ronda Ray came swishing back and forth between Bob and the Dairy parents poised at their well-fastened seats; she was passing out the coasters, and the cocktail napkins again, and flicking a damp towel over the edges of the tables. Frank peeked in from the door to the hall; Mother and the Uricks seemed paralyzed in the kitchen doorway; Father had lost none of the glitter he absorbed from the bar mirror, but he stared at his father, old Iowa Bob, as if he feared that the retired coach was about to say something crazy.

'Of *course* the chairs are screwed down!' Bob said, sweeping his arm toward the sky, as if he were giving his last halftime speech—and this were the game of his life. 'At the Hotel New Hampshire,' said Iowa Bob, 'when the shit hits the fan, nobody gets blown away!'

'Ya-*hoo!*' the Texan cried again, but everyone else seemed to have stopped breathing.

'Just hold on to your seats!' said Coach Bob. 'And nothing will ever hurt you here.'

'Ya-*hoo!* Thank *God* the chairs are screwed down!' the big-hearted Texan cried. 'Let's all drink to that!'

The wife of the man from Connecticut gave an audible sigh of relief.

'Well, I guess, we'll just have to speak up if we're all going to be friends and *talk* to each other!' the Texan said.

'Yes!' said the New Jersey woman, a little breathlessly.

Father was still staring at Iowa Bob, but Bob was just fine—he turned and winked at Frank in the hall doorway, and bowed to Mother and the Uricks, and Ronda Ray came through the room again and gave the old coach a saucy stroke across his cheek, and the Texan watched Ronda as if he'd forgotten all about chairs—screwed down or not screwed down. Who cares if the chairs can't be moved? he was thinking to himself—because Ronda Ray had more moves than Harold Swallow, and she was into the spirit of opening night, like everyone else.

'Ya-hoo,' Franny whispered in my ear, but I sat at the bar watching Father make the drinks. He looked more concentrated with energy than I had ever seen him before, and the gradual volume of voices came over me—and always would: I will remember that restaurant and bar, in *that* Hotel New Hampshire, as a place that was always so loud with talk, even if there weren't many people there. Like the Texan said, everyone had to speak up if they were going to sit so far apart.

And even after the Hotel New Hampshire had been open long enough so that we recognized many of our customers, from the town, as 'regulars'—those who were at the bar every night until closing time, just before which old Iowa Bob would appear for a nightcap before he turned in—even during those familiar evenings, with those familiar few, Bob could still pull his favorite trick. 'Hey, pull up your chair,' he'd say to someone, and someone would always be fooled. For a moment, forgetting where he or she was, someone would give a little lift, a little grunt, a little perplexed strain would pass across a face, and Iowa Bob would laugh and cry out, '*Nothing* moves at the Hotel New Hampshire! We're screwed down here—for *life!*'

That opening night, after the bar and restaurant was closed and everyone had gone to bed, Franny and Frank and I met at the switchboard and did a bed check on each of the rooms with the unique squawk-box system. We could hear who slept soundly, and who snored; we could detect who was still up (reading), and we were surprised (and disappointed) to discover no couples were talking, or making love.

Iowa Bob slept like a subway, rumbling miles and miles underground. Mrs. Urick had left a stockpot simmering, and Max was playing his usual static. The New Jersey couple was reading, or one of them was: the slow turning of pages, the short breaths of the nonsleeper. The Connecticut pair wheezed and whinnied and whopped in their sleep; their room was a boiler room of sound. Massachusetts, Rhode Island, Pennsylvania, New York, and Maine all gave off the sounds of their various habits of repose.

Then we switched on the Texan. 'Ya-hoo,' I said to Franny. 'Whoo-pee,' she whispered back.

We expected to hear his cowboy boots striking the floor; we expected to hear him drinking out of his hat, or sleeping like a horse—his long legs cantering under the covers, his big hands strangling the bed. But we heard nothing.

'He's dead!' Frank said, making Franny and me jump.

'Jesus, Frank,' Franny said. 'Maybe he's just out of his room.'

'He's had a heart attack,' Frank said. 'He's overweight and he drank too much.'

We listened. Nothing. No horse. No creaking of boots. Not a breath.

Franny switched the Texan's room from Receiving to Broadcasting. 'Ya-hoo?' she whispered.

And then it came to us—all three of us (even Frank) seemed to grasp it. It took Franny about one second to switch to Ronda Ray's 'dayroom.'

'You want to know what a *dayroom* is, Frank?' she asked.

And on came the unforgettable sound.

As Iowa Bob said, we *are* on a big cruise, across the world, and we're in danger of being swept away, at any time.

Frank and Franny and I gripped our chairs.

'*Ooooooooooo!*' gasped Ronda Ray.

'*Hoo, hoo, hoo!*' the Texan cried.

And later he said, 'I sure appreciate this.'

'Phooey,' Ronda said.

'No, I do, I really *do*,' he said. We heard him peeing—like a horse, it went on forever. 'You don't know how hard it is for me to hit that little bitty toilet up on the fourth floor,' he said. 'It's so far down,' the Texan said, 'I have to take aim before I shoot.'

'Ha!' cried Ronda Ray.

'Ya-*hoo!*' the Texan said.

'Dis*gus*ting,' Frank said, and went to bed, but Franny and I stayed up until the only sounds on the squawk box were the sounds of sleep.

In the morning it was raining, and I made a point of holding my breath every time I ran by the second-floor landing—not wanting to disturb Ronda, and knowing what she thought of my 'breathing.'

133

Blue in the face, I passed the Texan climbing between three and four.

'Ya-hoo!' I said.

'Morning! Morning!' he cried. 'Staying in shape, huh?' he said. 'Good for you! Your body's got to last you all your life, you know.'

'Yessir,' I said, and ran up and down some more.

About the thirtieth trip I was beginning to bring back the Black Arm of the Law, and the sight of Franny's missing fingernail—how so much pain seemed focused on this bleeding tip of her hand, and perhaps distracted her from the rest of her body—when Ronda Ray blocked my way on the second-floor landing.

'Whoa, boy,' she said, and I stopped. She was wearing one of her nightgowns, and if the sun had been shining, the light would have shot right through the material and lit her up for me—but it was a gloomy light, that morning, and the dim stairwell revealed very little of her. Just her moves, and her absorbing odor.

'Good morning,' I said. 'Ya-hoo!'

'Ya-hoo to you, John-O,' she said. I smiled and ran in place.

'You're *breathing* again,' Ronda told me.

'I was trying to hold my breath for you,' I panted, 'but I got too tired.'

'I can hear your fucking *heart*,' she said.

'It's good for me,' I said.

'It's not good for *me*,' Ronda said. She put her hand on my chest, as if she were reading my heartbeat. I stopped running in place; I needed to spit.

'John-O,' said Ronda Ray, 'if you *like* to breath this hard and make your heart pound, you should come to see *me* the next time it rains.'

And I ran up and down the stairs about forty more times. It will probably never rain again, I thought. I was too tired to eat anything at breakfast.

'Just have a banana,' said Iowa Bob, but I looked away from it. 'And an orange or two,' Bob said. I excused myself.

Egg was in the bathroom and he wouldn't let Franny in.

'Why don't Franny and Egg take their baths together?' Father asked. Egg was six, and in another year he would probably be too embarrassed to take a bath with Franny. He was fond of baths now because of all the tub toys he possessed; when you used the bathroom after Egg had been there, the bathtub looked like a children's beach—abandoned during an air raid. Hippos, boats, frogmen, rubber birds, lizards, alligators, a shark with a wind-up mouth, a seal with wind-up flippers, a ghastly yellow turtle—every conceivable imitation of amphibious life, sodden and dripping on the tub floor and crunching on the bathmat, underfoot.

'Egg!' I would scream. 'Come clean up your shit!'

'*What* shit?' Egg would cry.

'Honestly, your *language*,' Mother said—repeatedly, to us all.

Frank had taken to peeing against the trash barrels at the delivery entrance in the morning; he claimed he could never get to the bathroom when he wanted to. I went upstairs and used the bathroom attached to Iowa Bob's room, and used the weights there, too, of course.

'What a racket to wake up to!' old Bob complained. 'I never thought this is how retirement would be. Listening to someone peeing and weight-lifting. What an alarm clock!'

'You like to get up early, anyway,' I told him.

'It's not *when* that I mind,' said the old coach. 'It's *how*.'

And we slipped through November that way—a freak snow-fall early in the month: it really should have been rain, I knew. What did it mean that it *wasn't* rain? I wondered, thinking of Ronda Ray and her dayroom.

It was a dry November.

Egg had a run of ear infections; he seemed partially deaf most of the time.

'Egg, what did you do with my green sweater?' Franny asked.

'What?' Egg said.

'My green sweater!' Franny screamed.

'I don't have a green sweater,' Egg said.

'It's *my* green sweater!' Franny shouted. 'He dressed his bear in it yesterday—I saw it,' Franny told Mother. 'And now I can't find it.'

'Egg, where's your bear?' Mother asked.

'Franny doesn't have a bear,' Egg said. 'That's *my* bear.'

'Where's my running hat?' I asked Mother. 'It was on the radiator in the hall last night.'

'Egg's bear is probably wearing it,' Frank said. 'And he's out doing wind sprints.'

'What?' Egg said.

Lilly also had medical problems. We had our annual physicals just before Thanksgiving and our family doctor—an old geezer named Dr. Blaze, whose fire, Franny remarked, was almost out

135

—discovered during a routine check that Lilly hadn't grown in a year. Not a pound, not a fraction of an inch. She was exactly the same size she'd been when she was nine, which was not much bigger than she'd been at eight—or (checking the records) at seven.

'She's not growing?' Father asked.

'I've said so, for years,' Franny said. 'Lilly *doesn't* grow —she just *is*.'

Lilly seemed unimpressed by the analysis; she shrugged. 'So I'm small,' she said. 'Everyone's always saying so. So what's the matter with being small?'

'Nothing, dear,' Mother said. 'You can be as small as you want, but you should be growing—just a little.'

'She's going to be one of those who shoots up all at once,' said Iowa Bob, but even he looked doubtful. Lilly didn't impress you as the sort who would ever 'shoot up.'

We made her stand back to back with Egg; at six, Egg was almost as big as Lilly at ten, and he certainly looked more solid.

'Stand still!' Lilly said to Egg. 'Stop standing on your toes!'

'What?' said Egg.

'Stop standing on your toes, Egg!' Franny said.

'They're *my* toes!' Egg said.

'Maybe I'm dying,' Lilly said, and everyone shivered, especially Mother.

'You are *not* dying,' Father said, sternly.

'Frank's the only one who's dying,' Franny said.

'No,' said Frank. 'I have already died. And the living bore me to death.'

'Stop it,' Mother said.

I went to lift weights in Iowa Bob's room. Every time the weights rolled off the end of the barbell, one of them struck the closet door, and it opened, and out fell something. Coach Bob was terrible about the closet; he just threw everything in there loose. And one morning when Iowa Bob dropped a few weights, one of them rolled into the closet and out rolled Egg's bear. The bear was wearing my running hat, Franny's green sweater, a pair of Mother's nylons.

'Egg!' I screamed.

'What?' Egg screamed.

'I found your damn bear!' I yelled.

'It's *my* bear!' Egg yelled back.

'Jesus God,' Father said, and Egg went to Dr. Blaze to have

his ears checked, again, and Lilly went to Dr. Blaze to have her size checked, again.

'If she hasn't grown in two years,' Franny said, 'I doubt she's grown in the last two days.' But there were tests that could be run on Lilly, and old Dr. Blaze was apparently trying to figure out what the tests were.

'You don't eat enough, Lilly,' I said. 'Don't worry about it, but just try to eat a little more.'

'I don't like to eat,' Lilly said.

And it wouldn't rain—not a drop! Or when it rained, it was always in the afternoon, or in the evening. I would be sitting in Algebra II, or in the History of Tudor England, or in Beginning Latin, and I would hear the rain fall, and despair. Or I would be in bed, and it was dark—dark in my room and throughout the Hotel New Hampshire, and all of Elliot Park—and I would hear it raining and raining, and I'd think: *Tomorrow!* But in the morning, the rain would have turned to snow, or would have petered out; or it would be dry and windy again, and I would run my wind sprints in Elliot Park—Frank passing me en route to the bio lab.

'Nuts, nuts, nuts,' Frank would grumble.

'Who's nuts?' I asked.

'You're nuts,' he said. 'And Franny's *always* nuts. And Egg is deaf, and Lilly's weird,' Frank said.

'And you're perfectly normal, Frank?' I asked, running in place.

'At least I don't play with my body as if I were a rubber band,' Frank said. I knew, of course, that Frank played with his body—plenty—but Father had already assured me, in one of his heart-to-heart talks about boys and girls, that everyone masturbated (and *ought* to, from time to time), and so I decided to be friendly to Frank and not tease him about his beating off.

'How's it coming with stuffing the dog, Frank?' I asked him, and he became immediately serious.

'Well,' he said. 'There are a few problems. The *pose,* for example, is very important. I'm still deciding on the best possible pose,' he said. 'The actual body has been properly treated, but the pose really worries me.'

'The *pose?*' I said, trying to imagine what poses Sorrow ever had. He seemed to have slept and farted in a variety of casual positions.

'Well,' Frank explained. 'There are certain classic poses in taxidermy.'

'I see,' I said.

'There's the "cornered" pose,' Frank said, and he recoiled from me, suddenly, putting his forepaws up to defend himself and raising his hackles. 'You know?' he asked.

'God, Frank,' I said. 'I don't think *that* one would be too appropriate to Sorrow.'

'Well, it's a classic,' Frank said. 'And *this* one,' he said, turning sideways to me, and appearing to sneak along the limb of a tree, snarling over his shoulder. 'This is the "stalking" pose,' he said.

'I see,' I said, wondering if in this pose poor Sorrow would be supplied with a branch to stalk on. 'You know, he was a *dog*, Frank,' I said, 'not a cougar.'

Frank frowned. 'Personally,' he said, 'I favor the "attack" pose.'

'Don't show me,' I said. 'Surprise me.'

'Don't worry,' he said. 'You won't recognize him.'

That is precisely *what* worried me—that no one *would* recognize poor Sorrow. Least of all Franny. I think Frank had forgotten the purpose of what he was doing—he was so carried away with the *project* of it; he was getting three credits of independent study in biology for the task, and Sorrow had taken on the proportions of a term paper for a course. I could not imagine Sorrow, ever, in an 'attack' pose.

'Why not just curl Sorrow up in a ball, the way he used to sleep,' I said, 'with his tail over his face and his nose in his asshole?'

Frank looked disgusted, as usual, and I was tired of running in place; I did a few more wind sprints across Elliot Park.

I heard Max Urick yell at me from his fourth-floor window in the Hotel New Hampshire. 'You goddamn fool!' Max cried across the frozen ground, the dead leaves, and startled squirrels in the park. Off the fire escape, at *her* end of the second floor, a pale green nightgown waved in the gray air: Ronda Ray must have been sleeping in the blue one this morning, or in the black one—or in the shocking-orange one. The pale green one flapped at me like a flag, and I ran a few more wind sprints.

When I went to 3F, Iowa Bob was already up; he was doing his neck bridge routine, down on his back on the oriental rug, a pillow under his head. He was into a high neck bridge—with the barbell, at about 150 pounds, held straight over his head. Old Bob had a neck as big as my thigh.

'Good morning,' I whispered, and his eyes rolled back, and the barbell tilted, and he hadn't screwed the little things that hold the weights on tight enough, so that a few of the weights rolled off one end, and then the other, and Coach Bob shut his eyes and cringed as the weights dropped on either side of his head and went rolling off everywhere. I stopped a couple with my feet, but one of them rolled into the closet door, and it opened, of course, and out came a few things: a broom, a sweat shirt, Bob's running shoes, and a tennis racquet with his sweatband wrapped around the handle.

'Jesus God,' said Father, from downstairs in our family's kitchen.

'Good morning,' Bob said to me.

'Do you think Ronda Ray is attractive?' I asked him.

'Oh boy,' said Coach Bob.

'No, really,' I said.

'Really?' he said. 'Go ask your father. I'm too old. I haven't looked at girls since I broke my nose—the last time.'

That must have been in the line, at Iowa, I knew, because old Bob's nose had quite a number of wrinkles in it. He never put his teeth in until breakfast, too, so that his head in the early mornings looked astonishingly bald—like some strange, featherless bird, his empty mouth gaping like the lower half of a bill under his bent nose. Iowa Bob had the head of a gargoyle on the body of a lion.

'Well, do you think she's *pretty?*' I asked him.

'I don't think about it,' he said.

'Well, think about it now!' I said.

'Not exactly "pretty," ' said Iowa Bob. 'But she's sort of appealing.'

'Appealing?' I asked.

'Sexy!' said a voice over Bob's intercom—Franny's voice, of course; she had been listening to the squawk boxes at the switchboard, as usual.

'Damn kids,' said Iowa Bob.

'Damn it, Franny!' I said.

'You should ask *me,*' Franny said.

'Oh boy,' said Iowa Bob.

So it was that I came to tell Franny the story of Ronda Ray's apparent offer on the stairwell, her interest in my hard breathing, and in my beating heart—and the plan for a rainy day.

'So? Do it,' said Franny. 'But why wait for the rain?'

'Do you think she's a whore?' I asked Franny.

'You mean, do I think she charges money?' Franny said.

That thought had not occurred to me—'whore' being a word that was used all too loosely at the Dairy School.

'Money?' I said. 'How much do you think she charges?'

'I don't know *if* she charges,' Franny said, 'but if I were you, that's something I'd want to find out.' At the intercom, we switched to Ronda's room and listened to her breathing. It was her awake-but-just-lying-there-breathing sound. We listened to her a long while, as if we would understand from what we heard the possible *price* attached to her. Franny finally shrugged.

'I'm going to take a bath,' she said, and she gave a twirl to the room dial, and the intercom listened to the empty rooms. 2A, not a sound; 3A, nothing; 4A, nothing at all; 1B, nothing; 4B, Max Urick and his static. Franny was leaving the switchboard to go draw her bath and I gave the room dial a twirl: to 2C, 3C, 4C, then switching fast to 2E, 3E . . . *and there it was* . . . and on to 4E, where there was nothing.

'Wait a minute,' I said.

'What was *that?*' Franny said.

'Three E, I think,' I said.

'Try it again,' she said. It was the floor above Ronda Ray, and at the opposite end of the hall from her; it was across the hall from Iowa Bob, who was out.

'Do it,' Franny said. We were scared. We had *no* guests in the Hotel New Hampshire, but there had been one hell of a sound from 3E.

It was Sunday afternoon. Frank was in the bio lab and Egg and Lilly were at the movie matinee. Ronda Ray was just sitting in her room, and Iowa Bob was out. Mrs. Urick was in the kitchen, and Max Urick was playing his radio behind the static.

I put on 3E and Franny and I heard it again.

'*Ooooooooooo!*' went the woman.

'*Hoo, hoo, hoo!*' went the man.

But the Texan had gone home, long ago, and there was no woman staying in 3E.

'*Yike, yike, yike!*' said the woman.

'*Muff, muff, muff!*' said the man.

It was as if the crazy intercom system had made them up! Franny held my hand, tightly. I tried to switch it off, or move it to another, calmer room, but Franny wouldn't let me.

'*Eeeep!*' the woman cried.

'Nup!' said the man. A lamp fell. Then the woman laughed, and the man began to mutter.

'Jesus God,' my father said.

'Another lamp,' Mother said, and went on laughing.

'If we were guests,' Father said, 'we'd have to pay for it!'

They laughed at this as if Father had said the funniest thing in the world.

'Turn it off!' Franny said. I did.

'It's kind of funny, isn't it?' I ventured to say.

'They have to use the hotel,' Franny said, 'just to get away from *us!*'

I couldn't see what she was thinking.

'God!' Franny said. 'They really *love* each other—they really *do!*' And I wondered why I had taken such a thing for granted, and why it seemed to surprise my sister so much. Franny dropped my hand and wrapped her arms around herself; she hugged herself, as if she were trying to wake herself up, or get warm. 'What am *I* going to do?' she said. 'What's it going to be like? What happens next?' she asked.

But I could never see as far as Franny could see. I was not really looking beyond that moment; I had even forgotten Ronda Ray.

'You were going to take a bath,' I reminded Franny, who seemed in need of reminding—or some other advice.

'What?' she said.

'A bath,' I said. '*That's* what was going to happen next. You were going to take a bath.'

'Ha!' Franny cried. 'The hell with that!' she said. 'Fuck the bath!' said Franny, and went on hugging herself, and moving in place, as if she were trying to dance with herself. I couldn't tell whether she was happy or upset, but when I began to fool with her—to dance with her, and push her, and tickle her under the arms, she pushed and tickled and danced back, and we ran out of the switchboard room and up the stairwell to the second-floor landing.

'Rain, rain, rain!' Franny started yelling, and I became terribly embarrassed; Ronda Ray opened the door to her day-room, and frowned at us.

'We're having a rain dance,' Franny told her. 'Want to dance with us?'

Ronda smiled. She had on a shocking-orange nightgown. There was a magazine in her hand.

'Not right now,' she said.

141

'Rain, rain, it's going to rain!' Franny went off dancing.

Ronda shook her head at me—but nicely—and then shut her door.

I chased Franny outside into Elliot Park. We could see Mother and Father at the window by the fire escape in 3E. Mother had opened the window to call to us.

'Go get Egg and Lilly at the movies!' she said.

'What are you doing in *that* room?' I called back.

'Cleaning it!' said Mother.

'Rain, rain, rain!' Franny screamed, and we ran downtown to the matinee.

Egg and Lilly came out of the movies with Junior Jones.

'It's a *kids'* movie,' Franny said to Jones. 'How come *you* went?'

'I'm just a big kid,' Junior said. He held her hand while we all walked home, and Franny took a stroll with him through the Dairy School grounds; I continued toward home with Egg and Lilly.

'Does Franny love Junior Jones?' Lilly asked, seriously.

'Well, she *likes* him, anyway,' I said. 'He is her friend.'

'What?' said Egg.

It was almost Thanksgiving. Junior was staying with us for Thanksgiving vacation, because his parents didn't send him enough money to go home. And several of the foreign students at the Dairy School—who lived too far away to go home for Thanksgiving—would be joining us for Thanksgiving dinner. Everyone liked having Junior around, but the foreign students, whom nobody knew, had been Father's idea—and Mother had gone along, saying it was the kind of thing Thanksgiving was originally for. Maybe, but we children did not care for the invasion. Guests in the hotel were one thing, and there was one of those staying with us—a famous Finnish doctor, supposedly, who was there to visit his daughter at the Dairy School. She was one of the foreigners coming to dinner. The others included a Japanese whom Frank knew from his taxidermy project; the Japanese had been sworn to secrecy over the stuffing of Sorrow, Frank had told me, but the boy's English was so bad that he could have blurted out the truth and no one would have understood him. Then there were two Korean girls, whose hands were so pretty and small Lilly would never take her eyes from them—not for the entire dinner. They perhaps kindled an interest in eating that had been absent in Lilly before, however, because they ate lots of things with their little fingers—in such a delicate and beautiful way that Lilly began to play with her food in this fashion, and eventually even ate some. Egg, of course, would spend the day shouting 'What?' to the tragically incomprehensible Japanese boy. And Junior Jones would eat, and eat, and eat —making Mrs. Urick nearly detonate with pride.

'Now, *there* is an appetite!' said Mrs. Urick, admiringly.

'If I was as big as that, I'd eat like that, too,' Max said.

'No you wouldn't,' said Mrs. Urick. 'You don't have it in you.'

Ronda Ray did not wear her waitress uniform; she sat and ate with the family, jumping up to clear the dishes and serve things from the kitchen, along with Franny and Mother and the big blond girl from Finland whose famous father was visiting her.

The Finnish girl was enormous and made swooping movements around the table that made Lilly cringe. She was a big blue-and-white ski-sweater sort of girl, who kept hugging her father, a big blue-and-white ski-sweater sort of man.

'Ho!' he kept crying, at the arrival of new food from the kitchen.

'Ya-hoo,' Franny whispered.

'Holy cow,' said Junior Jones.

Iowa Bob sat next to Jones at the table; their end of the table was nearest the television above the bar, so that they could watch the football game in progress through our dinner.

'If that's a clip, I'll eat my plate,' Jones would say.

'Eat your plate,' Coach Bob would say.

'What's a "clip"?' the famous Finnish doctor would ask, only it sounded like 'Wot's a clop?'

Iowa Bob would then offer to demonstrate a clip, on Ronda, who was willing, and the Korean girls giggled shyly to themselves, and the Japanese struggled—with his turkey, with his butter knife, with Frank's mumbling explanations, with Egg's shouts of 'What!' all the time, with (apparently) everything.

'This is the loudest dinner I've ever eaten,' Franny said.

'What?' Egg cried.

'Jesus God,' said Father.

'Lilly,' Mother said. '*Please* eat. Then you'll grow.'

'What's that?' said the famous Finnish doctor, only it sounded like 'Wot's dot?' He looked at Mother and Lilly. 'Who's not growing?' he asked.

'Oh, it's nothing,' Mother said.

'It's me,' said Lilly. 'I've stopped growing.'

'No you haven't, dear,' Mother said.

143

'Her growth appears to be arrested,' Father said.

'Ho, *arrested!*' the Finn said, staring at Lilly. 'Not growing, eh?' he asked her. She nodded in her small way. The doctor put his hands on her head and peered into her eyes. Everyone stopped eating, except the Japanese boy and the Korean girls.

'How do you say?' the doctor asked, and then said something unpronounceable to his daughter.

'Tape measure,' she said.

'Ho, a tape measure?' the doctor cried. Max Urick ran and got one. The doctor measured Lilly around her chest, around her waist, around her wrists and ankles, around her shoulders, around her head.

'She's all right,' Father said. 'It's nothing.'

'Be quiet,' Mother said.

The doctor wrote down all the figures.

'Ho!' he said.

'Eat up your food, dear,' Mother told Lilly, but Lilly was staring at the figures the doctor had written on his napkin.

'How do you say?' the doctor asked his daughter, and said another unpronounceable word. This time the daughter drew a blank. 'You don't *know?*' her father asked her. She shook her head. 'Where's the dictionary?' he asked her.

'In my dorm,' she said.

'Ho!' he said. 'Go and get it.'

'Now?' she said, and looked wistfully at her second serving of goose and turkey and stuffing, heaped upon her plate.

'Go, go!' her father said. 'Of *course* now. Go! *Ho!* Go!' he said, and the big blue-and-white ski-sweater girl was gone.

'It's—how you say?—a pathological condition,' the famous Finnish doctor said, calmly.

'A pathological condition?' Father said.

'A pathological condition of arrested growth,' said the doctor. 'It's common, and there's a variety of causes.'

'A pathological condition of arrested growth,' Mother repeated.

Lilly shrugged; she imitated the way the Korean girls skinned a drumstick.

When the big, blond, out-of-breath girl was back, she looked stricken to see that Ronda Ray had cleared her plate; she handed the dictionary to her father.

'Ho!' Franny whispered across the table to me, and I kicked her under the table. She kicked me back; I kicked back at her and kicked Junior Jones by mistake.

144

'Ow,' he said.

'Sorry,' I said.

'Ho!' said the Finnish doctor, putting his finger on the word. 'Dwarfism!' he exclaimed.

It was quiet at the table, except for the sound of the Japanese struggling with his creamed corn.

'Are you saying she's a *dwarf?*' Father asked the doctor.

'Ho, *yes!* A dwarf,' the doctor said.

'Bull*shit*,' said Iowa Bob. 'That's no dwarf—that's a little girl! That's a *child,* you moron!'

'What is "moron"?' the doctor asked his daughter, but she wouldn't tell him.

Ronda Ray brought out the pies.

'You're no dwarf, dear,' Mother whispered to Lilly, but Lilly just shrugged.

'So what if I am?' she said, bravely. 'I'm a good kid.'

'Bananas,' said Iowa Bob, darkly. And no one knew if he meant that as a cure—'Just feed her bananas!'—or if he was stating a euphemism for 'bullshit.'

Anyway, that was Thanksgiving, 1956, and we careened on toward Christmas in that fashion: pondering size, listening to love, giving up baths, hoping to properly pose the dead —running and lifting and waiting for rain.

It was a morning in early December when Franny woke me. It was still dark in my room, and the snorkling sound of Egg's breathing reached me through the open connecting doorway; Egg was still asleep. There was someone's softer, controlled breathing nearer to me than Egg, and I was aware of Franny's smell—a smell I hadn't known for a while: a rich but never rank smell, a little salty, a little sweet, strong but never syrupy. And in the darkness I knew that Franny had been cured of taking baths. It was overhearing my Mother and Father that did it; I think that made her own smell seem perfectly natural to Franny again.

'Franny?' I whispered, because I couldn't see her. Her hand brushed my cheek.

'Over here,' she said. She was curled against the wall and the headboard of my bed; how she could squeeze in beside me without waking me, I'll never know. I turned toward her and smelled that she'd brushed her teeth. 'Listen,' she whispered. I heard Franny's heartbeat and mine, and Egg deep-sea diving in the adjoining room. And something else, as soft as Franny's breath.

'It's *rain,* dummy,' Franny said, and wormed a knuckle into my ribs. 'It's raining, kid,' she told me. 'It's your big day!'

'It's still dark,' I said. 'I'm still sleeping.'

'It's dawn,' Franny hissed in my ear; then she bit my cheek and started tickling me under the covers.

'Cut it out, Franny!' I said.

'Rain, rain, rain,' she chanted. 'Don't be chicken. Frank and I have been up for hours.'

She said that Frank was at the switchboard, playing with the squawk-box system. Franny dragged me out of bed and made me brush my teeth and put on my track clothes, as if I were going to run wind sprints on the stairs, as usual. Then she took me to Frank at the switch-board, and the two of them counted out the money and told me to hide it in one of my running shoes —a thick wad of bills, mostly ones and fives.

'How can I run with that in my shoe?' I asked.

'You're not going to *run,* remember?' Franny said.

'How much is it?' I asked.

'First find out if she charges,' Franny said. '*Then* worry if you have enough.'

Frank sat at the controls of the switchboard like the crazed operator of some flight-control tower at an airport under attack.

'And what are *you* guys going to do?' I asked.

'We're just looking out for you,' Frank said. 'If you really start embarrassing yourself, we'll call for a fire drill or something.'

'Oh, great!' I said. 'I don't need this.'

'Look, kid,' Franny said. 'We got the money, we have a right to listen.'

'Oh boy,' I said.

'You'll do just fine,' Franny said. 'Don't be nervous.'

'What if it's all a misunderstanding?' I asked.

'That's actually what I think it is,' Frank said. 'In which case,' he said, 'just take the money out of your shoe and run your wind sprints up and down the stairs.'

'You pill, Frank,' Franny said. 'Shut up and give us the bed check.'

Click, click, click, click: Iowa Bob was a subway again, miles underground; Max Urick slept behind his static, with a static all his own; Mrs. Urick and a stockpot or two were simmering; the guest in 3H   the grim aunt of a student at the Dairy School,

146

whose name was Bower—slept with a snore like the sound of a chisel being sharpened.

'And . . . good morning, Ronda!' Franny whispered, as Frank turned on *her* room. Oh, the delicious sound of Ronda Ray asleep! A sea breeze blowing through silk! I felt my armpits start to sweat.

'Get the hell up there,' Franny said to me, 'before it stops raining.'

Fat chance of that, I knew, glancing out the portal windows on the stairwell: Elliot Park was submerged, the water flooding over the curbs and carving ditches through the playground equipment; the gray sky was teeming rain. I pondered running a few laps, up and down the stairs—not necessarily for old times' sake, but thinking that this might be the most familiar way to wake Ronda up. But when I was standing in the hall outside her door, my fingers tingled, and I was already breathing hard —harder than I knew, Franny told me, later; she said that she and Frank could hear me over the intercom, even before Ronda got up and opened the door.

'It's either John-O or a runaway train,' Ronda whispered before she let me in, but I couldn't talk. I was already out of breath, as if I'd been running the stairs all morning.

It was dark in her room, but I could see that she was wearing the blue one. Her morning breath was slightly sour—but it smelled nice to me, and *she* smelled nice to me, although I would think, later, that her smell was simply Franny's smell taken several stages too far.

'Goodness, what cold knees—from wearing those pants without the legs!' said Ronda Ray. 'Come in here and get warm.'

I stumbled out of my shorts, and she said, 'Goodness, what cold arms—from wearing that shirt without the sleeves!' And I struggled out of that, too. I got out of my running shoes, managing to conceal the wad of money by stuffing it into the toe of one shoe.

And I wonder if it wasn't making love under the squawk-box system that colored my feelings about sexual intercourse from that moment on. Even now—when I'm almost forty—I am inclined to whisper. I remember begging Ronda Ray to whisper, too.

'I could have screamed at you to "speak up!" ' Franny told me later. 'It made me so damn mad—all that silly *whispering!*'

But there were other things I might have told Ronda Ray if I

147

hadn't known that Franny could hear. I never really thought about Frank, although I would always tend to see him—throughout our lives, together and apart—as stationed at an intercom, somewhere, listening in on love. I imagine Frank as listening in on love with the same displeased expression he wore for most of his tasks: a vague but widespread distaste, even bordering on disgust.

'You're quick, John-O, you're very quick,' Ronda Ray told me.

'Please whisper,' I told her, talking in a muffled voice into her wildly colorful hair.

I owe my sexual nervousness to this initiation—a feeling I have never quite escaped: that I've got to watch what I say and do, somehow, or risk betraying Franny. It is because of Ronda Ray, in that first Hotel New Hampshire, that I *always* imagine Franny is listening in?

'It sounded a little subdued,' Franny told me later. 'But I'm sure that's okay—for the first time.'

'Thank you for not coaching, from the sidelines,' I told her.

'Did you really think I would?' she asked me, and I apologized; but I never knew what Franny would or wouldn't do.

'How's it coming with the dog, Frank?' I kept asking, as Christmas bore down upon us all.

'How's it coming with the whispering?' Frank asked. 'I notice it's been raining a lot, lately.'

Or, if it didn't really rain a lot—that year, just before Christmas—I admit I took the liberty of interpreting snow as almost rain; or even a cloudy morning that threatened to be rain or snow, sometime later. And it was one of those times, very near to Christmas—when I'd long ago given Frank and Franny back the wad of money I'd stuffed in my shoe—that Ronda Ray asked me, 'Do you know, John-O, that it's customary to *tip* a waitress?' And I got the picture; I wondered if Franny overheard me that morning—or overheard the subsequent crinkling of bills.

I spent my Christmas money on Ronda Ray.

I bought a little something for Mother and Father, of course. We were not big on gifts at Christmas—the idea was to give something silly. I think I got Father an apron to wear behind the bar at the Hotel New Hampshire; it was one of those aprons with a stupid slogan on it. I think I got Mother a china bear. Frank always got Father a tie and Mother a scarf, and Mother gave the

148

scarves to Franny, who wore them every which way, and Father gave the ties back to Frank, who liked ties.

For Christmas, 1956, we made something special for Iowa Bob: a framed, blown-up photograph of Junior Jones scoring Dairy's only touchdown against Exeter. That was not so silly, but everything else was. Franny bought Mother a sexy dress that Mother would never wear. Franny was hoping Mother would give it to her, but Mother would never have allowed Franny to wear it, either.

'She can wear it for Father when they visit old Three E,' Franny told me, in a grouchy mood.

Father bought Frank a bus driver's uniform, because Frank was so fond of uniforms; Frank would wear it when he played doorman at the Hotel New Hampshire. On those rare occasions when we had more than one overnight guest, Frank liked to pretend that there was always a doorman at the Hotel New Hampshire. The bus driver's uniform was the good old Dairy death-gray color; the pants and the jacket sleeves were too short for Frank, and the cap was too large, so that Frank had an ominous, seedy-funeral-parlor look to him when he let in the guests.

'Welcome to the Hotel New Hampshire!' he practiced saying, but it always sounded as if he didn't mean it.

No one knew what to get Lilly—certainly not a dwarf, or an elf, or anything little.

'Give her *food!*' Iowa Bob suggested, a few days before Christmas. My family never went in for all this organized Christmas shopping shit, either. It was always down-to-the-last-minute with us, although Iowa Bob made a big deal about the tree that he chopped down in Elliot Park one morning: it was too large to stand up in the restaurant of the Hotel New Hampshire without being cut in half.

'You chopped down that lovely tree in the park!' Mother said.

'Well, we own the park, don't we?' Coach Bob said. 'What else do you do with trees?' He was from Iowa, after all, where you can see for miles—sometimes, without a tree in sight.

It was on Egg that we lavished the most presents, because he was the only one of us who was the prime age for Christmas that year. And Egg was very fond of *things*. Everyone got him animals and balls and tub toys and outdoor equipment—most of it junk that would be lost or outgrown or broken or under the snow before the winter was over.

149

Franny and I found a jar of chimpanzee teeth in an antique store in Dairy, and we bought the teeth for Frank.

'He can use them in one of his stuffing experiments,' Franny said.

I was just as glad that we would not be giving Frank the teeth *before* Christmas, because I feared that Frank might try to use them in his version of Sorrow.

'Sorrow!' Iowa Bob screamed aloud one night, just before Christmas, and we all sat up in our beds with our hair itching. 'Sorrow!' the old man called from his room; his barbells clanked across the floor. His door opened and we heard him bellow down the deserted third-floor hall. 'Sorrow!' he called.

'The old fool is having a bad dream,' Father said, thumping upstairs in his bathrobe, but I went into Frank's room and stared at him.

'Don't look at me,' Frank said. 'Sorrow's still down at the lab. He's not finished.'

And we all went upstairs to see what was the matter with Iowa Bob.

He had 'seen' Sorrow, he said. Coach Bob had smelled the old dog in his sleep, and when he woke up, Sorrow was standing on the old oriental rug—his favorite—in Bob's room. 'But he looked at me with such *menace,*' old Bob said. 'He looked like he was going to *attack!*'

I stared at Frank again, but Frank shrugged. Father rolled his eyes.

'You were having a nightmare,' he told his old dad.

'Sorrow was in this room!' Coach Bob said. 'But he didn't *look* like Sorrow. He looked like he wanted to *kill* me.'

'Hush, hush,' Mother said, and Father waved us out of the room; I heard him start talking to Iowa Bob that way I'd heard Father talk to Egg, or to Lilly—or to any of us children, when we were younger—and I realized that Father often talked to Bob that way, as if he thought his father was a child.

'It's that old rug,' Mother whispered to us kids. 'It's got so much dog hair on it that your grandfather can still smell Sorrow in his sleep.'

Lilly looked frightened, but Lilly often looked frightened. Egg was staggering around as if he were asleep on his feet.

'Sorrow is dead, isn't he?' Egg asked.

'Yes, yes,' Franny said.

'What?' Egg said, in such a loud voice that Lilly jumped.

'Okay, Frank,' I whispered in the stairwell. 'What *pose* did you put Sorrow in?'

'Attack,' he said, and I shuddered.

I thought that the old dog, in resentment for the terrible pose he'd been condemned to, had come back to haunt the Hotel New Hampshire. He'd gone to Iowa Bob's room because Bob had Sorrow's rug.

'Let's put Sorrow's old rug in Frank's room,' I suggested, at breakfast.

'I don't want that old rug,' Frank said.

'I *do* want that old rug,' said Coach Bob. 'It's perfect for my weights.'

'That was some dream you had last night,' Franny ventured to say.

'That was no dream, Franny,' Bob said, grimly. 'That was Sorrow—in the flesh,' said the old coach, and Lilly shivered so hard at the word 'flesh' that she dropped her cereal spoon with a clatter.

'What is *flesh?*' Egg asked.

'Look, Frank,' I said to Frank, out in frozen Elliot Park—the day before Christmas. 'I think you better let Sorrow stay down at the lab.'

Frank looked ready to 'attack' at this suggestion. 'He's all ready,' Frank said, 'and he's coming home tonight.'

'Do me a favor and don't gift-wrap him, okay?' I said.

'Gift-wrap him?' Frank said, with only mild disgust. 'Do you think I'm crazy?'

I didn't answer him, and he said, 'Look, don't you understand what's going on? I've done such a good job with Sorrow that Grandfather has had a *premonition* that Sorrow's come home,' Frank said.

It would always amaze me, how Frank could make pure idiocy *sound* logical.

And so we came to the night before Christmas. Not a creature was stirring, as they say. Just a stockpot or two. Max Urick's ever-present static. Ronda Ray was in her room. And there was a Turk in 2B—a Turkish diplomat visiting his son at the Dairy School; he was the only student at the Dairy School who had not gone home (or to *someone's* home) for Christmas. All the presents were hidden with care. It was our family tradition to bring everything out and put it under the bare tree on Christmas morning.

Mother and Father, we knew, had hidden all our presents in

151

3E—a room they visited happily and often. Iowa Bob had stored his gifts in one of the tiny fourth-floor bathrooms, which were not called 'fit for dwarfs,' not anymore—not since the dubious diagnosis of Lilly's possible affliction. Franny showed me all the presents she got—including modeling, for me, the sexy dress she bought for Mother. That prompted me to show her the nightgown I bought for Ronda Ray, and Franny promptly modeled it. When I saw it on her, I knew I should have gotten it for Franny. It was snow-white, a color not available in Ronda's collection.

'You should have gotten this for *me!*' Franny said. 'I love it!'

But I would never catch on to what I should do about Franny, in time; as Franny said, 'I'll always be a year ahead of you, kid.'

Lilly hid her gifts in a small box; all her gifts were small. Egg didn't get anyone any gifts, but he searched endlessly through the Hotel New Hampshire for all the gifts people had gotten for him. And Frank hid Sorrow in Coach Bob's closet.

'*Why?*' I would ask him, and ask him, later.

'It was just for one night,' Frank said. 'And I knew that Franny would never look there.'

On Christmas Eve, 1956, everyone went to bed early and no one slept—another family tradition. We heard the ice groaning under the snow in Elliot Park. There were times when Elliot Park could creak like a coffin changing temperature—being lowered into the ground. Why is it that even the Christmas of 1956 felt a little like Halloween?

There was even a dog barking, late at night, and although the dog could not have been Sorrow, all of us who were awake thought of Iowa Bob's dream—of his 'premonition,' as Frank called it.

And then it was Christmas morning—clear, windy, and cold —and I ran my forty or fifty wind sprints across Elliot Park. Naked, I was no longer as 'chubby' as I looked with my running clothes on—as Ronda Ray was always telling me. Some of the bananas were turning hard. And Christmas morning or no Christmas morning, a routine is a routine: I joined Coach Bob for a little weight lifting before the family gathered for Christmas breakfast.

'You do your curls while I do my neck bridges,' Iowa Bob told me.

'Yes, Grandfather,' I said, and I did as I was told. Feet to feet on Sorrow's old rug, we did our sit-ups; head to head, our

152

push-ups. There was only one long barbell, and the two short dumbbells for the one-arm curls. We traded the weights back and forth—it was a kind of wordless morning prayer for us.

'Your upper arms, your chest, your neck—that all looks pretty good,' Grandpa Bob told me, 'but your forearms could stand some work. And put maybe a flat twenty-five-pounder on your chest when you do your sit-ups—you're doing them too easily. And bend your knees.'

'Yup,' I said, out of breath in my Ronda Ray way.

Bob put the long barbell up; he cleaned it neatly about ten times, then he pumped a few standing presses with it—it seemed to me he had about 160 or 180 on the bar when the weights slid off one end and I got out of their way, and then about fifty or seventy-five pounds came sliding off the other end of the bar, and old Iowa Bob cried, 'Shit! Goddamn thing!' The weights rolled across the room. Father, downstairs, hollered up at us.

'Jesus God, you crazy weight lifters!' he yelled. 'Tighten those *screws!*'

And one of the weights rolled into the door of Bob's closet, and the door opened, of course, and out came the tennis racquet, Bob's laundry bag, a vacuum cleaner hose, a squash ball, and Sorrow—stuffed.

I tried to say something, although the dog alarmed me nearly as much as it must have alarmed Iowa Bob; at least *I* knew what it was. It was Sorrow in Frank's 'attack' pose. It was a pretty good attack pose, all right, and a better job of stuffing a black Labrador retriever than I would have thought Frank capable of. Sorrow was screwed down to a pine board—as Coach Bob would have said, 'Everything is screwed down in the Hotel New Hampshire; in the Hotel New Hampshire, we're screwed down for *life!*' The fierce dog slid rather gracefully out of the closet, landing firmly on all four feet and looking ready to spring. His black fur was so glossy it must have been recently oiled, and his yellow eyes caught the bright morning light—and the light caught the gleam in his old yellow teeth, which Frank had polished white for the occasion. The dog's hackles were drawn back farther than I ever saw old Sorrow's hackles drawn back, when Sorrow had been alive, and a shiny sort of spittle—very convincing stuff—seemed to brighten the dead dog's gums. His black nose looked wet and healthy, and I could almost smell his fetid halitosis reaching out to Iowa Bob and me. But *this* Sorrow looked much too serious to fart.

This Sorrow meant business, and before I could get my breath

153

back and tell my grandfather that it was only a Christmas present for Franny—that it was only one of Frank's awful projects from down at the bio lab—the old coach slung his barbell at the savage attack dog and threw his wonderful lineman's body back against me (to protect me, no doubt; that must have been what he meant to do).

'Holy cow!' said Iowa Bob, in a strangely small voice, and the weights clattered on all sides of Sorrow. The snarling dog was unfazed; he remained poised for the kill. And Iowa Bob, who was past the end of his last season, dropped dead in my arms.

'Jesus God, are you throwing those weights around *on purpose?*' Father screamed upstairs to us. 'Jesus God!' Father cried. 'Take a day off, will you? It's Christmas, for Christ's sake. Merry Christmas! Merry Christmas!'

'Merry fucking Christmas!' shouted Franny, from downstairs.

'Merry Christmas!' said Lilly, and Egg—and even Frank.

'Merry Christmas!' Mother called softly.

And was it Ronda Ray I heard chiming in? And the Uricks —already setting up for Christmas breakfast in the Hotel New Hampshire? And I heard something unpronounceable—it might have been the Turk in 2B.

In my arms, which I realized had grown very strong, I held the former Big Ten star, who was as heavy and meaningful, to me, as our family bear, and I stared into the short distance that separated us from Sorrow.

6

Father Hears from Freud

Coach Bob's Christmas present—the framed, blown-up photograph of Junior Jones scoring Dairy's only touchdown against Exeter—was given to Franny, who also inherited 3F, Iowa Bob's old room. Franny wanted nothing to do with Frank's version of Sorrow, which Egg dragged to his room; he hid the stuffed dog under his bed, where Mother discovered it, with a shriek, several days after Christmas. I know that Frank would have liked to have Sorrow back—for further experimenting with the facial expression, or the pose—but Frank had kept to himself, and to his room, since scaring his grandfather to death.

Iowa Bob was sixty-eight when he died, but the old lineman was in first-rate shape; without a fright of Sorrow's magnitude, he might have lived for another decade. Our family made every effort not to let the responsibility for the accident weigh too heavily on Frank. 'Nothing weighs too heavily on Frank,' Franny said, but even Franny tried to cheer him up. 'Stuffing Sorrow was a sweet *idea,* Frank,' Franny told him, 'but you must realize not everybody has your *taste.*'

What she might have told him was that taxidermy, like sex, is a very personal subject; the manner in which we impose it on others should be discreet.

Frank's guilt, if guilt was what he felt, was apparent only by his exaggerated absence; Frank was always more absent than the rest of us, but his usual silence grew even quieter. Even so, Franny and I felt that only Frank's sulking prevented him from asking for Sorrow.

Mother, against Egg's protests, instructed Max Urick to dispose of Sorrow, which Max accomplished by merely upending the paralyzed beast in one of the trash barrels at the delivery entrance. And one rainy morning, from Ronda Ray's room, I was startled to see the soggy tail and rump of Sorrow protruding from the mouth of the barrel; I could imagine the rubbish man, with his Department of Sanitation truck, being similarly startled —thinking suddenly to himself: My God, when they're through with their pets at the Hotel New Hampshire, they just throw them out with the garbage!

'Come back to bed, John-O,' said Ronda Ray, but I just stared through the rain, which was turning to snow—falling over the row of barrels crammed with Christmas wrappings, ribbons and tinsel, the bottles and cartons and cans of the restaurant business, the bright and dull scraps of food, of interest to the birds and dogs, and one dead dog of interest to no one. Well, almost no one. It would have broken Frank's heart to see Sorrow come to this degrading end, and I looked out at the snow thickening over Elliot Park and saw another member of my family who was still keenly interested in Sorrow. I saw Egg, in his ski parka and ski hat, dragging his sled to the delivery entrance. He moved quickly over the slick coating of snow, his sled grating on the driveway, which was still bare and dotted with puddles. Egg knew where he was going—a quick look into the basement windows and he was safely past Mrs. Urick's scrutiny; a glance to the fourth floor, but Max was not guarding the trash barrels. Our family's rooms didn't overlook the delivery entrance, and Egg knew that left only Ronda Ray who could see him. But she was in bed, and when Egg glanced up at her window, I ducked out of sight.

'If you'd rather be out running, John-O,' Ronda groaned, 'go run.'

And when I looked out the window again, Egg was gone; Sorrow had gone with him. The efforts to bring Sorrow back from the grave were not over, I knew; I could only guess where the beast might reappear.

When Franny moved to Iowa Bob's room, Mother rearranged the rest of us. She put Egg and me together, where Franny and Lilly had been, and she gave Lilly my old room *and* Egg's adjoining room—as if, illogically, Lilly's so-called dwarfism needed to be accommodated not only with privacy but with a larger space. I complained, but Father said I would have a 'maturing' influence on Egg. Frank's secret quarters were unchanged, and the barbells still resided in Iowa Bob's room, which gave me more reason to visit Franny, who liked to watch me lift. So when I lifted, now, I was not thinking just of Franny —my only audience!—but with a little extra effort I could bring back Coach Bob. I was lifting for both of us.

I suppose that, by salvaging Sorrow from the inevitable

156

journey to the dump, Egg might have been resurrecting Iowa Bob in the only way Egg could do it. What 'maturing' influence I was expected to have on Egg remained a mystery to me, though it was tolerable sharing a room with him. His clothes bothered me most of all, or not his clothes but his habits with clothes: Egg didn't dress himself, he costumed himself. He changed costumes several times a day, the discarded clothing always dominating a central area of our room and accumulating there, after several days, before Mother would rampage through the room and ask me if I couldn't urge Egg to be more tidy. Perhaps Father meant 'tidying' when he said 'maturing.'

For my first week of sharing a room with Egg, I was less concerned with his messiness than I was anxious to discover where he had hidden Sorrow. I did not want to be startled by that shape of death again, although I think the shape of death is always startling to us—it is *meant* to be startling—and not even proper anticipation can prepare us enough for it. This, at least, was true of Egg and Sorrow.

The night before New Year's Eve, with Iowa Bob not dead a week, and Sorrow missing from the garbage for only two days, I whispered across the darkness of our room to Egg; I knew he wasn't asleep.

'Okay, Egg,' I whispered. 'Where is he?' But it would always be a mistake to *whisper* to Egg.

'What?' Egg said. Mother and Dr. Blaze said that Egg's hearing was improving, although Father referred to Egg's 'deafness,' not to his 'hearing,' and concluded that Dr. Blaze must be deaf himself to think of Egg's condition as 'improving.' It was rather like Dr. Blaze's opinion of Lilly's dwarfism: that it was improving, too, because Lilly *had* grown (a little). But everyone else had grown much more, and the impression, therefore, was that Lilly was growing *smaller*.

'Egg,' I said more loudly. 'Where is Sorrow?'

'Sorrow is dead,' Egg said.

'I know he's dead, damn it,' I said, 'but *where*, Egg? Where is Sorrow?'

'Sorrow is with Grandpa Bob,' said Egg, who was right about that, of course, and I knew there would be no cajoling the whereabouts of the stuffed terror out of Egg.

'Tomorrow is New Year's Eve,' I said.

'Who?' Egg said.

'New Year's Eve!' I said. 'We're having a party.'

'Where?' he asked.

'Here,' I said. 'In the Hotel New Hampshire.'

'What room?' he said.

'The *main* room,' I said. 'The big room. The restaurant, dummy.'

'We're not having a party in this room,' Egg said.

With Egg's costumes all around, there was hardly room for a party in our room, I knew, but I let this observation pass. I was almost asleep when Egg spoke again.

'How would you dry something that's wet?' Egg asked.

And I thought to myself of the likely *condition* of Sorrow, after God knows how many hours in the open trash barrel, in the rain and snow.

'What is it that's wet, Egg?' I asked.

'Hair,' he said. 'How would you dry hair?'

'*Your* hair, Egg?'

'Anybody's hair,' Egg said. 'Lots of hair. More hair than mine.'

'Well, with a hair dryer, I suppose,' I said.

'That thing Franny has?' Egg asked.

'Mother has one, too,' I told him.

'Yeah,' he said, 'but Franny's is bigger. I think it's *hotter*, too.'

'Got a lot of hair to dry, huh?' I said.

'What?' Egg said. But it wasn't worth repeating; an aspect of Egg's deafness was Egg's ability to choose when not to hear.

In the morning I watched him take off his pajamas, under which he wore—and had slept in—a full suit of clothes.

'It's good to be ready—right, Egg?' I asked.

'Ready for what?' he asked. 'There isn't any school today —it's still vacation.'

'Then why'd you wear your clothes to bed?' I asked him, but he let that pass; he was rummaging through various piles of costumes. 'What are you looking for?' I asked him. 'You're already dressed.' But whenever Egg detected that the tone I took toward him was a teasing one, he ignored me.

'See you at the party,' he said.

Egg loved the Hotel New Hampshire; perhaps he loved it even more than Father, because Father loved most of all the idea of it; in fact, Father seemed daily more and more unsure of the actual success of his venture. Egg loved all the rooms, the stairwells, the great unoccupied emptiness of the former all-girl's school. Father knew we were unoccupied a little too much of the time, but that was fine with Egg.

Guests would occasionally bring odd things they had found in their rooms to breakfast. 'The room was very clean,' they would begin, 'but someone must have left this . . . this *something*.' The right rubber arm of a cowboy; the wrinkled, webbed foot of a dried toad. A playing card, with a face drawn over the face of the jack of diamonds; the five of clubs with the word 'Yuck' written across it. A small sock with six marbles in it. A costume change (Egg's policeman's badge pinned to his baseball uniform) hanging in the closet of 4G.

On the day of New Year's Eve, the weather was that thawing kind—a mist spreading over Elliot Park, and yesterday's snow already melting and revealing the gray snow of a week ago. 'Where were you this morning, John-O?' Ronda Ray asked me, as we were fussing with the restaurant for the New Year's Eve party.

'It wasn't raining,' I pointed out. A weak excuse, I knew —and she knew. I was hardly being unfaithful to Ronda—there was no one to be unfaithful with—but I dreamed of an imaginary someone else, about Franny's age, all the time. I had even asked Franny for a date with one of her friends, someone she would recommend—although Franny was in the habit of saying that her friends were too old for me, now; by which she meant that they were sixteen.

'No weight lifting this morning?' Franny asked me. 'Aren't you afraid you'll get out of shape?'

'I'm in training for the party,' I said.

For the party, we expected that three or four Dairy students (who were cutting their Christmas break short) would be spending the night in the hotel, among them Junior Jones, who was Franny's date, and a sister of Junior Jones, who was *not* a Dairy student. Junior was bringing her with him for me—I was terrified that Junior Jones's sister was going to be as big as Junior Jones, and I was also eager to know if this was the sister who'd been raped, as Harold Swallow had told me; it seemed unjustly important to know. Was I to have a large, raped girl for a date or a large, *un*raped girl?—for either way, I was sure, she would have to be huge.

'Don't be nervous,' Franny said to me.

We dismantled the Christmas tree, which brought tears to my father's eyes, because it had been Iowa Bob's tree; Mother had to leave the room. The funeral had seemed so subdued to us children—it was the first funeral we had ever seen, being too young to remember what was done about Latin Emeritus and my

159

mother's mother; the bear called State o' Maine had not been given a funeral. I think that considering the noise attached to the death of Iowa Bob, we expected the funeral to be louder, too —'at least the sound of barbells falling,' I said to Franny.

'Be serious,' she said. She seemed to think she was growing much older than me, and I was afraid she was right.

'Is this the sister who was raped?' I asked Franny suddenly. 'I mean, which sister is Junior bringing?' By Franny's look at me, I guessed that this question also put years between us.

'He only has one sister,' Franny said, looking straight at me. 'Does it matter to you that she was raped?'

Of course I didn't know what to say: that it *did!* That one would not discuss rape with someone who'd been raped, as opposed to launching into the subject right away with someone who hadn't? That one would look for the lasting scars in the personality, or not look for them? That one would *assume* lasting scars in the personality, and speak to the person as to an invalid? (And how did one speak to an invalid?) That it didn't matter? But it did. I knew why, too. I was fourteen. In my inexpert years (and I would always be inexpert on the subject of rape), I imagined that one would *touch* a person who'd been raped a little differently, or a little less; or that one would not touch her at all. I said that to Franny, finally, and she stared at me.

'You're wrong,' she said, but it was the way she said to Frank, 'You're an asshole,' and I felt that I would probably always be fourteen, too.

'Where is Egg?' Father bellowed. 'Egg!'

'Egg never does any work,' Frank complained, sweeping the dead needles from the Christmas tree aimlessly about the restaurant.

'Egg is a little boy, Frank,' Franny said.

'Egg could be more mature than he is,' Father said. And I (who was to be the maturing influence) . . . I knew very well why Egg was out of earshot. He was in some empty room of the Hotel New Hampshire, contemplating the terrible mass of wet black Labrador retriever, which was Sorrow.

When the last of Christmas had been swept and dragged out of the Hotel New Hampshire, we considered what decorations would be appropriate for New Year's Eve.

'No one feels very much like New Year's Eve,' Franny said. 'Let's not decorate anything at all.'

'A party is a party,' said Father, gamely, although we

suspected he felt the least like a party of us all. Everyone knew whose idea a New Year's Eve party had been: Iowa Bob's.

'There won't be anybody coming, anyway,' Frank said.

'Well, speak for yourself, Frank,' Franny said. 'I have some friends coming.'

'There could be a hundred people here and you'd still stay in your room, Frank,' I said.

'Go eat another banana,' Frank said. 'Go take a run—to the moon.'

'Well, I like having a party,' Lilly said, and everyone looked at her—because, of course, we had not seen her until she spoke; she was getting so small. Lilly was almost eleven, but she now seemed substantially smaller than Egg; she barely came up to my waist and she weighed less than forty pounds.

So we all rallied to the occasion: as long as Lilly was looking forward to a party, we would try to get in the mood.

'So how should we decorate the restaurant, Lilly?' Frank asked her; he had a way of bending over when he spoke to Lilly, as if he were addressing a baby in a carriage and what he had to say were pure gibberish.

'Let's not decorate anything at all,' Lilly said. 'Let's just have a good time.'

We all stood still, facing this prospect as we might face a death sentence, but Mother said, 'That's a wonderful idea! I'm going to call the Matsons!'

'The Matsons?' Father said.

'And the Foxes, and maybe the Calders,' Mother said.

'Not the Matsons!' Father said. 'And the Calders already asked *us* to a party—they have a New Year's party every year.'

'Well, we'll just have a few friends,' Mother said.

'Well, there will be the usual customers, too,' Father said, but he didn't look too sure, and we looked away from him. The 'usual customers' were such a small cluster of cronies; for the most part, they were the drinking friends of Coach Bob. We wondered if they'd ever show up again—and on New Year's Eve we doubted it.

Mrs. Urick didn't know how much food to have on hand; Max wondered if the entire parking lot should be plowed, or just the usual few spaces. Ronda Ray seemed in the spirit for a New Year's party of her own; she had a dress she wanted to wear —she'd told me all about it. I already knew the dress: it was the sexy dress Franny had bought Mother for Christmas; Mother had given it to Ronda. Having seen Franny model it, I was anxious about how Ronda would ever cram herself into it.

Mother had arranged to have a live band. 'An *almost* live band,' Franny said, because she'd heard the band before. They played to the Hampton Beach crowd in the summers, but during the regular year most of them were still in high school. The electric guitarist was a high school hood named Sleazy Wales; his mother was the lead singer and acoustic guitarist—a strapping, loud woman named Doris, whom Ronda Ray fervently called a slut. The band was named either after Doris or after the mild hurricane of some years before—which was also named Doris. The band was called, naturally, Hurricane Doris, and it featured Sleazy Wales and his mother and two of Sleazy's high school pals; acoustic bass and drums. I think that the boys worked in the same auto garage after school, because the band's uniforms consisted of garage mechanics' clothes—on the boys —with their names sewn on the breast alongside the GULF insignia. Their names were Danny, Jake, Sleazy—and all of them were GULF. Doris wore whatever she wanted to—dresses that even Ronda Ray would have thought immodest. Frank, of course, called Hurricane Doris 'disgusting.'

The band favored Elvis Presley numbers—'with lots of slow stuff if there's a lot of grown-ups in the crowd,' Doris told my mother over the phone, 'and the faster shit if the crowd's young.'

'Oh boy,' Franny said. 'I can't wait to hear what Junior thinks of Hurricane Doris.'

And I dropped several glass ashtrays that I was supposed to be distributing to the tables, because *I* couldn't wait to see what Junior Jones's sister would think of *me*.

'How old is she?' I asked Franny.

'If you're lucky, kid,' Franny teased me, 'she'll be about twelve.'

Frank had returned the mop and broom to the first-floor utility closet and had discovered, in the closet, a clue to the existence of Sorrow. It was the board, the cut-to-size plank, upon which Sorrow had been mounted in his attack pose. There were four neat screw holes in the board, and the trace of the dog's paw prints; he'd been screwed by his paws to the plank.

'Egg!' Frank screamed. 'You little thief, Egg!'

So Egg had removed Sorrow from his stand, and was perhaps at this very moment refashioning Sorrow's pose into something closer to his own version of our old pet.

'It's a good thing Egg never got hold of State o' Maine,' Lilly said.

'It's a good thing *Frank* didn't get hold of State o' Maine,' Franny noted.

'There's not going to be much room for dancing,' said Ronda Ray, wearily. 'We can't move any of the chairs out of the way.'

'We'll dance around the chairs!' Father cried, optimistically.

'Screwed down for life,' Franny murmured, but Father heard her, and he wasn't ready to hear any of Iowa Bob's old lines played back to him—not just yet. He looked very hurt, then he looked away. I remember New Year's Eve of 1956 as a time when everyone did a lot of 'looking away.'

'Oh, damn,' Franny whispered to me, and looked—actually —ashamed.

Ronda Ray gave Franny a quick hug. 'You just got to grow up a little, honey,' she said to her. 'You got to find out: grown-ups don't bounce back as fast as kids.'

We could hear Frank wailing for Egg in the stairwell. Frank didn't 'bounce back' so well, either, I thought. But Frank, in a way, was never a kid.

'Shut up your noise!' yelled Max Urick from the fourth floor.

'Come down and help us with the party—both of you!' Father cried.

'Kids!' Max bellowed.

'What does he know about kids?' Mrs. Urick grumbled.

Then Harold Swallow called from Detroit. He wasn't coming back to Dairy early, after all; he was going to miss the party. He said that he just remembered that New Year's Eve depressed him and he always ended up watching the whole thing on television. 'I might as well do that in Detroit,' he said. 'I don't have to take no airplane to Boston and ride in no car with Junior Jones and a whole crowd, just to stay in a funny hotel to watch New Year's Eve on TV.'

'We won't turn on the TV,' I told him. 'It would conflict with the band, anyway.'

'Well,' he said. 'Then I'd miss it. I better stay in Detroit.' There was never very much logic to the conversations one had with Harold Swallow; I never knew what to say next to him.

'Sorry about Bob,' Harold said, and I thanked him and reported to the others.

'Nasty isn't coming, either,' Franny said. 'Nasty' was the Boston boyfriend of Franny's friend Ernestine Tuck of Greenwich, Connecticut. Ernestine was called Bitty by everyone but

163

'Franny and Junior Jones. Apparently her mother had called her a 'little bitty' one terrible night and the name, as they say, stuck. Ernestine didn't seem to mind it, and she tolerated Junior Jones's version of her name, too: she had wondrous breasts and Junior called her *Titsie* Tuck, and Franny did, too. Bitty Tuck odolized Franny so much that she would endure any insult from her; and everyone in the world, I used to think, would simply have to accept insults from Junior Jones. Bitty Tuck was rich and pretty and eighteen, and not a bad person—she was just so easy to tease —and she was coming for New Year's Eve because she was what Franny called a party girl, and Franny's only female friend at the Dairy School. At eighteen, Bitty was very sophisticated —in Franny's opinion. The plan, Franny explained to me, was that Junior Jones and his sister were driving their own car from Philadelphia; they would pick up Titsie Tuck in Greenwich, en route, and then pick up Titsie's boyfriend, Peter ('Nasty') Raskin, in Boston. But now, Franny said, Nasty was not allowed to come—because he had insulted an aunt at a family wedding. Titsie had decided to come with Junior and his sister, anyway.

'Then there will be an extra girl—for Frank,' Father said, in his well-meaning way, and several shapes of death passed above us all, in silence.

'Just so there isn't a girl for me,' said Egg.

'Egg!' Frank yelled, making us all jump. None of us knew that Egg was with us, or when he'd arrived, but he had changed his costume and was pretending to straighten up things in a busy fashion about the restaurant, as if he'd been working right along with the rest of us, all day.

'I want to talk to you, Egg,' Frank said.

'What?' said Egg.

'Don't shout at Egg!' Lilly said, and drew Egg aside in her irritating, motherly fashion. We noticed that Lilly had taken an interest in mothering Egg as soon as Egg grew bigger than she was. Frank followed them into a corner of the room, hissing at Egg like a barrel of snakes.

'I know you've got him, Egg,' Frank was hissing.

'What?' Egg said.

Frank didn't dare say 'Sorrow' with Father in the restaurant, and none of us would allow Egg to be bullied; Egg was safe, and he knew it. Egg was wearing his infantry combat uniform; Franny had told me that she thought Frank probably wished he had a uniform like that, and that it made Frank mad every time Egg wore a uniform—and Egg had several. If Frank's love of

164

uniforms seemed odd, it seemed natural enough for Egg to love them; no doubt Frank resented this.

Then I asked Franny how Junior Jones's sister was going to get back to Philadelphia once New Year's was over and the Dairy School started again. Franny looked puzzled, and I explained that I didn't think Junior was going to drive his sister all the way back to Philadelphia, and then come right back to Dairy for school, and he wouldn't be allowed to keep a car at Dairy. That was against school rules.

'She'll drive herself back, I suppose,' Franny said. 'I mean, it's her car—or I think it is.'

Then it dawned on me that Junior Jones's sister, since they were bringing *her* car, had to be old enough to drive. 'She's got to be at least sixteen!' I said to Franny.

'Don't be frightened,' Franny said. 'How old do you guess Ronda is?' she whispered.

But the thought of an older girl was intimidating enough without imagining a *huge* older girl: a bigger, older, once-raped girl.

'It's reasonable to assume that she'll be black, too,' Franny said to me. 'Or didn't that occur to you, either?'

'That doesn't bother me,' I said.

'Oh, *every*thing bothers you,' Franny said. 'Titsie Tuck is eighteen and she bothers the hell out of you, and she'll be here, too.'

That was true: Titsie Tuck referred to me, publicly, as 'cute' —in her rich, rather condescending way. But I don't mean that; she was nice—she just never regarded me at all, unless it was to joke with me; she was intimidating to me in the way someone who never remembers your name can be intimidating. 'In this world,' Franny once observed, 'just when you're trying to think of yourself as memorable, there is always someone who forgets that they've met you.'

It was an up-and-down day at the Hotel New Hampshire, getting ready for New Year's Eve: I remember that something more pronounced than even the usual weave of silliness and sadness seemed to hang over us all, as if we'd be conscious, from time to time, of hardly mourning for Iowa Bob at all—and conscious, at other times, that our most necessary responsibility (not just in spite of but *because of* Iowa Bob) was to have fun. It was perhaps our first test of a dictum passed down to my father from old Iowa Bob himself; it was a dictum Father preached to us, over and over again. It was so familiar to us, we wouldn't dream of not behaving as if we believed it, although we probably never knew—until much later—whether we believed it or not.

The dictum was connected with Iowa Bob's theory that we were all on a big ship—'on a big cruise, across the world.' And in spite of the danger of being swept away, at any time, or perhaps because of the danger, we were not *allowed* to be depressed or unhappy. The way the world worked was *not* cause for some sort of blanket cynicism or sophomoric despair; according to my father and Iowa Bob, the way the world worked —which was badly—was just a strong incentive to live purposefully, and to be determined about living well.

'Happy fatalism,' Frank would speak of their philosophy, later; Frank, as a troubled youth, was not a believer.

And one night, when we were watching a wretched melodrama on the TV above the bar in the Hotel New Hampshire, my mother said, 'I don't want to see the end of this. I like happy endings.'

And Father said, 'There are no happy endings.'

'Right!' cried Iowa Bob—an odd mixture of exuberance and stoicism in his cracked voice. 'Death is horrible, final, and frequently premature,' Coach Bob declared.

'So what?' my father said.

'Right!' cried Iowa Bob. 'That's the point: So what?'

Thus the family maxim was that an unhappy ending did not undermine a rich and energetic life. This was based on the belief that there *were* no happy endings. Mother resisted this, and Frank was morose about it, and Franny and I were probably believers of this religion—or if, at times, we doubted Iowa Bob, the world would always come up with something that seemed to prove the old lineman right. We never knew what Lilly's religion was (no doubt it was a small idea, kept to herself), and Egg would be the retriever of Sorrow, in more than one sense. Retrieving Sorrow is a kind of religion, too.

The board that Frank had found with the paw prints on it and the Sorrow holes in it, looking like the abandoned crucifix of a four-footed Christ, seemed ominous to me. I talked Franny into a bed check, although she said Frank and I were nuts—Egg, she said, had probably wanted to keep the *board* and had thrown the *dog* away. Of course the intercom revealed nothing, since Sorrow—whether he was thrown away or hidden—was no longer breathing. There was a strange blowing sound, like the

166

rushing of air, from 4A—at the opposite end of the hall from Max Urick's static—but Franny said there was probably a window open: Ronda Ray had made up that bed for Bitty Tuck, and the room had probably been stuffy.

'Why are we putting Bitty way up on the fourth floor?' I asked.

'Because Mother thought she'd be here with Nasty,' Franny said, 'and that way—stuck up on the fourth floor—they could have some privacy from you kids.'

'From *us* kids, you mean,' I said. 'Where's Junior sleeping?'

'Not with me,' Franny said crisply. 'Junior and Sabrina have their own rooms on the second floor.'

'Sa-*bree*-na?' I said.

'That's it,' Franny said.

Sabrina Jones! I thought, and experienced a cataclysmic closing of the throat. Seventeen and six-foot-six, I imagined; goes about 185, stripped and towel-dried—and she can bench-press 200 pounds.

'They're here,' Lilly came and told us at the switchboard, in her wispy voice. The sight of the size of Junior Jones always took Lilly's breath away.

'How big is she?' I asked Lilly, but of course everyone looked enormous to Lilly; I would have to see Sabrina Jones for myself.

Frank, indulging in a moment of overt self-consciousness, had dressed himself in his bus driver's uniform and was playing doorman at the Hotel New Hampshire. He was carrying Bitty Tuck's luggage into the lobby; Bitty Tuck was the kind of girl who had luggage. She wore a sort of man's suit, but it had been tailored for a woman, and even a sort of man's dress shirt, with a button-down collar and tie, and everything—except the breasts, which were extraordinary, as Junior Jones had observed: they were impossible to conceal even in the most mannish costume. She flounced into the lobby behind Frank, who was sweating with her luggage.

'Hi, John-John!' she said.

'Hi, Titsie,' I said, not meaning to let her nickname slip out, because only Junior and Franny could call her Titsie and not receive her scorn. She looked at me scornfully and rushed past me, embracing Franny with the strange shrieks her kind of girl seems to have been born making.

'The bags go to 4A, Frank,' I said.

'Jesus, not now they don't,' Frank said, collapsing with Bitty's luggage in the lobby. 'It will take a team effort,' he said.

'Maybe some of you fools will get excited enough to actually have *fun* doing it, during the party.'

Junior Jones loomed in the lobby, looking capable of *hurling* Bitty Tuck's luggage up four floors—including Frank with the bags, I thought.

'Hey, the fun is here,' said Junior Jones. 'Here's the fun, man.'

I tried to see past him, or around him, to the doorway. For a terrified second I actually looked *above* him, as if his sister, Sabrina, might be towering there.

'Hey, Sabrina,' said Junior Jones. 'Here's your weight lifter.'

In the doorway was a slender Negress, about my height; her high, floppy-brimmed hat perhaps made her appear a little taller —and she wore heels. Her suit—a woman's suit—was every ounce as fashionable as Bitty Tuck's attire; she wore a cream-colored silky blouse with a wide collar, and it was open down her long throat to just a glimpse of the red lace of her bra; she wore rings on every finger, and bracelets, and she was a wondrous bitter-chocolate color, with wide bright eyes and a wide mouth smiling, full of strange but handsome teeth; she smelled so nice, and from so far away, that even Bitty Tuck's shrieks were diminished by the scent of Sabrina Jones. She was, I guessed, about twenty-eight or thirty, and she looked a little surprised to be introduced to me. Junior Jones, who was awfully quick for his size, moved far away from us fast.

'*You're* the weight lifter?' said Sabrina Jones.

'I'm only fifteen years old,' I lied; I would be fifteen very soon, after all.

'Holy cow,' said Sabrina Jones; she was so pretty I couldn't look at her. 'Junior!' she yelled, but Junior Jones was hiding from her—all the many pounds of him.

He had obviously needed a ride from Philadelphia, and not wanting to disappoint Franny by not showing up for New Year's Eve, he had acquired his *older* sister, and his sister's car, under the pretense of getting her a date with me.

'He told me Franny had an *older* brother,' Sabrina said, sorrowfully. I suppose Junior might have been thinking of Frank. Sabrina Jones was a secretary in a law firm in Philadelphia; she was twenty-nine.

'Fif*teen*,' she whistled through her teeth, which were not the bright white of her brother's gleaming mouth; Sabrina's teeth were perfectly sized and very straight, but they had a pearly, oyster hue to them. They were not unattractive teeth, but they were the only visibly flawed part of her. In my insecurity, I needed to notice them. I felt cloddish—full of bananas, as Frank would say.

'There's going to be a live band,' I said, and regretted saying so, immediately.

'Hot dog,' said Sabrina Jones, but she was nice; she smiled. 'Do you dance?' she asked.

'No,' I admitted.

'Oh well,' she said; she was really trying to be a good sport. 'You *do* lift weights?' she asked.

'Not as much as Junior,' I said.

'I'd like to drop a few weights on Junior's head,' she said.

Frank lurched through the lobby, struggling with a trunk full of Junior Jones's winter clothes; he couldn't seem to navigate successfully past Bitty Tuck's luggage, at the foot of the stairs, and so he dropped the trunk there—startling Lilly, who was sitting on the bottom step, watching Sabrina Jones.

'This is my sister Lilly,' I said to Sabrina, 'and that was Frank,' I said, pointing to Frank's back as he slunk away. We could hear Franny and Bitty Tuck shrieking somewhere, and I knew that Junior Jones would be speaking to my father—offering his condolences for Coach Bob.

'Hello, Lilly,' Sabrina said.

'I'm a dwarf,' Lilly said. 'I'm not ever going to grow any bigger.'

This information must have seemed, to Sabrina Jones, to fit rather perfectly with her disappointment at discovering my age; Sabrina did not appear shocked.

'Well, that's interesting,' she said to Lilly.

'You *are* going to grow, Lilly,' I said. 'At least, you're going to grow a *little,* and you're *not* a dwarf.'

Lilly shrugged. 'I don't mind,' she said.

A figure passed swiftly across the landing at the turn of the staircase—he had a tomahawk, he wore war paint and little else (a black loincloth with colored beads decorating the hips).

'That was Egg,' I said, watching the dazzled eyes of Sabrina Jones, her pretty mouth parted—as if attempting speech.

'That was a little Indian boy,' she said. 'Why's he called Egg?'

'I know why!' Lilly volunteered; sitting on the stairs, she raised her hand—as if she were in class, waiting to be called on. I was glad she was there; I never liked explaining Egg's name. Egg had been Egg from the beginning, dating from Mother's pregnancy, when Franny had asked her what the name of the new baby was going to be. 'Right now it's just an *egg,*' Frank had said, darkly—his wisdom of biology was always shocking, to us all. And so, as Mother grew and grew, the egg was called Egg with increasing conviction. Mother and Father were hoping for a third girl, only because it was going to be an April baby and they both liked the name April for a girl; they were undecided about a boy's name, Father not caring for his own name, Win, and Mother—despite her fondness for Iowa Bob—not really liking the idea of a Robert, Jr. By the time it was clear that the egg was a boy, he was—in our family—already an Egg, and the name (as they say) stuck. Egg *had* no other name.

'He began as an egg, and he's still an egg,' Lilly explained to Sabrina Jones.

'Holy cow,' Sabrina said, and I wished that something powerfully distracting would happen in the Hotel New Hampshire . . . to distract me from my embarrassment at how (it always struck me) our family must appear to outsiders.

'You see,' Franny would explain, years later, 'we *aren't* eccentric, we're *not* bizarre. To each other,' Franny would say, 'we're as common as rain.' And she was right: to each other, we were as normal and nice as the smell of bread, we were just a family. In a family, even exaggerations make perfect sense; they are always *logical* exaggerations, nothing more.

But my embarrassment with Sabrina Jones made me embarrassed for us all. My embarrassment even included people beyond my family. I was embarrassed for Harold Swallow every time I spoke with him; I was always afraid someone would make fun of him and hurt his feelings. And on New Year's Eve at the Hotel New Hampshire, I was embarrassed for Ronda Ray, wearing the dress Franny bought for Mother; I was even embarrassed for the almost live band, the terrible rock group called Hurricane Doris.

I recognized Sleazy Wales as a punk who had threatened me, years ago, in the Saturday matinee. He had wadded up a ball of bread, gray with the oil and grime from his auto-mechanic life; he'd stuck the wad of bread under my nose.

'Wanna eat that, kid?' he asked.

'No thanks,' I said. Frank leaped up and ran into the aisle, but Sleazy Wales gripped my arm and held me in my seat. 'Don't move,' he said. I promised I wouldn't, and he took a long nail out of his pocket and drove it through the wad of bread. Then he made a fist around the bread with the nail protruding savagely between his middle and ring fingers.

'Wanna get your fucking eyes poked out?' he asked me.

'No thanks,' I said.

'Then get the fuck out of here!' he said; even then I was embarrassed for him. I went to find Frank—who, whenever he was frightened at the movies, always stood by the water cooler. Frank frequently embarrassed me, too.

At the Hotel New Hampshire, on New Year's Eve, I saw at once that Sleazy Wales didn't recognize me. Too many miles, too much weight lifting, too many bananas had come between us; if he threatened me with bread and nails again, I could simply hug him to death. He didn't seem to have grown since the Saturday matinee. Scrawny and gray-skinned, his whole face the tone of a dirty ashtray, he hunched his shoulders forward in his GULF shirt and tried to walk as if each arm weighed one hundred pounds. I estimated that his whole body, plus wrenches and a few other heavy tools, couldn't weigh more than 130. I could have bench-pressed him an easy half-dozen times.

Hurricane Doris didn't seem especially disappointed at the absence of a crowd; and perhaps the boys were even grateful to have fewer people staring at them, as they dragged their bright, cheap equipment from outlet to outlet, plugging in.

The first thing I heard Doris Wales say was, 'Move the mike back, Jake, and don't be an asshole.' The acoustic bass (called Jake), another greasy splinter in a GULF shirt, cringed over the microphone as if he lived in terror of electrical shock—and of being an asshole. Sleazy Wales gave the other boy in the band a lovable punch in the kidneys; a fat drummer named Danny, the boy absorbed the punch with dignity—but with obvious pain.

Doris Wales was a woman with straw-blond hair whose body appeared to have been dipped in corn oil; then she must have put her dress on, wet. The dress grabbed at all her parts, and plunged and sagged over the gaps in her body; a lover's line of hickeys, or love bites—'love-sucks,' Franny called them—dotted Doris's chest and throat like a violent rash; the welts were like wounds from a whip. She wore plum-colored lipstick, some of which was on her teeth, and she said, to Sabrina Jones and me, 'You want hot-dancin' music, or slow-neckin' music? Or both?'

'Both,' said Sabrina Jones, without missing a beat, but I felt certain that if the world would stop indulging wars and famines and other perils, it would still be possible for human beings to

171

embarrass each other to death. Our self-destruction might take a little longer that way, but I believe it would be no less complete.

Doris Wales, some months after the hurricane that was her namesake, first heard Elvis Presley's 'Heartbreak Hotel' when she was actually *in* a hotel. She told Sabrina and me that this had been a religious experience.

'You understand?' Doris said. 'I was shacked up with this guy, in an actual hotel, when this *song* comes over the radio. That song told me how to *feel*,' Doris explained. 'That was about half a year ago,' she said. 'I haven't been the same since.'

I wondered about the guy who'd been shacked up with Doris Wales when she had her experience; where was he now? Had *he* been the same since?

Doris Wales sang *only* Elvis Presley songs; when it was appropriate, she changed the *he's* to *she's* (and vice versa); this improvisation and the fact, as Junior Jones noted, that she was 'no Negro,' made listening to her almost unbearable.

In a gesture of making peace with his sister, Junior Jones asked Sabrina to dance the first dance; the song, I remember, was 'Baby, Let's Play House,' during which Sleazy Wales several times overpowered his mother's voice with his electricity. 'Jesus God,' Father said. 'How much are we paying them?'

'Never mind,' Mother said. 'Everyone can have a good time.'

It seemed unlikely, although Egg appeared to be having a good time; he was wearing a toga, and Mother's sunglasses, and he was keeping clear of Frank, who lurked at the edge of light, among the empty tables and chairs—no doubt grumbling, to himself, his disgust.

I told Bitty Tuck that I was sorry I'd called her Titsie—that it had just slipped out.

'Okay, John-John,' she said, feigning indifference—or worse: feeling true indifference for me.

Lilly asked me to dance, but I was too shy; then Ronda Ray asked me, and I was too shy to refuse. Lilly looked hurt, and refused a gallant invitation from Father. Ronda Ray swung me violently around the floor.

'I know I'm losing you,' Ronda told me. 'My advice: when you're going to pull out on someone, tell them first.'

I was hoping Franny would cut in, but Ronda wheeled us into Junior and Sabrina, who were clearly arguing.

'Switch!' Ronda cried, gaily, and took Junior away.

Hurricane Doris, in an unforgettable transition of slopped-together sound, crushed instruments, and Doris's strident voice, switched gears and gave us 'I Love You Because'—a slow, close-dancing number, through which I trembled in the steady arms of Sabrina Jones.

'You're not doing so bad,' she said. 'Why don't you put a move on that Tuck girl—your sister's friend?' she asked me. 'She's about your age.'

'She's eighteen,' I said, 'and I don't know how to put a move on anybody.' I wanted to tell Sabrina that although my relationship with Ronda Ray was carnal, it had hardly been a learning experience. With Ronda, there was no foreplay; sex was immediate and genital, but Ronda refused to let me kiss her on the mouth.

'That's how the worst germs get spread around,' Ronda assured me. *'Mouths.'*

'I don't even know how to kiss anybody,' I told Sabrina Jones, who seemed puzzled at what—for her—was a non sequitur.

Franny, who didn't care for the way Ronda Ray was dancing the slow number with Junior, cut in on them, and I held my breath—hoping Ronda wasn't going to come after me.

'Relax,' said Sabrina Jones. 'You feel like a ball of wire.'

'I'm sorry,' I said.

'Never apologize to the opposite sex,' she said. 'Not if you want to get anywhere.'

'Get anywhere?' I said.

'Beyond the kissing,' Sabrina said.

'I can't get *to* the kissing,' I explained to her.

'That's easy,' Sabrina said. 'To get to the kissing, all you have to do is act like you know how to kiss: then someone will let you start.'

'But I *don't* know how,' I said.

'That's easy,' Sabrina said. 'Just practice.'

'Nobody to practice with,' I said—but I thought, fleetingly, of Franny.

'Try it with Bitty Tuck,' Sabrina whispered, laughing.

'But I have to look like I know how,' I said. 'And I don't.'

'We're back to that,' Sabrina said. 'I'm too old to let you practice with me. It wouldn't be good for either of us.'

Ronda Ray, cruising the dance floor, spotted Frank behind the empty tables, but Frank fled before she could ask him to dance. Egg was gone, so Frank had probably been waiting for an excuse to go corner Egg alone. Lilly was dancing, stoically, with one of

173

Father and Mother's friends, Mr. Matson, an unfortunately tall man—although, if he had been short, he couldn't have been short enough for Lilly. They looked like an awkward, perhaps unmentionable animal act.

Father danced with Mrs. Matson and Mother stood at the bar, talking with an old crony who was at the Hotel New Hampshire nearly every night—a drinking friend of Coach Bob's; his name was Merton, and he was the foreman at the lumberyard. Merton was a wide, heavy man with a limp and mighty, swollen hands; he listened half-heartedly to my mother, his face stricken with the absence of Iowa Bob; his eyes, feasting on Doris Wales, seemed to think that the band was inappropriate so soon after Bob's ultimate retirement.

'Variety,' said Sabrina Jones in my ear. 'That's the secret to kissing,' she said.

' "I love you for a hundred thousand reasons!" ' crooned Doris Wales.

Egg was back; he was in his Big Chicken costume; then he was gone again. Bitty Tuck looked bored; she seemed unsure about cutting in on Junior and Franny. And she was so sophisticated, as Franny would say, that she did not know how to talk with Ronda Ray, who had fixed herself a drink at the bar. I saw Max Urick gawking out of the kitchen doorway.

'Little bites, and a little bit of tongue,' said Sabrina Jones, 'but the important thing is to move your mouth around.'

'Do you want a drink?' I asked her. 'I mean, you're old enough. Father put a case of beer in the snow, out at the delivery entrance, for us kids. He said he couldn't let us drink at the bar, but *you* can.'

'Show me the delivery entrance,' said Sabrina Jones. 'I'll have a beer with you. Just don't get fresh.'

We left the dance floor, fortunately just in time to miss Doris Wales's slamming transition to 'I Don't Care If the Sun Don't Shine'—the speed of which prompted Bitty Tuck to cut in on Franny for a dance with Junior. Ronda looked sullenly upon my leaving.

Sabrina and I startled Frank, who was pissing on the trash barrels at the delivery entrance. In a gesture of Frank-like awkwardness, Frank pretended to be pointing out the beer to us. 'Got an opener, Frank?' I asked, but he had vanished into the mist of Elliot Park—the ever-dreary fog, which in the winter was our dominant weather.

Sabrina and I opened our beers at the reception desk in the

lobby, where Frank had permanently hung a bottle opener from a nail on a length of twine; it was for opening his Pepsi-Colas when he was on phone duty at the desk. In a clumsy effort to sit beside Sabrina, on the trunk of Junior's winter clothes, I spilled some beer on Bitty Tuck's luggage.

'You could introduce yourself to her affections,' Sabrina was saying, 'by offering to take all those bags to her room.'

'Where are *your* bags?' I asked Sabrina.

'For one night,' Sabrina said, 'I don't pack a bag. And you don't have to offer to show me to *my* room. I can find it.'

'I could show it to you, anyway,' I said.

'Well, do it,' she said. 'I got a book to read. This is one party I don't need,' she added. 'I might as well get ready for a long drive back to Philadelphia.'

I walked with her to her room on the second floor. I had no illusions of making a move on her, as she would say; I wouldn't have had the courage, anyway. 'Good night,' I mumbled at her door, and let her slip away. She was not gone long.

'Hey,' she said, opening her door before I had left the hall. 'You'll never get anywhere not trying. You didn't even *try* to kiss me,' she added.

'I'm sorry,' I said.

'Never apologize!' Sabrina said. She stood close to me in the hallway and let me kiss her. 'First things first,' she said. 'Your breath smells nice—that's a start. But stop shaking, and you shouldn't make tooth contact at the beginning; and don't try to *ram* me with your tongue.' We tried again. 'Keep your hands in your pockets,' she told me. 'Watch the tooth contact. Better,' she said, backing up, into her room; she motioned me to follow. 'Don't get fresh,' she said. 'Hands in the pockets at all times; two feet on the floor.' I stumbled toward her. We made tooth contact quite violently; she snapped her head back, away from me, and when I looked at her, incredibly, I saw that she held a row of her front upper teeth in her hand. 'Shit!' she cried. 'Watch the tooth contact!' For a horrible moment I thought I had knocked her teeth out, but she turned her back to me and said, 'Don't look at me. False teeth. Turn out the light.' I did, and it was dark in her room.

'I'm sorry,' I said, hopelessly.

'Never apologize,' she murmured. 'I was raped.'

'Yes,' I said, knowing all along that this would surface. 'So was Franny.'

'So I heard,' said Sabrina Jones. 'But they didn't knock her teeth out with a pipe. Am I right?'

'Yes,' I said.

'It's the kissing that gets me, every fucking time,' Sabrina said. 'Just when it gets good, my uppers loosen up—or some clod makes too much tooth contact.'

I didn't apologize; I reached to touch her but she said, 'Keep your hands in your pockets.' Then she came up close to me and said, 'I'm going to help you if you help me. I'll teach you all about kissing,' she said, 'but you've got to tell me something I always wanted to know. I was never with anyone I dared to ask. I try to keep it a secret.'

'Yes,' I agreed, terrified—not knowing to what I was agreeing.

'I want to know if it's *better* with my damn teeth *out*,' she said, 'or if it's gross. I always thought it would be gross, so I never tried it.' She went into the bathroom and I waited for her, in the dark, watching the line of light framing the bathroom door —until the light went out and Sabrina was back beside me.

Warm and mobile, her mouth was a cave in the world's heart. Her tongue was long and round and her gums were hard but never painful in the nips she took. 'A little less lip,' she mumbled, 'a little more tongue. No, not *that* much. That's disgusting! Yes, a little biting is fine. That's nice. Hands back in the pockets—*I mean it*. Do you like this?'

'Oh yes,' I said.

'Really?' she asked. 'Is it really better?'

'It's *deeper!*' I said.

She laughed. 'But *better,* too?' she asked.

'Wonderful,' I confessed.

'Hands back in the pockets,' Sabrina said. 'Don't get out of control. Don't be sloppy. Ouch!'

'Sorry.'

'Don't apologize. Just don't bite so *hard*. Hands in the pockets. I mean it. Don't get fresh. *In the pockets!*'

And so forth, until I was pronounced initiated, and ready for Bitty Tuck, and the world, and sent on my way from Sabrina Jones's room; hands still in my pockets, I collided with the door to 2B. 'Thank you!' I called to Sabrina. In the hall light, without her teeth, she dared to smile at me—a rose-brown, rose-blue smile, so much nicer than the odd, pearly cast of her false teeth.

She had sucked on my lips to make them swell, she had told me, and I walked pouting into the restaurant of the Hotel New

Hampshire, aware of the powers of my mouth, ready to make kissing history with Bitty Tuck. But Hurricane Doris was groaning its way through 'I Forgot to Remember to Forget'; Ronda Ray slumped at the bar in a stupor, Mother's new dress slipped up to the knot of muscle at Ronda's hip, on which a bruise, in the shape of a thumbprint, stared at me. Merton, the lumberyard foreman, was swapping stories with my father—I knew the stories would be about Iowa Bob.

' "I forgot to remember to forget," ' moaned Doris Wales.

Poor Lilly, who would always be too small to feel comfortable at a party—although she would continue to anticipate parties, with pleasure—had gone to bed. Egg, wearing ordinary clothes, sat sulking in one of the screwed-down chairs; his little face was gray, as if he had eaten something that had disagreed with him, as if he was *willing* himself to stay awake till midnight—as if he had lost Sorrow.

Frank, I imagined, was out drinking the cold beer in the snow stacked by the delivery entrance, or sucking Pepsi-Colas at the reception desk in the lobby, or perhaps at the intercom—listening to Sabrina Jones reading a book and humming with her marvelous mouth.

Mother, and the Matsons, were watching Doris Wales without reserve. Only Franny was free for dancing—Bitty Tuck was out on the floor, with Junior Jones.

'Dance with me,' I said to Franny, grabbing her.

'You can't dance,' Franny said, but she allowed me to drag her out on the floor.

'I can *kiss*,' I whispered to Franny, and tried to kiss her, but she pushed me away.

'Switch!' she cried to Junior and Bitty Tuck, and Bitty was in my arms and instantly bored.

'Just be dancing with her when it's midnight,' Sabrina Jones had advised. 'At midnight you get to kiss who you're with. Once you kiss her, she'll be hooked. Just don't blow the first one.'

'Have you been drinking, John-John?' Bitty asked me. 'Your lips are all puffy.'

And Doris Wales, hoarse and sweating, gave us 'Tryin' to Get to You,' one of those clumsy numbers, not slow and not fast, forcing Bitty Tuck to decide whether or not to dance close. Before she'd made her choice, Max Urick leaped out of the kitchen in his sailor's cap with a referee's whistle clenched in his teeth; he blew the whistle so shrilly that even Ronda Ray moved, a little, at the bar. 'Happy New Year!' shrieked Max, and

177

Franny stood on her toes and gave Junior Jones the sweetest kiss, and Mother ran to find Father. Merton, the lumberyard foreman, looked once at the dozing Ronda Ray; he then thought better of it. And Bitty Tuck, with a bored shrug, gave me her superior smile, again, and I remembered every lushness of the cavernous mouth of Sabrina Jones; I made, as they say, my move. A little tooth contact, but nothing offensive; the penetration of the tongue past the teeth, but only a flicker of ramming it farther; and the teeth skating under the upper lip. There were Bitty Tuck's wondrous, much-discussed breasts, like soft fists pushing my chest away, but I kept my hands in my pockets, forcing nothing; she was always free to pull away, but she didn't choose to break contact.

'Holy cow,' observed Junior Jones, momentarily breaking Bitty Tuck's concentration.

'Titsie!' Franny said. 'What are you doing to my brother?' But I held Titsie Tuck in touch a little longer, lingering over her lower lip, and nipping her tongue, which she'd given me, suddenly, too much of. There was a slight awkwardness, as I removed my hands from my pockets, because Bitty had decided that 'Tryin' to Get to You' was suitable for close dancing.

'Where'd you learn how to do that?' she whispered, her breasts like two warm kittens curled against my chest. We left the dance floor before Hurricane Doris could change the tempo.

There was a draft in the lobby, where Frank had left the door to the delivery entrance open; we could hear him outside in the dark slush, urinating—with great force—against a trash barrel. The floor beneath the bottle opener on the braid of twine was littered with beer-bottle caps. As I lifted Bitty Tuck's luggage in my arms, she said, 'Aren't you going to make two trips?' I heard Frank's sharp belch, a primitive gong announcing that the turn of the year was past, and I seized the luggage tighter and started climbing—four stories up, Bitty following.

'Geez,' she said. 'I knew you were strong, John-John, but you could get a job on *television*—kissing like that.' And I wondered what she imagined: my mouth as an advertisement, smooching a camera, point-blank?

I thus distracted myself from my lower-back pain, was grateful I had skipped this morning's bench presses and one-arm curls, and bore Bitty Tuck's luggage to 4A. The windows were open, but I couldn't hear the rushing-of-air sound I had heard over the intercom hours before; I guessed that the wind had

178

dropped. The luggage seemed to explode from my arms, which felt pounds lighter, and Bitty Tuck angled me toward her bed.

'Do it again,' she said. 'I bet you can't. I bet it was beginner's luck.' So I kissed her again, encouraging a little more tooth contact, and more mischief with the tongue.

'Jesus,' mumbled Bitty Tuck, touching me. 'Get your hands out of your pockets!' she said. 'Oh, wait, I have to use the bathroom.' And when she flicked on the bathroom light, she said, 'Oh, it was nice of Franny to leave me her hair dryer!' And I, for the first time, *smelled* the room—an odor more distinctive than a swamp: it was a burnt smell, yet strangely wet, as if fire and water had joined unpleasantly. I knew that the rushing-of-air sound I had heard on the intercom had been the hair dryer, but before I could get to the bathroom to prevent Bitty Tuck from looking farther, she said, 'What's that wrapped up in the shower curtain? *Gaaaaaaaaa!*' Her scream froze me in motion between her bed and the bathroom door. Even Doris Wales, four floors below and wailing her way through 'You're a Heartbreaker,' must have heard it. Sabrina Jones told me later that her book flew from her hands. Ronda Ray jerked bolt upright on the barstool, for at least a passing second; Sleazy Wales, Junior Jones told me, thought the source of the scream was his amplifier, but nobody else was fooled.

'Titsie!' Franny cried.

'Jesus God!' said Father.

'Holy cow!' said Junior Jones.

I was the first to get Bitty out of the bathroom. She had fainted sideways against the child-sized toilet and had wedged herself under the child-sized sink. The grown-up–sized bathtub, half-full of water, had caught her eye as she was inserting her diaphragm—which, in those days, was very sophisticated. Floating in the tub of water was the shower curtain, and Bitty had leaned forward and raised the curtain just enough to see the grizzly, submerged head of Sorrow—looking like a murder victim: a drowned dog, the ghastly fierceness of his last snarling fight with death slipping from his face under the water.

The discoverer of the body is rarely spared. It was fortunate Bitty's heart was young and strong; I could feel it pounding through her bosom when I put her on the bed. Thinking it a plausible way to revive her, I kissed her, and although it roused her eyes open for a bright moment, she only screamed again —even louder.

179

'It's just Sorrow,' I told her, as if this would explain everything.

Sabrina Jones was the first to get to 4A, since she was only traveling from the second floor. She glared at me, as if I'd been clearly a part of a rape case, and she said to me, 'You must have done something I never showed you!' She no doubt thought Bitty was the victim of bad kissing.

It had been Egg who'd done the wrong, of course. He had turned the hair dryer on Sorrow in Bitty's bathroom, and the terrible dog had caught fire. In a panic, Egg had thrown the burning beast in the bathtub and covered it with water. The fire thus extinguished, Egg had opened the windows to clear the scorched smell from the room, and at the peak of his tiredness, just before midnight—and fearing capture from the ever-prowling Frank—Egg had covered the carcass with the shower curtain, for the sodden dog was now too heavy with water for Egg to be able to lift him; Egg had gone to our room and changed into ordinary clothes to await his eventual punishment.

'My God,' Frank said, morosely, when he saw Sorrow, 'I think he's really ruined; I think he's beyond repair.'

Even the boys from Hurricane Doris trooped into Bitty's bathroom to pay their respects to the dreadful Sorrow.

'I wanted to make him nice again!' Egg cried. 'He *was* nice once,' Egg insisted, 'and I wanted him to be nice again.'

Frank, with a sudden wealth of pity, seemed to understand something about taxidermy for the first time.

'Egg, Egg,' Frank reasoned with the sobbing child. '*I* can make him nice again. You should have let me. I can make him *anything*,' Frank claimed. 'I *still* can,' he said. 'You want him nice, Egg? I'll make him nice.' But Franny and I stared into the bathtub and felt great doubt. That Frank had taken a harmless, farting Labrador retriever and made him a killer was one thing; but to reassemble this truly disgusting body, matted and burned and bloated in the bathtub, was a miracle of perversion that we doubted even Frank was capable of.

Father, on the other hand, was ever the optimist; he seemed to think all of this would be excellent 'therapy' for Frank—and, no doubt, a further maturing influence on Egg.

'If you can restore the dog, and make him nice, son,' Father told Frank, with inappropriate solemnity, 'that would make us all very happy.'

'I think we should throw it away,' Mother said.

'Ditto,' said Franny.

180

'I *tried*,' Max Urick complained.

But Egg and Frank began to whoop and cry. Perhaps Father saw that in the restoration of Sorrow lay Frank's forgiveness; salvaging Sorrow could possibly restore Frank's self-esteem; and perhaps by refashioning Sorrow, for Egg—by making Sorrow 'nice'—Father thought that a bit of Iowa Bob would be returned to us all. But as Franny would say, years later, there was never any such thing as 'nice sorrow'; by definition, sorrow would never be nice.

Could I blame my father for trying? Or Frank for being the agent of such depressing optimism? And there was no blaming Egg, of course; we would, none of us, ever blame Egg.

Only Lilly had slept through it all, perhaps already inhabiting a world not quite like ours. Doris Wales and Ronda Ray had not climbed four flights of stairs to see the body, but when we found them in the restaurant, they seemed almost sobered by the experience—even second-hand. Whatever hopes for even a mini-seduction that might have been on Junior Jones's mind were dashed by the interruption to the music; Franny kissed Junior good night and went to her own room. And Bitty Tuck, although she loved my kisses, could not forgive the intrusion upon her privacy in the bathroom—both Sorrow's and mine. I suppose she resented, most of all, the ungainly position I'd discovered her in—'Fainted while diaphragming herself!' as Franny would later characterize the scene.

I found myself alone with Junior Jones at the delivery entrance, drinking up the cold beer and watching out into Elliot Park for any other New Year's Eve survivors. Sleazy Wales and the boys in the band had gone home; Doris and Ronda were draped upon the bar—a kind of camaraderie had suddenly risen, in a blurry fashion, between them. And Junior Jones said, 'No offense to your sister, man, but I am very horny.'

'Ditto,' I said, 'and no offense to yours.'

The laughter of the women in the restaurant reached us, and Junior said, 'Want to try to hustle them ladies at the bar?' I didn't dare tell Junior the repugnance of that idea, to me —having already been hustled by one of them—but I felt badly later at how quickly I was willing to betray Ronda Ray. I told Junior that she could be hustled very easily, and it would only cost him money.

Later, I drank another beer and listened to Junior carrying Ronda to the stairwell at the hall's far end, away from me. And after another beer, or two, I heard Doris Wales, all alone, start to sing 'Heartbreak Hotel,' without the music, and occasionally forgetting the words of her religion—and occasionally slurring the rest. Lastly came the unmistakable sound of her throwing up in the bar sink.

After a while she found me in the lobby, at the open door to the delivery entrance, and I offered her the last cold beer. 'Sure, why not?' she said. 'It helps to cut the phlegm. That damn "Heartbreak Hotel,"' she added. 'It always moves me too much.'

Doris Wales was wearing her knee-high cowboy boots and carrying her thin-strapped green high heels in her hand; in her other hand she dallied her coat, a sad-flecked tweed with a skimpy fur collar. 'It's just muskrat,' she said, rubbing it against my cheek. She gripped the throat of her beer bottle in the hand with her high-heeled shoes and drank nearly all of it down. The hickey on her tilted throat appeared to have been made by a red-hot fifty-cent piece. She dropped the beer bottle at her feet and kicked it out the door, where it rolled toward the trash barrels at the delivery entrance. She stepped closer to me and thrust her thigh between my legs; she kissed me on the mouth, a kiss like nothing Sabrina Jones had shown me; it was a kiss like a wedge of soft fruit being mashed past my teeth and tongue until I gagged; her kiss tasted, lingeringly, of vomit and beer.

'I'm picking Sleazy up at this party,' she said. 'Wanna come?'

It reminded me of when Sleazy offered to force-feed me the ball of bread or poke out my eyes with the nail in the movies. 'No thanks,' I said.

'Chicken shit,' she said, and belched sharply. 'Kids today have no *spunk.*' Then she slammed me to her chest and hugged me to her body, hard as a man's but with her breasts sliding between us like two fresh-caught fish in loose bags; her tongue lolled along my jawline before skidding into my ear. 'You squirrel dink,' she whispered, then pushed me from her.

She fell in the slush near the delivery entrance, but when I helped her to her feet, she shoved me into the trash barrels and walked into the darkness of Elliot Park, unassisted. I waited for her to pass out of the darkness and into the pale lamplight from the single streetlight, and then pass into the darkness again; when she came briefly under the light, I called to her.

'Good night, Mrs. Wales, and thank you for the music!' She gave me the finger, slipped, almost fell again, and lurched out of the light—cursing at something, or someone, she encountered there. 'What the fuck?' she said. 'Cram it, will you?'

I turned away from the light and threw up in the emptiest trash barrel. When I looked back at the streetlight again, a figure was just veering under it, and I thought it was Doris Wales, returning to abuse me. But it was someone from another New Year's Eve party, for whom home was in another direction. It was a man, or a reasonably grown-up teen-ager, and although he was weaving under the spell of alcohol, he maintained slightly better footing in the slush than Doris Wales.

'Cram it yourself, lady!' he cried into the darkness.

'Chicken shit!' called Doris, from the dark and far away.

'Whore!' the man yelled, then lost his balance and sat down in the slush. 'Shit,' he said, to no one in particular; he couldn't see me.

It was then that I noticed how he was dressed. Black slacks and shoes, black cummerbund and bow tie—and a white dinner jacket. Of course I knew he was not *the* man in the white dinner jacket; he was lacking the necessary dignity, and whatever voyage he was on, or interrupting, it was not an exotic voyage. Also, it was New Year's Eve, and not the season—in New England—for white dinner jackets. The man was inappropriately dressed, and I knew this was no eccentric habit of distinction. In Dairy, New Hampshire, it could only mean that the moron had gone to the rental tuxedo shop after all the *black* jackets had been taken. Or else he didn't know the difference between summer and winter formal dress in our town; he was either a young clod coming from a high school dance or an older clod coming from an older dance (which had been no less sad and wasteful than anything a high school could engender). He was not *our* man in the white dinner jacket, but he reminded me of him.

Then I noticed that the man had stretched out in the slush under the streetlight and had gone to sleep there. The temperature was right around freezing.

I felt, at last, that New Year's Eve had come to something: there seemed to be a purpose for my having taken part in it at all —a purpose beyond the simultaneously vague and concrete sensations of lust. I lifted the man in the white dinner jacket and carried him to the lobby of the Hotel New Hampshire; he was easier to carry than Bitty Tuck's luggage; he didn't weigh much, although he was a man, not a teen-ager—in fact, he looked older than my father, to me. And when I searched him for some identification, I found I had been right about the rental clothes.

PROPERTY OF CHESTER'S MEN'S STORE, said the label in the white dinner jacket. The man, although he looked reasonably distinguished—at least for Dairy, New Hampshire—carried no wallet, but he had a silver comb.

Perhaps Doris Wales had mugged him in the dark, and that was what they'd been yelling about. But no, I thought: Doris would have taken the silver comb, too.

It seemed a good trick, to me, to arrange the man in the white dinner jacket on the couch in the lobby of the Hotel New Hampshire—so that early in the morning I might be able to surprise Father and Mother. I could say, 'There's someone who came for the last dance—last night—but he was too late. He's waiting to see you, in the lobby.'

I thought that was a terrific idea, but I felt—since I had been drinking—that I should really wake up Franny and show her the man in the white dinner jacket, who was peacefully passed out on the couch; Franny would inform me if she thought this was a *bad* idea. She would like it, too, I was sure.

I straightened the black bow tie of the man in the white dinner jacket and folded his hands upon his chest; I buttoned the waist button of his jacket, and straightened his cummerbund, so that he wouldn't look sloppy. The only thing missing was the tan, and the black cigarette box—and the white sloop outside the Arbuthnot-by-the-Sea.

That was not the sound of the sea outside the Hotel New Hampshire, I knew; it was the sound of the slush in Elliot Park, freezing and thawing and refreezing; and those were not the gulls calling, but dogs—alley dogs, ripping into the trash, which was everywhere. I hadn't noticed, until I arranged the man in the white dinner jacket on the couch, how shabby our lobby was —how the presence of an all-girls' school had never left the building: the ostracism, the anxiety of being considered (sexually) second-best, the too-early marriages, and other disappointments, that waited ahead. The almost elegant man in the white dinner jacket looked—in the Hotel New Hampshire—like someone from another planet, and I suddenly didn't want my father to see him.

I ran into the restaurant for some cold water; Doris Wales had broken a glass at the bar, and Ronda Ray's oddly sexless working shoes were scuffed under a table, where she must have kicked them—when she started dancing, and making her move for Junior Jones.

If I woke up Franny, I thought, Franny might catch on that Junior was with Ronda, and wouldn't that hurt her?

I listened at the stairwell and felt a flash of interest in Bitty Tuck returning to me—the thought of seeing her, asleep—but when I listened to her on the intercom, she was snoring (as deep and wallowing a sound as a pig in mud). The book of reservations hadn't a single name marked down; there was nothing until the summer, when the circus called Fritz's Act would arrive and (no doubt) appall us all. The petty-cash box, at the reception desk, wasn't even locked—and Frank, in his boredom during phone duty, had used the sharp end of the bottle opener to gouge his name into the armrest of the chair.

In the gray, after-the-party stench of New Year's Day, I felt that I should spare my father the vision of the man in the white dinner jacket. I thought that, if I could wake the man, I could employ Junior Jones to *scare* the man away, but I would have been embarrassed to disturb Junior with Ronda Ray.

'Hey, get up!' I hissed at the man in the white dinner jacket.

'Snorf!' he shouted, in his sleep. *'Ack! A whore!'*

'Be quiet!' I whispered fiercely to him.

'Gick?' he said. I seized him around the chest and squeezed him. *'Fuh!'* he moaned. 'God help me.'

'You're all right,' I said. 'But you have to leave.'

He opened his eyes and sat up on the couch.

'A young thug,' he said. 'Where have you taken me?'

'You passed out, outside,' I said. 'I brought you in so you wouldn't freeze. Now you have to leave.'

'I have to use the bathroom,' he said, with dignity.

'Go outside,' I said. 'Can you walk?'

'Of course I can walk,' he said. He went toward the delivery entrance, but stopped on the threshold. 'It's dark out there,' he said. 'You're setting me up, aren't you? How many of them are there—out there?'

I led him to the front lobby door and turned on the outside light. I'm afraid that this was the light that woke up Father. 'Good-bye,' I told the man in the white dinner jacket, 'and Happy New Year.'

'This is Elliot Park!' he cried, indignantly.

'Yes,' I said.

'Well, this is that funny hotel, then,' he concluded. 'If it's a hotel, I want a room for the night.'

I thought it best not to tell him that he didn't have any money on him, so I said instead, 'We're full. No vacancies.'

The man in the white dinner jacket stared at the desolate lobby, gawked at the empty mail slots, and at the abandoned trunk of Junior Jones's winter clothes lying at the foot of the dingy stairs. 'You're *full?*' he said, as if some truth about life in general had occurred to him, for the first time. 'Holy cow,' he said. 'I'd heard this place was going under.' It wasn't what I wanted to hear.

I steered him toward the main door again, but he bent down and picked up the mail and handed it to me; in our haste to prepare for the party, no one had been to the mail slot at the front lobby door all day; no one had picked up the mail.

The man walked only a little way out the door, then came back.

'I want to call a cab,' he informed me. 'There's too much violence out there,' he said, gesturing, again, to life in general; he couldn't have meant Elliot Park—at least not now, not since Doris Wales had gone.

'You don't have enough money for a cab,' I informed him.

'Oh,' the man in the white dinner jacket said. He sat down on the steps in the cold, foggy air. 'I need a minute,' he said.

'What for?' I asked him.

'Have to remember where I'm going,' he said.

'Home?' I suggested, but the man waved his hand above his head.

He was thinking. I looked at the mail. The usual bills, the usual absence of letters from unknowns requesting rooms. And one letter that stood out from the rest. It had pretty foreign stamps: *Österreich* said the stamps—and a few other exotic things. The letter was from Vienna, and it was addressed to my father in a most curious way:

> Win Berry
> Graduate of Harvard
> Class of 194?
> U.S.A.

The letter had taken a long time to reach my father, but the postal authorities had found one among them who knew where Harvard was. My father would say later that getting that letter was the most concrete thing going to Harvard ever did for him; if he'd gone to some less-famous school, the letter would never have been delivered. 'That's a good reason,' Franny would say, later, 'to wish he'd gone to a less-famous school.'

But, of course, the alumni network at Harvard is efficient and vast. My father's name and 'Class of 194?' was all they needed to discover the right class, '46, and the correct address.

'What's going on?' I heard my father calling; he had come out of our family's second-floor rooms and was on the landing, calling down the stairwell to me.

'Nothing!' I said, kicking the drunk on the steps in front of me, because he was falling asleep again.

'Why's the front light on?' Father called.

'Get going!' I said to the man in the white dinner jacket.

'I'm happy to meet you!' the man said, cordially. 'I'll just be trotting along now!'

'Good, good,' I whispered.

But the man walked only to the bottom step before he seemed overcome with *thought* again.

'Who are you talking to?' Father called.

'No one! Just a drunk!' I said.

'Jesus God,' said Father. 'A drunk isn't no one!'

'I can handle it!' I called.

'Wait till I get dressed,' Father said. 'Jesus God.'

'Get going!' I yelled at the man in the white dinner jacket.

'Good-bye! Good-bye!' the man called, happily waving to me from the bottom step of the Hotel New Hampshire. 'I had a wonderful time!'

The letter, of course, was from Freud. I knew that, and I wanted to see what it said before I let my father see it. I wanted to talk with Franny about it, for hours—and even with Mother —before I let Father see it. But there wasn't time. The letter was brief and to the point.

IF YOU GOT THIS, THEN YOU WENT TO HARVARD LIKE YOU PROMISED ME [Freud wrote]. YOU GOOD BOY, YOU!

'Good night! God bless you!' cried the man in the white dinner jacket. But he would walk no farther than the perimeter of light; where the darkness of Elliot Park began, he stopped and waved.

I flicked off the light so that if Father came, Father couldn't spot the apparition in formal attire.

'I can't see!' the drunk wailed, and I turned the light on again.

'Get out of here or I'll beat the shit out of you!' I screamed at him.

'That's no way to handle it!' I heard Father yelling.

187

'Good night, bless you all!' cried the man; he was still in the circle of light when I cut the light off him, again, and he made no protest. I kept the light off. I finished Freud's letter.

I FINALLY GOT A SMART BEAR [Freud wrote]. IT MADE ALL THE DIFFERENCE. I HAD A GOOD HOTEL GOING, BUT I GOT OLD. IT COULD STILL BE A <u>GREAT</u> HOTEL [Freud added], IF YOU AND MARY COME HELP ME RUN IT. I GOT A SMART BEAR, BUT I NEED A SMART HARVARD BOY LIKE YOU, TOO!

Father stormed into the wretched lobby of the Hotel New Hampshire; in his slippers he stumbled over a beer bottle, which he kicked, and his bathrobe flapped in the wind from the open door.

'He's gone,' I said to Father. 'Just some drunk.' But Father snapped on the outside light—and there, waving, on the rim of the light, was the man in the white dinner jacket. 'Good-bye!' he called, hopefully. 'Good-bye! Good luck! Good-bye!' The effect was stunning: the man in the white dinner jacket stepped out of the light and was gone—as gone as if he were gone to sea—and my father gaped into the darkness after him.

'Hello!' Father screamed. 'Hello? *Come back!* Hello?'

'Good-bye! Good luck! Good-bye!' called the voice of the man in the white dinner jacket, and my father stood staring into the darkness until the wind chilled him and he shivered in his bathrobe and slippers; he let me pull him inside.

Like any storyteller, I had the power to end the story, and I could have. But I didn't destroy Freud's letter; I gave it to Father, while the vision of the man in the white dinner jacket was still upon him. I handed over Freud's letter—like any storyteller, knowing (more or less) where we would all be going.

7

Sorrow Strikes Again

Sabrina Jones, who taught me how to kiss—whose deep and mobile mouth will have a hold on me, always—found the man who could fathom her teeth-in-or-out mystery; she married a lawyer from the same firm in which she was a secretary and had three healthy children ('Bang, Bang, Bang,' as Franny would say).

Bitty Tuck, who fainted while diaphragming herself—whose wondrous breasts and modern ways would, one day, seem not nearly as unique as they seemed to me in 1956—survived her encounter with Sorrow; in fact, I heard (not long ago) that she is still unmarried, and still a party girl.

And a man named Frederick Worter, who was only a hair over four feet tall, and forty-one years old, and who was better known to our family as 'Fritz'—whose circus, called Fritz's Act, was an advance booking for a summer that we looked forward to with curiosity and dread—*bought* the first Hotel New Hampshire from my father in the winter of 1957.

'For a song, I'll bet,' Franny said. But we children never knew how much Father sold the Hotel New Hampshire for; since Fritz's Act was the only advance booking for the summer of 1957, my father had written to Fritz first—warning the diminutive circus king of our family's move to Vienna.

'Vienna?' Mother kept muttering, and shaking her head at my father. 'What do you know about *Vienna?*'

'What did I know about motorcycles?' Father asked. 'Or bears? Or hotels?'

'And what have you *learned?*' Mother asked him, but my father had no doubt. Freud had said that a smart bear made all the difference.

'I know that Vienna isn't Dairy, New Hampshire,' Father said to Mother; and he apologized to Fritz of Fritz's Act—saying that he was putting the Hotel New Hampshire up for sale, and that

189

the circus might need to seek other lodgings. I don't know if the circus called Fritz's Act made my father a good offer, but it was the first offer, and Father took it.

'Vienna?' said Junior Jones. 'Holy cow.'

Franny might have protested the move, for fear that she would miss Junior, but Franny had discovered Junior's infidelity (with Ronda Ray, on New Year's Eve), and she was being cool to him.

'Tell her I was just horny, man,' Junior told me.

'He was just horny, Franny,' I said.

'Clearly,' Franny said. 'And you surely know all about what *that's* like.'

'Vienna,' said Ronda Ray, sighing under me—probably from boredom. '*I'd* like to go to Vienna,' she said. 'But I suppose I have to stay here—where I might be out of a job. Or else work for that bald midget.'

Frederick 'Fritz' Worter was the bald midget, a runt figure who visited us one snowy weekend; he was especially impressed with the size of the fourth-floor bathroom facilities—and with Ronda Ray. Lilly, of course, was most impressed with Fritz. He was only a little bigger than Lilly, although we tried to assure Lilly (and, mainly, ourselves) that she would continue to grow —a little—and that her features (we hoped) would not ever appear so out of proportion. Lilly was pretty: tiny but nice. But Fritz had a head several sizes too large for his body; his forearms sagged like slack calf muscles obscenely grafted to the wrong limbs; his fingers were sawed-off salamis; his ankles were swollen over his little doll's feet—like socks with wrecked elastic.

'What kind of circus do you have?' Lilly asked him, boldly.

'Weird acts, weird animals,' Franny whispered in my ear, and I shivered.

'*Little* acts, *little* animals,' Frank mumbled.

'We're just a small circus,' Fritz told Lilly, meaningfully.

'Meaning,' said Max Urick—after Fritz was gone—'that they'll all fit just fine on the fucking fourth floor.'

'If they're all like him,' said Mrs. Urick, 'they won't eat very much.'

'If they're all like *him,*' said Ronda Ray, and rolled her eyes —but she didn't continue; she decided to let it pass.

'I think he's cute,' said Lilly.

But Fritz of Fritz's Act gave Egg nightmares—great shrieks that stiffened my back and tore muscles in my neck; Egg's arm

lashed out and bashed the bedside lamp, his legs thrashed under
the sheets, as if the bedclothes were drowning him.

'Egg?' I cried. 'It's just a dream! You're having a dream!'

'A *what?*' he screamed.

'A dream!' I yelled.

'Midgets!' Egg shouted. 'They're under the bed! They're
crawling all around! They're all over, everywhere!' he howled.

'Jesus God,' Father said. 'If they're just midgets, why does he
get so upset?'

'Hush,' Mother said, ever fearful of hurting Lilly's little
feelings.

And I lay under the barbell in the morning, sneaking a look at
Franny getting out of bed—or getting dressed—and thinking of
Iowa Bob. What would *he* have said about going to Vienna?
About Freud's hotel that somehow *needed* a smart Harvard boy?
About the differences a smart bear might make—to *anyone's*
prospects for success? I lifted and thought. 'It doesn't matter,'
Iowa Bob would have said. 'Whether we go to Vienna or stay
here, it won't matter.' Under all that weight, that's what I
thought Coach Bob would have said. 'Here or there,' Bob would
have said, 'we're screwed down for life.' It would be *Father's*
hotel—whether in Dairy or in Vienna. Would nothing, ever,
make us more or less exotic than we were? I wondered, with the
weight wonderfully taut and rising, and Franny in the corner of
my eye.

'I wish you'd take those weights to another room,' Franny
said. 'So I can get dressed by myself, sometimes—for Christ's
sake.'

'What do you think about going to Vienna, Franny?' I asked
her.

'I think it will be more sophisticated than staying here,'
Franny said. Completely dressed now, and always so sure of
herself, she looked down at me where I struggled to let my last
bench press down slowly and levelly. 'I might even get a room
without barbells in it,' she added. 'Even one without a weight
lifter in it,' Franny said, blowing lightly into the armpit of my
left (and weaker) arm—and getting out of the way when the
weights slid first to the left, then to the right, off the bar.

'Jesus God!' Father shouted upstairs to me, and I thought that
if Iowa Bob had still been with us, he would have said that
Franny was wrong. Whether Vienna was more sophisticated, or
less—whether Franny had a room with barbells or a room with

191

lace—we were inhabitants of one Hotel New Hampshire after another.

Freud's hotel—or our imperfect picture of Freud's hotel, via air mail—was called the Gasthaus Freud; it was unclear, from Freud's correspondence, whether or not the *other* Freud had ever stayed there. We only knew it was 'centrally located,' according to Freud—'in the First District!'—but in the all-gray black-and-white photograph that Freud sent, we could barely make out the iron double door, sandwiched between the display cases of a kind of candy store. KONDITOREI, said one sign; ZUCKERWARDEN, said another; SCHOKOLADEN, promised a third; and over it all—bigger than the faded letters saying, GASTHAUS FREUD —was the word BONBONS.

'What?' said Egg.

'*Bonbons*,' said Franny. 'Oh boy.'

'Which is the door to the candy store, and which is the door to the hotel?' Frank asked; Frank would always think like a doorman.

'I think you have to live there to know,' Franny said.

Lilly got a magnifying glass and deciphered the name of the street, in funny script, under the street number on the hotel's double door.

'Krugerstrasse,' she decided, which at least matched the name of the street in Freud's address. Father bought a map of Vienna from a travel agency and we located Krugerstrasse—in the First District, as Freud had promised; it appeared very central.

'It's only a block or two from the opera!' Frank cried, enthusiastically.

'Oh boy,' Franny said.

The map had little green areas for parks, thin red and blue lines where the streetcars ran, and ornate buildings—grossly out of proportion to the street—to indicate the places of interest.

'It looks like a kind of Monopoly board,' Lilly said.

We noted cathedrals, museums, the town hall, the university, the Parliament.

'I wonder where the gangs hang out,' said Junior Jones, looking over the streets with us.

'The *gangs?*' said Egg. 'The *who?*'

'The tough guys,' said Junior Jones. 'The guys with guns and blades, man.'

'The gangs,' Lilly repeated, and we stared at the map as if the streets would indicate their darkest alleys to us.

'This is *Europe*,' Frank said, with disgust. 'Maybe there *aren't* gangs.'

'It's a city, isn't it?' Junior Jones said.

But on the map it looked like a toy city, to me—with pretty places of interest, and all the green spots where nature had been arranged for pleasure.

'Probably in the parks,' said Franny, biting her lower lip. 'The gangs hang out in the parks.'

'Shit,' I said.

'There won't be any gangs!' Frank cried. 'There will be music! And pastry! And the people do a lot of bowing, and they dress differently!' We stared at him, but we knew he'd been reading up on Vienna; he'd gotten a head start on the books Father kept bringing home.

'Pastry and music and people *bowing* all the time, Frank?' Franny said. 'Is that what it's like?' Lilly was using her magnifying glass on the map now—as if people would spring to life, in miniature, on the paper; and they'd either be bowing, and dressed differently, or they'd be cruising in gangs.

'Well,' Franny said. 'At least we can be pretty sure there won't be any *black* gangs.' Franny was still angry with Junior Jones for sleeping with Ronda Ray.

'Shit,' Junior said. 'You better hope there *are* black gangs. Black gangs are the best gangs, man. Those white gangs have inferiority complexes,' Junior said. 'And there's nothing worse than a gang with an inferiority complex.'

'A *what?*' said Egg. No doubt he thought that an inferiority complex was a weapon; sometimes, I guess, it *is*.

'Well, I think it's going to be *nice*,' said Frank, grimly.

'Yes, it *will* be,' Lilly said, with a humorlessness akin to Frank's.

'I can't see it,' Egg said, seriously. 'I can't see it, so I don't know *what* it's going to be like.'

'It'll be okay,' Franny said. 'I don't think it's going to be great, but it'll be all right.'

It was odd, but Franny seemed the most influenced by Iowa Bob's philosophy—which, to a degree, had become Father's philosophy. This was odd because Franny was frequently the most sarcastic to Father—and the most sarcastic about Father's plans. Yet when she was raped, Father had said to her—*incredibly!* I thought—that when *he* had a bad day, he tried to see if he could construe it as the luckiest day of his life. 'Maybe this is the luckiest day of your life,' he had said to her; I was

193

amazed that she seemed to find this reverse thinking useful. She was a kind of parrot of other tidbits of Father's philosophy. 'It was just a little event among so many,' I heard her say—to Frank, about scaring Iowa Bob to death. And once, about Chipper Dove, I heard Father say, 'He probably had a most unhappy life.' Franny actually agreed with him!

I felt much more nervous about going to Vienna than Franny seemed to feel, and I was ever conscious of what feelings Franny and I didn't absolutely share—because it mattered to me that I stay close to her.

We all knew that Mother thought the idea was crazy, but we could not ever make her disloyal to Father—although we tried.

'We won't understand the language,' Lilly said to Mother.

'The *what?*' Egg cried.

'The language!' Lilly said. 'They speak German in Vienna.'

'You'll all go to an English-speaking school,' Mother said.

'There will be weird kids in a school like that,' I said. 'Everyone will be a foreigner.'

'*We'll* be the foreigners,' Franny said.

'In an English-speaking school,' I said, 'the whole place will be full of misfits.'

'And people from the government,' said Frank. 'Diplomats and ambassadors will send their kids there. The kids will be all fucked up.'

'Who could be more fucked up than the kids at the Dairy School, Frank?' Franny asked.

'Whoa!' said Junior Jones. 'There's fucked up and then there's *foreign* and fucked up.'

Franny shrugged; so did Mother.

'We'll still be a *family*,' Mother said. 'The main part of your lives will be your family—just like now.'

And that seemed to please everyone. We busied ourselves with the books Father brought from the library, and the travel agency brochures. We reread the short but elated messages from Freud:

GOOD YOU COMING! BRING ALL KIDS AND PETS! LOTS OF ROOM. CENTRALLY LOCATED. GOOD SHOPPING FOR GIRLS (HOW MANY GIRLS?) AND PARKS FOR THE BOYS AND PETS TO PLAY IN. BRING MONEY. MUST RENOVATE—WITH YOUR ASSISTANCE. YOU'LL LIKE THE BEAR. A SMART BEAR MAKES ALL THE DIFFERENCE. NOW WE CAN WORK ON THE AMERI-CAN AUDIENCE. WHEN WE UPGRADE THE CLIENTELE, THEN

WE'LL HAVE A HOTEL TO BE PROUD OF. I HOPE YOUR
ENGLISH STILL GOOD IS. HA HA! BEST TO LEARN A LITTLE
GERMAN, YOU KNOW? REMEMBER MIRACLES DON'T GET
BUILT IN A NIGHT, BUT IN A COUPLE NIGHTS EVEN BEARS
CAN BE QUEENS. HA HA! I GOT OLD—THAT WAS THE
PROBLEM. NOW WE'LL BE OKAY. NOW WE SHOW THE
BASTARDS SONSOFBITCHES AND COCKSUCKER NAZIS WHAT A
GOOD HOTEL IS! HOPE THE KIDS DON'T HAVE COLDS, AND
DON'T FORGET TO GIVE PETS NECESSARY SHOTS.

Since Sorrow was our only pet—and he needed help, but not a
shot—we wondered if Freud thought we still had Earl.

'Of course not,' Father said. 'He's just speaking generally,
he's just trying to be helpful.'

'Make sure Sorrow gets his shots, Frank,' Franny said, but
Frank was getting better about Sorrow; he could occasionally be
teased about the new restoration, and he seemed to be committed
to the task of refashioning Sorrow—in a cheerful pose—for Egg.
We were not allowed to see the gross dog's transformation, of
course, but Frank himself seemed ever cheerful—upon returning
from the bio lab—so that we could only hope that, this time,
Sorrow would be 'nice.'

Father read a book about Austrian anti-Semitism and wondered if Freud had made the right decision in naming the hotel
the Gasthaus Freud; Father wondered, from what he read, if the
Viennese even *liked* the other Freud. He also couldn't help
wondering who the 'bastards sonsofbitches and cocksucker
Nazis' were.

'*I* can't help wondering how *old* Freud is,' Mother said. They
determined that if he'd been in his middle or late forties in 1939,
he would be only in his middle sixties now. But Mother said that
he *sounded* older. In his messages to us, she meant.

HI! QUICK IDEA: YOU THINK IT BEST TO RESTRICT CERTAIN
ACTIVITIES TO CERTAIN FLOORS? MAYBE HAVE CERTAIN
KIND OF CLIENTELE ON FOURTH FLOOR, OTHER KIND IN
BASEMENT? DELICATE MATTER TO DISCRIMINATE, YOU
THINK? CURRENT DAYTIME AND NIGHTTIME CLIENTELE OF
DIFFERENT—I WON'T SAY 'WARRING'—INTERESTS. HA HA!
ALL THAT WILL CHANGE WITH REMODELING. AND ONCE
THEY STOP THE FUCKING DIGGING UP THE STREET. JUST A
FEW MORE YEARS OF WAR RESTORATION, THEY SAY. WAIT
TILL YOU MEET THE BEAR: NOT JUST SMART, BUT <u>YOUNG</u>!

195

WHAT A TEAM WE'LL BE TOGETHER! WHAT YOU MEAN, 'IS
FREUD A REALLY WELL-LIKED NAME IN VIENNA!' DID YOU
GO TO HARVARD OR NOT??!! HA HA.

'He doesn't sound necessarily *older*,' said Franny, 'but he
sounds crazy.'

'He just doesn't use English very well,' Father said. 'It's not
his language.'

So we studied German. Franny and Frank and I took courses
at the Dairy School, and brought the records home to play to
Lilly; Mother worked with Egg. She started by just getting him
familiar with the names of the streets and the places of interest
on the tourist map.

'Lobkowitzplatz,' Mother would say.

'What?' Egg would say.

Father was supposed to be teaching himself, but he seemed to
be making the least progress. 'You kids *have* to learn it,' he kept
saying. '*I* don't have to go to school, meet new kids, all of that.'

'But we're going to an English-speaking school,' Lilly said.

'Even so,' Father said. 'You'll need the German more than I
will.'

'But *you're* going to run a hotel,' Mother said to him.

'I'm going to start off going after the American audience,'
Father said. 'We're trying to drum up an *American* clientele,
first—remember?'

'Better all brush up on our American, too,' said Franny.

Frank was getting the German more quickly than any of us. It
seemed to suit him: every syllable was *pronounced*, the verbs
fell like grapeshot at the ends of sentences, the umlauts were a
form of dressing up; and the whole idea of words having *gender*
must have appealed to Frank. By the late winter he was
(pretentiously) chatting in German, purposefully bewildering us
all, correcting our attempts to answer him, then consoling our
failures by telling us that *he'd* take care of us when we were
'over there.'

'Oh boy,' Franny said. 'That's the part that really gets to me.
Having *Frank* take us all to school, talk to the bus drivers, order
in the restaurants, take all the phone calls. Jesus, now that I'm
finally going abroad, I don't want to be dependent on *him!*'

But Frank seemed to flower at the preparations for moving to
Vienna. No doubt he was encouraged by having been given a
second chance with Sorrow, but he also seemed genuinely
interested in *studying* Vienna. After dinner he read aloud to us,

selected excerpts from what Frank called the 'plums' of Viennese history; Ronda Ray and the Uricks listened too—curiously, because they knew they *weren't* going and their future with Fritz's Act was unclear.

After two months of history lessons, Frank gave us an oral examination on the interesting characters around Vienna at the time of the Crown Prince's suicide at Mayerling (which Frank had earlier read to us, in full detail, moving Ronda Ray to tears). Franny said that Prince Rudolf was becoming Frank's hero —'because of his clothes.' Frank had portraits of Rudolf in his room: one in hunting costume—a thin-headed young man with an oversized moustache, draped with furs and smoking a cigarette as thick as a finger—and another in uniform, wearing the Order of the Golden Fleece, his forehead as vulnerable as a baby's, his beard as sharp as a spade.

'All right, Franny,' Frank began, 'this one is for you. He was a composer of genius, perhaps the world's greatest organist, but he was a hick—a complete rube in the imperial city—and he had a stupid habit of falling in love with young girls.'

'Why is that stupid?' I asked.

'Shut up,' said Frank. 'It's stupid, and this is Franny's question.'

'Anton Bruckner,' Franny said. 'He was stupid, all right.'

'Very,' said Lilly.

'Your turn, Lilly,' said Frank. 'Who was "the Flemish peasant"?'

'Oh, come on,' said Lilly, 'that's too easy. Give it to Egg.'

'It's too hard for Egg,' Franny said.

'*What* is?' Egg said.

'Princess Stephanie,' said Lilly, tiredly, 'the daughter of the King of Belgium, and Rudolf's wife.'

'Now Father,' Frank said.

'Oh boy,' Franny said, because Father was almost as bad at history as he was at German.

'Whose music was so widely loved that even peasants copied the composer's beard?' Frank asked.

'Jesus, you're strange, Frank,' Franny said.

'Brahms?' Father guessed, and we all groaned.

'Brahms had a beard *like* a peasant's,' Frank said. 'Whose beard did the peasants *copy?*'

'Strauss!' Lilly and I yelled.

'The poor drip,' said Franny. 'Now I get to ask *Frank* one.'

197

'Shoot,' said Frank, shutting his eyes tight and scrunching up his face.

'Who was Jeanette Heger?' Franny asked.

'She was Schnitzler's "Sweet Girl," ' Frank said, blushing.

'What's a "Sweet Girl," Frank?' Franny asked, and Ronda Ray laughed.

'*You* know,' said Frank, still blushing.

'And how many acts of love did Schnitzler and his "Sweet Girl" make between 1888 and 1889?' Franny asked.

'Jesus,' said Frank. 'A lot! I forget.'

'Four hundred and sixty-four!' cried Max Urick, who'd been present at all the historical readings, and never forgot a fact. Like Ronda Ray, Max had never been educated before; it was a novelty for Max and Ronda; they paid better attention at Frank's lessons than the rest of us.

'I've got another one for Father!' Franny said. 'Who was Mitzi Caspar?'

'Mitzi Caspar?' Father said. 'Jesus God.'

'Jesus God,' said Frank. 'Franny only remembers the *sexual* parts.'

'Who was she, Frank?' Franny asked.

'I know!' said Ronda Ray. 'She was Rudolf's "Sweet Girl"; he spent the night with her before killing himself, with Marie Vetsera, at Mayerling.' Ronda had a special place in her memory, and in her heart, for Sweet Girls.

'*I'm* one, aren't I?' she had asked me, after Frank's rendering of Arthur Schnitzler's life and work.

'The sweetest,' I had told her.

'Phooey,' said Ronda Ray.

'*Where* did Freud live beyond his means?' Frank asked, to any of us who knew.

'*Which* Freud?' Lilly asked, and we all laughed.

'The Sühnhaus,' Frank said, answering his own question. 'Translation?' he asked. 'The Atonement House,' he answered.

'Fuck you, Frank,' said Franny.

'Not about sex, so she didn't know it,' Frank said to me.

'Who was the last person to touch Schubert?' I asked Frank; he looked suspicious.

'What do you mean?' he asked.

'Just what I said,' I said. 'Who was the last person to *touch* Schubert?' Franny laughed; I had shared this story with her, and I didn't think Frank knew it—because I had taken the pages out of Frank's book. It was a sick story.

'Is this some kind of joke?' Frank asked.

When Schubert had been dead, for sixty years, the poor hick Anton Bruckner attended the opening of Schubert's grave. Only Bruckner and some scientists were allowed. Someone from the mayor's office delivered a speech, going on and on about Schubert's ghastly remains. Schubert's skull was photographed; a secretary took notes at the investigation—noting that Schubert was a shade of orange, and that his teeth were in better shape than Beethoven's (Beethoven had been resurrected for similar studies, earlier). The measurements of Schubert's brain cavity were recorded.

After nearly two hours of 'scientific' investigation, Bruckner could restrain himself no longer. He grabbed the head of Schubert and hugged it until he was asked to let it go. So Bruckner touched Schubert last. It was Frank's kind of story, really, and he was furious not to know it.

'Bruckner, again,' Mother answered, quietly, and Franny and I were amazed that *she* knew; we went from day to day thinking that Mother knew nothing, and then she turned up knowing it all. For Vienna, we know, she had been secretly studying—knowing, perhaps, that Father was unprepared.

'What trivia!' said Frank, when we had explained the story to him. 'Honestly, what trivia!'

'All history is trivia,' Father said, showing again the Iowa Bob side of himself.

But Frank was usually the source of trivia—at least concerning Vienna, he hated to be outdone. His room was full of drawings of soldiers in their regimentals: Hussars in skin-tight pink pants and fitted jackets of a sunny-lake blue, and the officers of the Tyrolean Rifle in dawn-green. In 1900, at the Paris World's Fair, Austria won the Most Beautiful Uniform Prize (for Artillery); it was no wonder that the *fin de siècle* in Vienna appealed to Frank. It was only alarming that the *fin de siècle* was the *only* period Frank really learned—and taught to us. All the rest of it was not as interesting to him.

'Vienna won't be like *Mayerling,* for Christ's sake,' Franny whispered to me, while I was lifting weights. 'Not *now.*'

'Who was the master of the song—as an art form?' I asked her. 'But his beard was plucked raw because he was so nervous he never let the hairs alone.'

'Hugo Wolf, you asshole,' she said. 'Don't you see? Vienna isn't *like* that anymore.'

199

HI!

Freud wrote to us.

YOU ASKED FOR A FLOOR PLAN? WELL I HOPE I KNOW WHAT
YOU MEAN. THE JOURNAL FOR THE SYMPOSIUM ON EAST-
WEST RELATIONS OCCUPIES THE SECOND FLOOR—THEIR
DAYTIME OFFICES—AND I LET THE PROSTITUTES USE THE
THIRD FLOOR, BECAUSE THEY'RE ABOVE THE OFFICES, YOU
SEE, WHICH ARE NEVER USED AT NIGHT. SO NOBODY
COMPLAINS (USUALLY). HA HA! THE FIRST FLOOR IS OUR
FLOOR, I MEAN THE BEAR AND ME—AND YOU, ALL OF YOU,
WHEN YOU COME. SO THERE'S THE FOURTH AND FIFTH FOR
THE GUESTS, WHEN WE GET THE GUESTS. WHY YOU ASK?
YOU HAVE A PLAN? THE PROSTITUTES SAY WE NEED AN
ELEVATOR, BUT THEY MAKE LOTS OF TRIPS. HA HA! WHAT
YOU MEAN, HOW OLD AM I? ABOUT ONE HUNDRED! BUT
VIENNESE ANSWER IS BETTER: WE SAY, 'I KEEP PASSING THE
OPEN WINDOWS.' THIS IS AN OLD JOKE. THERE WAS A
STREET CLOWN CALLED KING OF THE MICE: HE TRAINED
RODENTS, HE DID HOROSCOPES, HE COULD IMPERSONATE
NAPOLEON, HE COULD MAKE DOGS FART ON COMMAND. ONE
NIGHT HE JUMPED OUT HIS WINDOW WITH ALL HIS PETS IN
A BOX. WRITTEN ON THE BOX WAS THIS: 'LIFE IS SERIOUS
BUT ART IS FUN!' I HEAR HIS FUNERAL WAS A PARTY. A
STREET ARTIST HAD KILLED HIMSELF. NOBODY HAD SUP-
PORTED HIM BUT NOW EVERYBODY MISSED HIM. NOW WHO
WOULD MAKE THE DOGS MAKE MUSIC AND THE MICE PANT?
THE BEAR KNOWS THIS, TOO: IT IS HARD WORK AND GREAT
ART TO MAKE LIFE NOT SO SERIOUS. PROSTITUTES KNOW
THIS TOO.

'Prostitutes?' Mother said.
'What?' said Egg.
'Whores?' said Franny.
'There are whores in the hotel?' Lilly asked. So what *else* is
new? I thought, but Max Urick looked more than usually
overcome with sullenness at the thought of staying behind;
Ronda Ray shrugged.
'Sweet Girls!' said Frank.
'Well, Jesus God,' Father said. 'If they're there, we'll just get
them out.'

Wo bleibt die alte Zeit
und die Gemütlichkeit?

Frank went around singing.

Where is the old time?
Where is the Gemütlichkeit?

It was the song Bratfisch sang at the Fiacre Ball; Bratfisch had been Crown Prince Rudolf's personal horse-cab driver—a dangerous-looking rake with a whip.

Wo bleibt die alte Zeit?
Pfirt di Gott, mein schönes Wien!

Frank went on singing. Bratfisch had sung this after Rudolf murdered his mistress and then blew out his own brains.

Where is the old time?
Fare thee well, my beautiful Vienna!

HI!

Freud wrote.

DON'T WORRY ABOUT THE PROSTITUTES. THEY'RE <u>LEGAL</u> HERE. IT'S JUST BUSINESS. THAT EAST-WEST RELATIONS BUNCH IS THE BUNCH TO WATCH. THEIR TYPEWRITERS BOTHER THE BEAR. THEY COMPLAIN A LOT AND THEY TIE UP THE PHONES. DAMN POLITICS, DAMN INTELLECTUALS, DAMN INTRIGUE.

'Intrigue?' Mother said.
'A language problem,' Father said. 'Freud doesn't know the language.'
'Name one anti-Semite for whom an actual square, a whole *Platz*, in the city of Vienna has been named,' Frank demanded. 'Name just one.'
'Jesus God, Frank,' Father said.
'No,' Frank said.
'Dr. Karl Lueger,' Mother said, with such a dullness in her voice that Franny and I felt a chill.

'Very good,' said Frank, impressed.

'Who thought all Vienna was an elaborate job of concealing sexual reality?' Mother asked.

'Freud?' said Frank.

'Not *our* Freud,' said Franny.

But *our* Freud wrote to us:

ALL VIENNA IS AN ELABORATE JOB OF CONCEALING SEXUAL REALITY. THIS IS WHY PROSTITUTION IS LEGAL. THIS IS WHY WE BELIEVE IN BEARS. OVER AND OUT!

I was with Ronda Ray one morning, thinking wearily of Arthur Schnitzler fucking Jeanette Heger 464 times in something like eleven months, and Ronda asked me, 'What does he mean, it's "legal"—prostitution is *legal*—what's he mean?'

'It's not against the law,' I said. 'In Vienna, apparently, prostitution is not against the law.'

There was a long silence from Ronda; she moved, awkwardly, out from under me.

'Is it legal *here?*' she asked me; I could see she was serious —she looked frightened.

'*Everything's* legal in the Hotel New Hampshire!' I said; it was an Iowa Bob thing to say.

'No, *here!*' she said, angrily. 'In America. Is it legal?'

'No,' I said. 'Not in New Hampshire.'

'*No?*' she cried. 'It's against the *law? It is?*' she screamed.

'Well, but it happens, anyway,' I said.

'*Why?*' Ronda yelled. 'Why is it against the law?'

'I don't know,' I said.

'You better go,' she said. 'And you're going to Vienna and leaving me *here?*' she added, pushing me out the door. 'You better go,' she said.

'Who worked for two years on a fresco and called it *Sçhweinsdreck?*' Frank asked me at breakfast. *Schweinsdreck* means 'pig shit.'

'Jesus, Frank, it's breakfast,' I said.

'Gustav Klimt,' Frank said, smugly.

And there went the winter of 1957: still lifting the weights, but going easy on the bananas; still visiting Ronda Ray, but dreaming of the imperial city; learning irregular verbs and the mesmerizing trivia of history; trying to imagine the circus called Fritz's Act and the hotel called Gasthaus Freud. Our mother seemed tired, but she was loyal; she and my father appeared to rely on more frequent visits to old 3E, where the differences between them perhaps appeared easier to solve. The Uricks were wary; a cautious streak had developed in them, because they no doubt felt abandoned—'to a dwarf,' Max said, but not around Lilly. And one morning in early spring, with the ground in Elliot Park still half-frozen but turning spongy, Ronda Ray refused to take my money—but she accepted me.

'It's not legal,' she whispered, bitterly. 'I'm no criminal.'

It was later that I discovered she was playing for higher stakes.

'Vienna,' she whispered. 'What will you do there without me?' she asked. I had a million ideas, and almost as many pictures, but I promised Ronda I would ask Father to consider bringing her along.

'She's a real worker,' I told Father. Mother frowned. Franny started choking on something. Frank mumbled about the weather in Vienna—'Lots of rain.' Egg, naturally, asked what we were talking about.

'No,' Father said. 'Not Ronda. We can't afford it.' Everyone looked relieved—even me, I confess.

I broke the news to Ronda when she was oiling the top of the bar.

'Well, there was no harm in asking, right?' she said.

'No harm,' I said. But the next morning, when I stopped and breathed a little outside her door, it seemed that there had been some harm.

'Just keep running, John-O,' she said. 'Running is legal. Running is free.'

I then had an awkward and vague conversation with Junior Jones about lust; it was comforting that he didn't seem to understand it any better than I did. It was a frustration to us both that Franny had so many other opinions on the subject.

'Women,' said Junior Jones. 'They're very different from you and me.' I nodded, of course. Franny seemed to have forgiven Junior for his lust with Ronda Ray, but a part of her remained aloof to him; she appeared, at least outwardly, indifferent to leaving Junior for Vienna. Perhaps she was torn between not wanting to miss Junior Jones too much and remaining hopeful but calm about the possible adventure that Vienna could be for her.

She was detached when asked about it, and I found myself, that spring, more often stuck with Frank; Frank was in high gear. His moustache resembled, nervously, the facial excesses of the departed Crown Prince Rudolf, although Franny and I liked to call Frank the King of Mice.

'Here he comes! He can make dogs fart on command! Who is it?' I would cry.

' "Life Is Serious But Art Is Fun!" ' Franny would shout. 'Here is the hero of the street clowns! Keep him away from the open windows!'

'King of the Mice!' I yelled.

'Drop dead, both of you,' Frank said.

'How's it coming with the dog, Frank?' I asked; this would win him over, every time.

'Well,' Frank said, some vision of Sorrow crossing his mind and making his moustache quiver, 'I think Egg will be pleased —although Sorrow may seem a little tame, to the rest of us.'

'I doubt it,' I said. Looking at Frank, I could imagine the Crown Prince, moodily en route to Mayerling—and the murder of his mistress, and the killing of himself—but it was easier to think of Freud's street artist leaping out a window with his box of pets: the King of Mice dashed to the ground and a city that ignored him, once, now mourning him. Somehow, Frank looked the part.

'Who will make the dogs make music and the mice pant?' I asked Frank over breakfast.

'Go lift a few weights,' he said. 'And drop them on your head.'

So Frank journeyed back to the bio lab; if the King of Mice could make dogs fart on command, Frank could make Sorrow live in more than one pose—so perhaps he *was* a kind of Crown Prince, like Rudolf, Emperor of Austria to Be, King of Bohemia, King of Transylvania, Margrave of Moravia, Duke of Auschwitz (to mention only a few of Rudolf's titles).

'Where is the King of Mice?' Franny would ask.

'With Sorrow,' I would say. 'Teaching Sorrow to fart on command.'

And passing each other in the halls of the Hotel New Hampshire, I would say to Lilly, or Franny would say to Frank, 'Keep passing the open windows.'

'*Schweinsdreck*,' Frank would say.

'Show off,' Franny would say back to him.

'Pig shit to you, Frank,' I'd say.

'*What?*' Egg would shout.

And one morning Lilly asked Father, 'Will we leave before

the circus called Fritz's Act moves in, or will we get to see them?'

'I hope to *miss* seeing them,' Franny said.

'Won't we overlap, at least a day?' Frank asked. 'I mean for the passing of the keys, or something?'

'*What* keys?' Max Urick asked.

'What *locks?*' said Ronda Ray, whose door was shut to me.

'Perhaps we'll coincide for about ten or fifteen minutes,' Father said.

'I want to see them,' Lilly said, seriously. And I looked at Mother, who looked tired—but nice: she was a soft, rumpled woman, whom Father clearly loved to touch. He was always burrowing his face in her neck, and cupping her breasts, and hugging her from behind—which she only pretended to resent (in front of us children). When he was around Mother, Father was remindful of those dogs whose heads are always thrust in your lap, whose snouts take comfort in armpits and crotches—I don't mean, at all, that Father was crude with her, but he was always making contact: hugging and hanging on tight.

Of course, Egg did this with Mother, too, and Lilly—to a degree—though Lilly was more dignified, and holding back of herself, since her smallness had become such an item. It was as if she didn't want to appear any smaller than she was by acting too young.

'The average Austrian is three to four inches shorter than the average American, Lilly,' Frank informed her, but Lilly appeared not to care—she shrugged; it was Mother's move, independent and pretty. In their different ways both Franny and Lilly had inherited the motion.

Sometime that spring I saw Franny use it: just a single deft shrug, with a hint of some involuntary ache behind it—when Junior Jones told us that he would be accepting the football scholarship from Penn State in the fall.

'I'll write you,' Franny told him.

'Sure, and *I'll* write *you*,' he told her.

'I'll write you more,' said Franny. Junior Jones tried to shrug, but it didn't come off.

'Shit,' he told me, when we were throwing rocks at a tree in Elliot Park. 'What does Franny want to *do*, anyway? What does she think is going to happen to her over there?'

'Over there' was what we all called it. Except Frank: he now spoke of Vienna the German way. '*Wien*,' he said.

'*Veen*,' Lilly said, shuddering. 'It sounds like something a

lizard would say.' And we all stared at her, waiting for Egg to
say his 'What?'

Then the grass came out in Elliot Park, and one warm night,
when I was sure Egg was asleep, I opened the window and
looked at the moon and the stars and listened to the crickets and
the frogs, and Egg said, 'Keep passing the open windows.'

'You awake?' I said.

'I can't sleep,' Egg said. 'I can't see where I'm going,' he
said. 'I don't know what it'll be like.'

He sounded ready to cry, so I said, 'Come on, Egg. It will be
great. You've never lived in a *city*,' I said.

'I know,' he said, sniffling a little.

'Well, there's more to do than there is to do here,' I promised
him.

'I have a lot to do here,' he said.

'But this will be so *different*,' I told him.

'Why do the people jump out of windows?' he asked me.

And I explained to him that it was just a story, although the
sense of a metaphor might have been lost on him.

'There are spies in the hotel,' he said. 'That's what Lilly said:
"Spies and low women." '

I imagined Lilly thinking that 'low women' were short, like
her, and I tried to reassure Egg that there was nothing frightening
about the occupants of Freud's hotel; I said that Father would
take care of everything—and heard the silence with which both
Egg and I accepted *that* promise.

'How will we get there?' Egg asked. 'It's so far.'

'An airplane,' I said.

'I don't know what that's like, either,' he said.

(There would be two airplanes, actually, because Father and
Mother would never fly on the same plane; many parents are like
that. I explained that to Egg, too, but he kept repeating, 'I don't
know what it'll be like.')

Then Mother came into our room to comfort Egg and I fell
back to sleep with them talking together, and woke up again as
Mother was leaving; Egg was asleep. Mother came over to my
bed and sat down beside me; her hair was loose and she looked
very young; in fact, in the half-dark, she looked a lot like
Franny.

'He's only seven,' she said, about Egg. 'You should talk to
him more.'

'Okay,' I said. 'Do *you* want to go to Vienna?'

And of course, she shrugged—and smiled—and said, 'Your father is a good, good man.' For the first time, really, I could see them in the summer of 1939, with Father promising Freud that he *would* get married, and he *would* go to Harvard—and Freud asking Mother one thing: to forgive Father. Was *this* what she had to forgive him for? And was rooting us out of the terrible town of Dairy, and the wretched Dairy School—and the first Hotel New Hampshire, which wasn't so hot a hotel (though nobody said so)—was *that* so bad a thing that Father was doing, really?

'Do you *like* Freud?' I asked her.

'I don't really *know* Freud,' Mother said.

'But Father likes him,' I said.

'Your father likes him,' Mother said, 'but he doesn't really know him, either.'

'What do you think the bear will be like?' I asked her.

'I don't know what the bear is *for*,' Mother whispered, 'so I couldn't guess what it could be *like*.'

'What *could* it be for?' I asked, but she shrugged again —perhaps remembering what Earl had been like, and trying to remember what Earl could have been *for*.

'We'll all find out,' she said, and kissed me. It was an Iowa Bob thing to say.

'Good night,' I said to Mother, and kissed her.

'Keep passing the open windows,' she whispered, and I was asleep.

Then I had a dream that Mother died.

'No more bears,' she said to Father, but he misunderstood her; he thought she was asking him a question.

'No, *one* more bear,' he said. 'Just one more. I promise.'

And she smiled and shook her head; she was too tired to explain. There was the faintest effort of her famous shrug, and the intention of a shrug in her eyes, which rolled up and out of sight, suddenly, and Father knew that the man in the white dinner jacket had taken Mother's hand.

'Okay! No more bears!' Father promised, but Mother was aboard the white sloop, now, and she went sailing out to sea.

In the dream, Egg wasn't there; but Egg was there when I woke up—he was still sleeping, and someone else was watching him. I recognized the sleek, black back—the fur thick and short and oily; the square back of his blundering head, and the half-cocked, no-account ears. He was sitting on his tail, as he used to do—in life—and he was facing Egg. Frank had probably

207

made him smiling, or at least panting, witlessly, in that goofy way of dogs who repeatedly drop balls and sticks at your feet. Oh, the moronic but happy *fetchers* of this world—that was our old Sorrow: a fetcher and a farter. I crept out of bed to face the beast—from Egg's point of view.

I could see at a glance that Frank had outdone himself at 'niceness.' Sorrow sat on his tail with his forepaws touching and modestly hiding his groin; his face had a dippy, glazed happiness about it, his tongue lolled stupidly out of his mouth. He looked ready to fart, or wag his tail, or roll idiotically on his back; he looked like he was dying to be scratched behind his ears—he looked like a hopelessly slavish animal, forever in need of fondling attention. If it weren't for the fact that he was dead, and that it was impossible to banish from memory Sorrow's *other* manifestations, *this* Sorrow looked as harmless as Sorrow ever could have looked.

'Egg?' I whispered. 'Wake up.' But it was Saturday morning —Egg's morning for sleeping in—and I knew Egg had slept badly, or only a little, through the night. Out the window I saw our car driving between the trees of Elliot Park, treating the soggy park like a slalom course—at slow speed—and I knew that meant Frank was at the wheel; he'd just gotten his driver's license, and he liked to practice by driving around the trees in Elliot Park. Also, Franny had just gotten her learner's permit and Frank was teaching her to drive. I could tell it was Frank at the wheel because of the stately progress of the car through the trees, at limousine speed, at *hearse* speed—that was the way Frank always drove. Even when he drove Mother to the supermarket, he drove as if he were bearing the coffin of a queen past throngs of mourners seeking one last look. When Franny drove, Frank yelped beside her, cringing in the passenger seat; Franny liked to go fast.

'Egg!' I said more loudly, and he stirred a little. There was a slamming of doors outside, a changing of drivers in our car in Elliot Park; I could tell Franny had taken the wheel when the car began to careen between the trees, great slithers of the spring mud flying—and the wild, half-seen gestures of Frank's arms waving in what is popularly called the death seat.

'Jesus God!' I heard Father yell, out another window. Then he shut the window and I heard him raving at Mother—about the way Franny drove, about having to replant the grass in Elliot Park, about having to chip the mud off the car with a chisel—and while I was still watching Franny racing among the trees, Egg opened his eyes and saw Sorrow. His scream jammed my thumbs against the windowsill and made me bite my tongue. Mother ran into the room to see what was the matter and greeted Sorrow with a shriek of her own.

'Jesus God,' said Father. 'Why does Frank have to *spring* the damn dog on everyone? Why can't he just say, "Now I'm going to show you Sorrow," and carry the damn thing into a room —when we're all *ready* for it, for Christ's sake!'

'Sorrow?' said Egg, peering from under his bedclothes.

'It's just Sorrow, Egg,' I said. 'Doesn't he look nice?' Egg smiled cautiously at the foolish-looking dog.

'He *does* look nice,' Father said, suddenly pleased.

'He's *smiling!*' Egg said.

Lilly came into Egg's room and hugged Sorrow; she sat down and leaned back against the upright dog. 'Look, Egg,' she said, 'you can use him like a backrest.'

Frank came in the room, looking awfully proud.

'It's terrific, Frank,' I said.

'It's really nice,' said Lilly.

'A remarkable job, son,' Father said; Frank was just beaming. Franny came in the room, talking before she came in.

'Honestly, Frank is such a chicken shit in the car,' she complained. 'You'd think he was giving me stagecoach lessons!' Then she saw Sorrow. 'Wow!' she cried. And why did we all wait so quietly for what Franny would say? Even when she was not quite sixteen, my whole family seemed to regard her as the real authority—as the last word. Franny circled Sorrow, almost as if she were another dog—sniffing him. Franny put her arm around Frank's shoulder, and he stood tensed for her verdict. 'The King of Mice has produced a fucking *masterpiece*,' Franny announced; a spasm of a smile crossed Frank's anxious face. 'Frank,' Franny said to him sincerely, 'you've really done it, Frank. This really *is* Sorrow,' she said. And she got down and patted the dog—the way she used to, in the old days, hugging his head and rubbing behind his ears. This seemed completely reassuring to Egg, who began to hug Sorrow without reserve. 'You may be an asshole in an automobile, Frank,' Franny told him, 'but you've done an absolutely first-rate job with Sorrow.'

Frank looked as if he were going to faint, or just fall over, and everyone began talking at once, and pounding Frank on the back, and poking and scratching Sorrow—everyone but Mother, we suddenly noticed; she was standing by the window, looking out at Elliot Park.

'Franny?' she said.

'Yes,' Franny said.

'Franny,' Mother said, 'you're not to drive like that in the park again—do you understand?'

'Okay,' Franny said.

'You may go out to the delivery entrance, *now,*' Mother said, 'and get Max to help you find the lawn hose. And get some buckets of *hot, soapy* water. You're going to wash all the mud off the car before it dries.'

'Okay,' Franny said.

'Just look at the park,' Mother told her. 'You've torn up the new grass.'

'I'm sorry,' Franny said.

'Lilly?' Mother said, still looking out the window—she was through with Franny, now.

'Yes?' Lilly said.

'Your room, Lilly,' Mother said. 'What am I going to say about your room?'

'Oh,' Lilly said. 'It's a mess.'

'For a *week* it's been a mess,' Mother said. 'Today, please, don't leave your room until it's better.'

I noticed that Father slunk quietly away, with Lilly—and Franny went to wash the car. Frank seemed bewildered that his moment of success had been cut so short! He seemed unwilling to leave Sorrow, now that he had re-created him.

'Frank?' said Mother.

'Yes!' Frank said.

'Now that you're finished with Sorrow, perhaps *you* could straighten up *your* room, too?' Mother asked.

'Oh, sure,' Frank said.

'I'm sorry, Frank,' Mother said.

'Sorry?' Frank said.

'I'm sorry, but I don't like Sorrow, Frank,' Mother said.

'You don't *like* him?' Frank said.

'No, because he's *dead,* Frank,' Mother said. 'He's very *real,* Frank, but he's dead, and I don't find dead things amusing.'

'I'm sorry,' Frank said.

'Jesus God!' I said.

'And *you,* please,' Mother said to me, 'will you watch your *language?* Your language is terrible,' Mother told me. 'Especially when you pause to consider that you share a room with a

seven-year-old. I am tired of the "fucking" this and the "fucking" that,' Mother said. 'This house is not a locker room.'

'Yes,' I said, and noticed that Frank was gone—the King of
Mice had slipped away.

'Egg,' Mother said—her voice winding down.

'What?' Egg said.

'Sorrow is not to leave your room, Egg,' Mother said. 'I don't
like to be *startled*,' she said, 'and if Sorrow leaves this room—if
I see him anyplace but where I expect to see him, which is right
here—then that's it, then he's gone for good.'

'Right,' said Egg. 'But can I take him to Vienna? When we
go, I mean—can Sorrow come?'

'I suppose he'll *have* to come,' Mother said. Her voice had the
same resignation in it that I'd heard in her voice in my dream
—when Mother had said, 'No more bears,' and then drifted
away on the white sloop.

'Holy cow,' said Junior Jones, when he saw Sorrow sitting on
Egg's bed, one of Mother's shawls around Sorrow's shoulders,
Egg's baseball cap on Sorrow's head. Franny had brought Junior
to the hotel to see Frank's miracle. Harold Swallow had come
along with Junior, but Harold was lost somewhere; he'd made a
wrong turn on the second floor, and rather than come into our
apartment, he was wandering around the hotel. I was trying to
work at my desk—I was studying for my German exam, and was
trying *not* to ask Frank for help. Franny and Junior Jones went
off looking for Harold, and Egg decided against Sorrow's
present costume; he undressed the dog and started over.

Then Harold Swallow found his way to our door and peered in
at Egg and me—and at Sorrow sitting naked on Egg's bed.
Harold had never seen Sorrow before—dead or alive—and he
called the dog over to the doorway.

'Here, dog!' he called. 'Come here! Come on!'

Sorrow sat smiling at Harold, his tail itching to wag—but
motionless.

'Come on! Here, doggy!' Harold cried. 'Good dog, nice
doggy!'

'He's supposed to stay in this room,' Egg informed Harold
Swallow.

'Oh,' said Harold, with an impressive roll of his eyes to me.
'Well, he's very well behaved,' Harold Swallow said. 'He ain't
budging, is he?'

And I went to take Harold Swallow down to the restaurant,

211

where Junior and Franny were looking for him; I saw no reason to tell Harold that Sorrow was dead.

'That your little brother?' Harold asked me, about Egg.

'Right,' I said.

'And you got a nice dog, too,' Harold said.

'Shit,' Junior Jones said to me, later; we were standing outside the gymnasium, which the Dairy School had tried to decorate like a building of parliament—for the weekend of Junior's graduation. 'Shit,' Junior said, 'I'm really worried about Franny.'

'Why?' I asked.

'Something's bothering her,' Junior said. 'She won't sleep with me,' he said. 'Not even as just a way of saying good-bye, or something. She won't even do it *once!* Sometimes I think she doesn't *trust* me,' Junior said.

'Well,' I said. 'Franny's only sixteen, you know.'

'Well, she's an *old* sixteen, you know,' he said. 'I wish you'd speak to her.'

'*Me?*' I said. 'What should I say?'

'I wish you'd ask her why she won't sleep with me,' Junior Jones said.

'Shit,' I said, but I asked her—later: when the Dairy School was empty, when Junior Jones had gone home for the summer (to whip himself into shape for playing football at Penn State), when the old campus, and especially the path through the woods that the football players always used, reminded Franny and me of what seemed like *years* ago (to us). 'Why didn't you ever sleep with Junior Jones?' I asked her.

'I'm only sixteen, John,' Franny said.

'Well, you're an *old* sixteen, you know,' I said, not exactly sure what this might mean. Franny shrugged, of course.

'Look at it this way,' she said. 'I'll see Junior again; we're going to write letters, and all that. We're staying friends. Now, someday—when I'm older, and if we *do* stay friends—it might be the perfect thing to do: to sleep with him. I wouldn't want to have used it up.'

'Why couldn't you sleep with him *twice?*' I asked her.

'You don't get it,' she said.

I was thinking it had to do with her having been raped, but Franny could always read me like a book.

'No, kid,' she said. 'It's got nothing to do with being raped. Sleeping with someone is very different—provided it *means* something. I just don't know what it would *mean*—with Junior.

212

Not yet. *Also*,' she said, with a big sigh—and she paused. 'Also,' she said, 'I don't have exactly a lot of experience, but it seems that once someone—or *some* people—get to have you, you don't ever hear from them again.'

Now, it seemed to me, she *had* to be talking about her rape; I was confused. I said, 'Who do you mean, Franny?' And she bit her lip a while.

Then she said, 'It surprises me that I have not heard one word —not a single word—from Chipper Dove. Can you imagine that?' she asked. 'All this time and not one word.'

Now I was *really* confused; it seemed amazing to me that she would have thought she'd *ever* hear from *him*. I couldn't think of anything to say, except a stupid joke, so I said, 'Well, Franny, I don't suppose you've written to him, either.'

'Twice,' Franny said. 'I think that's enough.'

'*Enough?*' I cried. 'Why the fuck did you write him at *all?*' I yelled.

She looked surprised. 'Why, to tell him how I was, and what I was doing,' she said. I just stared at her, and she looked away. 'I was *in love* with him, John,' she whispered to me.

'Chipper Dove raped you, Franny,' I said. 'Dove and Chester Pulaski and Lenny Metz—they gang-banged you.'

'It's not necessary to say that,' she snapped at me. 'I'm talking about Chipper Dove,' she said. 'Just him.'

'He raped you,' I said.

'I was in love with him,' she said, keeping her back to me. 'You don't understand. I was *in love*—and maybe I still am,' she said. 'Now,' she added, brightly, 'would you like to tell Junior *that?* Do you think *I* should tell Junior that?' she asked. 'Wouldn't Junior just love that?' she asked.

'No,' I said.

'No, I thought not, too,' Franny said. 'So I just thought that —under the circumstances—I wouldn't sleep with him. Okay?' she asked.

'Okay,' I said, but I wanted to tell her that certainly Chipper Dove had not loved *her*.

'Don't tell me,' Franny said. 'Don't tell me that he didn't love *me*. I think I know. But do you know what?' she asked me. 'One day,' Franny said, 'Chipper Dove might fall in love with me. And you know what?' she asked.

'No,' I said.

'Maybe if that happens, *if* he falls in love with me,' Franny said, 'Maybe—by then—I won't love him anymore. And then

213

I'll *really* get him, won't I?' She asked me. I just stared at her; she was, as Junior Jones had observed, a very *old* sixteen indeed.

I felt suddenly that we all couldn't get to Vienna soon enough —that we all needed time to grow older, and wiser (if that's what really was involved in the process). I know that I wanted a chance to pull even with Franny, if not ever ahead of her, and I thought I needed a new hotel for that.

It suddenly occurred to me that Franny might have been thinking of Vienna in somewhat the same way: of *using* it—to make herself smarter and tougher and (somehow) grown-up *enough* for the world that neither of us understood.

'Keep passing the open windows,' was all I could say to her, at the moment. We looked at the stubbly grass on the practice field, and knew that in the fall it would be punctured everywhere with cleats, churned by knees striking the ground, and clawing fingers—and that, *this* fall, we would not be in Dairy to see it, or to look away from it. Somewhere else all that—or something like it—would be going on, and we would be watching, or taking part in, whatever it was.

I took Franny's hand and we walked along the path the football players always used, pausing only briefly by the turn we remembered—the way into the woods, where the ferns were; we didn't need to see them. 'Bye-bye,' Franny whispered to that holy and unholy place; I squeezed her hand—she squeezed back, then she broke our grip—and we tried to speak only German to each other, all the way back to the Hotel New Hampshire. It would be our new language very soon, after all, and we weren't very good at it. We both knew that we needed to get better in order to be free of Frank.

Frank was taking his hearse-driving tour through the trees when we returned to Elliot Park. 'Want a lesson?' he asked Franny. She shrugged, and Mother sent them both on an errand —Franny driving, Frank praying and flinching beside her.

That night, when I went to bed, Egg had put Sorrow in my bed —and dressed him in my running clothes. Getting Sorrow out of my bed—and getting Sorrow's *hair* out of my bed—I thoroughly woke myself up again. I went down to the restaurant and bar to read. Max Urick was having a drink, sitting in one of the screwed-down chairs.

'How many times did old Schnitzler give it to Jeanette What's Her Name?' Max asked me.

'Four hundred and sixty-four,' I said.

'Isn't that something!' he cried.

When Max stumbled upstairs to bed, I sat listening to Mrs. Urick putting away some pans. Ronda Ray was not around; she was out—or maybe she was in; it hardly mattered. It was too dark to take a run—and Franny was asleep, so I couldn't lift weights. Sorrow had ruined my bed for a while, so I just tried to read. It was a book about the 1918 flu—about all the famous and the unfamous people who were wiped out by it. It seemed like one of the saddest times in Vienna. Gustav Klimt, who once called his own work 'Pig shit,' died; he had been Schiele's teacher. Schiele's wife died—her name was Edith—and then Schiele himself died, when he was very young. I read a whole chapter in the book about what pictures Schiele *might* have painted if the flu hadn't got him. I was beginning to get the rather fuzzy idea that the whole book was about what Vienna might have become if the flu hadn't come to town, when Lilly woke me up.

'Why aren't you sleeping in your room?' she asked. I explained about Sorrow.

'I can't sleep because I can't imagine what my room *over there* is going to be like,' Lilly explained. I told her about the 1918 flu, but she wasn't interested. 'I'm worried,' Lilly admitted. 'I'm worried about the violence.'

'*What* violence?' I asked her.

'In Freud's hotel,' Lilly said. 'There's going to be violence.'

'*Why*, Lilly?' I asked.

'Sex and violence,' Lilly said.

'You mean the whores?' I asked her.

'The *climate* of them,' Lilly said, sitting pretty in one of the screwed-down chairs, rocking slightly in her seat—her feet, of course, not reaching the floor.

'The climate of whores?' I said.

'The climate of sex and violence,' Lilly said. 'That's what it sounds like to me. That whole city,' she said. 'Look at Rudolf —killing his girl friend, then killing himself.'

'That was in the last century, Lilly,' I reminded her.

'And that man who fucked that woman four hundred and sixty-four times,' Lilly said.

'Schnitzler,' I said. 'Almost a century ago, Lilly.'

'It's probably worse now,' Lilly said. 'Most things are.'

That would have been Frank—who told her that—I knew.

'And the flu,' said Lilly, '*and* the wars. And the Hungarians,' she said.

215

'The revolution?' I asked her. 'That was last year, Lilly.'

'And all the rape in the Russian Sector,' Lilly said. 'Franny will get raped again. Or I will,' she said, adding, 'if someone *small* enough catches me.'

'The occupation is over,' I said.

'A violent climate,' Lilly repeated. 'All the repressed sexuality.'

'That's the *other* Freud, Lilly,' I said.

'And what will the bear do?' Lilly asked. 'A hotel with whores and bears and spies.'

'Not *spies*, Lilly,' I said. I knew she meant the East-West relations people. 'I think they're just intellectuals,' I told her, but this didn't appear to comfort her; she shook her head.

'I can't stand violence,' Lilly said. 'And Vienna *reeks* of it,' she said; it was as if she'd been studying the tourist map and had found all the corners where Junior Jones's *gangs* hung out. 'The whole place *shouts* of violence,' Lilly said. 'It absolutely *broadcasts* it,' Lilly said; it was as if she had taken these words into her mouth to suck on them: *reeks, shouts, broadcasts.* 'The whole idea of going over there just *shivers* with violence,' Lilly said, shivering. Her tiny knees gripped the seat of the screwed-down chair, her slender legs whipped back and forth, violently fanning the floor. She was only eleven, and I wondered where she'd found all the *words* she used, and why her imagination seemed much older than she was. Why were the women in our family either wise, like Mother, or an '*old* sixteen'—as Junior Jones said of Franny—or like Lilly: small and soft, but bright beyond her years? Why should *they* get all the brains? I wondered, thinking of Father; although Mother and Father were both thirty-seven, Father seemed ten years younger to me—'and ten years dumber,' Franny said. And what was *I?* I wondered, because Franny—and even Lilly—made me feel I would be fifteen forever. And Egg was immature—a seven-year-old with five-year-old habits. And Frank was Frank, the King of Mice, able to bring back dogs from the dead, able to master a different language, and able to put the oddities of history to his personal use; but in spite of his obvious abilities, I felt that Frank—in many other categories—was operating with a mental age of four.

Lilly sat with her head down and her little legs swinging. 'I *like* the Hotel New Hampshire,' Lilly said. 'In fact, I *love* it; I don't want to leave here,' she said, the predictable tears in her eyes. I gave her a hug and picked her up; I could have bench-pressed Lilly while the seasons changed. I carried her back to her room.

'Think of it this way,' I told her. 'We'll just be going to *another* Hotel New Hampshire, Lilly. The same thing, but another country.' But Lilly cried and cried.

'I'd rather stay with the circus called Fritz's Act,' she bawled. 'I'd rather stay with them, and I don't even know what they *do!*'

Soon we *would* know what they did, of course. Too soon. It was summer, then, and before we were packed—before we'd even made the airplane reservations—the four-foot forty-one-year-old named Frederick 'Fritz' Worter paid us a visit. There were some papers to sign, and some of the other members of Fritz's Act wished to have a look at their future home.

One morning, when Egg was sleeping beside Sorrow, I looked out our window at Elliot Park. At first nothing seemed strange; some men and women were getting out of a Volkswagen bus. They were all, more or less, the same size. We were still a hotel, after all, and I thought they might be guests. Then I realized that there were *five* women and *eight* men—yet they quite comfortably spilled out of *one* Volkswagen bus—and when I recognized Frederick 'Fritz' Worter as one of them, I realized that they were all the same size as *him*.

Max Urick, who'd been shaving while looking out his fourth-floor window, screamed and cut himself. 'A fucking *busload* of midgets,' he told us later. 'It's not what you expect to see when you're just getting up.'

It is impossible to say what Ronda Ray might have done, or said, if *she* had seen them; but Ronda was still in bed. Franny, and my barbells, were lying untouched in Franny's room; Frank —whether he was dreaming, studying German, or reading about Vienna—was in a world of his own. Egg was sleeping with Sorrow, and Mother and Father—who would be embarrassed about it, later—were having fun in old 3E.

I ran into Lilly's room, knowing she would want to see the arrival of at least the *human* part of Fritz's Act, but Lilly was already awake and watching them through her window; she was wearing an old-fashioned nightgown that Mother had bought her in an antique store—it completely enveloped Lilly—and she was hugging her Raggedy Ann doll to her chest. 'It's a *small* circus, just like Mr. Worter said,' Lilly whispered, adoringly. In Elliot Park we watched the midgets gathering beside the Volkswagen bus; they were stretching and yawning; one of the men did a handstand; one of the women did a cartwheel. One of them started moving on all fours, like a chimpanzee, but Fritz clapped his hands, scolding such foolishness; they drew together, like a miniature football team having a huddle (with two extra players); then they started marching, in an orderly fashion, toward our lobby door.

Lilly went to let them in; I went to the switchboard to make the announcement. To 3E, for example: 'New owners arriving —all thirteen of them. Over and out.' To Frank: *'Guten Morgen! Fritz's Act ist hier angekommen. Wachs du auf!'* And to Franny: 'Midgets! Go wake up Egg so he won't be frightened; he'll think he *dreamed* them. Tell him thirteen midgets are here, but it's safe!'

Then I ran up to Ronda Ray's room; I was better at giving her messages in person. 'They're *here!*' I whispered, outside her door.

'Keep running, John-O,' Ronda said.

'There's thirteen of them,' I said. 'Only five women and *eight* men,' I said. 'There's at least three men for you!'

'What *size* are they?' Ronda Ray asked.

'That's a surprise,' I said. 'Come see.'

'Keep running,' Ronda said. *'All* of you—keep running.'

Max Urick went and hid with Mrs. Urick in the kitchen; they were shy about being introduced, but Father dragged them out to meet the midgets, and Mrs. Urick marched the midgets through her kitchen—showing off her stockpots, and how plain-but-good everything smelled.

'They *are* small,' Mrs. Urick conceded later, 'but there's a lot of them; they'll have to eat *something.*'

'They'll never reach all the lights,' Max Urick said. 'I'll have to change all the switches.' Grumpily, he moved off the fourth floor. It was clear that the fourth floor was the one the midgets wanted—'suited to their tiny washing and tiny peeing,' Max grumbled, but not around Lilly. Franny thought Max was only angry that he was moving closer to Mrs. Urick; but he moved no nearer to her than the third floor, where, (I imagined), he would be forever blessed to hear the patter of little feet above him.

'Where will the animals go?' Lilly asked Mr. Worter. Fritz explained that the circus would use the Hotel New Hampshire only for their summer quarters; the animals would stay outside.

'What kind of animals are they?' Egg asked, clutching Sorrow to his chest.

'Live ones,' said one of the lady midgets, who was about

218

Egg's size and appeared to be intrigued with Sorrow; she kept patting him.

It was the end of June when the midgets made Elliot Park look like a fairground; the once-brightly-colored canvases, now faded to pastels, flapped over the little stalls, fringed the merry-go-round, domed the big tent where the main acts would be performed. Kids from the town of Dairy came and hung around our park all day, but the midgets were in no hurry; they set up the stalls; they changed the position of the merry-go-round three times—and refused to hook up the engine that ran it, even to test it out. One day a box arrived, the size of a dining-room table; it was full of large spools of different-colored tickets, each spool as big as a tire.

And Frank drove carefully through the now crowded park, circling the little tents and the one big tent, telling the kids from the town to move on. 'It opens the Fourth of July, kids,' Frank would say, officiously—his arm hanging out the window of the car. 'Come back then.'

We would be gone by then; we hoped that the animals might arrive before we had to leave, but we knew, in advance, we were going to miss opening night.

'We've seen all the things they do, anyway,' Franny said.

'Mainly,' Frank said, 'they just go around looking *small*.'

Lilly burned. She pointed out the handstands, the juggling acts, the water and fire dance, the eight-man standing pyramid, the blind baseball team skit; and the smallest of the lady midgets said she could ride bareback—on a dog.

'Show me the dog,' said Frank. He was sour because Father had sold Fritz the family car, and Frank now needed Fritz's permission to drive the car around Elliot Park; Fritz was generous about the car, but Frank hated to ask.

Franny liked to take her driving lessons with Max Urick in the hotel pickup, because Max was nervy about Franny driving fast. 'Gun it,' he would encourage her. 'Pass that sucker—you've got plenty of room.' And Franny would come back from a lesson, proud that she had laid nine feet of rubber around the bandstand or twelve feet around the corner of Front Street verging with Court. 'Laying rubber' was what we said in Dairy, New Hampshire, for leaving a black stain on the road with squealing tires.

'It's disgusting,' Frank said. 'Bad for the clutch, bad for the tires, nothing but juvenile showing off—you'll get in trouble,

219

you'll get your learner's permit revoked, Max will lose his license (which he probably *should*), you'll run over someone's dog, or a small child, some dumb hoods from the town will try to drag-race you, or follow you home and beat the shit out of you. Or they'll beat the shit out of *me,*' Frank said, 'just because I know you.'

'We're going to Vienna, Frank,' Franny said. 'Get in your licks at the town of Dairy while you can.'

'*Licks!*' said Frank. 'Disgusting.'

HI!

Freud wrote.

> YOU ALMOST HERE! GOOD TIME TO COME. PLENTY OF TIME FOR KIDS TO GET ADJUSTED BEFORE SCHOOL STARTS. EVERYONE LOOKING FORWARD TO YOU COMING. EVEN PROSTITUTES! HA HA! WHORES HAPPY TO TAKE MATERNAL INTEREST IN KIDS—REALLY! I SHOW THEM ALL THE PICTURES. SUMMER A GOOD TIME FOR WHORES: LOTS OF TOURISTS, EVERYONE IN GOOD MOOD. EVEN EAST-WEST RELATIONS ASSHOLES SEEM CONTENT. THEY NOT SO BUSY IN SUMMER —DON'T START TYPING UNTIL 11 A.M. POLITICS TAKE SUMMER VACATIONS, TOO. HA HA! IT <u>NICE</u> HERE. NICE MUSIC IN PARKS. NICE ICE CREAM. EVEN BEAR IS HAPPIER —GLAD YOU COMING, TOO. BEAR'S NAME, BY THE WAY, IS SUSIE. LOVE FROM SUSIE AND ME, FREUD.

Susie?' Franny said.

'A bear named *Susie?*' Frank said. He seemed irritated that it wasn't a German name, or that it was a female bear. It was a disappointment to most of us, I think—a kind of anticlimax before we'd really gotten started. But moving is like that. First the excitement, then the anxiety, then the letdown. First we took a cram course on Vienna, then we started missing the old Hotel New Hampshire—in advance. Then there was a period of *waiting*—interminable, and perhaps preparing us for some inevitable disappointment on that day of simultaneous departure and arrival, which the invention of the jet plane makes possible.

On the first of July we borrowed the Volkswagen bus belonging to Fritz's Act. It had funny hand controls, for braking and acceleration, because the midgets couldn't reach the foot pedals; Father and Frank argued over who would be more dexterous at driving the unusual vehicle. Finally, Fritz offered to drive the first shift to the airport.

Father, Frank, Franny, Lilly, and I were in the first shift. Mother and Egg would meet us in Vienna the next day; Sorrow would fly with them. But the morning we were leaving, Egg was up before me. He was sitting on his bed in a white dress shirt, and with his best dress pants and black dress shoes, and wearing a white linen jacket; he looked like one of the midgets—in their skit about crippled waiters in a fancy restaurant. Egg was waiting for me to wake up so that I could help him tie his tie. On the bed beside him, the great grinning dog, Sorrow, sat with the frozen idiot glee of the truly insane.

'You go *tomorrow,* Egg,' I said. *'We* go today, but you and Mother don't go until tomorrow.'

'I want to be ready,' Egg said, anxiously. I tied his tie for him —to humor him. He was dressing up Sorrow—in an appropriate flying costume—when I brought my bags down to the Volkswagen bus. Egg and Sorrow followed me downstairs.

'If you've room,' Mother said to Father, 'I wish one of you would take the dead dog.'

'No!' Egg said. 'I want Sorrow to stay with me!'

'You know, you can *check* him through with the bags,' Fritz said. 'It's not necessary to carry him on board.'

'He can sit in my lap,' Egg said. And that was that.

The trunks had been sent ahead of us.

The carry-on and check-through bags were packed.

The midgets were waving.

Hanging from the fire escape, at Ronda Ray's window, was her orange nightgown—once shocking, now faded, like the canvas for Fritz's Act.

Mrs. Urick and Max stood at the delivery entrance; Mrs. Urick had been scouring pans—she had her rubber gloves on —and Max was holding a leaf basket. 'Four hundred and sixty-four!' Max called.

Frank blushed; he kissed Mother. 'See you soon,' he said.

Franny kissed Egg. 'See you soon, Egg,' Franny said.

'What?' said Egg. He had undressed Sorrow; the beast was naked.

Lilly was crying.

'Four hundred and sixty-four!' Max Urick screamed, witlessly.

Ronda Ray was there, a little orange juice on her white

waitress uniform. 'Keep running, John-O,' she whispered, but nicely. She kissed me—she kissed everyone but Frank, who had crawled into the Volkswagen bus to avoid the contact.

Lilly kept crying; one of the midgets was riding Lilly's old bicycle. And just as we were leaving Elliot Park, the animals for Fritz's Act arrived. We saw the long flat-bed trailers, the cages, and the chains. Fritz had to stop the bus for a moment; he ran around, giving everyone directions.

In our own cage—in the Volkswagen bus—we peered at the animals; we had been wondering if they would be dwarf species.

'Ponies,' Lilly said, blubbering. 'And a chimpanzee.' In a cage with red elephants painted on its side—like a child's bedroom wallpaper—a big ape was shrieking.

'Perfectly ordinary animals,' Frank said.

A sled dog circled the bus, barking. One of the lady midgets began to ride the dog.

'No tigers,' said Franny, disappointed, 'no lions, no elephants.'

'See the bear?' said Father. In a gray cage, with nothing painted on it, a dark figure sat swaying in place, rocking to some sad inner tune—its nose too long, its rump too broad, its neck too thick, its paws too short to ever be happy.

'That's a bear?' Franny said.

There was a cage that looked full of geese, or chickens. It was mostly a dog and pony circus, it seemed—with one ape and one disappointing bear: mere tokens toward the exotic hopefulness in us all.

Looking back on them, in Elliot Park, as Fritz returned to the bus and drove us forward—to the airport and to Vienna—I saw that Egg still held in his arms the most exotic animal of them all. With Lilly crying beside me, I imagined I saw—in the chaos of moving midgets and unloading animals—a whole circus called Sorrow, instead of Fritz's Act. Mother waved, and Mrs. Urick and Ronda Ray waved with her. Max Urick was yelling, but we couldn't hear him. Franny's lips, in time with his, whispered, 'Four hundred and sixty-four!' Frank was already reading the German dictionary, and Father—who was not a man for looking back—sat up front with Fritz and talked rapidly about nothing at all. Lilly wept, but as harmlessly as rain. And Elliot Park disappeared: my last look caught Egg in motion, struggling to run among the midgets, Sorrow held like an idol above his head —an animal for all those other, *ordinary* animals to worship.

Egg was excited, and yelling, and Franny's lips—in time with his—whispered, 'What? What? What?'

Fritz drove us to Boston, where Franny had to shop for what Mother called 'city underwear'; Lilly wept her way through the lingerie aisles; Frank and I cruised the escalators. We were at the airport much too early. Fritz apologized for not being able to wait with us; his animals needed him, he said, and Father wished him well—thanking him, in advance, for driving Mother and Egg to the airport tomorrow. Frank was 'approached' in the men's room at Logan International, but he refused to describe the incident to Franny and me; he continued to say only that he had been 'approached.' He was indignant about it, and Franny and I were furious with him for not spelling it out to us in more detail. Father bought Lilly a plastic carry-on flight bag, to cheer her up, and we boarded the plane before dark. I think we took off about 7 or 8 P.M.: the lights of Boston, on a summer night, were half on and half off, and there was enough daylight left to see the harbor clearly. It was our first time on an airplane, and we loved it.

We flew all night across the ocean. Father slept the whole way. Lilly would not sleep; she watched the darkness, and reported sighting what she said were two ocean liners. I dozed and woke, dozed and woke again; with my eyes shut, I watched Elliot Park turning into a circus. Most places we leave in childhood grow less, not more, fancy. I imagined returning to Dairy, and wondered if Fritz's Act would improve or run down the neighborhood.

We landed in Frankfurt at quarter to eight in the morning. Maybe it was quarter to nine.

'Deutschland!' Frank said. He led us through the Frankfurt airport to our connecting flight to Vienna, reading all the signs out loud, speaking amiably to all the foreigners.

'We're the foreigners,' Franny kept whispering.

'Guten Tag!' Frank hailed all the passing strangers.

'Those people were French, Frank,' Franny said. 'I'm sure of it.'

Father almost lost the passports, so we attached them with two stout rubber bands to Lilly's wrist; then I carried Lilly, who seemed exhausted from her tears.

We left Frankfurt at quarter to nine, or maybe quarter to ten, and arrived in Vienna about noon. It was a short, choppy flight in a smaller plane; Lilly saw some mountains and was frightened; Franny said she hoped it would be smoother weather, the next day, for Mother and Egg; Frank vomited twice.

'Say it in German, Frank,' Franny said, but Frank felt too terrible to answer her.

We had a day and a night and the next morning to get the Gasthaus Freud ready for Mother and Egg. Our flight had totaled about eight hours in the air—about six or seven from Boston to Frankfurt, and another hour or so to Vienna. The flight that Mother and Egg were taking was supposed to leave Boston slightly later in the evening of the next day and fly to Zürich; their connecting flight, to Vienna, would take about an hour, and Boston to Zürich—like our flight to Frankfurt—was scheduled for about seven hours. But Mother and Egg—and Sorrow —landed short of Zürich. Less than six hours out of Boston, they struck the Atlantic Ocean a glancing blow—off the coastline of that part of the continent called France. In my imagination, later (and illogically), it was some slight consolation to know that they did not fall in darkness, and to imagine that there might—in *their* minds—have been some hopefulness implied by the vision of solid ground in the distance (though they did not reach the ground). It is too unlikely to imagine that Egg was sleeping, although anyone would hope so; knowing Egg, he would have been wide-awake the whole way—Sorrow jouncing on his knees. Egg would have had the window seat.

What went wrong, we were told, went wrong quickly; but surely there would have been time to blurt out some advice—in some language. And time for Mother to kiss Egg, and squeeze him; time for Egg to ask, 'What?'

And though we had moved to the city of Freud, I must say that dreams are vastly overrated: my dream of Mother's death was inexact, and I would never dream it again. Her death—by some considerable stretch of the imagination—might have been initiated by the man in the white dinner jacket, but no pretty white sloop sailed her away. She shot from the sky to the bottom of the sea with her son beside her screaming, Sorrow hugged to his chest.

It was Sorrow, of course, that the rescue planes saw. Searching for the sunken wreckage, trying to spot the first debris upon the surface of the gray morning water, someone saw a dog swimming. Closer examination convinced the rescue crew that the dog was just another victim; there were no survivors, and how could the rescue crew have known that *this* dog was already dead? This knowledge of what led the rescue crew to the bodies came as no surprise to my surviving family. We had learned this fact of Sorrow, previously, from Frank: Sorrow floats.

It was Franny who said, later that we must all watch out for whatever form Sorrow would take *next;* we must learn to recognize the different poses.

Frank was silent, pondering the responsibilities of resurrection—always a source of mystery to him, and now a source of pain.

Father had to identify the bodies; he left us in Freud's care and traveled by train. Later, he wouldn't speak often of Mother or Egg; he was not a backward-looking man, and his need to care for us no doubt prevented him from such indulgent and dangerous reflection. No doubt it would have crossed his mind that *this* was what Freud wanted Mother to forgive my father for.

Lilly would weep, knowing all along that Fritz's Act would have been smaller and easier to live with—all around.

And *I?* With Egg and Mother gone—and Sorrow in an unknown pose, or in disguise—I knew we had arrived in a foreign country.

8

Sorrow Floats

Ronda Ray, whose breathing first seduced me over an intercom —whose warm, strong, heavy hands I can still feel (occasionally) in my sleep—would never leave the first Hotel New Hampshire. She would remain faithful to Fritz's Act, and serve them well—perhaps discovering, as she grew older, that waiting on midgets and making their beds were altogether preferable to the services she'd rendered to more fully grown adults. One day Fritz would write us that Ronda Ray had died—'in her sleep.' After losing Mother and Egg, no death would ever strike me as 'appropriate,' though Franny said that Ronda's was.

It was more appropriate, at least, than the unfortunate passing of Max Urick, who succumbed to life in the Hotel New Hampshire in a bathtub on the third floor. Perhaps Max never got over his irritation at having to give up the smaller bathroom equipment, and his cherished hideaway on the fourth floor, because I imagine him plagued by the sense, if not by the actual sound, of the midgets living over his head. I always thought it was probably the same bathtub where Egg attempted to conceal Sorrow that finally did in Max—having come close to doing the job on Bitty Tuck. Fritz never explained which tub it was, just that it was on the third floor; Max had appeared to suffer a stroke while bathing—he subsequently drowned. That an old sailor who'd come back from the deep so many times should end it all in a bathtub was a source of anguish to poor Mrs. Urick, who found Max's leaving so *in*appropriate.

'Four hundred and sixty-four,' Franny would go on saying, whenever we mentioned Max.

Mrs. Urick is still the cook for Fritz's Act today—perhaps a testament to the food, and to the life, of plainness but goodness. One Christmas Lilly would send her a pretty handwritten scroll with these words from an anonymous poet, translated from the

Anglo-Saxon: 'They who live humbly have angels from heaven to carry them courage and strength and belief.'

Amen.

Fritz of Fritz's Act surely had similar angels looking after him. He would retire in Dairy, making the Hotel New Hampshire his year-round home (when he no longer hit the road, and the winter circus circuit, with the younger midgets). Lilly would get sad whenever she thought of him, because if it had been Fritz's size that first impressed her, it was the vision of staying in Fritz's Hotel New Hampshire (instead of going to Vienna) that Lilly imagined whenever she thought of Fritz—and Lilly would therefore imagine how all our lives might have been different if we had not lost Mother and Egg. No 'angels from heaven' had been on hand to save them.

But, of course, we had no such vision of the world when we first saw Vienna. *'Freud's* Vienna,' as Frank would say—and we knew which Freud he meant.

All over Vienna (in 1957) were the gaps between the buildings, were the buildings collapsed and airy, the buildings left as the bombs had left them. In some rubbled lots, often the perimeters of playgrounds abandoned by children, one had the feeling of unexploded bombs buried in the raked and orderly debris. Between the airport and the outer districts, we passed a Russian tank that had been firmly arranged—in concrete—as a kind of memorial. The tank's top hatch was sprouting flowers, its long barrel was draped with flags, its red star faded and speckled by birds. It was permanently parked in front of what looked like a post office, but our cab flew by too fast for us to be sure.

Sorrow floats, but we arrived in Vienna before our bad news arrived, and we were inclined toward a cautious optimism. The war damage was more contained as we approached the inner districts; on occasion, even the sun shone through the elaborate buildings—and a row of stone cupids leaned off a roof over us, their bellies pockmarked by machine-gun fire. More people appeared in the streets, though the outer districts resembled one of those old sepia photographs taken at a time of day before everyone was up—or after everyone had been killed.

'It's spooky,' Lilly ventured; out of fright, she had finally stopped crying.

'It's *old,*' Franny said.

'Wo ist die Gemütlichkeit?' Frank sang, cheerfully—looking around for some.

'I think your mother will like it here,' Father said, optimistically.

'Egg won't like it,' Franny said.

'Egg won't be able to *hear* it,' Frank said.

'Mother will hate it, too,' Lilly said.

'Four hundred and sixty-four,' Franny said.

Our driver said something unintelligible. Even Father could tell it wasn't German. Frank struggled to talk with the man and discovered he was Hungarian—from the recent revolution. We searched the rearview mirror, and our driver's dull eyes, for signs of lasting wounds—imagining them, if not seeing them. Then a park burst beside us, on our right, and a building as lovely as a palace (it *was* a palace), and out a courtyard gate came a cheerful fat woman in a nurse's uniform (clearly a nanny) pushing in front of her a double-seater baby carriage (someone had had twins!), and Frank read an idiot statistic from a mindless travel brochure.

'A city of fewer than one and a half million people,' Frank read to us, 'Vienna still has more than three hundred coffee-houses!' We stared out of our cab at the streets, expecting them to be stained with coffee. Franny rolled down her window and sniffed; there was the diesel rankness of Europe, but no coffee. It would not take us long to learn what coffeehouses were for: for sitting a long time, for homework, for talking to whores, for darts, for billiards, for drinking more than coffee, for making plans—for our escape—and of course for insomnia, and for dreams. But then we were dazzled by the fountain at the Schwarzenbergplatz, we crossed the Ringstrasse, jolly with streetcars, and our driver began chanting to himself, 'Kruger-strasse, Krugerstrasse,' as if by this repetition the little street would leap out at us (it did), and then: 'Gasthaus Freud, Gasthaus Freud.'

The Gasthaus Freud did *not* leap out at us. Our driver slowly drove right by it, and Frank ran into the Kaffe Mowatt to ask directions; it was then pointed out to us—the building we had missed. Gone was the candy store (although the signs for the former Konditorei—BONBONS, and so forth—were leaning against the window, inside). Father assumed this meant that Freud—in preparation for our arrival—had begun the expansion plans, had bought out the candy store. But, upon closer inspection, we realized that a fire had destroyed the Konditorei and must have at least threatened the inhabitants of the adjacent Gasthaus Freud. We entered the small, dark hotel, passing the new sign by the gutted candy store; the sign, Frank translated, said: DON'T STEP ON THE SUGAR.

'Don't step on the *sugar,* Frank?' Franny said.

'That's what it says,' Frank said, and indeed, entering cautiously into the lobby of the Gasthaus Freud, we felt a certain stickiness on the floor (no doubt from those feet that had already trafficked on the sugar—the hideous glaze from the candy melted in the fire). And now the ghastly smell of burnt chocolate overwhelmed us. Lilly, staggering with her little bags, stumbled into the lobby first, and screamed.

We were expecting Freud, but we had forgotten Freud's bear. Lilly had not expected to see it in the lobby—loose. And none of us expected to see it on the couch by the reception desk, its short legs crossed while it rested its heels on a chair; it appeared to be reading a magazine (an apparently 'smart bear' as Freud had claimed), but Lilly's scream startled the pages right out of its paws and it gathered itself together in a bearlike fashion. It swung itself off the couch and ambled sideways toward the reception desk, not really looking at us, and we saw how small it was—squat, but short; no longer or taller than a Labrador retriever (we all were thinking), but considerably denser, thick-waisted, big-assed, stout-armed. It rose up on its hind legs and gave the bell on the reception desk a terrible clout, bashing the bell so violently that the little *ping!* was muffled by the thump of the animal's paw.

'Jesus God!' said Father.

'Is that *you?*' cried a voice. 'Is that Win Berry?'

The bear, impatient that Freud had still not emerged, picked up the bell on the reception desk and whistled it across the lobby; the bell struck a door with great force—with the sound of a hammer banging an organ pipe.

'I hear you!' Freud cried. 'Jesus God! Is that *you?*' And he came out of the room with open arms—a figure as strange to us children as any bear. It was the first time we children realized that Father had *learned* his 'Jesus God!' from Freud, and perhaps the contrast this information made with Freud's body was what surprised us; Freud's body bore no resemblance to my father's athletic shape and movements. If Fritz had allowed his midgets to vote, Freud might have been admitted to their circus —he was only slightly larger than they were. His body seemed stricken with something like an abridged history of his former power; he was now simply solid and compact. The black hair we'd been told about was white and long with the fly-around

quality of corn silk. He had a cane like a club, like a baseball bat
—which we realized, later, *was* a baseball bat. The strange patch
of hair that grew on his cheek was still the size of an average
coin, but its color was as gray as a sidewalk—the nondescript
and neglected color of a city street. But the main thing (about
how Freud had aged) was that he was blind.

'Is that *you?*' Freud called across the lobby, facing not Father
but the ancient iron post that began the banister of the staircase.

'Over here,' my father said, softly. Freud opened his arms
and groped toward my father's voice.

'Win Berry!' Freud cried, and the bear swiftly rushed to him,
caught the old man's elbow with its rough paw, and propelled
him in my father's direction. When Freud slowed his pace,
fearful of chairs out of place, or feet to trip over, the bear butted
him with its head from behind. Not just a smart bear, we
children thought: here was a Seeing Eye bear. Freud now had a
bear to see for him. Unquestionably, this was the kind of bear
who could change your life.

We watched the blind gnome hugging my father; we watched
their awkward dance in the dingy lobby of the Gasthaus Freud.
As their voices softened, we could hear the typewriters going at
it from the third floor—the radicals making their music, the
leftists writing up their versions of the world. Even the typewriters sounded sure of themselves—at odds with all those other,
flawed versions of the world, but sure they were right, absolutely believing it, every word tap-tap-tapping into place, like
fingers drumming impatiently on tabletops, fingers marking time
between speeches.

But wasn't this better than arriving at night? Admittedly, the
lobby would have looked better cared for under the mellow glow
of inadequate lighting and the forgiveness of darkness. But
wasn't it better (for us children) to hear the typewriters, and see
the bear—better than to hear (or imagine) the lunging of beds,
the traffic of the prostitutes going up and down the stairs, the
guilty greetings and good-byes (going on all night) in the lobby?

The bear nosed between us children. Lilly was wary of it (it
was bigger than she was), I felt shy, Frank tried to be friendly
—in German—but the bear had eyes only for Franny. The bear
pressed its broad head against Franny's waist; the bear jabbed its
snout in my sister's crotch. Franny jumped, and laughed, and
Freud said, 'Susie! Are you being nice? Are you being rude?'
Susie the bear turned to him and made a short run at him, on all
fours; the bear butted the old man in the stomach—knocking him

230

to the floor. My father seemed inclined to intervene, but Freud
—leaning on the baseball bat—got back to his feet. It was hard
to tell if he was chuckling. 'Oh, Susie!' he said, in the wrong
direction. 'Susie's just showing off. She don't like criticism,'
Freud said. 'And she's not so fond of men as she is of the *girls*.
Where *are* the girls?' the old man said, his hands held out in two
directions, and Franny and Lilly went to him—Susie the bear
following Franny, nudging her affectionately from behind.
Frank, suddenly obsessed with making friends with the bear,
tugged the animal's coarse fur, stammering, 'Uh, you must be
Susie the bear. We've all heard a lot about you. I'm Frank.
Sprechen Sie Deutsch?'

'No, no,' said Freud, 'not German. Susie don't like German.
She speaks *your* language,' Freud said in Frank's general
direction.

Frank, oafishly, bent down to the bear, tugging its fur again.
'Do you shake hands, Susie?' Frank asked, bending down, but
the bear turned to face him; the bear stood up.

'She's not being rude, is she?' Freud cried. 'Susie, be nice!
Don't be rude.' Standing up, the bear wasn't as tall as any of us
—except she was taller than Lilly, and she was taller than Freud.
The bear's snout came to Frank's chin. They stood face to face,
for a moment, the bear shifting its weight on its hind legs,
shuffling like a boxer.

'I'm Frank,' Frank said nervously to the bear, holding out his
hand; then, with both hands, he tried to grasp the bear's right
paw and shake it.

'Keep your hands to yourself, kid,' the bear said to Frank,
cuffing Frank's arms apart with a swift, short blow. Frank,
reeling backwards, stumbled on the reception bell—which made
a quick *ping!*

'How'd you do that?' Franny asked Freud. 'How'd you make
it talk?'

'Nobody makes me talk, honey,' Susie the bear said, nuzzling
Franny's hip.

Lilly screamed again. 'The bear talks, the bear talks!' she
cried.

'She's a *smart* bear!' Freud shouted. 'Didn't I tell you?'

'The bear talks!' Lilly screamed, hysterically.

'At least I don't scream,' Susie the bear said. Then she
dropped all semblance of bearlike mannerisms; she walked
upright, and sullenly, back to the couch—where Lilly's first
scream had disturbed her. She sat down and crossed her legs and

put her feet on the chair. It was *Time* magazine that she was reading, a rather out-of-date issue.

'Susie's from Michigan,' Freud said, as if this explained everything. 'But she went to college in New York. She's very smart.'

'I went to Sarah Lawrence,' the bear said, 'but I dropped out. What an elitist crock of shit,' she said—of Sarah Lawrence —the world of *Time* magazine passing impatiently through her paws.

'She's a *girl* ' Father said. 'It's a girl in a bear suit!'

'A *woman*,' Susie said. 'Watch it.' It was only 1957; Susie was a bear ahead of her time.

'A woman in a bear suit,' Frank said, with Lilly sliding against me and clutching my leg.

'There are no smart bears,' Freud said, ominously. 'Except this kind.'

Upstairs, the typewriters were quarreling over our stunned silence. We regarded Susie the bear—a smart bear, indeed; and a Seeing Eye bear, too. Knowing she was not a real bear suddenly made her appear larger; she took on new power before us. She was more than Freud's eyes, we thought; she might be his heart and mind, too.

Father viewed the lobby, while his old, blind mentor leaned on him for support. And what was Father seeing *this* time? I wondered. What castle, what palace, what deluxe-class possibility looming larger and larger—as he passed over the sagging couch where the she-bear sat, passed over the imitation Impressionists: the pink, bovine nudes fallen in flowers of light (on the clashing floral wallpaper)? And the easy chair with its stuffing exploding (like the bombs to be imagined under all the debris in the outer districts); and the one reading lamp too dim to dream by.

'Too bad about the candy store,' Father said to Freud.

'Too bad?' Freud cried. '*Nein, nein, nicht* too bad! It's *good*. The place is gone, and they had no insurance. We can buy them up—cheap! Give ourselves a lobby people will *notice*—from the street!' Freud cried, though of course there was nothing his own eyes would notice, or could. 'A very fortunate fire,' Freud said, 'a fire perfectly timed for your arrival,' Freud said, squeezing my father's arm. 'A brilliant fire!' Freud said.

'A smart bear's sort of fire,' said Susie the bear, cynically tearing her way through the old issue of *Time*.

'Did you set it?' Franny asked Susie the bear.

232

'You bet your sweet ass, honey,' Susie said.

Oh, there once was a woman who had also been raped, but when I told her Franny's story, and how it seemed to me that Franny had handled it—by *not* handling it, perhaps, or by denying the worst of it—this woman told me that Franny and I were wrong.

'Wrong?' I said.

'You bet your ass,' this woman said. 'Franny was raped, not beaten up. And those bastards *did* get the "her in her"—as your bullshit black friend calls it. What's *he* know? A rape expert because he's got a sister? *Your* sister robbed herself of the only weapon she had against those punks—their semen. And nobody stopped her from washing herself, nobody made her *deal* with it —so she's going to be dealing with it all her life. In fact, she sacrificed her own integrity by not fighting her attackers in the first place—and *you,'* this woman said to me, 'you conveniently diffused the rape of your sister and robbed the rape of *its* integrity by running off to find the hero instead of staying on the scene and *dealing* with it yourself.'

'A rape has integrity?' Frank asked.

'I went to get help,' I said. 'They just would have beaten the shit out of me and raped her, anyway.'

'I've got to talk to your sister, honey,' this woman said. 'She's into her own amateurish psychology and it won't work, believe me: I know rape.'

'Whoa!' Iowa Bob said, once. '*All* psychology is amateurish. Fuck Freud, and all that!'

'*That* Freud, anyway,' my father had added. And I would think, later: Maybe *our* Freud, too.

Anyway, this rape-expert woman said that Franny's apparent reaction to her own rape was bullshit; and knowing that Franny still wrote letters to Chipper Dove made me wonder. The rape-expert woman said that rape simply wasn't like that, that it didn't have that effect—at all. She knew, she said. It had happened to her. And in college she'd joined a kind of club of women who'd all been raped, and they had agreed among themselves *exactly* what it was like, and what were the *exactly* correct responses to have to it. Even before she started talking to Franny, I could see how desperately important this woman's private unhappiness was to her, and how—in her mind—the only credible reaction to the event of rape was *hers*. That someone else might have responded differently to a similar abuse

233

only meant to her that the abuse couldn't possibly have been the same.

'People are like that,' Iowa Bob would have said. 'They need to make their own worst experiences universal. It gives them a kind of support.'

And who can blame them? It is just infuriating to argue with someone like that; because of an experience that has denied them their humanity, they go around denying another kind of humanity in others, which is the truth of human variety—it stands alongside our sameness. Too bad for her.

'She probably has had a most unhappy life,' Iowa Bob would have said.

Indeed: this woman *had* had a most unhappy life. This rape-expert woman was Susie the bear.

'What's this "little event among so many" bullshit?' Susie the bear asked Franny. 'What's this "luckiest day of my life" bullshit?' Susie asked her. 'Those thugs didn't just want to *fuck* you, honey, they wanted to take your strength away, and you let them. Any woman who accepts a violation of herself so *passively* . . . how you can actually *say* that you knew, somehow, Chip Dove would be "the first." Sweetheart! You have *minimized* the *enormity* of what has happened to you—just to make it a little easier to take.'

'Whose rape is it?' Franny asked Susie the bear. 'I mean, you've got yours, I've got mine. If I say nobody got the me in me, then nobody got it. You think they get it every time?'

'You bet your sweet ass, honey,' Susie said. 'A rapist is using his prick as a weapon. Nobody uses a weapon on you without *getting* you. For example,' said Susie the bear, 'how's your sex life these days?'

'She's only sixteen,' I said. 'She's not supposed to have such a great sex life—at sixteen.'

'I'm not confused,' Franny said. 'There's sex and then there's rape,' she said. 'Day and night.'

'Then how come you keep saying Chipper Dove was "the first," Franny?' I asked her quietly.

'You bet your ass—that's the point,' said Susie the bear.

'Look,' Franny said to us—with Frank uncomfortably playing solitaire and pretending not to listen; with Lilly following our conversation like a championship tennis match that demanded reverence for every stroke. 'Look,' Franny said, 'the point is I own my own rape. It's mine. I *own* it. I'll deal with it my way.'

'But you're *not* dealing with it,' Susie said. 'You never got

234

angry enough. You've got to get angry. You've got to get savage about all the facts.'

'You've got to get obsessed and stay obsessed,' said Frank, rolling his eyes and quoting old Iowa Bob.

'I'm serious,' said Susie the bear. She was *too* serious, of course—but more likable than she at first appeared. Susie the bear would finally get rape right, after a while. She would run a very fine rape crisis center, later in her life, and she would write in the very first line of advice in the rape-counseling literature that the matter of 'Who Owns the Rape' is the most important matter. She would finally understand that although her anger was essentially healthy for her, it might not have been the healthiest thing for Franny, at the time. 'Allow the Victim to Ventilate,' she would wisely write in her counseling newsletter—and: 'Keep Your own Problems Separate from the Problems of the Victim.' Later, Susie the bear would really become a rape-expert woman—she of the famous line 'Watch Out: the real issue of each rape may not be *your* real issue; kindly consider there might be more than one.' And to all her rape counselors she would impart this advice: 'It is essential to understand that there is no one way that victims respond and adjust to this crisis. Any one victim might exhibit all, none, or any combination of the usual symptoms: guilt, denial, anger, confusion, fear, or something quite different. And problems might occur within a week, a year, ten years, or never.'

Very true; Iowa Bob would have liked this bear as much as he liked Earl. But in her first days with us, Susie was a bear on the rape issue—and on a lot of other issues, too.

And we were forced into an intimacy with her that was unnatural because we would suddenly need to turn to her as we would turn to a mother (in the absence of our own mother); after a while, we would turn to Susie for other things. Almost immediately this smart (though harsh) bear seemed more all-seeing than the blind Freud, and from our first day and night in our new hotel we turned to Susie the bear for *all* our information.

'Who are the people with the typewriters?' I asked her.

'How much do the prostitutes charge?' Lilly asked her.

'Where can I buy a good map?' Frank asked her. 'Preferably, one that indicates walking tours.'

'Walking tours, Frank?' Franny said.

'Show the children their rooms, Susie,' Freud instructed his smart bear.

Somehow, we all went first to Egg's room, which was the

235

worst room—a room with two doors and no windows, a cube with a door connecting it to Lilly's room (which was only one window better) and a door entering the ground-floor lobby.

'Egg won't like it,' Lilly said, but Lilly was predicting that Egg wouldn't like any of it: the move, the whole thing. I suspect she was right, and whenever I think of Egg, now, I tend to see him in his room in the Gasthaus Freud that he never saw. Egg in an airless, windowless box, a tiny trapped space in the heart of a foreign hotel—a room unfit for guests.

The typical tyranny of families: the youngest child always gets the worst room. Egg would not have been happy in the Gasthaus Freud, and I wonder now if any of us could have been. Of course, we didn't have a fair start. We had only a day and a night before the news of Mother and Egg would settle over us, before Susie became *our* Seeing Eye bear, too, and Father and Freud began their duet in the direction of a grand hotel—a successful hotel, at the very least, they hoped; if not a great hotel, at least a good one.

On the day of arrival, Father and Freud were already making plans. Father wanted to move the prostitutes to the fifth floor, and move the Symposium on East-West Relations to the fourth floor, thereby clearing floors two and three for guests.

'Why should the paying guests have to climb to the fourth and fifth floors?' Father asked Freud.

'The prostitutes,' Freud reminded my father, 'are also paying guests.' He didn't need to add that they also made a number of trips every night. 'And some of their clients are too old for all those stairs,' Freud added.

'If they're too old for the stairs,' Susie the bear said, 'they're too old for the dirty action, too. Better to have one croak on the stairs than to have one give up the ship in bed—on top of one of the smaller girls.'

'Jesus God,' said Father. 'Maybe give the prostitutes the second floor, then. And make the damn radicals move to the top.'

'Intellectuals,' Freud said, 'are in notorious bad shape.'

'Not all these radicals are intellectuals,' Susie said. 'And we should have an elevator, eventually,' she added. 'I'm for keeping the whores close to the ground and letting the thinkers do the climbing.'

'Yes, and put the guests in between,' Father said.

'*What* guests?' Franny asked. She and Frank had checked the registration; the Gasthaus Freud had no guests.

236

'It's just the candy fire,' Freud said. 'It smoked out the guests. Once we get the lobby right, the guests will pour in!'

'And the fucking will keep them awake all night, and the typewriters will wake them up in the morning,' said Susie the bear.

'A kind of bohemian hotel,' Frank said, optimistically.

'What do you know about bohemians, Frank?' Franny asked.

In Frank's room was a dressmaker's dummy, formerly the property of a prostitute who had kept a permanent room in the hotel. It was a stoutish dummy, upon which perched the chipped head of a mannequin Freud claimed had been stolen from one of the big department stores on the Kärntnerstrasse. A pretty but pitted face with her wig askew.

'Perfect for all your costume changes, Frank,' Franny said. Frank sullenly hung his coat on it.

'Very funny,' he said.

Franny's room adjoined mine. We shared a bath with an ancient bathtub in it; the tub was deep enough to stew an ox in. The W.C. was down the hall and directly off the lobby. Only Father's room had its own bath and its own W.C. It appeared that Susie shared the bath Franny and I shared, although she could enter it only through one of our rooms.

'Don't sweat it,' Susie said. 'I don't wash a whole lot.'

We could tell. The odor was not exactly bear, but it was acrid, salty, rich, and strong, and when she took her bear's head off, and we first saw her dark, damp hair—her pale, pockmarked face, and her haggard, nervous eyes—we felt more comfortable with her appearance as a bear.

'What you see,' Susie said, 'are the ravishments of acne—my teen-age misery. I am the original not-bad-if-you-put-a-bag-over-her-head girl.'

'Don't feel bad,' said Frank. 'I'm a homosexual. I'm not in for such a hot time as a teen-ager, either.'

'Well, at least you're attractive,' said Susie the bear. 'Your whole family is *attractive*,' she said, darting a mean look at us all. 'You may get discriminated against, but let me tell you: there's no discrimination quite like the Ugly Treatment. I was an ugly kid and I just get uglier, every fucking day.'

We couldn't help staring at her in the bear costume without the head; we wondered, of course, if Susie's own body was as burly as a bear's. And when we saw her later in the afternoon, sweating in her T-shirt and gym shorts, doing squats and knee bends against the wall of Freud's office—warming up for her role when the radicals checked out for the day and the prostitutes came on at night—we could see she was physically suited to her particular form of animal imitation.

'Pretty chunky, huh?' she said to me. Too many bananas, Iowa Bob might have said; and not enough road work.

But—to be fair—it was hard for Susie to go anywhere *not* dressed, and performing, as a bear. Exercise is difficult when dressed as a bear.

'I can't blow my cover or we're in trouble,' she said.

Because how could Freud ever keep order without her? Susie the bear was the enforcer. When the radicals were bothered by trouble-makers from the Right, when there were violent shouting matches in the hall and on the staircase, when some new-wave fascist started screaming, 'Nothing is free!'—when a small mob came to protest in the lobby, carrying the banner that said the Symposium on East-West Relations should move . . . farther East—it was at these times that Freud needed her, Susie said.

'Get out, you're making the bear hostile!' Freud would shout.

Sometimes it took a low growl and a short charge.

'It's funny,' Susie said. 'I'm not really so tough, but no one tries to fight a bear. All I have to do is grab someone and they roll into a ball and start moaning. I just sort of *breathe* on the bastards, I just kind of lay a little weight on them. No one fights back if you're a bear.'

Because of the radicals' gratitude for this bearish protection, there was really no problem telling the radicals to move upstairs. My father and Freud explained their case in midafternoon. Father offered me as a typewriter mover, and I began carrying the machines up to the empty fifth-floor rooms. There were a half-dozen typewriters and a mimeograph machine; the usual office supplies; a seeming excess of telephones. I got a little tired with the third or fourth desk, but I hadn't been doing my usual weight lifting—while we were traveling—and so I appreciated the exercise. I asked a couple of the younger radicals if they knew where I could get a set of barbells, but they seemed very suspicious—that we were Americans—and either they didn't understand English or they chose to speak their own language. There was a brief protest from an older radical, who struck up what appeared to be quite a lively argument with Freud, but Susie the bear started whining and rolling her head around the old man's ankles—as if she were trying to blow her nose on the cuffs of his pants—and he calmed down and climbed the stairs, even though *he* knew Susie wasn't a real bear.

'What are they writing?' Franny asked Susie. 'I mean, is it one of those newsletter kind of things, is it propaganda?'

'Why do they have so many phones?' I asked, because we hadn't heard the phones ringing, not once—not all day.

'They make a lot of outgoing calls,' Susie said. 'I think they're into threatening phone calls. And I don't read their newsletters. I'm not into their politics.'

'But what *are* their politics?' Frank asked.

'To change fucking everything,' Susie said. 'To start again. They want to wipe the slate clean. They want a whole new ball game.'

'So do I,' said Frank. 'That sounds like a good idea.'

'They're scary,' said Lilly. 'They look right over you, and they don't see you when they're looking right at you.'

'Well, you're pretty short,' said Susie the bear. 'They sure look at *me*, a lot.'

'And one of them looks at Franny, a lot,' I said.

'That's not what I mean,' said Lilly. 'I mean they don't see *people* when they look at you.'

'That's because they're thinking about how everything could be different,' Frank said.

'People, too, Frank?' Franny asked. 'Do they think *people* could be different? Do *you?*'

'Yeah,' said Susie the bear. 'Like we could all be dead.'

Grief makes everything intimate; in our grieving for Mother and Egg, we got to know the radicals and whores as if we had always known them. We were the bereft children, motherless (to the whores), our golden brother slain (to the radicals). And so —to compensate for our gloom, and the added gloom of the conditions in the Gasthaus Freud—the radicals and whores treated us pretty well. And despite their day-and-night differences, they bore more similarities to each other than *they* might have supposed.

They both believed in the commercial possibilities of a simple ideal: they both believed they could, one day, be 'free.' They both thought that their own bodies were objects easily sacrificed for a cause (and easily restored, or replaced, after the hardship of the sacrifice). Even their names were similar—if for different reasons. They had only code names, or nicknames, or if they used their real names, they used only their first names.

Two of them actually shared the same name, but there was no confusion, since the radical was male, the whore was female,

239

and they were never at the Gasthaus Freud at the same time. The name was Old Billig—*billig*, in German, means 'cheap.' The oldest whore was called this because her prices were substandard for the district of the city she strolled; the Krugerstrasse whores, although Krugerstrasse was in the First District, were themselves a sort of subdistrict to the Kärntnerstrasse whores (around the corner). If you turned off the Kärntnerstrasse onto our tiny street, it was as if you were lowering yourself (by comparison) into a world without light, one street off the Kärntnerstrasse you lost the glow of the Hotel Sacher, and the grand gleam of the State Opera, and you noticed how the whores wore more eyeshadow, how their knees buckled, slightly, or their ankles appeared to cave in (from standing too long), or how they appeared to be thicker in the waist—like the dressmaker's dummy in Frank's room. Old Billig was the captain of the Krugerstrasse whores.

Her namesake, among the radicals, was the old gentleman who had argued most ferociously with Freud about moving to the fifth floor. *This* Old Billig had earned his 'cheap' designation for his reputation of leading a hand-to-mouth existence—and his history of being what the other radicals called 'a radical's radical.' When there were Bolsheviks, he was one; when the names changed, he changed his name. He was at the forefront of every movement, but—somehow—when the movement ran amok or into terminal trouble, Old Billig took up the rear position and discreetly trailed away out of sight, waiting for the next forefront. The idealists among the younger radicals were both suspicious of Old Billig and admiring of his endurance —his survival. This was not unlike the view held of Old Billig, the whore, by *her* colleagues.

Seniority is an institution that is revered and resented in and out of society.

Like Old Billig the radical, Old Billig the whore was the most argumentative with Freud about changing floors.

'But you're going *down*,' Freud said, 'you'll have to climb one *less* flight of stairs. In a hotel with no elevator, the second floor is an *improvement* over the third.'

I could follow Freud's German, but not Old Billig's answer. Frank told me that she protested on the grounds of having too many 'mementos' to move.

'Look at this boy!' Freud said, groping around for me. 'Look at his muscles!' Freud, of course, 'looked' at my muscles by feeling them; squeezing and punching me, he shoved me in the general direction of the old whore. 'Feel him!' Freud cried. 'He can move every memento you got. If we gave him a day, he could move the whole hotel!'

And Frank told me what Old Billig said. 'I don't need to feel any more muscles,' Old Billig told Freud, declining the offer to squeeze me. 'I feel muscles in my frigging *sleep,*' she said. 'Sure he can move the mementos,' she said. 'But I don't want nothing broken.'

And so I moved Old Billig's 'mementos' with the greatest of care. A collection of china bears that rivaled Mother's collection (and after Mother's death, Old Billig would invite me to visit her room in the daylight hours—when she was off duty, and gone from the Gasthaus Freud—and I could spend a quiet time alone with her bears, remembering Mother's collection, which perished with her). Old Billig also liked plants—plants that leaped out of those pots designed to resemble animals and birds: flowers springing from the backs of frogs, ferns sprawling over a grove of flamingos, an orange tree sprouting from the head of an alligator. The other whores mostly had changes of clothes and cosmetics and medicines to move. It was strange to think of them as having only 'night rooms' at the Gasthaus Freud—as opposed to Ronda Ray having her 'dayroom'; it struck me how dayrooms and night rooms were used for similar purposes.

We met the whores that first night we helped them move from the third to the second floor. There were four whores on the Krugerstrasse, plus Old Billig. Their names were Babette, Jolanta, Dark Inge, and Screaming Annie. Babette was called Babette because she was the only one who spoke French; she tended to get most of the French customers (the French being most sensitive about speaking any language but French). Babette was small—and therefore Lilly's favorite—with a pixie face that the somber light in the lobby of the Gasthaus Freud could cause to look (at certain angles) unpleasantly rodentlike. In later years I would think of Babette as probably anoretic, without knowing it—none of us knew what anorexia was, in 1957. She wore flowery prints, very summerlike dresses—even when it wasn't summer—and she had a funny kind of overpowdered sense about her (as if, if you touched her, a small puff of powder would blast through her pores); at other times, her skin had a waxiness about it (as if, if you touched her, your finger might leave a dent). Lilly told me once that Babette's smallness was an important part of her (Lilly's) growing up, because Babette helped Lilly realize that small people could actually have sex with large people and not be altogether destroyed. That's how Lilly liked to put it: 'Not *altogether* destroyed.'

Jolanta called herself Jolanta because she said it was a Polish name and she was fond of Polish jokes. She was square-faced, strong-looking, as big as Frank (and nearly as awkward); she gave off a heartiness that you suspected of being false—as if, in the middle of a booming good joke, she might turn suddenly sour and produce a knife from her handbag or grind a wineglass into someone's face. She was broad-shouldered and heavy-breasted, solid in her legs but not fat—Jolanta had the robust charm of a peasant who'd been strangely corrupted by a sneaky sort of city violence; she looked erotic, but dangerous. In my first days and nights at the Gasthaus Freud it was *her* image I most often masturbated to—it was Jolanta I had the greatest trouble speaking to, not because she was the most coarse but because I was the most afraid of her.

'How can you recognize a Polish prostitute?' she asked me. I had to ask Frank for a translation. 'Because she pays *you* to fuck *her*,' Jolanta said. This I understood without Frank's help.

'Did you get it?' Frank asked me.

'Jesus, yes, Frank,' I said.

'Then laugh,' Frank said. 'You'd better laugh.' And I looked at Jolanta's hands—she had the wrists of a farmer, the knuckles of a boxer—and laughed.

Dark Inge was not a laugher. She'd had a most unhappy life. More important, she had not lived very *much* of her life, yet; she was only eleven. A mulatto—with an Austrian mother and a black American G.I. for her father—she'd been born at the start of the occupation. Her father had left with the occupying powers, in 1955, and nothing he'd told Inge or her mother about the treatment of black people in the United States had made them want to go with him. Dark Inge's English was the best among the whores, and when Father left for France—to identify the bodies of Mother and Egg—it was Dark Inge we spent most of our sleepless nights with. She was as tall as I was, although she was only Lilly's age, and the way they dressed her up made her look as old as Franny. Lithe and pretty and mocha-colored, she worked as a tease; she was not a real whore.

She was not allowed to stroll the Krugerstrasse without another whore beside her, unless she strolled the Krugerstrasse with Susie the bear; when any man wanted her, he was told he could only look at her—and touch himself. Dark Inge was not old enough to be touched, and no man was allowed to be alone in a room with her. If a man wanted to be with her, Susie the bear kept them company. It was a simple system, but it worked. If a man looked as if he was about to touch Dark Inge, Susie the bear would make the necessary sounds and gestures preparatory to a charge. If the man asked Dark Inge to take off too many clothes, or if he insisted she *look* at him while he masturbated, Susie the bear would get restless. 'You're making the bear hostile,' Dark Inge would warn the man, who would leave—or else finish masturbating quickly, while Dark Inge looked away.

All the whores knew that Susie the bear could get to their rooms in a matter of seconds. All it required was some cry of distress, because Susie—like any well-trained animal—knew all their voices by heart. Babette's nasal little yelp, Jolanta's violent bellow, Old Billig's shattering 'mementos.' But to us children the worst customers were the shame-faced men who masturbated to only the most modest glimpses of Dark Inge.

'I don't think *I* could beat off with a bear in my room,' Frank said.

'I don't think you could beat off with *Susie* in your room, Frank,' Franny said.

Lilly shuddered, and I joined her. With Father in France —with those bodies most important to us—we viewed the body traffic in the Gasthaus Freud with that detachment peculiar to mourners.

'When I get old enough,' Dark Inge told us, 'I can charge for the real thing.' It surprised us children that 'the real thing' cost more money than beating off while watching Inge.

Dark Inge's mother was planning to get Inge out of the business by the time her daughter was 'old enough.' Dark Inge's mother planned to retire her daughter before her daughter came of age. Dark Inge's mother was the fifth lady of the night in the Gasthaus Freud—the one called Screaming Annie. She made more money than any other whore on the Krugerstrasse, because she was working for a respectable retirement (for her daughter *and* for herself).

If you wanted a frail flower, or a little French, you asked for Babette. If you wanted experience, and a bargain, you got Old Billig. If you courted danger—if you liked a touch of violence —you could take your chances with Jolanta. If you were ashamed of yourself, you could pay to steal a look at Dark Inge. And if you desired the ultimate deception, you went with Screaming Annie.

As Susie the bear said, 'Screaming Annie's got the best fake orgasm in the business.'

Screaming Annie's fake orgasm could jar Lilly out of her worst nightmares, it could cause Frank to sit bolt upright in bed and howl in terror at the dark figure of the dressmaker's dummy lurking at the foot of his bed, it could rip me out of the deepest sleep—suddenly wide-awake, with an erection, or grabbing my own throat to feel where it was slashed. Screaming Annie, in my opinion, was an argument—all by herself—for *not* having the whores occupy the floor most immediately above our own.

She could even stir Father out of his grief—even upon his immediate return from France. 'Jesus God,' he would say, and come to kiss each of us, and see if we were safe.

Only Freud could sleep through it. 'Leave it to Freud,' Frank said, 'to not be fooled by a fake orgasm.' Frank thought himself very clever for this oft-repeated remark—because, of course, he meant the *other* Freud, not our blind manager.

Screaming Annie could sometimes fool even Susie the bear, who would grumble, 'God, that's got to be a *real* one.' Or, worse, Susie would occasionally confuse a fake orgasm with a possible scream for *help*. *'That's* nobody *coming,* for Christ's sake!' Susie would roar, reminding me of Ronda Ray. 'That is somebody *dying!'* And she would go bawling down the second-floor hall, throw herself against Screaming Annie's door, charge the wrecked bed with her terrifying snarls—causing Screaming Annie's mate to fly, or faint, or wither on the spot. And Screaming Anne would say, mildly, 'No no, Susie, nothing's wrong. He's a *nice* man.' By which time it was often too late to revive the man—at the very least reduced to a cringing, shrunken shape of fear.

'That's the ultimate guilt trip,' Franny used to say. 'Just when some guy's about to get off, a bear busts into the room and starts mauling him.'

'Actually, honey,' Susie told Franny, 'I think some of them get off on *that.'*

Were there actually some customers at the Gasthaus Freud who could *only* come when attacked by a bear? I wondered. But we were too young; we would never know some things about that place. Like the ghouls of all our Halloweens past, the clientele in the Gasthaus Freud would never be quite real for us. At least not the whores, and their customers—and not the radicals.

244

Old Billig (the *radical* Old Billig) was the first to arrive. Like Iowa Bob, he said he was too old to waste what was left of his life asleep. He got there so early in the morning that he occasionally passed the last whore on his way in, her way out. This was inevitably Screaming Annie, working the hardest hours —to save herself and her dark daughter.

Susie the bear slept in the early morning hours. There was little whore trouble after dawn, as if the light kept people safe —if not always honest—and the radicals never started quarreling before midmorning. Most of the radicals were late sleepers. They wrote their manifestos all day, and made their threatening phone calls. They harassed each other—'in the absence of more tangible enemies,' Father would say of them. Father, after all, was a capitalist. Who else could even imagine the perfect hotel? Who but a capitalist, and a basic non-rocker of the boat, would even *want* to live in a hotel, to manage a non-industry, to sell a product that was sleep—not work—a product that was at least rest if not recreation? My father thought the radicals were more ludicrous than the whores. I think that after the death of my mother my father felt familiar with the confusions of lust and loneliness; perhaps he was even grateful for 'the business'—as the whores called their work.

He was less sympathetic to the world-changers, to the idealists bent on altering the unpleasantries of human nature. This surprises me, now, because I think of Father as simply another kind of idealist—but of course Father was more determined to outlive unpleasantries than change them. That my father would never learn German also kept him isolated from the radicals; by comparison, the whores spoke better English.

The radical Old Billig knew one phrase of English. He liked to tickle Lilly, or give her a lollipop, while he teased her. 'Yankee go home,' he would say to her, lovingly.

'He's a sweet old fart,' Franny said. Frank tried to teach Old Billig another English phrase that Frank thought Billig would like.

"Imperialist dog,' Frank would say, but Billig got this hopelessly confused with 'Nazi swine,' and it always came out strange.

The radical who spoke the best English used the code name Fehlgeburt. It was Frank who first explained to me that *Fehlgeburt* means 'miscarriage' in German.

'As in "miscarriage of justice," Frank?' Franny asked.

'No,' Frank said. 'The other kind. The *baby* kind of miscarriage,' Frank said.

Fräulein Fehlgeburt, as she was called—Miss Miscarriage, to us children—had never been pregnant, thus had never miscarried; she was a university student whose code name was 'Miscarriage' because the only other woman on the staff of the Symposium on East-West Relations had the code name 'Pregnant.' *She* had been. Fräulein Schwanger—for *schwanger* means 'pregnant' in German—was an older woman, Father's age, who was famous in Viennese radical circles for a past pregnancy. She had written a whole book about being pregnant, and another book—a kind of sequel to the first—about having an abortion. When she was first pregnant she had worn a bright red sign saying 'pregnant' on her chest—SCHWANGER!—under which, in letters of the same size, was the question 'ARE YOU THE FATHER?' It had made a sensational book jacket, too, and she had donated all her royalties to various radical causes. Her subsequent abortion—and *that* book—had made her a popular subject for controversy; she could still draw a crowd when she gave a speech, and she was a loyal donator of the proceeds. Schwanger's abortion book—published in 1955, simultaneously with the end of the occupation—had made the expulsion of this unwanted child symbolic of Austria's freeing herself from the occupying powers. 'The father,' Schwanger wrote, 'could have been Russian, French, British, or American; at least to my body, and to my way of thinking, he was an unwanted foreigner.'

Schwanger was close to Susie the bear; the two shared a great many rape theories together. But Schwanger would also befriend my father; she appeared to be the most consoling to him, after my mother's loss, not because there was anything 'between' them (as they say) but because the calmness of her voice—the steady, soft cadence of her speech—was the most like my mother's of all the voices in the Gasthaus Freud. Like my mother, Schwanger was a gentle persuader. 'I'm just a realist,' she had a way of saying, so innocently—though her hopes for wiping the slate clean, for starting a new world, from scratch, were as fervent as the fire dreams of any of the radicals.

Schwanger took us children with her, several times a day, for coffee with milk and cinnamon and whipped cream at the Kaffee Europa on Kärntnerstrasse—or to the Kaffee Mozart at Albertinaplatz Zwei, just behind the State Opera. 'In case you don't know it,' Frank would say, later—and over and over, *'The Third Man* was filmed at the Kaffee Mozart.' Schwanger couldn't have

246

cared less; it was the whipped cream that drove her away from the clatter of typewriters and the heat of debate, it was the calm of the coffeehouse that got to her. 'The only worthwhile institution in our society—a shame that the coffeehouse will have to go, too,' Schwanger told Frank, Franny, Lilly, and me. 'Drink up, dears!'

When you wanted whipped cream, you asked for *Schlagobers*, and if Schwanger meant 'pregnant' to the other radicals, she meant pure *Schlagobers* to us children. She was our motherlike radical with a weakness for whipped cream; we really liked her.

And young Fräulein Fehlgeburt, whose major at the University of Vienna was American literature, adored Schwanger. We thought she seemed actually proud to be code-named 'Miscarriage,' perhaps because we thought that *Fehlgeburt*, in German, could also mean 'Abortion.' I'm sure this can't be true, but in Frank's dictionary, at least, the word for miscarriage and abortion was the same word, *Fehlgeburt*—which symbolizes perfectly our out-of-itness with the radicals, our failure to ever understand them. Every misunderstanding has at its center a breakdown of language. We never actually understood what these two women *meant*—the tough and motherlike Schwanger marshaling forces (and money) for causes that struck us children as left of reason, but able to soothe us with her gentle and most logical *voice*, and her *Schlagobers;* and the waiflike, stuttering, shy university student of American literature, Miss Miscarriage, who read aloud to Lilly (not just to comfort a motherless child but to improve her English). She read so well that Franny, Frank, and I would almost always listen in. Fehlgeburt liked to read to us in Frank's room, so it appeared that the dressmaker's dummy was listening, too.

It was from Fräulein Fehlgeburt, in the Gasthaus Freud—with our father in France, with out mother and Egg dragged from the cold sea (under the marker buoy that was Sorrow)—that we first heard the whole of *The Great Gatsby;* it was that ending, with Miss Miscarriage's lilting Austrian accent, that really got to Lilly.

' "Gatsby believed in the green light, the orgiastic future that year by year recedes before us. It eludes us then, but that's no matter," ' Fehlgeburt read, excitedly, ' "—tomorrow we will run faster, stretch out our arms farther . . ."!' Miss Miscarriage read. ' "And one fine morning—" ' Fehlgeburt paused; her

saucerlike eyes seemed glazed by that green light Gatsby saw
—maybe by the orgiastic future, too.

'What?' Lilly said, breathlessly, and a little echo of Egg was
in Frank's funny room with us.

' "So we beat on," ' Fehlgeburt concluded, ' "boats against
the current, borne back ceaselessly into the past." '

'Is that *it?*' Frank asked. 'Is it *over?*' He was squinting, his
eyes were shut so tight.

'Of course it's *over,* Frank,' Franny said. 'Don't you know an
ending when you hear one?'

Fehlgeburt looked drained of her blood, her childlike face
with a sad grown-up's frown, a strand of her lank blond hair
wrapped nervously around a neat pink ear. Then Lilly started in,
and we couldn't stop her. It was late afternoon, the whores
hadn't come around, but when Lilly started in, Susie the bear
thought Screaming Annie was faking an orgasm in a room she
didn't belong in. Susie burst into Frank's room, knocking the
dressmaker's dummy over and causing poor Fräulein Fehlgeburt
to yip in alarm. But even that intrusion couldn't stop Lilly. Her
cry seemed caught in her throat, her grief seemed to be
something she was sure to choke on; we could not believe such a
small body could generate so much trembling, could orchestrate
so much sound.

Of course, we were all thinking, it's not that the *book* moved
her so much—it's that bit about being 'borne back ceaselessly
into the past,' it's *our* past that's moving her, we were all
thinking; it's Mother, it's Egg, and how we won't ever be able to
forget them. But when we calmed her down, Lilly blurted out
suddenly that it was *Father* she was crying for. 'Father is a
Gatsby,' she cried. 'He *is!* I know he is!'

And we all started in on her, at once. Frank said, 'Lilly, don't
let that "orgiastic future" stuff get you down. It's not exactly
what Iowa Bob meant when he was always saying how Father
lives in the future.'

'It's a rather different future, Lilly,' I said.

'Lilly,' Franny said. 'What's "the green light," Lilly? I mean,
for *Father*: what's *his* green light, Lilly?'

'You see, Lilly,' Frank said, as if he were bored, 'Gatsby was
in love with the *idea* of being in love with Daisy; it wasn't even
Daisy he was in love with, not anymore. And Father hasn't got a
Daisy, Lilly,' Frank said, choking up just a little—because it had
probably just occurred to him that Father didn't have a *wife*
anymore, either.

248

But Lilly said, 'It's the man in the white dinner jacket, it's Father, he's a Gatsby. "It eluded us then, but that's no matter —" ' Lilly quoted to us. 'Don't you *see?*' she shrieked. 'There's always going to be an *It*—and *It* is going to elude us, every time. It's going to *always* get away,' Lilly said. 'And Father's not going to stop,' she said. 'He's going to keep going after it, and it's always going to get away. Oh, damn it!' she howled, stamping her little foot. 'Damn it! Damn it!' Lilly wailed, and she was off again, unstoppable—a match for Screaming Annie, who could only fake an orgasm; Lilly, we suddenly understood, could fake death itself. Her grief was so real that I thought Susie the bear was going to take her bear's head off and pay a little human reverence, but Susie prowled through Frank's room in her strictly bearish fashion; she bumped out the door, leaving us to deal with Lilly's anguish.

Lilly's *Weltschmerz*, as Frank would come to call it. 'The *rest* of us have anguish,' Frank would say. 'The rest of us have grief, the rest of us merely *suffer*. But *Lilly*,' Frank would say, 'Lilly has true *Weltschmerz*. It shouldn't be translated as "world-weariness," ' Frank would lecture us, 'that's much too mild for what Lilly's got. Lilly's *Weltschmerz* is like "world-*hurt*," ' Frank would say. 'Literally "world"—that's the *Welt* part—and "hurt," because that's what the *Schmerz* part really is: pain, real ache. Lilly's got a case of *world-hurt,*' Frank concluded, proudly.

'Kind of like *sorrow*, huh, Frank?' Franny asked.

'Kind of,' Frank said, stonily. Sorrow was no friend of Frank's: not anymore.

In fact, the death of Mother and Egg—with Sorrow in Egg's lap, and rising from the deep to mark the grave—convinced Frank to give up trying to properly pose the dead; Frank would give up taxidermy in all its forms. All manifestations of resurrection were to be abandoned by him. 'Including religion,' Frank said. According to Frank, religion is just another kind of taxidermy.

As a result of Sorrow's tricking him, Frank would come down very hard on *belief* of any kind. He would become a greater fatalist than Iowa Bob, he would become a greater nonbeliever than Franny or me. A near-violent atheist, Frank would turn to believing only in Fate—in random fortune or random doom, in arbitrary slapstick and arbitrary sorrow. He would become a preacher *against* every bill of goods anyone ever sold: from politics to morality, Frank was always for the opposition. By which Frank meant 'the opposing forces.'

'But what exactly do these forces oppose, Frank?' Franny asked him, once.

'Just oppose every prediction,' Frank advised. 'Anything anybody's for, be against it. Anything anybody's against, be for it. You get on a plane and it doesn't crash, that means you got on the right plane,' Frank said. 'And that's *all* it means.'

Frank, in other words, went 'off.' After Mother and Egg went away, Frank went ever farther away—somewhere—he went into a religion more vastly lacking in seriousness than even the established religions; he joined a kind of anti-everything sect.

'Or maybe Frank *founded* it,' Lilly said, once. Meaning nihilism, meaning anarchy, meaning trivial silliness and happiness in the face of gloom, meaning depression descending as regularly as night over the most mindless and joyful of days. Frank believed in *zap!* He believed in surprises. He was in constant attack and retreat, and he was equally, constantly, wide-eyed and goofily stumbling about in the sudden sunlight —tripping across the wasteland littered with bodies from the darkness of just a moment ago.

'He just went crazy,' Lilly said. And Lilly should know.

Lilly went crazy, too. She seemed to take Mother's and Egg's deaths as a personal punishment for some failure deep within herself, and so she resolved she would change. She resolved, among other things, to *grow*.

'At least a little,' she said, grimly determined. Franny and I were worried about her. Growth seemed unlikely for Lilly, and the strenuousness with which we imagined Lilly pursuing her own 'growth' was frightening to Franny and me.

'I want to change, too,' I said to Franny. 'But *Lilly*—I don't know. Lilly is just Lilly.'

'Everyone knows that,' Franny said.

'Everyone except Lilly,' I said.

'Precisely,' Franny said. 'So how are *you* going to change? You know something better than growing?'

'No. Not better,' I said. I was just a realist in a family of dreamers, large and small. I knew I *couldn't* grow. I knew I would never really grow up; I knew my childhood would never leave me, and I would never be quite adult enough—quite responsible enough—for the world. The goddamn *Welt*, as Frank would say. I couldn't change enough, and I knew it. All I could do was something that would have pleased Mother. I could give up swearing, I could clean up my language—which had upset Mother so. And so I did.

'You mean you're not going to say "fuck" or "shit" or "cock-sucker" or even "up yours" or "in the ear" or *any*thing, anymore?' Franny asked me.

'That's right,' I said.

'Not even "asshole"?' Franny asked.

'Right,' I said.

'You asshole,' Franny said.

'It makes as much sense as anything else,' Frank reasoned.

'You dumb prick,' Franny baited me.

'I think it's rather noble,' Lilly said. 'Small, but noble.'

'He lives in a second-rate whorehouse with people who want to start the world over and he wants to clean up his *language*,' Franny said. 'Cunthead,' she told me. 'You wretched fart,' Franny said. 'Beat your meat all night and dream of tits, but you want to sound *nice*, is that it?' she asked.

'Come on, Franny,' Lilly said.

'You little turd, Lilly,' Franny said. Lilly started to cry.

'We've got to stick together, Franny,' Frank said. 'This sort of abuse is not helpful.'

'You're as queer as a cat fart, Frank,' she told him.

'And what are *you*, honey?' Susie the bear asked Franny. 'What makes you think you're so tough?'

'I'm not so tough,' Franny said. 'You dumb bear. You're just an unattractive girl, with zits—with zit *scars*: you're scarred by zits—and you'd rather be a dumb bear than a human being. You think that's tough? It's fucking *easier* to be a bear, isn't it?' Franny asked Susie. 'And to work for an old blind man who thinks you're smart—and beautiful, too, probably,' Franny said. 'I'm *not* so tough,' Franny said. 'But I *am* smart. I can get by. I can *more* than get by,' she said. 'I can get what I want—when I know what it is,' she added. 'I can see how things *are*,' Franny said. 'And *you*,' she said, speaking to us all—even poor Miss Miscarriage—'you keep waiting for things to become something else. You think *Father* doesn't?' Franny asked me, suddenly.

'He lives in the future,' Lilly said, still sniffling.

'He's as blind as Freud,' Franny said, 'or he soon will be. So you know what I'm going to do?' she asked us. 'I'm *not* going to clean up my language. I'm going to aim my language wherever I want,' she told me. 'It's the one weapon I've got. And I'm only going to grow when I'm ready to, or when it's time,' she told Lilly. 'And I'm not *ever* going to be like *you*, Frank. No one else

251

will ever be like you,' she added, affectionately. 'And I'm not going to be a bear,' she told Susie. 'You sweat like a pig in that stupid costume, you get your rocks off making people uneasy, but that's because *you're* uneasy just being *you*. Well, I'm easy being me,' Franny said.

'Lucky you,' Frank said.

'Yes, lucky you, Franny,' Lilly said.

'So what if you're beautiful?' said Susie. 'You're also a bitch.'

'From now on, I'm mainly a *mother*,' Franny said. 'I'm going to take care of you fuckers—you, you, and you,' Franny said, pointing to Frank and Lilly and me. 'Because Mother's not here to do it—and Iowa Bob is gone. The shit detectors are gone,' Franny said, 'so I'm left to detect it. I point out the shit—that's my role. *Father doesn't know what's going on,*' Franny said, and we nodded—Frank, Lilly, and I; even Susie the bear nodded. We knew this was true: Father was blind, or he soon would be.

'Even so, I don't need *you* to mother *me*,' Frank said to Franny, but he didn't look so sure.

Lilly went and put her head in Franny's lap; she cried there —comfortably, I thought. Franny, of course, knew that I loved her—hopelessly, and too much—and so I didn't have to make a gesture or say anything to her.

'Well, I don't need a sixteen-year-old straightening me out,' said Susie the bear, but her bear's head was off; she held it in her big paws. Her ravaged complexion, her hurt eyes, her too-small mouth betrayed her. She put her bear's head back on; that was her only authority.

The student, Miss Miscarriage, serious and well intentioned, seemed at a loss for words. 'I don't know,' she said. 'I don't know.'

'Say it in German,' Frank encouraged her.

'Just spit it out any way you can,' Franny said.

'Well,' Fehlgeburt said. 'That passage. That lovely passage, that *ending*—to *The Great Gatsby*—that's what I mean,' she said.

'Get to it, Fehlgeburt,' Franny said. 'Spit it out.'

'Well,' Fehlgeburt said. 'I don't know, but—somehow—it makes me want to go to the United States. I mean, it's against my politics—your country—I know that. But that *ending,* all of it—somehow—is just so *beautiful.* It makes me want to *be* there.

I mean, there's no *sense* to it, but I would just like to be in the United States.'

'So you think *you'd* like to be there?' Franny said. 'Well, I wish we'd never left.'

'Can we go back, Franny?' Lilly asked.

'We'll have to ask Father,' Frank said.

'Oh boy,' Franny said. And I could see her imagining that moment, waltzing a little reality into Father's dreams.

'Your country, if you'll forgive me,' said one of the other radicals—the one they called simply Arbeiter (*Arbeiter* means 'worker' in German), 'your country is really a *criminal* place,' Arbeiter said. 'If you'll forgive me,' he added, 'your country is the ultimate triumph of corporate creativity, which means it is a country controlled by the *group*-thinking of corporations. These corporations are without humanity because there is no one personally responsible for their use of power; a corporation is like a computer with profit as its source of energy—and profit as its necessary fuel. The United States is—you'll forgive me —quite the worst country in the world for a humanist to live in, I thing.'

'Fuck what you think,' Franny said. 'You raving asshole,' she said. 'You *sound* like a computer.'

'You think like a transmission,' Frank told Arbeiter. 'Four forward gears—at predetermined speeds. One speed for reverse.'

Arbeiter stared. His English was a little plodding—his mind, it would occur to me, later, was about as versatile as a lawn mower.

'And about as poetic,' Susie the bear would say. No one liked Arbeiter—not even the impressionable Miss Miscarriage. Her weakness—among the radicals—was her fondness for literature, especially for the romance that is American literature. ('Your silly *major*, dear,' Schwanger always chided her.) But Fehlgeburt's fondness for literature was her strength—to us children. It was the romantic part of her that wasn't quite dead; at least, not yet. In time, God forgive me, I would help to kill it.

'Literature is for dreamers,' Old Billig would tell poor Fehlgeburt. Old Billig the radical, I mean. Old Billig the whore *liked* dreams; she told Frank once that dreams were *all* she liked —her dreams and her 'mementos.'

'Study economics, dear,' Schwanger told Fehlgeburt—that's what Miss Pregnant told Miss Miscarriage.

'Human usefulness,' Arbeiter lectured to us, 'is directly

related to the proportion of the whole population involved in decisions.'

'In the *power*,' Old Billig corrected him.

'In the powerful decisions,' Arbeiter said—the two men stabbing like hummingbirds at a single small blossom.

'Bullfuck,' Franny said. Arbeiter's and Old Billig's English was so bad, it was easy to say things like 'Take it in the ear' to them all the time—they didn't get it. And despite my vow to clean up my language, I was sorely tempted to say these things to them; I had to content myself, vicariously, by listening to Franny speak to them.

'The eventual race war, in America,' Arbeiter told us, 'will be misunderstood. It will actually be a war of class stratification.'

'When you fart, Arbeiter,' Franny asked him, 'do the seals in the zoo stop swimming?'

The other radicals were rarely a part of our group discussions. One spent himself on the typewriters; the other, on the single automobile that the Symposium of East-West Relations owned among themselves: all six of them, they could just fit. The mechanic who labored over the decrepit car—the ever-ailing car, useless in any getaway, we imagined, and probably never to be called upon for a getaway, Father thought—was a sullen, smudge-faced young man in coveralls and a navy-blue streetcar conductor's cap. He belonged to the union and worked the main-line Mariahilfer Strasse *Strassenbahn* all night. He looked sleepy and angry every day, and he clanked with tools. Appropriately, he was called Schraubenschlüssel—a *Schraubenschlüssel* is a wrench. Frank liked to roll Schraubenschlüssel's name off his tongue, to show off, but Franny and Lilly and I insisted on the translation. We called him Wrench.

'Hi, Wrench,' Franny would say to him, as he lay under the car, cursing. 'Hope you're keeping your mind clean, Wrench,' Franny would say. Wrench knew no English, and the only thing we knew about Wrench's private life was that he had once asked Susie the bear for a date.

'I mean, virtually *nobody* asks me out,' Susie said. 'What an asshole.'

'What an asshole,' Franny repeated.

'Well, he's never actually *seen* me, you know,' Susie said.

'Does he know you're *female?*' Frank asked.

'Jesus God, Frank,' Franny said.

'Well, I was just *curious*,' Frank said

'That Wrench is a real weirdo, I can tell,' Franny said. 'Don't go out with him, Susie,' Franny advised the bear.

'Are you kidding?' Susie the bear said. 'Honey, I don't go out. With *men*.'

This seemed to settle almost passively at Franny's feet, but I could see Frank edging uncomfortably near to, and then away from, its presence.

'Susie is a lesbian, Franny,' I told Franny, when we were alone.

'She didn't exactly say that,' Franny said.

'I think she is,' I said.

'So?' Franny said. 'What's Frank? The grand banana? And Frank's okay.'

'Watch out for Susie, Franny,' I said.

'You think about me too much,' she repeated, and repeated. 'Leave me alone, will you?' Franny asked me. But that was the one thing I could never do.

'All sexual acts actually involve maybe four or five different sexes,' the sixth member of the Symposium on East-West Relations told us. This was such a garbling of Freud—the *other* Freud—that we had to beg Frank for a second translation because we couldn't understand the first.

'That's what he said,' Frank assured us. 'All sexual acts actually involve a bunch of *different* sexes.'

'Four or five?' Franny asked.

'When we do it with a woman,' the man said, 'we are doing it with ourselves as we will become, and with ourselves in our childhoods. And, it goes without saying, with the self our lover will become, and with the self of her childhood.'

' "It goes without saying"?' Frank asked.

'So every time there's one fuck there's four or five people actually at it?' Franny asked. 'That sounds exhausting.'

'The energy spent on sex is the only energy that doesn't require replacement by the society,' the rather dreamy sixth radical told us. Frank struggled to translate this. 'We replace our sexual energy ourselves,' the man said, looking at Franny as if he'd just said the most profound thing in the world.

'No kidding,' I whispered to Franny, but she seemed a little more mesmerized than I thought she should have been. I was afraid she liked this radical.

His name was Ernst. Just Ernst. A normal name, but just a first name. He didn't argue. He crafted isolated, meaningless sentences, spoke them quietly, went back to the typewriter. When the radicals left the Gasthaus Freud in the late afternoon, they seemed to flounder for hours in the Kaffee Mowatt (across the street)—a dark and dim place with a billiard table and dart boards, and an ever-present solemn row of tea-with-rum drinkers playing chess or reading the newspapers. Ernst rarely joined his colleagues at the Kaffee Mowatt. He wrote and wrote.

If Screaming Annie was the last whore to go home, Ernst was the last radical to leave. If Screaming Annie often met Old Billig when the old radical was arriving for his morning's work, she often met Ernst when Ernst was finally calling it quits. He had an eerie other-worldliness about him; when he talked with Schwanger, their two voices would get so quiet that they would almost always end up whispering.

'What's Ernst write?' Franny asked Susie the bear.

'He's a pornographer,' Susie said. 'He's asked me out, too. And *he's* seen me.' That quieted us all for a moment.

'What sort of pornography?' Franny asked, cautiously.

'How many sorts are there, honey?' Susie the bear asked. 'The worst,' Susie said. 'Kinky acts. Violence. Degradation.'

'Degradation?' Lilly said.

'Not for you, honey,' Susie said.

'Tell me,' Frank said.

'Too kinky to tell,' Susie said to Frank. 'You know German better than I do, Frank—*you* try it.'

Unfortunately, Frank tried it; Frank translated Ernst's pornography for us. I would ask Frank, later, if he thought Ernst's pornography was the start of the *real* trouble—if we had been able to ignore it, somehow, would things have gone downhill just the same? But Frank's new religion—his *anti*-religion—had already taken over all his answers (to all the questions).

'Downhill?' Frank would say. 'Well, that *is* the eventual direction, of course—I mean, regardless. If it hadn't been the pornography, it would have been something else. The point is we are *bound* to roll downhill. What do you know that rolls *up?* What starts the downward progress is immaterial,' Frank would say, with his irritating offhandedness.

'Look at it like this,' Frank would lecture me. 'Why does it seem to take more than half a lifetime to get to be a lousy teen-ager? Why does childhood take forever—when you're a child? Why does it seem to occupy a solid three-quarters of the whole trip? And when it's over, when the kids grow up, when you suddenly have to face facts . . . well,' Frank said to me, just recently, 'you know the story. When we were in that first Hotel New Hampshire, it seemed we'd go on being thirteen and fourteen and fifteen forever. For fucking *forever*, as Franny would say. But once we left the first Hotel New Hampshire,' Frank said, 'the rest of our lives moved past us twice as fast. That's just how it is,' Frank claimed, smugly. 'For half your life, you're fifteen. Then one day your twenties begin, and they're over the next day. And your thirties blow by you like a weekend spent with pleasant company. And before you know it, you're thinking about being fifteen again.

'Downhill?' Frank would say. 'It's a long *up*hill—to that fourteen-year-old, fifteen-year-old, sixteen-year-old time of your life. And from then on,' Frank would say, 'of course it's all downhill. And anyone knows downhill is faster than uphill. It's *up*—until fourteen, fifteen, sixteen—then it's *down*. Down like water,' Frank said, 'down like sand,' he would say.

Frank was seventeen when he translated the pornography for us; Franny was sixteen, I was fifteen. Lilly, who was eleven, wasn't old enough to hear. But Lilly insisted that if she was old enough to listen to Fehlgeburt reading *The Great Gatsby*, she was old enough to hear Frank translating Ernst. (With typical hypocrisy, Screaming Annie wouldn't allow her daughter, Dark Inge, to hear a word of it.)

'Ernst' was his Gasthaus Freud name, of course. In the pornography, he went by a lot of different names. I do not like to describe the pornography. Susie the bear told us that Ernst taught a course at the university called 'The History of Eroticism Through Literature,' but Ernst's pornography was not erotic. Fehlgeburt had taken Ernst's erotic literature course, and even she admitted that Ernst's own work bore no resemblance to the truly erotic, which is never pornographic.

Ernst's pornography gave us headaches and dry throats. Frank used to say that even his eyes got dry when he read it; Lilly stopped listening after the first time; and I felt cold, sitting in Frank's room, the dead dressmaker's dummy like a curiously nonjudgmental schoolmistress overhearing Frank's recitation—I got cold from the floor up. I felt something cold passing up my pants legs, through the old drafty floor, through the foundation of the building, from the soil beneath all light—where I imagined were the bones from ancient Vindobona, and instruments of torture popular among invading Turks, whips and cudgels and tongue-depressors and dirks, the vogue chambers of horror of the Holy Roman Empire. Because Ernst's pornography was not about sex: it was about pain without hope, it was about death without a single good memory. It made Susie the bear storm out to take a bath, it made Lilly cry (of course), it made me sick to my stomach (twice), it made Frank hurl one of the books at the dressmaker's dummy (as if the dummy had written it)—it was the one called *The Children on the Ship to Singapore*; they never got to Singapore, not even one precious child.

But all it did to Franny was make her frown. It made her think about Ernst; it made her seek him out and ask him—for starters —why he did it.

'Decadence enhances the revolutionary position,' Ernst told her, slowly—Frank fumbling to translate him exactly. 'Everything that is decadent speeds up the process, the inevitable revolution. At this phase it is necessary to generate disgust. Political disgust, economic disgust, disgust at our inhuman institutions, and moral disgust—disgust at ourselves, as we've allowed ourselves to become.'

'Speaking for himself,' I whispered to Franny, but she was just frowning; she was concentrating too hard on him.

'The pornographer is, of course, *most* disgusting,' Ernst droned on. 'But, you see, if I were a communist, who would I want for the government in power? The most liberal? No. I would desire the most repressive, the most capitalistic, and most *anti*-communist government possible—for then I would thrive. Where would the Left be without the help of the Right? The more stupid and right-wing everything is, the better for the Left.'

'Are you a communist?' Lilly asked Ernst. In Dairy, New Hampshire, Lilly knew, this was not such a hot thing to be.

'That was just a necessary phase,' Ernst said, speaking of communism and himself—and to us children—as if we *all* were past history, as if something vast were in motion and we were either being dragged after it or being blown away in its exhaust. 'I am a pornographer,' Ernst said, 'because I am serving the revolution. *Personally*,' he added, with a limp wave of his hand, 'well . . . *personally*, I am an aesthete: I reflect upon the erotic. If Schwanger mourns for her coffeehouses—if she is sad about her *Schlagobers*, which the revolution must also consume—I mourn for the erotic, for it must be lost, too. Sometimes after the revolution,' Ernst sighed, 'the erotic might reappear, but it will never be the same. In the new world, it will never mean as much.'

'The new world?' Lilly repeated, and Ernst shut his eyes as if this were the refrain in his favorite piece of music, as if with his mind's eye he could already see it, 'the new world,' a totally different planet—brand-new brings dwelling there.

I thought he had rather delicate hands for a revolutionary; his long, slender fingers probably were a help to him, at the typewriter—at his piano, where Ernst played the music for his opera of gigantic change. His cheap and slightly shiny navy-blue suit was usually clean but wrinkled, his white shirts were well washed but never pressed; he wore no tie; when his hair grew too long, he cut it too short. He had an almost athletic face, scrubbed, youthful, determined—a boyish kind of handsomeness. Susie the bear, and Fehlgeburt, told us that Ernst had a reputation as a lady-killer among his students at the university. When he lectured on erotic literature, Miss Miscarriage remarked, Ernst was quite passionate, he was even playful; he was not the limp, low-key, sort of lazy-weary, sluggish (or at least lethargic) talker he was when his subject was the revolution.

He was quite tall; though not solid, he was not frail, either. When I saw him hunch his shoulders, and turn the collar of his suit jacket up—about to go home from the Gasthaus Freud, after a no-doubt saddening and disgusting day's work—I was struck how in profile he reminded me of Chipper Dove.

Dove's hands never looked like a quarterback's hands, either —too delicate, again. And I could remember seeing Chipper Dove shrug his shoulder pads forward and trot back to the huddle, thinking about the next signal—the next order, the next command—his hands like songbirds lighting on his hip pads. Of course I knew then who Ernst was: the quarterback of the radicals, the signal caller, the dark planner, the one the others gathered around. And I knew then, too, what it was that Franny saw in Ernst. It was more than a physical resemblance to Chipper Dove, it was that cocksure quality, that touch of evil, that hint of destruction, that icy leadership—that was what could sneak its way into my sister's heart, that was what captured the *her in her*, that was what took Franny's strength away.

'We all want to go back home,' I told Father. 'To the United States. We want America. We don't like it here.'

Lilly held my hand. We were in Frank's room, again—Frank nervously boxing with the dressmaker's dummy, Franny on Frank's bed, looking out the window. She could see the Kaffee Mowatt, across the Krugerstrasse. It was early morning, and someone was sweeping the cigarette butts out the door of the coffeehouse, across the sidewalk, and into the gutter. The radicals were not the nighttime company of the Kaffee Mowatt; at night the whores used the place to get off the street—to take a break, to play some billiards, to drink a beer or a glass of wine, or get picked up—and Father allowed Frank and Franny and me to go there to throw some darts.

'We miss home,' Lilly said, trying not to cry. It was still summer, and Mother and Egg had departed too recently to permit our dwelling for long on phrases that concerned *missing* anyone or anything.

'It's not going to work here, Dad,' Frank said. 'It looks like an impossible situation.'

'And now's the time to leave,' I said, 'before we start school, before we all have our various commitments.'

'But I already have a commitment,' Father said, softly. 'To Freud.'

Did an old blind man equal *us?* we wanted to shout at him, but Father didn't allow us to linger on the subject of his commitment to Freud.

'What do *you* think, Franny?' he asked her, but Franny continued to stare out the window at the early morning street. Here came Old Billig, the radical—there went Screaming Annie, the whore. Both of them looked tired, but both of them were very Viennese in their attention to form: they both managed a hearty greeting we could hear through the open summer window in Frank's room.

'Look,' Frank said to Father. 'For sure we're in the First District, but Freud neglected to tell us that we live on just about the worst street in the whole district.'

'A kind of one-way street,' I added.

'No parking, either,' said Lilly. There was no parking because the Krugerstrasse seemed to be used for delivery trucks making back-door deliveries to the fancy places on the Kärntnerstrasse.

Also, the district post office was on our street—a sad, grimy building that hardly attracted potential customers to our hotel.

'Also the prostitutes,' Lilly whispered.

'Second-class,' said Frank. 'No hope of advancement. We're only a block off the Kärntnerstrasse but we'll never *be* the Kärntnerstrasse,' Frank said.

'Even with a new lobby,' I told Father, 'even if it's an *attractive* lobby, there's no one to see it. And you're still putting people between whores and revolution.'

'Between sin and danger, Daddy,' Lilly said.

'Of course it doesn't matter, in the long run, I suppose,' Frank said; I could have kicked him. 'I mean, it's downhill either way —it doesn't matter exactly *when* we leave, it's just evident that we *will* leave. This is a downhill hotel. We can leave when it's sinking, or after it's sunk.'

'But we want to leave *now*, Frank,' I said.

'Yes, we *all* do,' Lilly said.

'Franny?' Father asked, but Franny looked out the window. There was a mail truck trying to get around a delivery truck on the narrow street. Franny watched the mail come and go, waiting for letters from Junior Jones—and, I suppose, from Chipper Dove. She wrote them both, a lot, but only Junior Jones wrote her back.

Frank, continuing with his philosophical indifference, said, 'I mean, we can leave when the whores all fail their medical checkups, we can leave when Dark Inge is finally old enough, we can leave when Schraubenschlüssel's car blows up, we can leave when we're sued by the first guest, or the last—'

'But we *can't* leave,' Father interrupted him, 'until we make it *work*.' Even Franny looked at him. 'I mean,' Father said, 'when it's a *successful* hotel, then we can *afford* to leave. We can't just leave when we have a failure on our hands,' he said, reasonably, 'because we wouldn't have anything to leave *with*.'

'You mean money?' I said. Father nodded.

'You've already sunk the money in *here*?' Franny asked him.

'They'll be starting the lobby before the summer is over,' Father said.

'Then it's not too late!' cried Frank. 'I mean, *is* it?'

'*Un*sink the money, Daddy!' Lilly said.

Father smiled benevolently, shaking his head. Franny and I looked out the window at Ernst the pornographer; he was moving past the Kaffee Mowatt, he looked full of disgust. He kicked some garbage out of his way when he crossed the street, he moved as purposefully as a cat after a mouse, but he looked forever disappointed in himself for arriving at work later than Old Billig. He had at least three hours of pornography in him before he broke for lunch, before he gave his lecture at the university (his 'aesthetic hour,' he called it), and then he would face the tired, mean-spirited hours of the late afternoon, which he told us children he reserved for 'ideology'—for his contribution to the newsletter of the Symposium on East-West Relations. What a day he had ahead of himself! He was already full of hate for it, I could tell. And Franny couldn't take her eyes off him.

'We should leave now,' I said to Father, 'whether we're sunk or unsunk.'

'No place to go,' Father said, affectionately. He raised his hands; it was almost a shrug.

'Going to no place is better than staying here,' Lilly said.

'I agree,' I said.

'You're not being logical,' Frank said, and I glared at him.

Father looked at Franny. It reminded me of the looks he occasionally gave Mother; he was looking into the future, again, and he was looking for forgiveness—in advance. He wanted to be excused for everything that *would* happen. It was as if the power of his dreaming was so vivid that he felt compelled to simply act out whatever future he imagined—and we were being asked to tolerate his absence from reality, and maybe his absence from our lives, for a while. That is what 'pure love' is: the future. And that's the look Father gave to Franny.

'Franny?' Father asked her. 'What do *you* think?'

Franny's opinion was the one we always waited for. She looked at the spot in the street where Ernst had been—Ernst the pornographer, Ernst the 'aesthete' on the subject of erotica, Ernst the lady-killer. I saw that the *her in her* was in trouble; something was already amiss in Franny's heart.

'Franny?' Father said, softly.

'I think we should stay,' Franny said. 'We should see what it's like,' she said, facing us all. We children looked away, but Father gave Franny a hug and a kiss.

'Atta girl, Franny!' he said. Franny shrugged; she gave Father Mother's shrug, of course—it could get to him, every time.

Someone has told me that the Krugerstrasse, today, is mostly closed to all but pedestrian traffic, and that there are *two* hotels on the street, a restaurant, a bar, *and* a coffeehouse—even a movie theater and a record store. Someone has told me that it's a posh street, now. Well, that's just so hard to believe. And I wouldn't ever want to see the Krugerstrasse again, no matter how much it has changed.

Someone has told me that there are fancy places on the Krugerstrasse itself, now: a boutique and a hairdresser, a bookstore and a record store, a place that sells furs and a place that sells bathroom fittings. This is utterly amazing.

Someone has told me that the post office is still there. The mail goes on.

And there are still prostitutes on the Krugerstrasse; no one has to tell me that prostitution still goes on.

The next morning I woke up Susie the bear. 'Earl!' she said, fighting out of sleep. 'What the fuck is it now?'

'I want your help,' I said to her. 'You've got to save Franny.'

'Franny's real tough,' said Susie the bear. 'She's beautiful and tough,' said Susie, rolling over, 'and she doesn't need me.'

'You impress her,' I said; this was a hopeful lie. Susie was only twenty, only four years older than Franny, but when you're sixteen, four years is a big difference. 'She likes you,' I said; *this* was true, I knew. 'You're at least older, like an older sister to her, you know?' I said.

'Earl!' Susie the bear said, staying in disguise.

'Maybe you *are* weird,' Frank told Susie, 'but Franny can be more influenced by you than she can be influenced by *us*.'

'Save Franny from what?' Susie the bear asked.

'From Ernst,' I said.

'From pornography itself,' said Lilly, shuddering.

'Help her get the *her in her* back,' Frank begged Susie the bear.

'I don't normally mess with underage girls,' Susie said.

'We want you to *help* her, not mess with her,' I said to Susie, but Susie the bear only smiled. She sat up in her bed, her costume disheveled on the floor of her room, her own hair like bear hair with its stiff and erratic directions, her hard face like a wound above her ratty T-shirt.

'Helping someone is the same as messing with someone,' said Susie the bear.

'Will you please *try?*' I asked her.

'And *you* ask *me* where the *real* trouble began,' Frank would say to me, later: 'Well, it didn't start with the pornography—not in my opinion,' Frank would say. 'Not that it matters, of course, but I know what started the trouble that got to *you*,' Frank would tell me.

Like the pornography, I don't wish to describe it, but Frank and I had only a very brief picture—we had only the quickest glimpse of it, though we saw more than enough. It started one evening in August, when it was so hot Lilly had woken up Frank and me and asked for a glass of water—as if she were a baby again—one evening when it was too hot for the men on the Krugerstrasse to think of whores, and so it was quiet in the Gasthaus Freud. There were no customers to make Screaming Annie scream, there was no one even interested enough to grunt with Jolanta, to whimper with Babette, to strike a bargain with

263

Old Billig, or even look at young Dark Inge. It was too hot to sit in the Kaffee Mowatt; the whores sat on the stairs in the cool, dark lobby of the Gasthaus Freud—now under construction. Freud was in bed, asleep, of course; he could not see the heat. And Father, who saw the future more clearly than the moment, was asleep, too.

I went in Frank's room and boxed the dressmaker's dummy around for a while.

'Jesus God,' Frank said, 'I'll be glad when you find some barbells and you leave my dummy alone.' But he couldn't sleep, either; we shoved the dressmaker's dummy back and forth between us.

There was no mistaking the sound for Screaming Annie—or for any of the whores. The sound seemed to bear no relationship to sorrow; there was too much light in the sound to have anything to do with sorrow, there was too much of the music of water in the sound to make Frank and me think of fucking for money, or even of lust—there was too much light and water music for lust, either. Frank and I had never heard this sound before—and in my memory, which is a forty-year-old's memory now, I do not remember another recording of this song; no one would ever sing quite exactly *this* song to me.

It was the song Susie the bear made Franny sing. Susie went through Franny's room to use the bathroom. Frank and I went through my room to get to the same bathroom; through the bathroom door we could peek into Franny's room.

The head of the bear on the rug at the foot of Franny's bed was at first unnerving, as if someone had severed Susie from her head when she'd first intruded. But the bear's head was not the focal point of Frank's and my attention. It was Franny's sound that drew us—both keen and soft, as nice as Mother, as happy as Egg. It was a sound almost without sex in it, although sex was the song's subject, because Franny lay on her bed with her arms flung over her head and her head thrown back, and between her long, slightly stirring legs (treading water, as if she were very buoyant), in my sister's dark lap (which I shouldn't have seen) was a headless bear—a headless bear was lapping there, like an animal eating from a fresh kill, like an animal drinking in the heart of a forest.

This vision frightened Frank and me. We didn't know where to go after seeing this, and for no reason, with nothing on our minds—or with too much on them—we stumbled into the lobby. There all the whores on the stairs greeted us; the heat and their own boredom, their inactivity, seemed to make them unusually glad to see us, although they always seemed to be pretty glad to see us. Only Screaming Annie looked disappointed to see us—as if she'd thought, for a moment, we might be 'business.'

Dark Inge said, 'Hey, you guys, you look like you seen a ghost.'

'Something you ate, dears?' asked Old Billig. 'It's too late for you to be up.'

'Your hard-ons keeping you awake?' Jolanta asked.

'*Oui, oui,*' sang Babette. 'Bring *us* your hard-ons!'

'Stop that,' said Old Billig. 'It's too hot to fuck, anyway.'

'Never too hot,' Jolanta said.

'Never too cold,' said Screaming Annie.

'Do you want to play cards?' Dark Inge asked us. 'Crazy eights?'

But Frank and I, like windup soldiers, did a few awkward turns at the foot of the stairs, reversed direction, made our way back to Frank's room—and then, like magnets, we were drawn to Father.

'We want to go home,' I said to him. He woke up, and took both Frank and me into his bed with him, as if we were still small.

'Please, let's go home, Dad,' Frank whispered.

'As soon as we're successful here,' Father assured us. 'Just as soon as we make it—I promise.'

'*When?*' I hissed at him, but Father put a headlock on me, and kissed me.

'Soon,' he said. 'This place is going to take off—soon. I can feel it.'

But we would be in Vienna until 1964; we would stay there seven years.

'I grew *old* there,' Lilly would say; she would be eighteen years old by the time we left Vienna. Older, but not a whole lot bigger—as Franny would say.

Sorrow floats. We knew that. We shouldn't have been so surprised.

But the night that Susie the bear made Franny forget about pornography—that night she made my sister sing so well —Frank and I were struck by a resemblance stronger than the resemblance Ernst the pornographer bore to Chipper Dove. In Frank's room with the dressmaker's dummy pushed against Frank's door, Frank and I lay whispering in the darkness.

'Did you *see* the bear?' I said.

'You couldn't see her head,' Frank said.

'Right,' I said. 'So it was just the bear suit, really—Susie was sort of hunched up.'

'Why was she still wearing the bear suit?' Frank asked.

'I don't know,' I said.

'Probably they were just starting,' Frank reasoned.

'But the way the bear *looked*,' I said. 'Did you see?'

'I know,' Frank whispered.

'All that fur, the body sort of curled,' I said.

'I know what you're saying,' Frank said. 'Stop it.'

In the darkness we both knew what Susie the bear had looked like—we had both seen whom she resembled. Franny had warned us: she'd told us to be on the lookout for Sorrow's new poses, for Sorrow's new disguises.

'Sorrow,' Frank whispered. 'Susie the bear is Sorrow.'

'She *looked* like him, anyway,' I said.

'She's Sorrow, I know it,' Frank said.

'Well, for the moment, maybe,' I said. 'For *now* she is.'

'Sorrow,' Frank kept repeating, until he fell asleep. 'It's Sorrow,' he murmured. 'You can't kill it,' Frank mumbled. 'It's sorrow. It floats.'

9

The Second
Hotel New Hampshire

The last renovation in the new lobby of the Gasthaus Freud was my father's idea. I imagine him standing one morning in front of the post office on the Krugerstrasse, looking up the street at the new lobby—the candy store completely absorbed, the old signs, like tired soldiers' rifles, leaning against the scaffolding that the workmen were taking down. The signs said: BONBONS, KONDITOREI, ZUCKERWAREN, SCHOKOLADEN, and GASTHAUS FREUD. And my father saw then that they should *all* be thrown away: no more candy store, no more Gasthaus Freud.

'The Hotel New Hampshire?' said Screaming Annie, always the first whore to arrive (and the last to leave).

'Change with the times,' said Old Billig, the radical. 'Roll with the punches, come up smiling. "The Hotel New Hampshire" sounds okay to me.'

'Another phase, another phase,' said Ernst the pornographer.

'A brilliant idea!' Freud cried. 'Think of the American clientele—how it will hook them! And no more anti-Semitism,' the old man said.

'No more guests staying away because of their anti-Freudian tendencies, I suppose,' Frank said.

'What the fuck else did you think he'd call it?' Franny asked me. 'It's Father's hotel, isn't it?' she asked.

Screwed down for life, as Iowa Bob would have said.

'I think it's sweet,' Lilly said. 'It's a nice touch, sort of small, but sweet.'

'Sweet?' Franny said. 'Oh boy, we're in trouble: Lilly thinks it's *sweet*.'

'It's sentimental,' Frank said, philosophically, 'but it doesn't matter.'

I thought that if Frank said something *didn't matter* again, I would scream. I thought I could fake more than an orgasm if

267

Frank said that again. But once more I was saved by Susie the bear.

'Look, kids,' Susie said. 'Your old man's made a step in a *practical* direction. Do you realize how many tourists from the U.S. and England are going to find that name reassuring?'

'This is true,' Schwanger said, pleasantly. 'This is a city of the *East* to the British and to the Americans. The very shape of some of the churches—the dreaded onion-shaped dome,' Schwanger said, 'and its implications of a world incomprehensible to Westerners . . . depending on how *far* West you come from, even Central Europe can *look* East,' Schwanger said. 'It's the *timid* souls who'll be attracted here,' Schwanger predicted, as if she was composing another pregnancy and abortion book. 'The Hotel New Hampshire will ring bells for them—bells that sound like *home*.'

'Brilliant,' Freud said. 'Bring us the timid souls,' Freud said, sighing, reaching his hands out to pat the heads that were nearest to him. He found Franny's head and patted it, but the big soft paw of Susie the bear brushed Freud's hand away.

I would get used to that—that possessive paw. This is a world where what strikes us, at first, as ominous can grow to become commonplace, even reassuring. What seems, at first, reassuring can grow to become ominous, too, but I had to accept that Susie the bear was a good influence on Franny. If Susie could keep Franny from Ernst, I had to be grateful—and was it too much to hope that Susie the bear might even convince Franny that she should stop writing to Chipper Dove?

'Do you think you are a lesbian, Franny?' I asked her, in the safety of the darkness on the Krugerstrasse—Father was having trouble with the pink neon flasher: HOTEL NEW HAMPSHIRE! HOTEL NEW HAMPSHIRE! HOTEL NEW HAMPSHIRE! Over and over again.

'I doubt it,' Franny said, softly. 'I think I just like Susie.'

I was thinking, of course, that since Frank knew he was a homosexual, and now Franny was involved with Susie the bear, maybe it was only a matter of time before Lilly and I discovered our similar inclinations. But, as usual, Franny was reading my mind.

'It's not like that,' she whispered. 'Frank is *convinced*. I'm not convinced of anything—except, maybe, that this is easier for me. Right now. I mean, it's easier to love someone of your own sex. There's not quite so much to commit yourself to, there's not

268

so much to risk,' she said. 'I feel *safer* with Susie,' she whispered. 'That's all, I think. Men are so *different*,' Franny said.

'A phase,' Ernst went around saying—about everything.

While Fehlgeburt, encouraged by everyone's response to *The Great Gatsby*, started reading *Moby-Dick* to us. Because of what happened to Mother and Egg, hearing about the ocean was difficult for us, but we got over that; we concentrated on the whale, especially on the different harpooners (we each had our favorite), and we kept a sharp eye on Lilly, waiting for her to identify Father with Ahab—'or maybe she'll decide Frank is the white whale,' Franny whispered. But it was *Freud* Lilly identified for us.

One night when the dressmaker's dummy stood at attention, and Fehlgeburt was droning, like the sea—like the tide—Lilly said, 'Can you hear him? Ssshhh!'

'What?' Frank said, like a ghost—like Egg would have said, we all knew.

'Cut it out, Lilly,' Franny whispered.

'No, listen,' Lilly said. And for a moment we thought we were below decks, in our seamen's bunks, listening to Ahab's artificial leg restlessly pacing above us. A wooden whack, a bonelike thud. It was just Freud's baseball bat; he was limping his blind way on the floor above us—he was visiting one of the whores.

'Which one does he see?' I asked.

'Old Billig,' said Susie the bear.

'The old for the old,' Franny said.

'It's sort of sweet, I think,' Lilly said.

'I mean it's Old Billig *tonight*,' said Susie the bear. 'He must be tired.'

'He does it with *all* of them?' Frank said.

'Not Jolanta,' Susie said. 'She scares him.'

'She scares *me*,' I said.

'And not Dark Inge, of course,' Susie said. 'Freud can't see her.'

It did not occur to me to visit the whores—one or all. Ronda Ray had not really been like them. With Ronda Ray, it was just sex with a fee attached; in Vienna, sex was a business. I could masturbate to my imagination of Jolanta; that was exciting enough. And for love . . . well, for love there was always my imagination of Franny. And in the late summer nights, there was also Fehlgeburt. *Moby-Dick* being such a monster of a reading experience, Fehlgeburt had taken to staying later in the evenings. Frank and I would walk her home. She rented a room in an ill-kept building behind the Rathaus, near the university, and she did not like crossing the Kärntnerstrasse or the Graben alone at night, because she would occasionally be mistaken for a whore.

Anyone who mistook Fehlgeburt for a whore must have had a great imagination; she was so clearly a student. It was not that she wasn't pretty, it was that her prettiness clearly wasn't an issue—for her. What plain good looks she had—and she had them—she either suppressed or neglected. Her hair was straggly; on the rare occasions when it was clean, it was simply uncared for. She wore blue jeans and a turtleneck, or a T-shirt, and about her mouth and eyes was the kind of tiredness that suggests too much reading, too much writing, too much thinking—too many of those things larger than one's own body, and its care or pleasures. She seemed about the same age as Susie, but she was much too humorless to be a bear—and her loathing for the nighttime activities in the Hotel New Hampshire surely bordered on what Ernst would have called 'disgust.' When it was raining, Frank and I would walk her no farther than the streetcar stop on the Ringstrasse at the opera; when it was nice, we walked her through the Plaza of Heroes and up the Ring toward the university. We were just three kids fresh from thinking about whales, walking under the big buildings in a city too old for all of us. Most nights it was as if Frank weren't there.

'Lilly is only eleven,' Fehlgeburt would say. 'It's wonderful that she loves literature. It could be her salvation. That hotel is no place for her.'

'*Wo ist die Germütlichkeit?*' Frank was singing.

'You're very good with Lilly,' I told Miss Miscarriage. 'Do you want a family of your own, someday?'

'Four hundred and sixty-four!' Frank sang.

'I wouldn't want children until after the revolution,' Fehlgeburt said, humorlessly.

'Do you think Fehlgeburt likes me?' I asked Frank, when we were walking home.

'Wait till we start school,' Frank suggested. 'Find a nice young girl—your own age.'

And so, although I lived in a Viennese whorehouse, my sexual world was probably like the sexual world for most Americans who were fifteen in 1957; I beat off to images of a dangerously violent prostitute, while I kept walking a young

270

'older' girl to her home—waiting for the day I might dare to kiss her, or even hold her hand.

I expected that the 'timid souls'—the guests who (Schwanger had predicted) would be drawn to the Hotel New Hampshire —would remind me of myself. They didn't. They came occasionally in buses: odd groups on organized tours—and some of the tours were as odd as the groups. Librarians from Devon, Kent, and Cornwall; ornithologists from Ohio—they had been observing storks at Rust. They were so regular in their habits that they all went to bed before the whores started working; they slept right through the nightly rumpus and were often off on a tour in the morning before Screaming Annie wrapped up her last orgasm, before the radical Old Billig walked in off the street —the new world shining in his old mind's eye. The groups were the oblivious ones, and Frank could sometimes make extra money by marching them off on 'walking tours.' The groups were easy—even the Japanese Male Choral Society, who discovered the whores as a group (and used them as a group). What a loud, strange time that was—all that screwing, all that singing! The Japanese had a great many cameras with them and took everyone's picture—all of our family pictures, too. In fact, Frank would always say it's a shame that the *only* photographs we have of our time in Vienna come from that one visit of the Japanese Male Choral Society. There is one of Lilly with Fehlgeburt—and a book, of course. There's a touching one of the two Old Billigs; they look like what Lilly would call a 'sweet' old couple. There's Franny leaning on the stout shoulder of Susie the bear, Franny looking a little thin, but sassy and strong—'strangely confident' is how Frank describes Franny in this period. There's a curious one of Father and Freud. They appear to be sharing the baseball bat—or they appear to have been squabbling over the bat; it is as if they'd been fighting over who was up next, and they'd interrupted their brawl only long enough for the picture to be taken.

I'm standing with Dark Inge. I remember the Japanese gentleman who asked Inge and me to stand beside each other; we had been sitting down, playing crazy eights, but the Japanese said the light wasn't right and so we had to stand. It's a slightly unnatural moment; Screaming Annie is still sitting down—at that part of the table where the light was generous—and overly powdered Babette is whispering something to Jolanta, who is standing a little back from the table with her arms folded across her impressive bosom. Jolanta could never learn the rules to crazy eights. In this picture, Jolanta looks like she's about to break up the game. I remember that the Japanese were afraid of her, too—perhaps because she was so much bigger than any of them.

And what distinguishes all these photographs—our only pictorial record of Vienna, 1957–64—is that all these people familiar to us have to share the photographs with a Japanese or two, with a total stranger or two. Even the photograph of Ernst the pornographer leaning against the car outside. Arbeiter is leaning against the fender with him—and those legs protruding from under the grille of the old Mercedes, those legs belong to the one called Wrench; Schraubenschlüssel never got more than his legs in a picture. And surrounding the car are Japanese —strangers none of us would see again.

Might we have known, then—had we looked at that photograph closely—that this was no ordinary car? Who ever heard of a Mercedes, even an old one, that needed so much mechanical attention? Herr Wrench was always under the car, and crawling around in it. And why did the one car belonging to the Symposium on East-West Relations need so much care when it was so rarely driven anywhere? Looking at it, now, of course . . . well, the photograph in obvious. It is hard to look at that photograph and not recognize that old Mercedes for what it was.

A bomb. A constantly wired and rewired, ever-ready bomb. The whole car was a bomb. And those unrecognizable Japanese that populate all of our only photographs . . . well, now it's easy to see these strangers, those foreign gentlemen, as symbolic of the unknown angels of death which would accompany that car. To think that for years we children told each other jokes about how bad a mechanic Schraubenschlüssel must be in order to be constantly fussing with that Mercedes! When all the while he was an *expert!* Mr. Wrench, the bomb expert; for almost seven years that bomb was ready—every day.

We never knew what they were waiting for—or what moment would have been *ripe* for it, had we not forced their hand. We have only the Japanese pictures to go on, and they make a murky story.

'What do you remember of Vienna, Frank?' I asked him—I ask him all the time. Frank went into a room to be alone with himself, and when he came out he handed me a short list:

1. Franny with Susie the bear.
2. Going to buy your damn barbells.

272

3. Walking Fehlgeburt home.
4. The presence of the King of Mice.

Frank handed me this list and said, 'Of course, there's more, but I don't want to get into it.'

I understand, and of course I remember going to buy my barbells, too. We *all* went. Father, Freud, Susie, and we children. Freud went because he knew where the sports shop was. Susie went because Freud could help her remember where the shop was by shouting at her in the streetcar. 'Are we past that hospital-supply place on Mariahilfer?' Freud would cry. 'It's the second left, or the third, after that.'

'Earl!' Susie would say, looking out the window. The *Strassenbahn* conductor would caution Freud, saying, 'I hope it's safe—it's not tied: the bear. We don't usually let them on if they're not tied.'

'*Earl!*' Susie said.

'It's a smart bear,' Frank told the conductor.

In the sports shop I bought 300 pounds of weights, one long barbell, and two dumbbell bars for the one-arm curls.

'Deliver them to the Hotel New Hampshire,' Father said.

'They don't deliver,' Frank said.

'They don't deliver?' Franny said. 'Well, we can't *carry* them!'

'Earl!' Susie said.

'Be nice, Susie!' Freud shouted. 'Don't be rude!'

'The bear would really appreciate it if these weights were *delivered,*' Frank told the man in the sports shop. But it didn't work. We should have seen then that the power of a bear in getting things to work out for us was diminishing. We distributed the weights as best we could. I put seventy-five on each of the short dumbbell bars and carried one in each hand. Father and Frank and Susie the bear struggled with the long bar, and another 150 pounds. Franny opened doors and cleared the sidewalk, and Lilly held on to Freud; she was his Seeing Eye bear for the trip home.

'Jesus God!' Father said, when they wouldn't let us on the *Strassenbahn*.

'They let us on to get *out* here!' Franny said.

'It's not the bear they mind,' Freud said. 'It's the long barbell.'

'It looks dangerous, the way you're carrying it,' Franny told Frank, Susie, and Father.

273

'If you'd kept working with the weights, like Iowa Bob,' I told Father, 'you could carry it by yourself. You wouldn't make it look so *heavy.*'

Lilly had noticed that the Austrians permitted bears on streetcars, but not barbells; she also noticed that the Austrians were liberal in regard to skis. She suggested we buy a ski bag and put the long barbell in it; then the streetcar conductor would think the barbell was just some very heavy pair of skis.

Frank suggested someone go get Schraubenschlüssel's car.

'It never runs,' Father said.

'It must be ready to run by now,' Franny said. 'That asshole's been fixing it for years.'

Father hopped the streetcar and went home to ask for the car. And shouldn't we have known by the radicals' quick refusal that a *bomb* was parked outside our new hotel? But we thought it was all merely an aspect of the rudeness of the radicals; we carried all that weight home. I finally had to leave the others, and the long barbell, at the Kunsthistorisches Museum. They wouldn't let a barbell in the museum, either—nor would they let in a bear. 'Brueghel wouldn't have minded,' Frank said. But they had to kill time on the street corner. Susie danced a little; Freud tapped his baseball bat; Lilly and Franny sang an American song—they passed the time by making a little money. Street clowns, Viennese specialties, 'the presence of the King of Mice,' as Frank would say—Frank passed the hat. It was the hat from the bus driver's uniform Father had bought Frank—the seedy-funeral-parlor cap that Frank wore when he played doorman at the Hotel New Hampshire. Frank wore it all the time in Vienna —our imposter King of Mice, Frank. We all thought often of the sad performer with his unwanted rodents who one day stopped passing the open windows, who made the leap, taking his poor mice with him. LIFE IS SERIOUS BUT ART IS FUN! He made his statement; the open windows he had kept passing for so long —they finally drew him.

I jogged home with the 150 pounds.

'Hi, Wrench,' I said to the radical under the car.

I ran back to the Kunsthistorisches Museum and trotted home with seventy-five more pounds. Father, Frank, Susie the bear, Franny, Lilly, and Freud brought home the remaining seventy-five. So then I had weights, then I could evoke the first Hotel New Hampshire—and Iowa Bob—and some of the foreignness of Vienna disappeared.

We had to go to school, of course. It was an American school near the zoo in Hietzing, near the palace at Schönbrunn. For a while Susie would accompany us on the streetcar each morning, and meet us when school was over. It was a great way to meet the other kids—to be delivered and brought home by a bear. But Father or Freud had to come with Susie because bears were not allowed on the streetcars alone, and the school was near enough to the zoo so that people in the suburbs were more nervous about seeing a bear than were the people in the city.

It would only occur to me, later, that we all did Frank a great disservice by not acknowledging his sexual discretion. For seven years in Vienna, we never knew who his boyfriends were; he told us that they were boys at the American School—and being the oldest of us, and in the most advanced German course, Frank was often at school the longest, and alone. His proximity to the excess of sex in the second Hotel New Hampshire must have inclined Frank to discretion in much the same manner that I was convinced of whispering by my intercom initiation with Ronda Ray. And Franny had her bear for the moment—and her rape to get over, Susie kept telling me.

'She's over it,' I said.

'*You're* not,' Susie said. 'You've still got Chipper Dove on your mind. And so does she.'

'Then it's Chipper Dove Franny's not done with,' I said. 'The rape's over.'

'We'll see,' said Susie. 'I'm a smart bear.'

And the timid souls kept coming, not in overwhelming numbers; overwhelming numbers of timid souls would probably have been a contradiction—although we could have used the numbers. Even so, we had a better guest list than we had in the first Hotel New Hampshire.

The tour groups were easier than the individuals. There's something about an individual timid soul that is much more timid than a group of them. The timid souls who traveled alone, or the timid couples with the occasional timid children—these seemed to be the most easily upset by the day-and-night activity between which they were anxious guests. But in our first three or four years in the second Hotel New Hampshire, only one guest actually complained—that was how truly timid *these* timid souls were.

The complainer was an American. She was a woman traveling with her husband and her daughter, who was about Lilly's age. They were from New Hampshire, but not from the Dairy part of the state. Frank was working the reception desk when they checked in—late afternoon, after school. Right away, Frank noticed, the woman started braying about missing some of the 'clean, plain old honest-to-goodness *decency*' that she apparently associated with New Hampshire.

'It's the old plainness-but-goodness bullshit,' Franny would say, recalling Mrs. Urick.

'We've been robbed all over Europe,' the New Hampshire woman's husband told Frank.

Ernst was in the lobby, explaining to Franny and me some of the weirder positions of 'Tantric union.' This was pretty hard to follow in German, but although Franny and I would never catch up to Frank's German—and Lilly was, conversationally, almost as good as Frank within a year—Franny and I learned a lot at the American School. Of course, they didn't teach coitus there. That was Ernst's line, and although Ernst gave me the creeps, I couldn't stand to see him talking to Franny alone, so whenever I saw him talking to her, I tried to listen in. Susie the bear liked to listen in, too—with a paw touching my sister somewhere, a nice big paw that Ernst could see. But the day the Americans from New Hampshire checked in, Susie the bear was in the W.C.

'And *hair* in the bathrooms,' the woman said to Frank. 'You wouldn't believe some of the filth we've been exposed to.'

'We've thrown the guidebooks away,' her husband said to Frank. 'There's no trusting them.'

'We're trusting our instincts now,' the woman said, looking over the new lobby of the Hotel New Hampshire. 'We're looking for some *American* touches.'

'I can't wait to get home,' the daughter said, in a mousy little voice.

'I've got a nice pair of rooms on the third floor,' Frank said; 'adjoining rooms,' Frank added. But he was worrying if that wasn't too close to the whores underneath—only a floor away. 'Then again,' Frank said, 'the view from the fourth is better.'

'The heck with the view,' the woman said. 'We'll take the adjoining rooms on three. And no *hair*,' she added, menacingly, just as Susie the bear shuffled into the lobby—saw the little girl guest, and gave a show-off toss of her head and a low, bearish huff and snort.

'Look, a *bear*,' the little girl said, holding her father's leg.

Frank hit the bell a sharp *ping!* 'Luggage carrier!' Frank hollered.

I had to tear myself away from Ernst's description of the Tantric positions.

'The *vyanta* group has two main positions,' he was saying, blandly. 'The woman leans forward till she touches the ground with her hands, while the man takes her from behind, standing —that's the *dhenuka-vyanta-asana,* or cow position,' Ernst said, with his liquid stare at Franny.

'Cow position?' Franny said.

'Earl!' Susie said, disapprovingly, putting her head in Franny's lap—playing the bear for the new guests.

I started upstairs with the luggage. The little girl couldn't take her eyes off the bear.

'I have a sister about your age,' I told her. Lilly was out taking Freud for a walk—Freud no doubt lecturing to her about all the sights he couldn't see.

That was how Freud gave us tours. The baseball bat on one side, one of us children, or Susie, on the other. We steered him through the city, shouting out the names of the street corners when we arrived. Freud was getting deaf, too.

'Are we on Blutgasse?' Freud would cry out. 'Are we on Blood Lane?' he would ask.

And Lilly or Frank or Franny or I would holler, '*Ja!* Blutgasse!'

'Take a right,' Freud would direct us. 'When we get to Domgasse, children,' he'd say, 'we must find Number Five. This is the entrance to the Figaro House, where Mozart wrote *The Marriage of Figaro.* What year, Frank?' Freud would cry.

'Seventeen eighty-five!' Frank would shout back.

'And more important than Mozart,' Freud would say, 'is the first coffeehouse in Vienna. Are we still on Blutgasse, children?'

'*Ja!* Blood Lane,' we would say.

'Look for Number *Six,*' Freud would cry. 'The first coffeehouse in Vienna! Even Schwanger doesn't know this. She loves her *Schlagobers,* but she's like all these political people,' Freud said. 'She's got no sense of *history.*'

It was true that we learned no history from Schwanger. We learned to love coffee, chased with little glasses of water; we learned to like the soft dirt of newspapers on our fingers. Franny and I would fight over the one copy of the *International Herald Tribune.* In our seven years in Vienna, there was always news of Junior Jones in there.

'Penn State thirty-five, Navy six!' Franny would read, and we'd all cheer.

And later, it would be the Cleveland Browns 28, the New York Giants 14. The Baltimore Colts 21, the poor Browns 17.

Although Junior rarely imparted any more news than this to Franny—in his occasional letters—it was somehow special, hearing about him so indirectly, through the football scores, several days late, in the *Herald Tribune*.

'At Judengasse, turn right!' Freud would instruct. And we would follow Jews' Lane to the church of St. Ruprecht.

'The eleventh century,' Frank would murmur. The older the better for Frank.

And down to the Danube Canal; at the foot of the slope, on Franz Joself-Kai, was the monument Freud led us to rather often: the marble plaque memorializing those murdered by the Gestapo, whose headquarters had been on that spot.

'Right here!' Freud screamed, stamping and whacking with the baseball bat. 'Describe the plaque to me!' he cried. 'I've never seen it.'

Of course: because it was in one of the camps that he went blind. They had performed some failed experiment on his eyes in the camp.

'No, not *summer* camp,' Franny had to tell Lilly, who had always been afraid of being sent to summer camp and was unsurprised to hear that they tortured the campers.

'Not *summer* camp, Lilly,' Frank said. 'Freud was in a *death* camp.'

'But Herr Tod never found me,' Freud said to Lilly. 'Mr. Death never found me at home when he called.'

It was Freud who explained to us that the nudes in the fountain at the Neuer Markt, the Providence Fountain—or the Donner Fountain, after its creator—were actually copies of the original. The originals were in the Lower Belvedere. Designed to portray water as the source of life, the nudes had been condemned by Maria Theresa.

'She was a bitch,' Freud said. 'She founded a Chastity Commission,' he told us.

'What did they do?' Franny asked. 'The *Chastity* Commission?'

'What *could* they do?' Freud asked. 'What can those people *ever* do? They couldn't do anything to stop the sex, so they fucked around with a few fountains.'

Even the Vienna of Freud—the *other* Freud—was notorious for being unable to do anything to stop the sex, though this didn't stop the Victorian counterparts of Maria Theresa's Chastity Commission from trying. 'In those days,' Freud pointed out, admiringly, 'whores were allowed to make arrangements in the aisles of the Opera.'

'At intermissions,' Frank added, in case we didn't know.

Frank's favorite tour with Freud was the Imperial Vault—the *Kaisergruft* in the catacombs of the Kapuzinerkirche. The Hapsburgs have been buried there since 1633. Maria Theresa is there, the old prude. But not her heart. The corpses in the catacombs are heartless—their hearts are kept in another church; their hearts are to be found on another tour. 'History separates everything, eventually,' Freud would intone in the heartless tombs.

Good-bye, Maria Theresa—and Franz Josef, and Elizabeth, and the unfortunate Maximilian of Mexico. And, of course, Frank's prize lies with them: the Hapsburg heir, poor Rudolf the suicide—he's also there. Frank always got especially gloomy in the catacombs.

Franny and I got gloomiest when Freud directed us along Wipplingerstrasse to Füttergasse.

'Turn!' he'd cry, the baseball bat trembling.

We were in the Judenplatz, the old Jewish quarter of the city. It had been a kind of ghetto as long ago as the thirteenth century; the first expulsion of the Jews, there, had been in 1421. We knew only slightly more about the recent expulsion.

What was hard about being there with Freud was that this tour was not so visibly historical. Freud would call out to apartments that were no longer apartments. He would identify whole buildings that were no longer there. And the *people* he used to know there—they weren't there, either. It was a tour of things we couldn't see, but Freud saw them still; he saw 1939, and before, when he'd last been in the Judenplatz with a working pair of eyes.

The day the New Hampshire couple and their child arrived, Freud had taken Lilly to the Judenplatz. I could tell because she was depressed when she came back. I had just taken the bags and the Americans to their rooms on the third floor, and I was depressed, too. I had been thinking all the way upstairs about Ernst describing the 'cow position' to Franny. The bags weren't especially heavy because I was imagining that they were Ernst, and I was carrying *him* up to the top of the Hotel New Hampshire, where I was going to drop him out a window on the fifth floor.

The woman from New Hampshire ran her hand briefly up the banister and said, 'Dust.'

Schraubenschlüssel passed us on the landing of the second floor. He was smeared with grease from his fingertips to his biceps; he had a coil of copper wire around his neck like a hangman's noose and in his arms he lugged an obviously heavy box-shaped thing that resembled a giant battery—a battery too big for a Mercedes, I would recall, much later.

'Hi, Wrench,' I said, and he grunted past us; in his teeth he held, quite delicately—for him—some kind of glass-wrapped little fuse.

'The hotel's mechanic,' I explained, because it was the easiest thing to say.

'Not very clean,' said the woman from New Hampshire.

'Is there an automobile on the top floor?' her husband asked.

As we turned down the third-floor corridor, searching in the half-dark for the correct rooms, a door opened up on the fifth floor, the clamor of a kind of eleventh-hour typing reached us —Fehlgeburt, perhaps, either bringing a manifesto to a close or writing her thesis on the romance that is at the heart of American literature—and Arbeiter screamed down the stairwell.

'Compromise!' Arbeiter shrieked. 'You represent nothing so strongly as you represent *compromise!*'

'Each time is its *own* time!' Old Billig hollered back. Old Billig the radical was leaving for the day; he crossed the third-floor landing while I was still fumbling with the luggage and keys.

'You blow the way the wind blows, old man!' Arbeiter yelled. This was in German, of course, and I suppose—for the Americans, who didn't understand German—it might have seemed more ominous in that language than it was. I thought it was pretty ominous, and *I* understood it. 'One day, old man,' Arbeiter concluded, 'the wind's going to blow you away!'

Old Billig the radical stopped on the landing and yelled back up to Arbeiter. 'You're crazy!' he screamed. 'You'll kill us all! You have no *patience!*' he shouted.

And somewhere between the third and fifth floors, moving softly, her gentle figure generous with *Schlagobers*, the good Schwanger tried to soothe them both, trotting downstairs a few steps toward Old Billig, and talking in a whisper, trotting upstairs a few steps toward Arbeiter—with whom she had to speak up a little.

'Shut up!' Arbeiter snapped at her. 'Go get pregnant again,' he said to her. 'Go get another abortion. Go get some *Schlagobers,*' he abused her.

280

'Animal!' Old Billig cried; he started back upstairs. 'It is possible to remain a gentleman, but not *you!*' he screamed up at Arbeiter. 'You are not even a *humanist!*'

'Please,' Schwanger was soothing. '*Bitte, bitte.* . . .'

'You want *Schlagobers?*' Arbeiter roared at her. '*I* want *Schlagobers* running all over the Kärntnerstrasse,' he said, crazily. 'I want *Schlagobers* stopping the traffic on the Ring. *Schlagobers* and blood,' he said. 'That's what you'll see: over everything. Oozing over the streets!' said Arbeiter. '*Schlagobers* and blood.'

And I let the timid Americans from New Hampshire into their dusty rooms. Soon it would be dark, I knew, and the shouting matches upstairs would cease. And downstairs the groaning would start, the bed-rocking, the constant flushing of the bidets, the pacing of the bear—policing the second floor—and the baseball bat of Freud, whumping steadily, room to room.

Would the Americans go to the Opera? Would they return to see Jolanta muscling a brave drunk upstairs—or rolling him down? Would someone be kneading Babette, like dough, in the lobby, where I played cards with Dark Inge and told her about the heroics of Junior Jones? The Black Arm of the Law made her happy. When she was 'old enough,' she said, she was going to make a bundle, then go visit her father and see for herself how bad it was for blacks in America.

And at what hour of the night would Screaming Annie's first fake orgasm send the daughter from New Hampshire scurrying into her parents' room through the adjoining door? Would they three huddle in one bed until morning—overhearing the tired bargains made with Old Billig, the mean thudding of Jolanta wrecking someone?

Screaming Annie had told me what she would do to me if I ever touched Dark Inge.

'I keep Inge away from the men in the street,' she confided. 'But I don't want her thinking she's *in love,* or something. I mean, in a way, that's worse—*I* know. That really fucks you up. I mean, I'm not letting anyone *pay* her for it—not ever—and I'm not letting you sneak in for free.'

'She's only my sister Lilly's age,' I said. 'To me.'

'Who cares how old *she* is?' Screaming Annie said. 'I'm watching *you.*'

'You're old enough to get a rod, occasionally,' Jolanta told me. 'I've seen it. I got an eye for seeing *rods.*'

'If you get a hard-on, you might use it,' Screaming Annie

said. 'And I'm just telling you, if you want to use it, don't use it on Dark Inge. Use it on her and you lose it,' Screaming Annie told me.

'That's right,' Jolanta said. 'Use it with us, never with the kid. Use it with the kid and we'll finish you. Lift all the weights you want, sometime you got to fall asleep.'

'And when you wake up,' said Screaming Annie, 'your rod will be gone.'

'Got it?' Jolanta asked.

'Sure,' I said. And Jolanta leaned close to me and kissed me on the mouth. It was a kiss as threatening with lifelessness as the New Year's Eve kiss, tinged with vomit, that I had received from Doris Wales. But when Jolanta finished this kiss, she pulled away suddenly with my lower lip trapped in her teeth —just until I screamed. Then her mouth released me. I felt my arms lift up all by themselves—the way they do when I've been curling the one-arm dumbbells, for half an hour or so. But Jolanta was backing away from me very watchfully, her hands in her purse. I looked at the hands and the purse until she was out of my room. Screaming Annie was still there.

'Sorry about the bite,' she said. 'I really didn't tell her to do it. She's just mean, all by herself. You know what she's got in the purse?' I didn't want to know.

Screaming Annie would know. She lived with Jolanta—Dark Inge had told me. In fact, Dark Inge told me, not only were her mother and Jolanta girl friends of the lesbian kind, but Babette also lived with a woman (a whore who worked the Mariahilfer Strasse). Only Old Billig actually preferred men; and, Dark Inge told me, Old Billig was so old she preferred nothing at all—most of the time.

So I stayed strictly nonsexual with Dark Inge; in fact, it wouldn't have occurred to me to even *think* of her sexually if her mother hadn't brought it up. I stayed strictly to my imagination: of Franny, of Jolanta. And of course my shy, stumbling courtship of Fehlgeburt, the reader. The girls at the American School all knew I lived in '*that* hotel on the Krugerstrasse'; I was not in the same class of Americans that they were in. People say that in America most Americans are not at all class-conscious, but I know about the Americans who live abroad, and they are wildly conscious about what *kind* of Americans they are.

Franny had her bear, and, I suppose, she had her imagination as much as I had mine. She had Junior Jones and his football scores; she must have had to work hard to imagine him past the ends of the games. And she had her correspondence with Chipper Dove, she had her rather one-sided imagination concerning him.

Susie had a theory about Franny's letters to Chipper Dove. 'She's afraid of him,' Susie said. 'She's actually terrified of ever seeing him again. It's *fear* that makes her do it—write to him all the time. Because if she can address him, in a normal voice—if she can *pretend* that she's having a normal relationship with him —well . . . then he's no rapist, then he never did actually *do it* to her, and she doesn't want to *deal* with the fact that he *did*. Because,' Susie said, 'she's afraid that Dove or someone like him will rape her *again*.'

I thought about that. Susie the bear might not have been the smart bear Freud had in mind, but she was a smart bear on her own terms.

What Lilly once said about her has stayed with me. 'You can make fun of Susie because she's afraid to simply be a human being and have to *deal*—as she would say—with other human beings. But how many human beings feel that way and don't have the imagination to do anything about it? It may be stupid to go through life as a bear,' Lilly would say, 'but you'll have to admit it takes imagination.'

And we were all familiar with living with imagination, of course. Father thrived there; imagination was his own hotel. Freud could see only there. Franny, composed in the present, was also looking ahead—and I was always, for the most part, looking at Franny (for signals, for some vital signs, for directions). Of us all, Frank was perhaps the most successfully imaginative; he made up his own world and kept to himself there. And Lilly, in Vienna, had a mission—which was to keep her safe, for a while. Lilly had decided to grow. It had to be with her imagination that she would do this, because we noted few physical changes.

What Lilly did in Vienna was *write*. Fehlgeburt's reading had gotten to her. Lilly wanted to be a writer, of all things, and we were embarrassed enough for her that we never accused her of it —although we knew she was doing it, all the time. And she was embarrassed enough by it so that she never admitted it, either. But each of us knew that Lilly was *writing* something. For nearly seven years, she wrote and wrote. We knew the sound of her typewriter; it was different from the radicals'. Lilly wrote very slowly.

'What are you doing, Lilly?' someone would ask her, knocking on her ever-locked door.

'Trying to grow,' Lilly would say.

And that was our euphemism for it, too. If Franny managed to say she was beaten up, when she'd been raped—if Franny could get away with *that*, I thought—then Lilly ought to be allowed to say she was 'trying to grow' when she was (we all knew) 'trying to write.'

And so when I told Lilly that the New Hampshire family included a little girl just her age, Lilly said, 'So what? I've got some growing to do. Maybe I'll introduce myself, after supper.'

One of the curses of timid people—in bad hotels—is that they're often too timid to *leave*. They're so timid they don't even dare to complain. And with their timidity comes a certain politeness; if they check out because a Schraubenschlüssel has frightened them on the stairs, because a Jolanta has bitten someone in the face in the lobby, because a Screaming Annie has inched them closer to death with her howls—even if they find bear hair in the bidet, they still apologize.

Not the woman from New Hampshire, however. She was more feisty than your average timid guest. She lasted through the early evening pickups of the whores (the family must have been dining out). The family lasted past midnight without a complaint; not even an inquiring phone call to the front desk. Frank was studying with the dressmaker's dummy. Lilly was trying to grow. Franny was at the desk in the lobby, and Susie the bear was cruising there—her presence made the whores' customers their usual peaceful selves. I was restless. (I was restless for seven years, but this night I was especially restless.) I had been playing darts at the Kaffee·Mowatt with Dark Inge and Old Billig. It was another slow night for Old Billig. Screaming Annie found a customer crossing the Kärntnerstrasse and turning down Krugerstrasse a little past midnight. I was waiting my turn at the darts when Screaming Annie and her furtive male companion peeked into the Mowatt; Screaming Annie saw Dark Inge with me and Old Billig.

'It's after midnight,' she said to her daughter. 'You go get some rest. It's a school day tomorrow.'

So we all walked back to the Hotel New Hampshire more or less together. Screaming Annie and her customer a little ahead of us. Inge and I on either side of Old Billig, who was talking about the Loire Valley in France. 'It's where I'd like to retire,'

284

she said, 'or go for my next holiday.' Dark Inge and I knew that Old Billig always spent her holidays—*every* holiday—with her sister's family in Baden. She took a bus or a train from a stop opposite the Opera; Baden would always be much more accessible to Old Billig than France.

When we walked into the hotel, Franny said that all the guests were in. The New Hampshire family had gone to bed about an hour ago. A youthful Swedish couple had gone to bed even earlier. Some old man from Burgenland hadn't left his room all night, and some British bicycle enthusiasts had come in drunk, double-checked their bicycles in the basement, attempted to be sportive with Susie the bear (until she growled), and were now, no doubt, passed out in their rooms. I went to my room to lift weights—passing Lilly's door at the magical instant her light went out; she had stopped growing for the night. I did some forearm curls with the long barbell, but I didn't have much interest in it; it was too late. I was just lifting because I was bored. I heard the dressmaker's dummy slam off the wall between my room and Frank's; something Frank was studying had made him cross, and he was taking it out on the dummy—or he was just bored, too. I knocked on the wall.

'Keep passing the open windows,' Frank said.

'Wo ist die Gemütlichkeit?' I sang, half-heartedly.

I heard Franny and Susie the bear slipping past my door.

'Four hundred and sixty-four, Franny!' I whispered.

I heard the solid *thock* of Freud's baseball bat, falling out of a bed above me. Babette's bed, I could tell. Father, as usual, was sleeping soundly—dreaming well, no doubt; dreaming on and on. A man's voice blurted out something on the landing of the second floor, and I heard Jolanta respond. She responded by throwing him down the stairs.

'Sorrow,' I heard Frank murmur.

Franny was singing the song Susie could make her sing, so I tried to concentrate on the fight in the lobby. It was an easy fight for Jolanta, I could tell. All the pain came from the man.

'You got a cock like a wet sock and you tell me it's *my* fault?' Jolanta was saying. This was followed by the sound of the man absorbing a blow—the heel of the hand into the jowl? I guessed. Hard to be sure, but there was the sound of the man falling again —that was clear. He said something, but his words seemed strangled. Was Jolanta choking him? I wondered. Should I interrupt Franny's song? Was this a job for Susie the bear?

And then I heard Screaming Annie. I think everyone on the

Krugerstrasse heard Screaming Annie. I think that even some fashionable people who'd been to the Opera, and who were just leaving the Sacher Bar and walking home along the Kärntnerstrasse, must have heard Screaming Annie.

One November day in 1969—five years after we left Vienna —two seemingly unrelated bits of news made morning headlines in the city. As of the seventeenth of November, 1969, it was announced, prostitutes were to be *barred* from strolling on the Graben and the Kärntnerstrasse—and from all the side streets off the Kärntnerstrasse, too, *except* the Krugerstrasse. The whores had owned these streets for 300 years, but after 1969 they would be given only the Krugerstrasse. In my opinion, the people in Vienna gave up on trying to save the Krugerstrasse *before* 1969. In my opinion, it was Screaming Annie's fake orgasm on the night the New Hampshire family was staying with us that determined the official decision. That particular fake orgasm *finished* the Krugerstrasse.

And on the same day in 1969 when the Austrian officials made their announcements about limiting the Kärntnerstrasse prostitutes to the Krugerstrasse, the newspapers also revealed that a new bridge over the Danube had *cracked;* a few hours after the ceremonies that opened the bridge, the bridge cracked. The official word on the fault of the crack put the blame on the poor sun. In my opinion, the sun was not to blame. Only Screaming Annie could crack a bridge—even a new bridge. There must have been a window open somewhere where she was working.

I believe that Screaming Annie faking an orgasm could raise the corpses of the heartless Hapsburgs out of their tombs.

And that night when the timid New Hampshire family was visiting us, Screaming Annie got off what was surely the record fake orgasm for the duration of our stay in Vienna. It was a seven-year orgasm. It was followed so closely by the single short yelp of her male companion that I reached a hand out of my bed and grabbed one of my barbells for support. I felt the dressmaker's dummy in Frank's room fly off the wall, and Frank himself stumbled clumsily toward his door. Franny's fine song was nipped in the upswing and Susie the bear, I knew, would be frantically searching for her head. For all the growing Lilly might have accomplished before she turned out her light, I knew she probably lost an inch in the single moment of recoiling from Screaming Annie's terrible sound.

'Jesus God!' Father called out.

The man Jolanta was beating up in the lobby found the sudden strength necessary to break free and lunge out the door. And other prostitutes passing by on the Krugerstrasse—I can only imagine them reconsidering their profession. Whoever called this 'the gentle occupation'? they must have been thinking.

Someone was whimpering. Babette, frightened, and thrown out of rhythm with Freud? Freud, seeking his baseball bat, as a weapon? Dark Inge, finally afraid for her mother? And it seemed that one of the radicals' typewriters—way up on the fifth floor —all by itself *moved* itself off a typing table and crashed to the floor.

In less than a minute, we were in the lobby, moving up the stairs to the second floor. I had never seen Franny look so deeply disturbed; Lilly went to her and hung on her hip. Frank and I fell in line, like soldiers, wordlessly drawn to the devastating cry. It was over now, and the silence Screaming Annie left behind was almost as bloodcurdling as her bellow. Jolanta and Susie the bear led the way upstairs—like bouncers moving in, grimly, on some unsuspecting rowdies.

'Trouble,' Father was muttering. 'That sounded like trouble.'

On the second-floor landing we met Freud and his baseball bat, leaning on Babette.

'We can't have any more of *that*,' Freud was saying. 'No hotel can survive it, no matter *what* class of clientele—that's too much, it's just more than anyone can bear.'

'Earl!' said Susie, bristling for a fight. Jolanta had her hands in her purse again. The whimpering continued and I realized it was Dark Inge, too frightened even to investigate her mother's incredible noise.

When we got to Screaming Annie's door, we saw that the New Hampshire family were not as timid as they had first appeared. The daughter certainly looked half-dead with fright, but she was standing almost on her own, leaning only slightly on her trembling father. He was in his pajamas and a red-and-black-striped robe. He held the shaft of a bedside lamp in his hand, the electrical cord wrapped around his wrist, the light bulb and shade removed—to make it a more efficient weapon, I suppose. The woman from New Hampshire stood closest to the door.

'It came from there,' she announced to us all, pointing to Screaming Annie's door. 'Now it's stopped. They must be dead.'

'Stand back,' her husband said to her, the lamp leaping up and down in his hand. 'It's not a sight for women or children, I'm sure.'

The woman glared at Frank, because—I guess—he had been the man at the desk who had officially admitted her to this madhouse. 'We're *Americans*,' she said, defiantly. 'We've never been exposed to anything this *sordid* before, but if one of you doesn't have the *guts* to go in there, *I* will.'

'You *will?*' Father said.

'It's clearly a murder,' the husband said.

'Nothing could be clearer,' the woman said.

'With a *knife*,' the daughter said, and cringed, involuntarily —she twitched against her father. 'It must have been a knife,' she almost whispered.

The husband dropped the lamp, then snatched it up again.

'Well?' the woman said to Frank, but Susie the bear pushed forward.

'Let the bear in!' Freud said. 'Don't mess with the guests, just let the bear in!'

'*Earl!*' said Susie. The husband, thinking Susie might attack him and his family, poked the lamp, threateningly, in Susie's face.

'Don't make the bear hostile!' Frank warned him, and the family retreated.

'Be careful, Susie,' Franny said.

'Murder,' murmured the New Hampshire woman.

'Something unspeakable,' her husband said.

'A knife,' the daughter said.

'It was just a fucking *orgasm*,' Freud said. 'Haven't you ever *had* one, for Christ's sake?' Freud blundered forward with his hand on Susie's back; he struck the door a blow with his baseball bat, then fumbled for the knob. 'Annie?' he called. I noticed Jolanta close behind Freud, like his larger shadow—her fierce hands in her dark purse. Susie made a convincing *snorfle* at the base of the door.

'An orgasm?' said the woman from New Hampshire—her husband automatically covered the daughter's ears.

'My God,' Franny would say later. 'They would bring their daughter to see a murder, but they wouldn't even let her *hear* about an orgasm. Americans sure are strange.'

Susie the bear shouldered the door, knocking Freud off balance. The end of his Louisville Slugger skidded along the hall floor, but Jolanta caught the old man and propped him up against the doorjamb, and Susie roared into the room. Screaming Annie was naked, except for her stockings and her garter belt; she was smoking a cigarette, and she leaned over the completely unmoving man on his back on the bed and blew smoke into his face; he didn't flinch, or cough, and he was naked except for his ankle-length dark green socks.

'Dead!' gasped the woman from New Hampshire.

'*Tod?*' whispered Freud. 'Somebody tell me!'

Jolanta took her hands out of her purse and sunk a fist in the man's groins. His knees snapped up all by themselves and he coughed; then he went flat again.

'He's not dead,' Jolanta said, and muscled her way out of the room.

'He just passed right out on me,' Screaming Annie said. She seemed surprised. But I would think, later, that there was no way you could keep both sane and conscious when you were deluded into thinking that screaming Annie was coming. It was probably safer to pass out than to hang on and go home crazy.

'Is she a *whore?*' the husband asked, and this time it was the woman from New Hampshire who covered her daughter's ears; she tried to cover the girl's *eyes,* too.

'What are you, *blind?*' Freud asked. 'Of course she's a whore!'

'We're *all* whores,' Dark Inge said, coming from nowhere and hugging her mother—glad to see she was all right. 'What's wrong with that?'

'Okay, okay,' Father said. 'Everyone back to bed!'

'These are your *children?*' the New Hampshire woman asked Father; she wasn't sure which of us to indicate with her sweep of the hand.

'Well, *some* of them are,' Father said, amiably.

'You should be ashamed,' the woman told him. 'Exposing children to this sordid life.'

I don't think it had occurred to Father that we were being 'exposed' to anything particularly 'sordid.' Nor was the New Hampshire woman's tone of voice anything Father ever would have heard from my mother. But nonetheless my father seemed suddenly stricken by this accusation. Franny said later that she could see in the genuine bewilderment on his face—and then the growing look of something as close to guilt as we would ever see in him—that despite the sorrow Father's dreaming might cause us, we would always prefer him dreamy to guilty; we could accept him as being *out of it,* but we couldn't like him as much if he were truly a worrier, if he had been truly 'responsible' in the way that fathers are expected to be responsible.

'Lilly, you shouldn't be here, darling,' Father said to Lilly, turning her away from the door.

'I should think *not*,' said the husband from New Hampshire, now struggling to keep both his daughter's eyes *and* ears covered at the same time—but unable to tear himself away from the scene.

'Frank, take Lilly to her room, please,' Father said, softly. 'Franny?' Father asked, 'are you okay, dear?'

'Sure,' Franny said.

'I'm sorry, Franny,' Father said, steering her down the hall. 'For everything,' he added.

'He's *sorry!*' said the woman from New Hampshire, facetiously. 'He exposes his children to such disgusting filth as this and he's *sorry!*' But Franny turned on her. We might criticize Father, but no one else could.

'You dead cunt,' Franny said to the woman.

'Franny!' Father said.

'You useless twat,' Franny told the woman. 'You sad wimp,' she told the man. 'I know just the man to show *you* what's "disgusting," ' she said. '*Aybha*, or *gajâsana*,' Franny said to them. 'You know what *that* is?' But *I* knew; I could feel my hands start to sweat. 'The woman lies prone,' Franny said, 'and the man lies on top of her pressing his *loins* forward and curving the small of his back.' The woman from New Hampshire shut her eyes upon mention of the word 'loins'; the poor husband seemed to be trying to cover the eyes and ears of his entire family at once. 'That's the elephant position,' Franny said, and I shuddered. The 'elephant position' was one of the two main positions (with the cow position) in the *vyanta* group; it was the elephant position that Ernst spoke of in the dreamiest way. I thought I was going to be sick, and Franny suddenly started to cry. Father took her down the hall, quickly—Susie the bear, worriedly but ever bearlike, went whining after them.

The customer who'd passed out when Screaming Annie finished the Krugerstrasse came to. He was awfully embarrassed to find Freud, me, the New Hampshire family, Screaming Annie, her daughter, and Babette all looking at him. At least, I thought, he was spared the bear—and the rest of my family. Late as usual, Old Billig wandered in; she'd been asleep.

'What's going on?' she asked me.

'Didn't Screaming Annie wake you, too?' I asked her.

'Screaming Annie doesn't wake me up anymore,' Old Billig said. 'It's those damn world planners up on the fifth floor.'

I looked at my watch. It was still before two in the morning. 'You're still asleep,' I whispered to Old Billig. 'The radicals don't come this early.'

'I'm wide-awake,' Old Billig said. '*Some* of the radicals never went home last night. Sometimes they stay all night. And they're usually quiet. But Screaming Annie must have disturbed them. They dropped something. Then they were hissing like snakes, trying to pick whatever it was up.'

'They shouldn't be here at *night*,' Freud said.

'I've seen enough of this sordidness,' the New Hampshire woman said, seeming to feel ignored.

'I've seen it all,' Freud said, mysteriously. '*All* the sordidness,' he said. 'You get used to it.'

Babette said she'd had enough for one night; she went home. Screaming Annie put Dark Inge back to bed. Screaming Annie's embarrassed male companion tried to leave as inconspicuously as possible, but the New Hampshire family watched him all the way out of the hotel. Jolanta joined Freud and Old Billig and me at the second-floor landing. We listened up the stairwell, but the radicals—if they were there—were quiet now.

'I'm too old for the stairs,' Old Billig said, 'and too smart to poke my nose where I'm not wanted. But they're up there,' she said. 'Go see.' Then she turned back to the street—to the gentle occupation.

'I'm blind,' Freud admitted. 'It would take me half the night to climb those stairs, and I wouldn't see anything if they *were* there.'

'Give me your baseball bat,' I said to Freud. 'I'll go see.'

'Just take me with you,' Jolanta said. 'Fuck the bat.'

'I need the bat, anyway,' Freud said. Jolanta and I said good night to him and started up the stairs.

'If there's anything to it,' Freud said, 'wake me up and tell me about it. Or tell me about it in the morning.'

Jolanta and I listened for a while on the third-floor landing, but all we could hear was the New Hampshire family sliding every object of furniture against their doors. The youthful Swedish couple had slept through it all—apparently used to some kind of orgasm; or used to murder. The old man from Burgenland had possibly died in his room, shortly after checking in. The bicyclists from Great Britain were on the fourth floor, and probably too drunk to be aroused, I thought, but when Jolanta and I paused on the fourth-floor landing and listened for the radicals, we encountered one of the British bicyclists there.

291

'Bloody strange,' he whispered to us.

'What is?' I said.

'Thought I heard a bloody scream,' he said. 'But it was *down*stairs. Now I hear them dragging the body round *up*stairs. Bloody odd.'

He looked at Jolanta. 'Does the tart speak English?' he asked me.

'The tart's with me,' I said. 'Why not just go back to bed?' I was perhaps eighteen or nineteen on this night, I think; the effects of the weight lifting, I noticed, were beginning to impress people. The British bicyclist went back to bed.

'What do you think is going on?' I asked Jolanta, nodding upstairs, toward the silent fifth floor.

She shrugged; it was nowhere near Mother's shrug, or Franny's shrug, but it was a woman's shrug. She put her big hands in the deadly purse.

'What do I care what's going on?' she asked. 'They might change the world,' Jolanta said of the radicals, 'but they won't change *me*.'

This somehow reassured me, and we climbed to the fifth floor. I hadn't been up there since I'd helped move the typewriters and office equipment, three or four years ago. Even the hall looked different. There were a lot of boxes in the hall, and jugs—of chemicals or wine? I wondered. More chemicals than they needed for the one mimeograph machine, anyway—if they were chemicals. Fluids for the car, I might have thought; I didn't know. I did the unsuspecting thing; I knocked on the first door Jolanta and I came to.

Ernst opened it; he was smiling. 'What's up?' he asked. 'Can't sleep? Too many orgasms?' He saw Jolanta just behind me. 'Looking for a more private room?' he asked me. Then he asked us in.

The room adjoined two others—I remembered that it was once joined to only *one* other—and its furnishings looked substantially different, although, over the years, I had not seen a single large item carried in or out; just those things I assumed Schraubenschlüssel needed for the car.

Schraubenschlüssel was in the room, and Arbeiter—the ever-working Arbeiter. It must have been one of the large battery-type boxes that Old Billig and I had heard fall off a table, because the typewriters were in another part of the room; clearly no one had been typing. There were some maps—or maybe they were blueprints spread about, and there was the automobilelike

292

equipment one associates with service garages, not offices: chemical things, electrical things. The radical Old Billig, who'd called Arbeiter crazy, was not there. And my sweet Fehlgeburt, like a good student of American literature, was either home reading or home asleep. In my opinion, just the *bad* radicals were there: Ernst, Arbeiter, and Wrench.

'That was one hell of an orgasm tonight!' Schraubenschlüssel said, leering at Jolanta.

'Another fake,' Jolanta said.

'Maybe *that* one was real,' Arbeiter said.

'Dream on,' Jolanta said.

'You've got the tough one following you around, eh?' Ernst said to me. 'You've got the tough piece of meat with you, I see.'

'All you do is write about it,' Jolanta said to him. 'You probably can't get it up.'

'I know just the position for you,' Ernst told her.

But I didn't want to hear it. I was frightened of them all.

'We're going,' I said. 'Sorry to disturb you. We just didn't know anyone was here at night.'

'The work backs up if we don't occasionally stay late,' Arbeiter said.

With Jolanta at my side, her strong hands hugging something in her purse, we said good night. And it was *not* my imagination that—just as I was leaving—I caught sight of another figure in the shadows of the farthest adjoining room. She also had a purse, but what she had in her purse was out—in her hand, and trained on Jolanta and me. It was just a glimpse I had of her, and her gun, before she slipped back in the shadows and Jolanta closed the door. Jolanta didn't see her; Jolanta just kept watching Ernst. But I saw her: our gentle, motherlike radical, Schwanger —with a gun in her hand.

'What do you have in your purse, anyway?' I asked Jolanta. She shrugged. I said good night to her, but she slipped a big hand down the front of my pants and held me a moment; I'd hopped out of bed and into some clothes so fast that I'd not taken the time for underwear. 'You going to send me out on the street again?' she asked me. 'I want just one more trick before I call it a night.'

'It's too late for me,' I said, but she could feel me growing hard in her hand.

'It doesn't *feel* too late,' she said.

'I think my wallet's in another pair of pants,' I lied.

'Pay me later,' Jolanta said. 'I'll trust you.'

293

'How much?' I asked, when she squeezed harder.

'For you, only three hundred Schillings,' she said. For *everyone*, I knew, it was three hundred Schillings.

'It's too much,' I said.

'It doesn't *feel* like too much,' she said, giving me a sharp twist; I was *very* hard at the moment, and it hurt.

'You're hurting me,' I said. 'I'm sorry, but I don't want to.'

'You *want to*, all right,' she said, but she let me go. She looked at her watch; she shrugged again. She walked down the stairs to the lobby with me; I said good night to her again. When I went to my room and she went out on the Krugerstrasse, Screaming Annie was coming back in—with another victim. I lay in bed wondering if I could fall soundly enough asleep so that the next fake orgasm would leave me alone; then I thought I'd never make it, so I lay awake waiting for it—after which, I hoped, I'd have plenty of time for sleep. But this one was a long time coming; I began to imagine that it had already happened, that I had dozed off and missed it, and so—like life itself—I believed that what was *about* to happen had already taken place, was already over, and I allowed myself to forget it, only to be surprised by it moments later. Out of that soundest sleep—right when you've first fallen off—Screaming Annie's fake orgasm dragged me.

'Sorrow!' Frank cried in his dreams, like poor Iowa Bob startled by his 'premonition' of the beast who would do him in.

I swear I could feel Franny tense in her sleep. Susie snorted. Lilly said, 'What?' The Hotel New Hampshire shuddered with the silence following a thunderclap. Perhaps it was later, actually in my sleep, that I heard something heavy being carried downstairs, and out the lobby door, to Schraubenschlüssel's car. At first I mistook the cautious sound for Jolanta carrying a dead customer out to the street, but she wouldn't have bothered about trying to be quiet. I am just imagining this, I said in my sleep, when Frank knocked on the wall.

'Keep passing the open windows,' I whispered. Frank and I met in the hall. We watched the radicals loading the car through the lobby window. Whatever they were loading looked heavy and still; at first I thought it might be the body of Old Billig—the radical—but they were being too careful with whatever it was for the thing to be a body. Whatever it was required propping up in the backseat, between Arbeiter and Ernst. Then Schrauben-schlüssel drove whatever it was away.

Through the window of the departing car, Frank and I saw the mysterious thing in silhouette—slightly slumped against Ernst, and bigger than him, and tilting away from Arbeiter, whose arm was ineffectually wrapped around it, as if he were hopelessly trying to reinterest a lover who was leaning toward someone else. The thing—whatever it was—was quite clearly not human, but it was somehow strangely animal in its appearance. I'm sure, now, of course, that it was completely mechanical, but its *shape* seemed animal in the passing car—as if Ernst the pornographer and Arbeiter held a *bear* between them, or a big dog. It was just a carload of sorrow, as Frank and I—and all of us—would learn, but its mystery plagued me.

I tried to describe it (and what Jolanta and I had seen on the fifth floor) to Father and Freud. I tried to describe the feeling of it all to Franny and Susie the bear, too. Frank and I had the longest talk about Schwanger. 'I'm sure you're mistaken about the gun,' Frank said. 'Not Schwanger. She might have been there. She might have wanted you to *not* associate her with *them,* and so she was hiding from you. But she wouldn't have a gun. And certainly she would never have pointed it at you. We're like her children—she's told us! You're imagining again,' Frank said.

Sorrow floats; seven years in a place you hate is a long time. At least, I felt, Franny was safe; that was always the main thing. Franny was in limbo. She was taking it easy, marking time with Susie the bear—and so I felt comfortable treading water, too.

At the university, Lilly and I would major in American literature (Fehlgeburt would be so pleased). Lilly majored in it, of course, because she wanted to be a writer—she wanted to grow. I majored in it as yet another indirect way of courting the aloof Miss Miscarriage; it seemed the most romantic thing to do. Franny would major in world drama—she was always the heavyweight among us; we would never catch up. And Frank took Schwanger's motherly and radical advice; Frank majored in economics. Thinking of Father and Freud, we all realized someone *ought* to. And Frank would be the one to save us, in time, so we would all be grateful to economics. Frank actually had a dual major, although the university would give him only a degree in economics. I guess I could say that Frank *minored* in world religions. 'Know thine enemy,' Frank would say, smiling.

For seven years we *all* floated. We learned German, but we spoke only our native language among ourselves. We learned literature, drama, economy, religion, but the sight of Freud's baseball bat could break our hearts for the land of baseball (though none of us was much interested in the game, that Louisville Slugger could bring tears to our eyes). We learned from the whores that, outside the Inner City, the Mariahilfer Strasse was the most promising hunting-ground for ladies of the night. And every whore spoke of getting out of the business if she was ever demoted to the districts past the Westbahnhof, to the Kaffee Eden, to the one-hundred-Schilling standing fucks in the Gaudenzdorfer Gürtel. We learned from the radicals that prostitution wasn't even officially *legal*—as we had thought —that there were registered whores who played by the rules, got their medical checkups, trafficked in the right districts, and that there were 'pirates' who never registered, or who turned in a *Büchl* (a license) but continued to practice the profession: that there were almost a thousand registered whores in the city in the early 1960s; that decadence was increasing at the necessary rate for the revolution.

Actually *what* revolution was supposed to take place we never learned. I don't know if all the radicals were sure, either.

'Got your *Büchl?*' we children would ask each other, going to school—and, later, going to the university.

That, and—'Keep passing the open windows': the refrain from our King of Mice song.

Our father seemed to have lost his *character* when our mother was lost to him. In seven years, I believe, he grew to be more of a presence and less of a person—for us children. He was affectionate; he could even be sentimental. But he seemed as lost to us (as a father) as Mother and Egg, and I think we sensed that he would need to endure some more concrete suffering before he would gain his character back—before he could actually *become* a character again: in the way Egg had been a character, in the way Iowa Bob had been one. I sometimes thought that Father was even less of a character than Freud. For seven years we missed our father, as if he had been on that plane. We were waiting for the hero in him to take shape, and perhaps doubting its final form—for with Freud as a model, one had to doubt my father's vision.

In seven years I would be twenty-two; Lilly, trying to grow and grow, would grow to be eighteen. Franny would be twenty-three—with Chipper Dove still 'the first,' and Susie the bear her one-and-only. Frank, at twenty-four, grew a beard. It was almost as embarrassing as Lilly's wanting to be a writer.

Moby-Dick would sink the *Pequod* and only Ishmael would

296

survive, again and again, to tell his tale to Fehlgeburt, who told it to us. In my years at the university, I used to press upon Fehlgeburt my desire to hear her read *Moby-Dick* aloud to me. 'I can never read this book by myself,' I begged her. 'I have to hear it from you.'

And that, at last, provided me with entrance to Fehlgeburt's cramped, desultory room behind the Rathaus, near the university. She would read to me in the evenings, and I would try to coax out of her why some of the radicals chose to spend the night in the Hotel New Hampshire.

'You know,' Fehlgeburt would tell me, 'the single ingredient in American literature that distinguishes it from other literatures of the world is a kind of giddy, illogical hopefulness. It is quite technically sophisticated while remaining ideologically naïve,' Fehlgeburt told me, on one of our walks to her room. Frank would eventually take the hint, and no longer accompany us —though this took him about five years. And the evening Fehlgeburt told me that American literature was 'quite technically sophisticated while remaining ideologically naïve' was *not* the evening I first tried to kiss her. After the line 'ideologically naïve,' I think a kiss would have seemed out of place.

The night I first kissed Fehlgeburt we were in her room. She had just read that part when Ahab refuses to help the captain of the *Rachel* search for the lost son. Fehlgeburt had no furniture in her room; there were too many books, and a mattress on the floor —a mattress for a single bed—and a single reading lamp, also on the floor. It was a cheerless place, as dry and as crowded as a dictionary, as lifeless as Ernst's logic, and I leaned across the uncomfortable bed and kissed Fehlgeburt on the mouth. 'Don't,' she said, but I kept kissing her until she kissed me back. 'You should go,' she said, lying down on her back and pulling me on top of her.

'Now?' I said.

'No, *now* it is not necessary to go,' she said. Sitting up, she started to undress; she did it the way she usually marked her place in *Moby-Dick*—uninterestedly.

'I should go *after?*' I asked, undressing myself.

'If you want,' she said. 'I mean you should go from the Hotel New Hampshire. You and your family. *Leave,*' she said. 'Leave before the fall season.'

'What fall season?' I asked her, completely naked now. I was thinking about Junior Jones's fall season with the Cleveland Browns.

'The Opera season,' Fehlgeburt said, naked herself—at last.
She was as thin as a novella; she was no bigger than some of the
shortest stories she had ever read to Lilly. It was as if all the
books in her room had been feeding on her, had consumed—not
nourished—her.

'The Opera season will start in the fall,' Fehlgeburt said, 'and
you and your family must leave the Hotel New Hampshire by
then. Promise me,' she said, halting me from moving farther up
her gaunt body.

'Why?' I asked.

'Please leave,' she said. When I entered her, I thought it was
the sex that brought her tears on, but it was something else.

'Am I the first?' I asked. Fehlgeburt was twenty-nine.

'First and last,' she said, crying.

'Do you have anything to protect you?' I asked, inside her. 'I
mean, you know, so you don't get *schwanger?*'

'It doesn't matter,' she said, in Frank's irritating fashion.

'Why?' I asked, trying to move cautiously.

'Because I'll be dead before the baby's born,' she said. I
pulled out. I sat her up beside me, but she—with surprising
strength—pulled me back on top of her; she took me in her hand
and *put* me back inside her. 'Come *on*,' she said, impatiently
—but it was not the impatience of desire. It was something else.

'Fuck me,' she said, flatly. 'Then stay the night, or go home. I
don't care. Just leave the Hotel New Hampshire, please *leave* it
—please make sure Lilly, especially, leaves it,' she begged me.
Then she cried harder and lost what slight interest she'd ever had
in the sex. I lay still inside her, growing smaller. I felt cold—I
felt the draft of coldness from under the ground, like the
coldness I remembered feeling when Frank first read to us from
Ernst's pornography.

'What are they doing on the fifth floor at night?' I asked
Fehlgeburt, who bit into my shoulder, and shook her head, her
eyes closed tightly in a violent squint. 'What are they planning?'
I asked her. I grew so small I slipped completely outside of her. I
felt her shaking and I shook, too.

'They're going to blow up the Opera,' she whispered, 'at one
of the peak performances,' she whispered. 'They're going to
blow up *The Marriage of Figaro*—something popular like that.
Or something heavier,' she said. 'I'm not sure which performance—*they're* not sure. But one that's full-house,' Fehlgeburt
said. 'The whole Opera.'

'They're crazy,' I said; I didn't recognize my voice. It

sounded creaky; it was like Old Billig's voice—Old Billig the whore *or* Old Billig the radical.

Fehlgeburt shook her head back and forth under me; her stringy hair whipped my face. 'Please get your family out,' she whispered. 'Especially Lilly,' she said. 'Little Lilly,' she blubbered.

'But they're not going to blow up the hotel, too, are they?' I asked Fehlgeburt.

'Everyone will be involved,' she said ominously. 'It has to involve everyone, or it's no good,' she said, and I heard Arbeiter's voice behind hers, or Ernst's all-embracing logic. A phase, a necessary phase. Everything. *Schlagobers,* the erotic, the State Opera, the Hotel New Hampshire—everything had to go. It was all decadent, I could hear them intoning. It was full of disgust. They would litter the Ringstrasse with *art*-lovers, with old-fashioned idealists silly and irrelevant enough to like *opera.* They would make some point or other by this kind of everything-bombing.

'Promise me,' Fehlgeburt whispered in my ear. 'You'll get them out. Your family. Everybody in it.'

'I promise,' I said. 'Of course.'

'Don't tell anyone I told you,' she said to me.

'Of course not,' I said.

'Please come back inside me, now,' Fehlgeburt said. 'Please come inside me. I want to feel it—just once,' she added.

'Why just *once?*' I asked.

'Just do it,' she said. 'Do everything to me.'

I did everything to her. I regret it; I am forever guilty for it; it was as desperate and joyless as any sex in the second Hotel New Hampshire ever was.

'If you think you're going to die before you'll even have time to have a baby,' I told Fehlgeburt, later, 'why don't you leave when *we* leave? Why don't you get away before they do it, or before they try?'

'I can't,' she said, simply.

'Why?' I asked. Of these radicals in our Hotel New Hampshire I would always be asking *why.*

'Because I drive the car,' Fehlgeburt said. 'I'm the driver,' she said. 'And the car's the main bomb, it's the one that starts all the rest. And someone has to drive it, and it's *me—I* drive the bomb,' Fehlgeburt said.

'Why *you?*' I asked her, trying to hold her, trying to get her to stop shaking.

'Because I'm the most expendable,' she said, and there was Ernst's dead voice again, there was Arbeiter's lawn-mower-like process of *thought*. I realized that in order for Fehlgeburt to believe this, even our gentle Schwanger would have had to convince her.

'Why not Schwanger?' I asked Miss Miscarriage.

'She's too important,' Fehlgeburt said. 'She's *wonderful*,' she said, admiringly—and full of loathing for herself.

'Why not Wrench?' I asked. 'He's obviously good with cars.'

'That's why,' Fehlgeburt said. 'He's too necessary. There will be other cars, other bombs to build. It's the hostage part I don't like,' she blurted out suddenly. 'It's not necessary, this time,' she added. 'There will be better hostages.'

'Who are the hostages?' I asked.

'Your family,' she said. 'Because you're Americans. More than Austria will notice us, then,' she said. 'That's the idea.'

'Whose idea?' I asked.

'Ernst's,' she said.

'Why not let Ernst be the driver?' I asked.

'He's the idea man,' Fehlgeburt said. 'He thinks it all up. Everything,' she added. Everything, indeed. I thought.

'And Arbeiter?' I asked. 'He doesn't know how to drive?'

'He's too loyal,' she said. 'We can't lose anyone that loyal. I am not so loyal,' she whispered. 'Look at me!' she cried. 'I'm telling *you* all this, aren't I?'

'And Old Billig?' I asked, winding down.

'He's not trustworthy,' Fehlgeburt said. 'He doesn't even know the plan. He's too slippery. He thinks of his own survival.'

'That's *bad?*' I asked her, brushing her hair back, off her streaked face.

'At *this* phase, that's bad,' Fehlgeburt said. And I realized what she was: a *reader*, only a reader. She read other people's stories just beautifully; she took direction; she followed the leader. Why I wanted to hear her read *Moby-Dick* was the same reason the radicals had made her the driver. We both knew she would do it; she wouldn't stop.

'Have we done everything?' Fehlgeburt asked me.

'What?' I said, and winced—and would wince, forever, to hear that echo of Egg. Even from myself.

'Have we done everything, *sexually?*' Fehlgeburt asked. 'Was that it? Was that everything?'

I tried to remember. 'I think so,' I said. 'Do you want to do more?'

'Not especially,' she said. 'I just wanted to have done it all once,' she said. 'If we've done it all, you can go home—if you want,' she added. She shrugged. It was not Mother's shrug, not Franny's, not even Jolanta's shrug. This was not quite a human movement; it was less a twitch than it was a kind of electrical pulsation, a mechanical lurch of her taut body, a dim signal. The dimmest, I thought. It was a nobody-home sign; it was an 'I'm-not-in, don't-call-me-I'll-call-you signal. It was a tick of a clock, or of a time bomb. Fehlgeburt's eyes blinked once at me; then she was asleep. I gathered my clothes. I saw she hadn't bothered to mark the spot where she stopped reading in *Moby-Dick;* I didn't bother to mark it, either.

It was after midnight when I crossed the Ringstrasse, walking from the Rathausplatz down the Dr. Karl Renner–Ring and into the Volksgarten. In the beer garden some students were shouting at each other in a friendly way; I probably knew some of them, but I didn't stop for a beer. I didn't want to talk about the *art* of this or that. I didn't want to have another conversation about *The Alexandria Quartet*—about which was the best of those novels, and which was the worst, and why. I didn't want to hear about who benefited the most from their correspondence—Henry Miller or Lawrence Durrell. I didn't even want to talk about *Die Blechtrommel,* which was the best thing there was to talk about —perhaps *ever*. And I didn't want to have another conversation about East-West relations, about socialism and democracy, about the long-term effects of President Kennedy's assassination —and, being an American, what did I think of the racial question? It was the end of the summer of 1964; I hadn't been in the United States since 1957, and I knew less about my country than some of the Viennese students knew. I also knew less about Vienna than any of them. I knew about my family, I knew about *our* whores, and *our* radicals; I was an expert on the Hotel New Hampshire and an amateur at everything else.

I walked all the way through the Heldenplatz—the Plaza of Heroes—and stood where thousands of cheering fascists had greeted Hitler, once. I thought that fanatics would always have an audience; all one might hope to influence was the *size* of the audience. I thought I must remember this perception, and test it against Frank, who would either take it over as his own perception, or revise it, or correct me. I wished I'd read as much as Frank; I wished I'd tried to grow as hard as Lilly. In fact, Lilly had sent off the efforts of her growth to some publisher in New York. She wasn't even going to tell us, but she had to borrow money from Franny for the postage.

'It's a novel,' Lilly said, sheepishly. 'It's a little autobiographical.'

'How little?' Frank had asked her.

'Well, it's really *imaginative* autobiography,' Lilly said.

'It's a *lot* autobiographical, you mean,' Franny said. 'Oh boy.'

'I can't wait,' Frank said. 'I bet I come off like a real loon.'

'No,' Lilly said. 'Everyone is a hero.'

'We're *all* heroes?' I asked.

'Well, you all *are* heroes, to me,' Lilly said. 'So in the book you are, too.'

'Even Father?' Franny asked.

'Well, he's the most imagined,' Lilly said.

And I thought that Father had to be the most imagined because he was the least real—he was the least *there* (of any of us). Sometimes it seemed Father was less with us than Egg.

'What's the book called, dear?' Father had asked Lilly.

'Trying to Grow,' Lilly had admitted.

'What else?' Franny said.

'How far's it go?' Frank asked. 'I mean, where's it *stop?'*

'It's over with the plane crash,' Lilly said. 'That's the end.'

The end of reality, I thought: just short of the plane crash seemed like a perfectly good place to stop—to me.

'You're going to need an agent,' Frank said to Lilly. 'That will be me.'

Frank *would* become Lilly's agent; he would become Franny's agent, and Father's agent, and even my agent, too—in time. He hadn't majored in economics for nothing. But I didn't know that on that end-of-the-summer evening in 1964 when I left Fehlgeburt, poor Miss Miscarriage, asleep and no doubt dreaming of her spectacular sacrifice; her *expendable* nature was virtually all I could see when I stood alone in the Plaza of Heroes and recalled how Hitler had made so many people seem expendable to such a mob of true believers. In the quiet evening I could almost hear the mindless din of *'Sieg Heil!'* I could see the absolute self-seriousness of Schraubenschlüssel's face when he tightened down the nut and washer on an engine-block bolt. And what else had he been tightening down? I could see the dull glaze of devotion in Arbeiter's eyes, making the statement to the press

302

upon his triumphant arrest—and our motherlike Schwanger sipping her *Kaffee mit Schlagobers,* the whipped cream leaving its pleasant little moustache upon her downy upper lip. I could see the way Schwanger braided Lilly's pigtail, humming to Lilly's lovely hair the way Mother had hummed; how Schwanger told Franny that she had the world's most beautiful skin, and the world's most beautiful hands; and I had bedroom eyes, Schwanger said—oh, I was going to be dangerous, she warned me. (Having just left Fehlgeburt, I felt not very dangerous.) There would always be a little *Schlagobers* in Schwanger's kisses. And Frank, Schwanger said, was a genius; if only he would consider politics more thoughtfully. All this affection did Schwanger shower on us—all this with a gun in her purse. I wanted to see Ernst in the cow position—with a cow! And in the elephant position! With you know what. They were as crazy as Old Billig said; they would kill us all.

I wandered on the Dorotheergasse toward the Graben. I stopped for a *Kaffee mit Schlagobers* at the Hawelka. A man with a beard at the table beside me was explaining to a young girl (younger than him) about the death of representational painting; he was describing the exact painting wherein this death of the whole art form had occurred. I didn't know the painting. I thought about the Schieles and the Klimts that Frank had introduced me to—at the Albertina and at the Upper Belvedere. I wished Klimt and Schiele were able to talk to this man, but the man was now addressing the death of rhyme and meter in poetry; again, I didn't know the poem. And when he moved on to the novel, I thought I'd better pay up and leave. My waiter was busy, so I had to listen to the story of the death of plot and characterization. Among the many deaths the man described, he included the death of sympathy. I was beginning to feel sympathy die within me when my waiter finally got to my table. Democracy was the next death; it came and went more quickly than my waiter could produce my change. And socialism passed away before I could figure the tip. I stared at the man with the beard and felt like lifting weights; I felt that if the radicals wanted to blow up the Opera, they should pick a night when only this man with the beard was there. I thought I'd found a substitute driver for Fehlgeburt.

'Trotsky,' the young girl with the bearded man blurted out, suddenly—as if she were saying, 'Thank you.'

'Trotsky?' I said, leaning over their table; it was a small, square table. I was curling seventy-five pounds, on one arm, on each of the dumbbells in those days. The table wasn't nearly that heavy, so I picked it up, carefully, with one hand, and lifted it over my head the way a waiter would raise a tray. 'Now, good old Trotsky,' I said. ' "If you want an easy life," good old Trotsky said, "you picked the wrong century to be born in." Do you think that's true?' I asked the man with the beard. He said nothing, but the young girl nudged him, and he perked up a little.

'*I* think it's true,' the girl said.

'*Sure* it's true,' I said. I was aware of the waiters nervously watching the drinks and the ashtray sliding slightly on the table over my head, but I was not Iowa Bob; the weights never slid off the bar when I lifted, not anymore. I was better with weights than Iowa Bob.

'Trotsky was killed with a pickax,' the bearded fellow said, morosely, trying to remain unimpressed.

'But he's not *dead*, is he?' I asked, insanely—smiling. 'Nothing's *really* dead,' I said. 'Nothing he *said* is dead,' I said. 'The paintings that we can still see—they're not dead,' I said. 'The characters in books—they don't die when we stop reading about them.'

The man with the beard stared at the place where his table was supposed to be. He was really quite dignified, I thought, and I knew I was in a bad mood and wasn't being fair; I was being a bully, and I felt ashamed. I gave the table back to the couple; nothing spilled.

'I see what you mean!' the girl called after me, as I was leaving. But I knew I had kept no one alive, not ever: not those people in the Opera, because sitting among them was surely that shape Frank and I had seen in the car, driven away between Ernst and Arbeiter, that animal shape of death, that mechanical bear, that dog's head of chemistry, that electrical charge of sorrow. And despite what Trotsky said, he was dead; Mother and Egg and Iowa Bob were dead, too—despite *everything* they said, and everything they meant to us. I walked out on the Graben, feeling more and more like Frank, feeling anti-everything; I felt out of control. It's no good for a weight lifter to feel out of control.

The first prostitute I passed was not one of *ours*, but I'd seen her before—at the Kaffee Mowatt.

'*Guten Abend*,' she said.

'Fuck you,' I told her.

'Up yours,' she told me; she knew that much English, and I

304

felt lousy. I was using bad language, again. I had broken my promise to Mother. It was the first and last time I would break it. I was twenty-two years old and I started to cry. I turned down Spiegelgasse. There were whores there, but they weren't *our* whores, so I didn't do anything. When they said, 'Guten Abend,' I said, 'Guten Abend' back. I didn't answer the other things they said. I cut across the Neuer Markt; I felt the vacancies in the chests of the Hapsburgs in their tombs. Another whore called to me.

'Hey, don't cry!' she called to me. 'A big strong boy like you —don't cry!'

But I hoped I was crying not just for myself but for them all. For Freud calling out the names who'd never answer in the Judenplatz; for what Father couldn't see. For Franny, for I loved her—and I wanted her to be as faithful to me as she had proved she could be to Susie the bear. For Susie, too, because Franny had shown me that Susie wasn't ugly at all. In fact, Franny had almost convinced Susie of this. For Junior Jones, who was suffering the first of the knee injuries that would force his retirement from the Cleveland Browns. For Lilly who tried so hard and for Frank who'd gone so far away (in order to be closer to life, he said). For Dark Inge, who was eighteen—who said she was 'old enough,' though Screaming Annie insisted she wasn't—who before this year was over would run away, with a man. He was as black as her father and he took her to an Army-base town in Germany; she would later become a whore there, I would be told. And Screaming Annie would scream a slightly different song. For *all* of them! For my doomed Fehlgeburt, even for the deceiving Schwanger—for both Old Billigs; they were optimists; they were china bears. For everyone —except Ernst, except Arbeiter, except that *wrench* of a man, except for Chipper Dove: I hated them.

I brushed past a whore or two signaling me off the Kärntner-strasse. A tall, stunning whore—out of the league of our Krugerstrasse whores—blew me a kiss from the corner of the Annagasse. I walked right by the Krugerstrasse without looking, not wanting to see one of them, or all of them, waving to me. I passed the Hotel Sacher—which the Hotel New Hampshire would never be. And then I came to the Staatsoper, I came to the house of Gluck (1714–87, as Frank would recite); I came to the State Opera, which was the house of Mozart, the house of Haydn, of Beethoven and Schubert—of Strauss, Brahms, Bruckner, and Mahler. This was the house that a pornographer playing with politics wanted to blow sky-high. It was huge; in seven years, I had never been in it—it seemed classier than I was, and I was never the music fan that Frank was, and never the lover of drama that Franny was (Frank and Franny went to the Opera all the time; Freud took them. He loved to listen; Franny and Frank described it all to him). Like me, Lilly had never been to the Opera; the place was too big, Lilly said; it frightened her.

It frightened *me*, now. It is too *big* to blow up! I thought. But it was the *people* they wanted to blow up, I knew, and people are more easily destroyed than buildings. What they wanted was a spectacle. They wanted what Arbeiter had shouted to Schwanger: they wanted *Schlagobers* and blood.

On the Kärntnerstrasse across from the Opera was a sausage vendor, a man with a kind of hot-dog cart selling different kinds of *Wurst mit Senf und Bauernbrot*—a kind of sausage with mustard on rye. I didn't want one.

I knew what I wanted. I wanted to grow up, in a hurry. When I'd made love to Fehlgeburt I had told her, *'Es war sehr schön,'* but it wasn't. 'It was very nice,' I had lied, but it wasn't anything; it wasn't enough. It had been just another night of weight lifting.

When I turned down the Krugerstrasse, I had already decided that I would go with the first one who approached me—even if it was Old Billig; even if it was Jolanta, I bravely promised myself. It didn't matter; maybe one by one I would try them all. I could do anything Freud could do, and Freud had done it all —our Freud *and* the other Freud, I thought; they had simply gone as far as they could.

Nobody I knew was in the Kaffee Mowatt, and I didn't recognize the figure standing under the pink neon: HOTEL NEW HAMPSHIRE! HOTEL NEW HAMPSHIRE! HOTEL NEW HAMPSHIRE!

It's Babette, I thought, vaguely repulsed—but it was just the sickly-sweet diesel breeze of the last night of summer that made me think of her. The woman saw me and started walking toward me—aggressively, I thought; hungrily, too. And I was sure it was Screaming Annie; I momentarily wondered how I would hold together during her famous fake orgasm. Maybe—given my fondness for whispering—I could ask her not to do it at all, I could simply tell her I *knew* it was a fake and it simply wasn't necessary, not for *my* benefit. The woman was too slender to be Old Billig, but she was too solid to be Screaming Annie, I realized; she was too well built to be Screaming Annie. So it was Jolanta, I thought; at last I would find out what she kept in her

306

evil purse. In the time ahead, I thought—shuddering—I might
even have to *use* what's in Jolanta's purse. But the woman
approaching me was not *solid enough* for Jolanta; this woman
was too well built in the *other* way—she was too sleek, too
youthful in her movements. She ran toward me on the street and
caught me in her arms; she took my breath away, she was so
beautiful. The woman was Franny.

'Where have you *been?*' she asked me. 'Gone all day, gone
all night,' she scolded me. 'We've all been *dying* to find you!'

'Why?' I asked. Franny's smell made me dizzy.

'Lilly's going to get *published!*' Franny said. 'Some publisher
in New York is really going to buy her book!'

'How much?' I said, because I was hoping it might be
enough. It might be our ticket out of Vienna—the ticket that the
second Hotel New Hampshire would never buy us.

'Jesus God,' Franny said. 'Your sister has a *literary* success
and you ask "How much?"—you're just like Frank. That's just
what Frank asked.'

'Good for Frank,' I said. I was still trembling; I had been
looking for a prostitute and had found my sister. She wouldn't
let go of me, either.

'Where *were* you?' Franny asked me; she pushed my hair
back.

'With Fehlgeburt,' I said, sheepishly. I would never lie to
Franny.

Franny frowned. 'Well, how was it?' she asked, still touching
me—but like a sister.

'Not so great,' I said. I looked away from Franny. 'Awful,' I
added.

Franny put her arms around me and kissed me. She meant to
kiss me on the cheek (like a sister), but I turned toward her,
though I was trying to turn away, and our lips met. And that was
it, that was all it took. That was the end of the summer of 1964;
suddenly it was autumn. I was twenty-two, Franny was twenty-
three. We kissed a long time. There was nothing to say. She was
not a lesbian, she still wrote to Junior Jones—and to Chipper
Dove—and I had never been happy with another woman; not
ever; not yet. We stayed out on the street, out of the light cast by
the neon, so that no one in the Hotel New Hampshire could see
us. We had to break up our kissing when a customer of Jolanta's
came staggering out of the hotel, and we broke it up again when
we heard Screaming Annie. In a little while her dazed customer
came out, but Franny and I still stayed on the Krugerstrasse.

Later, Babette went home. Then Jolanta went home, taking Dark Inge with her. Screaming Annie came out and back, out and back, like the tide. Old Billig the whore went across the street to the Kaffee Mowatt and dozed on a table. I walked Franny up to the Kärntnerstrasse, and down to the Opera. 'You think of me too much,' Franny started to say, but she didn't bother to finish. We kissed some more. The Opera was so big beside us.

'They're going to blow it up,' I whispered to my sister. 'The Opera—they're going to blow it up.' She let me hold her. 'I love you terribly much,' I told her.

'I love you, too, *damn it,*' Franny said.

Although the weather was feeling like fall, it was possible for us to stand there, guarding the Opera, until the light came up and the real people came out to go to work. There was no place we could go, anyway—and absolutely nothing, we knew, that we should do.

'Keep passing the open windows,' we whispered to each other.

When we finally went back to the Hotel New Hampshire, the Opera was still standing there—safe. Safe for a while, anyway, I thought.

'Safer than *we* are,' I told Franny. 'Safer than love.'

'Let me tell you, kid,' Franny said to me, squeezing my hand. *'Everything's* safer than love.'

10

A Night at the Opera:
Schlagobers and Blood

'Children, children,' Father said to us, 'we must be very careful. I think this is *the turning point,* kids,' our father said, as if we were still eight, nine, ten, and so forth, and he was telling us about meeting Mother at the Arbuthnot-by-the-Sea—that night they first saw Freud, with State o' Maine.

'There's always a turning point,' Frank said, philosophically.

'Okay, supposing there is,' Franny said, impatiently, 'but what is this particular turning point?'

'Yeah,' said Susie the bear, looking Franny over very carefully; Susie was the only one who'd noticed that Franny and I were out all night. Franny had told her we'd gone to a party near the university with some people Susie didn't know. And what could be safer than having your brother, and a weight lifter, for an escort? Susie didn't like parties, anyway; if she went as a bear, there was no one she could talk to, and if she didn't go as a bear, no one seemed interested in talking to her. She looked sulky and cross. 'There's a lot of shit to deal with in a hurry, as I see it,' said Susie the bear.

'Exactly,' Father said. 'That's the typical turning-point situation.'

'We can't blow this one,' Freud said. 'I don't think I got many more hotels left in me.' Which might be a good thing, I thought, trying to keep my eyes off Franny. We were all in Frank's room, the conference room—as if the dressmaker's dummy were a soothing presence, were a silent ghost of Mother or Egg or Iowa Bob; somehow the dummy was supposed to radiate signals and we were supposed to catch the signals (according to Frank).

'How much can we get for the novel, Frank?' Father asked.

'It's Lilly's book,' Franny said. 'It's not *our* book.'

'In a way, it is,' Lilly said.

'Precisely,' Frank said, 'and the way I understand publishing,

309

it's out of her hands now. Now is whether we either get taken or we make a killing.'

'It's just about growing up,' Lilly said. 'I'm sort of surprised they're interested.'

'They're only five thousand dollars interested, Lilly,' Franny said.

'We need fifteen or twenty thousand to leave,' Father said. 'If we're going to have a chance to do anything with it, back home,' he added.

'Don't forget: we'll get something for *this* place,' Freud said, defensively.

'Not after we blow the whistle on the fucking bombers,' said Susie the bear.

'There will be such a scandal,' Frank said, 'we won't get a buyer.'

'I told you: we'll get the police on *our* ass if we blow the whistle at all,' Freud said. 'You don't know our police, their Gestapo tactics. They'll find something we're doing wrong with the whores, too.'

'Well, there's a lot that *is* wrong,' Franny said. We couldn't look at each other; when Franny talked, I looked out the window. I saw Old Billig the radical crossing the street. I saw Screaming Annie dragging herself home.

'There's no way we *can't* blow the whistle,' Father said. 'If they actually think they can blow up the Opera, there's no talking to them.'

'There never *was* any talking to them,' Franny said. 'We just listened.'

'They've always been crazy,' I said to Father.

'Don't you *know* that, Daddy?' Lilly asked him.

Father hung his head. He was forty-four, a distinguished gray appearing on the thick brown hair around his ears; he had never worn sideburns, and he had his hair cut in a uniform, mid-ear, mid-forehead, just-covering-the-back-of-his-neck way; he never thinned it. He wore bangs, like a little boy, and his hair fit his head so dramatically well that from a distance we were some-times fooled into thinking that Father was wearing a helmet.

'I'm sorry, kids,' Father said, shaking his head. 'I know this isn't very pleasant, but I feel we're at *the turning point*.' He shook his head some more; he looked really lost to us, and it was only later that I would remember him on Frank's bed, in that dressmaker's dummy of a room, as looking really quite hand-some and in charge of things. Father was always good at

310

creating the illusion that he was in charge of things: Earl, for example. He hadn't lifted the weights, like Iowa Bob, or like me, but Father had kept his athletic figure, and certainly he had kept his boyishness—'too fucking *much* boyishness,' as Franny would say. It occurred to me that he must be lonely; in seven years, he hadn't had a date! And if he used the whores, he was discreet about it—and in *that* Hotel New Hampshire, who could be *that* discreet?

'He can't be seeing any of them,' Franny had said. 'I'd simply know it, if he was.'

'Men are sneaky,' Susie the bear had said. 'Even nice guys.'

'So he's not doing it; that's settled,' Franny had said. Susie the bear had shrugged, and Franny had hit her.

But in Frank's room, it was Father who brought up the whores.

'We should tell *them* what we're going to do about the crazy radicals,' Father said, '*before* we tell the police.'

'Why?' Susie the bear asked him. 'One of them might blow the whistle on *us*.'

'Why would they do that?' I asked Susie.

'We should tell them so they can make other plans,' Father said.

'They'll have to change hotels,' Freud said. 'The damn police will close us down. In this country, you're guilty by association!' Freud cried. 'Just ask any Jew!' Just ask the *other* Freud, I thought.

'But suppose we were *heroes*,' Father said, and we all looked at him. Yes, that would be nice, I was thinking.

'Like in Lilly's book?' Frank asked Father.

'Suppose the police thought that we were heroes for uncovering the bomb plot?' Father asked.

'The police don't think that way,' Freud said.

'But suppose, as *Americans*,' Father said, 'we told the American Consulate, or the Embassy, and someone over there passed on the information to the Austrian authorities—as if this whole thing had been a really top-secret, first-class kind of intrigue.'

'This is why I love you, Win Berry!' Freud said, tapping time to some interior tune with his baseball bat. 'You really *are* a dreamer,' Freud told my father. '*This* is no first-class intrigue! This is a second-class hotel,' Freud said. 'Even *I* can see that,' he said, 'and in case you haven't noticed, I'm blind. And those aren't any first-class terrorists, either,' Freud said. 'They can't

311

keep a perfectly good car running!' he shouted. 'I, for one, don't believe they know *how* to blow up the Opera! I actually think we're perfectly safe. If they *had* a bomb, they'd probably fall downstairs with it!'

'The whole car is the bomb,' I said, 'or it's the *main* bomb —whatever that means. That's what Fehlgeburt said.'

'Let's talk to Fehlgeburt,' Lilly said. 'I trust Fehlgeburt,' she added, wondering how the girl who had virtually been her tutor for seven years had actually become so convinced of destroying herself. And if Fehlgeburt had been Lilly's tutor, Schwanger had been Lilly's nanny.

But we wouldn't see Fehlgeburt again. I assumed it was me she was trying not to see; I assumed she was seeing the others. At the end of the summer of 1964—as 'the fall season' loomed —I was doing my best not ever to be alone with Franny, and Franny was trying hard to convince Susie the bear that although nothing had changed between them, Franny thought it was best that they be 'just good friends.'

'Susie's so insecure,' Franny told me. 'I mean, she's really sweet—as Lilly would say—but I'm trying to let her down without undermining what little confidence I might have given her. I mean, she was just beginning to like herself, just a little. I had her almost believing she wasn't ugly to look at; now that I'm rejecting her, she's turning into a bear again.'

'I love you,' I told Franny, with my head down, 'but what are we going to *do*?'

'We're going to love each other,' Franny said. 'But we're not going to *do* anything.'

'Not *ever*, Franny?' I asked her.

'Not now, anyway,' Franny said, but her hand trailed across her lap, across her tight-together knees, and into my lap—where she squeezed my thigh so hard I jumped. 'Not *here*, anyway,' she whispered, fiercely, then let me go. 'Maybe it's just *desire*,' she added. 'Want to try the desire on someone else and see if the thing between us goes away?'

'Who else is there?' I said. It was late afternoon, in her room. I would not dare be in Franny's room after dark.

'Which one do you think about?' Franny asked me. I knew she meant the whores.

'Jolanta,' I said, my hand involuntarily flying from my side and knocking a lampshade askew. Franny turned her back to me.

'Well, you know who *I* think about, don't you?' she asked.

'Ernst,' I said, and my teeth chattered—I was so cold.

'Do you like that idea?' she asked me.

'God, no,' I whispered.

'You and your damn whispering,' Franny said. 'Well, I don't like you with Jolanta, either.'

'So we won't,' I said.

'I'm afraid we *will*,' she said.

'*Why*, Franny?' I said, and I started across her room toward her.

'No, stop!' she cried, moving so that her desk was partially between us; there was a fragile standing lamp in the way.

Years later, Lilly would send us both a poem. When I read the poem, I called up Franny to see if Lilly had sent *her* a copy; of course she had. The poem was by a very good poet named Donald Justice, and I would one day hear Mr. Justice read his poems in New York City. I liked all of them, but I sat holding my breath while he was reading, half hoping he would read the poem Lilly sent to Franny and me, and half fearing he would. He didn't read it, and I didn't know what to do after the reading. People were speaking to him, but they looked like his friends —or maybe they were just other poets. Lilly told me that poets have a way of looking like they're all one another's friends. But I didn't know what to do; if Franny had been with me, we would have just waltzed right up to Donald Justice and he would have been completely bowled over by Franny, I think—everyone always is. Mr. Justice looked like a real gentleman, and I don't want to suggest that he would have been falling all over Franny. I thought that, like his poems, he would be both candid and formal, austere, even grave—but open, even generous. He looked like a man you'd ask to say an elegy for someone you'd loved; I think he could have done a heartbreaker for Iowa Bob, and—looking at him after his reading in New York, with some very smart-looking admirers around him—I wished he could have written and spoken some sort of elegy for Mother and for Egg. In a way, he *did* write an elegy for Egg; he wrote a poem called 'On the Death of Friends in Childhood,' which I have taken rather personally as an elegy for Egg. Frank and I both love it, but Franny says it makes her too sad.

ON THE DEATH OF FRIENDS IN CHILDHOOD
We shall not ever meet them bearded in heaven,
Nor sunning themselves among the bald of hell;
If anywhere, in the deserted schoolyard at twilight,
Forming a ring, perhaps, or joining hands

In games whose very names we have forgotten.
Come, memory, let us seek them there in the shadows.

But when I saw Mr. Justice in New York, I was thinking chiefly about Franny and the poem 'Love's Stratagems'—that was the name of the poem Lilly sent Franny and me. I didn't even know what to say to Mr. Justice. I was too embarrassed to even shake his hand. I suppose I would have told him that I wished I'd read the poem 'Love's Stratagems' when I was in Vienna with Franny, at the dead end of the summer of 1964.

'But would it have mattered, anyway?' Franny would ask me, later. 'Would we have believed it—then?'

I don't even know if Donald Justice had written 'Love's Stratagems' by 1964. But he must have; it seems written for Franny and me.

'It doesn't matter,' as Frank would say.

Anyway, years later, Franny and I would get 'Love's Stratagems' in the mail from dear little Lilly, and one night we would read it aloud to each other over the telephone. I tended to whisper when I read something that was good aloud, but Franny spoke up loud and clear.

> LOVE'S STRATAGEMS
> *But these maneuverings to avoid*
> *The touching of hands,*
> *These shifts to keep the eyes employed*
> *On objects more or less neutral*
> *(As honor, for the time being, commands)*
> *Will hardly prevent their downfall.*
>
> *Stronger medicines are needed.*
> *Already they find*
> *None of their stratagems have succeeded,*
> *Nor would have, no,*
> *Not had their eyes been stricken blind,*
> *Hands cut off at the elbow.*

Stronger medicines were needed, indeed. Had *our* hands been cut off at the elbow, Franny and I would have touched each other with the *stumps*—with whatever we had left, stricken blind or not.

But that afternoon in her room we were saved by Susie the bear.

'Something's up,' Susie said, shuffling in. Franny and I waited; we thought she meant *us*—we thought she knew.

Lilly knew, of course. Somehow she must have.

'Writers know everything,' Lilly said once. 'Or they should. They *ought* to. Or they ought to shut up.'

'Lilly must have known from the beginning,' Franny said to me, long distance, the night we discovered 'Love's Stratagems.' It was not a good connection; there was crackling on the line—as if Lilly were listening in. Or Frank were listening in—Frank was, as I have said, born to the role of listening in on love.

'Something's up, you two,' Susie the bear repeated, menacingly. 'They can't find Fehlgeburt.'

'Who's "they"?' I asked.

'The porno king and his whole fucking gang,' Susie said. 'They're asking *us* if we've seen Fehlgeburt. And last night they were asking the whores.'

'Nobody has seen her?' I said, and there was the growingly familiar cold draft up the pants legs again, there was the whiff of dead air from the tombs holding the heartless Hapsburgs.

How many days had we waited for Father and Freud to bicker over finding a buyer for the Hotel New Hampshire *before* they blew the whistle on the would-be bombers? And how many nights had we wasted, arguing about whether we should tell the American Consulate, or the Embassy, and have *them* tell the police—or whether we should just tell the Austrian police straightaway? When you're in love with your sister, you lose a lot of perspective on the real world. The goddamn *Welt,* as Frank would say.

Frank asked me, 'What floor does Fehlgeburt live on? I mean, you've seen her place. How high up is she?'

Lilly, the writer, tuned right in on the question, but it didn't make sense to me—yet. 'It's the first floor,' I said to Frank, 'it's just one flight up.'

'Not high enough,' Lilly said, and then I got it. Not high enough to jump out the window, is what she meant. If Fehlgeburt had at last decided *not* to keep passing the open windows, she would have to have found another way.

'That's it,' Frank said, taking my arm. 'If she's pulled a King of Mice, she's probably still there.'

It was more than a little shortness of breath I felt, crossing the Plaza of Heroes and heading up the Ring toward the Rathaus; that's a long way for a wind sprint, but I was in shape. I felt a little out of breath, there can be no doubt of that, but I felt a *lot*

315

guilty—though it couldn't have been simply *me;* I couldn't even have been Fehlgeburt's main reason to stop passing the open windows. And there was no evidence, they said later, that she had done much of anything after I'd gone. Maybe she'd read a little more *Moby-Dick,* because the police were very thorough and even noted where she'd marked her place. And I know, of course, that the place she'd stopped reading was *un*marked when I left. Curiously, she'd marked it just where she *had* stopped when she'd been reading to me—as if she had reread that entire evening before adopting the open-window policy. Fehlgeburt's form of open-window policy had been a neat little gun I never knew about. The suicide note was simple and addressed to no one, but I knew it was meant for me.

The night you
saw Schwanger
you didn't see
me. I have a
gun, too! 'So
we beat on . . .'

Fehlgeburt concluded, quoting Lilly's favorite ending.

I never actually saw Fehlgeburt. I waited in the hall outside her door—for Frank. Frank was not in such good shape and it took him a while to meet me outside Fehlgeburt's room. Her room had a private entrance up a back staircase that people in the old apartment house used only when they were bringing out their garbage and trash. I suppose they thought the smell was from someone's garbage and trash. Frank and I didn't even open her door. The smell outside her door was already worse than Sorrow ever smelled to us.

'I told you, I told you all,' Father said. 'We're at the turning point. Are we ready?' We could see that he didn't really know what to do.

Frank had returned Lilly's contract to New York. As her 'agent,' he had said, he could not accept so uncommitted an offer for what was clearly a work of genius—'genius still blooming,' Frank added, though he'd not read *Trying to Grow;* not yet. Frank pointed out that Lilly was only eighteen. 'She's got a lot of growing to do, still,' he concluded. Any publisher would do well to get into the gargantuan building of literature that Lilly was going to construct (according to Frank)—'on the ground floor.'

Frank asked for fifteen thousand dollars—and another fifteen thousand dollars was to be promised, for advertising. 'Let's not let a little economics stand between us,' Frank reasoned.

'If we know Fehlgeburt is dead,' Franny reasoned, 'then the radicals are going to know it, too.'

'It takes just a sniff,' Frank said, but I didn't say anything.

'I've almost got a buyer,' Freud said.

'Someone *wants* the hotel?' Franny asked.

'They want to convert it to offices,' Freud said.

'But Fehlgeburt is dead,' Father said. 'Now we have to tell the police—tell them everything.'

'Tell them tonight,' Frank said.

'Tell the Americans,' Freud said, 'and tell them tomorrow. Tell the *whores* tonight.'

'Yes, warn the whores tonight,' Father agreed.

'Then in the morning, *early*,' Frank said, 'we'll go to the American Consulate—or the Embassy. Which is it?'

I realized I didn't know which was for what, or who was for whom. We realized Father didn't know, either. 'Well, there are a number of us, after all,' Father said, sheepishly. 'Some of us can tell the Consulate, some of us can tell the ambassador.' It was apparent to me, then, how little any of us had really mastered about living abroad: we didn't even know if the American Embassy and the American Consulate were in the same building—for all we knew, a consulate and an embassy might be the same thing. It was apparent to me, then, what the seven years had done to Father: he had lost the decisiveness he must have had that night in Dairy, New Hampshire, when he took my mother walking in Elliot Park and snowed her with his vision of converting the Thompson Female Seminary to a hotel. First he'd lost Earl—the provider of his education. And when he lost Iowa Bob, he lost Iowa Bob's instincts, too. Iowa Bob was a man trained to pounce on a loose ball—a valuable instinct, especially in the hotel business. And now I could see wha̱ sorrow had cost Father.

'His marbles,' Franny would say later.   ꞏꞏꞏnk would

'He wasn't playing with a full deck of card̲   ꞏꞏꞏoved to tell him that
say.

'It's going to be okay, Pop,' Fran̲ṉu̲d.
afternoon in the former Gastha̲   ꞏre home free!'

'Sure, Dad,' said Frank

'I'm going to make millions, Daddy,' Lilly said.

'Let's take a walk, Pop,' I said to him.

'Who'll tell the whores?' he asked, bewilderedly.

'Tell one, you've told them all,' Franny said.

'No,' said Freud. 'Sometimes they're secretive with each other. I'll tell Babette,' Freud said. Babette was Freud's favorite.

'I'll tell Old Billig,' said Susie the bear.

'I'll tell Screaming Annie,' my father said; he seemed in a daze.

Nobody offered to tell Jolanta anything, so I said I'd tell her. Franny looked at me, but I managed to look away. I saw that Frank was concentrating on the dressmaker's dummy; he was hoping for some clear signals. Lilly went to her room; she looked so small, I thought—she *was* so small, of course. She must have been going to her room to try growing some more—to write and write. When we had our family conferences in that second Hotel New Hampshire, Lilly was still so small that Father seemed to forget she was eighteen; he would occasionally just pick her up and sit her in his lap, and play with her pigtail. Lilly didn't mind; the only thing she liked about being so small, she told me, was that Father still handled her as if she were a child.

'Our child author,' as Frank, the agent, would occasionally refer to her.

'Let's take a walk, Pop,' I said again. I wasn't sure if he'd heard me.

We crossed the lobby; someone had spilled an ashtray on the sagging couch that faced the reception desk, and I knew it must have been Susie's day to clean the lobby. Susie was well intentioned, but she was a slob; the lobby looked like hell when it was Susie's day to clean it.

Franny was standing at the foot of the staircase, staring up the stairwell. I couldn't remember when she'd changed her clothes, but she suddenly seemed dressed up, to me. She was wearing a dress. Franny was not a blue jeans and T-shirt sort of person she liked loose skirts and blouses—but she was not big on with either, and she was wearing her pretty dark green one,

'It's fan, shoulder straps.

be cold.' I told her. 'That's a summer dress. You'll

'I'm not going out,' looked at her bare shoulders id, still staring up the stairwell. I felt cold for her. It was late afternoon, but we both knew Ernst hadn't called it quits—he was still at work, up on the fifth floor. Franny started up the stairs. 'I'm just going to reassure him,' she said to me, but not looking at me—or at Father. 'Don't worry, I won't tell him what we know—I'll play dumb. I'm just going to try to find out what he knows,' she said.

'He's a real creep, Franny,' I said to her.

'I know,' she said, 'and you think about me too much.'

I took Father out on the Krugerstrasse. We were too early for the whores, but the working day was long over: the commuters were safe in the suburbs, and only the elegant people, killing time before dinner—or before the Opera—were out strolling.

We walked down the Kärntnerstrasse to the Graben and did the obligatory gawking at St. Stephen's. We wandered into the Neuer Markt and stared at the nudes in the Donner Fountain. I realized that Father knew nothing about them, so I gave him an abbreviated history of Maria Theresa's repressive measures. He seemed genuinely interested. We walked by the lush scarlet and gold entrance that the Ambassador Hotel made into the Neuer Markt; Father avoided looking at the Ambassador, or he watched the pigeons shitting in the fountain, instead. We walked on. It wouldn't grow dark for a little while. When we passed the Kaffee Mozart, Father said, 'That looks like a nice place. That looks a lot nicer than the Kaffee Mowatt.'

'It is,' I said, trying to conceal my surprise that he'd never been there.

'I must remember to come here, one day,' he said.

I was trying to make the walk come out another way, but we ended up at the Hotel Sacher just as the light in the sky was beginning to go—and just as they were turning on the lights in the Sacher Bar. We stopped to watch them light the bar; it is simply the most beautiful bar in the world, I think. *'In den ganzen Welt,'* Frank says.

'Let's have a drink here,' Father said, and we went in. I was a little worried about how he was dressed. I looked all right myself; that is how I always look—all right. But Father suddenly appeared a little shabby to me. I realized that his pants were completely unironed that his legs were as round as ~~home~~ —only baggy; he had lost weight in Vienna ~~up that his belt~~ cooking had made him a little thin, and it ~~his~~ 's belt; Father was was too long—in fact, I noticed, it ~~faded~~ gray-and-white pin-just borrowing it. He wore ~~a~~—it had been mine, I realized, striped shirt, which was

319

before the latest stages of the weight lifting had altered my upper body; it wouldn't fit me now, but it wasn't a bad shirt, only faded and a bit wrinkled. What was wrong was that the shirt was striped and the jacket was checkered. Thank God Father never wore a necktie—I shuddered to think what sort of tie Father would wear. But then I realized that no one in the Sacher was going to be snotty to us, because I saw for the first time what my father really looked like. He looked like a very eccentric millionaire; he looked like the richest man in the world, but a man who didn't give a dam. He looked like that very wealthy combination of generosity and fecklessness; he could wear anything and look like he had a million dollars in his pocket —even if his pocket had a hole in it. There were some terribly well dressed and well-to-do people at the Sacher Bar, but when my father and I came in, they all looked at him with a heartbreaking kind of envy. I think Father could see that, although he could see very little of the real world; and certainly he was naïve about the way the women looked at him. There were people at the Sacher Bar who'd spent over an hour dressing themselves and my father was a man who had lived in Vienna for seven years and had not spent a total of even fifteen minutes buying his clothes. He wore what my mother had bought for him, and what he borrowed from Frank and me.

'Good evening, Mr. Berry,' the bartender said to him, and then I realized that Father came here all the time.

'*Guten Abend,*' Father said. That was about it for Father's German. He could also say '*Bitte*' and '*Danke*' and '*Auf Wiedersehen.*' And he had a great way of bowing.

I had a beer and my father had 'the usual.' Father's 'usual' was an appalling, glopped-up drink that had some kind of whiskey or rum at its heart but resembled an ice cream sundae. He was no drinker; he just sipped a little of it and spent hours toying with the rest. He was not there for the drinking.

The best looking people in Vienna stopped in off the street, and the guests from the Hotel Sacher made their plans or met their dinner companions at the Sacher Bar. Of course, the der Wlnder never knew that my father lived at the terrible Hotel yacht, I suppo-shire, a few minutes—slow walking—away. I won- the Imperial. And I at least the Bristol or the Ambassador or needed the white dinner jacket that Father had never actually ok the part.

'Well,' Father said to me, quietly, in the Sacher Bar. 'Well, John, I'm a failure. I've let you all down.'

'No you haven't,' I told him.

'Now it's back to the land of the free,' Father said, stirring his nauseating drink with his index finger, then sucking his finger. 'And no more hotels,' he said, softly. 'I'm going to have to get a *job*.'

He said it the way someone might have said that he was going to have to have an *operation*. I hated to see reality hemming him in.

'And you kids are going to have to go to school,' he said. 'To college,' he added, dreamily.

I reminded him that we had all *been* to school and to college. Frank and Franny and I even had finished our university degrees; and why did Lilly need to finish hers—in American literature —when she had already finished a novel?

'Oh,' he said. 'Well, maybe we'll *all* have to get jobs.'

'That's all right,' I said. He looked at me and smiled; he leaned forward and kissed me on the cheek. He looked so absolutely perfect that no one in the bar could have possibly thought—even for a moment—that I was this middle-aged man's young lover. This was a father-and-son kiss and they looked at Father with even more envy than they had heaped upon their vision of him when he walked in.

He took forever to finish playing with his drink. I had two more beers. I knew what he was doing. He was *absorbing* the Sacher Bar, he was getting his last good look at the Hotel Sacher; he was imagining, of course, that he owned it—that he lived here.

'Your mother,' he said, 'would have loved all this.' He moved his hand only slightly, then rested it in his lap.

She would have loved all *what?* I wondered. The Hotel Sacher and the Sacher Bar—oh yes. But what *else* would she have loved? Her son Frank, growing a beard and trying to decipher his mother's message—her meaning—from a dressmaker's dummy? Her littlest daughter Lilly trying to grow? Her biggest daughter Franny trying to find out everything that a porno to pher knew? And would she have loved *me?* I wonder too! That who cleaned up his language, but wanted more t̶ ̶ make love to his own sister. And Franny ̶ ̶ ̶ was why she'd gone to Ernst, of co̶ ̶arted to cry, but he said

Father couldn't have known ̶e so bad,' he reassured me. all the right things. 'It ̶

'Human beings are remarkable—at what we can learn to live with,' Father told me. 'If we couldn't get strong from what we lose, and what we miss, and what we want and can't have,' Father said, 'then we couldn't ever get strong *enough*, could we? What else makes us strong?' Father asked.

Everyone at the Sacher Bar watched me crying and my father comforting me. I guess that's just one of the reasons it's the most beautiful bar in the world, in my opinion: it has the grace to make no one feel self-conscious about any unhappiness.

I felt better with Father's arm around my shoulder.

'Good night, Mr. Berry,' the bartender said.

'*Auf Wiedersehen*,' Father said: he knew he'd never be back.

Outside, everything had changed. It was dark. It was the fall. The first man who passed us, walking in a hurry, was wearing black slacks, black dress shoes, and a white dinner jacket.

My father didn't notice the man in the white dinner jacket, but I didn't feel comfortable with this omen, with this reminder; the man in the white dinner jacket, I knew, was dressed for the Opera. He must have been hurrying to be on time. The 'fall season,' as Fehlgeburt had warned me, was upon us. You could feel it in the weather.

The 1964 season of the New York Metropolitan Opera opened with Donizetti's *Lucia di Lammermoor*. I read this in one of Frank's opera books, but Frank says he doubts very much that the season would have opened with *Lucia* in Vienna. Frank says it's likely something more Viennese would have opened the season—'Their beloved Strauss, their beloved Mozart; even that Kraut, Wagner,' Frank says. And I don't even know if it was opening night when Father and I saw the man in the white dinner jacket. It was only clear that the State Opera was open for business.

'The 1835 Italian version of *Lucia* first opened in Vienna in 1837,' Frank told me. 'Of course, it's been back a few times since then. Perhaps most notably,' Frank added, 'with the great Adelina Patti in the title role—and most particularly the night her dress caught fire, just as she was beginning to sing the mad ~ne.'

hard to mad scene, Frank?' I asked him.

she was beginning see it to believe it,' Frank said, 'and it's a little gas flares, in those days, then. But Patti's dress caught fire just as mad scene the stage was lit with must have stood too close to one. And do you know what the great Adelina Patti did?' Frank asked me.

'No,' I said.

'She ripped off her burning dress and kept singing,' Frank said. 'In Vienna,' he added. 'Those were the days.'

And in one of Frank's opera books I read that Adelina Patti's *Lucia* seemed fated for this kind of disturbance. In Bucharest, for example, the famous mad scene was interrupted by a member of the audience falling into the pit—upon a woman—and in the general panic, someone shouted 'Fire!' But the great Adelina Patti cried, 'No fire!'—and went on singing. And in San Francisco, one weirdo threw a bomb onto the stage, and once more the fearless Patti riveted the audience to their seats. Despite the fact that the bomb exploded!

'A small bomb,' Frank has assured me.

But it was no small bomb that Frank and I had seen riding to the Opera between Arbeiter and Ernst; that bomb was as weighty as Sorrow, that bomb was as big as a bear. And it's doubtful that Donizetti's *Lucia* was at the Vienna Staatsoper the night Father and I said *auf Wiedersehen* to the Sacher. I like to think it was *Lucia* for my own reasons. There is a lot of blood and *Schlagobers* in that particular opera—even Frank agrees—and somehow the mad story of a brother who drives his sister crazy and causes her death, because he forces her on a man she doesn't love . . . well, you can see why this particular version of blood and *Schlagobers* would seem especially appropriate, to me.

'*All* so-called serious opera is blood and *Schlagobers*,' Frank has told me. I don't know enough about opera to know if that is true; all I know is that I think *Lucia di Lammermoor* should have been playing at the Vienna State Opera the night Father and I walked back to the Hotel New Hampshire from the Hotel Sacher.

'It doesn't matter, really—which opera it was,' Frank is always saying, but I like to think it was *Lucia*. I like to think that the famous mad scene was not yet under way when Father and I arrived at the Hotel New Hampshire. There was Susie the bear in the lobby—*without* her bear's head on!—and she was crying. Father walked right by Susie, without appearing to notice how upset she was—and out of costume!—but my father was used to unhappy bears.

He walked right upstairs. He was going to tell Screaming Annie the bad news about the radicals, the bad news for the Hotel New Hampshire. 'She's probably with a customer, or out on the street,' I said to him, but Father said he would just wait for her outside her room.

I sat down with Susie.

'She's still with him,' Susie sobbed. If Franny was still with Ernst the pornographer, I knew, it meant she was more than *talking* to him. There was no reason to pretend to be a bear anymore. I held Susie's bear head in my hands, I put it on, I took it off. I could not sit there in the lobby, waiting for Franny, like a whore, to be finished with him—to come down to the lobby again—and I knew I was helpless to interfere. I would have been too late, as always. There was no one around as fast as Harold Swallow, this time; there was no Black Arm of the Law. Junior Jones *would* rescue Franny again, but he was too late to save her from Ernst—and so was I. If I'd stayed in the lobby with Susie, I would have just cried with her, and I'd been crying entirely too much, I thought.

'Did you tell Old Billig?' I asked Susie. 'About the bombers?'

'She was only worried about her fucking china bears,' Susie said, and went on crying.

'I love Franny, too,' I told Susie, and gave her a hug.

'Not like I do!' Susie said, stifling a cry. Yes, *like you do,* I thought.

I started upstairs, but Susie misunderstood me.

'They're somewhere on the third floor,' Susie said. 'Franny came down for a key, but I didn't see which room.' I looked at the reception desk; you could tell it was Susie the bear's night to watch after the reception desk, because the reception desk was a big mess.

'I'm looking for Jolanta,' I said to Susie. 'Not Franny.'

'Going to tell her, huh?' Susie asked.

But Jolanta wasn't interested in being told.

'I've got something to tell you,' I said outside her door.

'Three hundred Schillings,' she said, so I slipped it under the door.

'Okay, you can come in,' Jolanta said. She was alone; a customer had just left her, apparently, because she was sitting on her bidet, naked except for her bra.

'You want to see the tits, too?' Jolanta asked me. 'The tits cost another hundred Schillings.'

'I want to *tell* you something,' I said to her.

'That costs another hundred, too,' she said, washing herself with the mindless lack of energy of a housewife washing dishes.

I gave her another hundred Schillings and she took her bra off. 'Undress,' she commanded me.

I did as I was told, while saying, 'It's the stupid radicals. They've ruined everything. They're going to blow up the Opera.'

'So what?' Jolanta said, watching me undress. 'Your body is basically wrong,' she told me. 'You're basically a little guy with big muscles.'

'I may need to borrow what's in your purse,' I suggested to her, '—just until the police take care of things.' But Jolanta ignored this.

'You like it standing up, against the wall?' she asked me. 'Is that how you want it? If we use the bed—if I have to lie down —it's one hundred Schillings extra.' I leaned against the wall and closed my eyes.

'Jolanta,' I said. 'They're really serious. Fehlgeburt is *dead*,' I said. 'And these crazy people have a bomb, a big bomb.'

'Fehlgeburt was born dead,' Jolanta said, dropping to her knees and sucking me into her mouth. Later, she put a prophylactic on me. I tried to concentrate, but when she stood up against me and stuffed me inside her, slamming me against the wall, she immediately informed me that I wasn't tall enough to do it standing up. I paid her another hundred Schillings and we tried it on the bed.

'Now you're not *hard* enough,' she complained, and I wondered if my failure to be hard enough would cost me another hundred Schillings.

'Please don't let on to the radicals that you *know* about them,' I said to Jolanta. 'And it would probably be better for you if you got out of here for a while—no one really knows what will become of the hotel. We're going back to America,' I added.

'Okay, okay,' she said, shoving me off her. She sat up in bed, she crossed the floor and sat back down on the bidet. '*Auf Wiedersehen*,' she said.

'But I didn't *come*,' I said.

'Whose fault is that?' she asked me, washing and washing herself, again and again.

I suppose, if I *had* come, it would have cost me another hundred Schillings. I watched her broad back rocking over the bidet; she was rocking with slightly more intensity than she had moved with when she was under me. Since her back was to me, I took her purse off the bedside table and looked in it. It looked like Susie the bear had been taking care of it. There was a tube

325

of some kind of ointment that had opened; the inside of Jolanta's purse was sticky with a sort of creme. There was the usual lipstick, the usual packages of prophylactics (I noticed I had forgotten to take mine *off*), the usual cigarettes, some pills, perfume, tissues, change, a fat wallet—and little jars of assorted *junk*. There wasn't a knife, not to mention a gun. Her purse was an empty threat, her purse was a bluff; she was mock-sex, and now—it seemed—she was only mock-violence, too. Then I felt the jar that was quite a bit larger than the rest—it was quite an uncomfortable size, really. I pulled it out of her purse and looked at it; Jolanta turned and screamed at me.

'My *baby!*' she screamed. 'Put my baby down!'

I almost dropped it—this large jar. And in the murky fluid, swimming there, I saw the human fetus, the tiny tight-fisted embryo that had been Jolanta's only flower, nipped in the bud. In her mind—the way an ostrich comforts its head in the sand —was this embryo a kind of mock-weapon for Jolanta? Was it what she reached in her purse for, what she put her hands on when the going got rough? And what unlikely comfort was it to her?

'Put my baby down!' she cried, advancing toward me, naked —and dripping from her bidet. I put the bottled fetus gently on the pillow of her bed, and fled.

I heard Screaming Annie announcing her false arrival when I opened and closed Jolanta's door. It appeared that Father was giving her the bad news. I sat on the second-floor landing, not wanting to see Susie the bear in the lobby, and not daring to seek out Franny on the floor above. Father came out of Screaming Annie's room; he wished me a good night, with a hand on my shoulder, and went down the stairs to go to bed.

'Did you tell her?' I called after him.

'It didn't seem to matter to her,' Father said. I went and knocked on Screaming Annie's door.

'I already know,' she told me, when she saw who it was.

But I hadn't been able to *come* with Jolanta; something else took possession of me outside Screaming Annie's door. 'Well, why didn't you say so?' Screaming Annie said, when I had still said nothing. She took me inside her room and shut the door. 'Like father, like son,' she said. She helped me undress; she was already undressed herself. No wonder she had to work so hard, I realized—because she didn't know the system of charging for all the 'extras' that Jolanta charged for. Screaming Annie just did it all for a flat four hundred Schillings.

326

'And if you don't come,' she told me, 'that's *my* fault. But you'll come,' she assured me.

'Please,' I said to her, 'if it's all the same to you, I wish you *wouldn't* come. I mean, I wish you wouldn't pretend to. I would appreciate a *quiet* ending,' I begged her, but she was already beginning to make curious sounds under me. And then I heard a sound that scared me. It resembled nothing I'd ever heard from Screaming Annie; it was not the song Susie the bear had coaxed out of Franny, either. For an awful second—because there was so much *pain* in the sound—I thought it was the song Ernst the pornographer was making Franny sing, and then I realized it was *my* sound, it was my own wretched singing voice. Screaming Annie started singing with me, and in the vibrating silence that followed our awesome duet I heard what was clearly Franny's voice yelling—so close by she must have been standing on the second-floor landing—'Oh, *Christ,* would you hurry up and get it *over with!*' Franny screamed.

'Why did you do it?' I whispered to Screaming Annie, who lay panting under me.

'Do what?' she said.

'The fake orgasm,' I said. 'I asked you not to.'

'That was no fake,' she whispered. But before I had a moment to even consider this news as a compliment, she added, 'I *never* fake an orgasm. They're *all* real,' Screaming Annie said. 'Why in hell do you think I'm such a wreck?' she asked me. And why, of course, did I think she was so convinced about not wanting her dark daughter in the 'business'?

'I'm sorry,' I whispered.

'I hope they *do* blow up the Opera,' Screaming Annie said. 'I hope they get the Hotel Sacher, too,' she added. 'I hope they wipe out all the Kärntnerstrasse,' she added. 'And the Ringstrasse, and everyone on it. All the *men,*' whispered Screaming Annie.

Franny was waiting for me on the second-floor landing. She didn't look any worse than I did. I sat down beside her and we asked each other if we were 'all right.' Neither one of us provided very convincing answers. I asked Franny what she found out from Ernst, and she shivered. I put my arm around her and we leaned against the banister of the staircase together. I asked her again.

'I found out about everything, I think,' she whispered. 'What do you want to know?'

'Everything,' I said, and Franny shut her eyes and put her head on my shoulder and turned her face against my neck.

'Do you still love me?' she asked.

'Yes, of course I do,' I whispered.

'And you want to know everything?' she asked. I held my breath, and she said, 'The cow position? You want to know about that?' I just held her; I couldn't say anything. 'And the elephant position?' she asked me. I could feel her shaking; she was trying very hard not to cry. 'I can tell you a few things about the elephant position,' Franny said. 'The main thing about it is, it *hurts*,' she said, and she started to cry.

'He hurt you?' I asked her softly.

'The elephant position hurt me,' she said. We sat quietly for a while, until she stopped shaking. 'Do you want me to go on?' she asked me.

'Not about that,' I said.

'Do you still love me?' Franny asked.

'Yes, I can't help it,' I said.

'Poor you,' said Franny.

'Poor you, too,' I told her.

There is at least one terrible thing about lovers—real lovers, I mean: people who are in love with each other. Even when they're supposed to be miscrable, and comforting each other, even then they will relish their every physical contact in a sexual way; even when they're supposed to be in a kind of mourning, they can get aroused. Franny and I simply couldn't have gone on holding each other on the stairs; it was impossible to touch each other, at all, and not want to touch everything.

I suppose I should be grateful to Jolanta for breaking us up. Jolanta was on her way out to the street, looking for someone else to abuse. She saw Franny and me sitting on the stairs and aimed her knee so that it struck me in the spine. 'Oh, excuse me!' she said. And, to Franny, Jolanta added, 'Don't get involved with him. He can't come.'

Franny and I, without a word, more or less followed Jolanta down to the lobby—only Jolanta went through the lobby and out onto the Krugerstrasse, while Franny and I went to have a look at Susie the bear. Susie was sleeping on the couch that had the ashtray spilled on it; there was an almost serene look on her face —Susie wasn't nearly as ugly as she thought she was. Franny had told me that Susie's little joke about being the original not-bad-if-you-put-a-bag-over-her-head girl was not so funny; the two men who had raped her *had* put a bag over her head

—'So we don't have to look at you,' they told her. This kind of cruelty might make a bear out of anyone.

'Rape really puzzles me,' I would later confess to Susie the bear, 'because it seems to me to be the most brutalizing experience that can be survived; we can't, for example, survive our own murder. And I suppose it's the most brutalizing experience I can imagine because I can't imagine *doing* it to someone, I can't imagine wanting to. Therefore, it is such a foreign feeling: I think that's what seems so brutalizing about it.'

'*I* can imagine doing it to someone,' Susie said. 'I can imagine doing it to the fuckers who did it to me,' she said. 'But that's because it would be simply revenge. And it wouldn't work, doing it to a fucking *man*,' Susie said. 'Because a man probably would enjoy it. There are men who think *we* actually enjoy getting raped,' Susie said. 'They can only think that,' she said, 'because they think *they* would like it.'

But in the ash-gray lobby of the second Hotel New Hampshire, Franny and I simply tried to put Susie the bear back together again, and get her to go to her own room to sleep. We got her on her feet, and found her head; we brushed the old cigarette butts (that she'd been lying in) off her shaggy back.

'Come on, come get out of your old suit, Susie,' Franny coaxed her.

'How *could* you—with Ernst?' Susie mumbled to Franny. 'And how could *you*—with *whores*?' she asked me. 'I don't understand either of you,' Susie concluded. 'I'm too old for this.'

'No, *I* am too old for this, Susie,' said Father gently, to the bear. We hadn't noticed him, standing in the lobby, behind the reception desk; we thought he had gone to bed. He wasn't alone, either. The gentle motherlike radical, our dear *Schlagobers,* our dear Schwanger, was with him. She had her gun out and she motioned us all back to the couch.

'Be a dear,' Schwanger said to me. 'Get Lilly and Frank. Wake them up nicely,' she added. 'Don't be rough, or too abrupt.'

Frank was lying in bed with the dressmaker's dummy stretched out beside him. He was wide-awake; I didn't have to wake him. 'I knew we shouldn't have waited,' Frank said. 'We should have blown the whistle right away.'

Lilly was also wide-awake. Lilly was writing.

'Here comes a new experience to write about, Lilly,' I joked with her, holding her hand as we walked back to the lobby.

'I hope it's just a *little* experience,' Lilly said.

They were all waiting for us in the lobby. Schraubenschlüssel was wearing his streetcar conductor's uniform; he looked very 'official.' Arbeiter had come dressed for work; he was so well dressed, in fact, that he wouldn't have looked out of place at the Opera. He was wearing a tuxedo—all black. And the quarter-back was there, the signal caller was there to lead them—Ernst the lady-killer, Ernst the pornographer, Ernst the star was there. Only Old Billig—Old Billig the radical—was missing. He blew the way the wind blew, as Arbeiter had observed: Old Billig was smart enough to have excluded himself from this end of the movement. He would still be around for the next show; for Ernst and Arbeiter, for Schraubenschlüssel and Schwanger, this was surely the gala (and maybe the final) performance.

'Lilly dear,' Schwanger said. 'Go fetch Freud for us. Freud should be here, too.'

And Lilly, once again cast in the role of Freud's Seeing Eye bear, brought the old blind believer to us—his Louisville Slugger tap-tap-tapping in front of him, his scarlet silk robe with the black dragon on the back was all he wore ('Chinatown, New York City, 1939!' he had told us).

'What dream is this?' the old man said. 'Whatever happened to democracy?'

Lilly seated Freud on the couch next to Father; Freud promptly whacked Father's shin with the baseball bat.

'Oh, sorry!' Freud cried. 'Whose anatomy is that?'

'Win Berry,' my father said softly; it was eerie, but that was the only time we children heard him speak his own name.

'Win Berry!' Freud cried. 'Well, nothing too bad can happen with Win Berry around!' No one looked so sure.

'Explain yourselves!' Freud shouted to the darkness he saw. 'You're all here,' the old man said. 'I can smell you, I can hear every breath.'

'It's really quite simple to explain,' Ernst said quietly.

'Basic,' said Arbeiter. 'Truly basic.'

'We need a driver,' Ernst said softly, 'someone to drive the car.'

'It runs like a dream,' Schraubenschlüssel said, worshipfully. 'It purrs like a kitten.'

'Drive it yourself, Wrench,' I said.

'Be quiet, dear,' Schwanger said to me; I just looked at her gun to confirm that it was pointed at me.

'Be quiet, weight lifter,' Wrench said; he had a short,

heavy-looking tool protruding from the front pants pocket of his streetcar conductor's uniform, and he rested his hand on the tool as if the tool were the butt of a pistol.

'Fehlgeburt was full of doubt,' Ernst said.

'Fehlgeburt is dead,' Lilly said—our family realist, the family writer.

'Fehlgeburt had a fatal case of romanticism,' Ernst said. 'She always questioned the *means*.'

'The ends *do* justify the means, you know,' Arbeiter interjected. 'That's basic, truly basic.'

'You're a moron, Arbeiter,' Franny said.

'And you're as self-righteous as any capitalist!' Freud told Arbeiter.

'But mainly a moron, Arbeiter,' said Susie the bear. 'A truly *basic* moron.'

'The bear would make a good driver,' Schraubenschlüssel said.

'Stick it in your ear, Wrench,' said Susie the bear.

'The bear is too hostile to be trusted,' Ernst said, so logically.

'You bet your sweet ass,' said Susie the bear.

'*I* can drive,' Franny said to Ernst.

'You *can't*,' I said. 'You never even got your driver's license, Franny.'

'But I know how to drive,' Franny said. 'Frank taught me.'

'I know how to drive better than you, Franny,' Frank said. 'If one of us has to drive, I'm a better driver.'

'No, *I* am,' Franny said.

'You *did* surprise me, Franny,' Ernst said. 'You were better at following directions than I thought you'd be—you were good at taking instructions.'

'Don't move, dear,' Schwanger said to me, because my arms were jerking—the way they do when I've been curling the long bar, for a long time.

'What's *that* mean?' Father asked Ernst; his German was so poor. '*What* directions—what instructions?' Father asked.

'He fucked me,' Franny told Father.

'Just sit tight,' Wrench said to my father, moving near him with his tool. But Frank had to translate for Father.

'Just stay where you are, Pop,' Frank said.

Freud was swishing the baseball bat as if he were a cat and the bat were his tail, and he tapped my father's leg with it—once, twice, thrice. I knew that Father wanted the bat. He was very good with the Louisville Slugger.

Occasionally, when Freud was napping, Father would take us to the Stadtpark and hit us some grounders. We all liked scooping up ground balls. A little game of good old American baseball in the Stadtpark, with Father whacking out the ground balls. Even Lilly liked playing. You don't have to be big to field a ground ball. Frank was the worst at it; Franny and I were good at fielding—in a lot of ways, we were about the same. Father would whack the sharpest grounders at Franny and me.

But Freud held the bat, now, and he used it to calm my father down.

'You slept with Ernst, Franny?' Father asked her, softly.

'Yes,' she whispered. 'I'm sorry.'

'You fucked my daughter?' Father asked Ernst.

Ernst treated it like a metaphysical question. 'It was a necessary phase,' he said, and I knew that at that moment I could have done what Junior Jones could do: I could have bench-pressed twice my own weight—maybe three or four times, fast; I could have pumped that barbell up and not felt a thing.

'My *daughter* was a necessary *phase?*' Father asked Ernst.

'This is not an emotional situation,' Ernst said. 'This is a matter of technique,' he said, ignoring my father. 'Although I'm sure you could do a good job of driving the car, Franny, Schwanger has asked us that each of you children be spared.'

'Even the weight lifter?' Arbeiter asked.

'Yes, he's a dear to me, too,' Schwanger said, beaming at me —with her gun.

'If you make my father drive that car, I'll *kill* you!' Franny screamed at Ernst, suddenly. And Wrench moved near to her, with his tool; if he had touched her, something would have happened, but he just stood near her. Freud's baseball bat kept time. My father had his eyes closed; he had such trouble following German. He must have been dreaming of hard ground balls spanked cleanly through the infield.

'Schwanger has asked us, Franny,' Ernst said, patiently, 'not to make you children motherless *and* fatherless, too. We don't want to hurt your father, Franny. And we *won't* hurt him,' Ernst said, 'as long as *someone else* does a good job of driving the car.'

There was a puzzled silence in the lobby of the Hotel New Hampshire. If we children were exempt, if Father was to be spared, and Susie the bear wasn't to be trusted, did Ernst mean he would use one of the *whores* for a driver? *They* couldn't be trusted—for sure. They were only concerned with themselves.

While Ernst the pornographer had been preaching his dialectic to us, the whores had been slipping past us in the lobby—the whores were checking out of the Hotel New Hampshire. A wordless team—friends in any crisis, thick as the thieves they were—they were helping Old Billig move her china bears. They were bearing their salves, their toothbrushes, their pills, perfumes, and prophylactics *away*.

'They were the rats abandoning the sinking ship,' as Frank would say, later. They were not touched with Fehlgeburt's romanticism; they were never anything larger than whores. They left us without saying good-bye.

'So who's the driver, you super shit?' Susie the bear asked Ernst. 'Who the hell's *left?*'

Ernst smiled; it was a smile full of disgust, and he was smiling at Freud. Although Freud could not see this, Freud suddenly figured it out. 'It's *me!*' he cried, as if he'd won a prize; he was so excited, the baseball bat tapped double time. '*I'm* the driver!' Freud cried.

'Yes, you are,' said Ernst, awfully pleased.

'Brilliant!' Freud cried. 'The perfect job for a blind man!' he shouted, the baseball bat like a baton, conducting, leading the orchestra—Freud's Vienna State Opera Band!

'And you love Win Berry, don't you, Freud?' Schwanger asked the old man, gently.

'Of course I do!' Freud cried. 'Like my own son!' Freud yelled, wrapping his arms around my father, the baseball bat snug between his knees.

'So if you drive the car properly,' Ernst said to Freud, 'no harm will come to Win Berry.'

'If you fuck it up,' Arbeiter said, 'we'll kill them all.'

'One at a time,' Schraubenschlüssel added.

'How can a blind man drive the car, you *morons?*' screamed Susie the bear.

'Explain how it works, Schraubenschlüssel,' Ernst said, calmly. And now it was Wrench's big moment, the moment he'd been living for—to *describe* every loving detail of his heart's desire. Arbeiter looked a little jealous. Schwanger and Ernst listened with the most benign expressions, like teachers proud of their prize pupil. My father, of course, didn't understand the language well enough to get all of it.

'I call it a sympathy bomb,' Wrench began.

'Oh, that's brilliant!' Freud cried out; then he giggled. 'A *sympathy* bomb! Jesus God!'

'Shut up,' Arbeiter said.

'There are actually *two* bombs,' Schraubenschlüssel said. 'The first bomb is the car. The whole car,' he said, smiling slyly. 'The car simply has to be detonated within a certain range of the Opera—quite close to the Opera, actually. If the car explodes within this range, the bomb in the Opera will explode, too—you might say "in sympathy" with the first explosion. Which is why I call it a sympathy bomb,' Wrench added, moronically. Even Father could have followed this part. 'First the car blows, and if it blows close enough to the Opera, then the *big* bomb—the one in the Opera—then *it* blows. The bomb in the car is what I call a *contact* bomb. The contact is the front license plate. When the front license plate is depressed, the whole car blows sky-high. Several people in its vicinity will be blown sky-high, too,' Schraubenschlüssel added.

'That's unavoidable,' Arbeiter said.

'The bomb in the Opera,' said Schraubenschlüssel, lovingly, 'is much more complicated than a contact bomb. The bomb in the Opera is a chemical bomb, but a very delicate kind of electrical impulse is required to *start* it. The fuse to the bomb in the Opera—in a quite remarkably sensitive way—*responds* to a very particular explosion within its range. It's almost as if the bomb in the Opera has *ears,*' Wrench said, laughing at himself. It was the first time we had heard Wrench laugh; it was a disgusting laugh. Lilly started to gag, as if she was going to be sick.

'*You* won't be hurt, dear,' Schwanger soothed her.

'All I have to do is drive the car, with Freud in it, right down the Ringstrasse to the Opera,' Schraubenschlüssel said. 'Of course, I have to be careful not to run into anything, I have to find a safe place to pull off to the side of the street—and then I get out,' Schraubenschlüssel said. 'When I'm out, Freud gets behind the wheel. Nobody will ask us to move on before we're ready; nobody in Vienna questions a streetcar conductor.'

'We know you know how to drive, Freud,' Ernst said to the old man. 'You used to be a mechanic, right?'

'Right,' said Freud; he was fascinated.

'I stand right next to Freud, speaking to him through the driver's side window,' said Wrench. 'I wait until I see Arbeiter come out of the Opera and cross the Kärntnerstrasse—to the other side.'

'To the *safe* side!' Arbeiter added.

'And then I just tell Freud to count to ten and floor it!'

Schraubenschlüssel said. 'I'll already have aimed the car in the right direction. Freud will simply floor it—he'll get up to as fast a speed as he can. He'll run smack into something—almost right away, no matter which way he turns. He's *blind!*' Wrench cried, enthusiastically. 'He *has* to hit something. And when he does, there goes the Opera. The sympathy bomb will respond.'

'The *sympathy* bomb,' my father said, ironically. Even Father understood the sympathy part.

'It's in a perfect place,' Arbeiter said. 'It's been there a long time, so we know no one knows where it is. It's very big but it's impossible to find,' he added.

'It's under the stage,' Arbeiter said.

'It's *built into* the stage,' Schraubenschlüssel said.

'It's right where they come out to take their fucking final bows!' Arbeiter said.

'Of course, it won't kill everyone,' Ernst said, simply. 'Everyone onstage will die, and probably most of the orchestra, and most of the audience in the first few rows of seats. And to those sitting safely back from the stage it will be truly *operatic,*' Ernst said. 'It will provide a very definite spectacle,' said Ernst.

'*Schlagobers* and blood,' Arbeiter teased Schwanger, but she just smiled—with her gun.

Lilly threw up. When Schwanger bent over to soothe her, I *might* have had an opportunity to grab the gun. But I wasn't thinking well enough. Arbeiter took the gun from Schwanger, as if—to my shame—he was thinking more clearly than I was. Lilly kept throwing up, and Franny tried to soothe her too, but Ernst went right on talking.

'When Arbeiter and Schraubenschlüssel come back here, and report on our success, then we'll know we won't have to harm this wonderful American family,' Ernst said.

'The American family,' Arbeiter said, 'is an institution that Americans dote on to the sentimental extreme that they dote on sports heroes and movie stars; they lavish as much attention on *the family* as they lavish on unhealthy food. Americans are simply *crazy* about the idea of the family.'

'And after we blow up the Opera,' Ernst said, 'after we destroy an institution that the Viennese worship to the *disgusting* extreme that they worship their coffeehouses—that they worship the *past*—well . . . after we blow up the Opera, we'll have possession of an American family. We'll have an American family as hostage. And a *tragic* American family, too. The mother and the youngest child already the victims of an

335

accident. Americans love accidents. They think disasters are *neat*. And here we have a father struggling to raise his four surviving children, and we'll have them all *captured*.'

Father didn't follow this very well, and Franny asked Ernst, 'What are your *demands*? If we're hostages, what are the demands?'

'No demands, dear,' Schwanger said.

'We demand nothing,' said Ernst, patiently—ever patiently. 'We'll already have what we want. When we blow up the Opera and we have you as our *prisoners*, we'll already have what we want.'

'An audience,' Schwanger said, almost in a whisper.

'Quite a wide audience,' Ernst said. 'An international audience. Not just a European audience, not just the *Schlagobers* and blood audience, but an *American* audience, too. The whole world will listen to what we have to say.'

'About *what*?' Freud asked. He was whispering, too.

'About everything,' Ernst said, so logically. 'We'll have an audience for everything we've got to say—about everything.'

'About the new world,' Frank murmured.

'Yes!' Arbeiter said.

'Most terrorists fail,' Ernst reasoned, 'because they take the hostages and *threaten* violence. But we're beginning with the violence. It is already established that we are capable of it. *Then* we take the hostages. That way everybody listens.'

Everyone looked at Ernst, which—of course—Ernst loved. He was a pornographer willing to murder and maim—not for a *cause*, which would be stupid enough, but for an *audience*.

'You're absolutely crazy,' Franny said to Ernst.

'You disappoint me,' Ernst said to her.

'What's that?' Father cried to him. 'What did you say to her?'

'He said I disappointed him, Pop,' Franny said.

'She *disappoints* you!' Father cried. 'My daughter disappoints *you!*' Father shouted at Ernst.

'Calm down,' Ernst said to Father, calmly.

'You fuck my daughter and then tell her she *disappoints* you!' Father said.

Father grabbed the baseball bat from Freud. He did this very quickly. He picked up that Louisville Slugger as if it had lived a lifetime in his hands, and he swung it levelly, getting his shoulders and hips into the swing, and following through with the swing—it was a perfect line-drive sort of swing, a level low liner that would still have been rising when it cleared the infield.

And Ernst the pornographer, who ducked too slowly, put his head in the position of a perfect letter-high fast ball to my father's fine swing of the bat. *Crack!* Harder than any ground ball Franny or I could have handled. My father caught Ernst the pornographer with the Louisville Slugger flat on the forehead and smack between the eyes. The first thing to strike the floor was the back of Ernst's head, his heels plopping down one at a time; it seemed like a full second after the head had hit the floor that Ernst's body settled down. A purple swelling the size of a baseball rose up between Ernst's eyes, and a little blood ran out of one of his ears, as if something vital but small—like his brain, like his heart—had exploded inside him. His eyes were open wide, and we knew that Ernst the pornographer could now see everything that Freud could see. He had gone out the open window with one swift crack of the bat.

'Is he dead?' Freud cried. I think if Freud hadn't cried out, Arbeiter would have pulled the trigger and killed my father; Freud's cry seemed to change Arbeiter's slow-moving mind. He stuck the barrel of the gun in my little sister Lilly's ear; Lilly trembled—she had nothing more to throw up.

'Please don't,' Franny whispered to Arbeiter. Father held the baseball bat tightly, but he held it still. Arbeiter had the big weapon now, and my father had to wait for the right pitch.

'Everyone stay calm,' Arbeiter said. Schraubenschlüssel could not take his eyes off the purple baseball on Ernst's forehead, but Schwanger kept smiling—at everyone.

'Calm, calm,' she crooned. 'Let's stay calm.'

'What are you going to do *now?*' Father asked Arbeiter, calmly. He asked him in English; Frank had to translate.

For the next few minutes, Frank would be kept busy as a translator because Father wanted to know *everything* that was going on. He was a hero; he was on the dock at the old Arbuthnot-by-the-Sea, except *he* was the man in the white dinner jacket—he was in charge.

'Give the bat back to Freud,' Arbeiter told my father.

'Freud needs his bat back,' Schwanger said to my father, stupidly.

'Give the bat up, Pop,' said Frank.

Father gave the Louisville Slugger back to Freud and sat down beside him; he put his arm around Freud and said to him, 'You don't *have* to drive that car.'

'Schraubenschlüssel,' Schwanger said. 'You're going to do it just the way we planned. Take Freud with you and get going,' she said.

'But I'm not at the Opera!' Arbeiter said, in a panic. 'I'm not there yet—to see if it's intermission, or to make sure it's *not*. Schraubenschlüssel has to see me walk out of the Opera so he knows it's okay, so he knows it's the right time.'

The radicals stared at their dead leader as if he would tell them what to do; they needed him.

'*You* go to the Opera,' Arbeiter told Schwanger. '*I'm* better with the gun,' he said. 'I'll stay here, and *you* go to the Opera,' Arbeiter advised her. 'When you're sure it's not intermission, walk out of the Opera and let Schraubenschlüssel see *you*.'

'But I'm not dressed for the Opera,' Schwanger said. '*You're* dressed for it,' she told Arbeiter.

'You don't have to be dressed for it to ask someone if it's intermission!' Arbeiter yelled at her. 'You look good enough to get in the door, and you can see for yourself if it's intermission. You're just an old lady—nobody hassles an old lady for how she's dressed, for Christ's sake'

'Stay calm,' Schraubenschlüssel advised, mechanically.

'Well,' our gentle Schwanger said, 'I'm not exactly an "old lady." '

'Fuck off!' Arbeiter cried at her. 'Get going. Walk up there, *fast!* We'll give you ten minutes. Then Freud and Schraubenschlüssel are on their way.'

Schwanger stood there as if she were trying to decide whether to write about pregnancy or another abortion book.

'Get going, you cunt!' Arbeiter yelled at her. 'Remember to cross the Kärntnerstrasse. And look for our car before you cross the street.'

Schwanger left the Hotel New Hampshire, composing herself —actually arranging her face in as motherly an expression as she could muster for the occasion. We would never see her again. I suppose she went to Germany; she might author a whole new book of symbols, one day. She might mother a new movement, somewhere else.

'You don't have to do this, Freud,' my father whispered.

'Of *course* I have to do it, Win Berry!' Freud said, cheerfully. He got up; he tapped his way with the baseball bat toward the door. He knew his way around pretty well, considering his total darkness.

'Sit down, you old fool,' Arbeiter told him. 'We've got ten minutes. Don't forget to get out of the car, you idiot,' Arbeiter told Schraubenschlüssel, but Wrench was still staring at the dead quarterback on the floor. I stared at him, too. For ten minutes. I realized what a terrorist is. A terrorist, I think, is simply another kind of pornographer. The pornographer pretends he is disgusted by his work; the terrorist pretends he is uninterested in the *means*. The *ends,* they say, are what they care about. But they are both lying. Ernst loved his pornography; Ernst worshiped the means. It is never the ends that matter—it is *only* the means that matter. The terrorist and the pornographer are in it *for* the means. The means is everything to them. The blast of the bomb, the elephant position, the *Schlagobers* and blood—they love it all. Their intellectual detachment is a fraud; their indifference is feigned. They both tell lies about having 'higher purposes.' A terrorist *is* a pornographer.

For ten minutes Frank tried to change Arbeiter's mind, but Arbeiter didn't have enough of a mind to experience a change. I think Frank only succeeded in confusing Arbeiter.

Frank was certainly confusing to *me*.

'You know what's at the Opera tonight, Arbeiter?' Frank asked.

'Music,' Arbeiter said, 'music and singing.'

'But it matters—*which* opera,' Frank lied. 'I mean, it's not exactly a full-house performance tonight—I hope you know that. It's not as if the Viennese have come in *droves*. It's not as if it's Mozart, or Strauss. It's not even Wagner,' Frank said.

'I don't care what it is,' Arbeiter said. 'The front rows will be full. The front rows are always full. And the dumb singers will be onstage. And the orchestra has to show up.'

'It's *Lucia,*' Frank said. 'Practically an empty house. You don't have to be a Wagnerian to know that Donizetti's not worth listening to. I confess to being something of a Wagnerian,' Frank confessed, 'but you don't have to share the Germanic opinion of Italian opera to know that Donizetti is simply insipid. Stale harmonies, lack of any dramatism appropriate to the music,' Frank said.

'Shut up,' Arbeiter said.

'Organ-grinder tunes!' Frank said. 'God, I wonder if *anyone* will show up.'

'They'll show up,' Arbeiter said.

'Better to wait for a big shot,' Frank said. 'Blow the place another night. Wait for an *important* opera. If you blow up *Lucia,*' Frank reasoned, 'the Viennese will *applaud!* They'll think your target was Donizetti, or, even better—*Italian* opera!

You'll be a kind of cultural hero,' Frank argued, 'not the villain you want to be.'

'And when you get your audience,' Susie the bear told Arbeiter, 'who's going to do the talking?'

'Your talker is dead,' Franny said to Arbeiter.

'You don't think *you* can hold an audience, do you, Arbeiter?' Susie the bear asked him.

'Shut up,' Arbeiter said. 'It's possible to have a bear ride in the car with Freud. Everyone knows Freud's got a thing for bears. It might be a nice idea to have a bear ride with him—on his last trip.'

'No change in the plan, not now,' said Schraubenschlüssel, nervously. 'According to plan,' he said, looking at his watch. 'Two minutes.'

'Go now,' Arbeiter said. 'It will take a while to get the blind man out the door and in the car.'

'Not me!' Freud cried. 'I know the way! It's my hotel, I know where the door is,' the old man said, hobbling on the baseball bat toward the door. 'And you've parked that damn car in the same place for years!'

'Go with him, Schraubenschlüssel,' Arbeiter told Wrench. 'Hold the old fucker's arm.'

'I don't need any assistance,' Freud said, cheerfully. 'Goodbye, Lilly dear!' Freud cried. 'Don't throw up, dear,' he urged her. 'And keep growing!'

Lilly gagged again, and shook; Arbeiter moved the gun about two inches away from her ear. He was apparently disgusted with her puking, though it was only a very small puddle that Lilly had managed; she was not even a big vomiter.

'Hang in there, Frank!' Freud called—to the entire lobby. 'Don't let anyone tell you you're queer! You're a *prince*, Frank!' Freud cried. 'You're better than Rudolf!' Freud yelled to Frank. 'You're more majestic than all the Hapsburgs, Frank!' Freud encouraged him. Frank couldn't speak, he was crying so hard.

'You're lovely, Franny my dear, Franny my sweetheart,' said Freud softly. 'One doesn't have to see to know how beautiful you are,' he said.

'*Auf Wiedersehen*, Freud,' Franny said.

'*Auf Wiedersehen*, weight lifter!' Freud cried to me. 'Give me a hug,' he asked me, holding out his arms, the Louisville Slugger like a sword in one hand. 'Let me feel how strong you are,' Freud said to me, and I went up to him and hugged him. That was when he whispered in my ear.

'When you hear the explosion,' Freud whispered, '*kill* Arbeiter.'

'Come on!' Schraubenschlüssel said, nervously. He grabbed Freud's arm.

'I love you, Win Berry!' Freud cried, but my father had his head in his hands; he would not look up from where he sat, sunk in the couch. 'I'm sorry I got you in the hotel business,' Freud said to my father. 'And the bear business,' Freud added. 'Good-bye, Susie!' Freud said.

Susie started to cry. Schraubenschlüssel steered Freud through the door. We could see the car, the Mercedes that was a bomb; it was parked against the curb almost in front of the door to the Hotel New Hampshire. It was a revolving door, and Freud and Schraubenschlüssel revolved through it.

'I don't need your assistance!' Freud was complaining to Wrench. 'Just let me *feel* the car, just get me to the fender,' Freud complained. 'I can find the door by myself, you idiot,' Freud was saying. 'Just let me touch the fender.'

Arbeiter was getting a stiff back, leaning over Lilly. He straightened up a little; he glanced at me, checking on where I was. He glanced at Franny. His gun wandered around.

'There it is, I've got it!' we heard Freud crying, cheerfully, outside. 'That's the headlight, right?' he asked Schraubenschlüssel. My father raised his head from his hands and looked at me.

'Of *course* that's the headlight, you old fool!' Schraubenschlüssel yelled at Freud. 'Get *in*, will you?'

'Freud!' Father screamed. He must have known, then. He ran to the revolving door. '*Auf Wiedersehen, Freud!*' Father cried. At the revolving door, Father saw the whole thing very clearly. Freud, with his hand feeling along the headlight, slipped toward the grille of the Mercedes instead of toward the door.

'The other way, you moron!' Schraubenschlüssel advised. But Freud knew exactly where he was. He tore his arm out of Wrench's grasp; he leveled the Louisville Slugger and started swinging. He was looking for the front license plate, of course. Blind people have a knack for knowing exactly where things that have always been are. It took Freud only three swings to locate the license plate, my father would always remember. The first swing was a little high—off the grille.

'Lower!' Father screamed, through the revolving door. '*Auf Wiedersehen!*'

The second swing hit the front bumper a little to the left of the license plate, and my Father yelled, 'To your right! *Auf*

Wiedersehen, Freud!' Schraubenschlüssel, Father said later, was already running away. He never got far enough away, however. Freud's third swing was on the money; Freud's third swing was the grand slam. What a lot for that baseball bat to go through in one night! That Louisville Slugger was never found. Freud was never entirely found, either, and Schraubenschlüssel's own mother would fail to identify him. My father was blasted back from the revolving door, the white light and glass flying in his face. Franny and Frank ran to help him, and I got my arms around Arbeiter just as the bomb blew—just as Freud had told me to do.

Arbeiter in his black tuxedo, dressed for the Opera, was a little taller than I was, and a little heavier; my chin rested firmly between his shoulder blades, my arms went around his chest, pinning his arms to his side. He fired the gun once, into the floor. I thought for a moment that he might be able to shoot my foot with it, but I knew I'd never let him raise the gun any higher. I knew Lilly was out of Arbeiter's range. He fired two more shots into the floor. I held him so tightly that he couldn't even locate my foot, which was right behind his foot. His next shot hit his own foot and he started screaming. He dropped the gun. I heard it hit the floor and saw Lilly grab it, but I wasn't paying much attention to the gun. I was concentrating on squeezing Arbeiter. For someone who'd shot himself in the foot, he stopped screaming pretty soon. Frank would tell me, later, that Arbeiter stopped screaming because he couldn't breathe. I wasn't paying much attention to Arbeiter's screaming, either. I concentrated on the squeezing. I imagined the biggest barbell in the world. I don't know, exactly, what I imagined I was doing to the barbell —curling it, bench-pressing it, dead-lifting it, or simply hugging it to my own chest. It didn't matter; I was just concentrating on its *weight*. I really concentrated. I made my arms believe in themselves. If I had hugged Jolanta this hard, she would have broken in two. If I had hugged Screaming Annie this hard, she would have been quiet. Once I had dreamed of holding Franny this tightly. I had been lifting weights since Franny was raped, since Iowa Bob showed me how; with Arbeiter in my arms, I was the strongest man in the world.

'A *sympathy* bomb!' I heard Father yelling. I knew he was in pain. 'Jesus God! Can you believe it? A fucking *sympathy* bomb!'

Franny later said that she knew, immediately: Father was blind. It was not just because of where he was standing when the

342

car blew up, or the glass that was blasted into his face as he stood at the revolving door; it was not all the blood in his eyes that Franny saw when she wiped his face enough to *see* what was wrong with him. 'I *knew* somehow,' she said. 'I mean, *before* I saw his eyes. I always knew he was as blind as Freud, or he would be. I knew he *would* be,' Franny said.

'*Auf Wiedersehen*, Freud!' Father was crying.

'Hold still, Daddy,' I heard Lilly saying to Father.

'Yes, hold still, Pop,' Franny said.

Frank had run up the Krugerstrasse to the Kärntnerstrasse, and around the corner up to Opera. He had to see, of course, if the *sympathy* bomb had responded—but Freud had possessed the vision to see that the Mercedes parked in front of the Hotel New Hampshire was too far from sympathy to make the Opera respond. And Schwanger must have just kept walking. Or maybe she decided simply to stay and watch the end of the opera; maybe it was one she liked. Maybe she wanted to be there, watching them all at the curtain call, taking their last bows above the unexploded bomb.

Frank said later that when he ran out of the Hotel New Hampshire to go see if the Opera was safe, he noticed that Arbeiter was a very vivid magenta color, that his fingers were still moving—or perhaps just twitching—and that he seemed to be kicking his feet. Lilly told me later that—while Frank was gone—Arbeiter turned from magenta to blue. 'A slateblue color,' Lilly, the writer, said. 'The color of the ocean on a cloudy day.' And by the time Frank got back from seeing if the Opera was safe, Franny told me that Arbeiter was completely motionless and a dead-white color—the color was all gone from his face. 'He was the color of a pearl,' Lilly said. He was dead. I had crushed him.

'You can let him go now,' Franny finally had to tell me. 'It's okay, it's going to be okay,' she whispered to me, because she knew how I liked whispering. She kissed my face, and then I let Arbeiter go.

I have not felt the same about weight lifting since. I still do it, but I'm very low-key about the lifting now; I don't like to push myself. A little light lifting, just enough to make me start feeling good; I don't like to strain, not anymore.

The authorities told us that Schraubenschlüssel's 'sympathy bomb' might even have worked if the car had been closer. The bomb authorities also implied that *any* explosion in the area might have set the sympathy bomb off at *any* time; I guess old

Schraubenschlüssel hadn't been as exact as he thought he was. A lot of nonsense was written about what the radicals had *meant*. An unbelievable amount of garbage would be written about the 'statement' they had been trying to make. And there wasn't enough about Freud. His blindness was noted, in passing; and that he had been in one of the camps. There was absolutely nothing about the summer of 1939, about State o' Maine and the Arbuthnot-by-the-Sea, about *dreaming*—or about the *other* Freud, and what *he* might have had to say about all this. There was a lot of idiocy about the *politics* of what had happened.

'Politics are always idiotic!' as Iowa Bob would have said.

And there was not enough about Fehlgeburt, how she could break your heart the way she read the ending of *The Great Gatsby*. They acknowledged that my father was a hero, of course. They seemed polite about the reputation that our second Hotel New Hampshire had enjoyed—'in its prime,' as Frank would refer to those sordid days.

When Father got out of the hospital, we gave him a present. Franny had written Junior Jones for it. Junior Jones had provided us with baseballs for seven years, so Franny knew that Junior could be counted on to find Father a new baseball bat. A Louisville Slugger all his own. He would need it, of course. And Father seemed touched by our present—by Franny's thoughtfulness, really, because the bat was Franny's idea. I think Father must have cried a little when he first reached out his hands and we placed the bat in them, and he felt what it was he held. We couldn't see if he cried, however, because the bandages were still on his eyes.

And Frank, who had always had to translate for Father, had to become his interpreter in other ways. When the people from the Staatsoper wanted to pay us a tribute, Frank had to sit next to Father—at the Opera—and whisper to him about the action on the stage. Father could follow the music, just fine. I don't even remember what opera it was. It wasn't *Lucia*, I know that much. It was a particularly farcical comic opera, because Lilly had insisted that we wanted no *Schlagobers* and blood. It was nice that the Vienna State Opera wanted to thank us for saving them, but we didn't want to sit through any *Schlagobers* and blood. We'd already seen *that* opera. That was the opera that played in the Hotel New Hampshire for seven years.

And so, at the opening of this merry farce of an opera —whatever it was—the conductor and the orchestra and all the singers pointed out my father in one of the front-row seats (that's where Father had insisted on sitting. 'So I can be sure to *see,*' he had said). And Father stood up and took a bow; he was great at bowing. And he waved the baseball bat to the audience; the Viennese loved the Louisville Slugger part of the story, and they were touched and applauded for a long time when Father waved the bat at them. We children felt very proud.

I often wonder if the New York publisher who wanted Lilly's book for five thousand dollars would have listened to Frank's demands *if* we hadn't all become famous—if we hadn't saved the Opera and murdered the terrorists in our good old American family kind of way. 'Who cares?' Frank asks, slyly. The point is, Lilly had not signed the five-thousand-dollar contract. Frank had gone for higher stakes. And when the publishers realized that *this* Lilly Berry was the little girl who'd had a gun held to her head, that little Lilly Berry was the youngest surviving (and certainly the smallest) member of *the* Berry family—the terrorist killers, the Opera savers—well . . . at that point, of course, Frank was in the driver's seat.

'My author is already at work on a new book,' Frank, the agent, said. 'We're in no hurry about any of this. As far as *Trying to Grow* is concerned, we're interested in the best offer.'

Frank would make a killing, of course.

'You mean we're going to be *rich?*' Father asked, sightlessly. When he was first blind, he had an awkward way of inclining his head too far forward—as if this might help him to see. And the Louisville Slugger was his ever-restless companion, his percussion instrument.

'We can do anything we want, Pop,' Franny said. '*You* can,' she added, to him. 'Just think of it,' she told Father, 'and it's yours.'

'Dream on, Daddy,' Lilly said, but Father seemed stupefied by all the options.

'*Anything?*' Father asked.

'You name it,' I told him. He was our hero again; he was our father—at last. He was blind, but he was in charge.

'Well, I'll have to think about it,' Father said, cautiously, the baseball bat playing all kinds of music—that Louisville Slugger in my father's hands was as musically complicated as a full orchestra. Though Father would never make as much noise with a baseball bat as Freud had made, he was more various than Freud could have dreamed of being.

And so we left our seven-year home away from home. Frank sold the second Hotel New Hampshire for a ridiculously high price. After all, it was a kind of historical landmark, Frank argued.

'I'm coming home!' Franny wrote to Junior Jones.

'I'm coming home,' she also wrote to Chipper Dove.

'*Why*, damn it, Franny?' I asked. '*Why write to Chipper Dove?*'

But Franny refused to talk about it; she just shrugged.

'I told you,' Susie the bear said. 'Franny's got to *deal* with it —sooner or later. You've *both* got to deal with Chipper Dove,' Susie said, 'and you're going to have to deal with *each other*, too,' said Susie the bear. I looked at Susie as if I didn't know what she was talking about, but Susie said, '*I'm* not blind, you know. I got eyes. And I'm a smart bear, too.'

But Susie wasn't being menacing. 'You two have got a real problem,' she confided in Franny and me.

'No shit,' Franny said.

'Well, we're being very careful,' I told Susie.

'For how long can anybody be *that* careful?' Susie asked. 'The bombs haven't all gone off,' Susie said. 'You two have a bomb between you,' said Susie the bear. 'You've got to be more than careful,' Susie warned Franny and me. 'The bomb between you two,' Susie said, 'can blow you both away.'

For once, it seemed, Franny had nothing to say; I held her hand; she squeezed me back.

'I love you,' I told her, when we were alone—which we should never have allowed ourselves to be. 'I'm so sorry,' I whispered, 'but I love you, I do.'

'I love you terribly much,' Franny said. And it was Lilly who saved us that time; despite the fact that we were all supposed to be packed and ready to leave, Lilly was writing. We heard the typewriter and could imagine our sister's little hands *blurring* over the keyboard.

'Now that I'm going to get published,' Lilly had said, 'I have to really get better. I've got to keep growing,' she said, a little desperately. 'My God, the next book has got to be bigger than the first. And the one after that,' she said, 'it will have to be even *bigger*.' There was a certain despair about the way she said this, and Frank said, 'Stick with me, kid. With a good agent, you've got the world by the balls.'

'But I still have to *do* it,' Lilly complained. 'I still have to write. I mean, now I'm *expected* to grow.'

And the sound of Lilly trying so hard to grow distracted Franny and me from each other. We went out in the lobby, where it was somewhat more public—where we felt safe. Two men had just been killed in that lobby, but it was a safer place for Franny and me than in our own rooms.

The whores were gone. I do not care, anymore, what became of them. They didn't care what became of us.

The hotel was empty; a dangerous number of rooms beckoned to Franny and me.

'One day,' I said to her, 'we'll *have* to. You know that. Or do you think it will change—if we wait it out?'

'It won't change,' she said, 'but maybe—one day—we'll be able to handle it. One day it might be a little *safer* than it feels right now.'

I doubted that it would ever be safe enough, and I was on the verge of trying to convince her to do it now, to *use* the second Hotel New Hampshire as it was meant to be used—to get it over with, to see if we were doomed or just perversely attracted to each other—but Frank was our savior . . . this time.

He brought his bags out into the lobby and startled the hell out of us.

'Jesus, Frank!' Franny screamed.

'Sorry,' he mumbled. Frank had his usual queer lot of things: his odd books, his peculiar clothes, and his dressmaker's dummy.

'Are you taking that dummy back to America, Frank?' Franny asked him.

'It's not as heavy as what *you two* are carrying,' Frank said. 'And it's a lot *safer*.'

So Frank knew too, we realized. At that time, Franny and I thought Lilly *didn't* know; and—regarding our own dilemma —we were grateful that Father was blind.

'Keep passing the open windows,' Frank said to Franny and me—the damn dressmaker's dummy, slung like a light log over his shoulder, had a distressing resemblance about it. It was the *falseness* of it that Franny and I noticed: the mannequin's chipped face, the obvious wig, and the stiff, unfleshly bust of the dummy—the fake bosom, the still chest, the rigid waist. In the bad light in the lobby of the second Hotel New Hampshire, Franny and I could be fooled into thinking we saw shapes of Sorrow when we saw nothing at all. But hadn't Sorrow taught us to be on guard, to look *everywhere?* Sorrow can take any shape in the world.

347

'You keep passing the open windows, too, Frank,' I said
—trying not to look too closely at his dressmaker's dummy.

'We've all got to stick together,' Franny said—as Father, in
his sleep, cried out, *'Auf Wiedersehen,* Freud!'

11

Being in Love with Franny;
Dealing with Chipper Dove

Love also floats. And, that being true, love probably resembles
Sorrow in other ways.

We flew to New York City in the fall of 1964—no separate
flights this time; we were sticking together, as Franny had
advised. The stewardess was troubled by the baseball bat, but
she let Father hold it between his knees—humane concessions
are made to the blind, in spite of 'regulations.'

Junior Jones was unable to meet our plane. Junior was playing
out his last season with the Browns—in a hospital in Cleveland.
'Man,' he said to me, over the phone, 'just tell your father I'll
give him my eyes if he'll give me his *knees*.'

'And what will you give *me* if I give you *my* knees,' I heard
Franny ask Junior over the phone. I didn't hear what he said to
her, but she smiled and winked at me.

We could have flown to Boston; I'm sure Fritz would have
met our plane, and let us stay for free at the first Hotel New
Hampshire. But Father had told us he never wanted to see Dairy,
New Hampshire, or that first Hotel New Hampshire again. Of
course Father wouldn't have 'seen' it if we'd gone there and
stayed there the rest of our lives, but we understood his
meaning. None of us had the stomach for seeing Dairy again,
and recalling when our family was whole—when each of us had
both eyes open.

New York was neutral territory—and for a while, Frank
knew, Lilly's publisher would put us up and entertain us.

'Enjoy yourselves,' Frank said to us. 'Just call room service.'
Father would behave like a child with room service, ordering
stuff he'd never eat, and ordering his usual undrinkable drinks.
He'd never stayed in a hotel with room service before; he
behaved as if he'd never been in New York before, either,
because he complained that all the room service personnel

couldn't speak English any better than the Viennese—they couldn't, of course, because they were foreigners.

'They're more foreign than the Viennese ever *dreamed* of being!' my father would cry. *'Sprechen Sie Deutsch?'* he'd yell into the phone. 'Jesus God, Frank,' Father would say, 'order us a proper *Frühstück*, would you? These people don't understand me.'

'This is New York, Pop,' Franny said.

'They don't speak German *or* English in New York, Dad,' Frank explained.

'What the hell *do* they speak?' Father asked. 'I order croissant and coffee and I get tea and toast!'

'Nobody knows what they speak here,' said Lilly, looking out the window.

Lilly's publisher put us up at the Stanhope on Eighty-first and Fifth Avenue; Lilly had asked to be near the Metropolitan Museum and I had asked to be near Central Park—I wanted to run. And so I ran around and around the Reservoir, four times around, twice a day—that last lap luxurious with pain, my head lolling, the tall buildings of New York appearing to topple over me.

Lilly looked out the windows of our suite on the fourteenth floor. She liked watching the people flood in and out of the museum. 'I think I'd like to live here,' she said softly. 'It's like watching a castle change kings,' Lilly whispered. 'And you can see the leaves change in the park, too,' Lilly noted. 'And whenever you visit me,' Lilly said to me, 'you can run around the Reservoir and reassure me that it's still there. I don't ever want to see it up close,' Lilly said weirdly, 'but it's comforting to have you report to me on the health of the water, the number of other runners in the park, the amount of horse shit on the bridle path. A writer has to know these things,' Lilly said.

'Well, Lilly,' Frank said, 'I think you'll be able to *afford* a permanent suite here, but you could get an apartment, instead, you know. You don't have to *live* at the Stanhope, Lilly,' Frank said. 'It might be more practical to get your own apartment.'

'No,' Lilly said. 'If I can afford it, I want to live here. Surely *this* family can understand why I might like to live in a hotel,' Lilly said.

Franny shivered. She didn't want to live in a hotel, she had told me. But Franny would stay with Lilly for a while—after the publisher stopped paying the tab and Lilly maintained her corner suite on the fourteenth floor, Franny would keep Lilly company for a while. 'Just so you have a chaperon, Lilly,' Franny teased her. But I knew it was Franny who needed the chaperon.

'And you know who I need a chaperon *from*,' Franny told me.

Frank and Father would be my chaperons; Father and I would move in with Frank. He found a palatial apartment on Central Park South. I could still run there, I could run through the entirety of Central Park, investigate the Reservoir for Lilly, arrive dripping with sweat and panting at the Stanhope, to report on the health of the water, and so forth, and to show myself to Franny—to get a glimpse of her.

These would not be permanent residences for Franny, Father, or me, but Frank and Lilly would become the kind of New Yorkers who affix themselves to certain parts of Central Park and never leave. Lilly would live at the Stanhope for the rest of her life, writing away, trying to grow up to the stature of the fourteenth floor; though small, she was ambitious. And Frank, the agent, would wheel and deal from his apartment, with its six telephones, at 222 Central Park South. They were both terribly industrious—Lilly and Frank—and I once asked Franny what she thought the difference between them was.

'About twenty blocks and the Central Park Zoo,' Franny said. That was the *distance* between them exactly, but Franny implied it was the *difference* between Lilly and Frank, too: a whole zoo and more than twenty blocks.

'And what's the difference between *us*, Franny?' I asked her, shortly after we'd arrived in New York.

'One difference between us is that I'll get over you, somehow,' Franny told me. 'That's just how I am: I get over things. And I'll get over you, too. But you won't get over me,' Franny warned me. 'I know you, my brother, my love,' she told me. 'And you won't get over me—at least, not without my help.'

She was right, of course; Franny was always right—and always one step ahead of me. When Franny would finally sleep with me, she would engineer it. She would know exactly why she was doing it, too—as a fulfillment of the promise she had made to *mother* us children now that Mother was gone; as the only way to take care of us; as the only way to save us. 'You and me need saving, kid,' Franny said. 'But especially *you* need it. You think we're in love, and maybe I think so, too. It's time to show you that I'm not so special. It's time to prick the bubble before it bursts,' Franny told me.

She chose the moment in the same way she chose *not* to sleep with Junior Jones—'to save it,' as she would say. Franny always had her plans and her reasons.

'Holy cow, man,' Junior Jones told me on the phone. 'Tell your sister to come see a poor wreck of a man in Cleveland. My knees are shot, but the rest of me works fine.'

'I'm not a cheerleader anymore,' Franny told him. 'Get your ass to New York, if you want to see me.'

'Man!' Junior Jones howled to me. 'Tell her I can't *walk*. I'm wearing two casts at a time! There's too *much* of me to haul around on crutches. And tell her I know what a shit-ass town New York is, man,' said Junior Jones. 'If I come to that town on crutches, some dudes will try to mug me!'

'Tell him that when he gets over his damn *football* phase, maybe he'll have time for me,' Franny said.

'Oh, man,' said Junior Jones. 'What does Franny *want?*'

'I want you,' Franny whispered to me, over the phone—when she had made up her mind about it. I was at 222 Central Park South, trying to answer all of Frank's phones. Father complained about the phones—they interfered with the radio he listened to all day—and Frank refused to get a secretary, much less a legitimate office.

'I don't need an office,' Frank said. 'I just need a mailing address and a few phones.'

'At least try an answering service, Frank,' I suggested, which he would grudgingly accept—one day. But that was after Father and I moved out.

In our first New York days, *I* was Frank's answering service.

'I want you terribly much,' Franny whispered to me, on the phone.

Franny was alone at the Stanhope. 'Lilly's out having a literary lunch,' Franny said. Maybe that would be one way Lilly would grow, I thought: having lots of literary lunches. 'Frank's wheeling and dealing,' Franny said. 'He's at lunch with her. They'll be tied up for hours. And you know where I am, kid?' Franny asked me. 'I'm in bed,' she said. 'I'm naked,' she added, 'and I'm fourteen fucking floors high—I'm high on you,' Franny whispered to me. 'I want you,' Franny said. 'Get your ass over here. Kid, it's now or never,' Franny said. 'We won't know if we can live without it until we try it.' Then she hung up. One of Frank's other phones was ringing. I let it ring. Franny must have known I was dressed for running; I was ready to run out the door.

'I'm going to take a run,' I told Father. 'A long one.' One I might never come back from! I thought.

'I won't answer a single phone call,' Father said grouchily. He was having trouble, at the time, making up his mind what to do. He would sit in Frank's splendid apartment with the Louisville Slugger and the dressmaker's dummy and he'd think and think all day.

'Anything?' he kept asked Frank. 'I can *absolutely*—in *all* sincerity—do *anything* I *want* to do?' Father would ask Frank, about fifty times a week.

'Anything, Pop,' Frank told him. 'I'll set it up.'

Frank had already set up a three-book contract for Lilly. He had negotiated an initial first printing of *Trying to Grow* —100,000 copies. He had optioned the film rights to Warner Brothers and had made a separate deal with Columbia Pictures for an original screenplay of the events leading up to the bomb that went off in front of the second Hotel New Hampshire—and the famous Opera bomb that didn't go off. Lilly was already working on the screenplay. And Frank had put through a contract for a television series to be based on life at the first Hotel New Hampshire (which Lilly was also authoring)—the series was to be based on *Trying to Grow,* and was not to be released until after the motion picture; the movie would be called *Trying to Grow,* the TV series would be called 'The First Hotel New Hampshire' (this, Frank pointed out, left room for future deals).

But who, I wondered, would ever dare to make a TV series out of the *second* Hotel New Hampshire? Who would *want* to? Franny wondered.

If Lilly had grown only a little (as the result of creating *Trying to Grow*), Frank had grown double time—for all of us (as the result of selling Lilly's effort). It had been no little effort for Lilly, we knew. And we were worried about how hard she was working, how much she was writing—how grimly she was trying to grow.

'Take it easy, Lilly,' Frank advised her. 'The cash flow is fast and furious—you're terrifically *liquid,*' said Frank, the economics major, 'and the future looks rosy.'

'Just coast for a while, Lilly,' Franny advised her, but Lilly took literature seriously—even if literature would never take Lilly quite seriously enough.

'I know I've been lucky,' Lilly said. 'Now I have to earn it,' she said—trying harder.

But one day in the winter of 1964—it was just before Christmas—Lilly was out at a literary lunch and Franny told me it was now or never. There were only about twenty blocks and a very small zoo between us. Any good middle-distance runner can get from Central Park South to Fifth Avenue and Eighty-first in a very short time. It was a winter day, brisk but gray. The New York City streets and sidewalks were cleared of snow —good footing for a fast, wintry run. The snow in Central Park looked old and dead, but my heart was very much alive and pounding in my chest. The doorman at the Stanhope knew me —the Berry family would be welcome at the Stanhope for years and years. The man at the reception desk—the alert, cheerful man with the British accent—said hello to me as I waited for the elevator (the elevators at the Stanhope are rather slow). I said hello back to him, scuffing my running shoes on the rug; over the years I would watch that man grow a little balder but no less cheerful. He would even deal cheerfully with the complainers (the European Lilly and I saw in a rage at the reception desk one morning, for example—a portly man in a barber-pole-striped robe; he was beshitted, head to toe. No one had told him about one of the Stanhope's features: their famous upward-flushing toilets. You should beware of them if you ever stay at the Stanhope. After you've done your business in the toilet, it's advisable to close the lid and stand well out of the way—I recommend kicking the flush handle with your foot. This portly European must have been standing directly over his mess—he must have thought he'd observe it all going away, when it suddenly was flung *up*, all over him. And the ever-cheerful man with the British accent, behind the reception desk, looked up at the beshitted guest who was raging at him and said, 'Oh dear. A little air in the pipes?' It was what he always said. 'A little air in the pipes?' the portly European bellowed. 'A lot of shit in my hair!' he howled. But that was another day).

The day I was there to make love to Franny, the elevator couldn't get there fast enough. I decided to run up to the fourteenth floor. I must have looked awfully eager when I arrived. Franny opened the door just a crack and peeked at me.

'Yuck,' she said. 'You'll have to take a shower!'

'Okay,' I said. She told me to hold the door open just a crack and give her time to get back to bed; she didn't want me to see her—not yet. I heard her bound across the suite and leap back into bed.

'Okay!' she called, and I went in, putting the DO NOT DISTURB sign on the door.

'Put the DO NOT DISTURB sign on the door!' Franny called to me.

'I already did,' I said, in the bedroom, looking at her; she was under the covers, looking just a little nervous.

'You don't have to take a shower,' she said. 'I *like* you all sweaty. At least I'm *used* to you that way.'

But I was nervous and I took a shower, anyway.

'Hurry up, you asshole!' Franny yelled at me. I took as fast a shower as I could and used the potentially upward-flushing toilet very cautiously. The Stanhope is a wonderful hotel, especially if you like to run in Central Park and enjoy watching the Met and its floods of visitors, but you have to watch out for the toilets. Coming from a family used to strange toilets—those toilets fit for dwarfs in the first Hotel New Hampshire, those tiny toilets used by Fritz's midgets to this day—I tend to be generous in my feelings toward the toilets at the Stanhope, although I know some people who say they'll never stay at the Stanhope again. But what's a little air in the pipes, or even a lot of shit in the hair, if you have good memories?

I came out of the bathroom, naked, and when Franny saw me, she covered her head with the sheet and said, 'Jesus God.' I slipped into bed beside her and she turned her back to me and began to giggle.

'Your balls are all wet,' she said.

'I dried myself!' I said.

'You missed your balls,' she said.

'Nothing like wet balls,' I said, and Franny and I laughed as if we were crazy. We were.

'I love you,' she tried to tell me, but she was laughing too hard.

'I want you,' I told her, but I was laughing so hard that I sneezed—right in the middle of telling her that I wanted her —and that broke us up for a while longer. It was like that as long as she kept her back to me and we lay together like the stereotypical love spoons, but when she turned to me, when she lay on top of me with her breasts against my chest—when she scissored her legs around me—everything changed. If it had been too funny when we started, now it was too serious, and we couldn't stop. The first time we made love, we were in a more or less conventional position—'nothing too Tantric, please,'

Franny had asked me. And when it was over, she said, 'Well, that was okay. Not great, but *nice*—right?'

'Well, it was better than "nice"—for me,' I said. 'But not quite "great"—I agree.'

'You agree,' Franny repeated. She shook her head, she touched me with her hair. 'Okay,' she whispered. 'Get ready for *great*.'

At one point, I must have held her too tightly. She said, 'Please don't hurt me.'

I said, 'Don't be frightened.'

She said, 'I am, just a little.'

'I am—a *lot*,' I said.

It is improper to describe making love to one's sister. Does it suffice to say that it became 'great,' and it got even greater? And later it grew worse, of course—later we got tired. About four o'clock in the afternoon Lilly knocked discreetly on the door.

'Is that a maid?' Franny called.

'No, it's me,' Lilly said. 'I'm not a maid, I'm a writer.'

'Go away and come back in an hour,' Franny said.

'Why?' Lilly asked.

'I'm writing something,' Franny said.

'No, you're not,' Lilly said.

'I'm trying to grow!' Franny said.

'Okay,' Lilly said. 'Keep passing the open windows,' she added.

In a sense, of course, Franny *was* writing something; she was the author of how our relationship would turn out—she took a mother's responsibility for it. She went too far—she made love to me too much. She made me aware that what was between us was *all* too much.

'I still want you,' she murmured to me. It was four-thirty in the afternoon. When I entered her, she winced.

'Are you sore?' I whispered.

'Of *course* I'm sore!' she said. 'But you better not stop. If you stop, I'll kill you,' Franny told me. She *would* have, too, I realized later. In a way—if I had *stayed* in love with her—she would have been the death of me; we would have been the death of each other. But she simply overdid it; she knew exactly what she was doing.

'We better stop,' I whispered to her. It was almost five o'clock.

'We better *not* stop,' Franny said fiercely.

'But you're sore,' I protested.

'I want to be sorer,' Franny said. 'Are *you* sore?' she asked me.

'A little,' I admitted.

'I want you a *lot* sore,' Franny said. 'Top or bottom?' she asked me grimly.

When Lilly knocked at the door again, I was on the verge of imitating Screaming Annie; if there'd been a new bridge around, I could have cracked it.

'Come back in an hour!' Franny yelled.

'It's seven o'clock,' said Lilly. 'I've been away for *three* hours!'

'Go have dinner with Frank!' Franny suggested.

'I had *lunch* with Frank!' Lilly cried.

'Go have dinner with Father!' Franny said.

'I don't even want to eat,' Lilly said. 'I've got to write—it's time to *grow*.'

'Take a night off!' Franny said.

'The whole night?' Lilly asked.

'Give me three more hours,' Franny said. I groaned quietly. I didn't think I had three more hours left in me.

'Aren't you getting hungry, Franny?' Lilly said.

'There's always room service,' Franny said. 'And I'm not hungry,' anyway.'

But Franny was insatiable; her hunger for me would save us both.

'No more, Franny,' I begged her. It was about nine o'clock, I think. It was so dark I couldn't see anymore.

'But you *love* me, don't you?' she asked me, her body like a whip—her body was a barbell that was too heavy for me.

At ten o'clock I whispered to her, 'For God's sake, Franny. We've got to stop. We're going to hurt each other, Franny.'

'No, my love,' she whispered. 'That's exactly what we're *not* going to do: hurt each other. We're going to be just fine. We're going to have a good life,' she promised me, taking me into her —again. And again.

'Franny, I *can't,*' I whispered to her. I felt absolutely blind with pain; I was as blind as Freud, as blind as Father. And it must have hurt Franny more than it hurt me.

'Yes you can, my love,' Franny whispered. 'Just once more,' she urged me. 'I know you've got it in you.'

'I'm finished, Franny,' I told her.

'*Almost* finished,' Franny corrected me. 'We can do it just once more,' she said. 'After this,' she told me, 'we're both

357

finished with it. This is the last time, my love. Just imagine trying to live every day like this,' Franny said, pressing against me, taking my last breath away. 'We'd go crazy,' Franny said. 'There's no living with this,' she whispered. 'Come on and *finish* it,' she said in my ear. 'Once more, my love. Last time!' she cried to me.

'Okay!' I cried to her. 'Here I come.'

'Yes, yes, my love,' Franny said; I felt her knees lock against my spine. 'Hello, good-bye, my love,' she whispered. 'There!' she cried, when she felt me shaking. 'There, there,' she said, soothingly. 'That's it, that's all she wrote,' she murmured. 'That's the end of it. Now we're free. Now that's over.'

She helped me to the bathrub. The water stung me like rubbing alcohol.

'Is that your blood or mine?' I asked Franny, who was trying to save the bed—now that she had saved us.

'It doesn't matter, my love,' Franny said cheerfully. 'It washes away.'

'This is a fairy tale,' Lilly would write—of our family's whole life. I agree with her; Iowa Bob would have agreed with her, too. *'Everything* is a fairy tale!' Coach Bob would have said. And even Freud would have agreed with him—*both* Freuds. Everything *is* a fairy tale.

Lilly arrived coincidentally with the room service cart and the bewildered New York foreigner who delivered our multi-course meal, and several bottles of wine, at about eleven in the evening.

'What are you celebrating?' Lilly asked Franny and me.

'Well, John just finished a long run,' Franny said, laughing.

'You shouldn't run in the park at night, John,' Lilly said, worriedly.

'I ran up Fifth Avenue,' I said. 'It was perfectly safe.'

'Perfectly safe,' Franny said, bursting out laughing.

'What's the matter with her?' Lilly asked me, staring at Franny.

'I think it's the luckiest day of my life,' Franny said, still giggling.

'It's been just a little event among so many for me,' I told her, and Franny threw a dinner roll at me. We both laughed.

'Jesus God,' Lilly said, exasperated with us—and seemingly revolted by the amount of food we had ordered.

'We *could* have had a most unhappy life,' Franny said. 'I

mean, all of us!' she added, attacking the salad with her fingers; I opened the first bottle of wine.

'I still *might* have an unhappy life,' Lilly said, frowning. 'If I have many more days like today,' she added, shaking her head.

'Sit down and dig in, Lilly,' said Franny, who sat down at the room service table and started in on the fish.

'Yes, you don't eat enough, Lilly,' I told her, helping myself to the frogs' legs.

'I had lunch today,' Lilly said. 'It was a rather gross lunch, too,' she said. 'I mean, the food was all right but the portions were too big. I only need to eat one meal a day,' Lilly said, but she sat down at the table with us and watched us eat. She picked an especially slender green bean out of Franny's salad, eating half of it and depositing the other half on my butter plate; she picked up a fork and poked at my frogs' legs, but I could tell she was just restless—she didn't want any.

'So what did you write today, Franny?' Lilly asked her. Franny had her mouth full, but she didn't hesitate.

'A whole novel,' Franny said. 'It was truly terrible, but it was something I just had to do. When I finished it, I threw it away.'

'You threw it away?' Lilly asked. 'Maybe some of it was worth saving.'

'It was all shit,' Franny said. 'Every word. John read a little of it,' Franny said, 'but I made him give it back so I could throw the whole thing out. I called room service and had them come pick it up.'

'You had room service throw it away for you?' Lilly said.

'I couldn't stand to even touch it any longer,' Franny said.

'How many pages was it?' Lilly asked.

'Too many,' Franny said.

'And what did you think of what *you* read of it?' Lilly asked me.

'Trash,' I said. 'There's only one author in our family.'

Lilly smiled, but Franny kicked me under the table; I spilled some wine and Franny laughed.

'I'm glad you have confidence in me,' Lilly said, 'but whenever I read the ending of *The Great Gatsby,* I have my doubts. I mean, that's just *so* beautiful,' Lilly said. 'I think that if I can't ever write an *ending* that perfect, then there's no point in *beginning* a book, either. There's no point in writing a book if you don't *think* it can be as good as *The Great Gatsby*. I mean, it's all right if you fail—if the finished book just isn't, somehow, very good—but you have to believe it *can* be very good before you start. And sometimes that damn ending to *The Great Gatsby* just wipes me out before I can get started,' Lilly said; her little hands were fists, and Franny and I realized that Lilly clutched what was left of a dinner roll in one of them. Lilly didn't like to eat, but she could somehow manage to mangle a whole meal while deriving no nourishment from it, whatsoever.

'Lilly, the worrier,' Franny said. 'You've got to just *do it, Lilly*,' Franny told her, kicking me under the table again as she said 'do it.'

I would go back to 222 Central Park South a wounded man. In fact, I wouldn't realize until after our enormous meal was over that I was in no condition to run for about twenty blocks and a zoo; I doubted that I could even walk. My private parts were in considerable pain. I saw Franny grimace when she got up from the table to get her purse; she was suffering the aftermath of our excesses, too—it was just as she had planned, of course: we would feel the pain of our lovemaking for days. And that pain would keep us sane; the pain would convince us both that awaiting us in this particular pursuit of each other was our certain self-destruction.

Franny found some money for a cab in her purse; when she gave me the money, she gave me a very chaste and sisterly kiss. To this day—between Franny and me—no other kind of kiss will do. We kiss each other now the way I imagine most brothers and sisters kiss. It may be dull, but it's a way to keep passing the open windows.

And when I left the Stanhope—on that night shortly before Christmas, 1964—I felt truly safe, for the first time. I felt fairly sure that all of us would keep passing the open windows—that we were all survivors. I guess, now, that Franny and I had been thinking only of each other, we had been thinking a little too selfishly. I think Franny felt that her invulnerability was infectious—most people who are inclined toward feelings of invulnerability *do* think this way, you know. And I tended to try to follow Franny's feelings, as exactly as I could manage.

I caught a cab going downtown at about midnight and rode it down Fifth Avenue to Central Park South; despite the agony of my private parts, I was sure I could walk to Frank's from there. Also, I wanted to look at the Christmas decorations in front of the Plaza. I thought of walking just a little out of my way so that I could look at the toys displayed in the windows of F. A. O. Schwarz. I thought of how Egg would have loved those windows; Egg had never been to New York. But, I thought, Egg had probably imagined better windows, full of more toys, all the time.

I limped along Central Park South. Number 222 is between the East Side and the West, but nearer to the West—a perfect place for Frank, I was thinking; and for us all, for all of us were the survivors of the Symposium on East-West Relations.

There is a photograph of Freud—of the *other* Freud—in his apartment in Vienna at 19 Berggasse. He is fifty-eight; it is 1914. Freud has an I-told-you-so sort of stare; he looks both cross and worried. He looks as emphatic as Frank and as anxious as Lilly. The war that would begin in August of that year would destroy the Austro-Hungarian Empire; that war would also convince Herr Professor Doktor Freud that his diagnosis of the aggressive and self-destructive tendencies in human beings had been quite correct. In the photograph one can imagine where Freud got his idea that the human nose was 'a genital formation.' Freud got that idea 'from the mirror,' as Frank says. I think Freud hated Vienna; to his credit, *our* Freud hated Vienna, too, as Franny was the first to point out. Franny also hated Vienna; she would always be a Freudian in her contempt for sexual hypocrisy, for example. And Frank would be a Freudian in the sense that he was anti-Strauss—'the *other* Strauss,' Frank would note; he meant Johann, the very Viennese Strauss, the one who wrote that dippy song: 'Happy is the man who forgets what he cannot change' (*Die Fledermaus*). But both our Freud and the other Freud were morbidly obsessed with what was forgotten —they were interested in what was repressed, in what we dreamed. That made them both very *un*-Viennese. And our Freud had called Frank a prince; Freud had said that no one should call Frank 'queer'; the other Freud had also endeared himself to Frank—when some mother wrote the good doctor and begged him to cure her son of his homosexuality, Freud brusquely informed her that homosexuality was not a disease; there was nothing to 'cure.' Many of the world's great men, the great Freud told this mother, had been homosexuals.

'That's right on target!' Frank was fond of shouting. 'Just look at me!'

'And look at *me*,' Susie the bear used to say. 'Why didn't he mention some of the world's great *women?* If you ask me,' Susie used to say, 'Freud's a little suspect.'

'*Which* Freud, Susie?' Franny would tease her.

'Either one,' Susie the bear used to say. 'Take your pick. One

361

of them carried a baseball bat, one of them had that thing on his lip.'

'That was cancer, Susie,' Frank pointed out, rather stiffly.

'Sure,' said Susie the bear, 'but Freud called it "this thing on my lip." He didn't call cancer cancer, but he called everyone *else* repressed.'

'You're too hard on Freud, Susie,' Franny told her.

'He's a *man,* isn't he?' Susie said.

'You're too hard on *men,* Susie,' Franny told her.

'That's right, Susie,' Frank said. 'You ought to *try* one!'

'How about *you,* Frank?' Susie asked him, and Frank blushed.

'Well,' Frank stammered, 'that's not the way I go—to be perfectly frank.'

'I think there's just someone else inside you, Susie,' Lilly said. 'There's someone else inside you who wants to get out.'

'Oh boy,' Franny groaned. 'Maybe there's a *bear* inside her that wants to get out!'

'Maybe there's a *man* inside her!' Frank suggested.

'Maybe just a nice woman is inside you, Susie,' Lilly said. Lilly, the writer, would always try to see the heroes in us all.

That night shortly before Christmas, 1964, I painfully inched my way along Central Park South; I started thinking about Susie the bear, and I remembered another photograph of Freud —*Sigmund* Freud—that I was fond of. In this one, Freud is eighty; in three years he would be dead. He is sitting at his desk at 19 Berggasse; it is 1936 and the Nazis would soon make him abandon his old study in his old apartment—and his old city, Vienna. In this photograph, a pair of no-nonsense eyeglasses are seriously perched on the genital formation of Freud's nose. He is not looking at the camera—he is eighty years old, and he hasn't much time; he is looking at his work, not wasting his time with us. Someone *is* looking at us in this photograph, however. It is Freud's pet dog, his chow named Jo-fi. A chow somewhat resembles a mutant lion; and Freud's chow has that glazed look of dogs who always stare stupidly into the camera. Sorrow used to do that; when he was stuffed, of course, Sorrow stared into the camera every time. And old Dr. Freud's little sorrowful dog is there in the photograph to tell us what's going to happen next; we might also recognize sorrow in the fragility of the knick-knacks that are virtually crowding Freud out of his study, off 19 Berggasse and out of Vienna (the city he hated, the city that hated him). The Nazis would stick a swastika on his door; that damn city never liked him. And on June 4, 1938, the eighty-two-year-old Freud arrived in London; he had a year left to live—in a foreign country. *Our* Freud, at the time, was one summer away from getting fed up with Earl; he would return to Vienna at the time when all those repressed suicides of the *other* Freud's day were turning into murderers. Frank has shown me an essay by a professor of history at the University of Vienna—a very wise man named Friedrich Heer. And that's just what Heer says about the Viennese society of Freud's time (and this may be true of *either* Freud's time, I think): 'They were suicides about to become murderers.' They were all Fehlgeburts, trying too hard to become Arbeiters; they were all Schraubenschlüssels, admiring a pornographer.

They were ready to follow the instructions of a pornographer's dream.

'Hitler, you know,' Frank loves to remind me, 'had a rabid dread of syphilis. This is ironic,' Frank points out, in his tedious way, 'when you remind yourself that Hitler came from a country where prostitution has always thrived.'

It thrives in New York, too, you know. And one winter night I stood at the corner of Central Park South and Seventh Avenue, looking into the darkness downtown; I knew the whores were down there. My own sex tingled with pain from Franny's inspired efforts to save me—to save us both—and I knew, at last, that I was safe from *them*; I was safe from both extremes, safe from Franny and safe from the whores.

A car took the corner at Seventh Avenue and Central Park South a little too fast; it was after midnight and this fast-moving car was the only car I could see moving on either street. A lot of people were in the car; they were singing along with a song on the radio. The radio was so loud that I could hear a very clear snatch of the song, even with the windows closed against the winter night. The song was not a Christmas carol, and it struck me as inappropriate to the decorations all over the city of New York, but Christmas decorations are seasonal and the song I heard just a snatch of was one of those universally bleeding-heart kind of Country and Western songs. Some trite-but-true thing was being tritely but truthfully expressed. I have been listening, for the rest of my life, for that song, but whenever I think I'm hearing it again, something strikes me as not quite the same. Franny teases me by telling me that I must have heard the Country and Western song called 'Heaven's Just a Sin Away.'

And indeed, that one would do; almost any song like that would suffice.

There was just this snatch of a song, the Christmas decorations, the winter weather, my painful private parts—and my great feeling of relief, that I was free to live *my life* now—and the car that was moving too fast tore by me. When I started across Seventh Avenue, when it looked safe to cross, I looked up and saw the couple coming toward me. They were walking on Central Park South in the direction of the Plaza—they were headed west to east—and it was inevitable, I would later think, that we should have met in the middle of Seventh Avenue on the very night of Franny's and my own *release*. They were a slightly drunk couple, I think—or at least the young woman was, and the way she leaned on the man made him weave a little, too. The woman was younger than the man; in 1964, at least, we would have called her a girl. She was laughing, hanging on her older boyfriend's arm; he looked about my age—actually he was a little older. He would have been in his late twenties on this night in 1964. The girl's laughter was as sharp and as splintering of the frigid night air as the sound of very thin icicles breaking away from the eaves of a house encased in winter. I was in a really good mood, of course, and although there was something too educated and insufficiently fisceral in the girl's cold, tingling laughter—and although my balls ached and my cock stung—I looked up at this handsome couple and smiled.

We had no trouble recognizing each other—the man and I. I could never forget the quality of the quarterback in his face, though I had not seen him since that Holloween night on the footpath the football players always used—and everyone else would have been well advised to *let* them use it, to let them have it for themselves. Some days when I was lifting weights, I could still hear him say, 'Hey, kid. Your sister's got the nicest ass at this school. Is she banging anybody?'

'Yes, she's banging *me*,' I could have told him that night on Seventh Avenue. But I didn't say anything to him. I just stopped and stood in front of him, until I was sure he knew who I was. He hadn't changed; he looked almost exactly as he'd always looked, to me. And although I thought I *had* changed—I knew the weight lifting had at least changed my *body*—I think that Franny's constant correspondence with him must have kept our family close to Chipper Dove's memory (if not close to his heart).

Chipper Dove stopped in the middle of Seventh Avenue, too. After a second or two he said, softly, 'Well, look who's here.'

Everything is a fairy tale.

I looked at Chipper Dove's girl friend and said, 'Watch out he doesn't rape you.'

Chipper Dove's girl friend laughed—that high-strung, over-strenuous laugh like breaking ice, that laugh of little icicles shattering. Dove laughed a little bit with her. The three of us stayed in the middle of Seventh Avenue; a taxi heading downtown and turning off Central Park South almost killed us, but only the girl friend flinched—Chipper Dove and I didn't move.

'Hey, we're in the middle of the street, you know,' the girl said. She was a *lot* younger than he was, I noticed. She skipped to the east side of Seventh Avenue and waited for us, but we didn't move.

'I've enjoyed hearing from Franny,' Dove said.

'Why haven't you written her back?' I asked him.

'Hey!' his girl friend screamed at us, and another taxi, turning downtown, blew its horn at us and dodged around us.

'Is Franny in New York, too?' Chipper Dove asked me.

In a fairy tale, you often don't know what the people *want*. Everything had changed. I knew I didn't know if Franny wanted to see Chipper Dove or not. I knew I never knew what was *in* the letters she'd written him.

'Yes, she's in the city,' I said cautiously. New York is a big place, I was thinking; this felt safe.

'Well, tell her I'd like to see her,' he said, and he started to move around me. 'Can't keep *this* girl waiting,' he whispered to me, conspiratorially; he actually winked at me. I caught him under the armpits and just picked him up; for a quarterback, he didn't weigh much. He didn't struggle, but he looked genuinely surprised at how easily I had lifted him. I wasn't sure what to do with him; I thought a minute—or it must have seemed like a minute to Chipper Dove—and then I put him back down. I simply placed him back in front of me in the middle of Seventh Avenue.

'Hey, you crazy guys!' his girl friend called; two cabs, appearing to be in a race with each other, passed on either side of us—the drivers kept their hands on their horns for a long way, heading downtown.

'Tell me *why* you would like to see Franny,' I told Chipper Dove.

'You've been doing a little work with the weights, I guess,' Dove said.

'A little,' I admitted. 'Why do you want to see my sister?' I asked him.

'Well, to apologize—among other things,' he mumbled, but I could never believe *him;* he had that ice-blue smile in his ice-blue eyes. He seemed only slightly intimidated by my muscles; he had an arrogance larger than most people's hearts and minds.

'You could have answered just one of her letters,' I told him. 'You could have apologized *in writing,* anytime.'

'Well,' he said, shifting his weight from foot to foot, like a quarterback settling himself, getting ready to receive the ball. 'Well, it's all so hard to say,' he said, and I almost killed him on the spot; I could take almost anything from him but *sincerity*—hearing him sound genuine was almost too much to bear. I felt a need to hug him—to hug him harder than I had hugged Arbeiter—but fortunately for both of us, he changed his tone. He was getting impatient with me.

'Look,' he said. 'By the *statute of limitations* in *this* country, I'm clear—short of murder. Rape *is* short of murder, in case you don't know.'

'*Just* short,' I said. Another cab almost killed us.

'Chipper!' his girl friend was screaming. 'Shall I get the police?'

'Look,' Dove said. 'Just tell Franny I'd be happy to see her —that's all. Apparently,' he said, with the ice-blue in his eyes slipping into his voice, 'apparently she'd like to see me. I mean, she's *written* me enough.' He was almost complaining about it, I thought—as if my sister's letters had been *tedious* for him!

'If you want to see her, you can tell her yourself,' I told him. 'Just leave a message for her—leave the whole thing up to *her:* if she wants to see you. Leave a message at the Stanhope,' I said.

'The Stanhope?' he said. 'She's just passing through?'

'No, she lives there,' I said. 'We're a hotel family,' I told him. 'Remember?'

'Oh yes,' he laughed, and I could see him thinking that the Stanhope was a big step up from the Hotel New Hampshire —from either Hotel New Hampshire, though he'd only known the first one. 'Well,' he said, 'so Franny lives at the Stanhope.'

'We *own* the Stanhope, now,' I told him. I have no idea why I lied, but I simply had to do *something* to him. He looked stunned, and that was at least a mildly pleasing moment; a green sports car came so close to him that his scarf was flapped by the

366

sudden passing wind. His girl friend ventured out in Seventh Avenue again; she cautiously approached us.

'Chipper, *please*,' she said softly.

'Is that the only hotel you own?' Dove asked me, trying to be cool about it.

'We own half of Vienna,' I told him. 'The controlling half. The Stanhope is just the first of many—in New York,' I told him. 'We're going to take over New York.'

'And tomorrow, the world?' he asked, that ice-blue lilt in his voice.

'Ask Franny all about it,' I said. 'I'll tell her she can expect to hear from you.' I had to walk away from him so I wouldn't hurt him, but I heard his girl friend ask him, 'Who's Franny?'

'My sister!' I called. 'Your friend raped her! He and two other guys gang-banged her!' I shouted. Neither Chipper Dove nor his girl friend laughed this time, and I left them in the middle of Seventh Avenue. If I'd heard the squeal of tires and brakes, and the thud of bodies making contact with metal, or with the pavement, I wouldn't have turned around. It was only when I recognized the pain in my private parts as actually belonging to me that I realized I had walked too far. I'd walked past 222 Central Park South—I was wandering around Columbus Circle —and I had to turn around and head east. When I saw Seventh Avenue again, I saw that Chipper Dove and his girl friend had gone. I even wondered, for a second, if I had only dreamed them.

I would have preferred to have dreamed them, I think. I was worried how Franny would handle it, how she might 'deal with it,' as Susie was always saying. I was worried about even mentioning to Franny that I had seen Chipper Dove. What would it mean to her, for example, if Dove *never* called? It seemed unfair—that on the very evening of Franny's triumph, and mine, I had to meet her rapist and tell him where my sister lived. I knew I was out of my league, I was over my head—I was back to zero, I had *no* idea what Franny wanted. I knew I needed some expert rape advice.

Frank was asleep; he was no rape expert, anyway. Father was also asleep (in the room I shared with him), and I looked at the Louisville Slugger on the floor by my Father's bed and knew what Father's rape advice would be—I knew that any rape advice from Father would involve swinging that bat. I woke Father up taking off my running shoes.

'Sorry,' I whispered. 'Go back to sleep.'

'What a long run you had,' he groaned. 'You must be *exhausted*.'

I was, of course, but I was also wide-awake. I went and sat at the desk in front of Frank's six phones. The resident rape expert (in the second Hotel New Hampshire) was only a phone call away; the rape advice I wanted was actually residing in New York City now. Susie the bear was living in Greenwich Village. Although it was one o'clock in the morning, I picked up the phone. At last the issue had presented itself. It didn't matter that it was almost Christmas, 1964, because we were back to Halloween, 1956. All Franny's unanswered letters finally deserved an answer. Although Junior Jones's Black Arm of the Law would one day provide New York City with its admirable services, Junior was still recovering from the thug game of football; he would spend three years in law school, and he'd spend another six starting the Black Arm of the Law. Although Junior *would* rescue Franny, he could be counted upon for his late arrivals. The issue of Chipper Dove had presented itself *now;* although Harold Swallow had never found him, Dove was out of hiding now. And in dealing with Chipper Dove, I knew, Franny would need the help of a smart bear.

Good old Susie the bear is a fairy tale, all by herself.

When she answered her telephone at 1 A.M. she was like a boxer springing off the ropes.

'Dumb-fuck! Creep-of-the-night! Pervert! Do you know what time it is?' Susie the bear roared.

'It's me,' I said.

'Jesus God,' Susie said. 'I was expecting an obscene call.' When I told her about Chipper Dove, she decided it *was* an obscene call. 'I don't think Franny's going to be happy that you told him where she lives,' Susie said. 'I think she wrote all those letters so she wouldn't ever hear from him again.'

Susie lived in a simply terrible place in Greenwich Village. Franny liked going down there to see her, and Frank occasionally dropped in—when he was in the vicinity (there was a very Frank-like bar around the corner from where Susie lived)—but Lilly and I hated the Village. Susie came uptown to see us.

In the Village, Susie could be a bear when she wanted to be; there were people down there who looked worse than bears. But when Susie came uptown, she had to look normal; they wouldn't have let her in the Stanhope, as a bear, and on Central Park South some policeman would have shot her—thinking her an escapee from the Central Park Zoo. New York was not Vienna, and although Susie was trying to break herself of the bear habit, she could revert to bearishness in the Village and nobody would even notice. She lived with two other women in a place that had only a toilet and a cold-water sink; Susie came uptown to bathe —preferring Lilly's suite at the Stanhope to the opulent bathroom at Frank's place at 222 Central Park South; I think Susie *liked* the potential danger of the upward-flushing toilets.

She was trying to be an actress in those days. The two women she shared the terrible apartment with were both members of something called the West Village Workshop. It was an actors' workshop; it was a place that trained street clowns. Frank said of it that if the King of Mice had still been alive, he could have gotten tenure at the West Village Workshop. But I thought that if there'd been such a thing as the West Village Workshop in Vienna, maybe the King of Mice would still be alive. There ought to be someplace where you can study street dancing, animal imitations, pantomime, unicycling, scream therapy, and acts of degradation that are only acts. Susie said the West Village Workshop was basically teaching her how to be as confident as a bear *without* the bear suit. It was a slow process, she admitted, and in the meantime—hedging her bets—she'd had the bear suit refashioned by an animal costume expert in the Village.

'You ought to see the suit now,' Susie was always telling me. 'I mean, if you think I looked like a real bear before, man . . . you haven't seen the whole story!'

'It *is* rather remarkable,' Frank had told me. 'There's even a *wet* look about the mouth, and the eyes are uncanny. And the *fangs,*' Frank said—always an admirer of costumes and uniforms, Frank would say, 'The fangs are great.'

'But we all want Susie to get *over* being a bear,' Franny said.

'We want the *bear in her* to emerge,' Lilly would say, and we'd all grunt and make other disgusting sounds together.

But when I told Susie that Franny and I had saved each other from each other—only to meet up again with Chipped Dove —Susie was all business; Susie was that ever-essential friend, the one who'll be a bear for you when the going gets rough.

'You at Frank's?' Susie asked.

'Yes,' I said.

'Hang in there, kid,' Susie said. 'I'll be right up. Warn the doorman.'

369

'Should I warn him about a bear or about *you*, Susie?' I asked her.

'One day, honey,' Susie said, 'the *real* me is going to surprise you.' One day, it was true, Susie *would* surprise me. But before Susie got up to 222 Central Park South, Lilly called me on one of Frank's six phones.

'What's wrong?' I said. It was nearly two in the morning.

'Chipper Dove,' Lilly whispered, in a frightened little voice. 'He called here! He asked for Franny!' That son of a bitch! I thought. He'd call up a girl he'd raped when she was *sleeping!* He must have wanted to be sure that Franny really *did* live at the Stanhope. So now he knew.

'What did Franny say to him?' I asked Lilly.

'Franny wouldn't talk to him,' Lilly said. 'Franny *couldn't* talk to him,' Lilly said. 'I mean, she couldn't get her mouth to work—no words came out,' Lilly said. 'I told him Franny was out and he said he'd call again. You better come over here,' Lilly said. 'Franny is *afraid*,' Lilly whispered. 'I've never seen Franny afraid,' Lilly added. 'She won't even go back to bed, she just keeps looking out the window. I think she thinks he's going to rape her *again*,' Lilly whispered.

I went to Frank's room and woke him up. He sat bolt upright in bed, throwing back the covers and flinging the dressmaker's dummy away from him. 'Dove,' was all I had whispered to him. 'Chipper Dove,' was all I had to say, and Frank woke up as if he were still banging the cymbals. We left a message for Father in the tape recorder next to his bed. We just said we were at the Stanhope.

Father was pretty good on the telephone; he counted the holes. Even so, Father still got a lot of wrong numbers, and they made him so cross that he invariably shouted to the persons on the receiving end of his calls—as if the wrong numbers had been *their* fault. 'Jesus God!' he would holler. 'You're the wrong number!' Thus, in this small way, did my Father and his Louisville Slugger terrorize a portion of New York.

Frank and I met Susie at the door of 222 Central Park South. We had to run up to Columbus Circle to find a cab. Susie was not wearing the bear suit. She was wearing old pants and a sweater over a sweater over a sweater.

'Of *course* she's afraid,' Susie told Frank and me as we sped uptown. 'But she's got to deal with it. *Fear* is one of the first phases, my dears. If she can get over the fucking fear, then she gets to the *anger*. And once she's angry,' Susie said, 'then she's

370

home free. Just look at me,' she declared, and Frank and I looked at her and didn't say anything. We were over our heads, and we knew it.

Franny was sitting wrapped in a blanket, her chair drawn up to the heat register; she peered out the window. The Metropolitan Museum stood in the pre-Christmas cold like a castle abandoned by its king and queen—so abandoned it looked cursed; even the peasants were staying away.

'How can I even go *out?*' Franny whispered to me. 'He could be *anywhere* out there,' she said. 'I don't *dare* go out,' she repeated.

'Franny, Franny,' I said, 'he won't touch you again.'

'Don't *tell* her things,' Susie said to me. 'That's not the way. Don't tell—*ask* her things. Ask her what she wants to do?'

'What do you want to do, Franny?' Lilly asked her.

'We'll do anything you want us to do, Franny,' Frank said.

'Think about what you *want* to have happen,' Susie the bear said to Franny.

Franny shivered, her teeth chattered. It was stifling in the suite, but Franny was bone-cold.

'I want to kill him,' Franny said, softly.

'Don't say anything,' Susie the bear whispered in my ear. There was nothing I could say, anyway. We sat in the room with Franny looking out the window for about an hour. Susie gave her a back rub to try to warm her up. Franny wanted to whisper something to me, so I bent down to her. 'Are you still sore?' she whispered. She wore a little smile and I smiled back at her and nodded. 'Me too,' she said, and smiled; but she looked right back out the window again, and she said, 'I wish he were dead.' In a little while she repeated, 'I simply can't go out, I can take all my meals here—but one of you will have to be here, all the time.' We assured her we would be. 'Kill him,' she repeated, just as it was getting light above the park. 'He could be *anywhere* out there,' she said, watching the light grow. 'The bastard!' she screamed, suddenly. 'I want to kill him!'

We took turns staying with her for a couple of days. We made up a story for Father—that Franny had the flu and she was staying in bed so that she'd be all better in time for Christmas. It was a reasonable lie, we thought. Franny had lied to Father about Chipper Dove before; she'd told him she was just 'beaten up.'

We didn't even have a plan—if Chipper Dove *did* call back, we had no idea how Franny even wanted to deal with it.

'Kill him,' she kept saying.

And Frank, waiting in the lobby with me for the Stanhope elevator to arrive, said, 'Maybe we *should* kill him. That would take care of it.'

Franny was our leader; when she was lost, we were all lost. We needed her judgment before we could settle on a plan.

'Maybe he'll never call again,' Lilly said.

'You're a writer, Lilly,' Frank said. 'You ought to know better. Of course he'll call.' Frank was making one of his anti-world statements—expressing one of his perverse theories that precisely what you don't *want* to happen *will*. As a writer, Lilly would one day share Frank's *Weltanschauung*.

But Frank was right about Chipper Dove; he called. It was Frank who answered the phone. Frank was very uncool about it; when he heard Chipper Dove's ice-blue voice, he twitched—he underwent such a spasm on the couch that he batted the standing lamp beside him, he sent the lampshade spinning, and Franny knew right away who it was. She started screaming, she ran out of the living room of the suite and into Lilly's bedroom (it was the closest hiding place), and Susie the bear and I had to run after her and hold her on Lilly's bed, trying to calm her down.

'Uh, no, she's not in right now,' Frank said to Chipper Dove. 'Want to leave a number where she can call you?' Chipper Dove gave Frank his number—two numbers, actually: his number at home, and his number at work. The thought that he had a job seemed to make Franny suddenly sane again.

'What does he *do?*' she asked Frank.

'Well,' Frank said. 'He just said he was with his uncle's firm. You know how everyone gets their rocks off the way they say "firm"—the fucking *firm,* whatever a *firm* is,' Frank said.

'It could be anything, Franny,' I said. 'A law firm, a business firm.'

'Maybe it's a rape firm,' Lilly said, and we had our first good sign in days. Franny laughed.

'Atta girl, Franny,' Frank encouraged her.

'That super shit of a human being!' Franny yelled.

'Atta girl, Franny,' said Susie the bear.

'That fuck-off in his uncle's fucking *firm!*' Franny said.

'That right,' I said.

And finally Franny said, 'I don't *care* about killing him. I just want to scare him,' she said. 'I want him to be *frightened,*' she said, shivering suddenly; she started crying. 'He really *scared* me!' she cried. 'I'm *still* afraid of him, for Christ's sake,' she said. 'I want to scare the bastard, I want to frighten him back!' Franny said.

'Now you're talking,' said Susie the bear. 'Now you're dealing with it.'

'Let's rape him!' Frank said.

'Who'd want to?' Lilly asked.

'I'd do it—for the *cause*,' Susie said. 'But even with me, I think he'd like it. Men are creeps that way,' Susie said. 'They could hate your guts but their *cocks* will still like you.'

'We *can't* rape him,' Franny said. So Franny was okay, I thought. She was our leader again.

'We can do anything we want,' Frank argued—Frank the agent, Frank the arranger.

'Even if we could figure out a way to rape him,' Susie said, 'even if we could find the perfect rapist for him, I still say it wouldn't be the same: the fucker would find a way to *enjoy* himself.'

And then Lilly, the author, spoke up. Our little Lilly, the creator: she had the best imagination. 'He wouldn't enjoy himself if he thought a *bear* was raping him,' Lilly said.

'Sodomy!' cried Frank, gleefully, clapping his hands—like the cymbals he'd once used on Chipper Dove. '*Sodomize* the bastard!' Frank cried.

'Wait a fucking minute!' said Susie the bear. 'Maybe *he'll* think it's a bear, but *I'll* still know it's *him*. I mean, anything for the *cause*,' Susie said, 'anything for *you*, honey,' Susie told Franny, 'but you'll have to give me some time to think this over.'

'But I don't think you'd have to really *do* it to him, Susie,' Franny said. 'I think you could scare him enough by *almost* doing it.'

'You could pretend to be a bear in heat, Susie,' Lilly said.

'A bear in heat!' howled Frank, with delight. 'That's it!' he shouted, wildly. 'A bear in heat goes berserk! You could wolf the bastard's *balls* right into your terrible bear's *mouth!*' Frank screamed at Susie. 'Make him think he's going to get *blown* by a bear! For the last time!' Frank added.

'I could take him right to the edge,' Susie the bear said.

'But no further, Susie,' Franny said. 'I just want to frighten him.'

'Scare him to death,' Frank said, exhausted.

'Not quite,' said Lilly. 'Scare him *almost* to death.'

'A bear in heat: that's brilliant, Lilly,' I said.

'Just give me a day,' Lilly said.

'For what, Lilly?' Susie asked.

'The script,' Lilly said. 'I'll need a day to get the script right.'

'I love you, Lilly,' Franny said, and gave her a hug.

'You all have to be very good actors,' Lilly said.

'I'm taking *lessons,* for Christ's sake!' Susie roared. 'And I'll bring my friends! Can you use two friends, Lilly?' Susie asked.

'If they're *women,* I can use them,' Lilly said frowning.

'Of *course* they're women!' Susie said, indignantly.

'Can *I* be in it?' Frank asked.

'You're not a woman, Frank,' I pointed out. 'Maybe Lilly wants all women.'

'Well, I'm a fag,' Frank said, huffily. 'And Chipper Dove knows that.'

'I can get a creat costume for Frank,' Susie told Lilly.

'You can?' Frank asked, excitedly. He hadn't had a chance to dress up in a while.

'Let me work on it,' Lilly said. Lilly the worker: she would always work a little *too* hard. 'It will have to be just perfect,' Lilly said. 'To be *believable,'* Lilly said, 'we'll have to get everything just right.'

And Franny asked, suddenly, 'Will I have to be in it, Lilly?' We could see she didn't want to be, or she was frightened to be in it; she wanted it to happen—she thought she wanted to *see* it, but she didn't know if she could actually take a *part.*

I held Franny's hand. 'You'll have to *call* him, Franny,' I said, and she shivered again.

'You'll just have to invite him here,' Lilly said. 'Once you get him here, you won't have to say much. You won't have to *do* anything, I promise,' Lilly said. 'But it's got to be you who calls him up.'

Franny looked out the window again. I rubbed her shoulders so she wouldn't be cold. Frank patted her hair; Frank had an irritating habit of showing his affection for human beings by patting them as if they were dogs.

'Come on, Franny,' Frank said. *'You* can do it, Franny.'

'You *got* to, honey,' Susie the bear told her softly, putting her friendly paw on Franny's arm.

'It's now or never, Franny. Remember?' I whispered to her. 'Let's just get this over with,' I told her, 'and then we can all return to the rest of the business—to the rest of our lives.'

'The rest of our lives,' Franny said, pleased. 'Okay,' she

whispered. 'If Lilly can write the script,' Franny said, 'I can make the fucking phone call.'

'Then all of you get out of here,' Lilly said. 'I've got to get to work,' she said, worriedly.

We all went to Frank's to have a party with Father. 'Not a word about this to Father,' Franny said. 'Let's keep Father out of it.'

Father, I knew, was out of it most of the time. But when we arrived at Frank's, Father had come to a small decision. From the myriad options in front of him, Father had failed to come up with what Iowa Bob would have called a game plan; he still didn't know what he wanted to *do*. Good fortune was an option unfamiliar to my father. But when we arrived at Frank's in a party mood, Father had at least accomplished a mini-decision.

'I want one of those Seeing Eye dogs,' Father said.

'But you've got us, Pop,' Frank told him.

'There's always someone around to take you anywhere you want,' I told him.

'It's not just that,' Father said. 'I need an animal around,' he said.

'Oh boy,' Franny said. 'Why not hire Susie?'

'Susie's got to stop being a bear,' Father said. 'We shouldn't keep encouraging her.' We all looked a little guilty, and Susie beamed—of course, Father couldn't see our faces. 'And besides,' Father said, 'New York is a terrible place for a bear. I'm afraid the bear days are over,' he sighed. 'But a good old Seeing Eye dog,' Father said. 'Well, you see,' he said, almost a little embarrassed to admit his loneliness, 'it would be someone for me to *talk* to. I mean, you have your own lives—or you *will* have,' Father said. 'I'd just like a dog, really. The Seeing Eye part of the dog isn't really what matters. I'd just like to have a nice dog. Can I?' he asked.

'Sure, Pop,' Frank said.

Franny kissed Father and told him we'd get him a dog for Christmas.

'So soon?' Father asked. 'I don't think you can *rush* getting a Seeing Eye dog,' Father said. 'I mean, it would be a problem to get a badly trained one.'

'Anything's possible, Pop,' Frank said. 'I'll take care of it.'

'Oh, for Christ's sake, Frank,' Franny said. 'We'll *all* get him a dog, if you don't mind.'

'One thing,' Father said. Susie the bear put her paw on my

375

hand, as if even Susie knew what was comimg. 'Just one thing,' Father said. We were very quiet, waiting for this. 'It mustn't look like Sorrow,' Father said. 'And *you've* got the eyes, so you've got to pick out the dog. Just make sure it in no way resembles Sorrow.'

And Lilly wrote the necessary fairy tale, and we each acted our parts. According to the fairy tale that Lilly wrote, we were perfect. On the last working day before Christmas, 1964, Franny took a deep breath and called Chipper Dove at his 'firm.'

'Hi, it's *me!*' she said to him, brightly. 'I absolutely *need* to have lunch with you, in the *worst* way,' Franny said to Chipper Dove. 'Yes, it's Franny Berry—and you can pick me up, anytime,' Franny said. 'Yes, at the Stanhope—Suite *fourteen-oh-one*.'

Then Lilly grabbed the phone away from Franny and said to Franny in a voice as crabby as any crabby nurse's voice—and plenty loud enough for Chipper Dove to hear—'Who are you making phone calls *to now?* You're nót supposed to make any more phone calls!' Then Lilly hung up the phone and we waited.

Franny went into the bathroom and threw up. She was okay when she came back out. She looked awful, but she was supposed to look awful. The two women from the West Village Workshop had done the makeup job on Franny; those women can work wonders. They took a beautiful woman and they *ravaged* her; they gave Franny a face with the lifelessness of chalk; they gave her a mouth like a gash, they gave my sister needles for eyes. And they dressed her all in white, like a bride. We were worried that Lilly's script might be too theatrical.

Frank stood looking out the window in his black leotard and lime-green caftan. He had just a little lipstick on.

'I don't know,' Frank said, worriedly. 'What if he doesn't come?'

Susie's two friends were there—the wounded women from the West Village Workshop. It had been *men*, Susie had told us, who had wounded them. The black one was named Ruthie: she resembled a near-perfect cloning of Junior Jones. Ruthie wore a sleeveless sheepskin vest, over nothing at all, and a pair of bright green bell-bottoms above which her belly wobbled. She had a long silver nail, almost as thick as a railroad spike, jabbed into her crazy hair. She held a long leather leash in one of her big black hands; at the end of the leash was Susie the bear.

It was a bear suit that was a victory of animal imagination.

Especially the mouth, as Frank had pointed out; especially the fangs. Their wet look. And the sad insanity of the eyes. (Susie actually 'saw' out of the mouth.)

The claws were a nice touch, too; they were the real thing, Susie proudly pointed out—the whole paws were the real thing. It somehow enhanced the reality of everything that Susie wore a muzzle. We'd bought the muzzle in an accessory shop for Seeing Eye dogs; it was a real muzzle.

We'd turned the thermostat on the heat register up as high as it would go because Franny complained of being cold. Susie said she liked the heat; she felt more like a bear if she sweated a lot, and inside the bear suit, we could tell, she was hot and dripping. 'I've never felt so much like a bear,' Susie said to us, pacing, down on all fours.

'You're all bear today, Susie,' I said to her.

'The *bear in you* gets out today, Susie,' Lilly told her.

Franny sat in the bridal dress on the couch, the candle burning in a sickly way on the table beside her. There were candles lit throughout the suite, and all the window shades were drawn. Frank had lit a little incense, so the whole suite smelled truly terrible.

The other woman from the West Village Workshop was a pale, plain-looking, very girlish type with straw-blond hair. She was dressed in the conventional uniform of a hotel maid, the same uniform worn by all the Stanhope maids, and she had a perfectly bored, expressionless gaze that matched her dull employment. Her name was Elizabeth Something, but in the Village she was called Scurvy. She was the best actress ever to graduate from the West Village Workshop—she was the queen of the Washington Square Park performers. She could have taught scream therapy to a whole backyard full of moles; she could have taught the moles how to scream so loud that the worms would leap right out of the ground. She was what Susie called a number one first-class hysteric. 'Nobody can do hysteria better than Scurvy,' Susie the bear had told us, and Lilly had written up a number one first-class hysteric role for her. Scurvy just sat in the suite, smoking a cigarette and looking as lifeless as a park bench bum.

I played around with the big barbell in the middle of the living room. Frank and Lilly had greased me all over; I was oily from head to toe and I smelled like a salad, but the oil made my muscles stand out in a special way. I was wearing this skimpy little thing called a singlet—it's that old-fashioned-looking, one-piece-bathing-suit thing that wrestlers and weight lifters wear.

'Keep warm,' Lilly coached me, 'keep lifting just enough to keep the veins standing out. When he walks in here, I want those veins *popping* right up there on the surface of your skin.'

'*If* he walks in here,' Frank fumed.

'He will,' Franny said, softly. 'He's very near,' she said, shutting her eyes. 'I know he's very near,' she repeated.

When the phone rang, everyone in the room jumped—everyone but Franny and the number one first-class hysteric named Scurvy; they didn't flinch. Franny let the phone ring a little. Lilly came out of the bedroom, all neatly dressed in her nurse's uniform; she nodded to Franny at about the fourth ring and Franny picked up the phone. She didn't say anything.

'Hello?' Chipper Dove said. 'Franny?' we heard him ask. Franny shivered, but Lilly kept nodding to her.

'Come up right away,' Franny whispered into the phone. 'Come up while my nurse is still out!' she hissed. Then she hung up; she gagged, and for a moment I thought she'd have to go throw up in the bathroom again, but she held it in; she was okay.

Lilly adjusted the tight, gray, mousy little bun of a wig she wore. She looked like an old nurse in a home for dwarfs; the women from the West Village Workshop had made up Lilly's face like a prune. She stepped into the closet that was nearest the main door to the suite and shut the door. When you were in the living room of the suite, it was easy to confuse the closet with the entrance and exit door.

Scurvy put a stack of clean linen on her arm and went outside the suite into the hall. 'Between five and seven minutes after he gets inside,' I told her.

'I don't need reminding,' she said, crossly. 'I can listen outside the door for my cue,' she told me contemptuously. 'I'm a fucking *pro*, you know.'

The West Village Workshop women had one thing in common, Susie had confided to me. They had all been raped.

I started lifting the weight. I did some fast lifting to pump the muscles full of blood. Susie the bear curled up at the foot of the couch farthest from Franny and pretended to go to sleep. She hid her paws and her muzzled snout; from the back she looked like a sleeping dog. The black woman named Ruthie—the huge woman who was Junior Jones's clone—plopped down in the dead center of the couch, right next to Franny. When the hibernating bear began to snore, Frank took off the caftan and hung it on a doorknob—he now wore just the black leotard—and went into Lilly's bedroom and put the music on. From the living room, you could see the bed through the bedroom's open door. When the music started, Frank started dancing on the bed. The music had been Frank's choice. Frank had no trouble making up his mind: he chose the mad scene from Donizetti's *Lucia*.

I looked at Franny and saw some tears squeeze their way out of the pinholes the makeup women had given her for eyes; the tears made messy tracks through the makeup caked upon her face. Franny knotted her fingers in her lap, and I knocked lightly on the closet door and whispered to Lilly: 'A masterpiece, Lilly,' I said. 'It's got all the indications of a masterpiece.'

'Just don't blow your lines,' Lilly whispered.

When Chipper Dove knocked on the door, my bicepses were standing right up there—the way Lilly wanted them—and the forearms were looking pretty good. I had a little sweat running over the oil, and in the bedroom Lucia was beginning to scream. Frank was so incredibly awkward, leaping on the bed, that I almost couldn't look at him.

'Come in!' Franny cried to Chipper Dove. When I saw the doorknob turn, I grabbed my side of the door and helped Chipper Dove inside—fast. I guess I snapped the door open a little harder than was necessary because Chipper Dove seemed to be propelled inside the room—on all fours. I hung the DO NOT DISTURB sign on the outside knob and closed the door behind him.

'Well, look who's here,' Franny said, in her best ice-blue voice.

'Holy cow!' cried Frank, at full height above the bouncing bed.

I rolled the barbell against the door, but Chipper Dove stood up—fairly calmly. He had that smile that wouldn't die; at least, it hadn't died *yet*.

'What's all this, Franny?' he asked her, casually, but Franny had come to the end of her lines. Franny's part of the script was over with. ('Well, look who's here.' That was all that was necessary for her to say.)

'We're going to rape you,' I said to Chipper Dove.

'Hey, look,' Dove said. 'That was never exactly what I'd call a *rape*,' he said. 'I mean, you really *liked* me, Franny,' he said to her, but Franny wasn't talking. 'I'm sorry about the other guys, Franny,' Dove added, but Franny's pinhole stare gave him nothing. 'Shit!' said Dove, turning to me. *'Who's* going to rape me?'

'Not me!' Frank screamed from the bedroom, bouncing higher and higher. 'I like fucking *mud puddles,* myself. I do it all the time!'

Chipper Dove still managed a smile. 'So it's the one on the couch?' he asked me, slyly. He stared at big Ruthie; he must have been remembering Junior Jones when he looked at her —she just stared back at him—but Chipper Dove even managed to smirk at her. 'I have nothing against black women,' Chipper Dove said, dividing his attention between Ruthie and me. 'In fact, I like a black woman now and then.' Ruthie raised up one cheek of her enormous ass and farted.

'You ain't fucking *me,'* she told Chipper Dove.

Dove directed his full attention to me. Almost all of his smile had left him, because I think he was beginning to suspect that *I* was the one appointed to rape him and he wasn't so fond of this idea.

'No, it's not *him,* you asshole!' Frank yelled from the bedroom, panting and leaping—higher and higher. 'He likes *girls,* like *you* do!' Frank yelled at Dove. 'Disgusting, disgusting, disgusting *girls!'* Frank hollered. He fell off the bed, but he was right back up and dancing, fiercely. Lucia was really sounding crazy.

'Are you trying to tell me it's the *dog?'* Chipper Dove asked me. 'Do you think I'll hold still for a fucking *dog!'* he snapped at me.

'What dog, man?' Ruthie asked Chipper Dove. Ruthie had a smile that was as terrible as Chipper Dove's.

'That dog right there,' Dove said, pointing to Susie the bear. Susie was curled up in a ball, snoring, her hairy back turned to Dove—her paws tucked in, her head tucked down. Ruthie stuck her big bare foot in Susie's crotch; she started *kneading* Susie with her foot. Susie started to groan.

'That ain't no *dog,* man,' Ruthie said, smiling—and obscenely kneading, kneading with her foot. Then Ruthie twisted her foot, sharply, in Susie's crotch and Susie the bear roared awake; she wheeled viciously on Ruthie, snapping at her. Dove saw the muzzle barely restraining her, he saw Ruthie bound out of the way of the long, striking claws. Ruthie threw the leash in Susie's face and ran to the far side of the room. Susie looked ready to charge after her, but Franny just reached out her hand.

She touched Susie just once and Susie calmed right down. The bear put her head in Franny's lap. Susie growled softly there.

'Earl! Earl!' she moaned.

'That's a *bear*,' Dove said.

'You bet your ass, man,' Ruthie said.

And Frank, sailing ever higher, singing his way into Lucia's song—and, seemingly, rising above even *her* madness—yelled out, 'That's a bear *in heat!*'

'That's a bear that *wants* you,' I said to Chipper Dove.

When Dove looked at the bear again, he saw that Franny had her hand on Susie exactly where a bear's private parts would be. Franny was rubbing the bear there, and Susie the bear got suddenly playful; she lolled her head around, she made the most disgusting noises. The West Village Workshop had simply worked wonders with Susie the bear; she'd been a smart bear before, but now she was a bear to be reckoned with.

'That bear's so horny,' Ruthie said, 'she'd even fuck *me*.'

'Hey, look,' said Chipper Dove. He was holding fast to the illusion that I was the only one among them who was sane. That was how he was reading it, now; I was his last hope. We had him right where Lilly wanted him when Scurvy, the maid, knocked on the door. I slung the barbell aside as if it weighed nothing at all. I yanked the door open so hard that Scurvy flew into the room in greater confusion and disarray than had marked Chipper Dove's entrance. Susie the bear growled—not liking too much sudden movement—and the terrified maid stared up at me.

'It says DO NOT DISTURB, you moron!' I yelled at her. I pulled her to her feet and tore open the front of her little maid's costume. She started to get hysterical right away. I held her upside down and shook her. Frank howled with delight.

'Black panties, black panties!' Frank shrieked on the bouncing bed.

'You're fired,' I told the sniveling maid. 'You don't come in when the sign says DO NOT DISTURB. If you can't learn *that*, you moron,' I told her, 'then you're fired.' I passed her, still holding her upside down, to Ruthie. Ruthie and Scurvy had been practicing this routine together all year, Susie had told me. It was a kind of apache dance. It was a kind of woman-raping-another-woman dance. Ruthie simply proceeded to maul Scurvy right there in front of Chipper Dove.

'I don't care if you *do* own the hotel!' Scurvy was crying. 'You're terrible disgusting people and I won't clean up after that bear again, *I won't, I won't*,' she moaned. Then she did an absolutely stunning job of *convulsing* under Ruthie—she gagged herself, she spewed, she gibbered. Ruthie left her in a ball, shriveled up and whining—with an occasional, absolutely chilling spasm.

Ruthie shrugged, and said to me, 'You got to get a tougher crew of maids than this white trash, man. Every time the bear rapes someone, the maids can't handle it. They just don't know how to *deal* with it.'

And when I looked at Chipper Dove, I saw—at last!—that his ice-blue looks had left him. He was staring at the bear: Susie was more and more responsive, under Franny's touch. Ruthie went up to the bear and took her muzzle off; Susie gave us a toothy smile. She was more bear than any bear; for this single performance of Lilly's script, Susie the bear could have convinced a *bear* that she was a bear. A bear in heat.

I don't even know if bears ever *get* in heat. 'It doesn't matter,' as Frank would say.

All that mattered was that Chipper Dove believed it. Ruthie started scratching Susie, cautiously, behind the ears. '*See* him? See him—*that* one, over there?' Ruthie said sweetly. And Susie the bear began to shuffle and sway; she started nosing her way toward Chipper Dove.

'Hey, look,' Dove started to say to me.

'Better not move suddenly,' I told him. 'Bears don't like any sudden movement.'

Dove froze. Susie, taking all the time in the world, started sniffing him over. Frank lay on the bed in the bedroom, exhausted. 'I'll give you some advice,' Frank said to Chipper Dove. 'You introduced me to mud puddles, so I'll give you some advice about bears,' Frank said.

'Hey, please,' Chipper Dove said softly, to me.

'The main thing,' Frank said, 'is *don't move*. Don't resist *anything*. The bear does not appreciate resistance of any kind.'

'Just kind of go with it, man,' Ruthie said, dreamily.

I stepped up to Dove and unbuckled his belt; he started to stop me, but I said, 'No sudden movements.' Susie the bear jabbed her snout into Dove's crotch the instant Dove's pants hit the rug with a soft flop.

'I recommend holding your breath,' Frank advised, from the bedroom.

And that was Lilly's cue. In she came. It looked to Dove as if she just walked in with her own key from the door to the hall.

We all stared at the dwarf nurse; Lilly looked cross.

382

'I had the feeling you were up to this again, Franny,' Lilly said to her patient. Franny curled up on the couch, putting her back to us all.

'You're her nurse, not her mother,' I snapped at Lilly.

'It's not *good* for her—this lunatic raping, raping, *raping* everyone!' Lilly shouted at me. 'Every time that damn bear is in heat, you just pull anyone you want in here and *rape* him—and I'm telling you it's not *good* for her.'

'But it's all Franny *likes*,' Frank said, peevishly.

'It's not *right* that she likes it,' Lilly pointed out, like a stubborn but good nurse, which she was.

'Aw, come *on*,' I said. '*This* one is special. This one raped *her!*' I cried to Lilly.

'He made me fuck a mud puddle!' Frank wailed.

'If we can just rape *this* one,' I pleaded with Lilly, 'we won't rape anybody else.'

'Promises, promises,' said Lilly, folding her little arms across her little breasts.

'We promise!' Frank shouted. 'Just one more. Just *this* one.'

'Earl!' Susie snorted, and I thought Dove was going to faint dead away. Susie snorted violently into Dove's crotch. Susie the bear seemed to be saying that she was especially interested in *this* one, too.

'Please, please!' Dove started to scream. Susie knocked his legs out from under him and laid her weight over his chest. She put a big paw—a *real* paw—right on his private parts. 'Please!' Dove said. 'Please don't! *Please!*'

And that was all Lilly wrote. That was where we were supposed to stop. Nobody had any more lines, except Lilly.

Lilly was just supposed to say, 'There will be no more rapes, *no more*—that's final.' And I was supposed to pick Dove up and dump him out in the hall.

But Franny got up off the couch and pushed everyone away; she walked over to Dove. 'That's enough, Susie,' Franny said, and Susie got off Dove. 'Put your pants back on, Chipper,' Franny said to him. He stood up but he fell; he struggled to his feet again and pulled his pants up. 'And the next time you take your pants *off*, for *anybody*,' Franny told Chipper Dove, 'I want you to think of me.'

'Think of *all* of us,' said Frank, coming out of the bedroom.

'Remember us,' I said to Chipper Dove.

'If you see us again,' big Ruthie told him, 'better go the other way. Any one of us might kill you, man,' she told him, matter-of-factly.

Susie the bear took her bear's head off; she would never *need* to wear it again. From now on, the bear suit was just for fun. She looked Chipper Dove right in the eye. The number one first-class hysteric named Scurvy got up off the rug and came over to look at Chipper Dove, too. She looked at him as if she was committing him to memory; then she shrugged, and lit a cigarette, and looked away.

'Don't pass any open windows!' Frank called down the hall to Dove, as he left us; he walked away holding the wall of the hall for support. We all couldn't help but notice that he'd wet his pants.

Chipper Dove moved like a man seeking the men's room in a hospital ward for the disoriented; he moved with the feeble lack of sureness of a man who wasn't sure what experience awaited him in the men's room—as if, even, he wouldn't be sure what to do when he arrived at the urinal.

But there was, in all of us, that initial sense of letdown that should be documented in any fair study of revenge. Whatever we had done, it would never be as awful as what he had done to Franny—and if it *had* been as awful, it would have been too much.

I would feel, for the rest of my life, as if I were still holding Chipper Dove by his armpits—his feet a few inches off the ground of Seventh Avenue. There was really nothing to do with him except put him down; there never *would* be anything to do with him, too—with our Chipper Doves we just go on picking them up and putting them down, forever.

And so, you'd think, that was that. Lilly had proven herself with a real opera, a genuine fairy tale. Susie the bear had played out the part; she had exhausted her bear's role; she would keep the bear suit only for its sentimental value, and for amusing children—and, of course, for Halloween. Father was about to get a Seeing Eye dog for Christmas. It would be his first of many Seeing Eye dogs. And once he had an animal to talk to, my father would finally figure out what he wanted to do with the rest of his life.

'Here comes the rest of our lives,' Franny said, with a kind of awed affection. 'The rest of our fucking lives is finally coming up,' she said.

That day Chipper Dove wandered out of the Stanhope and

back to his 'firm,' it seemed we *all* would be survivors—those of us who were left; it seemed we had made it. Franny was now free to find a life, Lilly and Frank had their chosen careers—or, as they say, their careers had chosen them. Father needed only a little time with the animal side of himself—to help him make up his mind. I knew that an American literature degree from an Austrian university didn't qualify *me* for very much, but what did I *have* to do but look after my father—but lift what weight I could lift off my brother and my sisters whenever the weight needed lifting?

What we had all forgotten in the pre-Christmas decorations, in our frenzy over dealing with Chipper Dove, was that shape that had haunted us from the beginning. As in any fairy tale, just when you think you're out of the woods, there is more to the woods than you thought; just when you think you're out of the woods, it turns out you're still *in* them.

How could we so quickly have forgotten the lesson of the King of Mice? How could we have put away that old dog of our childhood, our dear Sorrow, as neatly as Susie folded up her bear suit and said, 'That's it. That's over. Now it's a whole new ball game'?

There is a song the Viennese sing—it is one of their so-called *Heurigen* songs, the songs they sing to celebrate the first wine of the season. Typical of those people Freud understood so well, their songs are full of death wishes. The King of Mice himself, no doubt, once sang this little song.

> *Verkauft's mei G'wand, I Fahr in Himmel.*
> *Sell my old clothes, I'm off to heaven.*

When Susie the bear took her friends back to the Village, Frank and Franny and Lilly and I called up good old room service and ordered the champagne. As we tasted the very slight sweetness of our revenge on Chipper Dove, our childhood appeared like a clear lake—behind us. We felt we were free of sorrow. But one of us must have been singing that song, even then. One of us was secretly humming the tune.

LIFE IS SERIOUS BUT ART IS FUN!

The King of Mice was dead, but—for one of us—the King of Mice was not forgotten.

I am not a poet. I was not even the writer in our family.

385

Donald Justice would become Lilly's literary hero: he replaced even that marvelous ending of *The Great Gatsby,* which Lilly read to us too often. Donald Justice has most eloquently posed the question that flies to the heart of my hotel-living family. As Mr. Justice asks,

> *How shall I speak of doom, and ours in special,*
> *But as of something altogether common?*

Add doom to the list, then. Especially in families, doom *is* 'altogether common.' Sorrow floats; love, too; and—in the long run—doom. It floats, too.

12

The King of Mice
Syndrome; the Last
Hotel New Hampshire

Here is the epilogue; there always is one. In a world where love
and sorrow float, there are many epilogues—and some of them
go on and on. In a world where doom always muscles in, some
of the epilogues are short.

'A dream is a *disguised* fulfillment of a *suppressed* wish,'
Father announced to us over Easter dinner at Frank's apartment
in New York—Easter, 1965.

'You're quoting Freud again, Pop,' Lilly told him.

'Which Freud?' Franny asked, by rote.

'Sigmund,' Frank answered. 'From Chapter Four of *The
Interpretation of Dreams*.'

I should have known the source, too, because Frank and I
were taking turns reading to Father in the evening. Father had
asked us to read *all* of Freud to him.

'So what did you dream about, Pop?' Franny asked him.

'The Arbuthnot-by-the-Sea,' Father said. His Seeing Eye dog
spent every mealtime with her head in Father's lap; every time
Father reached for his napkin, he would deposit a morsel into the
dog's waiting mouth and the dog would raise her head—
momentarily—allowing Father access to his napkin.

'You should *not* feed her at the table,' Lilly scolded Father,
but we all liked the dog. She was a German shepherd with a
particularly rich golden-brown color that liberally interrupted the
black all over her body and dominated the tone of her gentle
face; she was particularly long-faced and high-cheekboned, so
that her appearance was nothing like a Labrador retriever's.
Father had wanted to call her Freud, but we thought there was
enough confusion among us concerning *which* Freud was meant

—by this remark or that. A *third* Freud, we convinced Father, would have driven everyone crazy.

Lilly suggested we call the dog Jung.

'What? That traitor! That anti-Semite!' Frank protested. 'Whoever heard of naming a *female* after *Jung?*' Frank asked. 'That's something only *Jung* would have thought of,' he said, fuming.

Lilly then suggested we call the dog Stanhope, because of Lilly's fondness for the fourteenth floor; Father liked the idea of naming his first Seeing Eye dog after a hotel, but he said he preferred naming the dog after a hotel he really liked. We all agreed, then, that the dog would be called 'Sacher.' Frau Sacher, after all, had been a woman.

Sacher's only bad habit was putting her head in Father's lap every time Father sat down to eat anything, but Father encouraged this—so it was really Father's bad habit. Sacher was otherwise a model Seeing Eye dog. She did not attack other animals, thus dragging my father wildly out of control after her; she was especially smart about the habits of elevators—blocking the door from reclosing with her body until my father had entered or exited. Sacher barked at the doorman at the St. Moritz but was otherwise friendly, if a trifle aloof, with Father's fellow pedestrians. These were the days before you had to clean up after your dog in New York City, so Father was spared that humiliating task—which would have been almost impossible for him, he realized. In fact, Father feared the passing of such a law years before anyone was talking about it. 'I mean,' he'd say, 'if Sacher shits in the middle of Central Park South, how am I suppoed to *find* the crap? It's bad enough to have to pick up dog shit, but if you can't *see* it, it's positively arduous. I won't do it!' he would shout. 'If some self-righteous citizen even *tries* to speak to me, even *suggests* that I am responsible for my dog's messes, I think I'll use the baseball bat!' But Father was safe —for a while. We wouldn't be living in New York by the time they passed the dog shit law. As the weather got nice, Sacher and my father would walk, unaccompanied, between the Stanhope and Central Park South, and my father felt free to be blind to Sacher's shitting.

At Frank's, the dog slept on the rug between Father's bed and mine, and I sometimes wondered, in my sleep, if it was Sacher I heard dreaming, or Father.

'So you dreamed about the Arbuthnot-by-the-Sea,' Franny said to Father. 'So what else is new?'

'No,' Father said. 'It wasn't one of the *old* dreams. I mean, your mother wasn't there. We weren't *young* again, or anything like that.'

'No man in a white dinner jacket, Daddy?' Lilly asked him.

'No, no,' Father said. 'I was old. In the dream I was even older than I am now,' he said; he was forty-five. 'In the dream,' Father said, 'I was just walking along the beach with Sacher; we were just taking a stroll over the grounds—all around the hotel,' he said.

'All around the *ruins*, you mean,' Franny said.

'Well,' Father said, slyly, 'of course I couldn't actually *see* if the Arbuthnot was still a ruin, but I had the feeling it was *restored*—I had the feeling it was all fixed up,' Father said, shoveling food off his plate and into his lap—and into Sacher. 'It was a brand-new hotel,' Father said, impishly.

'And you *owned* it, I'll bet,' Lilly said to him.

'You *did* say I could do *anything*, didn't you, Frank?' Father asked.

'In the dream you *owned* the Arbuthnot-by-the-Sea?' Frank asked him. 'And it was all fixed up?'

'Open for business as usual, Pop?' Franny asked him.

'Business as usual,' Father said, nodding; Sacher nodded, too.

'Is *that* what you want to do?' I asked Father. 'You want to own the Arbuthnot-by-the-Sea?'

'Well,' Father said. 'Of course we'd have to change the name.'

'Of course,' Franny said.

'The *third* Hotel New Hampshire!' Frank cried. 'Lilly!' he shouted. 'Just think of it! *Another* TV series!'

'I haven't really been working on the first series,' Lilly said, worriedly.

Franny knelt beside Father; she put her hand on his knee; Sacher licked Franny's fingers. 'You want to do it *again?*' Franny asked Father. 'You want to start all over again? You understand that you don't *have* to.'

'But what *else* would I do, Franny?' he asked her, smiling. 'It's the *last* one—I promise you,' he said, addressing all of us. 'If I can't make the Arbuthnot-by-the-Sea into something special, then I'll throw in the towel.'

Franny looked at Frank and shrugged; I shrugged, too, and Lilly just rolled her eyes. Frank said, 'Well, I guess it's simple enough to inquire what it costs, and who owns it.'

'I don't want to see him—if *he* still owns it,' Father said. 'I don't want to see the bastard.' Father was always pointing out to us the things he didn't want to 'see,' and we were usually restrained enough to resist pointing out to him that he couldn't 'see' anything.

Franny said she didn't want to see the man in the white dinner jacket, either, and Lilly said she saw him all the time—in her sleep; Lilly said she was tired of seeing him.

It would be Frank and I who would rent a car and drive all the way to Maine; Frank would teach me how to drive along the way. We would see the ruin that was the Arbuthnot-by-the-Sea again. We would note that ruins don't change a lot: what capacity for change is in a ruin has usually been exhausted in the considerable process of change undergone in order for the ruin to *become* a ruin. Once becoming a ruin, a ruin stays pretty much the same. We noted some more vandalism, but it's not much fun vandalizing a ruin, we supposed, and so the whole place looked almost exactly as it had looked to us in the fall of 1946 when we had all come to the Arbuthnot-by-the-Sea to watch Earl die.

We had no trouble recognizing the dock where old State o' Maine was shot, although that dock—and the surrounding docks —had been rebuilt, and there were a lot of new boats in the water. The Arbuthnot-by-the-Sea looked like a small ghost town, but what had once been a quaint fishing and lobstering village—alongside the hotel grounds—was now a scruffy little tourist town. There was a marina where you could rent boats and buy clam worms, and there was a rocky public beach within sight of the private beach belonging to the Arbuthnot-by-the-Sea. Since no one was around to care, the 'private' beach was hardly private anymore. Two families were having a picnic there when Frank and I visited the place; one of the families had arrived by boat, but the other family had driven right down to the beach in their car. They'd driven up the same 'private' driveway that Frank and I had driven up, past the faded sign that still said: CLOSED FOR THE SEASON!

The chain that once had blocked that driveway had long ago been torn down and dragged away.

'It would cost a fortune to even make the place habitable,' Frank said.

'Provided they even want to sell it,' I said.

'Who in God's name would want to *keep* it?' Frank asked.

It was at the realty office in Bath, Maine, that Frank and I found out that the man in the white dinner jacket still owned the Arbuthnot-by-the-Sea—and he was still alive.

'You want to buy old Arbuthnot's place!' the shocked realtor asked.

We were delighted to learn that there was an 'old Arbuthnot.'

'I only hear from his lawyers,' the realtor said. 'They've been trying to unload the place, for years. Old Arbuthnot lives in California,' the realtor told us, 'but he's got lawyers all over the country. The one I deal with most of the time is in New York.'

We thought, then, that it would simply be a matter of letting the New York lawyer know that we wanted it, but—back in New York—Arbuthnot's lawyer told us that Arbuthnot wanted to see us.

'We'll have to go to California,' Frank said. 'Old Arbuthnot sounds as senile as one of the Hapsburgs, but he won't sell the place unless he gets to *meet* us.'

'Jesus God,' Franny said. 'That's an expensive trip to make just to meet someone!'

Frank informed her that Arbuthnot was paying our way.

'He probably wants to laugh in your faces,' Franny told us.

'He probably wants to meet someone who's crazier than *he* is,' Lilly said.

'I can't believe I'm so lucky!' Father cried. 'To imagine that it's still available!' Frank and I saw no reason to describe the ruins—and the seedy new tourism surrounding his cherished Arbuthnot-by-the-Sea.

'He won't *see* any of it, anyway,' Frank whispered.

And I am glad that Father never got the chance to see old Arbuthnot, a terminal resident of the Beverly Hills Hotel. When Frank and I arrived at the Los Angeles airport, we rented our second car of that week and drove ourselves to meet the aged Arbuthnot.

In a suite with its own palm garden, we found the old man with an attending nurse, an attending lawyer (this one was a California lawyer), and what would prove to be a fatal case of emphysema. He sat propped up in a fancy hospital bed—he sat breathing very carefully alongside a row of air-conditioners.

'I like L.A.,' Arbuthnot gasped. 'Not so many Jews here as there are in New York. Or else I've finally gotten *immune* to Jews,' he added. Then he was flung off at a sharp angle on his hospital bed by a cough that seemed to attack him by surprise (and from the side); he sounded as if he were choking on a whole turkey leg—it seemed impossible he would recover, it seemed his persistent anti-Semitism would finally be the death of him (I'm sure that would have made Freud happy), but just as suddenly as the attack had seized him, the attack left him and he was calm. His nurse plumped up his pillows for him; his lawyer placed some important-looking documents upon the old man's chest and produced a pen for old Arbuthnot to hold in his trembling hand.

'I'm dying,' Arbuthnot said to Frank and me, as if this hadn't been obvious from our first glimpse of him. He wore white silk pajamas; he looked about one hundred years old; he couldn't have weighed more than fifty pounds.

'They say they're not Jews,' the lawyer told Arbuthnot, indicating Frank and me.

'Is *that* why you wanted to meet us?' Frank asked the old man. 'You could have found that out over the phone.'

'I may be dying,' he said, 'but I'm not selling out to the Jews.'

'My father,' I told Arbuthnot, 'was a dear friend of Freud.'

'Not *the* Freud,' Frank said to Arbuthnot, but the old man had begun coughing again and he didn't hear what Frank had to say.

'Freud?' Arbuthnot said, hacking and spewing. '*I* knew a Freud, too! He was a Jewish animal trainer. The Jews aren't good with animals, though,' Arbuthnot confided to us. 'Animals can tell, you know,' he said. 'They can always sense anything funny about you,' he said. 'This Freud *I* knew was a dumb Jewish animal trainer. He tried to train a bear, but the bear ate him!' Arbuthnot howled with delight—which brought on more coughing.

'A sort of anti-Semitic bear?' Frank asked, and Arbuthnot laughed so hard I thought his subsequent coughing would kill him.

'I was *trying* to kill him,' Frank said later.

'You must be crazy to want that place,' Arbuthnot told us. 'I mean, don't you know where *Maine* is? It's nowhere! There's no decent train service, and there's no decent flying service. It's a terrible place to drive to—it's too far from *both* New York and Boston—and when you *do* get there, the water's too cold and the bugs can bleed you to death in an hour. None of the really *class* sailors sail there anymore—I mean the sailors with money,' he said. 'If you have a little money,' Arbuthnot said, 'there's absolutely nothing to spend it on in Maine! They don't even have *whores* there.'

'We like it anyway,' Frank told him.

'They're not Jews, are they?' Arbuthnot asked his lawyer.

'No,' the lawyer said.

'It's hard to tell, looking at them,' Arbuthnot said. 'I used to be able to spot a Jew at first glance,' he explained to us. 'But I'm dying now,' he added.

'Too bad,' Frank said.

'Freud *wasn't* eaten by a bear,' I told Arbuthnot.

'The Freud *I* knew was eaten by a bear,' Arbuthnot said.

'No,' said Frank, 'the Freud you knew was a *hero.*'

'Not the Freud I knew,' old Arbuthnot argued, petulantly. His nurse caught some spittle dribbling off his chin and wiped him as absentmindedly as she might have dusted a table.

'The Freud we *both* know,' I said, 'saved the Vienna State Opera.'

'Vienna!' Arbuthnot cried. 'Vienna is full of Jews!' he yelled.

'There's more of them in Maine than there used to be,' Frank teased him.

'In L.A., too,' I said.

'I'm dying, anyway,' Arbuthnot said. 'Thank God.' He signed the documents on his chest and his lawyer handed them over to us. And that was how, in 1965, Frank bought the Arbuthnot-by-the-Sea and twenty-five acres on the coast of Maine. 'For a song,' as Franny would say.

An almost sky-blue mole was sprouting on old Arbuthnot's face and both his ears were painted a vivid purple with gentian violet, an old-fashioned fungicide. It was as if a giant fungus were consuming Arbuthnot from the inside out. 'Wait a minute,' he said, as we were leaving—his chest made a watery echo of his words. His nurse plumped up his pillows again; his lawyer snapped a briefcase shut; the cold of the room, from all the purring air-conditioners, made the place feel, to Frank and me, like the tomb—the *Kaisergruft*—for the heartless Hapsburgs in Vienna. 'What are your plans?' Arbuthnot asked us. 'What in hell are you going to *do* with that place?'

'It's going to be Special Commando Training Camp,' Frank told old Arbuthnot. 'For the Israeli Army.'

I saw Arbuthnot's lawyer crack a smile; it was the special sort of smile that would make Frank and me later look up the lawyer's name on the documents that had been handed over to us. The lawyer's name was Irving Rosenman, and despite the fact that he came from Los Angeles, Frank and I were pretty sure he was Jewish.

Old Arbuthnot didn't crack a smile. 'Israeli commandos?' he said.

'*Ratta-tat-tat-tat-tat!*' said Frank, imitating a machine gun. We thought that Irving Rosenman was going to throw himself into the air-conditioners to keep himself from laughing.

'The bears will get them,' Arbuthnot said, strangely. 'The bears will get *all* the Jews, in the end,' he said—the mindless hatred in his old face was as old-fashioned and as vivid as the gentian violet in his ears.

'Have a nice death,' Frank told him.

Arbuthnot started coughing; he tried to say something more but he couldn't stop coughing. He motioned the nurse over to him and she seemed to interpret his coughing without very much difficulty; she was used to it; she motioned us out of Arbuthnot's room, then she came outside and told us what Arbuthnot had told her to tell us.

'He said he's going to have the best death money can buy,' she told us, which—Arbuthnot had added—was more than Frank and I were going to get.

And Frank and I could think of no message to give the nurse to pass on to old Arbuthnot. We were content to leave him with the idea of Israeli commandos in Maine. Frank and I said good-bye to Arbuthnot's nurse and to Irving Rosenman and we flew back to New York with the third Hotel New Hampshire in Frank's pocket.

'That's just where you should keep it, Frank,' Franny told him. 'In your pocket.'

'You'll never make that old place into a hotel again,' Lilly told Father. 'It's had its chance.'

'We'll start out modestly,' Father assured Lilly.

Father and I were the 'we' Father meant. I told him I'd go to Maine with him and help him get started.

'Then you're as crazy as he is,' Franny had told me.

But I had an idea I would never share with Father. If, as Freud says, a dream is the fulfillment of a wish, then—as Freud also says—the same holds true for jokes. A joke is also the fulfillment of a wish. I had a joke to play on Father. And I have been playing it, now, for more than fifteen years. Since Father is more than sixty years old now, I think it's fair to say that the joke 'came off'; it's fair to say that I have gotten away with it.

The last Hotel New Hampshire was never—and never will be —a hotel. That is the joke I have played on Father for all these years. Lilly's first book, *Trying to Grow,* would make enough money so that we *could* restore the Arbuthnot-by-the-Sea; and when they made the movie version, we could have bought back the Gasthaus Freud, too. Maybe, by then, we could have afforded the Sacher; at least we could have bought the Stanhope. But I knew it wasn't necessary that the third Hotel New Hampshire be a *real* hotel.

'After all,' as Frank would say, 'the first two weren't *real* hotels, either.' The truth is, Father had always been blind, or Freud's blindness had proved to be contagious.

We had the debris cleaned off the beach. We had the 'grounds' more or less restored, which is to say we mowed the lawn again, and we even made an effort with one of the tennis courts. Many years later we put in a swimming pool, because Father liked to swim and it made me nervous to watch him in the ocean; I was always afraid he'd make a wrong turn and head out to sea. And the buildings that had been dormitories for the staff —where Mother and Father and Freud had once resided? We simply removed them; we had the wreckers come and drag them away. We had the ground leveled, and we paved it. We told Father it was a parking lot, although we never had very many cars around.

We put our hearts into the main building. We put a bar where the reception desk had been; we turned that lobby into a huge game room. We were thinking of the dart board and the billiard tables in the Kaffee Mowatt, so I suppose it's accurate to say—as Franny says—that we converted the lobby to a Viennese coffeehouse. It led into what had been the hotel restaurant, and the kitchen; we just knocked down some walls and made the whole thing into what the architect called 'a kind of country kitchen.'

'A huge kind,' Lilly said.

'A weird kind,' said Frank.

It was Frank's idea to restore the ballroom. 'In case we have a big party,' he argued, though we would never have a party so large that the so-called country kitchen couldn't handle it. Even with eliminating many of the bathrooms, even with turning the top floor into storage space, and the second floor into a library, we could sleep thirty-odd people—in complete privacy—if we'd ever gone through with it and bought enough beds.

At first Father seemed puzzled by how quiet it was: 'Where are the guests?' he'd ask, especially in summer, with the windows open, when you would expect to hear the children

395

—their high, light voices swept up from the beach and mingled with the cries of gulls and terns. I explained to Father that we did well enough in the summers to not even need to bother to stay open for business in the winter, but some summers he would question me about the surrounding silence orchestrated by the steady percussion of the sea. 'By my count, I can't imagine there's more than two or three guests around here,' Father would say, 'unless I'm going *deaf*, too,' he would add.

But we'd all explain to him how we were such a first-class *resort* hotel that we didn't really need to fill the place; we were getting such a stiff price for a room, we didn't need to fill every room to be making a bundle.

'Isn't that fantastic?' he'd say. 'It's what I knew this place *could* be,' he'd remind us. 'It needed only that proper combination of class and democracy. I always knew it could be *special*.'

Well, my family was a model of democracy, of course; first Lilly made the money, then Frank went to work with the money, and so the third Hotel New Hampshire had lots of *un*paying guests. We wanted as many people around as possible, because the presence of people, both their merry and quarrelsome sounds, helped further my father's illusions that we were at last a joint of distinction, operating wholly in the black. Lilly came and stayed as long as she could stand it. She never liked working in the library, although we offered her—virtually—the entire second floor. 'Too many books in the library,' she said; she felt, when she was writing, that the presence of other books dwarfed her little efforts. Lilly even tried writing in the ballroom, once —that vast space awaiting music and graceful feet. Lilly would write and write in there, but her tiny pecks upon her typewriter would never fill the empty dance floor—though she tried. How Lilly tried.

And Franny would come and stay, out of the public's scrutiny; Franny would use our third Hotel New Hampshire to collect herself. Franny would be famous—more famous than Lilly, too, I'm afraid. In the movie version of *Trying to Grow*, Franny got the part of playing herself. After all, she *is* the hero of the first Hotel New Hampshire. In the movie version, of course, she's the only one of us who seems authentic. They made Frank into your stereotypical homosexual cymbalist and taxidermist; they made Lilly 'cute,' but Lilly's smallness was never cute to us. Her size, I'm afraid, always seemed like a failed effort—no cuteness involved in the struggle, or in the

396

result. And they overplayed Egg: Egg the heartbreaker—Egg really was 'cute.'

They found some veteran Western actor to play Iowa Bob (Frank and Franny and I all remembered seeing this old duffer shot off a horse a million times); he had a way of lifting weights as if he were wolfing down a plate of flapjacks—he was completely unconvincing. And, of course, they cut out all the swearing. Some producer actually told Franny that profanity revealed a poor vocabulary and a lack of imagination. And Frank and Lilly and Father and I all loved to shout at Franny, then, and ask her what she had said to *that*. 'What an anal crock of shit, you dumb asshole!' she'd told the producer. 'Up yours —and in your ear, too!'

But even with the limitation imposed upon her language, Franny came across in *Trying to Grow*. Even though they cast Junior Jones in such a way that he came on like some self-conscious buffoon auditioning for a jazz band; even though the people playing Mother and Father were insipid and vague; and the one who was supposed to be *me!*—well, Jesus God. Even with these handicaps, Franny shone through. She was in her twenties when they shot the movie, but she was so pretty that she played sixteen just fine.

'I think the oaf they got to play *you*,' Franny told me, 'was supposed to exude an absolutely lifeless combination of sweetness and stupidity.'

'Well, I don't know, that's what you *do* exude, every now and then,' Frank would tease me.

'Like a kind of weight-lifting maiden aunt,' Lilly said to me. 'That's how they cast you.'

But in my first few years of looking after Father at the third Hotel New Hampshire, that is rather what I felt like much of the time: a kind of weight-lifting maiden aunt. With a degree in American literature from Vienna, I could do worse than become the caretaker of my father's illusions.

'You need a nice woman,' Franny said to me, long distance —from New York, from L.A., from the viewpoint of her rising stardom.

Frank would argue with her that perhaps what I needed was a nice *man*. But I was wary. I was happy setting up my father's fantasy. In the tradition established by the doomed Fehlgeburt, I would especially enjoy reading to Father in the evenings; reading aloud to someone is one of this world's pleasures. I would even succeed in interesting Father in lifting weights. You don't have

397

to see to do it. And in the mornings, now, Father and I have a wonderful time in the old ballroom. We've got mats spread out everywhere, and a proper bench for the bench presses. We've got barbells and dumbbells for every occasion—and we have the ballroom's splendid view of the Atlantic Ocean. If Father hasn't the means to see the view, he is content to feel the sea breeze wash over him as he lies lifting. Ever since squeezing Arbeiter, as I've said, I don't put quite as much into the weights, and Father has become sophisticated enough as a weight lifter to realize this; he chides me a little bit about it, but I enjoy just taking a light workout with him. I leave him to do the heavy lifting, now.

'Oh, I know you're still in shape,' he teases me, 'but you're no match for what you were in the summer of sixty-four.'

'You can't be twenty-two all your life,' I remind him, and we lift and lift for a while. On those mornings, with the Maine mist not yet burned off, and the sea damp settled upon us, I can imagine that I'm just starting the voyage all over again—I can believe I'm lying on the rug old Sorrow liked to lie on, and it's Iowa Bob beside me, instructing me, instead of me instructing my father.

I would be sneaking up on forty before I would try living with a woman.

For my thirtieth birthday, Lilly sent me a Donald Justice poem. She liked the ending and thought it applied to me. I was feeling cross at the time and fired back a note to Lilly, saying, 'Who is this Donald Justice and how come everything he says applies to *us?*' But it's a nice ending to any poem, and I *did* feel just like this at thirty.

> *Thirty today, I saw*
> *The trees flare briefly like*
> *The candles upon a cake*
> *As the sun went down the sky,*
> *A momentary flash,*
> *Yet there was time to wish*
> *Before the light could die,*
> *If I had known what to wish,*
> *As once I must have known,*
> *Bending above the clean,*
> *Candlelit tablecloth*
> *To blow them out with a breath.*

And, when Frank was forty, I would send him a birthday greeting with Donald Justice's 'Men at Forty' poem enclosed.

> *Men at forty*
> *Learn to close softly*
> *The doors to rooms they will not be*
> *Coming back to.*

Frank fired me back a note saying he stopped reading the damn poem right there. 'Close your own doors!' Frank snapped. 'You'll be forty soon enough. As for me, I bang the damn doors and come back to them all the fucking time!'

Bravo, Frank! I thought. He has always kept passing the open windows without the slightest trace of fear. It's what all the great agents do: they make the most incredible and illogical advice sound reasonable, they make you go ahead without fear, and that way you get it, you get more or less what you want, or you get something, anyway; at least you don't end up with nothing when you go ahead without fear, when you lunge into the darkness as if you were operating on the soundest advice in the world. Who would have thought Frank would have ended up so lovable? (He was such a rotten kid.) And I do not blame Frank for pushing Lilly too hard. 'It was *Lilly*,' Franny always said, 'who pushed Lilly too hard.'

When the damn reviewers liked her *Trying to Grow*—when they condescended to her with their superior forms of praise, saying how *in spite of* who she was, *the* Lilly Berry of that famous opera-saving family, she was really 'not a bad writer,' she was really very 'promising'—when they prattled on and on about the *freshness* of her *voice,* all it meant to Lilly was that now she had to get going; now she had to get serious.

But our little Lilly wrote her first book almost by accident; that book was only a euphemism for trying to grow, yet it insisted to her that she *was* a writer, when perhaps she was only a sensitive and loving reader, a lover of literature who thought she *wanted* to write. I think it was the writing that killed Lilly, because writing can do that. It just burned her up; she wasn't big enough to take the self-abuse of it, to take the constant chipping away —of herself. After the movie version of *Trying to Grow* made Franny famous, and after the TV series of 'The First Hotel New Hampshire' made Lilly Berry a household word, I suppose that Lilly wanted to 'just write,' as one is always hearing writers say.

399

I suppose she just wanted to be free to write *her* book, now. The problem was, it wasn't a very good book—the second one. It was called *The Evening of the Mind*, from a line she stole from her guru, Donald Justice.

> *Now comes the evening of the mind.*
> *Here are the fireflies twitching in the blood;*

and so on. She might have been wiser to take her title and make her book from another Donald Justice line:

> *Time a bow bent with his certain failure.*

She might have called her book *Certain Failure,* because it was just that. It was more than she could handle; it was over her head. It was about the death of dreams, it was about how hard the dreams die. It was a brave book, in that it departed from anything directly relatable to Lilly's little autobiography, but it departed to a country too foreign for her to grasp; she wrote a *vague* book that reflected how foreign the language she was only visiting was to her. When you write vaguely, you are always vulnerable. She was easily wounded when the critics—when the damn reviewers, with their dull, plodding cunning—jumped on her.

According to Frank, who was usually right about Lilly, she suffered the further embarrassment of writing a bad book that was adopted as *heroic* by a rather influential group of bad readers. A certain illiterate kind of college student was *attracted* to the vagueness of *The Evening of the Mind;* this kind of college student was relieved to discover that absolute obscurity was not only publishable but seemingly identified with seriousness. What some of the students liked best in her book, Frank pointed out, was what Lilly hated most about it—its self-examinations that led nowhere, its plotlessness, its people fading in and out of character, its absence of story. Somehow, among a certain university population, the obvious failure to be clear confirms that what any fool knows is a vice can be rearranged, by art, to resemble a virtue.

'Where in hell do these college kids *get* such an idea!' Franny would complain.

'Not *all* of them have this idea,' Frank would point out.

'They think what's forced and strained and *difficult* with a fucking capital D is *better* than what's straightforward, fluent,

400

and comprehensible!' Franny shouted. 'What the fuck's *wrong* with these people?'

'Only some of them are like that, Franny,' Frank would say.

'Just the ones who've made a cult out of Lilly's failure?' Franny asked.

'Just the ones who listen to their teachers,' Frank said, smugly —happily at home in one of his anti-everything moods. 'I mean, where do you think the college students *learn* to think that way, Franny?' Frank asked her. 'From their teachers.'

'Jesus God,' Franny would say.

She would not ask for a part in *The Evening of the Mind;* there was no way to make that book into a movie, anyway. Franny became a star with so much more ease than Lilly became a writer. 'Being a star is easier,' Franny would say. 'You don't have to do anything but be relaxed about who you are and trust that people will like you; you just trust that they'll get the *you in you*,' Franny said. 'You just be relaxed and hope that the *you in you* comes across.'

For a writer, I guess, the *you in you* needs more nourishment to emerge. I always wanted to write Donald Justice a letter about that, but I think that seeing him—only once, and from a distance —should suffice. If what's best and clearest in him *isn't* in his poems, he wouldn't be a very good writer. And since something good and strong in him *emerges* in his poems, it would probably be disappointing to meet him. Oh, I don't mean that he'd be a bum. He's probably a wonderful man. But he couldn't be as precise as his poems; his poems are so stately, he'd have to be a letdown. In Lilly's case, of course, her work was a letdown —and she knew it. She knew her work wasn't as lovable as she was, and Lilly would have preferred it the other way around.

What saved Franny was not just that being a star is easier than being a writer. What saved Franny, too, was that she didn't have to be a star alone. What Donald Justice knows is that you have to be a writer all alone, whether you *live* alone or not.

> *You would not recognize me.*
> *Mine is the face which blooms in*
> *The dank mirrors of washrooms*
> *As you grope for the light switch.*
>
> *My eyes have the expression*
> *Of the cold eyes of statues*
> *Watching their pigeons return*
> *From the feed you have scattered.*

401

'Jesus God,' as Franny has said. 'Who'd want to meet *him?*'

But Lilly was lovely to know—except, perhaps, to herself. Lilly wanted her words to be lovely, but her words let her down.

It's remarkable how Franny and I once thought of Frank as the King of Mice; we had Frank figured all wrong. We underestimated Frank, from the beginning. He was a hero, but he needed to get to that point in time when he would be signing all our checks, and telling us how much we could spend on this or that, in order for us to recognize the hero that Frank had always been.

No, Lilly was our King of Mice. 'We should have known!' Franny would wail, and wail. 'She was just too small!'

And so Lilly is lost to us, now. She was the sorrow we never quite understood; we never saw through her disguises. Perhaps Lilly never grew quite large enough for us to see.

She authored one masterpiece, which she never gave herself enough credit for. She wrote the screenplay for the movie starring Chipper Dove; she was the writer and director of that opera, in the grand tradition of *Schlagobers* and blood. She knew just how far to go with that story. It was *The Evening of the Mind* that didn't live up to her own expectations, and the difficulty she had trying to begin again—trying to write the book that would have been called, ambitiously, *Everything After Childhood*. That isn't even a Donald Justice line; that was Lilly's own idea, but she couldn't live up to it, either.

When Franny drinks too much, she gets pissed off at the power Donald Justice had over Lilly; Franny sometimes gets drunk enough to blame poor Donald Justice for what happened to Lilly. But Frank and I are always the first to assure Franny that it was *quality* that killed Lilly; it was the end of *The Great Gatsby,* which was not her ending, which was not an ending within her grasp. And once Lilly said, '*Damn* that Donald Justice, anyway! He's written all the good lines!'

He may have written the last line my sister Lilly read. Frank found Lilly's copy of Donald Justice's *Night Light*, opened to page 20, the page dog-eared many times, and the one line at the top of the page was circled and circled—in lipstick, once, and in several different tones of ink from several different ballpoint pens; even in lowly pencil.

I do not think the ending can be right.

402

That might have been the line that drove Lilly to it.

It was a February night. Franny was out on the West Coast; Franny couldn't have saved her. Father and I were in Maine; Lilly knew we went to bed early. Father was on his third Seeing Eye dog at the time. Sacher was gone, a victim of overeating. The little blond dog with the perky, yapping bark, the one that was hit by a car—its vice was chasing cars, fortunately *not* when Father was attached—that one was gone too; Father called her Schlagobers because she had a disposition like whipped cream. The third one was a farter, but only in this way did he bear an unpleasant resemblance to Sorrow; it was another German shepherd, but a male this time, and Father insisted that his name be Fred. That was also the name of the handyman at the third Hotel New Hampshire—a deaf retired lobsterman named Fred. Whenever Father called *any* dog—when he called Sacher, when he called Schlagobers—Fred the handyman would cry, 'What?' from whatever part of the hotel he was working in. The whole thing irritated Father so much (and so much, unspokenly, reminded us both of Egg) that Father always threatened to name the *next* dog Fred.

'Since that old fool Fred will answer whenever I call the dog, anyway, no matter *what* name I'm calling!' Father shouted. 'Jesus God, if he's going to be calling out "What?" all the time, we might as well get the name right.'

So Seeing Eye Dog Number Three was Fred. His only bad habit was that he tried to hump the cleaning woman's daughter whenever the little girl strayed from her mother's side. Fred would goofily pin the little girl to the ground, and start humping her, and the little girl would scream, 'No, Fred!' And the cleaning woman would holler, 'Cut it out, Fred!' and whack Fred with a mop or a broom, or with whatever was handy. And Father would hear the fracas and know what was going on, and he'd yell, 'Goddamn it, Fred, you horny bastard! Get your ass over here, Fred!' And the deaf handyman, the retired lobsterman, our *other* Fred, would cry out, 'What? What?' And I'd have to go find him (because Father refused) and tell him, 'NOT *YOU*, FRED! NOTHING, FRED!'

'Oh,' he'd say, going back to work. 'Thought somebody called.'

So it would have been hopeless for Lilly to call us in Maine. We wouldn't have been able to do much more for her than yell 'Fred!' a few times.

What Lilly tried to do was call Frank. Frank wasn't that far from her; he might have helped. We tell him, now, that he might have helped her *that* time, but in the long run, we know, doom floats. Lilly got Frank's answering service, anyway. Frank had replaced his live answering service with one of those mechanical services, with one of those infuriating recordings of himself.

HI! FRANK HERE—BUT ACTUALLY I'M NOT HERE (HA HA). ACTUALLY, I'M OUT. WANT TO LEAVE A MESSAGE? WAIT FOR THE LITTLE SIGNAL AND TALK YOUR HEART OUT.

Franny left many messages that made Frank cross. 'Go fuck a doughnut, Frank!' Franny would scream into the infuriating machine. 'It costs me *money* every time that fucking device answers me—I'm in fucking *Los Angeles,* Frank, you moron, you dip-shit, you turd in a birdbath!' And then she'd make all sorts of farting sounds, and very liquid kisses, and Frank would call me, disgusted, as usual.

'Honestly,' he'd say. 'I don't understand Franny at all. She just left the most disgusting message on my tape recorder! I mean, I *know* she thinks she's being funny, but doesn't she know that we've all heard quite enough of her vulgarity? At her age, it hardly becomes her any longer—if it ever did. You've cleaned up *your* language, I wish you'd make an effort to clean up *hers.*'

And on and on.

Lilly's message must have scared Frank. And he probably didn't come in from his evening date very long after she had called; he put the machine on and listened to his messages as he was brushing his teeth, getting ready to go to bed.

They were mostly business things. The tennis player he represents had gotten in some difficulty over a deodorant commercial. A screenwriter called to say that a director was 'manipulating' him, and Frank made a fast mental note—to the effect that this writer *needed* lots of 'manipulation.' A famous choreographer had bogged down in her autobiography; she was blocked in her childhood, she confided to Frank, who just kept brushing his teeth. He rinsed his mouth, turned off the bathroom light, and then heard Lilly.

'Hi, it's me,' she said, apologetically—to the machine. Lilly was always apologizing. Frank smiled and untucked his bedcovers; he always put his dressmaker's dummy in bed before he crawled in. There was a long pause on the machine and Frank

404

thought the thing was broken; it often was. But then Lilly added, 'It's just me.' Something about the tiredness in her voice made Frank check the time of night, and made him listen with some anxiety. In the pause that followed, Frank remembers whispering her name. 'Go on, Lilly,' he whispered.

And Lilly sang her little song, just a little snatch of a song; it was one of the *Heurigen* songs—a silly, sad song, a King of Mice song. Frank knew the song by heart, of course.

> *Verkauft's mei G'wand, I Fahr in Himmel.*
> *Sell my old clothes, I'm off to heaven.*

'Holy cow, Lilly,' Frank whispered to the recorder; he started getting dressed, fast.

'*Auf Wiedersehen*, Frank,' Lilly said, when her little song was over.

Frank didn't answer her. He ran down to Columbus Circle and caught an uptown cab. And even though Frank was no runner, I'm sure he made good time; I couldn't have done any better. Even if he'd been home when Lilly called, I always told him that it would take *anyone* longer to cover twenty blocks and a zoo than it takes to fall fourteen stories—the distance from the window of the corner suite on the Stanhope's fourteenth floor to the pavement at Eighty-first and Fifth Avenue. Lilly had a shorter trip to take than Frank's, and she would have beaten him to her destination—regardless; there was nothing he could have done. Even so, Frank said, he didn't say (or even think to himself), '*Auf Wiedersehen*, Lilly,' until after they'd shown him her little body.

She left a better note than Fehlgeburt had left. Lilly was not crazy. She left a serious suicide note.

Sorry,

said the note.

Just not big enough.

I best remember her little hands: how they leaped about in her lap, whenever she said anything thoughtful—and Lilly was always thoughtful. 'Not enough laughter in her, man,' as Junior Jones would say. Lilly's hands could not contain themselves; they danced to whatever she thought she heard—maybe it was the same music Freud tapped his baseball bat to, the same song Father is hearing now, the bat stirring gracefully at his tired feet. My father, the blind walker: he walks everywhere, he covers the grounds of the Hotel New Hampshire for hours every day, summer and winter. First Sacher led him, then Schlagobers, then Fred; when Fred developed his habit of killing skunks, we had to get rid of him. 'I *like* Fred,' Father said, 'but between the farting and the skunks, he'll drive the guests away.'

'Well, the *guests* aren't complaining,' I told Father.

'Well, they're just being polite,' Father said. 'They're showing their class, but it's loathsome, it's truly an imposition, and if Fred ever attacks a skunk when I'm *with* him . . . well, for Christ's sake, I'll *kill* him; it's the baseball bat for him, then.'

So we found a nice family who wanted a watchdog; they weren't blind, but they didn't care if Fred farted and smelled like a skunk.

And now Father walks with See Eye Dog Number Four. We got tired of naming them, and when Lilly died, Father lost a little more of his playfulness. 'I just am not up to naming another dog,' he said. 'Want to do this one?' But I wasn't up to a dog-naming either. Franny was shooting a film in France, and Frank—who was the hardest hit by Lilly's leaving us—was irritated at the whole idea of dogs. Frank had too much sorrow on his mind; he wasn't in a mood for naming dogs at all.

'Jesus God,' Frank said. 'Call it Number Four.'

My father shrugged and settled for just plain old 'Four.' So that now, in the twilight, when Father is searching for his walking companion, I hear him screaming the number four. 'Four!' he bellows. 'Goddamn it, Four!' And old Fred, the handyman, still cries out, 'What?' And Father goes on with his 'Four! Four! Four!' Like someone remembering a childhood game: that one where you throw up the ball and yell someone's number, and the one called has to try to catch the ball before the ball hits the ground. 'Four!' I hear Father calling, and I imagine some child running, arms held out for the ball.

Sometimes the child is Lilly, sometimes it's Egg.

And when Father has finally found Four, I watch out the window as Four leads my father carefully down to the docks; in the failing light, it's possible to mistake my father and his Seeing Eye dog for a much younger man on the dock—with a bear, perhaps; possibly they're fishing for pollack. 'It's no fun fishing when you can't see the fish come out of the water,' Father has told me. And so, with Four, Father just sits on the dock, welcoming the evening, until the fierce Maine mosquitoes drive him back to the Hotel New Hampshire.

There is even a sign: HOTEL NEW HAMPSHIRE. Father insisted on it, and although he can't see it—and wouldn't miss it, if I only pretended there was a sign—it is a concession I gladly make for him, although it is a nuisance, at times. Occasionally tourists get lost and find us; they see the sign and think we *are* a hotel. I have explained to Father a very complicated system that our 'success' in *this* hotel business has afforded us. When the lost tourists find us and ask for rooms, we ask them if they have reservations.

They say no, of course, but invariably—looking around themselves, at the silence, at the abandoned quality of peace we have achieved at the third Hotel New Hampshire—they ask, 'But surely you have vacancies?'

'No vacancies,' we always say. 'No reservations, no vacancies.'

Sometimes Father argues with me about this. 'But surely we have *room* for them,' he hisses. 'They seem very nice. There's a child or two, I can hear them quarreling, and the mother sounds tired—they've probably been doing too much driving.'

'Standards are standards, Pop,' I say. 'Really, what would our other guests think if we got too loose about this?'

'It's just so elitist,' he whispers, wonderingly. 'I mean, I always *knew* this was a special place, but, somehow, I never dreamed it would *actually* . . .' And he usually breaks off his sentence right there, smiling. And then he adds, 'Well, wouldn't your mother have loved all *this!*' The baseball bat waves, showing it all to Mother.

And I say, without the slightest tone of qualification in my voice, 'She sure would have, Pop.'

'If not every minute,' my father adds, thoughtfully, 'at least this part. At least the end.'

Lilly's end, considering her cult following, was as quiet as we could have it. I wish I'd had the courage to ask Donald Justice for an elegy but it was—as much as possible—a family funeral. Junior Jones was there; he sat with Franny, and I couldn't help but notice how perfectly they held each other's hands. It often takes a funeral to make you realize who has grown older. I noticed Junior had added a few gentle lines around his eyes; he was a very hardworking lawyer, now—we'd hardly heard from him when he was in law school; he disappeared almost as completely into law school as he had once disappeared into the bottom of a pile of Cleveland Browns. I guess law school and football are similarly myopic experiences. Playing in the line, Junior always said, had prepared him for law school. Hard work, but boring, boring, boring.

Now Junior ran the Black Arm of the Law, and I knew that when Franny was in New York, she stayed with him.

They were both stars, and maybe they were finally at ease with each other, I thought. But at Lilly's funeral, all I could think was how Lilly would have loved seeing them together.

Father, next to Susie the bear, kept the heavy end of his baseball bat on the floor between his knees—just swaying slightly. And when he walked—on Susie's arm, on the arm of Freud's former Seeing Eye bear—he carried the Louisville Slugger with great dignity, as if it were simply a stout sort of cane.

Susie was a wreck, but she held herself together at the funeral —for Father's sake, I think. She had worshiped my father ever since his miracle swing of the bat—the fabulous, instinctual swing that had batted Ernst the pornographer away. By the time of Lilly's suicide, Susie the bear had been around. She'd left the East Coast for the West, and then had come back East again. She ran a commune in Vermont for a while. 'I ran that fucker right into the ground,' she would tell us, laughing. She started a family counseling service in Boston, which blossomed into a day care center (because there was a greater need for one of those), which blossomed into a rape crisis center (as soon as day care centers were everywhere). The rape crisis center was not welcome in Boston, and Susie admits that not *all* the hostility was external. There were rape lovers and women haters everywhere, of course, and a variety of stupid people who were willing to assume that women who worked in a rape crisis center *had* to be what Susie called 'hardcore dykes and feminist troublemakers.' The Bostonians gave Susie and her first rape crisis center a rather hard time. Apparently, as a way of making their point, they even raped one of the rape crisis center employees. But, even Susie admits, some of the rape crisis women in those early days *were* 'hardcore dykes and feminist troublemakers,' they really *were* just man haters, and so *some* of the trouble at the rape crisis center was internal. Some of those women were simply anti-system philosophers without Frank's sense of humor, and if the law-enforcement personnel were antagonistic to women wanting to see a little rape justice—for a change—so were the women antagonistic to the law, in general, and nobody really did the *victim* much good.

Susie's rape crisis center, in Boston, was broken up when some of the man haters castrated an alleged rapist in a parking lot in Back Bay. Susie had come back to New York—she had gone back to family counseling. She specialized in child beatings—'dealing with,' as she would say, both the children and the beaters—but she was sick of New York City (she said it was no fun to live in Greenwich Village if you *weren't* a bear) and she was convinced that she had a future in rape crisis.

Having witnessed her performance at the Stanhope in 1964, I had to agree. Franny always said it was a better performance than any performance *Franny* would ever give, and Franny is very good. The way Franny held herself together for her one-line part in dealing with Chipper Dove must have given her the necessary confidence. In fact, in all her later films, Franny would make that old line live again: 'Well, look who's here.' She always finds a way to slip in that lovely line. She does not use her own name, of course. Movie stars almost never do. And Franny Berry isn't exactly the sort of name that people notice.

Franny's Hollywood name, her acting name, is one you know. This is our family's story, and it's inappropriate for me to use Franny's stage name—but I know that you know her. Franny is the one you always desire. She is the best one, even when she's the villain; she's always the real hero, even when she dies, even when she dies for love—or worse, for war. She's the most beautiful, the most unapproachable, but the most vulnerable, too, somehow—and the toughest. (She's why you go to the movie, or why you stay.) Others dream of her, now—now that she had freed me from dreaming about her in quite such a devastating way. Now I can live with what *I* dream about Franny, but there must be members of her audience who don't live so well with what they dream about her.

She made the adjustment to her fame very easily. It was an adjustment Lilly could never have made, but Franny made it easily—because she was always our family's star. She was used to being the main attraction, the center of everyone's attention—the one we waited for, the one we listened to. She was born to the leading role.

'And I was born to be a miserable fucking *agent*,' Frank said gloomily, after Lilly's funeral. 'I have agented even this,' he said, meaning Lilly's death. 'She wasn't big enough for all the shit I gave her to do!' he said, morosely; then he began to cry.

We tried to cheer him up, but Frank said, 'I'm always the fucking *agent,* damn it. I bring it all about—that's me. Look at Sorrow!' he howled. 'Who stuffed him? Who started the whole story?' Frank cried, crying and crying. 'I'm just the asshole agent,' he blubbered.

But Father reached out to Frank, the baseball bat as his antenna, and he said, 'Frank, Frank, my boy. *You're* not the agent of Lilly's trouble, Frank,' Father said. 'Who is the family dreamer, Frank?' Father asked, and we all looked at him. 'Well, it's *me—I'm* the dreamer, Frank,' Father said. 'And Lilly just dreamed more than she could *do,* Frank. She *inherited* the damn dreams,' Father said. 'From me.'

'But I was her agent,' Frank said, stupidly.

'Yes, but that doesn't matter, Frank,' Franny said. 'I mean, it matters that you're *my* agent, Frank—I really need you,' Franny told him. 'But *nobody* could be Lilly's agent, Frank.'

'It wouldn't have mattered, Frank,' I told him—because he was always saying this to me. 'It wouldn't have mattered who her agent was, Frank.'

'But it was me,' he said—he was so infuriatingly stubborn!

'Christ, Frank,' Franny said. 'It's easier to talk to your *answering* service.' That finally brought him around.

For a while we would have to endure the wall of worshipful wailers: Lilly's suicide cult—they were her fans who thought that Lilly's suicide was her ultimate statement, was the proof of her seriousness. This was ironic in Lilly's case, because Frank and Franny and I knew that Lilly's suicide—from Lilly's point of view—was the ultimate admission that she was not serious *enough.* But these people insisted on loving her for what she least loved in herself.

A group of Lilly's suicide fans even wrote to Franny, requesting that Franny travel to the nation's college campuses giving readings from Lilly's work—as Lilly. It was Franny the actress they were appealing to: they wanted Franny to play Lilly.

And we remembered Lilly's only writer-in-residence role, and her account of the only English Department meeting she ever attended. In the meeting, the Lecture Committee revealed that there was only enough money remaining for two more visits by moderately well-known poets, or one more visit by a well-known writer or a poet, *or* they could contribute *all* the remaining money toward the considerable expenses asked by a woman who was traveling the nation's campuses 'doing' Virginia Woolf. Although Lilly was the only person in this English Department who actually taught any of Virginia Woolf's books in her courses, she found that she was alone in resisting the department's wishes to invite the Virginia Woolf impersonator. 'I think Virginia Woolf would have wanted the money to go to a living writer,' Lilly said. 'To a *real* writer,' she added. But the department insisted that they wanted all the money to go to the woman who 'did' Virginia Woolf.

'Okay,' Lilly finally said. 'I'll agree, but only if the woman does it *all*. Only if she goes all the way.' There was a silence in the English Department meeting and someone asked Lilly if she was really serious—if she could possibly be in such 'bad taste' as to suggest that the woman come to the campus to commit suicide.

And my sister Lilly said, 'It is what my brother Frank would call disgusting that you—as teachers of literature—would actually spend money on an actress imitating a dead writer, whose work you do not teach, rather than spend it on a living writer, whose work you probably haven't read. Especially,' said Lilly, 'when you consider that the woman whose work is not being taught, and whose person is being imitated, was virtually *obsessed* with the difference between greatness and *posing*. And you want to *pay* someone to pose as *her?* You should be ashamed,' Lilly told them. 'Go ahead and bring the woman here,' Lilly added. 'I'll give her the rocks to put in her pockets; I'll lead her to the river.'

And that is what Franny told the group who wanted her to pose as Lilly and 'do' the nation's campuses. 'You should be ashamed,' Franny said. 'Besides,' she added, 'I am much too tall to play Lilly. My sister was really *short*.'

This, by the suicide fans, was construed as Franny's insensitivity—and by association, in various aspects of the news, our family was characterized as being indifferent to Lilly's death (for our unwillingness to take part in these Lilly *poses*). In frustration, Frank volunteered to 'do' Lilly at a public reading from the works of suicidal poets and writers. Naturally, none of the writers or poets were reading from their own work; various hired readers, sympathetic to the work of the deceased—or worse, sympathetic to their 'life-style,' which nearly always meant their 'death-style'—would read the work of the suicides as if they *were* the dead authors come back to life. Franny wanted no part of this, either, but Frank volunteered; he was rejected. 'On the grounds of "insincerity,"' he said. 'They surmised I was

411

insincere. Fucking *right* I was!' he shouted. 'They could all stand a fucking overdose of insincerity!' he added.

And Junior Jones would marry Franny—finally! 'This is a fairy tale,' Franny told me, long distance, 'but Junior and I have decided that if we save it any longer, we won't have anything worth saving.' Franny was sneaking up on forty at the time. The Black Arm of the Law and Hollywood had, at least, *Schlagobers* and blood in common. I suppose that Franny and Junior Jones would strike people—in their New York and their Los Angeles life—as 'glamorous,' but I often think that so-called glamorous people are just very busy people. Junior and Franny were consumed by their work, and they succumbed to the comfort of having each other's arms to fall exhausted into.

I was truly happy for them, and only sorry that they both announced that they would have no time for kids. 'I don't want children if I can't take care of them,' Franny said.

'Ditto, man,' said Junior Jones.

And one night Susie the bear told me that *she* didn't want children either, because the children she gave birth to would be ugly, and she wouldn't bring an ugly child into the world—not for anything, she said; it was simply the cruelest life one could expose a child to: the discrimination suffered by people who aren't good-looking.

'But you're *not* ugly, Susie,' I told her. 'You just take a little getting used to,' I told her. 'I think you're really attractive, if you want to know.' And I *did* think so; I thought Susie the bear was a hero.

'You're sick, then,' Susie said. 'I got a face like a hatchet, like a chisel with a bad complexion. And I got a body like a paper bag,' she said. 'Like a paper bag of cold oatmeal,' Susie said.

'I think you're very nice,' I told her, and I did; Franny had shown me how lovable Susie the bear was. And I had heard the song Susie the bear taught Franny to sing; I'd had some interesting dreams concerning Susie's teaching me a song like that. So I repeated to her, 'I think you're very nice.'

'Then you've got a *brain* like a paper bag of cold oatmeal,' Susie told me. 'If you think I'm very nice, you're a real sick boy.'

And one night when there were no guests in the Hotel New Hampshire, I heard a peculiar creeping sound; Father was as likely to walk around at night as he was likely to walk around in the daylight—because, of course, it was always nighttime for him. But wherever Father went, the Louisville Slugger trailed after him or searched ahead of him, and as he grew older his gait more and more resembled the gait of Freud, as if Father had psychologically developed a limp—as a form of kinship to the old interpreter of dreams. Also, wherever Father went, Seeing Eye Dog Number Four went with him! We were negligent about keeping Four's toenails clipped, so that Father, accompanied by Four, made quite a clatter.

Old Fred, the handyman, had a room on the third floor and slept like a stone at the bottom of the sea; he slept as soundly as the abandoned weirs, ruined by seals and now sunk in the mud flats, now rinsed by the tide. Old Fred was a sundown and sunup sort of sleeper; because he was deaf, he said, he didn't like to be up at night. Especially in summer, the Marine nights are vibrant with noise—at least when you compare the nights to the Maine *days*.

'The opposite of New York,' Frank liked to say. 'The only time it's quiet on Central Park South is about three in the morning. But in Maine,' Frank liked to say, 'about three in the morning is about the *only* time anything's going on. Fucking nature comes to life.'

It was about three in the morning, I noted—a summer night, with the insect world teeming; the seabirds sounded fairly restful but the sea was no less determined. And I heard this peculiar creeping sound. It was at first hard to tell if it was outside my window, which was open—though there was a screen—or if the sound was outside my door, in the hall. My door was open, too; and the outside doors to the Hotel New Hampshire were never locked—there were too many of them.

A racoon, I thought.

But then something much heavier than any raccoon shuffled across the bare floor at the landing to the stairs and softly padded down the carpeted hall toward my door; I could feel the *weight* of whatever it was—it was making the floorboards sigh. Even the sea seemed to quiet itself, even the sea seemed to listen to whatever it was—it was the kind of sound you hear in the night that makes the tide pause, that makes the birds (who never fly at night) float up to the sky and hang suspended as if they were painted there.

'Four?' I whispered, thinking that the dog might be on the prowl, but whatever was in the hall was too tentative to be

Seeing Eye Dog Number Four. Four had been in the hall before; old Four wouldn't be pausing at every door.

I wished I had Father's baseball bat, but when the bear lurched into my doorway I realized there was no weapon in the Hotel New Hampshire powerful enough to protect me from *this* intruder. I lay very still, pretending to be sound asleep—with my eyes wide open. In the flat, blurred, flannel-soft light of the predawn, the bear seemed huge. It stared into my room, at my motionless bed, like an old nurse taking a bed check in a hospital; I tried not to breathe, but the bear knew I was there. It sniffed, deeply; and very gracefully, on all fours, it came into my room. Well, why not? I was thinking. A bear began my life's fairy tale; it is fitting that a bear should end it. The bear shoved its warm face near mine and breathed in everything about me; with one purposeful sniff, it seemed to review my life's story —and in a gesture resembling commiseration, it placed its heavy paw on my hip. It was quite a warm summer night—for Maine —and I was naked, covered by just a sheet. The bear's breath was hot, and a little fruity—perhaps it had just been feeding in the wild blueberries—but it was surprisingly pleasant breath, if not exactly fresh. When the bear drew back the sheet and looked me over, I felt just the tip of the iceberg of fear that Chipper Dove must have felt when he truly believed that a bear *in heat* wanted him. But this bear rather disrespectfully snorted at what it saw. 'Earl!' said the bear, and rather roughly shoved me; it made room beside me for itself and crawled into my bed with me. It was only when it embraced me, and I identified the most distinctive component of its strange and powerful scent, that I suspected this was no ordinary bear. Mixed with the pleasure of its fruited breath, and the mustard-green sharpness of its summer sweat, I detected the obvious odor of *mothballs*.

'Susie?' I said.

'Thought you'd never guess,' she said.

'Susie!' I cried, and turned to her, returning her embrace; I had never been so happy to see her.

'Keep it down,' Susie ordered me. 'Don't wake up your father. I've been crawling all over this fucking hotel trying to find you. I found your father first, and someone who says "What?" in his sleep, and I met an absolute *moron* of a dog who didn't even know I was a bear—the fucker wagged his tail and went right back to sleep. What a watchdog! And fucking *Frank* gave me the directions—I don't think Frank should be trusted to give the directions to *Maine*, much less to *this* queer little part of

414

the wretched state. Holy cow,' said Susie, 'I just wanted to see you before it got light, I wanted to get to you while it was still dark, for Christ's sake, and I must have left New York about noon, yesterday, and now it's almost fucking dawn,' she said. 'And I'm exhausted,' she added; she started to cry. 'I'm sweating like a pig in this dumb fucking suit, but I smell so bad and look so awful I don't dare take it off.'

'Take it off,' I told her. 'You smell very nice.'

'Oh sure,' she said, still crying. But I coaxed her out of the bear head. She smudged her tears with her paws, but I held her paws and kissed her on the mouth for a while. I think I was right about the blueberries; that's what Susie tastes like, to me: wild blueberries.

'You taste very nice,' I told her.

'Oh sure,' she mumbled, but she let me help her out of the rest of the bear suit. It was like a sauna inside there. I realized that Susie was built like a bear, and she was as slick with sweat as a bear fresh out of a lake. I realized how I admired her—for her bearishness, for her complicated courage.

'I'm very fond of you, Susie,' I said, closing my door and getting back into bed with her.

'Hurry up, it will be light soon,' she said, 'and then you'll see how ugly I am.'

'I can see you now,' I said, 'and I think you're lovely.'

'You're going to have to work hard to convince me,' said Susie the bear.

For some years now I have been convincing Susie the bear that she is lovely. *I* think so, of course, and in a few more years, I think, Susie will finally agree. Bears are stubborn but they are sane creatures; once you gain their trust, they will not shy away from you.

At first Susie was so obsessed with her ugliness that she took every conceivable precaution against a possible pregnancy, believing that the worst thing on earth for her to do would be to bring a poor child into this cruel world and allow him or her to suffer the treatment that is usually bestowed upon the ugly. When I first started sleeping with Susie the bear, she was taking the Pill, and she also wore a diaphragm; she put so much spermicidal jelly on the diaphragm that I had to suppress the feeling that we were engaging in an act of overkill—to sperm. To ease me over this peculiar anxiety, Susie insisted that I wear a prophylactic, too.

'That's the trouble with men,' she used to say. 'You got to

arm yourself so heavily before you dare do it with them that you sometimes lose sight of the purpose.'

But Susie has calmed down, recently. She seems to feel that *one* method of birth control is adequate. And if the accident happens I can't help but hope that she will accept it bravely. Of course, I wouldn't push her to have a baby if she didn't want to; those people who want to make people have babies they don't want to have are ogres.

'But even if I weren't too ugly,' Susie protests, 'I'm too old. I mean, after forty you can have all sorts of complications. I might not just have an ugly baby, I might not even *have* a baby —I might give birth to a kind of *banana!* After forty, it's pretty risky.'

'Nonsense, Susie,' I tell her. 'We'll just get you in shape—a little light work with the weights, a little running. You're young at heart, Susie,' I tell her. 'The *bear in you,* Susie, is still a *cub.*'

'Convince me,' she tells me, and I know what that means. That's our euphemism for it—whenever we want each other. She will just say, out of the blue, to me, 'I need to be convinced.'

Or I will say to her, 'Susie, you look in need of a little convincing.'

Or else Susie will just say 'Earl!' to me, and I'll know exactly what she means.

When we got married, that's what she said when she came to her moment to say 'I do.' Susie said, 'Earl!'

'What?' the minister said.

'Earl!' Susie said, nodding.

'She *does,*' I told the minister. 'That means she does.'

I suppose that neither Susie nor I will ever, quite, get over Franny, but we have our love for Franny in common, and that's more to have in common than whatever thing it is that's held in common by most couples. And if Susie was once Freud's eyes, I now see for my father, so that Susie and I have the vision of Freud in common, too. 'You got a marriage made in heaven, man,' Junior Jones has told me.

That morning after I'd first made love to Susie the bear I was a little late meeting Father in the ballroom for our weight-lifting session.

He was already lifting hard when I staggered in.

'Four hundred and sixty-four,' I said to him, because this was our traditional greeting. Recalling that old rogue, Schnitzler,

Father and I thought it was a very funny way for two men living without women to greet each other.

'Four hundred and sixty-four, my eye!' Father grunted. 'Four hundred and sixty-four—like hell! I had to listen to you half the night. Jesus God, I may be blind, but I can *hear*. By my count you're down to about four hundred and fifty-eight. You haven't got four hundred and sixty-four left in you—not anymore. Who the hell is she? I've never imagined such an *animal!*'

But when I told him I'd been with Susie the bear, and that I very much hoped she would stay and live with us, Father was delighted.

'That's what we've been missing!' he cried. 'That's really perfect. I mean, you couldn't ask for a better hotel. I think you've handled the hotel business brilliantly! But we need a bear. Everybody does! And now that you've got the bear, you're home free, John. Now you've finally written the happy ending.'

Not quite, I thought. But, all things considered—given sorrow, given doom, given love—I knew things could be much worse.

So what is missing? Just a child, I think. A child is missing. I wanted a child, and I still want one. Given Egg, and given Lilly, children are all I am missing, now. I still might convince Susie, the bear, of course, but Franny and Junior Jones will provide me with my first child. Even Susie is unafraid for *that* child.

'*That* child is going to be a beauty,' Susie says. 'With Franny and Junior making it, how can it miss?'

'But how could *we* miss?' I ask her. 'As soon as you have it, believe me, it will be beautiful.'

'But just think of the *color*,' Susie says. 'I mean, with Junior and Franny making it, won't it be an absolutely gorgeous fucking color?'

But I know, as Junior Jones has told me, that Franny and Junior's baby might be *any* color—'I'll give it a range between coffee and milk,' Junior likes to say.

'*Any* color baby is going to be a gorgeous-colored baby, Susie,' I tell her. 'You know that.' But Susie just needs more convincing.

I think that when Susie *sees* Junior and Franny's baby, it will make her want one, too. That's what I hope, anyway—because I am almost forty, and Susie has already crossed that bridge, and if we're going to have a baby, we shouldn't wait much longer. I

417

think that Franny's baby will do the trick; even Father agrees —even Frank.

And isn't it just like Franny to be so generous as to offer to have a baby for *me?* I mean, from that day in Vienna when she promised us all that she was going to take care of us, that she was going to be our mother, from that day forth, Franny has stuck to her guns, Franny has come through—the hero in her has kept pumping, the hero in Franny could lift a ballroom full of barbells.

It was just last winter, after the big snow, when Franny called me to say that she was going to have a baby—just for me. Franny was forty at the time; she said that having a baby was closing the door to a room she wouldn't be coming back to. It was so early in the morning when the phone rang that both Susie and I thought it was the rape crisis center hot-line phone, and Susie jumped out of bed thinking she had another rape crisis on her hands, but it was just the regular telephone that was ringing, and it was Franny—all the way out on the West Coast. She and Junior were staying up late and having a party or two together; they hadn't gone to bed, yet, they said—they pointed out that it was still night in California. They sounded a little drunk, and silly, and Susie was cross with them; she told them that no one but a rape victim ever called us that early in the morning and then she handed the phone to me.

I had to give Franny the usual report on how the rape crisis center was doing. Franny has donated quite a bit of money to the center, and Junior has helped us get good legal advice in our Maine area. Just last year Susie's rape crisis center gave medical, psychological, and legal counsel to ninety-one victims of rape—or of rape-related abuse. 'Not bad, for Maine,' as Franny says.

'In New York and L.A., man,' says Junior Jones, 'there's about ninety-one thousand victims a year. Of *everything*,' he adds.

It wasn't hard to convince Susie that all those rooms in the Hotel New Hampshire could be used for something. We're a more than adequate facility for a rape crisis center, and Susie has trained several of the women from the college in Brunswick, so we always have a woman here to answer the hot-line phone. Susie has instructed me never to answer the hot-line phone. 'The last thing a rape victim wants to hear, when she calls for help,' Susie has told me, 'is a fucking *man's* voice.'

Of course it's been a little complicated with Father, who can't

418

see which phone is ringing. So Father, when he's caught off guard by a ringing phone, has developed this habit of yelling, 'Telephone!' Even if he's standing right next to it.

Surprisingly, although Father still thinks that the Hotel New Hampshire is a hotel, he is not bad at rape counseling. I mean, he knows that rape crisis is Susie's business—he just doesn't know that it's our only business, and sometimes he starts a conversation with a rape victim who's recovering herself with us at the Hotel New Hampshire, for a few days, and Father gets her confused with what he thinks is one of the 'guests.'

He might happen upon the victim, just composing herself down on one of the docks, and my father will tap-tap-tap his Louisville Slugger out onto the dock, and Four will wag his tail to let my father know that someone is there, and Father will start chatting. 'Hello, who's here?' he'll ask.

And maybe the rape victim will say, 'It's just me, Sylvia.'

'Oh yes, Sylvia!' Father will say, as if he's known her all his life. 'Well, how do you like the hotel, Sylvia?' And poor Sylvia will think that this is my father's very polite and indirect way of referring to the rape crisis center—'the hotel'—and she'll just go along with it.

'Oh, it's meant a lot to me,' she'll say. 'I mean, I really needed to talk, but I didn't want to feel I had to talk about anything until I was ready, and what's nice here is that nobody pressures you, nobody tells you what you *ought* to feel or ought to do, but they help you get to those feelings more easily than you might get to them all by yourself. If you know what I mean,' Sylvia will say.

And Father will say, 'Of course I know what you mean, dear. We've been in the business for years, and that's just what a good hotel does: it simply provides you with the space, and with the atmosphere, for what it is you *need*. A good hotel turns space and atmosphere into something generous, into something sympathetic—a good hotel makes those gestures that are like touching you, or saying a kind word to you, just when (and *only* when) you need it. A good hotel is always there,' my father will say, the baseball bat conducting both his lyrics and his song, 'but it doesn't ever give you the feeling that it's breathing down your neck.'

'Yeah, that's it, I guess,' Sylvia will say; or Betsy, or Patricia, Columbine, Sally, Alice, Constance, or Hope will say. 'It gets it all *out* of me, somehow, but not by force,' they'll say.

'No, never by force, my dear,' Father will agree. 'A good

419

hotel forces nothing. I like to call it just a *sympathy* space,'
Father will say, never acknowledging his debt to Schraubenschlüssel and his sympathy bomb.

'And,' Sylvia will say, 'everyone's nice here.'

'Yes, that's what I like about a good hotel!' Father will say,
excitedly. 'Everyone *is* nice. In a *great* hotel,' he'll tell Sylvia,
or anybody who'll listen to him, 'you have a right to *expect* that
niceness. You come to us, my dear—and please forgive me for
saying so—like someone who's been maimed, and we're your
doctors and your nurses.'

'Yes, that's right,' Sylvia will say.

'If you come to a great hotel in *parts,* in broken pieces,' my
father will go on and on, 'when you leave the great hotel, you'll
leave it *whole* again. We simply put you back together again, but
this is almost mystically accomplished—this is the sympathy
space I'm talking about—because you can't *force* anyone back
together again; they have to grow their own way. We provide
space,' Father will say, the baseball bat blessing the rape victim
like a magic wand. 'The space and the *light,*' my father will say,
as if he were a holy man blessing some other holy person.

And that's how you should treat a rape victim, Susie says;
they are holy, and you treat them as a great hotel treats every
guest. Every guest at a great hotel is an honored guest, and every
rape victim at the Hotel New Hampshire is an honored guest
—and holy.

'It's actually a good name for a rape crisis center,' Susie
agrees. 'The Hotel New Hampshire—that's got a little class to
it.'

And with the support of the county authorities, and a
wonderful organization of women doctors called the Kennebec
Women's Medical Associates, we run a real rape crisis center in
our unreal hotel. Susie sometimes tells me that Father is the best
counselor she's got.

'When someone's really fucked up,' Susie confides in me, 'I
send them down to the docks to see the blind man and Seeing
Eye Dog Number Four. Whatever he tells them must be
working,' Susie concludes. 'At least, so far, nobody's jumped
off.'

'Keep passing the open windows, my dear,' my father will tell
just about anyone. 'That's the important thing, dear,' he adds.
No doubt it is Lilly who lends such authority to my father's
advice. He was always good at advising us children—even when
he knew absolutely nothing about what was wrong. 'Maybe

420

especially when he knows absolutely nothing,' Frank says. 'I mean, he *still* doesn't know I'm queer and he gives me good advice all the time.' What a knack!

'Okay, okay,' Franny said to me on the phone, just last winter, just after the big snow. 'I didn't call you to hear the ins and outs of every rape in Maine—not *this* time, kid,' Franny told me. 'Do you still want a baby?'

'Of *course* I do,' I told her. 'I'm trying to convince Susie of it, every day.'

'Well,' Franny said, 'how'd you like a baby of mine?'

'But *you* don't want a baby, Franny,' I reminded her. 'What do you mean?'

'I mean Junior and I got a little sloppy,' Franny said. 'And rather than do the modern thing, we thought we knew the perfect mother and father for a baby.'

'Especially these days, man,' Junior said, on his end of the phone. 'I mean, Maine may be the last hideout.'

'Every kid should grow up in a weird hotel, don't you agree?' Franny asked.

'What I thought, man,' said Junior Jones, 'was that every kid should have at least one parent who does *nothing*. I don't mean to insult you, man,' Junior said to me, 'but you're just a perfect sort of *caretaker*. You know what I mean?'

'He means, you look after everybody,' Franny said, sweetly. 'He means, it's kind of like your *role*. You're a perfect father.'

'Or a mother, man,' Junior added.

'And when Susie's got a baby around, perhaps she'll see the light,' Franny said.

'Maybe she'll get brave enough to give it a shot, man,' said Junior Jones. 'So to speak,' he added, and Franny howled on her end of the phone. They'd obviously been cooking this phone call up together, for quite some time.

'Hey!' Franny said on the phone. 'Cat got your tongue? Are you there? Hello, hello?'

'Hey, man,' said Junior Jones. 'You passed out or something?'

'Has a bear got your balls?' Franny asked me. 'I'm asking you, do you want my baby?'

'That's not a frivolous question, man,' said Junior Jones.

'Yes or no, kid?' Franny said. 'I love you, you know,' she added. 'I wouldn't have a baby for just *anybody*, you know, kid.' But I couldn't speak, I was so happy.

421

'I'm offering you nine fucking months of my life! I'm offering you nine months of my beautiful *body*, kid!' Franny teased me. 'Take it or leave it!'

'Man!' cried Junior Jones. 'Your sister, whose body is desired by millions, is offering to change her *shape* for you. She's willing to look like a fucking Coke bottle just to give you a baby, man. I don't know exactly how I'm going to put up with it,' he added, 'but we *both* love you, you know. What do you say? Take it or leave it.'

'I *love* you!' Franny added to me, fiercely. 'I'm trying to give you what you *need*, John,' she told me.

But Susie the bear took the phone from me. 'For Christ's sake,' she said to Franny and Junior, 'you wake us up with what I'm sure is another fucking rape and now you've got him all red in the face and unable to *speak!* What the fuck is going on this morning, anyway?'

'If Junior and I have a baby,' Franny asked Susie, 'will you and John take care of it?'

'You bet your sweet ass, honey,' said my good Susie the bear.

And so the matter was decided. We're still waiting. Leave it to Franny to take longer than anybody else. 'Leave it to *me*, man,' says Junior Jones. 'This baby's going to be so big it needs a little more time in the cooker than most.'

He must be right, because Franny's been carrying my baby for almost ten months now. 'She's big enough to play for the Browns,' Junior Jones complains; I call him every night for a progress report.

'Jesus God,' Franny says to me. 'I just lie in bed all day, waiting to *explode*. I'm so bored. The things I suffer for you, my love,' she tells me—and we share a private laugh over that.

Susie goes around singing 'Any Day Now,' and Father is lifting more and more weight; Father is weight lifting with a frenzy these days. He is convinced the baby will be *born* a weight lifter, and Father says he's got to get in shape to handle it. And all the rape crisis women are being very patient with me —about the way I lunge for the phone when it rings (toward *either* phone). 'It's just the hot line,' they tell me. 'Relax.'

'It's probably just another rape, honey,' Susie reassures me. 'It's not your baby. Calm down.'

It's not at all that I'm anxious to discover if it will be a boy or a girl. For once I agree with Frank. It doesn't matter. Nowadays, of course, with the precautionary tests they take—especially with a woman Franny's age—they already *know* the sex of the child; or *someone* knows. Not Franny—she didn't want to know. Who wants to know such things in advance? Who doesn't know that half of pleasure lies in the wonder of anticipation?

'Whatever it is, it's going to be bored,' Frank says.

'Bored, Frank!' Franny howls. 'How *dare* you say my baby will be bored?'

But Frank is just expressing a typical New York City opinion of growing up in Maine. 'If the baby grows up in Maine,' Frank insists, 'it will *have* to be bored.'

But I point out to Frank that life is never boring in the Hotel New Hampshire. Not in the lighthearted first Hotel New Hampshire, not in the darkness of the dream that was the second Hotel New Hampshire, and not in our third Hotel New Hampshire, either—not in the *great* hotel we have at last become. No one is bored. And Frank finally agrees; he is a frequent and ever-welcome guest here, after all. He takes over the library on the second floor the way Junior Jones dominates the barbells in the ballroom when *he* is visiting, the way Franny's beauty graces every room when *she* is here—the good Maine air and the cold Maine sea: Franny graces it all. I fully expect that Franny's child will have a similar good influence.

To comfort her, I tried to read Franny a Donald Justice poem over the phone, the one called 'To a Ten-Months' Child.'

> Late arrival, no
> One would think of blaming you
> For hesitating so.
>
> Who, setting his hand to knock
> At a door so strange as this one,
> Might not draw back?

'Hold it right there,' Franny interrupted me. 'No more fucking Donald Justice, please. I've heard enough Donald Justice poems to get *pregnant* from them, or at least sick to my stomach.'

But Donald Justice is right, as usual. Who *wouldn't* hesitate to come into this world? Who wouldn't put off this fairy tale as long as possible? Already, you see, Franny's child is indicating a remarkable insight, a rare sensitivity.

And yesterday it snowed; in Maine we learn to take weather personally. Susie was investigating the alleged rape of a waitress in Bath, and I was worried about her driving back in the storm,

423

but Susie was safely home before dark and we both said how this storm reminded us of the big snow of last winter, of the day Franny called to tell us about her coming gift.

Father plays like a child in the snow. 'Snow is quite a wonder to the blind,' he said just yesterday, coming into the kitchen all covered with it; he'd been out in the drifts, literally rolling around with Seeing Eye Dog Number Four—they were both covered with it. It was a wild storm; by three-thirty in the afternoon we had to turn all the lights on. I stoked up the fires in two of the woodstoves. A bird, blinded by the snow, had flown through a windowpane in the ballroom and broken its neck. Four found it lying by the barbells and carried it all around the hotel before Susie could get it away from the dog. The snow melted off Father's boots and made the kitchen slippery. Father slipped in a puddle and whacked me in the ribs with the Louisville Slugger—which he always waves wildly whenever he is thrown off balance. We had a little argument about that. Just like a child, he won't knock the snow off his boots *before* he comes inside.

'I can't *see* the snow!' he complains, childishly. 'How the fuck do I knock it off if I can't see it?'

'Shut up, both of you,' Susie the bear told us. 'When there's a child in the house, you'll both have to stop *yelling*.'

I made some fresh pasta with a neat machine Frank brought from New York; it flattens the dough in sheets and cuts the pasta into any shape you want. It's important to have toys like that, if you live in Maine. Susie made a mussel sauce for the pasta. Father chopped up the onion for her; an onion never seems to bother Father's eyes. When we heard Four bark, we thought he'd found another poor bird. We saw a Volkswagen bus trying to make its way up our driveway in the storm; the bus was slithering and sliding. Whoever was driving the bus was either excited ('Another fucking rape,' said Susie, instinctively), or else it was someone from out of state. No Maine driver would have so much trouble driving in the snow, I thought, but it was hardly the tourist time of year at the Hotel New Hampshire. The bus couldn't make it all the way to the parking lot, but it got close enough for me to see the Arizona license plate.

'No wonder they can't drive,' I said—which is a typical Maine point of view toward out-of-staters.

'Yeah, well,' Susie said. 'You'd probably look like an idiot in an Arizona desert.'

'What's a desert?' Father asked, and Susie laughed.

The driver of the Arizona bus was walking through the snow toward us; he didn't even know how to walk in the snow—he kept falling down.

'They've had a rape all the way out in Arizona, Susie,' I told her. 'And you're so famous, they'll only talk to *you*.'

'Don't they know we're a *resort* hotel?' Father asked, peevishly. 'I'll tell whoever it is that we're closed for the season.'

The man from Arizona was sorry to hear that. He explained that he thought he was headed for the mountains, for some skiing —which he and his family had never tried before—but that he'd been given some bad directions or he got lost in the storm, and here he was at the ocean, instead.

'Wrong season for the ocean,' Father pointed out. The man could see that. He looked nice, but awfully tired.

'We *do* have enough room,' Susie whispered to me.

I didn't want to start taking in guests; in fact, what I loved best about *this* Hotel New Hampshire was that the only guests were in Father's mind. But when I saw all the little kids pile out of the Volkswagen bus and start playing in the snow, I had a change of heart. The mother looked awfully tired, too—nice but tired.

'What's *that?*' one of the kids was screaming.

'It's an ocean, I think,' the mother said.

'An *ocean!*' the children shouted.

'Is there a beach, too?' one of the kids cried.

'Under all that snow, I guess,' the mother told them.

So we invited the man and his wife and his four little children to be our guests in the Hotel New Hampshire, even though we were 'closed for the season.' It's easy to make more pasta; it's easy to stretch a mussel sauce.

Father got a little confused, showing our guests to their rooms. It was the first time he'd had to show a guest to a room in *this* Hotel New Hampshire, and it occurred to him, as he was hunting for linen in the library, that he didn't know where anything was. I had to help him, naturally, and I did a fair job of pretending that I showed guests to their rooms all the time.

'You'll have to forgive us if we seem a little unprofessional,' I told the father of the nice young family. 'When we're closed for the season, we get a little out of practice.'

'It's sweet of you to take us in,' the nice young mother said. 'The kids were disappointed not to see the skiing, but they've never seen an ocean, either, so it's a treat for them. And they can

425

get to the skiing tomorrow,' she added. She sounded like a good mother to me.

'I'm expecting a child myself,' I told her. Any day now.' And only later did Susie point out to me that my remark must have seemed odd, since even Susie was clearly not pregnant.

'What the hell must they have thought you *meant*, you moron!' Susie said.

But everything was fine. The kids had wonderful appetites, and after dinner I showed them how to make an apple pie. And while the pie was baking, I took them for a scary, wintry walk down to the snow-blown beach and the drifted-over docks; I showed them the violent waves bashing through the laces of ice that fringed the shore, I showed them that the sea in a storm is a great gray swell of water rolling, forever rolling. My father, of course, told the young husband and wife from Arizona all about the fabulous space for sympathy that a truly great hotel provides; he described our hotel to the nice people from Arizona, Susie told me, as if he were describing the Sacher.

'But it's as if we *are* the Sacher, to him,' the warm bear said in my arms that night, while the storm howled and the snow fell.

'Yes, my love,' I told her.

It was wonderful to lie in bed in the morning and hear the voices of the children; they had discovered the barbells in the ballroom, and Father was giving them pointers. Iowa Bob would have loved *this* Hotel New Hampshire, I thought.

That was when I woke up Susie and asked her to get into the bear suit.

'*Earl!*' she complained. 'I'm too old to be a bear anymore.' She is a bit of a bear in the early morning—my dear Susie.

'Come on, Susie,' I said. 'Do it for the kids. Think of what it will mean to them.'

'What?' Susie said. 'You want me to scare children?'

'No, no, Susie,' I said. 'Not *scare* them.' All I wanted her to do was dress up in the bear suit and walk outside, in the snow, around the hotel, and I would suddenly call out, 'Look! *Bear* tracks in the snow! And they're *fresh!*'

And the people, big and small, from Arizona would all come out and wonder over the *wilderness* they had stumbled upon, as if in a dream, and then I would cry, 'Look! There's the bear! Going around the woodpile!' And Susie would pause then —perhaps I could persuade her to give us a good *Earl!* or two —and she would disappear behind the woodpile, in her bearlike fashion, and slip in one of the back doors, and slip out of her

426

disguise, and come into the kitchen, saying, 'What's all this about a bear? You rarely see a bear around here anymore.'

'You want me to go outside in the fucking snow?' Susie asked.

'For the kids, Susie,' I said. 'What a treat it would be for them. First they see the ocean and then they see a *bear*. Everyone should see a bear, Susie,' I said. Of course she agreed. She was grouchy about it, but that made her performance all the better; Susie was always superb as a bear, and now she is getting convinced that she's a lovely human being, too.

And so we gave the strangers from Arizona a vision of a bear to take away with them. Father waved good-bye to them from the ballroom, after which he said to me, 'A bear, huh? Susie will catch her death, or at least pneumonia. And no one should be sick—no one should even have a cold—when the baby comes. I know more about babies than you do, you know. A *bear*,' he repeated, shaking his head, but I knew that the people from Arizona had been convinced; Susie the bear is a masterpiece of conviction.

The bear that paused by the woodpile, its breath a fog upon the bright, cold morning, its paws softly denting the fresh, untouched snow—as if it were the first bear on earth, and this the planet's first snow—*all* of it had been convincing. As Lilly knew, everything *is* a fairy tale.

So we dream on. Thus we invent our lives. We give ourselves a sainted mother, we make our father a hero; and someone's older brother, and someone's older sister—they become our heroes, too. We invent what we love, and what we fear. There is always a brave, lost brother—and a little lost sister, too. We dream on and on: the best hotel, the perfect family, the resort life. And our dreams escape us almost as vividly as we can imagine them.

In the Hotel New Hampshire, we're screwed down for life —but what's a little air in the pipes, or even a lot of shit in the hair, if you have good memories?

I hope this is a proper ending for you, Mother—and for you, Egg. It is an ending conscious of the manner of your favorite ending, Lilly—the one you never grew big enough to write. There may not be enough barbells in this ending to satisfy Iowa Bob, and not enough fatalism for Frank. There may not be enough of the nature of dreams in this ending for either Father or Freud. And not enough resilience for Franny. And I suppose it's not ugly enough for Susie the bear. It's probably not big enough for Junior Jones, and I know it's not nearly violent enough to please some of the friends and foes from our past; it might not merit so much as a moan from Screaming Annie—wherever she lies screaming now.

But this is what we do: we dream on, and our dreams escape us almost as vividly as we can imagine them. That's what happens, like it or not. And because that's what happens, this is what we need: we need a good, smart bear. Some people's minds are good enough so that they can live all by themselves —their *minds* can be their good, smart bears. That's the case with Frank, I think: Frank has a good, smart bear for a mind. He is not the King of Mice I first mistook him for. And Franny has a good, smart bear named Junior Jones. Franny is also skilled at keeping sorrow at bay. And my father has his illusions; they are powerful enough. My father's illusions are *his* good, smart bear —at last. And that leaves me, of course, with Susie the bear —with her rape crisis center and my fairy-tale hotel—so I'm all right, too. You have to be all right if you're expecting a baby.

Coach Bob knew it all along: you've got to get obsessed and stay obsessed. You have to keep passing the open windows.

THE END

THE WORLD ACCORDING TO GARP

BY JOHN IRVING

The most talked-about novel since *Catch-22*

'It is not easy to find words in which to convey the joy, the excitement, the passion this superb novel evokes. The imagination soars as Irving draws us inexorably into Garp's world, which is at once larger than life and as real as our own most private dreams of life and death, love lust and fear.'

Publishers Weekly

'Absolutely extraordinary ... a roller-coaster ride that leaves one breathless, exhausted, elated and tearful.'

Los Angeles Times Book Review

'Like all great works of art, Irving's novel seems to have always been there, a diamond sleeping in the dark, chipped out at last for our enrichment and delight ... as approachable as it is brilliant, *Garp* pulses with vital energy.'

Cosmopolitan

'A loopy novel of inspired anarchy.'

Mordecai Richler

'An extraordinary work, crammed with incidents, characters, feelings and craft ... John Irving moves into the front rank of America's young novelists.'

Time

0 552 11190 2   £1.95

SETTING FREE THE BEARS

BY JOHN IRVING

Siggy and Hannes are disenchanted students and exuberant fellow-conspirators. With their horny haunches astride a 700cc Royal Enfield, they roam the Austrian countryside, joined on their wild and uproarious adventures by the lovely, long-legged Callen, zeroing in on the Vienna Zoo and Siggy's life-long passion – setting free the bears ...

'The most nourishing, satisfying novel I have read in years. I admire the hell out of it.'

Kurt Vonnegut Jr.

'Sensual, moving, truly remarkable.'

Time

0 552 11191 0   £1.25

THE WATER-METHOD MAN

BY JOHN IRVING

A work of consummate artistry and comic invention, bizarre imagery and sharp social and psychological observation. John Irving's work escapes easy classification, but its original brilliance has already placed him at the front rank of contemporary American novelists.

'Brutal reality and hallucination, comedy and pathos. A rich, unified tapestry. Something of beauty.'

Time

'Irving's blend of gravity and play is unique, audacious.'

New Republic

'John Irving, it is abundantly clear, is a true artist. He is not afraid to take on great themes.'

Los Angeles Times

0 552 11266 6   £1.25

ZEN AND THE ART OF MOTOR CYCLE MAINTENANCE

BY ROBERT M. PIRSIG

This book has been hailed as one of the most unique and exciting books in the history of literature.

This book speaks directly to the confusions and agonies of existence. In the intimate detailing of a real-life odyssey – personal, philosophical – Robert M. Pirsig has written a touching, painful, and ultimately transcendent book of life.

This book is an autobiography of the mind and body. It takes the reader on a trip – in a literal, emotional and philosophical sense – that is not only unforgettable but also unlike anything you have previously experienced.

Not since CATCH 22 has a book been so overwhelmingly and universally praised.

0 552 10166 4   £1.95

SOMETHING HAPPENED BY JOSEPH HELLER

It was the madness of war which prompted the magnificent lunacy of CATCH 22; it is the malaise of modern America which inspires Joseph Heller's great new novel – a book as stunning and as splendidly unique as its predecessor.

'Mr Heller's disembowelments are ferocious, gory and memorable. In CATCH 22 he satirized the horrors of war: in *Something Happened* he has attempted something more ambitious and difficult – an expose of the horrors of prosperity and peace.'
Times Literary Supplement

'It is the anatomy of an American man – and through him of American society – written in depth and characterised by all the intelligence, frankness and wit which we would expect.'
Evening Standard

'. . . it would be a rare person who reads this book without many nods or shudders of recognition – Heller's book is another important contribution to contemporary self-consciousness.'
New Society

0 552 10220 2   £2.25

A SELECTED LIST
OF CORGI TITLES

WHILE EVERY EFFORT IS MADE TO KEEP PRICES LOW, IT IS SOMETIMES NECESSARY TO INCREASE PRICES AT SHORT NOTICE. CORGI BOOKS RESERVE THE RIGHT TO SHOW AND CHARGE NEW RETAIL PRICES ON COVERS WHICH MAY DIFFER FROM THOSE ADVERTISED IN THE TEXT OR ELSEWHERE.

THE PRICES SHOWN BELOW WERE CORRECT AT THE TIME OF GOING TO PRESS (SEPTEMBER '82)

☐	11552 5	**Just above my Head**	*James Baldwin* £1.95
☐	11564 9	**Another Country**	*James Baldwin* £1.95
☐	11340 9	**Good as Gold**	*Joseph Heller* £1.50
☐	10220 2	**Something Happened**	*Joseph Heller* £2.25
☐	09755 1	**Catch-22**	*Joseph Heller* £1.95
☐	11267 4	**The 158lb Marriage**	*John Irving* 95p
☐	11190 2	**The World According to Garp**	*John Irving* £1.95
☐	11191 0	**Setting Free the Bears**	*John Irving* £1.25
☐	10942 8	**Elephant Bangs Train**	*William Kotzwinkle* 85p
☐	10545 7	**Doctor Rat**	*William Kotzwinkle* 85p
☐	10166 4	**Zen and the Art of Motorcyle Maintenance**	*Robert M. Pirsig* £1.95
☐	11781 1	**Still Life with the Woodpecker**	*Tom Robbins* £1.50
☐	11827 3	**Even Cowgirls Get the Blues**	*Tom Robbins* £1.75
☐	11012 4	**When She Was Good**	*Philip Roth* £1.25
☐	11614 9	**Portnoy's Complaint**	*Philip Roth* £1.50

All these books are available at your bookshop or newsagent, or can be ordered direct from the publisher. Just tick the titles you want and fill in the form below.

CORGI BOOKS, Cash Sales Department, P.O. Box 11, Falmouth, Cornwall.

Please send cheque or postal order, no currency.

Please allow cost of book(s) plus the following for postage and packing:

U.K. CUSTOMERS. 45p for the first book, 20p for the second book and 14p for each additional book ordered, to a maximum charge of £1.63.

B.F.P.O. & EIRE. Please allow 45p for the first book, 20p for the second book plus 14p per copy for the next three books, thereafter 8p per book.

OVERSEAS CUSTOMERS. Please allow 75p for the first book plus 21p per copy for each additional book.

NAME (Block Letters) ....

ADDRESS ....

....